Praise for Kit Alloway

"A suspenseful riddle full of intrigue."   —*Publishers Weekly*
on *Dreamfire*

"Alloway's writing is rich and vivid, and the dynamics within the close-knit cast of characters make the danger even more delicious as readers watch for the outcome."   —*School Library Journal*
on *Dreamfire*

"With compelling characters, fraught relationships, and high stakes, the drama of this book carries us through and leaves us wanting more."   —New York *Daily News* on *Dreamfever*

"*Dreamfire* is an amazing fantasy novel with realistic characters who will grab readers from the first page, immersing them in a fantastic new universe. *Divergent* fans will be pleased with the unique concept. The twisty plot never dulls, leaving readers guessing 'til the end. Alloway is one author to be on the lookout for."
—*RT Book Reviews* on *Dreamfire*

"Patient readers will be richly rewarded with effective mystery, a charged romance (of course Will and Josh wind up together), and a cool alternative world detailed onto our current one in ways that make expected places and scenes unfamiliar and magical."
—*The Bulletin of the Center for Children's Books* on *Dreamfire*

"The nightmare vignettes are rivetingly chilling. A dark and exciting paranormal adventure that will keep patient genre fans up late."
—*Kirkus Reviews* on *Dreamfire*

Dreamworld

Dreamworld

kit alloway

st. martin's griffin 🦅 new york

DREAMFIRE. Copyright © 2015 by Kit Alloway. DREAMFEVER. Copyright © 2016 by Kit Alloway. All rights reserved. Printed in the United States of America. For information, address St. Martin's Press, 175 Fifth Avenue, New York, N.Y. 10010.

www.stmartins.com

Designed by Anna Gorovoy

The Library of Congress Cataloging-in-Publication Data is available upon request.

ISBN 978-1-250-12251-3 (trade paperback)

Our books may be purchased in bulk for promotional, educational, or business use. Please contact your local bookseller or the Macmillan Corporate and Premium Sales Department at 1-800-221-7945, extension 5442, or by e-mail at MacmillanSpecialMarkets @macmillan.com.

First Edition: January 2017

10 9 8 7 6 5 4 3 2 1

Dreamfire

For Mom and Dad,

my champions;

and Sara,

who makes a joyful noise

List of Characters

Family

Josh Weaver (Joshlyn Dustine Hazel Weavaros)
Deloise Weaver: Josh's younger sister
Lauren Weaver (Laurentius Weavaros): Josh and Deloise's father
Jona Weaver: Josh and Deloise's mother (deceased)
Kerstel Weaver: Lauren's wife, Josh and Deloise's stepmother
Dustine Borgenicht: Josh and Deloise's grandmother, Peregrine's estranged wife
Peregrine Borgenicht: Josh and Deloise's grandfather, Dustine's estranged husband

Friends

Winsor Avish: Josh's best friend
Whim Avish: Winsor's older brother
Saidy and Alex Avish: Whim and Winsor's parents
Haley McKarr (Micharainosa): Ian's twin brother
Ian McKarr (Hianselian Micharainosa): Haley's twin brother
Davita Bach: the local government representative
Young Ben Sounclouse: the local seer
Schaffer Sounclouse: Young Ben's great-grandson

The Outsider

Will Kansas: Josh's apprentice

One

The sewer wasn't the worst place for a nightmare, Josh Weaver admitted to herself as she fumbled with the boxy, rose-gold lighter in her hand. But it was hardly a warm afternoon in the park, either.

She stood knee-deep in very cold water that smelled of rotting fast food and gave off fumes like fresh asphalt. Her jeans were soaked—she'd slipped and fallen twice—and her black shirt was too thin to keep her warm. Around her legs, oily patterns floated on the surface of stagnant, brackish water as it flowed down the cramped concrete sewer tunnel and into the darkness.

Josh moved her lighter in a wide arc, which brought back the sharp pain in her right elbow where she'd slammed it against a ladder climbing down here. The ladder had been behind her a moment before; now it was gone. Like so many things in the Dream, it had vanished without reason.

When the lighter grew hot in her hand, she let the cap close with a click. The darkness was absolute—*No cheating,* it seemed to say—and while Josh had been in dark places lots of times, there was a bad vibe down here; it drove the adrenaline that made her hands want to grab a weapon and her legs ache to run. The feeling might just have been instinct, but Josh knew better than to ignore it. Instinct had saved her life too many times.

For a moment she hesitated, rubbing her numb fingertips against the warm metal lighter. Then she closed her eyes against the dark and broke Stellanor's First Rule of dream walking: *Never let the dreamer's fear become your own.*

Usually when Josh was inside the Dream universe, she kept the image of stone walls in the back of her mind. The walls—thick and high and impenetrable—protected her from the dreamers' emotions and made it possible for her to focus and not become paralyzed by terror or anxiety. But now Josh imagined a tiny hole in one wall, a well-worn hole the size of her pinky finger where a cork usually fit, and when she pulled the cork out, a slither of blue smoke came through.

A man in an old-fashioned coat. A gas can. A mask. A little boy wearing the gas mask, his face turning white, then blue, the mask pulling at his skin, sucking, sucking . . .

And something else, a hint of primal fear, like a match held to the woman's anxiety and ready to set it alight: *dreamfire.*

Josh jammed the cork back in the wall before the dreamfire could overwhelm her. She opened her eyes and flicked the lighter again.

So there's a bad guy down here somewhere, she thought. *Skippy.*

A sloshing noise came from one end of the tunnel, and Josh saw the dreamer come running—a woman in her early forties, nice-looking in a middle-class, soccer-mom kind of way.

"They're coming!" the woman warned Josh, stopping a few feet away. "I got them away from the children, but they're coming."

"Who's coming?" Josh asked.

"The men, with the gas masks. They put a mask on Paul and he turned all blue."

"You're dreaming," Josh calmly told the soccer mom. "You need to wake up."

Sometimes the best way to deal with dreamers was to point out that they were dreaming. Some would realize the truth of the statement and wake up, while an interesting few would gain conscious control over their own nightmare.

Soccer mom did neither.

"*Blue,*" the woman repeated, her eyes staring into the darkness.

Josh felt the dreamfire flickering against the walls in her mind, like flames burning just outside her field of vision.

All right, she thought, *this lady is not hearing me. We need an out.*

Unfortunately, there was no immediately apparent way to escape the dream. Josh needed a doorway, a manhole, an iron gate. Any kind of porthole, anything that would move them both to a different place.

"Don't worry about Paul—" she started to say, and the woman let out an operatic scream that echoed up and down the sewer tunnel in a wicked one-woman chorus.

Josh grimaced as the dreamer took off running, splashing through the water like a duck taking flight.

Before Josh could go after her, a gust of freezing air swept the back of her neck. She spun so fast her feet lost purchase on the greasy tunnel floor and she fell on her butt—again. The hand holding the Zippo slipped underwater.

But before the light went out, she caught a glimpse of the man who had been standing not five feet behind her.

Now she understood why the woman was so upset.

The man stood tall and wide enough to fill the tunnel. He wore a green-black leather trench coat that glistened like the shell of a beetle. Big green buttons ran down the front and a wide belt cinched the waist. On his head sat a matching felt fedora with a black band.

A gas mask covered his face, and two rubber tubes connected it to a huge canister that he wore on his back. The canister was so large that Josh could see it over his shoulder. It was made of something white and slick, like bone. The gas mask hid his face, but the two hands sticking out of the overlong sleeves were massive, and the fingers, thick as quarter rolls, were spread wide apart. Even in the meager half-second glimpse she got of him, Josh saw the muscles in the backs of his hands straining against the flesh as he forced his fingers farther away from each other. His hands must have hurt, spread so wide.

Josh sat in the water, in the dark, and listened to the gritty sound of the lighter flicking futilely. The man in the trench coat didn't make a sound, but she felt his presence somewhere nearby, like air pressure against her skin. He was close—how close? Which side? She hated not knowing where he was, because she was going to have to make a run for it and she needed to know which direction to run.

Some nightmares could be dealt with, resolved, like the one the week before when a man dreamt that he had started a grease fire in the kitchen while frying a couple of breaded tennis shoes. Josh had just walked in, grabbed a fire extinguisher, and put the fire out. Man relieved, nightmare over.

But this dream was too minimalist to work with; there were no possibilities for improvisation in the tunnel. The source of danger was obvious, but the means of defense were a mystery. What could she use against this canister-carrying menace?

Possibly nothing. Not all nightmares could be resolved, and if that was the case in this nightmare, Josh had only one option left.

According to what was formally known as Tao Sing's Dictum: *If you can't face a nightmare, run from it as fast as you possibly can.*

The man in the trench coat still didn't make a sound. Finally, the lighter's wick dried enough that the little flame burst into action, and Josh's throat shut as if a string had been yanked tight around it.

The face of the man in the trench coat was less than a foot from her own.

All she saw during that glance were his eyes, bulging from above the rubber rim of his gas mask. They were black. The man carrying the canister had black eyes, deep and yet shiny. They had no whites. They had no irises. They had no pupils. It was as if his eyelids opened onto deep space.

He peered at her. A feeling emanated from this man—no, this *creature*—that made it hard for Josh to focus. Part of the feeling was intense desire, not for her but for violence, and part of it was indifference. The thing living in the trench coat wanted to kill, but it didn't care what, and this deep, unconscious need to end life was the source of the woman's dreamfire.

Only the deepest fears could awaken dreamfire, and only the

strongest mental walls could stand against it. One moment of weakness would be enough to ignite a hysteria that would render Josh as powerless as the dreamer.

Josh began wondering if she'd have to kill the man.

This would hardly be her first time. But her father had once told her that even when he was in Vietnam, the killing hadn't seemed as real as Dream death did. Every sense was exaggerated—the sound of ribs cracking exploded in his ears, the blood was as thick as frosting, and it dried bright crimson, when it did finally dry.

And Dream death didn't always work. Once, Josh had blown a zombie's head off with a shotgun, watched it roll down a staircase, and felt his hands continue ripping her hair out. She'd had to break his body open like a lobster before he finally stopped coming at her.

The man in the trench coat struck her as the kind of guy who wasn't going to go down easily.

Then he spoke, the words muffled by the mask. No accent. No cadence. No real interest.

"You're Jona's daughter."

Josh was so startled she forgot to kick him. He knew her *mother?* Her mother had been dead for five years; Josh didn't bump into a lot of random people who had known her. And besides that, he was a nightmare, not a person—he shouldn't have been able to recognize Josh.

But while Josh stared at him with a tilted head, the man in the trench coat reached for a second gas mask dangling from his canister, and she remembered what the soccer mom had said.

They put a mask on Paul and he turned all blue.

That was when Josh remembered to kick him, leaning back on the hand that wasn't holding her lighter and using the leverage to get her right cross-trainer in under his chin.

His head snapped back. The felt hat flipped off his skull, revealing strands of gray-black hair twisted around a palm-sized bald spot.

Josh lashed out again. This time her heel caught him square in the breastbone and sent him flying into the side of the tunnel. His canister clanged against the wall.

She didn't waste any time. Before he could so much as finish sliding into the water, she was on her feet and running full-out through the tunnel. The water felt thick; it clung to her jeans as if trying to hold her back.

Move, move, move, she told herself.

The dreamer appeared around a bend in the tunnel, and Josh stumbled to a stop beside her. "I can't get this door open!" the woman screamed, knocking her fashion-ring-laden hand against a steel access door in the wall.

Finally, Josh thought at the sight of the door.

She listened for a moment, but between her own breath and soccer mom's gasps and sobs, she couldn't hear anything. Either the man in the trench coat wasn't following, or else he could move silently. She thought she could guess which.

Cold air gusted from the direction she had run.

"Don't panic," she told the woman, and braced her shoulder against the door. In the real world, she could never have knocked down a steel door, but this was the woman's dream, and it would respond to the woman's perceptions. If she thought Josh capable, the Dream would conform.

Josh launched herself at the door. Pain shot through her shoulder, but the hinges creaked.

"Harder," the woman urged.

Josh managed not to glare at her. She threw herself against the door again, so hard her arm moved in her shoulder socket. This time the door fell outward.

And kept falling. On the other side of the doorway stretched black emptiness. Josh grabbed the tunnel wall with her free hand to keep from tumbling into the void.

"I'm gonna die," the dreamer whispered.

If she hadn't felt sorry for the woman, Josh would have been annoyed. Why were people always so quick to assume that they were going to die? Josh had been in much worse situations than this one and made it out unharmed.

She relit her lighter with one hand while she pulled a makeup compact from her back pocket with the other. All of the facial powder had long ago fallen out of the hunter-green case. When she revved up the Zippo and reflected the light off the mirror and into the doorway, a shimmering surface appeared where the empty doorway had been a moment before. This filmy glaze, which dream walkers called the Veil, stretched across the doorframe like a huge soap bubble sparkling in the firelight.

"Through," Josh said.

"I'm gonna die."

The air that rushed over Josh's hair lifted it off her ears and slid icy fingers across her scalp. She turned without thinking.

The man in the green-black trench coat stood an arm's length away.

Josh raised her right foot, set it against the dreamer's waist, and kicked her through the doorway. Then she jumped after her.

Two

Josh stumbled on her way out of the Dream and ended up on her knees on the archroom's tile floor. At the same time, somewhere else in the world, the dreamer was probably bolting upright in bed.

Josh's younger sister, Deloise, rose from a chair that sat near the stone archway through which Josh had fallen. But instead of helping her up, Deloise put her manicured hands on her hips and said, "I've been looking everywhere for you! Do you have any idea what time it is?"

"Um . . ." Josh shook her head, trying to reorient herself. "Around six thirty?"

"Try eight twenty. You're going to be late to—oh, drat, Josh, you're wet. And you smell like you've been swimming in a septic tank."

Despite her attempt to appear disapproving, Deloise was smiling. She usually was. When Josh held out her hands, Deloise took them and tugged her sister up.

Deloise was—to her infinite pleasure—a full four inches taller than Josh, and at least four times as pretty. When people said her blond hair had good body, they were talking about the Venus de Milo's body, and when they said her brown eyes resembled a doe's, they were talking about Bambi's mom. And people were always talking, because not only was Deloise beautiful, she was wonderful. She preferred young children's nightmares, where she could soothe, reassure, and comfort, and she was well suited to the task. In the World, kids were unnaturally drawn to her, as if they knew subconsciously that she fought for them. And she was social, and funny, and enthusiastic, and sensitive, and . . . a hundred other things Josh was not.

Josh groaned as she got to her feet. A puddle was forming on the clean, white tile and her hand was red from where she had let the Zippo burn too long. Her entire body shimmered with the aftermath of passing through the Veil, scientifically called Veil dust but more commonly known as fairy dust.

Josh wiped her face of fairy dust with a white hand towel. "How late am I going to be, you think?" she asked. Her seventeenth birthday party was set to start at nine.

"You'll make it if you hurry. I ironed your outfit."

Deloise was already dressed in a dark blue dress with palm-sized white flowers printed on it. A white shrug covered her bare shoulders—Laurentius Weavaros did not approve of his daughters showing skin—and her left wrist was adorned with a pearl bracelet that matched the accents on her ballet flats. Like most dream walkers, Lauren believed that young women should dress modestly, and he wouldn't have been the only one frowning if Deloise had showed up in heels.

Deloise shut off the archroom lights while, ahead, Josh scrambled up the spiral stairs in her squishing shoes. "I only saw a minute of that nightmare, but the dreamer looked like she was caught up in some serious dreamfire," Deloise said, following.

"Yeah. The guy in the trench coat was gassing people to death. Although he was also *wearing* a gas mask. . . . And he said the strangest thing—"

Josh pushed open the door at the top of the steps and let herself into the kitchen pantry. Spice racks and soda caddies cleverly disguised the door to the basement. After Deloise closed it behind herself, only Josh's gritty gray footprints on the floor suggested the room held anything more than nonperishable foodstuffs.

In the kitchen, Josh and Deloise's stepmother, Kerstel, was preparing a tray of bruschetta and goat cheese. The girls' mother had died five years before while trying to open a new archway between the World and the Dream, and three years later, their father had married Kerstel. She was twenty years too young for him and better educated than he was, but she was smart and funny and a good cook, and she thought Josh was a responsible young person, so Josh didn't mind having her around. Deloise positively adored her.

Saidy Avish was assisting Kerstel with the finger foods. Saidy and her husband, Alex, lived on the house's second floor with their daughter, Winsor, who was—or had once been—Josh's best friend.

Saidy looked disparagingly at the mess Josh tracked on the floor and ordered her to remove her shoes. Kerstel said, "Josh, I *just* washed the floor," but she was laughing.

Barefoot, Josh followed Deloise down the hall and into the stairwell. Deloise floated up the steps, her ballet flats hardly indenting the carpet. "What were you saying?"

"Yeah, the guy in the trench coat. He said . . ." Josh hesitated, half wondering if she hadn't misheard the words through his mask. "He said I was Jona's daughter."

"What?" Deloise looked sharply at Josh over her shoulder, lost her balance, and had to grab the banister to keep from falling down the stairs. Josh put a hand on her sister's back until Deloise was moving forward again.

"That's impossible," Deloise said. "I mean, how could he know who you are?"

"He couldn't." Now that she had a moment to think, Josh found the man's recognition even more disturbing. He had been a figment of the nightmare, not a conscious being with a mind or a past. He had never met Josh's mother.

"I must have misheard him."

"Well, you should talk to Dad about it," Deloise advised. "Or Grandma. They'll know. You didn't break Stellanor's First Rule, did you?" She turned sharply again, her voice rising with alarm. "He might have been able to read your mind if you let the dreamer's fear take you over."

"I didn't break Stellanor," Josh said, although that's exactly what she had done. Yes, letting the dreamer's fear touch her was dangerous—especially when dreamfire was present—but sometimes it was the only way to get vital information. And she was careful. "I'll ask Grandma later," she said, and let the subject drop.

They reached the third floor. The house, originally a Greek-revival mansion, had been renovated and expanded several times, and now contained two three-bedroom apartments on the second floor and a four-bedroom apartment on the third. Because the Dream required monitoring, continuously but especially at night, and because the archway in the basement was the only one for miles around, it made sense for a number of dream walkers to share the house.

The Weavaroses lived on the third floor. The living room, once nothing more than four white walls and a couch, had flourished like a garden under Kerstel's care. Now the windows were dressed with brown velvet curtains and the taupe walls bore earth-toned textile art created by a local craftswoman. Alpaca throw blankets were piled in a wicker basket at the end of the couch, and the air smelled of Kerstel's favorite toasted-almond-scented candles.

Josh and Deloise's bedrooms were connected by a bathroom and sat between the master bedroom and an extra room used for storage and the collection of junk. Two weeks earlier, Kerstel had decided to clean out the junk room, but she had lacked answers when Josh asked about the unexpected change. "Just seemed like a good idea," she'd said finally.

Deloise said this meant Kerstel was pregnant, but Josh thought she probably just wanted the extra closet space.

Josh's own room was a wreck of textbooks and martial-arts books and clothing she couldn't be bothered to put away. Half a dozen blankets, none of which matched one another or the sheets on the bed, were heaped on the mattress and the window seat and the overstuffed recliner in the corner. Most of her possessions looked like they had been won in a street fight; even her hairbrush had a corner chipped off.

Winsor was sitting on the corner of the bed, leafing through a knife catalog. Her dark, layered hair shone in the ruddy light of the bedside table, and she smiled knowingly—and just a bit scornfully—as she looked up at Josh, blue eyes cutting through her overlong bangs.

Though not shy, Winsor's combination of intensity, obvious intelligence, and reserve often created a barrier between her and other people. She could appear cold without meaning to—at least, Josh thought she didn't mean to. If her family hadn't lived on the second floor, Josh considered it unlikely that they would ever have become friends. After a "wardrobe malfunction" at a middle school pool party, Winsor had developed great sympathy for dreamers trapped in shame and embarrassment nightmares. Josh couldn't count the number of times she'd had to pass up a perfectly terrifying monster chase because Winsor wanted to help some kid dreaming he was naked in his school cafeteria.

"I told Del you would be down there." Winsor shook her head. "Workaholic."

"I'm not a workaholic," Josh told her, although winter break had just ended, and she had worked like a sled dog the entire time. She fought the urge to flop down on the bed—she didn't want to contaminate her blankets with sewer sludge.

"You're a workaholic in dire need of a shower," Winsor replied.

Although her voice was light and she continued to smile, Josh detected a fine edge to her tone, like a very long, thin blade hidden beneath her words.

Nothing had been right between them since the summer before, and Josh was beginning to think that the damage to their friendship was irreparable.

"Yeah, yeah, yeah," Josh said. "I'm moving."

As Josh closed the door to the bathroom that connected her room to Deloise's, she heard her sister say, "Look at this place!" Winsor chuckled.

Josh leaned against the door and sighed. She was exhausted. No, she had been exhausted for weeks. She was beyond exhausted and into bone-tired. And now she had her birthday party to deal with.

Her image in the mirror was a mess. Smelly, grayish water dripped out of her short brown hair. Her mouth hung slack with fatigue, and her green eyes, too pale to begin with, were now the color of cheap pottery glaze.

She peeled off her thin black shirt, shivering, and tossed it into the hamper with the rest of her clothes. Her right shoulder was swollen and already turning purple. Only a dreamer's soul—or spirit or consciousness or whatever one wanted to call it—was present in the Dream, so a dreamer couldn't be killed or injured no matter what happened to them. But a dream walker entered the Dream body, mind, and spirit, and whatever injuries they sustained in the Dream remained real when they returned to the World.

Josh pulled the compact out of her pocket and tossed it onto the wicker dish on the counter, along with her Zippo. Engraved in the lighter's rose-gold plating, among the myriad scratches and dents, she could still make out the inscription: *To J.D. Love Always, Ian.*

Ian had been the only one who ever called her J.D.

For a moment Josh stared at the words, realizing it had been exactly one year since Ian had given her the lighter. Such an odd gift coming from him, so thoughtful. And it was all the more precious because it was one of the only things she had left of Ian.

Finally, she removed a long golden chain from around her neck and set it in the wicker dish. A tiny pendant hung from the chain—a plumeria blossom stamped on a golden disk. The plumeria represented the True Dream Walker, who had been the first person to enter the Dream and end nightmares. Josh wasn't really sure she believed in his legend—and she certainly didn't believe the tale that he would someday return—but she had grown up hearing the stories just like every other dream walker before her. Moreover, she believed in the ideals his legend stood for, and she wanted to wear the pendant tonight of all nights, when she accepted the mantle of responsibility he had—according to the stories—passed down to her. But she took it off so she could wear the only other necklace she owned: three jade teardrops, set an inch apart, hanging from a thin golden chain. Her grandmother had given it to her, and Deloise had shopped for Josh's outfit with it in mind.

Half an hour later, she was dry and dressed in a floor-length light-green skirt with a knit cream top that hung over her hips. Although the outfit didn't resemble the formal gowns most girls wore to their seventeenth-birthday parties—except one of the Grodonia girls, who had worn a black leather miniskirt, a blue-green corset, and a belly-button piercing so new it still dripped blood—Josh doubted anyone who knew her expected that she would arrive dressed for the prom. This was the only skirt she owned.

"Turn around," Deloise said after fastening the necklace behind Josh's neck.

Josh went back into the bathroom to look at herself. Deloise had done a good job; the color of the jade matched the shade of the skirt exactly and made Josh's eyes appear darker than they were, drawing out the features of her face.

"Oh, it's perfect," Deloise cooed, obviously pleased by this feminine touch. Winsor gave an indifferent nod of approval.

It *was* perfect—even Josh could see that. Which was precisely why she had asked Deloise to select an outfit for her. Deloise knew about things like details and accessories and the hidden implications of clothing.

"We're going to be late in four minutes," Winsor announced, standing up and smoothing her dress.

Deloise grinned. "Come on, birthday girl."

Josh took a deep breath and followed her sister through the bedroom door. She had faced hundreds of other people's nightmares; tonight she had to face her own.

They held the ceremony out on the lawn. Josh knew what to expect, but the sight of the stone pathway leading to a giant weeping willow tree in the moonlight, marked every yard by a glowing white candle, still made her suck in a breath.

"Oh," Deloise whispered, "I love this stuff!"

Paper lanterns hung from the branches of the ancient willow tree, casting a yellow glow over the grass. The air was chilly but not cold—unseasonably warm for January—and Josh was glad Deloise had picked a sweater for her to wear.

More than a hundred people had gathered around the tree. Josh had known most of them all her life—they were all part of the local dream-walker clan—but she was self-conscious with the knowledge that tonight everyone was looking at *her,* talking about *her.* Expecting something special from *her.*

She started to ask Deloise to stay with her and found that her sister had already vanished, along with Winsor. The crowd's chatter died down as everyone turned their attention to Josh, which only increased her desire to go running, but she forced her wooden feet in their dainty cream slippers to keep walking along the candle-marked path. Through the thin soles, she felt the sharp gravel path with each step.

She sat down on a stone chair placed at the bottom of the willow tree's trunk and forced herself to look up bravely into the crowd. At first the glare of candlelight in her eyes was too strong, but after a few seconds the faces began to make themselves known to her. She felt less anxious as she recognized people and returned their smiles—her martial-arts instructor, her cousins and aunts and uncles, her mother's best friend. Just as Josh recognized Young Ben Sounclouse, he stepped out of the circle and came toward her.

Young Ben had to be approaching a hundred years old. In his twenties, he had taken over as seer for a really old guy named Ben, and everyone had been calling him Young Ben ever since. His face was dappled with liver spots and he walked slowly, but he had quick eyes and good hearing aids. He was the local seer, one of a small group of dream walkers who kept histories, doled out wisdom, and—most important—wrote prophecies. Under the monarchy that had once ruled Europe, Asia, and North America, seers had garnered great respect, but since the revolution—led by none other than Josh's own grandfather—the seers had lost all of their political authority, and no one was quite sure how they fit into dream-walker culture anymore.

In the nineteen years since the overthrow, a permanent government had yet to be formed, and the junta that remained in power had thrown out the grand old ceremonies and elaborate rituals that the monarchs had loved. Coming-of-age parties—once a standard rite of passage with a well-known form—lacked their former ostentatious pomp.

Young Ben was wearing a Hawaiian-themed tux that didn't really fit—his beer belly was slumping over the cummerbund—and he held a heavy rosewood box. Jewels set into the lid caught the candlelight and glittered like colored stars. A lot of communities printed scrolls off computers and handed them out in sealed envelopes these days, but Young Ben still hand-wrote his on parchment and presented them in the same jeweled box he'd always used.

"Good evening," he said, standing next to Josh's chair. His ancient voice sounded like a record played with a barbed-wire needle, but it carried clearly between the branches. When he put his plump hand on Josh's shoulder, his touch was warm and firm with affection. "Welcome to Josh's birthday," he added, and easy laughter relaxed the atmosphere. "We're here tonight to welcome one of my favorite people into adulthood. Laurentius, Kerstel, you've done a wonderful job. You've given Josh every value a good dream walker needs, and I know Jona would be proud. I doubt there's one among us who hasn't been downright astonished by Josh's skills in the Dream, by her determination not just to end nightmares but to resolve them, or by her commitment to return night after night. I can't think of a higher compliment than to say that when Josh decides she's going to help a dreamer wake up, that person can know for certain that they aren't going to be abandoned to the monsters. And I don't know of a higher calling, or someone I'd rather see take it up." He gave the crowd a big smile. "Does anyone have anything they'd like to say?"

Josh—who was already hot-cheeked and sick to her stomach—wondered if that wasn't a little like saying, "If anyone has any reason why this child should not be allowed into adulthood, speak now or forever hold your peace."

And *this*, she realized, was what she was afraid of. Her deepest fear, her personal dreamfire, surrounded her in the form of friends and family. This was her moment of truth, and she was terrified that the truth was exactly what would be said.

For an instant, she thought she saw Ian's face in the crowd. Seven months ago he had been the one sitting beneath the wings of the willow tree, and she had been the one telling the crowd everything she loved about him.

He wasn't here tonight to tell her family the whole truth about what had happened to him. The evidence was right in front of them, but they didn't want to see it because Josh was their darling, their prodigy, proof of their success as a family and a community. They didn't want to think about Josh's mistakes.

She killed her boyfriend.

No one said that, or the other things she was afraid to hear. No one even made a joke at her expense. One by one, people rose to talk about her gifts, her abilities in-Dream unaccounted for by her training. They recalled her moments of glory—how at the age of eight she had resolved the first dream she ever walked without a word of instruction from her parents; how at twelve she had jumped out the window of a nine-story building and landed in a Dumpster, not a scratch on her or the old woman she had saved from a nightmare's burning apartment; how at fifteen she had dragged her own father, unconscious, out of the Dream after he was hit in the head with a hockey stick.

Everyone said nice things. But the longer Josh listened, the more apparent it became that no one was going to mention anything she had done outside the Dream. They spoke as if she existed to them only when she walked, only inside the Dream's nebulous fantasy world.

What else could they talk about? she wondered. *My so-so grades? My complete lack of social graces? Last summer?*

Her heart hurt at the thought of last summer. She felt the pain as an injured muscle—sore, battered, aching with every breath and beat. No one was going to bring up last summer, and she couldn't decide if she wanted them to or not, if it would be better to keep up this charade of her infallibility or to face what she had done. For a moment she even thought of stopping the ceremony and giving her own account of what had happened the night the cabin burned—wasn't that what a true adult would have done?—but the idea so frightened her that she only gripped the rough arms of the stone chair and swallowed hard.

When people finished talking, Young Ben stepped around to face Josh, and Laurentius and Kerstel fell in on either side of him. "Stand up," Ben whispered, after several seconds' pause, and Josh realized he had been waiting for her and scrambled to her feet.

"Joshlyn Dustine Hazel Weavaros," he announced, "from tonight on you will be an adult among us. I understand you wish to take your journeyer's vows?"

"I do," Josh said. This was the only part of the ceremony she had looked forward to.

"Just let her take her master's vows!" someone in the crowd called out, and laughter filled the yard.

Young Ben made a face like he was giving the idea some thought, then grew serious again. "Hold out your hands and repeat after me."

Josh held her hands out, palms up, and Ben dipped his finger in a vial of scented oil before tracing a spiral onto each palm. As he did so, he said, "*I do this night commit my body, mind, and heart to the protection and care of the Dream for a term of seven years.*"

Josh repeated the words. The oil on her palms smelled like cedar and sandalwood. Dream-walker children took a novice vow before they began training, but not many bothered to take a formal journeyer vow when they turned seventeen, and even fewer took a master vow at the age of twenty-five. Even those who dedicated the better parts of their lives to dream walking rarely took vows, but the words meant a great deal to Josh. She felt them sink into her body like warmth.

Ben rested his hands on her shoulders. "May the True Dream Walker himself watch over you, and may you always walk safely."

"Walk safely," a hundred voices echoed.

Young Ben took the rosewood box from Kerstel and held it out to Josh. He opened the lid.

Josh couldn't stop herself from pulling back a few inches, half expecting all the world's evils to come pouring from the box's mouth. When they didn't, she peered at the contents the way she would have looked at the sun—with her eyes fixed up against the inevitable pain.

But all she saw was a wooden box lined in black velvet and edged with gold tassel. A piece of parchment rested innocently inside, rolled tight and fastened with a green wax seal stamped *W*.

"Go on," Young Ben said.

Josh stared at the scroll for a long time, making out the depth of the stamp in the wax, the slight imperfections in the surface of the parchment.

"Go on, pick it up," Ben said. "It won't bite."

Chuckles came from those nearby, and even though Josh loved Young Ben, she shot him a hateful look. She rubbed her hands together to disperse the oil on her palms and then, overcoming her reluctance with speed, she snatched the scroll up from where it lay. The paper felt grainy against her fingertips, and she could smell the wax seal. It softened against her hot palm.

Inside the scroll was written the seer's vision of her life. A vision that would—no matter the actions taken against it—come to pass. Clues, hints, warnings . . . She wouldn't know unless she broke the seal.

Only three people knew what the scroll said inside: her parents and Young Ben, who had written it. Whether or not Josh ever learned what it contained was up to her now; it was her decision. She was being issued a challenge, and if she rose to it, then she would be a true adult.

She thought again of Ian, who had been given the same challenge and failed miserably. She had been partially responsible, and the idea that she was being given another chance to ruin a life unsettled her. As far as she was concerned, the scroll was a time bomb that would go off the moment she opened it.

She looked up at Young Ben and forced a smile that was overshadowed by her sense of dread. "Thanks," she managed to say.

Young Ben shouted, "Happy birthday!" and the crowd broke into hoots and agreements that filled the air like wishes floating up to the stars.

Never, Josh promised herself, deaf to the cheers around her.

I will never open this scroll.

Three

Although Josh's moment of reckoning had come and gone, and her scroll hadn't exploded in her hand, three hours later she still felt anxious. She sat on a couch between Deloise and Winsor in the long, badly lit basement of the house, surrounded by an assortment of unloved furniture, storage boxes, and training equipment. The basement was the only room big enough to hold a hundred people, so that's where Kerstel had set up a fabulous reception—Champagne, a two-tier cake, tables of finger food, even a silver samovar of hot chocolate kept warm by a little gas burner. No one had commented on the concrete wall with the bank-vault door at the far end of the room; everyone at the party knew what it protected.

After hours of food, drink, and chitchat, people were beginning to leave; dawn was on the way and the next day was a Friday. Those who weren't leaving were getting progressively more intoxicated, including Josh's father and Young Ben.

Josh scanned the crowd for a threat, just as she would have in the Dream. She passed her scroll from one hand to the other. She wasn't used to drinking, and she was beginning to suspect that a single piece of chocolate cake wasn't enough to soak up three glasses of Champagne. Her head had grown very hard to hold up, and knowledge that her reflexes were dulled made her even more anxious.

They'd drunk Champagne on Ian's birthday too, and when he'd kissed her the bubbles had made her lips feel like they were sparkling. He had held her hand all night, and when dawn had broken they had gone up to his room and cracked the seal on his scroll.

And he had never kissed her again.

"You're really not going to open it?" Deloise asked. She was being sensible and eating a handful of nuts to counteract all the sugar she'd ingested. "Come on, Josh, snap that seal. I want to know what it says."

"Win, is it just rude to ask someone what their scroll says, or is there actually a rule against it?"

Winsor covered a yawn with one hand and leaned back on the lumpy plaid couch. "Both. It's so rude there's a rule against it."

"What?" Deloise said. "You're making that up."

"It's the dream-walker version of the Ten Commandments," Winsor said, closing her eyes. She'd looked decidedly bored most of the evening. "First commandment: Don't ask anybody what their scroll says."

"What's the second commandment?"

"There's only one. It's that important." She yawned again. "But there's no point in nagging Josh to open it. She has a complex."

Sitting forward, Josh couldn't see Winsor, who was leaning back beside her. But she could feel the tip of that blade in Winsor's voice as if it were tracing words across her back.

"A complex?" Deloise repeated.

"She's afraid she won't be able to handle what's written inside. Some people can't, you know."

Josh was on her feet and a yard away before she realized she had moved. She caught sight of her grandmother among the lingering guests and called over her shoulder, "I'm going to go say hi to Grandma."

"That was mean," she heard Deloise tell Winsor.

Yeah, Josh agreed silently. *It was.*

But she didn't stay to defend herself because she believed she had no right to be angry. Not when she was the one who had caused so much damage.

Dustine Borgenicht greeted her granddaughter with a hug, stepping tremulously out from behind her walker, which had been made especially for Dustine from white pine and polished to a high shine for the celebration. Dustine wasn't a hugger, but then neither was Josh, and the exchange was somewhat awkward.

"Happy birthday, honey."

"Thanks, Grandma."

"And you're wearing my necklace," Dustine said. "Don't I feel special. You look beautiful." She frowned and reached out to adjust the necklace around Josh's throat. "Now, if I can just get through your sister's seventeenth, maybe I can die already."

"Grandma!"

Dustine chuckled at Josh's upset. "Sorry. No one told the bartender not to give us old folks wine tonight."

"I don't think there is a bartender."

"That explains it, then. Don't worry, dear, I'm not going anywhere." Her eyes narrowed. "Well, not permanently, but here comes your grandfather, and dueling at a birthday party would be rude. Cover for me."

Josh watched her grandmother scuttle off toward the far end of the basement a great deal faster than her walker would imply she could move. Questions about the man in the trench coat would have to wait till morning. When Josh turned around, her grandfather was grinning at her.

She didn't understand how her grandparents had ever decided to marry each other. They were both dominant and in-charge types, and Peregrine's know-it-all attitude clashed horribly with Dustine's need for control. Unfortunately, they were also the type of people who didn't get divorced; they had just been estranged ever since the overthrow of the monarchy. Dustine hadn't approved of her husband's actions during the coup—particularly the part where he burned the palace to the ground with the king and queen and infant princess still inside it—and had hardly spoken to him since.

Peregrine Borgenitch was shorter than his wife and always moved like he'd been drinking too much coffee. He wore a practiced smile beneath his overbright eyes.

"Happy birthday, Joshy!" he cried.

Joshy. Ugh.

"Thanks," Josh said weakly. He hugged her so hard she tasted the cake she'd eaten in the back of her throat.

"Been working hard?" he asked. "You're the best, you know, the best of all the little dream walkers around. I tell everybody on the junta the same thing."

"That's just . . . skippy," Josh mumbled. "Thanks."

"Anything for my granddaughter. Your mother would be so proud."

Actually, Josh thought, *Mom probably would have been pretty bored.* Jona had hated social events.

Peregrine made a show of opening his suit coat and pulling out a checkbook. "That's real gold leaf on these checks," he said smugly, and scribbled Josh's name on one. After scratching the date, he drew a perfect five and a zero in the amount box.

Then he turned to her, grinned conspiratorially, and added another zero.

Josh had to stop herself from sighing. Her father was the CEO of Strike on Box Records, a massive label responsible for the latest boy band and two of the slutty sixteen-year-old singers currently in high demand. Josh was no stranger to money.

"Thanks," she said again as she accepted the check. She'd tried to refuse one once, and Peregrine had insisted on adding yet another decimal place.

"Spend it on something you really want," he told her. "Don't just stick it in a bank account like your mother would have." He put his hand on her shoulder and leaned close. His breath smelled like old mustard. "Your mother was a wonderful person, Josh, but she wasn't much fun."

"Are you talking about me?" asked a female voice.

Great, Josh thought, sliding out from her grandfather's grasp. Who had put together this guest list?

"No, Davey," Peregrine replied with a condescending smile, "we all know how much fun you were back in the day."

Davita Bach was a titian beauty in her midforties. She was the government representative for all the dream walkers in Josh's hometown of Tanith, and Josh had never been certain whether she and Peregrine actually wanted to do each other harm or just enjoyed ribbing each other.

"Back in the day?" Davita repeated, laughing.

"Yes," Peregrine agreed, "before you sided with the monarchy and the revolution nearly destroyed your career."

Davita didn't seem to mind the disgusting barb—the same way she didn't mind that her continued allegiance to the few remaining members of the royal family meant she had no hope of ever advancing in dream-walker politics. Josh knew that at the end of the gold chain that vanished under Davita's blouse hung the Rousellarios' royal emblem, a star tetrahedron.

"Ah, yes," Davita said, "but if I hadn't landed here then I would never have had the chance to meet Josh and find out what a delightful and amazingly talented generation is going to take over when the junta finally steps down. Speaking of which, I got you a birthday present, Josh."

"You didn't have to do that," Josh told her.

"No," Davita agreed, "but I wanted to." She handed Josh a plain white envelope with an unsealed flap and nodded for her to open it.

After tucking her scroll under one arm, Josh removed a picture cut from a catalogue that showed a black mesh vest against a camouflage background. The caption read, "Finally, bulletproof protection for smaller people!"

"It's real Kevlar," Davita promised. "Deloise gave me your size, and they're making it special."

Peregrine lost his smile as he realized that Davita had upstaged him.

"Wow, Davita," Josh said, folding the picture up. She hugged the older woman quickly, and this time she didn't feel awkward at all. "This is so great of you!"

Davita smelled like jasmine and facial powder. "It won't be ready for at least a month, but I thought you wouldn't mind the wait."

"Of course not. Thank you."

Peregrine took the picture from Josh and examined it skeptically. "I would think that a girl as skillful as you wouldn't need fancy toys like bulletproof vests."

"Dimka's Adage: *Better to wear too many coats than freeze to death in a bush*," Josh quoted, and took the picture back.

Peregrine rolled his eyes, and Davita looped her arm through his. "Come on, old man, let's go argue politics with someone who cares. Happy birthday, Josh."

Josh watched Davita guide her grandfather away and tucked the envelope into the pocket of her skirt. This was the nicest thing that had happened all night.

Her grandmother had vanished, but she managed to find her father, who threw his arms around her. All this hugging was getting to be a nuisance; Josh felt like a psychiatrist's teddy bear.

"Hi, Dad," she said as she pulled away. "Hi, Ben."

Young Ben had discarded his tuxedo jacket and cummerbund.

He had a tumbler of scotch in his hand and a giddy expression on his face. "It's the birthday girl!"

Her father appeared equally intoxicated. "I'm glad to see you guys are enjoying yourselves without the help of chemical stimulants," Josh said, appraising them both. "It's important to remember that you can just say no."

Lauren peered at her with blurry eyes and said, "You should be getting to bed, Josh. It's late."

"I have to leave for school in a few hours. If I sleep now, I'll just be groggy all day."

"All right," Lauren agreed, "but you have to sleep sometime if you're going to stay awake tomorrow night."

"Why would I stay awake tomorrow night?" Josh was pretty certain she wasn't on the schedule to dream walk.

"To wait for your apprentice. He's coming tomorrow, isn't he?"

Josh stared at her father. His drunkenness was rapidly losing humor in her eyes. "What?"

"Your apprentice. At midnight thirty."

"Dad, that's not even a time, and I don't know what you're talking about."

Lauren glanced at the floor around his feet as if looking for something, then back at Josh. "Didn't you open your scroll?"

"*What?*"

Lauren's expression turned to one of absolute horror, but after a moment he laughed again, uneasily, as if he were trying to ward off approaching guilt.

"Oh my god," Josh said. "Where's Kerstel?"

Lauren pointed deeper into the basement.

Josh made a beeline for her stepmother, whom she found condensing the remaining snacks onto a single table. Josh knew her expression must have been dreadful, because she didn't even have to speak before Kerstel said, "What's wrong, hon?"

Josh didn't often reach out to people, but she found herself holding on to Kerstel's elbow like a toddler hanging on to a parent's pant leg.

"Does it say in my scroll that I'm going to have an apprentice who will arrive at twelve thirty tomorrow night?"

Kerstel glanced down at the scroll in Josh's hand. "Did you read it?"

"I didn't even open it. I'm never going to open it, but Dad's four sheets to the wind, and he just blurted it out. Tell me it isn't true."

Kerstel took a deep breath, and then she very evenly said, "It's true."

The world began to tilt. All the people shifted, and when Josh looked around, instead of defining the room by edges and contrasts, she started to see the planes of color made by suit jackets and white tablecloths. Her stomach rolled. She didn't realize she was falling over until Kerstel grabbed her shoulders.

"Oh my god," Josh breathed, sinking against an antique wardrobe. "Oh my god, oh my god."

"I'm going to get your father."

"I'm going to throw up, Kerstel. I don't want to throw up."

Kerstel pushed Josh's head down toward her knees. "You aren't going to throw up. Just don't think of a blue horse."

"A blue horse?"

Josh didn't know what that meant, but she did spend the next several minutes too distracted by trying *not* to think of a blue horse to throw up.

Across the basement, Kerstel spoke to Laurentius in a low voice accompanied by sharp gestures. The news sank into Josh's numbed brain like a lead pipe into quicksand. *I didn't ask for this,* she thought. *I'm not ready for this.*

When her father and Kerstel came back, she said without waiting, "What if I never open the scroll at all? What if I decide not to, like Winsor did?"

Lauren looked significantly less drunk than he had two minutes ago. He held out a hand to help her off the floor, but she ignored it.

"Reading the scroll wouldn't change anything except your knowing about it."

"But how is this even allowed? Don't you have to want to teach an apprentice? Don't you have to sign up for some sort of training—"

"Josh." He blinked hard, as if trying to clear his eyes of an alcoholic haze. "Some things are meant to be. We can't control them, no matter what we do."

"But then what's the point? I thought the scrolls were meant to help us get by, not give us assignments."

When he realized she wasn't going to stand up, Lauren knelt down in front of her. "You're not listening," he said with a kindness that bordered on pity. "If I hadn't told you that this boy was coming here tonight to learn dream walking, he still would have ended up here. You still would have taken him on as your apprentice. Whether you knew ahead of time or not, it would still happen."

Josh began to feel sick again. "Do the scrolls tell your destiny or control it?"

It was a question she and Ian had struggled with until the hour he died.

Lauren had no answer and could only shake his head. "It's a paradox," Kerstel said softly.

Josh stared into her father's eyes. They were so much like Deloise's, big and brown and . . . certain. They trusted. And Josh didn't. She didn't trust her scroll, or her destiny, or even her father at that moment.

But most of all, she didn't trust herself.

"What if I can't do it?" she asked. She knew she sounded pathetic. "What if I *can't*?"

Lauren covered her hands with his own. "Josh, you will figure it out. I've never seen you fail at anything."

She closed her eyes, wanting to contradict him. *You mean you've never seen me fail at anything in-Dream. But what about Ian? Remember when I failed Ian? Remember when Ian died?*

But she didn't say it because she didn't want to talk about Ian. She didn't want to know if her failure to protect him had been in her scroll as well, and if her father had decided not to warn her.

"I thought I would be in control of my life," she said. "Isn't that what being an adult is about? Making my own decisions?"

Her father didn't reply, only reached out to hug her. This time, she didn't push him away.

Four

"Okay," Josh said as Winsor pulled into the parking lot outside East Tanith High School. "We need a plan."

The main building of the high school looked exactly like the Army barracks from which it had been converted. In the growing seasons, the grounds crew did a cheering job with flower beds and well-trimmed trees, but today the gray concrete structure looked no warmer than the parking lot.

This might have accounted for the dejected expressions worn by many of the students lingering outside. Josh knew most of them by name if not personally. Elliot Meyers stood by the front doors, smoking a cigarette and grinding the toe of one shoe into the pavement as if he had a personal grudge against it. Will Kansas was arguing with the driver of the bus for the county home. Rose Cloud and Seagull were digging through the trash for aluminum cans to recycle. In stark contrast to their weary classmates, Kara Lisney and Kyle Finner were necking passionately on a bench.

None of them were Josh's friends. Although she'd gone to school in Tanith her entire life, she'd never been particularly popular, unlike Deloise. Since Ian's death last summer, Josh had withdrawn more and more, preferring the company of those few people who understood the full story of what had happened. She'd entirely lost touch with her few non–dream walker friends. After all, she couldn't explain to them about Ian's scroll, or the archway in the cabin, or the part she had played in the fire; the dream walkers operated in strict secrecy.

"A plan to do what, exactly?" Winsor asked.

Josh realized with dismay that Winsor and Deloise were both opening their doors and exiting the car. She hurried after them, still hoping to wrangle a planning session. "We need to be prepared for tonight."

"Why?" Winsor asked simply.

"What do you mean, 'why?'" Josh asked.

"Nice legs, Del," Elliot Meyers called as they passed him. "Thanks for having 'em."

"Fall down a well, Elliot," Deloise replied sweetly.

"The scroll said your apprentice would show up at your house at twelve thirty," Winsor reminded Josh. "It didn't say you had to do anything to make that happen. So there's no need to stress out. Just let fate run its course." They passed through the front doors of the school, and she turned away from Josh to head down the west-wing hallway, then stopped to look over her shoulder. The thin silver blade was back in her voice when she added, "*Trust* your scroll, Josh," before merging with the crowd of students.

Ouch. Josh had said the same thing to Ian more than once, and anger made the blood rush to the palms of her hands. She shut her eyes against the desire to say something cruel to Winsor.

She turned, expecting Deloise to offer comfort, but Deloise must have headed for her homeroom before Winsor's barb, because Josh realized she was standing alone in the lobby. With a sigh, she turned and headed for class.

Josh fell asleep in history class. The teacher was showing a documentary on the life of Pope Beautiful Wonderful Chastity III, and Josh dozed off. In the snug darkness, even her desktop felt like a feather pillow.

She woke up to a light tap on her arm. "Josh," someone whispered.

Bolting upright, she blinked and found the lights still off. The video continued to play on an old TV with bad color. None of the other students around appeared to be staring at her: Kara Lisney was passing a note to Camille Gothan; the Korean kid who never talked was drawing in his notebook; Will Kansas was taking a calculator apart. At first Josh thought she had imagined hearing her name, but then the guy at the desk next to hers whispered, "You were snoring."

"Oh. Thanks," she whispered back.

Louis Poston smiled.

And Josh knew.

It's Louis!

All need for sleep left her, and she saw him as clearly as if they had been sitting under stage lights. Louis Poston had been in Josh's class since they started high school. He was an excellent student but not arrogant, he was a little dorky but not socially inept, and he was an all-around easygoing guy.

Josh knew he would be easy to teach. And most important, she got the feeling he would *like* dream walking.

Louis caught her gaping at him and lifted his eyebrows. He was on the short side, a little round but not incapacitatingly so, and he had a nice, simple smile.

"Did I miss anything?" Josh asked quickly.

"Yeah, the pope quit the Church and founded Scientology. It was cool."

And he was funny to boot.

Josh smiled and sat back in her chair.

Crisis averted.

She grabbed Winsor at lunch and the two of them fell into chairs at their usual table in the back corner. The cafeteria was a grungy old room that smelled like years of hot lunches past and had developed a disturbing layer of sticky gray dust on the ceiling. The food was surprisingly edible.

Kids were scattered around tables throughout the room. Brianna

Selts was burning a lock of her hair with a lighter, hiding it from the lunch ladies with a notebook, and Will Kansas was trying to stuff a bunch of napkins back into the dispenser after accidentally freeing them all. Roth Purfin was playing footsie with Gretchen Mallory, while Johnny Packard tornado-whipped his potatoes with three taped-together forks. Lunch as usual.

As she dumped her backpack onto a spare chair, Josh realized once again how empty the back corner table felt. A year ago, Ian would have been sitting next to her, Winsor and Haley would have been passing notes, and Deloise and Whim would have been trading side dishes or gossip or playful insults.

Now it was just Josh and Winsor. Deloise was sitting with friends from her grade, as she had every day this year. Ian was dead. Haley was . . . gone. He had left town right after Ian's memorial service. Whim had taken off too.

Whim was Winsor's older brother, and the autumn before, he'd taken the money his grandfather left him and vanished. The only real signs of him were postcards from exotic international locales and frequent posts on his underground, anti-junta blog, *Through a Veil Darkly.*

It would be nice to have him around, Josh reflected. Whim always knew how to lighten things up.

But Whim was a touchy subject with Winsor these days, so instead of asking if she'd heard from her brother lately, Josh walked over to where Deloise was sitting, at a table of kind, pretty people. They greeted Josh with smiles and homemade brownies. Josh dragged Deloise back to their old corner haunt.

"Okay," Deloise said as she slipped onto a chair, "*that* was bad timing. Neil just asked for my number."

"I'm sure it will be the same number when you get back."

"Yeah, but now it's going to seem so . . . *deliberate* when I give it to him."

"Sorry, but I figured out who the apprentice is."

Unimpressed, Deloise lifted the top slice of bread on Josh's sandwich to see what was underneath. "Who?"

"Louis Poston."

Winsor scoffed. "You wish."

"Who's Louis Poston?" Deloise asked. She made a face at the sandwich and closed it.

"He delivers pizza for Serena's Pizzeria—he's one of their scooter delivery guys. He's been to the house a couple of times."

Deloise frowned and ate a French fry. "I don't remember him."

"And how exactly do you know it's Louis?" Winsor asked.

The tone of her voice made Josh feel small and stupid. She said weakly, "I . . . just know. I have a feeling."

Winsor rolled her eyes.

"Maybe she does know," Deloise said. "Maybe a teacher and an apprentice have, like, a psychic link."

"You just want it to be Louis because he's smart and he's not a jerk," Winsor told Josh.

"No," Josh protested. "I had a feeling. I really . . . did. He'll be there."

Winsor added, "You hope."

Through a Veil Darkly

This just in: A friend who works in an ER says that in the last month, three people have been brought to the same hospital after their loved ones were unable to fully wake them. Each case presented with fever, irregular heartbeat, and catatonia, and the patients have remained semicomatose due to frontal-lobe trauma.

What makes this story worthy of TaVD is that each of the patients appears to have become ill while asleep. All were reported to have gone to bed healthy. One woman says that she woke up and heard her husband making a choking sound and saw him scratching at his face, then called 911 when she was unable to wake him. Her story suggests a connection to a fourth case, that of an elderly man whose wife reported a similar scenario. He, however, died of cardiac arrest.

Sitting in her room in front of her laptop, Josh felt vaguely disappointed. Sometimes Whim's blog included a little vignette from his life or some hint as to where he'd been recently, but not today, and Josh wasn't convinced that this rumor he'd heard had anything to do with dream walking. Not that this had ever stopped Whim before; he had pages and pages devoted to proving that the thylacine wasn't really extinct. But there had to be more interesting occurrences in the Dream worth reporting on—

The thought made her recall the man in the trench coat, and moments later she was trudging downstairs to talk to her grandmother. She found Dustine in the living room, watching *The Barney Meadows Show* with an expression of staunch disapproval.

"That *man-child*," she said to Josh, pointing to a man in a white undershirt, "has slept with *both* of his girlfriend's sisters. Isn't that deplorable? His girlfriend did hit him with a chair, though, that was well done."

"Grandma," Josh said, taking the remote, "I don't think this show is for you."

"Don't change it. I like it. When Alex gets home, all he'll want to watch is game shows."

Winsor's father did have an inordinate affection for game shows. Josh sat down on the couch next to Dustine and—against a background of screaming and bleeped curses—described her encounter with the man in the trench coat. By the time she was done, Dustine had lost interest in her show and muted it herself.

"Hmm," Dustine said when Josh finished. She thought, tapping her short-filed nails on the knee of her polyester pants. "I see three possibilities. One is more likely than the others. First, someone who knew Jona and recognizes you is running around in the Dream, somehow causing nightmares."

"That doesn't seem very likely," Josh said. People couldn't survive for more than a day or two in the Dream—the constant need to fight off nightmares soon exhausted them and they would make a fatal mistake. Also, Josh didn't think that anyone who had known her mother was likely to run around in the Dream terrorizing dreamers.

"Second, the nature of the nightmare somehow involved mind reading, and the man read Jona's name out of your mind."

"Maybe," Josh said slowly. She wanted to dismiss the possibility outright because—having touched the dreamer's fear—she knew the nightmare hadn't involved mind reading. But she couldn't very well tell her grandmother that she'd broken Stellanor's First Rule of dream walking, so she told a partial lie instead. "The dreamer kept saying something about the man putting a gas mask on someone, and that person turning blue. It didn't sound like telepathy. And I don't remember thinking about Mom."

"Well, then we have to fall back on the third, most likely, possibility, which is that you misheard him."

"Oh." Josh fiddled with the plumeria pendant around her neck. She just didn't think she had misheard him; the tunnel had been dead quiet. "Well, I'll probably never see him again and it won't matter. I was just perplexed. Thanks for thinking it through with me."

"You were right to come to me with it," Dustine said, already turning the sound for her program back up. As Josh reached the doorway, she said, "Josh. When logic doesn't get you anywhere, trust your gut."

Josh smiled. "Thanks, Grandma."

"I saw a gate beyond the arch."

Josh opened her eyes. "What?" she said. Her voice was groggy, and she didn't know who she was talking to.

"I saw a gate beyond the arch," Ian said again.

Now she really was awake. The alarm clock was bleating like a lost lamb. Josh managed to knock it off the nightstand and onto the floor, where it continued to beep until she yanked the cord out of the wall.

"Bleh," she groaned, falling onto the unmade bed. She'd gone upstairs after talking to her grandmother and immediately fallen asleep in the armchair in her bedroom. Now her body felt hesitant to wake up, as if confused by the lack of sunlight. Her clothes had lost all of their stiffness and breathed with her.

Okay, clean clothes before Louis gets here.

But as she dragged herself into a sitting position, she remembered what she had thought she heard as she woke up. *I saw a gate beyond the arch.* She'd been hearing Ian say it for months, his voice cutting through the instant between sleeping and waking.

She stood up and started to get undressed, but the usual questions ran through her mind. *A gate beyond the arch? Beyond the arch that opens into the Dream? What sort of gate?*

There would be no sorting it out tonight—not when she had an apprentice to greet. Josh changed quickly into black jeans, a maroon shirt with half-length sleeves, and a black sweater. She grabbed the journal her father had given to her as a birthday gift: a sturdy, inch-thick book bound in black leather, and a golden ballpoint pen to go with it.

Josh debated a moment over the contents of the wicker basket on the bathroom counter. She wasn't planning to enter the Dream tonight, but better safe than sorry. She put the compact and Zippo in her pocket.

After collecting a blanket and her coat, Josh went out to the front porch. The night was chilly and the stars were still hidden by thin clouds. The porch swing was set at a right angle to the house, giving it a long arc. Josh sat down on the padded seat and chucked her shoes before tucking her feet under herself. Wrought-iron lanterns hung on either side of the front door, shedding just enough light by which to write.

~~Dear Diary,~~

I tried, but I can't write to a book. It feels weird, and more than enough things feel weird right now. I'm going to start over.

My name is Joshlyn Dustine Hazel Weavaros. This is my first journal.

I've never kept a journal before. I've read all the journals of famous dream walkers, but they're so formal and smart and everybody sounds like they know what they're doing. They always start with something like, "Today I turned seventeen years old and assumed the mantle of responsibility that is my birthright. From this day forth I will record all my deeds for future generations."

But I don't know what to write.

I don't feel like an adult.

I'm sitting on the front porch, waiting for my apprentice to arrive. Dad says it makes no difference if I know the apprentice is coming or not, but it does. It does to me. If he just showed up, fell through the ceiling, or saw somebody coming out of the Dream and flying through the archway, and said, "Hey, I'd like to learn that. Would you teach me, Josh?" then I would be like, "Yeah, I could show you a couple of things, if you're interested." And it would be . . . casual, or natural, or something. There wouldn't be this huge responsibility on me: You must have an apprentice. You must train the apprentice. You must keep the apprentice alive.

I can't handle that kind of pressure. And the worst part is that Dad and Kerstel keep saying I'll be great at it, I'll be fine, it's not a big deal. I'm not as good as everyone thinks I am. Just because I'm a good dream walker doesn't mean I'm a good teacher. It doesn't even mean I'm a good person.

I wish I had a role model or something, somebody who had an apprentice who could tell me how all this works. But I don't even know any apprentices. It's not like this happens every day. I think the only way to get an apprentice is to have one written into your scroll, and that's pretty rare. Not unheard-of, just rare.

Wait a sec. What am I talking about? Wasn't Grandma an apprentice?

"Am I interrupting?"

Josh glanced up and saw Winsor standing in front of her. Her shining hair caught the light and amplified it. "No," Josh said. "Sit down."

Winsor wore cotton pants and a faded T-shirt, and instead of a coat, she had wrapped a thick throw blanket around her shoulders. She looked a little run-down, a little less like her collected, unfathomable self. Faintly more approachable.

"Deloise woke me up," Winsor said. "She'll be down in a minute."

Josh nodded. She wasn't super-excited to see her friend, whom she assumed had showed up to gloat in the event that Louis didn't arrive.

Winsor hesitated before sitting down on the swing beside Josh. "I don't mind if you don't want me around for this."

For the first time in months, she didn't sound mocking or sarcastic. "Why wouldn't I want you around?" Josh asked.

"Because . . ." Winsor tilted her head, and then a ripple passed across her face, as if uncertainty lurked beneath her expression, disturbing her calm. "You might think that I'm trying to butt in where I don't belong. But . . . I know my place." She paused again and added, "In this."

Josh's gaze was drifting over the flagstones beneath her when she finally understood what Winsor meant. "Are you talking about what happened with Ian?" she asked, looking up.

Winsor's hands knotted together in a rare display of unease. "I realize that . . . I should have stayed out of your problems."

Because you hooked up with him behind my back? You think that might have been a bad idea? Really?

Josh spent so much time feeling guilty about what had happened to Ian that she sometimes forgot she had reasons to be angry. But she avoided confronting her own anger the same way she avoided confronting Winsor's—by saying nothing—because she was terrified of the damage she might do if she spoke.

When she failed to reply, Winsor said, as if by explanation, "I'm not apologizing."

Josh looked out over the dark yard so her friend wouldn't see the pain on her face. "Then don't apologize, Winsor."

Another minute passed in silence before Winsor let out a long breath between her teeth. "Josh, we can't just go on not talking about it forever."

"Yeah, we can."

"That's—"

The sound of tires on gravel jarred them both. "Is that our drive?" Winsor asked as Josh climbed swiftly off the swing and walked over to the porch's railing.

One headlight grew as it came near, closing in on the house with steady speed. "What time is it?" Josh asked.

"Twelve twenty-nine and forty-nine seconds. This has to be him."

"But it doesn't look like a car. . . ."

The front door opened. "He's here," Winsor said, and Deloise squealed with delight as she came to stand by Josh's side.

"I thought I'd missed it," she whispered.

They all waited breathlessly while the light turned, and then Winsor said, "It looks like a motorcycle."

But it wasn't a motorcycle. It was a motor scooter.

The scooter stopped in front of the porch, a padded green box strapped to the back. The person riding it put down the kickstand and turned off the engine.

Will Kansas took off his helmet.

Josh turned and glared at Deloise.

"You ordered *pizza*?"

Five

"Am I at the wrong house?" Will Kansas asked, seeing the look on Josh's face.

She barely heard him. She was still staring at Deloise in horrified disbelief.

"What?" Deloise asked. "You said you wanted it to be Louis. So I called Serena's Pizzeria and arranged for him to deliver a pizza to the house at twelve thirty. Win, what time is it?"

"Twelve thirty-one," Winsor said. Josh heard her distantly, as if from a great height.

"See? He's right on time."

"*That*," Josh said, pointing at Will and gritting her teeth to keep from shouting, "is *not* Louis Poston."

Deloise glanced toward the scooter. "Are you sure?"

"*I'm* sure," Will mentioned.

Josh finally looked at him. He was wearing jeans with the knees missing—torn so badly he was about to lose one pant leg—and had a Serena's Pizzeria shirt, unbuttoned, thrown over his tattered white tee. His toes poked out of the ends of his shoes and his auburn hair hadn't been combed.

But he held her gaze with eyes as steady and perceptive as an owl's.

"It's him," Winsor said, finally getting off the swing and walking to the edge of the porch.

"That's not Louis," Josh said again.

"No," Winsor said, lowering her voice. "I mean he's the apprentice. He showed up at exactly twelve thirty. No one else did."

"But Deloise ordered a pizza for twelve thirty. Of course he showed up then." Josh shook her head. "I can't believe you did this, Del."

Deloise hovered on the verge of tears as she realized what was happening. "Oh my gosh! Josh, I didn't mean to, they said they'd send Louis—"

"They did," Will interrupted, bringing everyone's attention back to him. "Louis got sick from some bad ravioli and asked me to cover for him. Is that a problem?"

Josh was starting to wonder if she hadn't eaten some of that ravioli herself. Her stomach was clenched so tight it could have fit inside a chicken egg.

"There's been a mistake," she said. "There's been some kind of mistake. Louis was supposed to—"

"Deliver the pizza, I know," Will told her. "Like I said, he's out sick." He raised the boxes. "But the pizza is fine. The pizza is right here."

"It's not a mistake," Winsor said.

"It has to be," Josh said in a near whisper.

"You never knew for sure that it was Louis."

"But . . ."

Winsor finally shrugged and gestured to Will. "He's here. Now."

Will watched each of them in turn, his eyes beginning to narrow. "Do you want this pizza or not?"

Josh turned to Deloise and muttered, "Just pay him already."

Deloise bit her lower lip. "My purse is upstairs," she admitted.

After closing her eyes until the urge to shove her sister out of the way passed, Josh stepped around Deloise and walked down the porch steps. She dug thirty dollars out of her back pocket and held it out to Will.

"Here," he said, sliding two pizza boxes out of the warmer. He handed them to Josh and took her money. "I've got change somewhere," he told her, digging through his own pockets.

Now that she stood closer to him, he appeared less generically scruffy and more distinctly poor. The belt holding his pants on looked like a hand-me-down from better days, and his shoes were falling apart because they were too small.

"Just keep the rest," she said. "Sorry for the confusion."

Will nodded. "Okay. Thanks. I'll tell Louis you were looking for him."

"No, don't . . . it's . . ." She sighed and would have thrown up her hands if she hadn't been holding the pizzas. "Don't tell Louis anything," she said. "It's not important."

From the way he looked at each of them, as if fixing the scene in his mind, she could tell that he didn't agree.

"Why don't you come in?" Winsor suggested.

Josh's eyes flew to her. "What?" she asked.

"It's late, and that's a lot of pizza," Winsor explained calmly. "Maybe Will could give us a hand eating it? He drove all the way out here, after all."

Josh sent her a *What the hell do you think you're doing?* look, but Winsor ignored it.

"Yeah," Will said, in a tone that meant, *no way*. He was watching them like a cop locked in a room with three suspected serial killers. "Nice offer and all, but it sounds like you guys have stuff to talk about."

"This is all my fault," Deloise burst out.

"Be *quiet*," Josh said.

"Are you trying to get with Louis?" Will asked. "'Cause you could just ask him out. He'd be cool."

"Oh my god, no."

Josh couldn't tell him the truth. She didn't know how the situation appeared from his perspective, but she was certain it was bizarre. And yet, he kept looking at her with his steadfast eyes and a complicated expression that—while it was suspicious—seemed to suggest he was willing to think the best of her if she'd just confide in him.

Don't look at me like that, she thought frantically.

"It's . . ." She stumbled over her words. If only he would look away. "We're recruiting. We need to hire someone. My family has a business, and we were hoping to get Louis out here and talk to him about it."

"You couldn't just call and ask him?"

"No, because . . ." At least now he didn't think she was trying to lure Louis into a date. She was gaining back some credibility. "It's a hard business to explain. We have a workshop here, and we thought Louis might understand better if we showed him."

Winsor nodded almost imperceptibly. Josh walked back up the front steps, still carrying the pizzas. Over her shoulder, she blurted out in a rush, "But since you're here you might as well have the job, so just come inside and I'll show you what to do."

She stopped at the door. She couldn't reach the handle and hold the bulky pizza boxes at the same time, so she stood there on the stoop, banging the boxes against the doorframe over and over as her hand lunged for the knob. She felt Will's eyes on her back.

"Okay," Will said finally. His voice was guarded now, as if he'd given up hope of coaxing the truth out of them. "I don't know what's really going on here, but I'll admit you've got my attention." Josh heard his steps brushing the grass as he walked up to the porch. "People at the pizzeria know where I am tonight," he added.

"Understood," Josh said. She finally pushed the pizza boxes into Deloise's arms and opened the front door. "Come inside," she said, gesturing to Will.

His steps weren't hesitant, but they were measured. "Nice house," he said. He thought to wipe his filthy shoes on the mat before stepping onto the living-room carpet.

The entire household—five people—was waiting in the living room. Even Josh's father had gotten out of bed to meet the apprentice. Except for Dustine—who sat, a queen in a rocking-chair throne—they were all standing and facing the door like badgers waiting outside a snake hole. Will stiffened visibly at the sight.

"You guys having a party?" he asked.

"The Avishes live here," Josh told him. "The house is a triplex."

She made quick introductions, aware that the warmth with which everyone greeted Will confused him further. Halfway through, he tilted his head toward Josh and whispered, "What's your name again?"

Wonderful. "Josh Weaver. This is Winsor, the blonde is Deloise."

"Deloise I know," he told her as Winsor's father clapped a hand around his.

"It's good to meet you, son," Alex said brightly. He was unstoppably sociable, which was partly where Winsor's brother got it. Of course, Whim generally managed to be less tedious and irritating. "It'll be nice to have some fresh blood around the place, and no one better to learn from than Josh!"

"Yeah," Will agreed in a voice anyone but Alex would have recognized as completely baffled. Alex began to wring Will's hand like it was a stiff doorknob.

Josh took a step back to whisper to Deloise, "I have no idea what to do," while Alex started off on a speech about having a positive work ethic.

"I guess . . . What would you have done with Louis?" Deloise whispered back.

"Sat him down at the kitchen table and told him I had a surprise. It would have been melodramatic but he would have listened. Will's likely to bolt at any time." She ran a hand through her hair. "I say we go for the shock tactic. Once we're in-Dream, he'll have to listen to us."

"What if he panics and runs off? We'll never find him if the Dream shifts."

"In which case we can recruit Louis tomorrow," Josh finished, with much more bravado than she felt. "Look, Will seems like he can keep his head on straight. I'll just take him downstairs and show him the archway. If we just tell him what's going on, he's going to think we're crazy."

"I guess. . . ." Deloise repeated.

"Go grab Winsor and meet us in the archroom."

"Okay." Deloise headed for the kitchen, where Winsor had vanished with the pizzas. Josh stepped forward so that she, Alex, and Will formed a triangle. "And in the end, those long hours count," Alex was saying. "Sure, we might not see it in this lifetime, but they count."

"I'm still not sure exactly what you do," Will began, and Josh quickly cut in.

"Which is why I think we should go down to the workroom," she said. "That way I can show you."

"The workroom?" Will asked. He eyed Josh skeptically. She had assumed that his auburn hair was dyed, but his eyelashes were the same color. "Downstairs?"

"Excellent idea," Alex told them.

Will seemed to consider that for a moment, and she wasn't sure what he was going to do. Then he shrugged. "O-kay," he said, breaking the syllables. "Let's go see the workroom."

Josh led him down the hallway, past the little library full of family histories and the diaries of dream walkers long dead, and down the staircase that led to the basement where, twenty-four hours before, she and a hundred guests had celebrated her birthday and put this whole mess in motion.

The archroom was built into the farthest corner of the basement. It had two entrances, one of which was the secret passage in the upstairs kitchen pantry. That one had been built when the house was designed back in the 1920s, and the bank-vault entrance had been added when the house was renovated, doubling its size, in 1953.

Josh had to type an access code into the panel on the wall before the steel door would open. Will gave her an odd look, but he didn't say anything as the basement filled with the sounds of internal bolts drawing back. Josh opened the door and beckoned him inside.

He stared at the white floor and curved white walls with obvious alarm. Josh knew they looked like every secret FBI interrogation room ever shown on television, but what the FBI didn't have in the middle of their rooms was a seven-foot-high archway made of straw mortar and chunks of stone. The two pillars grew from the foundations of the house straight up through the bleached tile floor. In front of the archway sat a metal folding chair, and beside that, a Bible-sized slab of what appeared to be red glass rested three feet aboveground atop a steel rod.

When the door closed with a hiss of air pressure, Will stepped gingerly across the floor to look more closely at the arch. Josh didn't want to show him any nightmares until she had Winsor and Deloise to back her up (despite the fact that they hadn't been too much help up until now) so she waited by the door while he made his examination.

"So this is your . . . workshop," Will said.

"Yeah."

He circled the archway, and the room fell silent. Josh didn't know what to say. They'd gone to school together since . . . ninth grade, at least, but they'd never run in the same circles, and obviously he didn't recognize her or else he wouldn't have asked her name.

"What kind of work do you do?" he asked without looking at her.

She was trying to come up with a response when she saw his hand moving toward the flat piece of red glass that was mounted near the archway. "No!" she heard herself shout, but Will's palm had already made full contact.

At first Josh clung to the hope that he wasn't in tune enough with the Dream for anything to happen. Then she saw him shut his eyes hard.

She had been joking about hurling him into the Dream as a shock tactic. It didn't seem funny now.

"Will," Josh said firmly, *"don't move."*

His eyes opened, but he didn't appear to register her. An image flickered across the soap-bubble Veil—a little boy in pajamas cowering in his bedroom.

How did he do that? Two seconds and he's already found a nightmare?

Under other circumstances, she would have been impressed.

Meepa the Albino Koala appeared on the Veil. Josh recognized her instantly—a number of children had endured nightmares about the internationally televised Australian puppet. In this dream, Meepa was so large that she filled an entire doorway, her rounded ears brushing the ceiling. Her eyes and nose, normally a dark pink, glowed bright red, and when she opened her mouth, her lips pulled taut over curved fangs.

"Oh god," Will whispered. "There's a kid . . ."

Meepa stalked the dark hallway, rays of red light pulsating from her eyes. In one hand, she carried a Louisville Slugger.

Josh tore her eyes away from the bizarre image just in time to see Will take two steps through the archway. "No!" she shouted again, but when she tried to grab him, she felt herself pulled forward, and they both tumbled into the Dream.

They landed hard in the middle of a living room. Will swore and rolled to his knees, his head hanging down as if he might throw up. Josh was already on her feet. The living room was tidy, lacking details as dreams often did. No pictures on the walls, no knickknacks. A long red couch overlapped an end table. The television loomed over the room, several times larger than was practical. The ceiling was cathedral height and the corners faded into gray oblivion.

Josh had enough experience to know that all of this—the couch and the end table occupying the same space, the disproportionate furniture, the colors that washed away as if they had never been fully thought through—indicated that they were in a child's dream. These were often the most unstable of dreams, and the Dream was unstable to begin with.

"Get up," she said to Will. She offered him her hand and he took it, groaning.

"What happened?"

There was no time to break the news gently. "We're in the middle of a child's nightmare about being attacked by Meepa the Albino Koala."

Will turned his head quickly from side to side, looking at everything around them as if to check her theory for himself. Enough light shone for her to see him clearly, but where it came from she couldn't have said; no lamps were on and pure blackness stretched beyond the window.

"That's what I saw back there?" Will asked. "Somebody's nightmare?"

"That archway is an entrance to the Dream world we all share. When you touched it, you were able to see inside. When you walked through the archway, you entered the Dream."

"But how—" he began, and she cut him off.

"There's no time. We have to get rid of the koala."

For a split second she thought he would argue, but he said, "What do you want me to do?"

"Get behind me. Stay out of the way."

"This doesn't even look like a real house," he said as she stepped past him and into the hallway.

"It could change at any moment. Be ready for anything. Keep your eyes out for a weapon."

"Here," he said, and pulled a pocketknife out of his jeans. Josh took it and opened the larger of the two blades, glad Will hadn't tried to keep it for himself. She was betting she had more knife-fighting training than he did.

Ten feet ahead of her Meepa stood in the doorway to a bedroom and looked inside, her red eye lasers sweeping the room. She lifted the baseball bat with one paw, and her free paw dragged three claws down the wall beside the door, shredding the wallpaper. Josh faced her, holding out the knife.

This close, the nightmare swept over her. Physically, Josh felt cold inside and out. But worse was the bone-deep terror emanating from the child she knew was hiding in the bedroom. It wasn't the fear she felt at a scary movie or when Deloise snuck up behind her; it was closer to dread. She knew what was going to happen if Meepa found her. She knew that there was absolutely nothing she could do about it. The inevitability was terrible.

Behind her, Will swore again as the fear hit him. His voice shook.

Josh blinked and imagined herself surrounded by strong stone walls. Before her father had ever let her enter the Dream, he'd taught her Stellanor's First Rule of dream walking: *Never let the dreamer's fear become your own.*

If Will had given her a chance to explain all this, she would have taught him Stellanor's First Rule.

As it happened, Will managed to knock Josh down while rushing to the dreamer's rescue.

"Don't!" she shouted as she hit the floor on her knees, then her stomach. She had to let go of the knife in order to keep from stabbing herself.

Will took a few fast steps before launching himself into the air with a hysterical war cry. He landed on Meepa's back with his arms around the koala's neck.

Meepa growled deep in her round belly. She spun, trying to throw Will off, and instead saw Josh on the floor. Josh rolled onto her back just before the Slugger hit the spot where she had been lying. The hallway carpet vanished so quickly Josh couldn't even fully register the change before the baseball bat was breaking the wood beneath. The floor wasn't made up of unfinished floorboards like one would normally find beneath a carpet, but mahogany, like a polished tabletop. It shone in the sourceless light.

A child's dream. Full of misinformation.

Meepa thrashed from side to side again, and this time she succeeded in flinging Will off. Although his momentum wasn't so very great, it threw him not just against the wall but all the way through it, creating a large hole.

Oh shit, Josh thought, but then she saw Will's hand appear out of the hole, so she scrambled to her feet to create a distraction.

"Hey!" she called. "Eucalyptus breath!" The taunt was dreadfully weak, but it was enough to bring Meepa thundering toward her. Josh dug in her pocket for her lighter. Between Meepa's thick, fuzzy legs, she saw a little boy in pajamas cowering just inside the bedroom doorway.

"Stay there!" Josh called to him, and when Will climbed back into the hallway through the hole in the wall, he stumbled over to stand in front of the dreamer.

That won him a lot of points with Josh.

Meepa's growl grew louder, like a scream trapped behind her teeth. *She's not nearly as articulate in person,* Josh thought as the puppet swung at her.

Crouching to duck the bat, Josh said calmly, "Will, your knife is on the floor." As she straightened up, she flipped open the lighter and extended a flame between herself and Meepa. Polyester burned, didn't it?

Meepa halted and, without warning, the dream changed. Josh, Will, Meepa, and the child all kept their relative positions, but now they stood on a football field at the fifty-yard line. The grass was too green, like in Easter candy commercials. Stands surrounded the field, but beyond that the world faded into nothingness. The little boy was wearing a helmet and full football gear in the Packers' colors.

The kid rushed Meepa from behind. He only came to Meepa's knees, but when his bare hands made contact with the massive koala, she fell flat on her face as if punched in the back. The baseball bat vanished from her hands. Handcuffs in one chubby fist, the kid climbed on top of Meepa and started cuffing her.

"You have to remain silent and right," the boy announced.

The air warmed suddenly. Josh let her lighter go out. Will lowered the knife in his hand.

The terror was gone. The nightmare was over. Relief and peace and gratefulness cradled them with hands like clouds.

Josh and Will stared at each other, both breathing hard, as the light above them grew brighter. Will grinned like they'd done something amazing together, and Josh wanted to grin back, but they fell out of the Dream before she had a chance.

The landing wasn't so hard this time. Josh felt the cool tile through the seat of her jeans and against the fist she had made around her lighter. She'd banged her right elbow when Will knocked her down, the same elbow she'd hit in-Dream the night before, and it hurt anew.

"Are you okay?" Deloise was asking. Her voice was high-pitched, scared. "Josh, talk to me. Open your eyes."

"Yeah, yeah," Josh said. The bright track lighting coming from the ceiling was creating an angelic halo of blond hair around Deloise's face and made Josh realize she was lying on her back on the archroom floor. "I'm all right."

Deloise helped her sit up. Will was sitting on the other side of the room, leaning against the wall. Winsor was righting a chair that had somehow been knocked over.

"Are *you* all right?" Josh asked him.

He nodded. Then he shook his head, and then he laughed, and then he said, "I might have a concussion—you look like you're glowing."

"It's not your head; it's called fairy dust. Del, hand him a towel."

From a small table against one wall, Deloise retrieved two white hand towels and handed them to Josh and Will. Josh wiped the fairy dust from around her nose and mouth, and watched to make sure Will followed suit. She didn't think that now was the time to bring it up, but breathing too much Veil dust could actually drive a person insane.

Afterward, she rolled her neck and felt it pop. "What happened?" Winsor asked her.

Deloise gave Josh a hand getting to her feet. "I was trying to think of what to say when he touched the looking stone. A nightmare popped up there instantly, and before I could even figure out how he'd done it, he was already walking into the Dream."

Deloise and Winsor exchanged impressed glances, which frustrated Josh. They were missing the point. She said to Will, "You nearly got us killed."

Just like that, she destroyed the camaraderie they'd begun to develop in the Dream. Will bristled at her. "What I did was see a little kid getting attacked by a seven-foot-tall puppet and try to help." He stood up as if readying himself for a fight.

"What matters is that you got out okay," Winsor said.

"Out of the *dream*," Will told her. "Just so that *I'm* clear on what's going on here, we got out of the *dream* okay."

Winsor merely nodded. Josh could tell that the blasé fashion with which everyone was handling this frustrated him, and suddenly she was aware that this would be the first of many encounters with him. If she was going to train him, they would be seeing a lot of each other. It might not be a bad idea to extend an olive branch.

"Win's right," she said. "All that matters is that we got out in one piece. Two pieces, I mean. I realize you were trying to help the kid, I just wasn't expecting you to jump in like that or I would have warned you not to touch the looking stone."

"You mean that piece of glass on the stick?" he asked.

"Yeah. It allowed you to see into the Dream."

"How did we get out?"

"We ended the nightmare. It dissolved and dumped us back here."

"You do this frequently?"

"A dozen times a night, sometimes more."

Will ran a hand over his head, sending shaggy auburn hair rustling around his face. "And you randomly recruit high school pizza-delivery guys to help you out?"

The comparative histories of the dream walkers and the rest of the world stretched out between them, eight miles long. There was so much to tell Will before Josh even got to the scrolls; how much of it would he believe?

"This is going to take a while to explain," she warned.

"Maybe we should go upstairs," Deloise suggested. "We still have all that pizza in the kitchen."

"What time is it?" Will asked, and Winsor held out her watch for him to read. "I have to go," he said. "I'm already going to be late."

"You can call your parents," Deloise offered.

Will's expression didn't have the malice that Josh—knowing his situation—expected. "Not really—I live at the county home. They're kind of strict about curfew."

"Oh." Deloise gave him a light smile, apologizing for herself without making a big deal, and Will returned it.

"I'll walk you out," Josh told him.

They walked in silence up to the living room, where the initial spectators had been joined by at least ten local dream walkers. Josh gave Alex a slight shake of the head when he started to stand up, and opened the front door.

Despite being on the front lawn, Josh felt like they finally had a little bit of privacy. Will seemed to feel the same way. As soon as he was standing on the grass outside the circles of illumination from the porch lights, he turned to Josh and laughed.

"I don't know what I saw in there," he told her, lifting his upturned hand toward the house. "I don't know what happened. I mean . . . I *felt* that kid's fear. He was terrified, and I *felt* it."

It's the worst feeling in the world, Josh agreed silently, but she only nodded.

"You do that a dozen times a night?" he asked.

"Sometimes more. It isn't always fighting big monsters. Sometimes it's talking to somebody, or just disrupting a situation enough that the fear goes away."

"But you get to feel what I felt just before we . . . came back to this world. You get to feel that relief a dozen times a night?"

She walked down the porch steps until she was standing with him on the lawn. They were on an even level now, and their shadows stretched across the grass like sunbathers. She uncrossed her arms and stuck her hands in her pockets. "Not always," she admitted. "Sometimes the best you can do is wake a person up or help them escape, and then you don't feel it. But when you resolve a nightmare—that's what we call it—that's the feeling it gives you."

Will was looking at her again, focusing on her entirely. "Who is 'we'?" he asked.

Saying the name was like giving him her heart in three syllables. "Dream walkers."

He repeated it with respect. "Dream walkers. And you're offering me a job? As a dream walker?"

"Yeah."

He pointed out the obvious while climbing onto his scooter. "Josh, you don't even know me."

She shrugged. "It's another thing I don't have time to explain." Seeing that he was about to drive off, she added, "You know you can't tell anyone about this, right? Not even Louis."

Will grinned like the street kid she thought he had once been. "I had a feeling there would be a confidentiality clause somewhere along the way. Don't worry, I'll keep it to myself."

"Thanks."

He started the scooter's engine.

"Wait a sec," Josh said. "We should set up a time to meet."

"I've got to go," Will said, already knocking his kickstand into place. "Don't worry! I'll find you!"

Josh watched helplessly as he sped off into the night.

"I'll find you," she thought. *He probably doesn't even remember my name.*

She walked back onto the porch and watched his taillight fade. Her journal, she realized, was still sitting on the flagstones where she'd left it earlier. She picked it up and ran her thumbs over the binding as she walked back into the house. She suddenly had a lot to write about.

The crowd of locals was all waiting for her in the living room. Deloise and Winsor hovered in the kitchen doorway. Kerstel, who had been serving coffee, muted the television.

"Well?" Dustine asked as Josh shut the front door.

Josh thought of how Will had instinctively operated the looking stone, how he'd jumped through the archway without a second thought, how he had responded to the child's terror with protective compassion.

"The Force is strong with him," she said, and the room broke into cheers.

Six

Will stood at the end of the hallway. Cheap flooring glared in the light of bare bulbs, but shadows grew in every corner. Doors with small windows and narrow slots lined both walls. Above the heavy deadbolt locks were numbers written on duct tape with thick-tipped Sharpies.

Will knew where he was. He'd come here once to see his mother, when he was seven or eight. The doctor kept saying that it wasn't a good idea, but his mother's boyfriend didn't listen. They came anyway, and part of Will never left.

This was Detox.

He tried the first door on his left. It was locked tight, so tight it didn't even rattle in the doorframe. He peered through the window, through two panes of glass and a layer of crisscrossing wires in between. A hysterical blond girl thrashed inside. She tore at her paper gown, at the mattress already in shreds, at her own skin. Her mouth opened and closed and muscles in her throat clenched, but the soundproof room contained her screams. Will looked away.

His mother was in one of these rooms. She was running out of water. He knew this because she had explained it once. "They take the bad people," she'd said, "and put them in little rooms, and they don't give them anything to drink. So the people die of thirst." Then she had given Will a bottle of vodka to keep under his pillow, just in case. There was always plenty to drink around the house.

He couldn't see into the second room. Something covered the window, blood or puke. He called for his mother and beat his fists on the door but got no response.

"Your tongue swells up," his mother had told him, and then stuck out her tongue. It had turned green from all the sweet minty stuff she was drinking, which made Will laugh. His mother shook him. "Are you listening to me? They don't give you anything to drink in Detox and your tongue swells up until it fills your mouth and you can't breathe!"

The third room contained a motionless old man. He sat on the edge of his bed wearing striped boxer shorts and stared at the wall. His beard had grown until it touched the floor.

Will thought the fourth room was empty and was about to walk away when he saw a foot sticking out from under the bed. "Mom!" he shouted. He slammed his palm against the metal door, then kicked it. "Mom!"

She was probably lying beneath the bed, staring at the underside of the mattress, listening to her own breathing as it grew slower . . . slower . . . until it dissipated like an ice cube dissolving.

"Will," said a voice behind him.

He shouted and spun so quickly that he lost his balance and fell against the wall. Because he expected to see his mother, it took him a long time to recognize the girl standing at arm's length, but she waited patiently until he said, "Josh?"

"Hi," she said.

Will straightened up slowly, glancing around. "What are you doing here?"

"You're having a nightmare." She was wearing a wrinkled green sweatshirt that clung to her body as if she had been sleeping in it, a theory supported by the sleep in her eyes, the crumpled jeans, and the flip-flops. "My stepmom woke me when she recognized you."

Josh Weaver was an odd-looking girl. She was very small, and her light-brown hair had been cut short but was beginning to grow down over her ears, giving her an elfin appearance at odds with her well-muscled limbs. Her expressions were both self-conscious and responsive, as if she thought she was hiding her emotions and didn't realize how clearly they showed. And Will knew what his mother would have said about her overly pale green eyes—"They ruin her entire face"—but he rather liked them.

He shook himself and said, "I'm dreaming?"

"Yeah, but that doesn't mean the danger isn't real." She pointed to door number five. "That room is full of cobras, and the door's unlocked."

Will approached the door slowly. Through the window, he saw what must have been a dozen cobras, all longer than he was tall, their hoods flared out, their fangs dripping an acid that burned small holes in the floor where it landed.

"Whoa!" Will shouted, and jumped back. He didn't like snakes. "Where did those come from? There are never snakes in this dream!"

Josh shrugged apologetically. "If your nightmare resolves completely, the Dream will kick me out into the archroom. So I planted the idea of the cobras, and your subconscious made it real."

Will calmed a little, but not much. "That seems kind of mean," he said, half joking.

Josh smiled. "Maybe a little. But I thought you might want to talk for a minute, since we didn't have much time earlier."

"Do we have a minute now?" He glanced at Room Five again.

"Oh, at least three or four." She gazed around the hallway. "What is this place?"

"Detox. I was looking for . . . someone."

"Did you find them?"

"No."

I never do.

He didn't elaborate, even though he wanted to connect with her and earn her trust. If he did, there were things she could tell him. She could show him another world hidden inside the one where he lived.

But she probably didn't want to hear about his alcoholic mother anyway.

She hesitated before asking, "Can we sit down?" He could tell she was nervous by the way she didn't wait for an answer before sliding down to the floor and drawing her legs up to her chest, and he couldn't help thinking it strange that she seemed so self-conscious and uncertain suddenly. The night before, when she'd been fighting that giant koala, she'd seemed as swift and sure as an action hero.

He sat beside her. "So tell me about dream walking."

"Dream walking." Suddenly she smiled. Not a practiced smile—

it was a little lopsided—but sweet, and truly happy. Only when he saw her smile did he realize how sad she had looked before, how deeply sadness was etched into the set of her eyes and mouth. But for a brief instant, she looked happy.

Dream walking makes her happy. I'll have to remember that.

"All right," she began, "stop me when you get bored, or before the snakes get loose. My family has been dream walking for hundreds of generations. I know because they kept diaries, family histories. Supposedly my great-whatever grandmother, Ha'azelle, helped build the first gateway into the Dream, but who knows if it's true. There are a few other families that go back as far as mine, but not many. Everybody born to a dream-walker family learns to walk as a kid, but some people leave to go to college and get jobs and do whatever. My father doesn't walk much because he's always working."

"So you're a sort of . . . culture? Like the Amish?"

"We're a community," she said. "We share a secret, and a responsibility."

"To end nightmares? Why?"

"The Dream is made up of subconscious emotion the same way our universe is made up of energy. Not only that, but the Dream is a fundamentally unstable universe struggling to stay in balance. It's continuously spilling into our world in small ways—mostly through people dreaming, but also through hallucinations, drug trips, even daydreams. If enough emotional turmoil were to build up in it, the Veil that separates the Dream from our world could tear." Will squinted to let her know he didn't understand, and she added, "Imagine nightmares walking into the World, all the rules of physics breaking down, and clouds of Veil dust causing rampant insanity."

"Wait, back up." Somehow, even after what he'd seen the night before, Will found this hard to accept. "You're saying that if dream walkers don't keep ending nightmares, the World will end?"

"Ultimately, yeah." Josh said this with disturbing calm, but something about this question made her pause, and her smile faded. She seemed to be considering something—not just the question; he felt her considering him as well. "Are you sure you want to know all this? Because you're actually under no obligation to become a dream walker."

He had thought about the situation as he rode from her house to the county home. He thought about how everything had changed when he left his mother to live with the state, and how everything would change again if he accepted this mysterious job offer.

And he thought about the fact that he really had nothing to lose. "I'm in," he said. "I might as well help save the World, right?"

"No, Will." Josh shook her head, clearly frustrated. The lines around her eyes that had vanished returned. "Look, forget about saving the World. People *die* dream walking, a lot of people. It's dangerous. It's scary. The things inside people's heads are ugly and they're hard to look at, and sometimes when you come out of that archway you feel dirty. And being a dream walker is—you'd be part of a whole other world, with rules and traditions and politics. *Lots* of politics. Some of the people in it aren't very nice." Her voice softened. "Even the nice ones are still just people."

Josh ducked her head, her expression becoming self-conscious again, and finished, "I just don't want you to think that your life will be better than it is now if you become a dream walker." Her green eyes, pale as seawater trapped in cupped hands, met his as if for emphasis. "Sometimes it's better not to know how the Universe works."

He wondered what had happened to make her contemplate such an idea. Despite his dad bailing and his mom drinking anything in liquid form, he'd never stopped being curious or wanting to investigate the world around him. On the contrary, he'd developed an insatiable desire to understand people and how they worked inside.

"Would you be the one teaching me?" he asked, and she nodded.

He was sitting in a dream with her, awake and aware in this phantasmagorical landscape where he had spent so many agonizing nights. She had walked in and with her mere presence ended the terror. He knew there would be danger, that he was putting his life in her hands. He didn't know what to make of this community she had spoken of, and he didn't really understand what knowing "how the Universe works" might mean.

But she was the first one to ever offer him an unlocked door in this hallway, in the endless hallway that his life seemed to be. She was the first to give him an out. And he knew that if he didn't take her offer, the mystery would haunt him for the rest of his life.

"Yes," he said.

Josh didn't look happy. He wasn't even sure he saw surprise in her face. She just nodded and said, "All right then. You're officially my apprentice."

They were both quiet for a moment, which was why Will was able to hear the sizzling behind him. He turned his head and saw that the cobra venom had melted the flooring under the door to Room Five, and the snakes were close to escaping. One had gotten far enough that he could see its tongue tasting the hallway air.

He and Josh jumped up at the same moment. "Talk's over," Josh said. She pulled a Zippo lighter and a compact out of her pocket. "Can you open that door?" she asked, gesturing to Room Six.

"It's locked," Will told her, but tried anyway. The knob turned easily in his hand, revealing an empty patient room.

Josh flipped the compact open, flicked the Zippo, and reflected the flame off the mirror and into the doorway. A shimmering film appeared.

"That's the Veil," she said. "Step through and you'll wake up. This is what we do with people when we can't resolve a nightmare. We end it."

Will paused before going through. Some gesture of appreciation was in order, some indication that he was glad to be part of this. Or that he at least thought he might not regret it later. But in the end he knew that the time wasn't right and that someday, when they could talk more easily to each other, he'd tell her.

So he just said, "You want to meet at school on Monday?"

One of the cobras shot out from under the door. "Don't worry—I'll find you," Josh said, grabbing Will and pulling him through the Veil.

He grinned, and then he fell and fell and landed on his back in bed.

Seven

The idea of Will as Josh's apprentice changed from distant fear to inevitable reality Monday afternoon when he rode home with her from school.

"You're too nervous," Deloise whispered to Josh as they climbed out of the car.

"I don't know what to say."

Josh had never felt so pressured. Everyone in the dream-walker community knew by now that she had an apprentice—they'd been calling all weekend like she'd just had a baby. Granted, it wasn't every day that an apprentice joined the dream-walker community, but did Josh's grandfather really need daily updates on Will's training?

As awkward as this was for her, it was probably worse for Will, although he was playing it pretty cool so far.

"It's not a date," Deloise whispered to her as they entered the house through the back door. "Just show him around. Explain how the Dream works."

"I've spent seventeen years trying to figure that out myself."

"Then you should have plenty to fill an afternoon with," Winsor remarked with a snort.

Kerstel was in the kitchen reading from her laptop and listening to Vivaldi. "Hey," she said as the kids walked in. She leaned over to turn down the music. "Nice to see you again, Will."

"Thank you," Will said politely.

Winsor went to the living room to do homework. Deloise immediately got a phone call and wandered up to her room.

Josh and Will stood awkwardly and stared at each other.

"So, um," Josh said, "I guess I'll show you around."

"Okay," Will said.

She led him through the first floor—the office/guest room, the library, Kerstel's office, and Dustine's bedroom, where she knocked lightly on the oak door.

"Come in!"

Dustine was sitting in a plastic deck chair next to the window with the television on. Josh saw her tucking a cardboard folder covered in tinfoil behind the dresser. "Getting your sun, Grandma?"

"Watch it." Dustine cackled. "I've got to keep up my color during the winter somehow." Her eyes were sharp as she looked Will over. "I take it you've agreed to apprentice. You're very, very lucky to have Josh as a teacher. I've lived eighty-seven years and never seen a more talented dream walker. Just the same, you have a long road ahead of you. *If* you make it."

Will stiffened and Josh felt the need to say, "Take it easy, Gran. He'll be fine."

"He could be the True Dream Walker himself and he wouldn't be good enough for you."

"All right, we just wanted to say hi," Josh said, deciding to let Will and Dustine get to know each other some other time. "We'd better get back to work."

Dustine nodded. "If you look in the top drawer of my dresser, I dug something out of the attic for you."

Josh glanced at her, but Dustine didn't give anything away. Inside the drawer, Josh found a bundle of cloth. "That's it," Dustine said. "Lasia used this wall quilt back when I was an apprentice. Give it to Will; he can study it. There's more there than meets the eye."

Josh touched the quilt with care. The fabric felt old and fragile, the stitches loosened by time. "Are you sure you want to give this away?"

Dustine shrugged. "I can see every detail in my mind. Go on and take it."

"Thank you," Will said as Josh handed him the quilt. "I'll take good care of it."

Dustine nodded, her eyes still on him. "You follow that quilt, and you'll do fine."

They slipped out before she could change her mind and decide that Will was hopeless. "That went well," he said as they walked up the stairwell.

"No, you did great. I should have warned you that she's kind of a grouch." They passed a landing with two doors. "So this," Josh said, "is the second floor." She touched one door. "The Avishes live in this apartment. That's Winsor and her parents. Winsor has an older brother, but he's been traveling the world since last summer, so it's just the three of them now."

"Is he planning to come back and dream walk again?"

"He didn't say. But probably. Why?" She glanced back at Will.

"Am I a replacement for him?"

She hadn't realized that Will didn't understand the finality of his role. Maybe she should have waited before introducing him to her grandmother. "No," she said. "Your apprenticeship has nothing to do with Whim."

He grinned. "Whim?"

"It's a nickname."

"For what?"

"Whimarian Travarres Nikolaas Avishara."

"Whoa," Will said. "Is that some kind of joke?"

Now it was Josh's turn to be amused. "No. Kids around here get a first name of their own, a second name after a mother's relative, a third name after a role model, and their father's last name." It took her a moment to figure out what she wanted to explain to him about the custom. "Knowing someone's full name is a gesture of respect," she told him. "Not that you'd ever call Whim by all that, but if you have to ask a person what their full name is, you probably don't know them that well. Out in the world, nearly all dream walkers shorten their names. It's not that weird—you do the same thing."

"Actually," Will said behind her, "Will Kansas *is* my full name."

"It's not William or Wilson or Wilfredo?"

"Nope. Just Will."

"Well." There were twenty-seven letters in her name and ten in his. She became very aware again that he was a stranger.

Much to Josh's relief, Will's thoughts didn't appear to have taken the same route as hers. "So if I'm not a replacement for Whim, why did you suddenly decide to get an apprentice?"

"Long story short, each dream-walker kid gets a prophecy written at their birth, and mine said I would have an apprentice who showed up exactly when you did."

After staring at her with the stunned expression of a dead fish, Will sputtered, "But I was just delivering a pizza. I wasn't even supposed to be there—Louis was."

"And Louis wouldn't have been there if Deloise hadn't ordered pizza. I thought it was Louis, so she went ahead and arranged for him to show up at the house at the right time . . ."

"And I showed up instead," Will finished. "I'm not supposed to be here."

Josh felt guilty. She'd gotten him into this; she didn't want him to feel unwelcome. "My father keeps telling me that fate doesn't make mistakes. Maybe Deloise and the pizza and you delivering for Louis was what was meant to happen all along."

Will leaned against the wall and rubbed the back of his neck. "I'm sorry, this is freaking me out a little."

"Sorry," Josh said, wishing she could reassure him, wishing she could reassure herself. Still rubbing his neck, Will looked at her from under his bangs. His blue eyes were wide with anxiety, but he smiled a forced smile. "It's okay. Did you want to show me your apartment?"

"Oh, yeah." Josh started up the stairs, but Will stopped her.

"Wait," he said, gesturing to the second door on the landing. "Where does this lead?"

She had been hoping he wouldn't ask. "There's another apartment here. But it's empty."

He didn't push. *He doesn't know there's anything to find,* she reminded herself. She wondered what would happen when he found out about Ian and Haley, and how long she was allowed to not mention them before it was actually keeping a secret.

After touring the Weavers' third-floor apartment, they went downstairs to the library, put the quilt Dustine had given them on the table, and unrolled it ever so carefully. Every stitch felt as breakable as the threads of a spider's web.

Josh opened the final fold and sucked in a deep breath. Will came around the table to see the quilt right side up, and they stood next to each other in total silence for more than a minute, staring.

"Someone spent months on this," Will said.

"More like years. This is . . . I can't believe I've never seen this."

The quilt was approximately three by four feet. It depicted three circles overlapping, each connected to the other by an archway. In the empty spaces of the corners, the quilt showed the contents of each world. The World: tiny women having tea; lions prowling between high grasses; a glittering fire built inside the smooth, curving walls of an igloo. The Dream: uniformed rats performing ballet; people running upside down as they fled from a manticore; machete-wielding clowns with painted mouths full of sharp metal teeth. Death: faceless human forms made of luminous golden silk who towered over the ash-colored people filing into their world. Every fabric type imaginable had been used, and each fingernail-sized bit of colored cloth looked like the stroke of a paintbrush.

Josh explained what each circle represented. Will, using a touch suitable for stroking a newborn baby's face, ran his fingertips reverently over the triangle where all three circles overlapped and said, "What's this black part?"

"Nothing. The diagram sort of fails here, because there is no place where all three worlds overlap." In examining the triangle, however, Josh realized that the fabric wasn't black but the darkest peacock green, and she understood what the quilt maker had been trying to show her. "I take that back—there are myths that a place where all three worlds overlap used to exist, and dream theorists think it could possibly exist, but no one's proven it."

She shook her head, amazed that the person who had made the quilt had thought to include a theoretical universe, and amazed by the care and complexity that had gone into the quilt's creation. Her grandmother had been right; the quilt was a beautiful teaching tool. Why hadn't Dustine ever showed it to Josh before? As far as

Josh knew, none of the other dream walkers who had been trained in this house had seen it either.

And why would Dustine suddenly share it now?

Setting the thought aside, Josh pulled a blank sheet of paper out of her backpack and drew a Venn diagram of the three universes, explaining as she went. "We can cross from one universe to another if we know how. Sometimes the boundaries are broken, sometimes the worlds spill into each other. Some of the boundaries are broken on purpose when we build archways." Between the World and the Dream, she drew arrows pointing both ways, but arrows only pointed into Death, never out of it. Will asked about them.

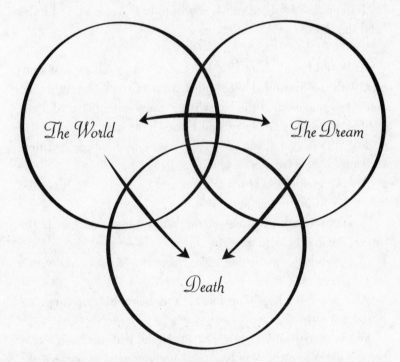

"You can only go into Death. You can't come back out."

"So you couldn't go into Death and bring someone back?"

"You can't . . ." She started and had to stop and swallow. Her chest began to ache. "You can't cross into Death without dying. Nobody comes back."

He doesn't know, Josh, she told herself. *Let it go—he doesn't know anything.*

Will simply nodded, and Josh knew for certain then that his question had been innocent, but that wound was already open, that Ian wound right in the center of her chest that bled with every heartbeat.

Her fingers walked across the quilt, tracing the passage from the World to Death.

Nobody comes back.

Josh reached for the quilt and began folding it, forcing the memories down. So her chest hurt. So what?

"I asked around about you at school today," Will said, and Josh's head shot up.

"You—?"

"Yeah. I'd heard about that house fire out in Charle last summer, with the fireworks, but I didn't connect you to it until today. Somebody told me that the guy who died was your boyfriend. I just wanted to say that I'm sorry, and I know that you're probably still dealing with it, and if, you know, you ever want to talk or anything, I'm a pretty good listener."

His expression was absolutely sincere, even when Josh blurted out, "I don't want to talk about it."

"I'm not trying to pressure you to," Will assured her. "Just, in the future, if you ever need to—"

"No," Josh said, panicking. "*No.* I thought you said you were a good listener."

Will raised his hands up like he was being held at gunpoint. "Okay. I'm sorry."

Josh couldn't think clearly. She knew she had just been bitchy but she didn't know how to backtrack without weakening what she felt was a desperately important message: *I don't want to talk about Ian—not today, not tomorrow, not ever.*

"It's all right," she said. She lifted her palms from the quilt and then allowed her fingertips to rest there again. "I think that's enough for today. Kerstel will give you a ride home."

She turned and headed for the basement before she had to watch Will's face fall.

Through a Veil Darkly

More weird news. Not only are people going into comas for no reason at all while they sleep, now people are worried about a new pair of villains roaming the Dream. One's really tall and sort of thin and the other's wider and shorter, but they both wear giant dark green trench coats and carry silver canisters on their backs. Some people say they're wearing gas masks, but others say they use the masks to suffocate dreamers. ("Just like the facehugger in *Alien*!" one girl said.)

If you've seen them, send me an e-mail about it with the subject "TCM." (That's Trench-Coat Men, in case you haven't had your coffee yet today.) Maybe we can figure out what book or movie our new friends are from.

Eight

The first afternoon Will spent at Josh's house, he figured the chances that he'd still be working with her a month later were around 2 percent.

Four days later, he'd increased the chances to 25 percent.

Josh didn't like the emotional stuff. She didn't want to talk about her feelings or her family or her past—definitely not her past. She didn't want to know why Will lived with the county (Mom drank,

Dad just didn't care) or if he was single (he'd broken up with his last girlfriend because she was obsessed with cross-country) or what he was into (he lived and breathed self-help books).

What Josh did like was dream walking and anything to do with it. When she talked about her work, she spoke easily. She explained concepts clearly. She was patient. She even gave examples from her own experience, which were as close to sharing personal stories as she ever came.

And she was *good*. From the moment she began instructing him, Will didn't doubt that she knew what she was talking about. Not just the ass-kicking stuff—although he was pretty sure she could name every bone and muscle in the body and apparently she was a black belt in three different forms of martial arts—but how to make decisions while in the Dream. She knew why she did what she did.

"There are only three ways to deal with a nightmare," she told him, the day after she showed him the quilt. "One: Resolve it. Two: Convince the dreamer that they're dreaming. Three: Bail."

"Bail?" Will had repeated. He was sitting on a trunk in the basement where the training equipment was stored. Josh was pacing in front of a dry-erase board that he and Josh had purchased and hung on the wall right after school.

"If the odds are stacked against you, get out of there. A certain amount of risk is inevitable, but don't take stupid chances and don't stick around if you can't resolve things. Remember Burkov's Tenet: *A dream walker's life is worth as many resolved dreams as seven to the seventh power.*"

"What does that actually mean?" Will asked.

"It means don't get killed."

She knew a seemingly inexhaustible store of sayings, all attributed to famous dream walkers of the glorious past. Will had been relieved to learn that Deloise and Winsor found this as irritating as he did.

"We work in quantity," Josh added.

"Back up," Will said. "Quantity?"

"Right, sorry, I jumped ahead there." She ran a hand through her hair. She had very little ego about the work she did or how she did it, which fascinated Will. "Where's my trimidion?"

She went to a wicker basket that held an assortment of odds and ends, and returned with a small pyramid made of bars like golden toothpicks in one hand, and a little round base with another, longer gold toothpick coming out of it in the other. After setting these on the trunk next to Will, she pulled the diagram of the three universes out of the piles of notes they were generating.

She started to speak and then paused, and the pause turned into a stilted question. "Are you religious?"

Since Josh didn't like to get personal, the question surprised Will. He did his best to answer it honestly. "I was raised Catholic, but I haven't been to church since I was like eight."

"But you probably believe in souls, right?"

He shrugged. "I guess I do believe people are more than just flesh and blood."

"All right. So when people fall asleep in the World, some part of them travels from the World to the Dream. You can think of it as a soul or a spirit or consciousness or whatever you want, just realize that it's people leaving the World and entering the Dream."

She pointed to the arrow on the diagram that showed this. Will felt himself frown without meaning to. He hadn't realized he'd still been thinking of dreams as something that took place inside people's heads; that was what all those psychology books he'd read told him, after all. That was what *science* told him.

"So at any given time, there are about half a billion people on the planet dreaming," Josh said. "The trimidion is basically a scale with three sides instead of two. Each corner represents one of the universes. They measure emotional turmoil, and we need to keep them roughly in balance. Now, the World is much more stable than the Dream. It destabilizes over decades, not hours like the Dream. Death always remains in perfect balance."

"So wouldn't the Dream throw everything completely out of whack, since it's full of nightmares?"

"Absolutely. Nobody's been able to measure how many dreams

are actually nightmares, but some psychologists think it might be as many as three-quarters. Dream theorists think it's much lower, closer to one-quarter. Regardless, that's a lot of emotional turmoil to mess with the balance."

Her whole job, Will reflected, as Josh continued talking, *is about keeping emotions from spilling over. That's got to mess her up.*

It explained a lot.

"Is that why you only try to resolve nightmares? Because they're the only ones that mess up the balance?"

"Um, yeah. Basically. Happy dreams can have the opposite effect and stabilize the Dream. Happy dreams do our job for us. But there's a lot of controversy over what sorts of dreams we should interfere with, if we should just try to end out-and-out nightmares or if we should get involved in any old unhappy dream. You should talk to Winsor if you're interested in that. She likes to resolve humiliation dreams. You know—you show up for class late, without your homework or your pants?"

Will nodded. That told him a *lot* about Winsor.

"But the long and the short of it is that we just don't have the manpower to deal with all the nightmares in the world, let alone go after embarrassment dreams and forgotten-homework dreams and running-late dreams."

"Why not recruit more people?"

"We can, but at some point we're going to have trouble maintaining secrecy."

This was something Will had been curious about. "Yeah, why the secrecy? Why not just come out and tell the World what you're doing? I mean, you're helping people. I know it would be crazy for a while, but in the long run everybody would probably be better off."

Josh thought for a minute. She ran her hand through her short hair, which was something Will had noticed she did when she was thinking. "This is complicated," she said. "We can't come out to the World because we have to protect the Dream from people who would want to manipulate it and use it for their own ends."

Whoa, Will thought.

"But that's a different conversation," Josh said before picking up where she'd left off. "Nightmares cause emotional turmoil in the Dream, which throws it out of balance with the World and Death. We monitor the balance between universes with this little thingy, which we call the trimidion."

She assembled the golden thingy. The pyramid balanced on a stand that stuck straight out of a flat base. Looking closely, Will made out tiny markings on the corners: an empty circle, a solid circle, and a spiral.

"What are those?" he asked.

"Labels, basically. The empty circle is the World. The solid circle is Death. The spiral is the Dream. When one of the universes is out of balance, that corner of the pyramid will hang closer to the stand."

The pyramid was, in fact, tilted so that the Dream's corner hung lower than the other two. "That's wild," Will said. "This thing definitively doesn't work on gravity."

"Um, no, it doesn't. Each dream walker has one. It tells us how close we are to keeping the Dream in balance on a local level. If it's hanging way too far, we all work extra shifts. If it's about level, we can take a few nights off."

Will straightened up from examining the trimidion. "But why is Death always in perfect balance?"

He realized too late that he probably shouldn't have brought up death, that it was one of the topics Josh didn't like to discuss, so he was surprised when she smiled enigmatically. "Nobody knows," Josh said. "It's a dream-theory mystery."

"Do you like mysteries?" he couldn't resist asking, suspecting she didn't.

"No," she said. "But I do like solving them."

After more than a week of learning dream theory and basic hand-to-hand combat techniques, Will went into his second nightmare with Josh.

Will watched as Josh touched the looking stone in the archroom.

Instantly, a vaporous image of a man with a bomb strapped to his chest appeared in the empty archway. Josh frowned at it, and another image took its place. She jumped from one dream to another as quickly as if she were changing TV stations with a remote.

"When can I learn how to use the looking stone?" Will asked, and she glanced at him.

"You didn't need any lessons last week."

"You just put your hand on the stone? There isn't any more to it?"

"There is for most people. But you must have some sort of knack for it. Believe me, if I'd known, I never would have let you near it." She frowned, then lifted her hand from the looking stone. "There is one thing we should discuss before we go in, one of those mysteries of dream theory: Chyman's Dilemma."

"Chyman's Dilemma," Will repeated, trying to commit the name to memory. "Okay. What's that?"

"When we go through the archway into the Dream, the archway sort of . . . keeps track of us. It's called *ligamus*. If we were in-Dream and Deloise walked into the archroom, she'd be able to see us in the Veil, and she'd be able to jump in and help. When we resolve a nightmare, we always come out the same archway we went into because of *ligamus*. But sometimes we don't manage to resolve a nightmare, and it ends on its own because the dreamer wakes up or starts having a different dream or whatever. In that case, the Dream shifts and dumps us in some other nightmare."

"You can't just open an exit before the Dream shifts?" Will asked. He didn't like the idea of being randomly dumped into a nightmare.

"There's almost never enough warning. If the Dream shifts with you in it, *ligamus* no longer applies. The Veil vanishes and the archway can't track you any longer."

"Why not?"

"Nobody knows. It's another dream-theory mystery, and it happens pretty frequently. Chyman's Dilemma is sort of the common cold of dream theory." She put her hand back on the looking stone, and after an instant, a nightmare popped up. "If we trigger Chyman's

Dilemma, resolving a nightmare will no longer cue the Dream to release us. We have to open an exit in order to leave. That's why you never, *ever* go into the Dream without your lighter and compact. Once you trigger Chyman's Dilemma, they're your only way out."

"What happens if you forget them and trigger Chyman's Dilemma?" Will asked.

From the guilty look on her face, Will understood that Josh had been hoping he wouldn't ask that question. "Then the only way to get out of the Dream is to find another dream walker who can open an exit for you. But the Dream is vast. The chances of finding another dream walker are very small."

"So if you get lost in the Dream . . . you die?"

Josh nodded and glanced away. "You die in a nightmare you're too tired to fight."

That is not good news, Will thought. He decided that remembering to take keys into the Dream was now the single most important thing in his life.

"Anyway," Josh said, obviously eager to change the subject, "if you do trigger Chyman's Dilemma and then open an exit, there's a small chance that the exit will lead to an archway other than this one, because *ligamus* no longer applies. But that pretty much only happens in cases of multiple shifts, and there's sort of an unspoken rule of hospitality regarding lost dream walkers who come out of the wrong archway."

Will could just imagine the look on the face of a Pakistani dream walker if Will and Josh suddenly walked out of his archway. But he supposed it had happened before.

Josh was staring through the archway at a nightmare in which an old man tried to crawl from his burning home. "By the way," she said, her voice strained, "what are you afraid of?"

Will blinked and wondered if he'd heard her right. "What?"

She fiddled with the pendant she wore, clearly uncomfortable discussing something so personal. "I was talking to my grandma last night, and she pointed out that it probably wouldn't be a good idea to go rushing into any nightmares full of things you fear. We should stick to things that don't freak you out too much, at least to start. So I thought I'd ask what you're afraid of."

Will compiled a list in his head: *Loneliness. Guilt. Being where I'm not wanted.*

Aloud, he said, "Drowning. You?"

"Birds," she replied immediately.

They didn't look at each other.

After a long silence, Josh asked, "How do you feel about mobs?"

"Fine. Great. I love mobs."

"Let's try this one, then."

Through the archway, Will saw a middle-aged woman running through a house. In each room, faces were pressed up against her windows; people were beating on the glass and screaming. The woman raced from one window to the next pulling curtains and blinds, but each opened up again as soon as she left the room.

Lots of doors, Will thought, trying to remember what Josh had taught him. *Plenty of easy exits.*

"Here's the plan," Josh said, speaking quickly. With one hand she touched her pocket to make sure she had her lighter and compact; Will doubted she was aware that she did it. "The dreamer's afraid of the mob getting into the house. We can't fight a whole mob, so we have to convince her that those people aren't a threat. I'm going to reassure her that the house is sturdy and will protect her, and if she believes me, the nightmare should resolve. Got it?"

"Got it. What do I do?"

"Observe. And try not to get killed."

Nice to feel needed, Will thought, but in truth he was relieved.

They jumped through the archway. Josh had explained that they could step through, but they'd just end up falling. If they jumped, they were more likely to land on their feet.

Josh pulled it off. Will landed on a coffee table, stumbled, and fell onto an overstuffed red couch. The dreamer, who was struggling with a Venetian blind, stopped muttering to herself and stared at them both.

"We're here to help," Josh said.

Will scrambled up from the couch. He looked around the living room, at all the faces pressed against the windows, and wondered how much pressure the glass could withstand before it would shatter. In his mind, he saw the glass bursting and the faces streaked with blood, and there wouldn't even be anyone who could help him. . . .

"The house is very strong," Josh continued. "There's no way those people can get inside. The doors have lots of locks and the windows are made of bulletproof glass. You're safe inside the house. They can't come in."

Suddenly, Will realized what was happening. He'd let the dreamer's fear take him over, just like he had in the Meepa nightmare.

You're safe in your egg, he told himself, practicing what Josh had taught him. *You are surrounded by the strong walls of your egg, and nothing can hurt you.*

He imagined the egg around him, not made of eggshell but of an iridescent energy force field that would incinerate anything that tried to pass through it. The fear passed.

The dreamer listened to Josh's reassurances, stared at her for a moment, and then gave a hopeless cry and ran into the next room.

Josh and Will looked at each other. "Well," she said. "That didn't work at all."

"What now?"

"Follow her. Improvise. But if that mob gets in, we need to abort immediately."

They found the woman in the kitchen, where the bright sunlight outside was obscured by dozens of faces pressed up against the window above the sink and the sliding-glass door. The sight of the door disturbed Will; faces were pressed against it even at floor level, as if people were lying on top of each other outside with only their heads touching the glass. The woman was muttering again: "Listening, like they can't hear anything . . ."

Josh quickly dragged a curtain over the door, darkening the room. "We're here to help," she said again.

The dreamer gave her a look that implied Josh was being ridiculous and then ran to the next room. As they followed her, Will glanced over his shoulder and saw the kitchen growing light again as the curtain over the sliding-glass door drew itself back.

They ran into a bedroom. "We can push this against the window," Josh said, pointing to a wardrobe. "It will work much better than the curtains."

"What's wrong with you?" the woman cried. To herself, she whispered, "Here I'm doing everything I can—they're all walking around like it's St. Patrick's Day—the bloody curtains won't stay shut—"

She ran back into the hallway. The bedroom curtains swished open as if by magic. Faces were pressed so hard against the glass that they were flattened and misshapen.

"This isn't working either," Josh said.

"I noticed," Will said. "What do you want to do?"

"I don't know. I need to think. . . ."

The woman ran past the bedroom door and they followed her into a parlor full of cream-colored furniture and dried roses in porcelain vases. All the available surfaces were decorated with tiny glass animals and seashells.

Josh sat down on the sofa and thought. Will didn't know how she could ignore the woman, or the flattened, slobbering faces crammed against the windows—they were starting to creep him out—or how she could be so calm just *knowing* that she was inside a nightmare. She might have been sitting on the couch in her own living room.

Will felt useless. If Josh didn't know what to do, he certainly didn't.

"If he tells me to calm down one more time—so help me God— all I'm asking is that he listen for ten minutes—look at that curtain rod, it will never hold—"

The woman was trying to move all the little glass unicorns and baby deer off the windowsill so she could pull the curtains without sending all her tchotchkes to the floor. Josh tried to help and the woman chucked a glass sea lion at her.

It hit Josh in the face. "Ouch!"

Will knew he couldn't help. He couldn't convince the woman that she was safe.

But he could listen.

Will was a good listener. He'd been reading self-help books since he was twelve years old—they had a lot to say about listening. He knew how to be patient and quiet and mirror what someone said to him.

He listened to the dreamer.

"So help me God—I've told them all a hundred times—"

"You've told them all a hundred times," he repeated.

The dreamer stopped moving glass animals to stare at him.

"All you're asking is that he listen for ten minutes," Will said. "That curtain rod is never going to hold. They're all walking around like it's bloody St. Patrick's Day."

"They keep telling me to calm down," she said.

"You shouldn't calm down," he said, and he saw that this was working, that she was focused on him instead of the mob. "This is no time to be calm!"

"Exactly!" she cried. "There is good reason to be upset!"

"Plenty of reasons!"

She waved her arms around, accidentally tossing glass animals in all directions. Josh ducked. "I have every right to be hysterical!"

"Damn right you do!"

"So help me God—"

And suddenly, in a cloud of warm relief and gratitude and a sense of having been heard, Josh and Will rolled out of the Dream and back into the archroom. Josh landed sitting down, Will on all fours.

Wait a second, Will thought. *I was just getting going.*

Josh was grinning at him, and she looked a little amazed as well. Her smile, covered in glittering fairy dust, appeared almost magical.

"That was . . ." she said. "I don't know how you did that. I don't even know *what* you did."

He tried not to be smug. "It's called active listening."

"Active listening," she repeated.

He nodded. "Yeah. We thought the nightmare was that she was afraid the mob would get into the house, but what she was afraid of was that no one would acknowledge that she had a good reason to be upset."

"That's a weird nightmare." Josh stood up. She was still smiling, and Will knew he'd earned a point in her mind. Maybe a couple of points. "That was good, Will."

She offered him a hand up. He accepted.

"It would have taken me at least two more minutes to figure that out," she added.

Nine

"So, listen, about this adoption thing . . ." Will said as he and Josh made their way down a poorly marked path through the woods.

Josh felt herself tense up at his words. "It's traditional for apprentices to join dream-walker families. Lots of apprentices don't have families, actually, so adoption is pretty common."

The tradition of apprenticeship among dream walkers had originated in a legend about the True Dream Walker. Supposedly he had once taken in a band of orphans called the Wussuri and turned them into ultimate nightmare-fighting champs. Josh knew she should have anticipated that her father and Kerstel would formally adopt Will, but somehow it had taken her as much by surprise as it had him.

"Yeah . . ." Will said. "I just don't want to be a burden."

Josh glanced over her shoulder at him. "It's not a burden; it's tradition." She felt like she should say something else, but all she could think to ask was, "Would you rather stay in the county home?"

"No, of course not. But I . . . If it's cool with you, then that's great."

She didn't look back this time. "It's cool with me," she said, which was a complete lie. It actually made her stomach knot up like a friendship bracelet. "We can increase your training schedule."

Above, the tree branches that twisted together like anxious fingers began to thin as they approached a clearing.

"Ah, is that what I think it is?" Will asked.

Ahead of them stood a cathedral made of gingerbread, complete with stained-glass windows of intricately cut hard candies, spice-drop bricks laid with frosting mortar, and candy-cane flying buttresses.

"If you think it's a church for the worshipers of Little Debbie, then you're probably right," Josh said. The graham-cracker pavement that led to the church door crunched beneath their steps.

She pushed open one of the massive licorice doors and her hand came away sticky.

Inside, she found chocolate-bar pews, a pulpit of cookies, and floral displays made from Twizzlers and Laffy Taffy. Even the air was sweet, and every step she took released another odor, because the floor was a beautiful mosaic made from jelly beans.

"I think I'm gonna throw up," she told Will.

"Really? 'Cause it seems like you eat a lot of sugar." She gave him an indignant look. "No offense. But you ate a king-sized Snickers right before we entered this nightmare, and you drank that giant root beer on the way home."

Josh knew this was an argument she would lose, but the idea that Will had observed her eating habits so closely freaked her out. "This place is still too much," she said.

She spotted the dreamer: a goth teenager kneeling on a root-beer barrel at the front of the church. As they walked toward her, Will broke a peanut-brittle armrest off a pew and started eating it. Josh glared at him and he offered her a piece.

The dreamer was mumbling prayers as they approached. Josh tried to make a lot of noise as she walked up—she smashed a lot of jelly beans—but the girl's eyes remained fervently closed.

"Hi," Josh said, kneeling beside her. No response. She touched the girl's shoulder.

"Ahhh!"

The dreamer, who was wearing a black skirt and low-cut top,

threw herself away from Josh while sending out a stupendous wave of fear. Josh had been so distracted by the candy that she had been forgetting to shield, and now she had to throw all her energy into protecting herself.

I'm safe behind my wall. No one can get to me here. There is no fear behind the wall.

Just as her nerves were settling, the girl screamed again, and Josh opened her eyes to see her pointing at Will. "You've eaten from the sacred house! Blasphemy, blasphemy! She will kill us all!"

"Oh," Will said. He carefully put down the armrest he'd been eating. "Whoops."

Josh gave Will a look.

"Who's going to kill us?" Josh asked the dreamer.

"The witch!"

"Oh, right, there's a witch in the story with the candy house. But she needs an oven to cook us in, right? So let's go destroy her oven before she gets here."

The girl shook her head. "She isn't going to cook us. She's going to turn us into candy!"

Then she pointed, and Josh noticed something she hadn't noticed before, or perhaps saw something that hadn't been there before. That strange sculpture at the front of the church—didn't it look a lot like someone trying to escape being sucked into a bubble-gum bog? And the huge gummy bear in the corner—wasn't his face strangely human? And the two chocolate soldiers wrapped in tinfoil who stood guard at the door—why did they look like they were screaming in terror?

"Crap," Josh said.

"We have to hide," the dreamer said. She ran out a side door, flinging it open so hard that some of the SweeTARTS decorations were knocked loose, and Josh and Will followed her into a small graveyard with white chocolate headstones. Between two rows, a casket made of chocolate peppermint bark and lined with marshmallows lay open.

"Get in!" the girl cried.

Will looked at Josh. "Is this a good idea?"

I do not want to get in that coffin with Will, Josh thought. "Look, you get in the coffin," she told the girl. "We're going to go hide somewhere else."

"No, you have to protect me! Please!"

Josh gritted her teeth. This was obviously the direction the nightmare wanted to go, and she knew there was no use in fighting. Reluctantly, she said, "All right, fine."

"You first," the girl told Will. He climbed in, then the girl instructed Josh to squeeze in on her side next to him. The only way this worked at all comfortably was if he put his arm around her and she rested her head on his chest.

Josh thought she was going to pull a muscle she was so tense. She was starting to get used to touching Will when she needed to correct his aim or show him how to move, but she wasn't ready to snuggle with him.

Then the girl climbed in, facedown, on top of him, and pulled the coffin shut.

Josh felt terribly self-conscious, aware of her thighs pressed against Will's, her breasts smashed against the side of his torso, his heartbeat beneath her ear. She kept finding excuses to lift her head up from his chest, and each time she did she felt awkward setting it down again.

"What's wrong?" he said.

"I thought I heard something," she lied.

She hadn't lain like this with anyone since Ian died, and the guilt was mixed with a confusing sense of contentment. She had to force her head down to Will's chest. But as the minutes passed, she began to relax, at least enough to close her eyes. The marshmallows beneath her were soft, softer than her own bed, and the rise and fall of Will's chest as he breathed created a soothing rhythm.

Will turned his face toward her, and she felt him inhale just a bit more deeply than he had before, his chest expanding a centimeter farther. *Did he just smell my hair?* she wondered, but before she could ponder the thought, she heard his heartbeat quicken directly beneath her ear.

This can't happen, she thought.

"I have to get out of here," she said, at the same time Will said, "Ah, miss?"

His tone of voice had gone from drowsy to alarmed. "I realize you're very anxious right now, and that we're in a very tight space, but in spite of that, I need you to observe certain personal boundaries."

What the hell does that mean? Josh thought, forgetting her own discomfort.

"My name is Sorsha, and personal space is just so . . ."

"Oh god!" Will cried.

"*Personal,*" Sorsha said.

"She just licked my neck, Josh. She's licking my neck, she's got her hands inside my shirt—OW! No biting!"

Josh had heard enough. She gave the coffin lid a hard kick.

It did not open.

"Well, that's just skippy," she muttered. She reached into the darkness and found Sorsha's gel-slicked ponytail. Then she jerked it, hard, until Sorsha's head snapped back and the girl squealed.

"Let go of my hair!" Sorsha whined.

"Let go of my nipples!" Will snapped.

Josh shoved her hand between their bodies, her own palm sweeping a large swath of Will's chest, and yanked Sorsha's hand out. Then she took charge of the ponytail again and tugged Sorsha far enough to one side that Will could grab the other roaming hand.

Now restrained, Sorsha settled for telling Will repeatedly that he was no fun.

"You sexually assaulted me in a chocolate coffin!" Will shot back.

"She'd probably never do that sort of thing if she were awake," Josh pointed out.

"I hope not," Will said.

"Wait, you mean I'm asleep?" Sorsha demanded.

At which point the peppermint bark broke into pieces, the marshmallows fell away, and they plunged into space.

Since they hadn't resolved the nightmare, Josh felt no sense of relief, no warm gratitude. All she felt was a jarring sensation, and then she was crashing to the floor of a minimart and bullets were flying and bags of potato chips were exploding and she was hissing, "Down! Stay down!"

"What happened?" Will cried, flat on the floor, hands over the back of his neck.

"Sorsha woke up."

"So why didn't the archway dump us out?"

"It only does that if we resolve the nightmare or—" She broke off while one of the glass doors to the freezer compartment behind them shattered, then finished. "—if we make an exit. Chyman's Dilemma, remember? Right now, we've just slid into some other part of the Dream."

Someone at the other end of the store yelled, "Twenties, idiot! The twenties!"

"What do we do?" Will asked.

Josh generally avoided nightmares involving guns. Chekhov's Principle, *One must not put a loaded rifle on the stage if no one is thinking of firing it,* had been intended for writers, but it worked just as well for dream walkers. If someone bothered to dream of a gun, they almost always bothered to dream of firing it.

Now Josh and Will were stuck in the middle of what appeared to be a very violent minimart robbery, and as the firing stopped briefly, they peeked up over the rack of snacks to survey the store. There was a front door to the shop, and that was it. Josh cursed. "We need an exit!"

"I don't see one," Will whispered.

"Wait a sec!" Josh hissed. "We can use the cooler doors."

"What? But they aren't real doors."

"No, we can use them. Didn't you read that article I gave you, 'Nontraditional Dream-Exit Strategies'?"

"Yeah, but these doors don't lead anywhere!"

"We can make them lead somewhere," Josh said, and sprang to her feet.

She opened one of the unbroken doors to the freezer compartment and began yanking out cases of beer. By the time anyone at the front of the store realized what she was doing, she had cleared enough space to step inside.

The cold air swept past Josh, eager to enter the warm store. She stood inside the compartment long enough to open and close the door, and then jumped back out. "See? Now it leads somewhere."

"Yeah, you're awesome," Will said, but he already had his lighter and compact out and was concentrating on opening the Veil. It shimmered into view, and Josh jumped through just as the gunfire started up again. Will followed.

But instead of landing in the archroom, they slammed into a pile of wooden beams on a concrete floor. Josh landed hard against Will and they both made sounds of protest.

They weren't in the Weaver-Avish house's basement. They were . . . somewhere half-burned, a sunken concrete basement surrounded by charred timber. The ceiling above them had burned away completely, and most of the walls had gone with it. Josh knew the building had burned some time ago, because the smell of smoke had departed.

"Are we still in-Dream?" Will asked.

"I don't think so . . . but maybe." Josh stood up and held out a hand to him, and he took it. "Help me up. I need to get a better view."

She gestured to a partially destroyed staircase. It was concrete, so it hadn't burned, but rubble covered the first four steps. Will got down on one knee, and Josh used his other knee to springboard herself onto the fifth step.

"I can see the ocean," she said, facing in the direction away from the trees. "I—oh my god." She looked around at the basement again and caught sight of broken mirrors beneath the wreckage. When her heart skipped a beat, it left her bloodless for a moment, and her chest filled with a feeling like suction. "We're in the cabin in Charle," she managed to say.

"The one that burned down last summer?" Will asked, and Josh felt another piercing, sick shock at the idea that he knew.

"Yeah," she mumbled.

Josh hadn't been here since Ian died. Was this Ian's way of punishing her for what she'd felt in the coffin a few minutes ago? The pain in her chest that woke up at his name felt like a muscle clenched so tight her chest would cave in around it.

He's dead, she reminded herself. *He's dead, and even if he weren't, he left me before he died. He doesn't care what I do.*

No matter how many times she repeated the thoughts, she couldn't bring herself to believe them.

Finally, she jumped down to a spot clear of rubble and explained to Will as much as she felt she had to explain.

"This was my mother's cabin." She kept her voice tight, neutral, but couldn't help rushing her words together. "Mom died here while trying to build a new archway. We assumed she died before finishing, but I guess we were wrong, because we seem to have just come out through it."

Josh busied herself peering at the air as if she could identify where the archway might hang.

"How old were you?" Will asked.

Why does he want to know that? Josh wondered, cringing.

"Twelve. But . . ."

She wanted to say, *It's all right, I'm over it. Kerstel is great.* Except it wasn't all right, not really, and she'd never be over it, even if it didn't haunt her the way Ian's death did. Sure, Kerstel was great, but she'd never be Jona Weaver. She'd never be Josh's *mom.*

"I was twelve when I went to live with the state," Will said, bringing Josh back to the burned-out basement. "I haven't heard from my mom since."

Josh understood that he was trying to connect with her, but their situations looked so different to her.

"That sucks," she said finally.

"Yeah." Will held her gaze, and she felt him trying to hang on to that connection, trying to make it important, but she turned away again.

"If the archway works," she said, "we can go back through it into the Dream, but we'll have to trigger Chyman's Dilemma again."

"What? You lost me."

"If we leave through this archway, *ligamus* will make sure we come back through this archway, so if we want to leave through a different one, we have to trigger Chyman's Dilemma to break *ligamus*."

"If we trigger Chyman's Dilemma and aren't connected to any archway, how can we be sure we'll come out through the one in your basement?"

"We can't be. But there's a rough geographic correspondence between the Dream and the World, and the house is only a hundred miles from here. Our chances are good."

They used a lighter and compact to open the archway, the edges of which had never been marked in stone and so hung jagged in the air. They had no looking stone, either, but they got lucky in that the first dream to appear was a teenage boy's SAT nightmare. Josh and Will took seats in the back of the classroom and watched as the poor guy ran into every possible test-taking misfortune: His pencils snapped, his erasers tore off, his calculator melted into a smoldering mess.

In order to trigger Chyman's Dilemma, they had to sit through a nightmare until it ended on its own. Josh wasn't fond of test taking herself, and watching the kid grow increasingly panicked was brutal. She'd had just about all she could take when the dreamer accidentally set his completed answer sheet on fire and wailed himself awake.

Josh and Will slid straight into a nightmare about evil Martian ghosts. After much firing of laser guns and the complete destruction of a space station, they earned their way out of the Dream . . .

And onto the archroom floor.

Josh found her father waiting for her, holding a stapled handful of papers in his hand. He had his eyebrows raised, and his unexpected presence made Josh anxious at a time when she was already emotionally drained.

"It's after seven," Laurentius said, sounding more concerned than angry. "How late do you two train at night?"

"Um," Josh said. His question startled her. "Usually not past dinner."

She caught Will mouthing *Eight thirty!* to Lauren.

"Good grief," Lauren said. He lifted the papers in his hand. Josh got just enough of a glimpse to realize it was her history test and that there was a lot of red pen on the first page. "I was thinking that we might need to have a talk about this, but now I realize how much time you're putting in, between training Will and keeping up your own skills. Just make a little more time to study before the next exam, all right?"

Josh nodded. "I will. I promise. We were just about to knock off for the night and go study anyway."

Lauren kissed her forehead and headed up the stairs to the pantry.

"So, when your dad finishes adopting me," Will said to Josh when they were alone, "can I blow off schoolwork to dream walk?"

"Oh, shut up," Josh said, amused and embarrassed at the same time. Then she grew more serious and said, "But I do expect you to reread that article on nontraditional dream-exit strategies."

"Yes, ma'am. Right *after* I do my reading for history."

"All right," Josh agreed. *"After."*

Ten

"So, where are we going?" Will asked as he and Josh drove out of Tanith.

"We're going to Braxton, where the headquarters of the junta are. The junta controls all the dream walkers on the North American continent. Their office keeps calling and demanding I bring you in to get registered as a dream walker."

"Isn't a junta a group that holds power after a revolution?" Will asked, adding mentally, *And aren't they usually part of a really scary, horrible military dictatorship?*

"We used to have a monarchy," Josh explained. "The Rousellarios. They didn't rule all the dream walkers in the world, but they ruled over most of Europe and Asia, and all of North America, and I think a good part of Africa."

"What happened to them?" Will asked.

"The short explanation is, my grandfather brought them down."

"Ah, that might be too short."

"All right. Let's see. For as long as anyone can remember, there's always been controversy about whether or not dream walkers are doing enough for humanity. The last few centuries, the theories about exactly what more we could be doing center around one idea called staging, which is going into the Dream and influencing dreamers' subconscious minds to make them happier and more peaceful."

"How does that work?" Will asked.

"There are a lot of possibilities. The simplest is called influential staging, and dream walkers do it all the time. It's where we put an idea in a dreamer's mind—you know, *This door is unlocked,* or when I tried to tell the woman in the mob dream that she would be safe. That can be a little risky for dream walkers, but it's not a big deal for dreamers. But what most people refer to as staging is where people go into the Dream in groups and actually act out scenes of happiness to change nightmares into joyful dreams."

"That sounds okay," Will said.

"It's not," Josh told him, a little too sharply. "Sorry. Yeah, it sounds okay—until you start thinking about ways you could abuse it. That's why the Rousellarios, the royal family, kept forbidding anyone to try it. Like, for centuries. Then twenty years ago, my grandfather, who is a despicable person, led a movement to get staging approved. His group was called the Lodestone Party, and they didn't just ask permission from the royal family, they prepared a whole proposal. They had shrinks and lawyers and social workers all involved. They wanted to stage dreams for the people of this country, Khuzegistan. Ever heard of it?"

"Ah, I know it's some tiny war-torn country in Asia."

"That's pretty much all you need to know. It's tiny, it's war-torn, it's in Asia. That was all true back then, too. The Khuzegi dream walkers begged the royal family to let the Lodestone Party try staging in their country. They even sent a choir of blind schoolchildren to sing at the palace. But the king and queen kept saying no.

"So Peregrine just went ahead and launched the project without their permission. The Khuzegi people worship some god nobody here has ever heard of, and the Lodestone Party went into nightmares dressed like the god and gave everybody messages of peace and love. The next morning the president declared military rule over, the war over, and the army disbanded. People were dancing in the streets and dismantling weapons to use as flowerpots."

"Wait," Will said. "I heard about this in school. Didn't this end really badly?"

"Yeah. A few days later, a foreign warlord got wind that Khuzegistan was completely defenseless, so he marched in with his guys and took the whole place over. Then he put everybody in camps and made them work in smelting factories, and years later NATO had to go in to clean up the mess. But before all that, the day after the staging, the dream-walker king declared Peregrine guilty of treason and put out a warrant for his arrest."

"Wait, he could just declare someone guilty of treason?" Will asked.

"I guess. I don't know much about the monarchy. Anyway, it gave Peregrine an excuse to stage a full-blown rebellion. He and a bunch of other Lodestones went to the palace, and *somehow* it got set on fire. It burned down with the king and queen and their baby daughter inside."

"That seems extreme."

"I think Peregrine was waiting for an excuse to revolt. He saw his chance and he took it."

"Yeah, but a baby? That's awful."

"Some people think the baby survived. Maybe that's just what they want to believe, but there are a lot of rumors that she's hidden away somewhere. The Rousellarios have a weird cult following now—Deloise has a bunch of books about them.

"So, the staging in Khuzegistan ended badly for everyone. There was one other incident of staging, back in the '60s, in this little town in Iowa called Maplefax. One guy was trying to stage dreams all by himself, and he accidentally ripped the Veil and the whole town went crazy from fairy dust. And those are just the instances where people were trying to do good. Part of the danger of staging is that not everyone will use it to create peace. People could use it to influence what dreamers buy, how they vote, decisions they have to make. Today you'll have to take Melrio's Oath, which says you promise to try not to influence dreamers beyond the scope of the Dream. But every few years you hear about somebody breaking the oath. One guy last year was going into women's dreams and convincing them he was their soul mate so they would sleep with him when they woke up."

Will shook his head. "That is really pathetic."

"Agreed."

"So you guys got the junta after the royal family burned up?"

"Yeah, but only in North America. It was supposed to be temporary and only hold power until a permanent government could be formed, but that was almost twenty years ago, and they're just now getting ready to hold elections. The junta has seven members, and Peregrine is one of them. He still leads the Lodestone Party, and they're still pushing for staging, but after what happened with Khuzegistan, the other members of the junta were worried enough that they always put off legalizing staging. The other big party is the Troth Party, which I guess I'm old enough to join now that I'm seventeen, and they say the way we've been doing things for hundreds of years is working just fine. The Dream is stable. The World hasn't ended yet. We're doing as much as we can without risking too much."

"So the reason you don't like staging is that you feel like it's dangerous and unnecessary?"

Josh thought for a long time before answering. "I don't think we have the moral right to manipulate people that way. I mean, keeping the Dream stable is necessary. If we didn't, the World would dissolve into chaos. And it's a kindness to people, a service, at the same time. But to say that we know what's best for other people and then force that vision into their subconscious minds . . . I don't think we have *that* right. My grandfather only wants staging because he loves having power over other people, not out of any desire for world peace."

"You decide what's best for me," Will pointed out, half joking.

Josh laughed. "I try. That's about all I can claim."

The car fell silent as they both reflected. Will agreed with Josh's concerns, and he could see dozens of ways staging could be abused that she hadn't even mentioned. But . . .

If he had been given the chance to go back in time and stage a dream that would make his mother stop drinking, no argument in the world would have stopped him.

Josh, as if hearing his thoughts, said, "I won't be mad at you if you decide to be a Lodestone. Whim agrees with them more than he does with me, and we're still friends."

"That's good to know."

After thinking a bit longer, Josh added, "But I will be mad if you decide you like and admire my grandfather."

Will laughed. "I'm sure I'll loathe him on sight."

At the junta's headquarters in downtown Braxton—a skyscraper made of gray granite and steel-framed windows—they were ushered to the registration office.

"Hello!" squealed a woman with brunette curls cropped short against her scalp. "Oh, this is so exciting! I was hoping I'd be here when you came in!"

"Sorry," Josh said, awkwardly drawing her shoulders up to ear level and cramming her hands into her pants pockets. "I—have we met?"

"Oh, no, honey. I've just heard so much about you over the years. And when I heard you were going to have an apprentice, well, we were all thrilled that you might pass some of that talent on." She looked at Will. "Do you know how lucky you are to be working with her?"

Will smiled because he didn't know what else to do. This was a decidedly weird reception. This woman had *heard* of Josh? He'd known Josh was a good dream walker, but he hadn't realized that people had *heard* of her.

In the woman's office, Josh produced affidavits from Davita, Young Ben, Dustine, and Josh herself, all attesting that they approved Will's entry into dream-walker society. He felt unexpectedly touched that Dustine had written a letter of support for him.

Then the whole process nearly fell apart when they discovered that Josh had forgotten to bring a copy of Will's birth certificate. However, after several uncomfortable moments, the woman said, "Well, let's just pretend you brought it, all right? I think the junta can trust that Josh Weaver's apprentice is who she says he is."

Although this raised more questions in Will's mind, he tried to concentrate as she speed-read him two pages of tiny type explaining exactly what he was and wasn't allowed to do in the Dream according to Melrio's Oath—which, more than anything else, gave him all sorts of ideas for devious things he could do in-Dream— after which he took a two-sentence oath.

She issued him a user ID and password for the dream walker's online database, then said, "This is completely optional, but if you like, we are offering to store ear prints, bone scans, and DNA for all dream walkers. I want to assure you that this information remains private and secure and will *only* be used in the event that your remains need to be identified. The junta has agreed that it cannot be accessed even by subpoena, and you have the right to destroy it at any time."

Will couldn't help feeling alarmed. "Is there a big need to identify remains?"

"No," Josh told him before the woman could answer. "It's mostly just an excuse for the junta to charge people a fifty-dollar storage fee every year. But Dad wrote the check for the registration fee for an extra fifty in case you want to do it."

"Did you do it?" he asked her.

She nodded. "Better safe than sorry, right?"

"Yeah, I guess. Okay then."

The bone scan only took ten minutes, the ear prints were just high-tech photographs, and the DNA sample only required a cheek swab. Finally, the woman opened a desk drawer, and said, "Just one more thing. Will Kansas, as a welcome gift from the dream-walker community, I hereby present you with this trimidion."

She held out a pyramid made of six silver sticks and a stand with a circular base and one long pole to balance the pyramid on. "May the True Dream Walker watch over you, that you always walk safely."

Will never would have anticipated how much the gift meant to him. Everything thus far had felt very official, like registering for school, but here was this little welcome gift being given to him by someone who, unlike Josh, was so excited that he was part of their world now.

"Thank you," he said. The trimidion was light in his hands.

"That's it." The woman stood up to shake their hands. "Please just let me say again how delighted I am to have gotten to meet you both."

Afterward, riding upstairs, Will caught Josh's eye in one of the elevator's mirrored walls and said, "So, here's a weird question: Are you famous?"

"What?" she said. "No." But she tried to sink under her shoulders again.

"Is it because your grandfather's on the junta?"

"No! Bleh. I only see him when I have to. I don't even tell people I'm related to him." She cringed as she continued, lowering her voice as if afraid their reflected images might hear her. "I'm not famous, exactly. Just . . . a few people know who I am from this study."

"What kind of study?"

"Some dream theorists were studying whether or not variables like age, race, gender, and all that had any influence on a dream walker's resolution rate. Peregrine heard about it and volunteered me, and . . . I sort of messed up their data."

"How?" Will asked when Josh trailed off.

Reluctantly, Josh admitted, "Everybody else was able to resolve a nightmare an average of sixty-four percent of the time. My resolution rate was eighty-eight percent."

A *24 percent* difference? Either the scientists who had conducted this study were incompetent, or else Josh was an outright prodigy.

But when Will thought back on their trips to the Dream together, he realized that 88 percent sounded right to him. Some afternoons they walked four or five nightmares and resolved every single one.

"This totally explains why I've been getting congratulation cards from people I don't know," he said as the elevator doors opened.

"You have?" Josh cringed. "How many?"

"Like, nearly a dozen. One lady sent a poem."

They stepped out onto the top floor, where Josh's equilibrium was restored by the news that her grandfather was at a press conference and would have to leave immediately afterward to catch a flight, negating the possibility of their visiting with him today.

"Please make sure to tell him we stopped by," Josh said firmly.

She was positively giddy on the ride back downstairs. *She really hates this guy,* Will thought.

"Let's stop in the press room and wave," she said. "He won't be able to do anything."

Will had never been to a press conference, or a press room, and was surprised by the large, voluptuous room filled with velvet curtains and upholstered chairs. At the front of the room, behind a podium on a stage, stood a man with a large bald head. His face was too big for his skull, with thick, wet lips that could have touched his chin and eyes that might have slid right down his cheeks for their weight. Small and very thin, he was not at all frail but overly animated, crossing and uncrossing his arms, putting his hands on his hips, tapping one foot, shifting his weight, pulling out a pocket watch on a chain to check the time, even as he answered questions from the dozen or so journalists gathered before him.

Josh slipped inside the doors and leaned against the back wall. Will followed.

"Mr. Hyde," Peregrine was saying, "Dracula, Hannibal Lecter—" Peregrine stumbled over his words as he caught sight of Josh's wave. He gave her a little nod before continuing. "Plus Darth Vader, terminators, the guy from *Harry Potter* who didn't have a nose, the *Jaws* shark—a few years ago I ran into Grendel's mother, for God's sake! And those are just the famous ones. Remember '97, when it took almost six months to figure out that a single copy of some Portuguese horror story had made its way into a middle school library in Savannah? Every kid in the seventh grade had read that book, they were passing it around like the flu, and everybody freaked out just like now with these trench-coat people. We *will* identify them, but it's going to take time, people."

He paused to take a question Will couldn't hear.

"That's a ludicrous suggestion," Peregrine replied. His voice dripped condescension. "This isn't a matter for the Gendarmerie, it's a matter for the Department of Media and Cultural Influences, and I assure you that every member of that department is working his ass off as we speak. People who are demanding an investigation are just pathetic conspiracy-mongers who are looking for a way to discredit me because they're afraid that one day, I might ask them to give back to a government that has done nothing but give to them. So they sit with their laptops and their fancy cappuccinos and they bitch and whine all over the Internet, and now you're at an official press conference asking if a rumor about a rumor on a blog is real. You're wasting time, people—"

The doors closed behind Josh and Will as they left the press room.

"So," Will said, "good news: I absolutely loathe your grandfather."

Josh held her hand up for a high five.

———

The only real light in the coffee shop came from a single spotlight aimed at the low stage. Beyond it, the tips of cigarettes burned red like the eyes of nocturnal animals. Just enough illumination passed beyond the stage to highlight the rims of whiskey glasses and reveal that many in the audience were smoking hookahs.

The woman in the spotlight was African American, fortyish, her hair in perfect curls, wearing black-rimmed cat-eye glasses, jeans, and a shimmery red top that seemed to have been woven around her body. Her guitar was stained auburn and had a pattern of sunbeams emanating from the sound hole.

Josh headed toward the smoky, dim seating area, and Will cautiously mounted the two steps to the stage. She'd agreed to let him handle this one alone—a simple stage-fright dream—and only get involved if needed.

As Will approached the woman on the stage, moving very slowly, she noticed him. Her fingers fumbled on the guitar's fretboard, and the chord she meant to play emerged warped and cringing. She gave a tiny shake of her head. *No. No.*

"I'm here to help," Will said, but he didn't think she could hear him above her own music.

He went to stand beside her and put his arm around her shoulder. He didn't know what her song was about exactly—despite the clarity of her singing, he couldn't make sense of the lyrics—but it sounded beautiful to him. With his free hand, he patted a rhythm out on his thigh. He'd always thought he would make a good drummer, and he thought the beat he was putting to this song was really bringing the music up a notch.

Then he stopped looking at the woman to glance out at the audience, and he felt frightened. The smoke from the hookahs seemed to make a solid golden wall in the circle of light cast around him, and beyond it glowed the crimson eyes of the animals watching him. He could hear an awful dragging sound accompanied by footsteps—step, step, drag. Step, step, drag.

Something terrible was happening. The woman didn't have stage fright; why had he made that assumption when he was using the looking stone? Why couldn't he stop tapping on his leg now that he'd started? Each touch reverberated through his entire body, weakening him. The wall of stage light could not protect him from the feral animals on the other side.

He looked down and saw that the woman had become ever so slightly transparent. When she sang, a swath of burgundy marked with stars flowed out of her mouth and was sucked into the darkness beyond the spotlight.

Frantically, Will looked down at his own hand, still tapping, tapping away, and yes, it was happening to him, too, a brushstroke of midnight blue shot through with green that stretched longer and longer as he lost more of himself to the creatures.

This was why the woman had been terrified. Because when she played a concert for people, she gave them a part of her soul.

But when she played for the devil, she had to give him all of it.

The smoke in the room began to clear, and there he was in the audience, Satan himself. Will had forgotten that Lucifer had been an angel once, but he saw now the decrepit remains of what once must have been beauty: two skeletal wings, their feathers mostly gone, one badly bent; refined features half eaten away by worms; long fingers reduced to claws with swollen knuckles. He bared his teeth—whittled down to pencil points—at Will and hissed, and blood sprayed the table before him. Then he opened his mouth and used his foot-long serpent's tongue to clasp the souls in the air and draw them into his mouth.

Will had never felt such intense fear. It raced along his nerves like flames tracing a line of gasoline, and when the lines met at the center of his chest, an explosion of terror filled him. He began to shriek, to scream utterly without reserve, every breath more fuel to the fire that rose out of his chest and ruined the air.

Suddenly Josh was standing in front of him, and though it took him an instant to recognize her, he felt a glimmer of hope. His soul changed its path to flow past her.

"Will," she said. "Stop screaming."

He hadn't realized he *was* still screaming. Stopping required too great an effort, though, so it wasn't until Josh pushed his jaw shut and sealed her palm over his mouth that the cycle of shrieking burned itself out.

"Good," Josh said, cautiously removing her hands. "Now, listen to me: You have gotten sucked into the dreamer's fear. None of this is real. You need to imagine your protective egg."

He had no idea what she was talking about. Luckily, Josh seemed to sense that, and after thinking hard for several seconds, she changed tactics.

"You remember that the Dream exists, right?"

"Yes," he whispered on his stripped-dry throat. "It must. There's a looking stone."

"Good! Yeah, there's a looking stone. And anything can happen in the Dream, right?"

He nodded.

"Do you remember earlier today, when we decided to go into a nightmare together? You used the looking stone. Which nightmare did you pick?"

He thought back, letting the memories present themselves to him like a movie, one frame at a time. "I picked one with a woman singing in a coffee sh—"

Josh waited.

"Oh," Will said. He glanced around, somehow impressed by how realistic everything appeared, and then looked back at Josh. "None of this is real."

His hand quit tapping. He looked down and saw that his flesh had become opaque again.

The woman next to him vanished completely. Her guitar fell to the stage.

"Let's get the hell out of here," Josh said.

Will expected her to be angry at him, but she just looked freaked out. Without saying anything, she took him upstairs to her apartment and made them both hot chocolate in a microwave. For a while, they just sat together on the couch, mugs in hand.

"Ah, I'm sorry," Will said finally.

"It's all right," Josh said tightly.

"I know I screwed up back there. I broke Stellanor, I let the dreamer's fear get to me."

"It's all right, I mean it." She ran a hand through her hair. He wondered if this was the end of his apprenticeship. "There was an unusual kind of fear in that nightmare, something called dreamfire. I should have realized it was there sooner and gotten you out right away."

"Dreamfire?"

"When a nightmare triggers one of a dreamer's deepest fears, we call the fear dreamfire. It has a different feel to it, and if someone gets caught in it, they almost never manage to pull themselves out again." Josh poked at the mini marshmallows in her hot chocolate, submerging each in turn. "I don't know what the dreamer was so afraid of tonight, though."

Will remembered the sensation of loss he'd felt as the blue light slipped out of his body, and the fear that had burst into hysteria. "She was afraid of losing her sense of self," he said.

"Maybe so. Look, every dream walker makes the mistake of getting caught up in the dreamer's fear. Every single one. It was bad luck that you got caught up in dreamfire on top of the usual fear. I'm just glad you survived it."

"Me too." Will thought a moment and then realized that her last comment might not have been hypothetical. "Wait, are you saying that you think that if you'd ended the nightmare, I would have died?"

Josh nodded her head grimly. "You were half-transparent by the time I got to you. I think that you were so in tune with the dreamer that whatever was happening to her began happening to you. If I'd ended the nightmare, I doubt you would have made it."

The magnitude of the danger he had faced hit him full-force then, and he had to push the hot chocolate away because he was overcome by nausea. "Take it easy," Josh said, and she dragged a small wicker trash can up next to the couch. "Everybody's all right."

"Yeah," Will said, mostly to remind himself. He swallowed against the lump in his throat. "You did a pretty amazing job of talking me down."

She waved the compliment away. "There was no psychological insight, I just used reasoning."

"Whatever it was, it saved my life, so give yourself a little credit."

She softened. "All right." Then she reached out, awkwardly, and put her arm around him. "You want to knock off for the rest of the day? Watch TV and eat cheese puffs or something?"

She'd never offered to let him skip training before. He nodded yes, but he didn't feel any better, and he said, "Josh, I don't know if I can go back in there."

This time, the anger he'd expected her to display never came at all. She just smiled, squeezed his shoulder, and said, "You'll be able to."

"I don't know—"

"*I* do. You care about people too much not to go back in."

Mystified, Will said, "What does that have to do with anything?"

"It has everything to with why we walk nightmares in the first place. You'll see another kid getting attacked by another Meepa, and you'll think about how scared he is, and you won't be able to stop yourself from running in to help, just like the first time."

Will stared at her, hardly able to believe what she'd said. Despite all the times it had seemed like she was barely aware of his presence, she had known something about him that he hadn't known about himself. Something good, even.

A little thrill ran through him at the knowledge that she thought about him.

"Maybe you're right," he said.

Eleven

Dear Diary (I'm trying to give that opening another try),

I keep thinking of how scared I was when Will was fading away. My voice was shaking so bad I'm surprised he could hear what I was saying. Then afterward, I could barely keep it together. I just wanted to hug him and tell him how glad I was that he'd made it out.

This is exactly what I was afraid would happen—I'd start caring about him and thinking of him as a friend, and then I'd get him killed. Why didn't I think to warn him about dreamfire? Would that even have helped? Once someone gets caught in it, they don't usually get out.

And he trusts me! He proved it today. That can only put him in worse danger. If he trusts me and I care about him enough that I can't think straight when he's in trouble, it's just a matter of time until something terrible happens.

Maybe I could explain all of this to him somehow. Maybe he'd understand that knowing he's my responsibility freaks me out so much that I can't keep him safe. He gets the psychological stuff so much better than I do. He's read all these books, and he throws around terms like "passive-aggressive" and "defense mechanism" like everyone knows them. But I'd have to tell him about Ian then, and I just can't do that. It's stupid. I know he shouldn't trust me, that I should warn him away from putting his faith in me.

But some part of me really likes that he does.

"Relax your shoulder," Josh said.

Will lowered his gun and used one hand to lift a pair of protective earmuffs from his ear. "What?" he asked.

"I said to relax your shoulder. Think of the gun as an extension of your arm, not as a deadly weapon you use to kill people."

"That's a big help."

Josh shrugged and leaned against the wall of their stall in the shooting range. She smiled to see him struggling with the hand-gun. He was in good shape—he could run forever—but he got nervous around guns.

He fired three rounds and then stopped to examine the paper figure in the distance. "That third shot grazed the left arm," Josh told him.

"Yeah, I'm sure a flesh wound will stop the Creature from the Black Lagoon from tearing me to pieces."

"If he's a lefty, it might."

Will smiled, but Josh could see him getting frustrated. "Come on," she said. "Let's go find Deloise and call it a day."

Three stalls over, Deloise had just blown the letter *D* into the cardboard target's chest.

"Hey," she said, gathering up her shells. "Am I good, or am I good?"

Will gazed wistfully at her mangled target. "We're lucky you aren't an assassin."

Deloise winked. "No one suspects us blondes."

Will was still living in the county home and would have to stay there until Lauren and Kerstel were approved as temporary guardians. That was supposed to happen very soon, but Josh was still reluctant to drop Will off at the county home. Over the last few weeks, making conversation with him had gotten easier every day: less tense, less terse, more familiar. Josh had been surprised to realize that she actually *liked* Will, and often after training she found herself thinking, *We didn't get any time to just hang out.*

Well, she was meant to be his teacher, not his friend. And it was just as well that they didn't become too close. . . .

"Don't worry about the shooting," she told Will as she put the car in park just outside the county home's front doors. "It's not an essential skill."

He shrugged. He was a guy; he didn't like thinking he was a naturally lousy shot. "Maybe I can learn how to throw a tomahawk instead," he suggested as he opened the door.

Josh watched him walk into the hospital-like building as Deloise climbed from the backseat to the front. "You think he's all right in there?" Josh asked. "I don't even know what happened to his parents, why he's living there."

"You could ask him," Deloise suggested practically.

"If I ask him questions, then he gets to ask me questions."

"You still haven't told him about Ian?" Deloise asked with a sigh.

"I don't know what to tell him. What would I say? That the house fire was my fault? That someone is *dead* because of me?"

By the time she stopped speaking, Josh's chest hurt. Ian's memory muscle seized up.

"You did what you could for Ian," Deloise told her.

"And it wasn't good enough. What does *that* say about the girl teaching Will?"

"Nobody blames you for what happened."

Josh didn't argue, just rubbed the cramp in her chest with one hand; but inside she thought, *Pretending doesn't change the past.*

"Winsor blames me."

"Winsor's dealing in her own way. Plus, these postcards from Whim are driving her nuts. He's always saying he's coming home and then not showing, and she was so close to him. . . ."

Josh turned onto the highway and said thoughtfully, "Closer to him than you are?"

"Of course. They're siblings. Whim and I are just friends."

And Josh could have said something about that, but she didn't.

They arrived home to the usual predinner bustle. Kerstel called Josh over to the stove, where a wok full of peppers sizzled. "How's my soon-to-be son? I missed seeing him today. Oh, and there's mail for you."

"He's fine. Can't shoot the broad side of a barn, but otherwise fine."

"The lawyer called," Kerstel said. "Unofficial word is that Lauren and I are approved. We'll probably hear for sure tomorrow, which means we can move Will in on Saturday."

"Oh," Josh said, startled. "That happened fast."

"Your grandfather pulled some strings."

"In the real government? I thought he could only pull strings in the dream-walker government."

"Apparently he knows someone in Family Services."

Does he have his finger in every pie in town? Josh wondered as she retrieved her card from the mail basket on the counter. Frowning, she ripped open the envelope and pulled the card free. The front cover showed a baby chicken saying, "I know I missed your birthday, but I made you a cake anyway. . . ." Inside, it read, "One for each day late," and showed the chick lying on its back, surrounded by dozens of half-eaten cakes.

"Who's it from?" Kerstel asked.

Someone had taken a red pen and drawn guts exploding from the chick's torso, as if its stomach had ruptured violently. "This could only have come from Whim. It says, 'Dear Josh, Hey! I hope you and Del and Winny are doing well. I'm sorry I couldn't make it back for your birthday, but I'm sure you had a great time and your scroll gave you winning lottery numbers.'"

Josh choked on the next word and fell silent.

> *Haley and I are heading back in your direction. I know I've written to Winsor a couple different times that I'm on my way home, but this time I mean it. Not sure about the date, so expect us any time. Happy birthday!*
> *Love and peanut brittle,*
> *Whim*

"That sounds like Whim," Kerstel agreed, unaware that she hadn't heard the entire message.

"Yeah." *What is he doing with Haley?* "He just wrote to say happy birthday."

Josh looked again at the exploding chick and felt a strange kinship. The discomfort she had lived with ever since Will came into her life closely resembled having eaten too much cake. She closed the card and put it back in the envelope, and moments later, she was in the Avishes' apartment, knocking on Winsor's bedroom door.

"Come in!" Winsor called.

Josh entered and found Winsor in her connected bathroom, removing a squishy pair of shoes. "Kiddie-pool nightmare," she explained.

"You have carrot shavings in your hair," Josh pointed out as she shut the bedroom door.

"Oh." Winsor peered at herself in the mirror. "There was also a Dumpster involved."

Josh sat down on the padded bench at the foot of the bed. The room was crowded with a bedroom set from the early 1900s, complete with a four-poster bed, a rolltop desk, and a wardrobe large enough to fit two grown men inside. Heavy red drapes had been pulled back around the bed and window.

"I got a card from Whim today."

Winsor glanced at the floor near Josh's feet, momentarily caught off guard. "Really," she said, and turned back to the wardrobe.

"Yeah. Did you know that he and Haley are traveling together?"

"He might have mentioned it at some point."

Josh waited while Winsor kicked off her garbage-soaked pants and stepped into a pair of white cotton shorts. As usual, she looked effortlessly sophisticated.

"Why didn't you tell me?" Josh asked. She didn't mean it to come out as an accusation, but it did.

"Why would I?" Winsor said, her tone growing sharp and narrow.

"Because they're my friends."

"Which is exactly why it's *your* job to keep up with them." Winsor gathered up her dirty clothes and chucked them into the bottom of the wardrobe.

"But you're the only one they write to."

Winsor shrugged.

Frustrated, Josh said, "I don't understand why you're being so . . ."

Winsor leaned both hands atop the dresser. Looking at Josh in the mirror, she said, "So *what*, Josh?"

Josh felt the knife in Winsor's voice as if the tip were just poking into the skin above her breastbone. "Nothing," she said, but she was angry and she knew her voice revealed it. "I just don't know when you're going to be finished punishing me."

Winsor shifted her eyes to her own reflection and began putting on a pair of gold earrings.

"I know you're still mad at me about Ian—" Josh said, trying one more time.

"*Still* mad about Ian?" Winsor demanded. Her eyes flew back to Josh. "Is Ian *still* dead, Josh?"

Josh shrank back on the bench, her anger turned to devastating shame. "I didn't mean it like that." She couldn't look at her friend. No matter what Winsor had done to Josh, she wasn't responsible for a death, and Josh was.

"Whatever you say," Winsor snapped. She picked up a brush and began whipping it through her hair.

Winsor's knife had torn into that sore spot in her chest where Ian's memory resided. Josh felt a droplet of something wet run between her breasts and assumed it was blood before realizing she was sweating.

"Sorry," she said in a half whisper. "I shouldn't have said anything."

"Probably not," Winsor agreed.

Josh got up from the bed and walked out of the room, trying to make her footsteps soundless, closing the door as softly as she could. But she couldn't help pressing one hand over the wound in her chest as she walked away.

Through a Veil Darkly

More bad news. The total number of people who have gone into comas while they're sleeping is up to seven. Some of them have heart arrhythmias, too. Now the Centers for Disease Control is investigating. A source says that the CDC can't decide whether or not what's happening is a communicable disease, because it's regional, but the victims don't know each other and have nothing in common.

Basically, everybody is at risk.

Twelve

Josh picked Will up from the county home for the last time that Saturday. After a leisurely lunch at the Grape & Leaf, Josh, Will, and Deloise went to an upscale department store and embarked on a shopping trip of such magnitude that Josh began to wonder exactly how many bedrooms Deloise thought Will planned to occupy.

"Don't look, don't look," she whispered to Will as they stood at the checkout. The cash register kept beeping, and the numbers on its screen kept growing larger. When Will's eyes got so big Josh was afraid his vision would suffer permanent damage, she grabbed his arm and forced him to turn away. "If Del doesn't buy it all, Kerstel will just send us back."

At the house, they unloaded the new furniture and spent the next two hours hauling and arranging and putting everything away. Josh sat on the walnut desk chair with its new cushion and watched Will hover while Deloise made the new bed. She'd chosen maroon and navy blue as the motif, right down to the contact paper she used to line each dresser drawer.

Afterward, the room looked as if it had come straight out of a catalogue. A deceptively idyllic photograph of Will's family—his parents and an older brother, taken when Will was around four years old—sat in a black frame next to the alarm clock on the nightstand. Will's books, which were all psychology or self-help, were propped between blue geode bookends on top of the dresser. The top desk drawer held a pack of lighters and two compacts with the powder knocked out. (Deloise kept the powder in a plastic box; it was, after all, her shade.)

"Well?" Deloise asked. "What do you think?"

Josh held her breath. She could tell that Will was overwhelmed from his shallow breathing, but she could also tell that it was important to Deloise that he liked the space she'd created for him.

"It's . . . great," Will managed, making Josh wince. But then he reached out and put a hand on Deloise's shoulder. "I'm just feeling a bit like Alice in Wonderland right now."

Deloise smiled forgivingly at him. "I know it's a change. I'm sure you're used to a more . . . minimalist decor style. But most of this stuff you really did need—like sheets and blankets and a trash can—and there's nothing wrong with having it all match if you're going to buy it anyway."

Will nodded, still gazing around like he was afraid to touch anything. Then he gave Deloise a smile. "It's really, really nice, Del. You did an amazing job. I don't know how to thank you. If the guys at the home saw this, they'd probably be so jealous they'd beat me up."

Deloise laughed. "I wish we could do this for everybody there. But since we can't, I'm glad you like it. Oh—wait, there's one more thing." She opened the closet and dragged out a very thin, four-by-five-foot package.

"Go ahead," she said, propping the wrapped gift against the bed and stepping back.

"Is it a billboard?" Will guessed.

"*Open* it."

Carefully, he found the taped corner on the back and pried it up. He managed to get the paper off in one piece—Josh would have ended up with just shreds in her hands—to reveal the quilt Dustine had given him, expertly pinned against a red background in a solid wood frame.

"Bet you were wondering what that nail in the wall was for, weren't you?" Deloise asked, but Josh and Will were both speechless. "Help me lift it up."

After a few minutes of maneuvering, they got the frame to hang on the appointed nail.

"It looks perfect," Deloise said, gathering up the wrapping paper.

And it did. Suddenly, the room had an identity—a focal point.

The phone in the other room rang and Deloise theatrically

clapped a hand to her forehead. *"That's* what I forgot to buy," she cried. "A phone for in here." She darted into her own bedroom.

The overwhelmed expression began to return to Will's face; a vertical line appeared between his eyebrows. Josh stood next to him and they stared at the quilt on the wall until she finally said, "So, Del went a little overboard, but this will work, right?"

Will shook his head instead of nodding, saying, "This is . . . I hate accepting charity, but—"

"This isn't charity," Josh said, turning to him.

"But thank you."

They looked at each other. "Thank you for all of this," Will said, glancing around the room and swallowing.

"You're welcome," Josh told him.

She didn't realize what her arms were doing until she was already hugging him. He hesitated, stiffening before allowing himself to step closer to her. He smelled like cheap detergent and some deodorant, original scent, not unpleasant or too strong.

Without thinking, she tilted her head back. She didn't even understand why she did so until she saw the surprise on Will's face: Ian would have kissed her then. But Will didn't know what to do, and Josh pulled away before he gave her what she'd instinctively asked for.

She put a few feet between them and jammed her hands in her pockets. Will was *looking* at her again, trying to make sense of that moment, and then Deloise blew in the door and the moment was gone.

"Hey," she said. "Winsor and I are going to walk a nightmare before dinner. You two want to come?"

"Yes," Josh and Will said at the same time.

"How do we know who the dreamer is when there are this many people around?" Will asked as they reached the top of the wooden waterslide tower. He tried not to look down; he, Josh, Deloise, and Winsor were nearly a hundred feet off the ground.

"It's not always easy," Josh replied. "That's why I usually take you into less crowded dreams."

They were standing a few feet from the launchpad for a water-slide that began eight stories off the ground. The air whipping around them reeked of chlorine. Below, an amusement park stretched for miles in every direction, punctuated by more giant waterslide towers. Some of them soared twenty, thirty stories high.

The platform was peopled by families and couples in bathing suits, a few children. As was common in the Dream, some of the people were faceless, indistinct figures made when the dreamer's mind ran out of ideas.

They creeped Will out.

"What's the dreamer afraid of?" Josh asked. "It's an amusement park. Everybody's having a good time."

"So we should look for something upsetting," Will said. "Maybe a haunted house."

"Mirror mansion," Deloise put in.

"Guess-Your-Weight," Winsor suggested.

"If the dreamer is afraid of heights," Deloise added, "we should get down now."

"And why is Deloise suggesting that?" Josh asked Will, but it was an easy test.

"Because the worst always happens in people's nightmares," he recited. "If the dreamer comes up here and is terrified that he'll fall, he probably will."

"Or the tower might collapse, taking all of us with it," Josh concluded.

"Are you in line?" a girl around fourteen asked Deloise. She wore a bright pink-and-yellow bikini, but tears streaked her sunburned face.

"No," Deloise said, at the same time Josh said, "That's her."

Will blinked. How could Josh know that?

"So it's my turn," the girl said miserably, and sat down in the shallow pool of water at the top of the slide.

Suddenly three men in Army fatigues charged up the staircase carrying preposterously oversized guns in their arms. Each soldier stood more than seven feet tall.

"Don't shoot me!" the girl screamed.

"Josh?" Will asked, fighting the urge to drop to his belly on the platform.

"Please don't make me go down," the girl begged. One of the men fired and the bullet sank into the wood next to her head with a sharp thud.

That cemented it—she was definitely the dreamer. However Josh had known, she had been exactly right, just as she always was. Will opened his mouth to ask what to do, but Josh shouted, "Meet me at the bottom!" and threw herself on top of the girl.

They vanished down the slide.

Will looked at Deloise and Winsor. He'd never been in-Dream with anyone besides Josh, and he felt her absence like a sort of nakedness. "Who's next?" he asked.

"We should go after the military guys," Winsor said.

"Wait, what?" Will asked. "Why?"

The military guys were, at that moment, starting to rappel down the side of the tower.

"They're the villains. We just need a knife and we can cut their lines," Winsor said.

"But we don't have a knife," Deloise pointed out.

"Wait!" Will cried, accidentally raising his voice. He couldn't believe how much time they were wasting; no wonder Josh's resolution rate was 24 percent higher than anyone else's. "You're forgetting Distay's Brocard: *A letter unopened is a message unsent.*"

He couldn't quite believe he had just repeated one of Josh's stupid mantras, especially when Deloise said, "I have no idea what that means!"

"It means that if you somehow find a knife and cut the military guys down, and they splat on the concrete but the dreamer doesn't see it because she's in the slide tunnel, she might not acknowledge that it happened and will just re-dream them."

Winsor laughed, but with scorn in her voice. "Oh my god—Josh really is teaching you to think like her." Still chuckling, she sat down on the launchpad and pushed herself into the blue tube.

Deloise followed her. "I love slides!" she cried.

That was nice for her, but Will had never been down a water-slide, and he hadn't been lying the day he'd told Josh he was afraid of drowning. He wasn't a terrific swimmer.

"A whole day of firsts," he muttered.

As he stepped onto the slide's launchpad, awkward in his tennis shoes, a flash of silver-white on the ground below caught his eye and he hesitated.

He squinted through the sunlight. *Is somebody down there wearing a gas tank?* he wondered. *That's weird.*

But weird was the norm in the Dream, so he ignored the uneasy feeling the figure gave him. As he turned away from the sight, his tennis shoes slipped in the water, and before he had time to get nervous, he was whirling down the slide.

Josh's left side was soaking wet, and her Zippo dug into her hip. She and the dreamer slipped and slid, flying up against the walls on the corkscrew turns and then soaring through the straight passages.

The girl cried and clawed Josh's arms. "We're going to be fine," Josh told her, although she suspected just the opposite. She was worried that the slide might end in a drop-off.

"Look!" she shouted, although there was really little sound besides the rushing of the water and the air whipping past. "When the slide ends, let go of me. Keep your body straight—"

The girl screamed, "The slide's gonna *end?*"

Josh swore mentally. *Yet another example of the dangers of staging,* she thought, *and now my only option is to keep staging.* If she could influence what the dreamer was thinking, the dreamer might unconsciously influence the Dream. "The water at the bottom of the slide is very deep!" Josh hollered. "At least thirty-five feet. If you just keep your body straight and hold your breath, you'll be fine."

"But what about the man in the trench coat?" the girl sobbed.

Josh looked at her, stunned, and the slide dropped them into the air.

They only fell about ten feet. Josh didn't even have time to wrestle free of the dreamer before she hit the water on her back. Shock ran through her rib cage and shook her heart and lungs roughly. Her mouth, nose, and throat filled with foul chemical water.

The girl thrashed as she tried to reach the surface. One thing had gone right: The water was at least thirty-five feet deep. Josh saw it in the moment before the sun went out.

Black water surrounded them. The dreamer kicked Josh in the stomach, causing her to exhale all the water she'd just sucked in. Josh fought the panic, fought her need to breathe. *Patience,* she reminded herself. *Patience will keep you from drowning.*

Siglau's Postulate: *Panic can only decrease one's chances of survival.*

But when Josh kicked toward where she thought the surface should be, her shoulder cracked against the bottom of the pool, and it became very hard not to panic. Blackness above, blackness below, blackness all around. She saw a vision of the last two minutes of her life: thrashing in the water, looking for some indication of light, of air, always hitting a wall or a floor, never finding an exit, and slowly suffocating in the silence underwater.

It could happen. In the Dream, there could be a pool without a surface.

But the dreamer isn't afraid of drowning; she's afraid of the soldiers. There has to be a way out.

Using every ounce of self-control she had, Josh stilled herself and let gravity show her which way was up. The meager breath of air in her lungs was enough to draw her toward the surface, feet first.

I'm upside down.

The blood rushed down from her head as she flipped over, planted one foot on the floor of the pool, and shot upward. Her head broke the surface and her ears filled with the sounds of splashing and people shouting to one another.

The pool became suddenly shallow, only three feet deep, and

the depth changed so fast that Josh managed to kick the cement. She coughed violently, spraying water from her nose and mouth. If she'd thought her chest hurt when she couldn't breathe, she had no concept of pain. She felt as if the air were full of splinters. She had definitely taken in a lot of water.

The dreamer stood a few feet away, waist-deep in water and crying. The sky had turned to nighttime darkness but the park glowed with blue and red carnival lights, and the Ferris wheel turned slowly in a ragged circle of yellow bulbs.

Behind her, a splash rose up, followed by the sound of swearing. Josh turned to see Will shaking the water from his hair. He grinned at her.

"That was awesome!" he said. Deloise swam up next to him, and they high-fived. Nearby, Winsor stood with her long shirt billowing around her.

"Everybody in one piece?" Josh asked.

Winsor nodded.

The dreamer screamed, and Josh looked toward the sound. A diving board extended off the side of the pool opposite the deposit from the slide. It was completely out of place, since anyone who jumped off it would break their neck in three feet of water.

Looming over them at the end of the diving board stood the man in the green-black trench coat. The purple lights of a game booth reflected off the giant canister on his back.

Josh had seen the same man in the sewer dream on her birthday.

And not just the same man, but *exactly* the same man.

Thanks to popular culture and mass media, lots of people had nightmares about the same things, but no two people ever remembered characters exactly as they had appeared on television or in a movie. Everyone forgot a detail here or there, and their subconscious minds filled in the blanks, producing a multitude of variations on a theme.

The man in the trench coat was not a variation. Josh remembered those needy, grasping hands that he extended over the water, the wide belt that fit around him like the straps of a straitjacket, and the strange gas tank on his back that was neither white nor silver. Even those empty, glistening eyes. The details were too perfect.

Without even thinking, Josh broke Stellanor's First Rule. She might have ignored this extraordinary coincidence, made excuses, come up with some rationale—if the dreamer's terror hadn't set off all the alarm bells inside her at once. Her instinct didn't just speak up; it exploded like a land mine.

Run, run, run!

He will kill you.

The dreamer had already swum to the diving board, sobbing but apparently unable to control her own motions. The man pulled her out of the water by her hair, causing her to scream, and then he dropped her on the end of the diving board, which bounced beneath her weight. With quick, coordinated gestures, he unhooked a second mask from the tank and jammed it against the dreamer's face. He twisted a knob on the mask and the girl began to twitch.

Josh suddenly recalled what the woman in the sewer dream had said: *They put a mask on Paul and he turned all blue.*

She could feel that the man was going to do something awful to the girl, something that had nothing to do with gas. Fear doused her as if from a flamethrower, but as a scream rose in her throat, she realized she had nearly lost herself in the dreamer's fear and pulled back.

This nightmare is full of dreamfire, she thought, and even after she had imagined jamming the cork back into her safety walls, pounding it into place with a mallet, frissons of anxiety ran up her spine like sparks on a wire. Her skin felt strangely warm.

No, wait, her skin wasn't warming, the pool water was hardening around her. For a moment it flashed opaque, and she felt concrete surrounding her legs. Then it slipped into water again, but around her matter itself began to flicker and melt.

This dream was coming undone.

Run, run, run! Josh's instinct wailed.

Josh's Rule: *Trust your gut.*

"Abort!" she shouted.

"Wait—what?" Will asked. Unlike Josh, he had never run into the man in the trench coat before. "What about the dreamer?"

"Forget her!"

Winsor and Deloise swam toward the pool's edge. They might not have followed Josh's reasoning, but they knew her well enough not to question when she called time.

Will questioned. "Why?"

Above them, the Ferris wheel came to a creaky halt. Its yellow lights flickered.

"I said abort!" Josh shouted, but Will continued to argue.

"He doesn't even have a weapon."

Winsor climbed out of the pool and ran toward the fun house nearby.

"I can save her!" Will said, and he swam away from Josh, closer to the diving board, where the dreamer continued to twitch, her skin white. The man in the trench coat crushed the gas mask to her face.

The spokes of the Ferris wheel began to wilt until the whole structure listed to one side. Beside it, the slide tower swayed. The wailing siren in Josh's head grew louder.

This was no time for Will to be a hero.

"Will!" Josh yelled. "Stop! Right now! *Stop!*"

She wanted to threaten him, to say she'd ground him or slap him or kick him out of her house. She was desperate enough that all those things sounded reasonable.

He must have heard the panic in her voice, because he stopped swimming and turned around. Before he could speak, Josh pointed to the fun house and shouted as if she were making an imperial decree: "*GO!*"

Looking like a whipped puppy, he went. Josh followed.

For a moment, she thought they would be okay. She and Will were swimming away from the man in the trench coat. Deloise was climbing out of the pool. At the fun house, Winsor had her lighter out and was readying her compact to open a porthole back to the World.

Then a second trench-coated figure stormed through the fun house door and knocked Winsor to the ground.

"Winsor!" Josh shouted. Deloise ran toward the fun house.

Will cursed and stopped swimming long enough for Josh to catch up with him. She shoved him hard between the shoulder blades and they took off together.

Run, Josh's gut said. *You don't know what you're fighting.*

The trench-coated figure wrestling with Winsor saw Deloise coming and turned his head sharply in her direction. A cotton candy machine exploded as Deloise passed it, and she hit the ground.

Did he just control the Dream?

Josh scrambled out of the pool, barely able to believe what she'd seen.

Winsor took advantage of the distraction to kick her assailant's legs out from under him. Lighter tucked in her fist, she punched him in the gut.

Deloise was already back on her feet. "Open the archway!" she called to Josh. "I'll help Winsor."

Josh nodded, although she didn't see a doorway besides the one Winsor and the man were wrestling in. As she turned her head to look around, she caught sight of Will.

He had retrieved the mallet from the strong-man booth. Holding it over his shoulder, he inched his way down the diving board behind the man in the trench coat. Josh wanted to shout at him again, but she was afraid of ruining his surprise. The dreamer, who had turned as gray as cigarette smoke, lay faceup on the edge of the diving board. Josh ran toward them even though she knew she would be too late to do anything.

"Look at the tower!" Deloise screamed.

The slide tower was bending at the waist and then straightening, bending then straightening. Never mind that no wooden structure should be so flexible—the whole thing was about to topple.

Will brought down the hammer. The wooden end, edges flared from so many poundings, caught the man's green felt hat at an angle and flung his head to his shoulder. He crashed into the water. The dreamer, still tethered to him by her gas mask, followed.

Something crashed. People screamed, and a static crackle filled the air. The dreamer surfaced without her mask, eyes wide open, mouth full of water. The creaking of the waterslide structure became a terrible groan. Josh didn't have time to look up, but she knew what was happening—the tower was finally giving way.

And then . . . something fell on her. Sound crashed around her, so much sound that it lost all distinction and became only a deafening rush. Something else landed on her, something heavier, and behind her eyelids she saw a flash of red.

Then there was quiet, and with the quiet came the pain. She didn't try to move, not even when she felt her left leg twisted back under her hip and the agony it sent through her knee. Cold water soaked her clothes, and her neck was wrenched to one side.

She thought time had passed, but she wasn't sure how much. At some point she must have passed out. She opened and closed one hand. All her fingers worked. She tried to call for help and choked.

People screamed and more water splashed against her legs. *Didn't anyone manage to wake that dreamer up?* Josh wondered. She could still smell the cotton candy and roasted peanuts.

"Josh, don't move!" someone called. She knew his voice, but she couldn't place it. Why couldn't she remember who he was? "We're going to get you out of there."

Suddenly something heavy was lifted off her head. "Don't move her," another voice ordered, and this one she at least recognized. "Wait until we have the back board."

"Del?" Josh asked, her voice hardly more than a croak.

"I see her," said the guy she couldn't place. His boot flew past her face, knocking away planks and sheets of curved plastic. When there was space, he crouched down in front of her. She finally saw his face, his pretty green-hazel eyes and curly black hair. "I've got you."

Her heartbeat fluttered in her ears.

"Ian?" she whispered.

Thirteen

Josh stared at the stain on the hospital room ceiling through the mess of wires, slings, and metal bars holding up her leg. The pillows under her head were flat and made her neck cramp. She was surprised she could still feel pain of any sort, what with all the drugs the doctor had pumped into her. She could feel her heart, too, the beats slowed to the pace of a funeral dirge from the meds as she lay in bed and rubbed her thumb over her plumeria pendant.

Deloise, Lauren, and Kerstel had finally gone home. Josh didn't know what time it was, but she felt certain that the witching hour had come and gone. Whim Avish—who had apparently arrived home just as the amusement-park nightmare was heating up—was going to stay the night at the hospital and make sure that Will, who had a concussion, didn't lapse into a coma before sunrise. Winsor had endured having her broken wrist set before leaving with her mother.

Josh didn't know where Haley McKarr had landed in all of the chaos.

How could I have thought he was Ian?

It had been easy, really. Ian and Haley were—no, *had been*—identical twins, and she hadn't seen either one of them for seven months. She hadn't expected Haley—or Whim, for that matter—to show up in a nightmare gone horribly wrong. And she hadn't expected Haley to have his hair cut like Ian's, or to be wearing one of Ian's shirts.

During the confusion of her rescue, Josh managed to call Haley "Ian" four more times.

In the ER, the cover story was that Josh had been standing next to an aboveground pool when a second-story deck collapsed on it. Will had been standing on the pool's ladder and hit his head when the structure fell apart. Winsor had broken her wrist trying to dig them out. Since they were all soaked in chlorine water, the story went over well.

Josh winced when she heard the hospital room door open. If that nurse was back to check her vitals again . . .

But it wasn't the nurse. Will stood in the doorway, his billowing hospital gown a black silhouette against the hall lights.

"Will?" she asked.

He didn't move. Josh couldn't see his face, but the way he stood reminded her of numerous dreamers: panicked, frozen. He looked like she had felt for the last six hours.

"Are you all right?" she asked finally.

"I'm sorry," he all but whispered.

"Come in."

He hesitated before stepping inside, closing the door, and walking to the bed. One hand trailed the wall to balance his wobbly steps. He half fell into the chair beside the bed.

"Do I look that bad?" Josh asked.

"What?"

In the light from the window's view of Tanith, she saw his face in hues of silver and gray, like she imagined aliens would look. Only without the overgrown auburn hair and the white bandage around his head.

"You nearly went running when you saw me," she told him.

"Oh, I'm sorry." He smiled with a wince and shook his head, which caused him to wince again. "It wasn't you. Just . . . for a second, you looked like my mother."

He and Josh had never talked about his parents, or why he had been a ward of the state. She hadn't wanted to pry, and she hadn't wanted to risk a session of quid pro quo, but tonight she asked anyway. Maybe the meds were messing with her judgment.

"Did your mother die in a hospital?"

He managed to catch himself before shaking his head again. "She didn't die. But she was in hospitals or rehab centers a lot, because of her drinking. One night she got confused about which bottle the rum was in and accidentally swallowed some cleaning fluid. Her kidneys were really messed up after that."

His hands shook while he poured a glass of water from the plastic pitcher on the tray table.

"Where is she now?"

"I don't know. Five years ago she left me with the state and took off. West, she said. Maybe California, although I sincerely doubt it."

He said the last with venom. Then his expression weakened, and he looked down.

"That's not fair," he said. "I shouldn't say it like that. I told her to leave me. I was the one who called the police."

Oh god, Josh thought. Part of her was screaming, *Don't ask, you don't want to know!* and the rest was snared by the raw pain in Will's voice.

"Did your father go with her?"

"Dad left when I was six. He lives in New York, with two more ex-wives and like a dozen kids."

Couldn't you have gone to him? She didn't let the words pass her lips; she didn't want to know this; she didn't want to hurt for him.

Will finished drinking the water and poured a second glass, then glanced at it and set it down. "I'm sorry," he said. "I know you don't want to hear that kind of shit."

Josh felt as if he'd slapped her. Was that the message her silence had given him, that his past was just a load of shit not worth her time?

"I'm sorry," he said again, before she could figure out a response. "I have a concussion—I'm not thinking straight."

Neither am I. Between her own exhaustion and the cool IV drugs slipping through her system, her heart felt too close to the surface tonight, her emotions too near. She was afraid that if she spoke, she wouldn't be able to control what she said and apologies and reassurances and secrets would pour from her mouth.

Maybe she wanted all that.

"How's your leg?" Will asked.

"Badly bruised cartilage and pulled muscles," she said, nearly whispering. The words felt useless, phony. She tried again. "Sorry about your mom. And your dad."

He looked away from his glass of water and back at her. "Thank you."

His eyes in the dim room were piercing, bright as if with fever. She knew that his reserve at that moment was as fragile as her own. What could she say that was comforting? The words never came to her, and she wondered if it would be easier to convey what she meant by touching him, if a hug would say what she couldn't. But she remembered earlier that day, when he had almost kissed her, and she feared going too far again.

"I'm sorry I didn't listen to you," Will said, oblivious to her thoughts, "when you told us to bail. I'm sorry I ignored you. Or, I guess it was actually more like I mutinied. I just . . . I had this bad feeling, this terrible feeling about that guy in the trench coat. It didn't even feel like dreamfire, more like . . . dread."

"It's all right," Josh said, relieved to be back in safe territory. She knew the feeling he meant; she'd had it too, when her gut was screaming like a tornado siren. The difference was that she'd run away from the danger and Will had run toward it.

He'd made a bad choice, but he'd done it for the right reasons.

"It's not all right," he said. "You're in the hospital because of me."

"I'm in the hospital because a slide fell on top of me. Even if you hadn't gone after the man in the trench coat, the slide still would have fallen."

"Next time I'll listen."

"I know."

Will put one elbow on the mattress and laid his chin in his hand. "Don't fall asleep," Josh reminded him, dangerously close to sleep herself.

He smiled weakly. "I won't. And I'll get out of here so that you can rest, but before I go . . . I'm sorry. I just want to tell you that again."

His voice was full of defeat. She used her leaden hand to tug his out from under his chin and then wrapped her fingers around his, willing to take the risk of touching him if it meant bringing him some comfort. "I know. Stop worrying."

His hand was cold and dry, hospitalized, but his grip was reassuring. *We almost died together tonight,* she thought.

"You hear me?" Josh asked.

"Yes."

"Good." As she closed her eyes she heard him stand up. His fingers whispered across the grainy wallpaper as he shuffled to the door.

"Josh?" he asked.

"Yeah?"

With no small awareness of the irony, he said, "Sweet dreams."

She smiled at the stained ceiling. "You too."

Fourteen

 Will was released from the hospital just before lunch, and Laurentius picked him up in a Mercedes that made the candy stripers swoon. The ride to the house was the first time Will had been alone with his adoptive father. He and Lauren didn't have much to talk about besides Josh, and ended up discussing every parent's favorite subject—college—which was okay until Will realized that Lauren was happy to pay for Will to go to any school he got into, which freaked him out and made him clam up.

At the house, Will wasn't sure what to do with himself. Josh was still in the hospital, and he felt like he needed her silent, unspoken permission to be here. He didn't live here; he had yet to spend one night in the bedroom Kerstel and Dustine had so carefully prepared for him.

He wandered down the hallway until he heard laughter coming from the office. Through the open door, he saw Winsor sitting in front of the computer and Deloise on the futon beside Whim, who was sprawled out like a lazy giraffe.

"Will," Whim said. "You're an eyewitness! Come in here and give us your two cents!"

Whimarian Travarres Nikolaas Avishara was very tall and very thin, with his sister's blue eyes and his father's sociability. He had little in the way of either muscle or fat, but he was both coordinated and nimble, and he smiled easily. In the eighteen hours Will had known him, he'd discovered that Whim also talked easily, and quickly, and constantly.

"My two cents on what?" Will asked, joining them.

"Deloise says that one of the trench-coat men in the amusement park controlled the Dream," Winsor explained. "She says he made a cotton-candy machine explode just by looking at it."

Whim proceeded to act this out, playing the parts of both the trench-coat man and the cotton-candy machine.

"I was trying to get to Winsor to help her," Deloise explained, ignoring Whim, "and when the guy saw me, he looked at the cotton-candy machine, like, really *hard*. Like he was mad at it. And then it just exploded and completely blocked my way."

"I thought nobody could alter the Dream except dreamers," Will said.

"Absolutely true," Winsor said.

"*Not* absolutely true!" Whim cried. "How quickly thou hast forgotten the learnings of thine childhood." He held up a single finger in point. "The True Dream Walker could have altered the Dream."

Winsor groaned. "All right: discounting the presence of imaginary people, no one can alter the Dream. Besides which, the park was already starting to fall apart by then, so the machine could have exploded on its own."

"However, we are anxious to hear your testimony before deciding the case," Whim added.

Will rubbed the back of his neck to stall for time. Everyone was talking so quickly, the way people who had known each other for a long time often did. He was having a hard time keeping up. "Ah, who's the True Dream Walker?"

"Your teacher, who wears his symbol around her neck at all times, hasn't told you about the TDW?" Whim asked with a laugh.

"The True Dream Walker opened the first archway to the Dream," Deloise explained to Will. Winsor's eyes narrowed, and Deloise quickly continued. "According to legend. And supposedly someday he'll return to bring permanent balance to the three universes."

"And Josh believes in him? That's what the flower charm is about?"

"Well," Deloise said, "I don't know if she really *believes* in him."

"He's more like her idol," Whim put in. "He's her guiding light."

The picture felt somehow incomplete to Will. He wondered if he would ever get the opportunity to talk to Josh about it; personal beliefs weren't at the top of the list of things she liked to discuss with him.

"So, about the cotton-candy machine," Deloise said.

Will shrugged. "I didn't see it happen, so I can't really vouch one way or the other."

Whim lifted Winsor's right hand—which was in a cast—into the air. "Sister, I declare you the winner of this debate. Would you like to make a victory speech?"

"No, I would not." Winsor carefully tugged her hand away. "Where is this drawing you were going to show me?"

Whim produced a very thin, very sleek laptop. "One of my many faithful readers says she saw the trench-coat men in a nightmare, and she did these drawings of them."

The first image showed a sinister man in a green-black trench coat. His shoulders were massive, hulking, and he reached out with hands that looked like rakes made of flesh. Black boots leaked green sewage water. The whole picture was overblown, a sort of caricature drawn with colored pencils. But the green hat with its black band and the overall feel were right.

The second image showed the man's rubber gas mask and the canister peeking over his shoulder. The artist hadn't gotten the tank's color quite right—it was too silver—but she'd included both gas masks.

"That's them!" Deloise cried. "Look at the eyes!"

The eyes were the clincher. No white, no irises, no pupils. Just a shining black expanse.

"It's the same guys," Winsor agreed.

"What does this mean?" Will asked.

Whim stabbed the trench-coat man's face decisively with one finger, causing the laptop's screen to blur. "I think they're connected to the sick people."

"Don't start with that again," Winsor snapped. "It's absurd."

"Not if you connect the dates—"

Ignoring them, Deloise said, "So, the trench-coat guys must be getting publicity from somewhere. Maybe comic books." She tilted the laptop's screen to get a better look at the images. "He looks like a comic-book character."

"What happens when we find out who he is?" Will asked.

"Then we know how to fight him," Winsor said. "He has to have a weak spot."

"So, you don't think there's any chance he's . . ." Will hesitated and then decided to admit what he'd been thinking. "That he's a real guy walking around in there?"

Deloise's eyes moved quickly from Will to Winsor, as if she, too, had wondered. Winsor didn't laugh, but she didn't seem to take the idea very seriously, either. "Highly unlikely."

"But definitely possible," Whim said. When Winsor shot him a look, he added, "According to modern dream theory."

"Don't be condescending," Winsor said tartly.

Whim sighed. "I'm not."

"You are! That's your Ha-Ha-Winsor-Can't-Take-a-Joke voice."

Whim sighed again, letting his head fall back on the futon's arm and his eyes roll at the same time. "Okay, Winsor, I'm sorry."

He's not sorry at all, Will thought, just as Winsor spun the desk chair to face Whim. Her nostrils flared, and she said, "You know what, Whim? My tolerance for taking crap from you is zero right now, because I've been taking crap from you for the last six straight months, so don't you—"

"Is that what this is about?" Whim asked, not bothering to sit up. "I sent letters—"

"You sent *postcards*. And now you show up with *Haley*?"

Will must have missed something. What did Haley have to do with this?

"Oh, I get it," Whim said with a morose smile. "You wanted me to drop him on the side of the highway before I came home."

"You could have called to say he was coming here. You know things are weird between us."

Whim chuckled. "Winsor, look, it's not my fault you cheated on him with Ian, okay?"

Will felt like he'd just walked onto the set of a soap opera. Winsor had dated *Haley*? And cheated on him with *Ian*?

"Golly," Deloise said, shoving Whim's legs off her lap and rising from the futon. "I don't think Will and I need to stick around for this. We probably have homework to do, or spaceships to build, or . . ."

"Baby seals to club," Will put in, although he was tempted to stay and see how much more he could find out.

"You're a jackass," Winsor told her brother, who laughed. Neither of them was paying Will or Deloise any attention as they escaped into the hallway.

Deloise yanked the office door shut behind them and blew out an exaggerated breath of relief. "I think I need my aura cleansed." She shook her head. "Before you came in, Whim admitted that he and Haley had been traveling around since last summer. Whim graduated last year, but Haley's missed more than half his junior year! I don't even think his mom knows—she probably thought he was living here and going to school with us."

Living here? Will wondered, and then remembered the empty second-floor apartment. "His apartment's still empty, isn't it?"

"Yeah. He slept in Josh's room last night." Deloise made a face that suggested she knew how Josh would feel about that. "Don't tell her, okay? 'Cause it would just upset her, and he's already acting, like . . . strange."

Will hadn't met Haley yet, so he couldn't help asking, "Strange how?"

Deloise glanced up and down the hall as if making sure no one would overhear them, then dragged Will into Kerstel's office. A desk with a towering hutch, an overburdened bookcase, and two filing cabinets were crammed into the tiny space.

Deloise pulled her cell phone out of her pocket, and a moment later she was showing Will a series of photographs. "Look at these," she said, holding the phone out to Will.

The similarities—and differences—between the twins were astonishing. They both had curly black hair and hazel eyes; they shared the same tall, slim frames. But Ian's hair was trimmed into a cap close around his skull, there were smile lines at the corners of his eyes, he carried a decent amount of muscle, and he was dressed in slightly preppy clothes that Will was sure Deloise appreciated. Ian jumped off the page, making Haley look like a pale afterimage left in his brother's wake. Aside from his greasy hair, Haley seemed to be wearing a black or navy-blue T-shirt and stained jeans in every picture, and he slouched so badly that he was more than an inch shorter than Ian. It was obvious from his uncertain and panicky expression that the camera made him nervous.

"You can see how different they looked, right? They always looked like that. I mean, nobody ever had trouble telling who was Haley and who was Ian." She stuck the phone back in her pocket. In a half whisper, she continued, "But when Haley showed up yesterday, he had his hair cut just like Ian's used to be, and he was wearing Ian's clothes. He was even standing like Ian. And Josh kept calling him Ian in the hospital, because she hit her head when the slide fell on her, and she called him Ian, like, ten times, and he didn't correct her once. One time he even answered her. Like, what *is* that? You're into psychology, right? That's not normal, is it?"

Hell, no! Will thought. Aloud, he said, "Well, grieving is its own thing, and twins have their own kind of bond, and maybe this is just how Haley is grieving. Everybody does it differently." Feeling that his answer was somehow insufficient, he added, "But no, frankly, it doesn't sound normal to me. Answering to Ian's name doesn't sound at all normal."

Deloise let out a long, theatrical sigh. "I'm so glad you said that.

I was feeling kind of guilty for being so creeped out by it. Thanks for letting me vent."

She hugged him, and Will couldn't help smiling. She was such a sweetheart.

"Hey," she said, releasing him, "let's go do something fun."

"You got a plan?"

"Let's make brownies and take them to Josh in the hospital."

Will grinned. "She'll probably eat them for breakfast tomorrow."

Deloise's jaw dropped and she smacked his arm. "She will! How did you know that?"

He opened the door to the hallway and then followed Deloise out. "Oh, I've learned a thing or two about her."

Through a Veil Darkly

I've been getting a ton of e-mails about the mystery illness that strikes sleeping victims. I ignored the first half dozen that suggested the illness had something to do with the trench-coat men, but then I noticed something interesting. The date of the first reported sighting of the TCM is only four days before the first victim fell ill of CSAD (that's what the CDC is calling it—catatonic sinoatrial dysfunction).

Then a source—someone I trust fully—got in touch with me to say that he had actually witnessed the eleventh victim, Simon Parish, being attacked by the TCM in-Dream. My source only recognized Parish after seeing him on the local news and learning he was the latest victim of CSAD. My source pointed out that the pink markings around Simon Parish's mouth and nose align perfectly with the placement of the gas mask the trench-coat man had fitted him with in-Dream.

I'm starting to think people are on to something.

ifteen

I saw a gate *beyond the arch.*

Josh blinked. Ian stood next to the window, his arms crossed and his eyes cloaked by sunglasses. She saw the dawn reflected in the lenses and heard waves splashing outside the cabin.

She was so glad to see him.

She untangled her pendant's chain from around her neck. "I don't remember letting go of your hand," she said as she reached for his arm.

Then she opened her eyes again.

"Josh?" Ian asked.

He was still standing next to the window, wearing ironed brown slacks and a sweater, but his sunglasses were gone and the room around them had changed. *Wait,* Josh thought. *We aren't at the cabin. We're in the office.* She remembered the night before, stumbling home from the hospital on crutches that chewed at her armpits and finding that Kerstel had made up the futon in the office so that Josh wouldn't have to climb all those stairs to her bedroom.

"Are you awake?" Ian asked.

She nodded and then shook her head. It wasn't Ian—it was *Haley* standing next to the window, *Haley* wearing Ian's green argyle sweater.

The happiness she had felt dropped down through her body like a weight, leaving behind a terrible sense of loss.

"Breakfast is ready in the kitchen," Haley told her. Then he paused before putting one bent knee on the foot of the futon and leaning his weight on it. If he hadn't hesitated before assuming his brother's stance, Josh wouldn't have been sure he was Haley at all.

"I'll be there in a couple of minutes," she said. She wanted him gone, needed a few moments to remind herself who was here—she couldn't use the word "alive"—and who wasn't.

"Do you need a hand getting dressed?" he asked.

Josh stared at him. Did she need a *hand* getting *dressed*?

"No, that's all right," she told him when she could speak again. "I'll be fine by myself."

He shrugged sheepishly. The gesture was reassuring, pure Haley, and she saw a notepad and pen tucked into his left pocket as he turned away.

"God bless obsessive-compulsive disorders," she muttered when he was gone, throwing back the covers, but inside she still felt torn up.

Truthfully, she could have used some help getting dressed. "You can be walking again in a couple of weeks if you just don't stress the joint," the doctor had told her, and to prove the point he had encased her leg in a huge metal and Velcro brace that ran from halfway up her thigh down to her ankle. It was a pain, but she already felt better than she had the morning before.

Of course, the morning before her father had told her that she wasn't allowed to dream walk until her knee was not only out of its brace but fully rehabbed.

"How am I going to train Will if we can't go into the Dream?" Josh had demanded.

"There are plenty of things to study here in the World," Lauren had replied. "There's dream theory, weapons skills, first aid—"

"But none of that can take the place of real experience, and it could be months before I finish physical therapy."

"Oh, I'm sure it won't be months," Lauren said. "A month, maybe."

That had not reassured Josh.

The kitchen was a noisy place. *Must mean Whim's home,* Josh thought, and smiled. Sure enough, he was flipping pancakes while Kerstel cut strawberries. He hadn't undergone a dramatic change since he'd been away, which comforted Josh, and his smile when he saw her was warm. He gave her a hug with his long, wiry arms.

Meanwhile, Deloise was reading the pancake mix's nutritional information, and Laurentius was on his way out the door. Josh had just sat down at the table with a cup of hot chocolate when Will suddenly appeared, out of breath, in the kitchen doorway. "Am I too late?" he asked.

"No," Josh told him, mystified, "we're still here." She felt startled to see him at this time of day, and also startled that everyone else was already used to his presence.

"I meant for breakfast."

Whim handed him a plate. "I'm afraid so. This will have to be lunch."

"Thank you," Will said, plopping down at the table. "Good morning, everybody." He looked down at the plate in front of him. "Who came up with the brilliant idea of putting strawberries in pancakes?"

Kerstel laughed and smoothed his hair down before going upstairs to shower.

Whim joined Will and the Weaver girls at the table and wolfed down three glasses of milk, a mug of coffee, and half a cup of butter with his seven pancakes. He had the metabolism of a puppy and an appetite to match; Josh had always suspected he had an extra thyroid hidden somewhere on his thin frame.

Winsor came down a few minutes before they needed to leave for school, dressed in designer jeans, a button-down poplin shirt, and a men's wool suit jacket. "You guys ready to go?" she asked, hoisting her leather messenger bag over her shoulder with her good arm.

Haley stepped uncertainly into the kitchen and held out a slip of paper to Josh. She couldn't quite look at it, but she pretended to and nodded. Then she jammed it into her pocket.

"By the way," he said, with perfect and utter confidence, "you look beautiful this morning."

Will talked through the silence that descended on the rest of the room and then caught himself. Haley smiled at Josh, then blushed and retreated from the room with stubby little steps.

Winsor set her cup of coffee down on the counter and said, "Okay, Whim, tell me."

Whim lifted his eyebrows. "Tell you what?"

"What is *up* with *Haley*?"

"*Seriously,*" Deloise added.

Whim shrugged and opened a Tupperware container of trail mix, largely composed of M&M's and honey-roasted peanuts. "In ten years, have you ever seen Haley without a piece of paper and a pen? I've still got notes from back when he wrote with a crayon."

"Not the notes," Winsor said, "the clothes. The amber-scented cologne. The haircut."

"Ian's ring," Deloise added. "Ian's car."

"The way he's hit on me twice this morning," Josh put in.

Will was wearing the expression that meant he was paying very careful attention to what was going on around him, and Josh was aware that she didn't really want to talk about this in front of him. But the situation resolved itself when Whim said simply, "Nothing's going on. Ian left all his stuff to Haley and he's using it."

"You don't think that's just a little strange?" Winsor asked, at the same time Will said quietly, "He didn't inherit *Josh*."

Whim put the trail mix back in the cupboard and rummaged around for something else. "I just got used to it. He's still Haley."

"We have to get going," Josh pointed out. "We're going to be late for homeroom."

But minutes later, sitting in the backseat of Winsor's car with her leg propped up across Will's lap—he insisted he didn't mind—Josh dug Haley's note out of her pocket. The page, torn from a steno pad, began to shake in her hand as she read.

January 25th
To: J. D. Weaver
From: H. McKarr

1. *Accident—You*
   a. *An aboveground swimming pool collapsed on top of you on Sat.*
   b. *You were treated for bruised cartilage in your right knee, internal bruises, and a lightly twisted neck Sat. night at St. Dymphna's Hospital.*
   c. *You were released Mon. night.*
2. *Accident—Others*
   a. *W. Kansas—concussion (released Sun.)*
   b. *Wi. Avish—broken wrist (treated and released Sat.)*
   c. *D. Weaver, H. McKarr, and Wh. Avish—unharmed*

3. Continued Treatment

  a. Your knee brace can be removed Fri.

  b. For pain, take Advil as prescribed.

4. Schoolwork

  a. Make-up work for Mon. will be due on Thurs.

5. Love

  a. I still love you.

Sixteen

"Deloise."

"Deloise Marigold Laurene Weavaros."

"Kerstel. And you have to spell it."

Will stared across the library table at Josh. "*Spell it?* Kersteleinaly Yseult Hyacinth Weavaros?"

Josh grinned. "Just because we can't dream walk right now doesn't mean I'm going to take it easy on you."

To avoid actually trying to spell Kerstel's name, he said, "I suppose your name is just as complicated."

Josh shrugged. "My name is a piece of cake compared to Kerstel's. Although not as easy as yours, obviously."

"Obviously," he agreed, but what he noticed was that she didn't actually give him her name.

"You should also know the full names of my father, Whim's parents, and my grandmother, because you live with them and it's respectful to learn."

Will sighed. "I think I liked training better when my life was in danger."

Josh frowned as if she didn't agree, but she said, "You could do some more of that Romanian circuit training."

He was still sore from the first time through the circuit. "Never mind, spelling is great."

Josh considered, then said, "There is one thing we could do. Come with me."

They headed for the basement.

"Can you make it?" he asked as they reached the top of the stairs.

"Hold my crutches. I am so sick of this brace!"

The Velcro straps on her knee brace protested as she peeled them back. She tugged the brace off and limped down the stairs. Will expected that at any moment her knee would buckle and she'd go tumbling, and he wondered if he should have tried to carry her. She probably wouldn't have appreciated the offer.

Safely on the basement floor, she took back her crutches and said, "You know, you should think about adding to your name. People might think you're holding out on them if you just say, 'Will Kansas.' They'd be offended."

"What would I add?" he asked, moving slowly to match her pace as they began the long trek across the basement.

"You're missing a member of your mother's family and a role model."

He thought of his mother's family and winced. Would he rather call himself after his shoplifting uncle Mitch or his disgruntled moonshiner grandpa Hank? "A family member's going to be tough."

"What about the role model?"

A name popped into his head. "Sigmund."

"Sigmund?"

"After Freud. Don't laugh. He might be outdated, but I would have ended up an alcoholic dropout if I hadn't discovered psychology and self-help books."

Josh smiled, but not in a mocking way. "Where did you get all those books?"

"Somebody gave my mother *How to Take Back Your Life* when she was in rehab one time, and she left it lying around the house. I wouldn't have read it except that Mom didn't pay the electric bill and we lost power for three weeks, and I didn't have anything else to do. Then I found a bunch more at this social worker's yard sale for a quarter each, and after that I was pretty hooked, so I started getting them at Goodwill."

"You want to be a psychiatrist?" Josh asked.

"Well, I hadn't planned on it because I didn't think I could afford to go to college, but . . ."

"Dad told you how much money he makes?"

"Yes. And basically that if I want to spend ten years in college and medical school, he thinks that's great." Will got nervous just thinking about the idea, which he knew from his reading was a result of his insecurities about admitting he wanted something because subconsciously he thought it would be taken away. Somehow, the knowledge didn't reassure him; he just wasn't sure he deserved any of this.

"What about you?" he asked.

Josh tucked her crutches and knee brace under one arm while she typed in the code for the vault door to the archroom. "There's a three-year college for dream walkers in Scotland called Kasari Academy. I thought maybe I'd send in my application and see what happens."

"You're worried you won't get in?"

"Sort of. They're pretty selective, and heavy on dream theory. My great-aunt Lasia went there. But even if I don't get in, I'll still dream walk full-time."

That she had never wanted to do anything besides dream walk was one of the few things Will knew about her. "You'll get in," he told her confidently as the archroom door swung open.

Inside the round room with its stone arch and metal chair, they came across Haley. He was sitting on the floor with his chin on his knees like a four-year-old, staring at the archway. One hand held a small steno pad and the other gripped a pen, but he hadn't written anything.

Josh stopped short in the doorway, and Will bumped into her from behind. "I'm sorry," he muttered at the same time she said, "Oh!"

Haley lifted his head. The pen slipped from his hand and rolled across the floor.

"We didn't mean to intrude," Josh said.

"S'okay," Haley told her. His voice trembled. "I was just sitting here. S'okay."

Once again, Will wondered exactly what was wrong with Haley. Why was he sitting on the floor—with a chair no more than two feet away—staring into an empty archway? Why was he holding a pen and paper as if he expected to take dictation from the Dream? Why did he write notes in the first place? He seemed like a nice enough guy, but when he wasn't imitating his dead twin, he was barely functional.

"We were only going to use the looking stone," Josh said.

Haley picked his pen up. "I'll go."

"No," Josh said quickly, "wait a sec. If we're not bothering you, it's no problem."

Haley's face was unreadable as he slid across the floor to lean against the wall.

They spent the next hour refining Will's searching skills. The exercise was physically easy but emotionally exhausting. After a long session, Will needed a while to remember who and where he was, as though he had touched so many minds that he had lost his own.

They moved quickly from one nightmare to the next, and Josh always asked three questions: *Who is the dreamer? What is the danger? Do we go in?*

Will answered as quickly as he could while Josh stood behind him, looking into the Veil. With his hand on the looking stone, he had some connection to the dreamer's fear, but that didn't mean he could always accurately sense what was happening in a nightmare. The number of times Josh corrected him, just by watching over his shoulder, amazed him.

"Who's the dreamer?" Josh asked again, a half hour or so into their session.

"A man, late middle age. He's dreaming he's in . . . China, I think. He's carrying something and running. He has to get it somewhere."

"No, try again."

Will closed his eyes, but all he could see was the man straining to run faster.

"He's not trying to get somewhere," Josh said. "He's being chased. Where's the danger?"

Will tried to aim his perception, and instead of focusing on the dreamer, he looked at what was behind him. "Oh no."

Josh's hand clamped around his shoulder. "What's wrong?"

"It's him. The man in the trench coat."

Through the archway, Josh watched a man in a green-black coat lumber down a narrow alley with painted walls on either side. *It is him,* she thought, taking in the heavy boots, the black-banded hat, the large, hunched shoulders. *He's right there.*

She wasn't aware that she was digging her fingernails into Will's shoulder until he shrugged to loosen her grip. "Sorry," she said. "Hold on to this dream, okay?"

"I've got it."

The man moved quickly toward the mouth of the alley, away from them. Josh had been forbidden to enter the Dream, but here was her chance to confront the man in the trench coat, to determine whether he was a figment of someone's imagination or a real person walking around in there, a person who recognized her. She didn't know when she'd get another chance like this.

I don't know what to do, she thought, and she felt a sick paralysis. The feeling was familiar, although it hadn't struck her in years. When she was younger—much younger—she used to feel like this—helpless and uncertain, like a rabbit darting back and forth between lines of traffic in the middle of a highway, every direction leading to danger, every choice the wrong one.

Unconsciously, Josh let her weight shift onto her injured leg. Pain shot out from her knee into her thigh and shin, and she shifted back with a cry. In the next instant, Haley was standing beside her, just the way Ian always had, and he looped Josh's arm around his neck to support her weight. His slouch was gone, his eyes wide open and focused. A hard line marked his jaw.

Ian, Josh thought, and felt a different sort of pain.

Because she wanted Ian in moments like this, needed Ian to tell her what to do when she turned into that rabbit on the highway, when she couldn't decide what was most important, when she couldn't live up to everyone's expectations. Will was waiting for her instructions, and she had no idea what to say.

She tightened her arm around Haley's neck. "What should I . . ."

Will turned toward them, his hand still on the looking stone. He frowned at the sight of them standing so close to the archway, and perhaps at the sight of Josh clinging to Haley—Josh didn't know which. She didn't have time to think about that.

Haley said, "J.D., look at me."

She did, and he looked back at her with perfect steadiness. In a voice as strong and clear as bulletproof glass, he said, "You're wasting time. You know what to do, so get on with it already."

Will said, "Josh, you can't go in there," but Josh barely heard him. All she heard was Ian's voice—confident, certain—cutting through her fears. He was short with her; even that was reassuring, because he wouldn't have dismissed her so quickly if he hadn't believed that she was overreacting.

"Josh," Will said urgently, but she and Haley were already moving.

"Whatever happens, stay here," Josh said to Will, as she and Haley stepped through the Veil, causing it to shiver.

Her ears filled with clanging bells and shouting in Chinese. The hot, spicy scents of seasoned meat wafted in the air, and grimy water ran down the center of the alley into a rusted grate. Ahead of her, the man in the trench coat had reached the street and was looking back and forth, searching for the dreamer.

Josh didn't hesitate before breaking Stellanor's First Rule of dream walking this time. In her mind, she yanked the cork from the stone wall of her mental defenses and let the dreamer's fear rush through, just long enough to get a sense of the situation.

A man, with a precious microchip in his pocket. Running, running. Already a block away.

Strangely, she felt the scorching anxiety of dreamfire. Predicting what fears would reach deep enough into a dreamer's subconscious to summon dreamfire was more or less impossible, but Josh wouldn't have expected that level of terror in a nightmare about a microchip. Yet she'd encountered dreamfire in each of the three nightmares where she'd seen the man in the trench coat.

She had no time then to ponder the connection. As she severed her link with the dreamer's fear, she saw the man in the trench coat turn left at the mouth of the alley.

"Hey!" she shouted.

The man turned, his eyes shadowed by the brim of his fedora, his face hidden behind the glossy gas mask. With slow, even steps, he began walking toward Josh and Haley. His heavy-soled boots sank into the water running down the alley.

Good, she thought, even as her gut began to scream, *Danger! Danger!*

Watching him come closer, Josh wondered if she had made a mistake. The man approached her without any indication that he feared the situation, and Josh supposed that a teenage girl being half held up by a teenage boy didn't look so imposing, but still . . . the man had recognized her before. Since he'd identified her as Jona's daughter, he had to know that she was a dream walker and that—whether he was a real person or a figment of someone's subconscious—she was going to want answers from him.

Haley held her tighter. Distantly, she smelled Ian's warm, rich amber cologne on his neck, and the scent reassured her.

"Who are you?" Josh demanded.

The man said nothing, but he began running toward them. Water splashed from his boots.

"Dammit," muttered Haley, who never cursed.

"Stop!" Josh shouted, but the man's speed increased. He was ten feet from them, seven feet, five . . .

"Clothesline!" Haley hissed, and shoved Josh away even as he found her hands.

Clothesline. A stupid old trick Josh and Ian had pulled together a hundred times, more because it amused them than anything else. They grabbed each other's hands, their arms forming a long line, and the man in the trench coat ran right into it. His boots slid on the wet cobblestones and he crashed onto his back, his gas tank clanging like a bell against the ground. Before the man had time to recover, Josh threw herself onto his chest and Haley clobbered his legs.

Then the man's hat fell back, and Josh found herself staring into those terribly empty black eyes.

"Who are you?" she demanded.

No reaction. She hadn't realized before how pale his skin was.

Finally, he said, "You're Jona's daughter."

Josh swallowed. He spoke from behind his gas mask, but this close, his words were clear. Josh knew she had heard him correctly.

"Did you know my mother?" she asked.

"Yes, before . . ."

His black eyes moved. Their coloration made them difficult to follow, but Josh thought they flicked from side to side, as if checking to make sure he was not overheard.

"Before Feodor . . ." the man whispered.

"Feodor? Who's—"

From behind her, Josh heard a shout. "Josh! Watch out!"

When she turned to look in the direction from which the shout had come, she saw Will standing at the far end of the alley, and the panic she'd felt before entering the Dream came back to her, worse, at the sight of him. He couldn't be here—not where even she wasn't supposed to be. She had to get him out immediately.

She was so caught up in her panic that she didn't see what Will had been warning her about. Something crashed into her from behind.

Another man, another trench coat. This man was thinner, wiry, but no less strong, and he knocked her onto her side. She fell, cracking her head against an aluminum garbage can that rang like a gong in her ears.

The man who had attacked her put one hand on her face and held her head to the ground—he wore black leather gloves, she noticed, unlike his partner—and with the other hand he dug into her hip. She thought at first that he was going for the fly of her jeans, and she reached up to poke his eyes out with her thumbs, but his arms were longer than hers, and besides, he wasn't unzipping her pants, just digging into her pocket.

Josh was fuzzy enough from the knock on the head that this seemed like a relief to her for a moment. In the precious second it took her to realize what he was actually doing, the man with the gloves jerked both her lighter and her compact out of her pocket.

Without her keys, she could be stranded in the Dream forever. She always carried them, even if she wasn't planning to enter the Dream, and she hoped to God that either Will or Haley was doing the same. Otherwise, they would become intimately familiar with Aivasian's Apothegm: *To be lost in the Dream is to be outlived by bubbles.*

I have to get out of here somehow, Josh thought, and that's when her mind cleared. Gloves sat back on his heels, and she rose up and punched him hard in the forehead above his gas mask. A clumsy blow—her fist form was so bad that her knuckles popped—but it was enough to knock him backward and onto her legs.

Josh scrambled out from beneath him, the pain in her knee continuous now, and when she tried to stand, her leg wouldn't hold her. She crawled forward on her hands and her good knee and hit Gloves in the face again. Out of the corner of her eye, she saw the larger man—the one she had clotheslined earlier—bring the garbage can down on Haley's head. Haley fell to the cobblestones, and Will rushed forward.

"No!" Josh shouted, but the aluminum can was already coming up again. It caught Will square in the chest and knocked him back against the wall.

Then Josh had to forget about Will and Haley, because she was blocking punches from Gloves, grabbing at his hands as they passed because he had her compact in one and her lighter in the other. She managed to catch the hand with the lighter and slam it against the ground. With the hard tip of her thumb, she dug into the pressure point on his outer wrist to make his fingers uncurl, and while she tried to pull the lighter from his grasp, he smashed her in the cheek with the compact so hard the plastic casing shattered and cut her skin.

Josh shouted wordlessly and hit Gloves in the face again, this time bringing the heel of her palm up into his mask, but he let his head roll back so that her blow rolled off.

He's had martial-arts training, Josh half thought, her other hand scrambling to find the compact on the ground beside her.

Then she stopped worrying about the lighter or the compact, because she realized that the man who had first attacked them had withdrawn a mask and rubber hose from the contraption on his back and was attempting to force the mask onto Haley's face, while Haley, half-conscious, feebly tried to fend him off. Will walked toward them with a section of broken two-by-four board.

"Will!" Josh screamed. "Open an exit! Do it now!"

Josh ducked a punch so powerful it crushed the concrete wall behind her.

She was fighting on her knees, and the already injured one landed on her compact as she moved. Shards of glass and plastic sliced through her jeans and into her skin, and a whole new kind of pain tore through the joint.

"But Haley—" Will said.

Josh bent over, trying to get off her knee, which now seemed more important than not getting hit. "Abort!" she shouted at Will, and then Gloves hit her in the back—a kidney shot, which was low of him, made worse by his phenomenal strength—and she doubled up from the nausea.

GET UP GET UP GET UP! her mind screamed.

She got up. Never mind her knee or her bleeding cheek, never mind the rising bile in her gullet, never mind the big man in the trench coat who was tightening the gas-mask straps over Haley's head. Josh straightened up with her weight on her good knee and, by moving slowly, deliberately gave Gloves an opening to swing at her again.

She was too small and he was too strong. She couldn't outmuscle him. Fine—that's why she'd been studying with Sensei Daiki since she was six years old.

Gloves jabbed. Josh ducked then swung, but without much force and without extending herself enough to give him any access to her body. As expected, he took her weak shot as a sign that he was gaining and threw a roundhouse. Josh ducked it and used the opportunity to roll him over her hip and slam him to the ground.

One of his legs landed bent, his foot close to his other knee. The position was ideal for a favorite jiujitsu move of Josh's—the Indian Death Lock. She grabbed both his ankles and arranged them as if he were sitting cross-legged. By hanging on to one of his legs, she immobilized both of them. Then she extended her own left leg until she could plant her foot under his chin and press down on his throat.

He scratched at her ankle, but his gloves saved her skin from gouging. Josh pushed down harder on his throat, and the fall must have knocked the wind out of him, because he passed out in less than thirty seconds. She remained in position at least that long again—even though her knee was screaming at her—just to make sure he was out, then stood up, breathing hard. She hadn't actually thrown someone twice her size in a while.

Turning, she saw Will holding an exit open in a doorway that led to the building next door. *Finally,* she thought.

The man pressing the mask to Haley's face saw what Will was doing at the same time as Josh did. He looked at the door and narrowed his fathomless eyes.

And the entire door vanished.

Just—gone. No doorway, no door, no doorknob. The red wall now extended, unblemished, deep into the alley.

Will's eyes locked with Josh's, and she knew they were thinking the same thing: *That's not possible.*

It wasn't possible for a figment of nightmare to alter the Dream.

Josh's mind was so completely unable to process the idea that it quit thinking entirely. Years of training took over, and she went into survival mode.

She looked at the trash around them and found a small microwave with a blackened interior. It smelled of melted plastic, and it weighed more than she expected as she lifted it and hopped over on one leg to the man in the trench coat. He had turned from the vanished doorway and was kneeling over Haley, who had revived enough to claw at the rubber mask on his face. When Haley saw Josh approaching, he intensified his struggle, and the man in the trench coat was entirely preoccupied when Josh dropped the microwave on him.

She tried to drop it on his head, but it was heavy and she was too tired to lift it that high. So she settled for dropping it on his stooped back, which sent him sprawling but failed to rupture the canister as she had hoped it would.

Josh might have held him down and gotten more information out of him, but Gloves was stirring, and she was afraid she and Haley wouldn't survive another encounter. So she just held her hand out to Haley.

Will had already run farther down the alley and opened a new exit. Josh hadn't had to tell him to do so; he'd just done it. Gratefully, she and Haley stumbled and limped through the exit Will held open.

When they were all standing in the archroom, dripping water onto the tile floor, she turned back and caught a glimpse of Gloves reaching for something small and golden on the ground.

My lighter, Josh thought. And then the archway closed.

Seventeen

They looked like they had been in a car accident. *No,* Will thought, *worse than a car accident.* A train derailment. A plane crash. A subway collapse. Not just an accident but some terrible shock.

Of the three of them, Will had come out the least injured. Josh's jeans were ripped over her knee, which dripped blood and glittered with reflective shards of mirror. Whatever that flower on her pendant was, it looked like a crimson rose now. Her cheek, already turning purple, had been scratched as if by an angry bear. She stood half bent over, one hand pressed to her back where she'd taken the kidney shot, and when she looked at Will, her eyes didn't quite focus.

Haley looked worse. For a moment before he and Josh had jumped into the Dream, Haley's face had been flushed with health, but now the circles and the paper-white cheeks had returned. Blood matted the black curls on his head and ran in thick streams down his temples. He had a pink outline around his nose and mouth— like a little kid who'd been drinking red juice—where the gas mask had been, and the mask must have been tight as hell, because the straps had left pink lines across his cheeks. Will didn't know what was in the canister, but Haley's breathing made a raspy, crackling sound as he sank to the floor and swallowed convulsively.

Josh looked at Will from beneath her lowered brows. "I told you to stay here."

Will just stared at her.

"I told you not to follow," she said through gritted teeth. "*Whatever happens*—those were my exact words. Why didn't you listen to me?"

Will couldn't believe she was actually going to chew him out. She had needed his help. Without it, she would never have been able to open an exit while fending off both men.

"If you hadn't gone in," she continued, "if I hadn't been looking at *you*, thinking about *you*, worrying about *you*—"

"You would have gotten clobbered," Will said, finally finding his voice. "You didn't even realize there was a second guy in there."

"I can handle getting hit!" she shouted. He'd never heard her raise her voice in anger before. "What I can't handle is trying to protect myself *and you* when you're somewhere you shouldn't be!"

Something about the way she kept spitting the word "you" made him feel like she hated him.

"How many times do we have to go over this? When I tell you to do something, do it! When I tell you not to do something, don't do it!" Now her voice was cracking, breaking down, and she was falling back against the wall, then wincing and trying to push herself away from it. "Do you hear me? Do you get it? This is the lesson, Will: *Don't ever disobey me!* Because if you do and you get killed, I'll—"

But she just shook her head, tears she wasn't conscious of dripping from her cheeks, and Will realized she wasn't angry at him. She was terrified.

He didn't know why she was so scared. He sensed that it had less to do with him—despite her constant use of the word "you"— than it did with the situation. Something in the Dream had triggered a memory or a deep-seated fear, Josh's own dreamfire, and she didn't know what to do with the fear besides shout at him.

The realization made it easier for him not to shout back. *I will not get into a screaming match with her,* Will told himself. *I will not turn into my father.*

"You're right," he said. "I'm sorry. I need to start doing what you tell me to do."

She didn't seem to know what to do with that, either. She looked at him strangely, wet her lips, and turned to Haley. "Are you all right?"

Haley didn't answer, though his breathing had begun to return to normal. He stretched out one arm to reach for his pad and pen where he'd left them on the floor, but when he'd collected them he didn't write anything, just held them to his chest like a teddy bear.

Will shut his eyes. *This is so screwed up.*

He wanted to comfort Josh. He wanted her to tell him whatever it was that had frightened her like this, if only so he could avoid triggering it again. Then he wanted to get a warm, wet washcloth and gently wash the blood off her face. He wanted to tell her how scared for her he had been.

But he knew her well enough to know that she wouldn't let him do any of that. They stood there in silence until she finally said, "Dad will freak if he finds out I went into the Dream, so here's what we're going to do. Will, wipe up the floor. Haley and I are going to go break the mirror in that big ugly armoire, and then we're going to tell everyone that we were showing you how to disarm somebody and we crashed into it. That's our story."

They were going to lie. Great. Will was going to lie to the nice people who were adopting him because Josh had a complex and had gone into the Dream when she shouldn't have. Wonderful.

He must have been giving her a look, because she barked, "*What? Go!*"

And Will, who had just promised to obey her, got up and went.

After cleaning the floor and helping to break the armoire—which turned out to be no easy task—and lying to Kerstel and watching Deloise pick the glass from Josh's knee, Will sat in the library alone. He didn't know what else to do with himself, so he just sat there drumming his fingers on the tabletop and replaying his last conversation with Josh in his head.

She had gone beyond not wanting him to get involved in her problems. Now she didn't even want him to care.

How he was supposed to not care, he didn't know.

"Will?"

He started, but it was only Dustine standing in the doorway. Her wooden walker shone in the library's yellow lights.

"Hi," he said.

Dustine smiled unexpectedly, as if she knew everything that had just happened to him and saw the folly of youth in it.

"Bumps in the road?" she asked. She maneuvered her walker between the table and the walls of books and took a seat across from him.

"Nope," he lied. Dustine hadn't been terribly warm to him during the last month—not the way Kerstel and Deloise had—but she hadn't been cold, either. He knew she had been watching him. "You heard about the armoire?"

She lifted an eyebrow. "Could have heard that thing fall two miles down the road. Heard a lot of shouting, too."

Shouting *before* the armoire fell, she meant. Will decided his best bet was just to say nothing, so that's what he did.

"You know," Dustine said, settling into the chair, "I wasn't born a dream walker."

"I think you mentioned it."

She nodded ruefully. "I was fifteen when I became an apprentice to Lasia Borgenicht, Josh and Deloise's great-aunt. Honestly, for a long time I thought I had entered my own personal nightmare and never woken up."

Leaning her elbows on the table, she looked at him squarely. "I'm not going to tell you my life story, Will. If you want to know it you can read my diaries when I'm dead, or you can call up Peregrine and hear his side of the story. What I want to tell you now is this: You will *always* be an outsider."

Will didn't know if the house around them was truly as still as it seemed then, or if he was simply unable to focus on anything but the old woman's face. Her eyes were a beautiful green—resembling Josh's but darker, as if the color had faded through the generations—and she didn't dodge his gaze the way Josh would have.

He wanted to say, "How did you know that?" He wanted to cry.

"It doesn't matter what you do, what you give them, or how hard you work. There will always be family stories you don't know and no one will ever trust your instincts and they will still leave you out of important conversations. They don't mean to do it; it's just automatic. Deloise won't be as thoughtless, because she's more sensitive than the others, and Kerstel comes from Savannah and knows a bit about what it's like to be an outsider, but Josh was born a dream walker through and through. All her loyalties are intact. You're going to be the new kid until the day you die."

Will turned his face away, breathing quickly through his mouth, hoping she wouldn't see the tears in his eyes.

"Josh doesn't know what she has in you," Dustine said, more softly than before. "And trust doesn't come easy to her to begin with.

I don't want you to think that you'll never be happy here, because you will. But there will always be a line between you and them, and you're going to have to walk it."

Will didn't move. When he failed to reply, Dustine reached out and ran the back of her cool, waxy fingers over his cheek. Then she stood up and took a few pained steps deeper into the library.

He wiped his eyes while she still had her back to him. Was his desperation to fit in so obvious that even Dustine had noticed?

She slid a book across the table to him, and Will looked up, startled. Dustine smiled more impishly, showing a little of the young woman she once had been. "I think you've been looking for this," she told him.

The edition was bound in gray cloth and had been labeled along the spine with a black Sharpie. He had no idea what it was, and he didn't know what to say. "Ah, thank you," he muttered.

Dustine only smiled again, as if his confusion were just one more step in the complicated joke she was playing. He waited until she had left the library before he picked up the book.

Most of the pages lay flush together; only the first few were rumpled. He tilted the spine to the light and made out the block letters:

HIANSELIAN AMBROSE DONOVAN MICHARAINOSA

Will tried to reform the name into something he might have heard in casual conversation. *What do you call a kid named Hianselian?*
Hianselian. Hansel. Hans. Hian.
Ian?

Will put the book down. He couldn't quite bear to touch it now, knowing who had written it.

He should have thought of it before—all the family diaries were here in the library. Some were so ancient they had to be kept in amber plastic bags and carried stickers reading DO NOT HANDLE WITHOUT GLOVES. The books and pages were as varied as their authors: ink in every color, lines forming Roman and Greek and Cyrillic alphabets, and brushstrokes arranged into beautiful, wispy characters. Sometimes a long life was chronicled in the pages of a slim pamphlet, or a few years written in such detail that they produced a dozen or more volumes.

Dustine hadn't been telling him to back off; she had been letting him know that Josh wasn't the only source of information available to him.

"Oh, man," he said. He didn't know if he felt better or worse now. He started to turn back the cover and heard the sound of Josh's crutches hitting the floor in the kitchen. Without thinking, he stood up, tucked the book under his shirt, and went into the hallway. He hit the stairs two at a time.

Will couldn't remember being this concerned about a pile of pages since he saw his first girlie magazine years before. He entered the Weavers' apartment without hesitation and gave Kerstel a quick, casual wave as he passed through the living room. For the first time, the bedroom he had been given didn't feel so large and empty; he realized the doorknob had no lock. He pulled down the shades for no logical reason and opened his math textbook on the bed for a cover.

For an instant, he wondered if he really wanted to read Ian's diary. Would beginning on a path of small deceptions be worth knowing what happened last summer?

But he knew Josh would never tell him. And he would keep on walking into traps the way he had today; he would keep on triggering her fears until the day came when the stress was too much for both of them and she told him to get out.

He pulled back the book's cover.

Glued to the inside cover was a column cut from a parchment scroll. Someone had blacked out two lines with a Sharpie:

Hianselian Ambrose Donovan Micharainosa

*Two boys born—alike as mirrors
flame and fount in eye of Seer.
This one burns his wick to ashes
and keeps burning, never still,*

brewing anger out of passion,
for a void he'll never fill.
~~[redacted]~~

One day of majority
gives these words all authority.
His own heart he will forsake
while grasping at the reins of life.
Is love made or what we make?
He will not take true love to wife.
Wrongly he thinks his pain greater
than the injury he pays her.

Another's love he will abuse,
"free and hardened heart" he proves.
On the wrong door he goes knocking
and is met by Queen's outcast.
A door evil is quick in locking—
there to be torn fore and aft,
and seek not of kith but kin
for a sound sanctum therein.

Death has her own tales to tell,
but those I do not know so well.

On the first page, a piece of notebook paper.

Dear Ian,
    I know you don't want to talk to me or see me or whatever, so I'm going
to write this down because it's important. Haley just gave me a note saying
you convinced your mom to move out. I know you're mad at me, but it's not
fair to punish your family. Haley couldn't say it, but he doesn't want to go.
I don't know what moving would do to him.

I don't know what else to say. If you have to leave me, I wish you wouldn't do it like this. You're taking the coward's way. You're better than this, I know you are.

Josh

On the second page, a note torn from a steno pad:

June 25th
To: I. McKarr
From: H. McKarr

1. Ring
    a. I returned the ring to the store.
    b. They gave me a full refund.
    c. The salesclerk sends her condolences.
2. Moving
    a. G. Carane has agreed to let us live with her.
    b. G. Carane lives in Baton Rouge, Louisiana.
    c. Baton Rouge is over six hundred and seventy (670) miles away.

The scroll and notes were glued into the journal. A small plastic baggie was stapled to the fourth page. It was full of ash, but the burning had been hurried enough that Will could sift through and find bits of photo paper.

There was one more letter.

Dear Ian,

If I could think of a way to make this easier for you, I would. I'm aware of how pathetic that must sound, but it's true and I mean it.

My whole bed is covered in these notes now. Writing takes longer than talking but I don't mind. Some things are hard to say out loud. I know because I've been trying to say them for months now.

You know what I want to write next but I'm not going to. I don't want to put you under any obligations and I don't want to add to your burdens. I know what trying to get over someone is like, for reasons that should be obvious to you, of all people. I know how you feel. Don't listen to Whim, he doesn't have a clue. His scroll says something about Deloise, and he's still working up the guts to tell her what it is.

As for Josh, all I can tell you for certain is that if you can't be with her because of your scroll, then you'd only be hurting you both by staying with her. She should be able to understand that.

I'm going to tuck this under your door and then go to bed, but if you decide to write back, there's one thing I have to ask: Do you think I'm a horrible person because of how I've treated Haley?

Okay, good night. Maybe we can continue this tomorrow night at the cabin.

> Yours,
> Winsor

The rest of the journal was empty.

Eighteen

She had almost gotten him killed. She had almost gotten them all killed.

Josh sat in history class the next day, stewing. She sat next to Louis Poston, and Will sat across the room, staring out the window at a day that had never really dawned. The sky was still dark, the fluorescent lights overhead helpless against the gloom. In the hush that filled the classroom, Camille Gothan had torn a nail while clipping it, and that Korean kid who never talked, Man-Shik, had unexpectedly produced a silk hankie to stop the bleeding. Brianna Selts had managed to take her bra off without removing her shirt, but then made the bad decision to hand it to Jay Appleton, who passed it around the classroom to be autographed.

Josh didn't know why she had decided to sit beside Louis. Maybe she was a glutton for punishment, sitting next to him and wishing that he had just done his damn job and delivered the pizza to her house five weeks before.

The grass is always greener, she reminded herself. If Louis had arrived instead of Will, the problems would have been the same. Or maybe worse. After all, Louis had parents who would have found it odd when he started spending so much time at Josh's house, doing things he couldn't talk about.

His parents would have been terribly upset if Josh had gotten Louis killed.

She already had one death on her hands. She couldn't handle another.

That morning, she had woken up with Ian's voice in her ears: *I saw a gate beyond the arch.* She had rolled right off the office futon, saying as she fell, "I don't remember letting go of your hand."

And she didn't, but she must have, because he had slipped out of her grasp and into the Dream, into that terrible, dark nightmare with the broken windows and the sound of distant explosions.

Then she had arrived at school to find all the hallways and classrooms decorated for Valentine's Day, which had been her and Ian's honorary anniversary because they'd been together for so long that neither of them could remember when they'd first started dating.

Sixth grade, Josh thought, *when he punched Eddie for calling me puny. Fourth grade, when he gave me his dessert every day at lunch. Kindergarten, when he asked me to hold some flowers he was picking for his girlfriend and then ran away.*

Ian had died because of her stupid, arrogant foolhardiness. She couldn't let the same thing happen to Will. She didn't even want to talk to him, look at him, think about him, do anything that might lead to caring about his well-being, because she was beginning to believe that she couldn't protect him.

She knew she had been so upset the day before because she already cared about him too much. Far, *far* too much.

She forced herself to glance at him, sitting two rows over and a seat ahead of her. Resting his chin on a propped palm, he stared out the gray-washed windows at the cloudy, drizzling day beyond.

At she watched, he lifted his head and turned to catch her staring at him. She winced, wondering if her gaze held some weight he could sense. His look for her was so earnest, an apologetic almost-smile on his lips, but too sad for a real smile. Then he glanced at Louis, sitting beside her, right between them, and whatever vestige of a smile he had worn slipped away. Josh opened her mouth to say, "No, wait, I didn't sit here because—"

But, of course, she had.

The bell rang. "See you, Josh," Louis said, and Josh mumbled some appropriate reply while shoving her book into her backpack. She fumbled with her crutches, hoping she could catch Will before he left the classroom. But Jay Appleton pushed past her, and she saw Will reach the front of the row. Before he could get away, she let her crutches clatter to the floor, dumped her backpack on the nearest desk, and hopped forward so that she could grab Will's arm too hard, her fingers digging into his sleeve.

"Sorry," she told him. "Sorry I yelled at you."

Then she hugged him.

Her apology was inelegant, she knew. She probably sounded like a third-grader being forced to make up after a playground mishap, but maybe Will didn't care, or maybe he knew that however plain her words, she meant them, because he didn't hesitate at all before hugging her back. He hugged her completely, his arms wrapped all the way around her back, and she was so relieved by his response that she pressed her face to his shoulder so he wouldn't see her expression.

"It's okay," he said. "Forget it."

"No, I was terrible to you."

"You were scared."

Oh god, did he see through her so easily?

"I *was* scared," she admitted, and for an instant, just a fleeting half thought, she considered telling him about all her fears and all her failures. But no—*no, no, no*—he would lose whatever faith he had left in her.

Reluctantly, she let go of Will and stepped back, one hand on a desk to steady herself. "I'll listen next time," he said, and he laughed ruefully. "I swear, one of these days I'm going to learn to listen to you."

Josh laughed with him. Despite her relief, though, she felt mystified by how easily their conflict had been resolved. Why did he always make things so easy for her? And *how*?

He swung her backpack onto his right shoulder, his own bag hanging from his left. He was smiling at her again, a real smile. He said, as if she had asked, "It's going to be fine, Josh."

She felt herself smile back. She wasn't sure she believed him, but she wanted to.

Josh had an idea during sixth period, but she had to wait until she and Will were alone at home in the library to bring it up.

"I was thinking," she said, "about the man in the trench coat."

"Which one of them?"

"The first guy we saw, that taller one, without gloves. Let's call him something."

"How about Snitch, since he's willing to talk? At least, relative to the other guy."

"Good. Snitch. I've been thinking of the other guy as Gloves. Anyway," she hesitated an instant before going on, "I don't think there's any doubt now that the two of them can alter the Dream."

She felt relieved when Will immediately said, "I think you're right. Which shouldn't be possible unless they're dreamers." Then he hesitated, just as she had. "Or, according to Whim, the True Dream Walker."

"The True Dream Walker is a legend. Did Whim get to that part?"

"Winsor made it pretty clear." Will rubbed the back of his neck; Josh had thought for a while that he had a disc problem before realizing it was a nervous gesture. "Whim also said that the True Dream Walker is your guiding light and that's why you wear his symbol."

Josh laughed. "He's not my guiding light. He's a legend. I wear his symbol because I believe in what his legend stands for, and I like to be reminded every time I go into the Dream."

She held the pendant out for Will to examine. "Supposedly, the True Dream Walker built the first archway to the Dream, and when he did, he gave the original dream walkers five charges: compassion, commitment, courage, modesty, and might. The plumeria has one petal for each charge, and because the petals form a spiral, it's also a symbol for the Dream."

Will peered at the pendant, then smiled. "That's nice."

Josh tucked the necklace back under her shirt. "Supposedly, someday the True Dream Walker will return and fix whatever causes the universes to slide out of balance. I don't know quite how he'll do that, but a lot of people think that our job will basically end when he returns."

"So, if Gloves is the True Dream Walker, he was trying to kill us because the World doesn't need us anymore?"

Josh heard surprising fervor in her own voice when she said, "*That thing* was not the True Dream Walker. I don't know what he was, but he wasn't the Dream Walker."

Will backed off. "You'd know better than I would."

"I don't know who those people were," she said. "I don't know why they can do what they do. But I don't think their ability is natural. Snitch mentioned a name: Feodor."

"You recognize it?" Will asked.

"I've never heard it before. I'm not even sure how to spell it. But there's a dream-walker database we could run the name Feodor through, at least to see if anything pops up."

Will nodded. "Let's do it."

They met up in the office after Will made a trip back to the kitchen for Oreos. "This place is starting to look like your bedroom," Will noted, sitting down on the messy, unmade futon.

"Kerstel brought down a bunch of my clothes. But I might have to send her up for some more, since I'm about to run out."

And since my knee is back to being nearly broken after yesterday, Josh added in her head. *I don't think I'll be moving back upstairs for quite a while.*

"I can get you some stuff," Will said.

Right, like she was going to ask him to fetch her clean panties and a bra. Josh made a noncommittal sound and logged onto the website for Dashiel Winters Consulting.

The website was a front for another very exclusive, very encrypted website for dream walkers. Josh typed her username and password, and then submitted a retinal scan.

The database searched official historical documents, declassified monarchy documents, the diaries of dead dream walkers that had been typed up (a project only recently begun), and a number of academic databases. After consulting the Internet on how to spell Feodor, twenty-six entries—and fourteen different spellings of six variations—popped up. Next to the title of each entry was a brief description, and Josh scrolled through them, removing the obvious misses from her list.

"Here's one," she said. She pointed to an entry labeled *Feodorik Jambulira Bronisławorin Kajażkołskiocsi.*

A grainy photograph of a small, intense man appeared beneath the biography. Will squinted at the photo as if he thought he was missing something. Josh felt the same way.

"What do the other files say about him?"

Josh read off the titles. "Awarded the Shotts Fellowship in 1949. Won the Hume Award for Dream Theory in 1952. Received the Star of Ha'azelle in 1955. These are like, the biggest awards a dream theorist can get. These are a huge deal. The Star of Ha'azelle was a medal that the queen gave out for special service to the Crown. Here's a list of stuff he published."

"That's a long list," Will noted.

"No kidding—oh my god! I've read *War and Rumors of War: A*

Compendium of Medieval Prophesies! Well, I read part of it. It's, like, five hundred pages long, and it's really boring. But I didn't realize this guy wrote it." She read down the list of publications again, more carefully this time, wondering what other titles she might recognize if she were better read in dream theory. Although she couldn't say, what she did notice was that there wasn't an area of dream work to which Feodor hadn't contributed. From *Implications of Planck's Law on Archway Creation* to *The Dream and Modern Theories of Evolution* to *Translations of Etruscan Dream Walking Records,* he appeared to have worked in every academic field.

But he returned to one topic over and over. "He wrote a lot about dream-walker ethics," Josh said.

Will pointed to an article title, "Why Staging Will Destroy Us." "Sounds like he agreed with the monarchy on staging."

"Look, there's no death date. It just says he was 'exiled by order of the monarchy.' I don't even know what that means. Outside of the monarchy's lands? There are dream walkers all over the world. So where did they exile him to, the moon?"

"Why would Snitch have mentioned him?"

Dustine walked down the hall, past the office door. "Grandma!" Josh called, and the old woman stopped.

"Yes, my dear, demanding child?"

"Do you know anything about a Polish dream walker named Feodor, uh, *ka-jazz-kol-skee*?"

"Kajażkolski," Dustine corrected. She pronounced it *ka-yazh-kow-skee*. "What about him?"

"His database bio says he was exiled. What does that mean?"

Dustine turned her walker, entered the office, and closed the door behind her. Will jumped up to offer her his seat, but she ignored it. "What do you want to know about him for, Joshlyn?"

Josh was not a good liar. She knew this, and she also knew that, even had she been an excellent liar, Dustine would have been the last person she could have fooled.

"I think he's related to the men in the trench coats. One of them said his name."

Dustine sucked in such a deep, sharp breath, arching her back as she did so, that Josh was afraid she was having a heart attack.

"Grandma!" Josh cried, springing to the old woman's side, but Dustine ignored her concern.

With flushed cheeks and hands clenched around her pine walker, she said, "Tell me what you know."

"Are you all right?" Josh demanded.

"Tell me!" Dustine insisted. "*Right now!*"

Josh glanced at Will, who looked petrified.

With some reluctance and lingering concern for her grandmother's well-being, Josh related what had happened the day before. She expected Dustine to be angry, but she didn't expect Dustine to say, "Go put on your shoes," and then pick up the library phone extension and dial from memory.

Josh and Will looked at each other again. "Wait a sec—what?" Josh asked.

"We're going to see Ben," Dustine said. Then, into the phone, she said, "It's me. I'm bringing Josh and Will over. It's about Feodor."

Nineteen

An hour later, Josh and Will were seated on a cat-hair-coated couch in a snug, extremely cluttered living room. They were each drinking chocolate milk, which Young Ben seemed to think was all the rage among young people. Ben was sitting in a recliner that retained a perfect imprint of his body when he got out of it. Dustine sat in another chair drinking rooibos tea from a mug that read PLUTO IS TOO A PLANET!

The ride to Young Ben's house had been nearly silent. Will had known from the way Josh pursed her lips the whole time that her grandmother's behavior was making her nervous. They had obviously stumbled upon something big. Either that, or they were both about to learn firsthand how someone got exiled from dream walking.

The doorbell rang, and Young Ben got up to answer it. A gray Persian climbed into Will's lap and looked at him expectantly. He gave in and petted her. Will had met Young Ben once before; the seer had come over to the house to welcome Will to the dream-walker community. After being somewhat intimidated by both Dustine and Davita, Will had been relieved to meet the easygoing old man.

Young Ben returned with Davita Bach, who wore a black suit with white piping. Her red hair was twisted off her neck with a long, pearl-ended stick. She kissed Dustine's cheek and said hello to Will and Josh, and then she looked meaningfully at the couch with its layer of cat hair, and Young Ben said, "I'll get a towel."

When Davita was seated on a large, clean towel, she said lightly, "So, Josh, I hear you and Will ran into something strange in-Dream yesterday."

She failed to point out that they weren't supposed to have been in-Dream, which made Will anxious. Adults only ignored what you had done wrong if something else was even worse.

He noticed, also, that she addressed herself exclusively to Josh.

Josh told Davita what had happened the day before, leaving out most of the fighting and that fact that Will had gone in after her against orders. The elders and Davita exchanged covert glances as Josh spoke. Will felt the tension in the room rise with a pressure like humidity.

"All right then," Davita said, as if coming to some decision. "We're going to tell you about Feodor, because if we don't I assume you'll keep digging, and there's a lot of wrong information about him floating around out there. Especially on the *Internet*." Davita gave Josh a hard stare that left Will assuming she was referring to Whim's blog.

"If you want to understand Feodor, you have to understand the atrocities Feodor'd lived through," Young Ben began. "He was born in Poland, and he was thirteen when World War II began. The Germans considered the Poles *untermensch,* subhuman, and planned to use them as slave labor until they died out. They killed Feodor's entire family, his entire community, and most of Poland's dream walkers."

"AB-Aktion," Dustine said in a grim tone.

"That's right, that's what they called it. Hitler wanted to destroy Poland's identity, so he killed politicians, teachers, professors, doctors, clergy, even athletes. Most of the dream walkers were well educated and had good jobs, so a lot of them ended up in camps, or they got worked to death on the railroads. Feodor managed to survive, even fought for the resistance in the Battle of Warsaw. After the war, Poland fell to the Communists, and Feodor immigrated to England and then to the US under the royal family's protection. He was a brilliant young man. He became a dream theorist and historian, and his interpretation of medieval prophecy is still the best around. But as time passed, I guess the memories started to get to him."

"His theories grew more and more bizarre," Davita explained. "He became fixated on the prophecies concerning the return of the True Dream Walker."

The True Dream Walker again, Will thought. *For a legend, people are really obsessed with this guy.*

"Finally, Feodor published a theory that if people used staging to deliberately destabilize the Dream to the point that it collapsed into the World on a large scale, then the True Dream Walker would be forced to appear and save us."

"Ah . . ." Josh said.

"Something about this theory seems off," Will suggested.

"Even people who were pro-staging," Dustine told Josh, "thought Feodor's idea was insane. But it played into a rumor people had been whispering for years that before Feodor's mother died, she had told him that his scroll said he would Temper the True Dream Walker."

Will didn't know what it meant to "Temper" someone, but the conversation was moving along without him.

"No one knows if the rumor was true," Dustine added. "The scroll was destroyed in the war, and Feodor's mother was killed."

"But when he wrote that article, about deliberately destabilizing the Dream," Ben said, "that was more or less the last straw. His employer fired him. The monarchy cut ties with him. His woman left him."

"What did he do?" Will asked.

"He disappeared," Davita said. "Nobody heard from him for years. Then, a little town in Iowa called Maplefax experienced a collapse of the Dream into the World."

"Wait a sec—Maplefax?" Josh asked. "*The* Maplefax?"

"Yes, *that* Maplefax. Feodor went there and started staging terrible dreams for the entire town. He may have murdered people in-Dream; we don't know. Maplefax was a very small, isolated town—actually an ideal prospect for staging. Except that when the Dream destabilized and collapsed into the World, the True Dream Walker didn't show up to save everyone."

Will vaguely remembered Josh mentioning Maplefax to him while they drove to the dream-walker headquarters a few weeks before. "You mean the Veil between the World and the Dream ripped?" he asked, jumping in before the conversation moved on.

"Precisely," Dustine said. "And the nightmares came marching out, two by two. At least forty people wandered into the Dream and were never seen again. Another two dozen were killed on this side, either by nightmares or by each other. Some others went mad from Veil dust. The FBI quarantined the entire town, which made it all the harder for us to get in there and repair the rip. The government saw some things we'd have preferred they'd not seen, but it wasn't the first time."

The room fell to silence. Will realized that the Persian in his lap was drinking the chocolate milk from his glass, and he gently nudged the cat off the couch. He set the milk on the coffee table.

"But why exile Feodor?" Josh asked. "Why not put him in jail?"

"He breathed too much Veil dust," Davita said, and Will thought she answered just an instant too quickly. "He was insane before, but after Maplefax he went stark raving mad. And he was dangerous—even when he slept."

Josh and Will glanced at each other.

"Ah," Will said, "how does that work?"

"He started lucid dreaming," Young Ben explained. "He'd realize he was dreaming and try to stage more nightmares. It was amazing how much havoc one man could wreak in the course of a few hours. That was when the monarchy realized they had to keep him out of the Dream entirely."

"But he had to sleep sometime," Josh said.

"Exactly. So the monarchy came up with a plan to cut off a part of the Dream—a corner, so to speak—and seal Feodor up in it. A pocket universe, they called it. He'd be stuck there, both when awake and asleep. No one else could enter or exit."

"But . . ." Josh said, her voice dazed, "that's . . ."

"Cruel," Will finished.

"Some thought so," Davita admitted. "Some thought we should have killed him outright. But the monarchy didn't believe in capital punishment."

"How long has he been there?"

"Since 1962."

Half a century alone, Will thought. *Without another person to talk to.*

"But Feodor's pocket universe was created from part of the Dream," Davita said. "The builders theorized that because it retained the properties of the Dream, Feodor would be able to shape it into whatever he wanted when he lucid dreamed. He could have made it heaven, if he liked."

Will wondered what a madman would have chosen to create, given godlike power over a whole universe. "Could he have collapsed his own universe?" Will asked. "Escaped?"

"No," Davita said. "The Dream itself is too vast for any sort of stability, but the small size of Feodor's universe made its boundaries incredibly strong. It was built with the intention of holding forever."

"He'd have to be awfully old by now," Josh said. "If he's even still alive."

Davita nodded and thought for a moment before saying, "We'll have to tell your grandfather about what happened to you yesterday."

"Great," Josh muttered, but her voice sounded more numb than angry.

"However," Dustine added, "I think we can forego telling your father, at least for the time being." She gave Josh a little wink.

"What should Josh and I do?" Will asked.

"Stay out of the Dream," Davita said firmly. "No exceptions, Josh. No excuse can justify going in there again—not until we know who those people are and what they're capable of, and not while you're still injured. You got away with it once, but there's no reason good enough to risk your life like that again."

"Or Will's life," Dustine said. The Persian jumped into her lap and she shoved the cat back onto the floor without taking her eyes off Josh's face. "You're responsible for his safety."

Josh turned her head away sharply, then nodded. She looked at Will as if frightened of him and the responsibility he represented, and he wanted to apologize. Why did he always want to apologize around her?

Maybe because she always seemed to be in pain. She wrapped her arms around herself, and Will saw something he'd never seen before on her face: shame.

She wore it the whole way home.

Twenty

I'm responsible for his safety. That's what she said.

But how could I have known, when I went into the Dream, how big the danger was? I knew I was going against Dad's rules. I knew I would get chewed out if I got caught. I even knew that the men in the trench coats weren't a normal part of the Dream. But how could I have possibly known

*that Snitch and Gloves were connected to some Polish mad scientist? I knew
I was getting into danger, but not that kind of danger. And I TOLD
Will NOT to come in after me.*

*But maybe none of that matters and I'm just making excuses. Grandma
is right. Thanks to fate and Deloise, Will is my responsibility. If he gets
hurt, it's nobody's fault but my own.*

*That scares the hell out of me. I have to do something to make the
Dream safe again, I have to help figure out who these guys are and how
they're connected to Feodor, but what can I do that won't put Will in even
worse danger? I just don't know how to protect him.*

If there really is a True Dream Walker, I hope he'll help me now.

Her leg took longer than expected to heal. Josh got the impression
from the throbbing pain that engulfed it for two days that her trek
through the Dream sans crutches might have been detrimental to
her recovery. She removed the brace for good on Friday, but it
wasn't until Sunday that she was able to bend her knee all the
way.

By the Wednesday after, she was walking without crutches. "I'm
going to move back into my room," she announced that morning,
but apparently no one was listening. Breakfast was in full swing;
Kerstel had gone all out and made complicated fruit shakes with
yogurt, and now she and Dustine were trying to leave the house.
Haley hovered next to the pantry and Whim rinsed dishes.

Josh stirred her shake—a combination of bananas, honey, and
coconut—a couple of times before silently handing it to Whim and
putting water on the stove for hot chocolate.

"Sounds great, hon," Kerstel said, digging through a basket
hanging next to the door. "Has anybody seen my keys?"

"We're going to be late," Dustine warned. She shrugged on a
rabbit fur coat that Deloise had once threatened to dye bloodred.

"Here," Haley said softly. As usual, a fine tremble made his words
sound uncertain. "You can take my car." He held an unadorned key
ring out to Kerstel.

"Oh, thank you, sweetheart. I'm sorry, but we have got to be on time. We'll be home before school lets out."

Josh watched her plant a kiss on Haley's cheek and rush Dustine out the back door. "Where are they going?"

"There was a call at three this morning," Whim said, sitting down beside her with the remains of her smoothie in his hand. "Apparently the junta is having an emergency meeting."

Will walked in through the hallway door, dressed in a gray flannel shirt and jeans that appeared rust-stained. He gave Josh a nod as he went to the fridge.

"Why?" Josh asked.

"I don't know. Despite the fact that you and I *are,* as you pointed out, technically adults, we weren't invited. Although my sources say it has to do with the trench-coat men. Both my parents went, and your father is meeting them in Braxton."

Josh stood up and went to the stove, where the kettle was near boiling. She and Will had agreed not to tell anyone else about what had happened the last time they went into the Dream, and unless Haley had told someone—a doubtful proposition—Deloise, Whim, and Winsor were in the dark. But Josh had a fairly good idea what the meeting in Braxton was about.

She caught Will's eye as they both pulled chairs out from the table and sat down. She inclined her head toward Whim and lifted her eyebrows. *Should we tell him?*

Will bit into an apple and gave her a look that said, *How should I know? He's your friend.*

Josh sipped her hot chocolate and then said, "Haley, come sit with us."

Haley, who looked surprised if not frightened, sank into a seat at the table like he was taking his place in the electric chair.

"All right, Whim," Josh said, "I have gossip. But this is *not* to end up on your blog."

"I can't promise that," Whim said immediately.

"Well, then I can't tell you," she bluffed. She started to stand up, and he raised a long-fingered hand.

"Hold your horses. Does this gossip have anything to do with the meeting in Braxton?"

"Let me put it this way: Will and Haley and I are the reason there *is* a meeting in Braxton."

"Hmm." Whim thought, stroking an imaginary goatee with a thumb and forefinger. "I'll make you a deal: I won't put it up on *Through a Veil Darkly* until I've gotten third-party sources to confirm enough of what you've said to make your info look like reasonable projection. We'll call it inevitable discovery."

That would have to do. It was actually a pretty good deal, coming from Whim. Josh sat down again.

She told Whim everything, beginning with the alleyway nightmare and ending with the meeting with the elders the day before. "So," she said afterward, "since I've just given you a big scoop, I need a favor."

"There's always a catch."

"I just need to know everything you can find out about Feodor. Anything that might not be in the official record."

"You underestimate me, my friend. *Through a Veil Darkly* already has a whole page devoted to Feodor. Maplefax is a legend, and one the junta has tried very hard to hide."

"Why?" Will asked.

"Because it's an example of just how badly staging can go wrong," Whim told him. "Peregrine doesn't want people thinking about that. He wants staging to become standard practice for dream walkers. But it's pretty hard to hide the self-destruction of an entire town."

"So what are the rumors?" Josh asked.

"Well, for starters, everybody agrees that Feodor went insane long before he breathed all that Veil dust. In fact, one of the guards who attended Feodor's hearing before the monarchy claims he didn't breathe any dust and was completely lucid, he just had no morals."

"He was a sociopath," Will clarified.

"Precisely. Then there's the pocket universe he got sent to: ironically, most people think Feodor was the one who invented the technology for that, back when he was working for Willis-Audretch."

"*What?*" Josh nearly shouted. "Davita didn't tell us that!"

"Who's Willis-Audretch?" Will asked.

Whim grinned. Haley looked at him with disapproval.

"They're dangerous," Haley said.

"They're the evil corporation you see in every movie about an evil corporation," Josh said.

"We don't know that they're evil," Whim said. "We just know that they're shady. And mysterious. And secretive. Willis-Audretch is the World's only dream-walker think tank. Their research institute has produced some brilliant minds, and some brilliant patents, and they're pretty serious about protecting both. Feodor was only, like, twenty-five when they hired him. The rumor is that he was inventing things for the royal family."

"What kind of things?" Josh asked suspiciously.

"Inter-archway highways. A system for mapping the Dream. A laser that would destroy nightmares. A Veil dust–filtering mask. Some sort of noncombustible jetpack that would let people fly in-Dream. Yeah, I don't believe that one either. There's also a rumor—and mind you, this one isn't super credible—that people go visit him in that pocket universe where he lives."

"They visit him? Why?"

"Probably to buy things he's building now. If he's still alive, that is. The grapevine is divided on that."

Josh thought while Will asked, "How do people find him? Aren't there any protections on his universe?"

Whim shrugged. "How would you lock the Dream, if you needed to? I think the pocket universe's best protection is that nobody knows how to get to it. Everywhere you open an archway automatically leads to the Dream."

So there's a chance he's still in touch with the World, Josh thought. *Still . . . infecting people with his madness.* She wasn't just horrified by the deaths at Maplefax but by the idea that someone had betrayed everything for which dream walking stood, every ideal in which she believed and that the True Dream Walker represented.

Particularly someone so talented and intelligent. How had Feodor lost his faith in their work?

"What does your rumor mill say about the story that Feodor's mother told him his scroll predicted he would Temper the True Dream Walker's return?" Josh asked.

Whim put off answering until he had upended the smoothie glass over his mouth and drained the last drops out. "Not much," he said, wiping his mouth with the back of his hand. "Supposedly she said the True Dream Walker would have to undergo the same Tempering ritual as monarchs, and that Feodor would help administer it."

"What's a Tempering ritual?" Will asked.

Distractedly, Josh explained. "Before a dream walker could become a monarch, he or she had to spend twenty-four hours in the Dream walking through nightmares without doing anything to resolve a single one. Just feeling the terror and suffering. It was supposed to teach compassion and make sure they understood why our work is so important."

"That's kind of intense."

Something began beeping, and Josh looked around to see what it was. Whim got up, opened the oven, and pulled out a picture-perfect pie-sized pastry of indeterminate type.

"What is *that*?" Will asked. "It smells amazing."

"That," Whim replied, setting the confection carefully on a trivet, "is German apple kuchen."

Josh checked the clock. "What time did you get up this morning?"

Will went to stand next to him and stared at the steaming apple cake. His eyes were large. "Can we eat it?" he asked in a hushed, reverent voice.

Whim looked at him scornfully. "Of course we can eat it. Go get some forks."

Josh had a feeling that all productive conversation was finished for the morning, which was just as well. "We need to leave for school. I'm going upstairs to grab Winsor and Deloise."

"Josh," Haley said.

She stopped getting up and looked at him instead.

"Be careful," he said. "With Feodor."

Haley looked like he wanted to say something more, but he didn't.

"All right," Josh replied. "I'll be careful."

But as she walked away, she got the feeling that whatever he hadn't said, she had needed to hear it.

Josh trekked up the stairs to the second floor—*I can too handle stairs,* she thought, although she sloshed some hot chocolate onto the carpet—and knocked on Winsor's door.

"Hey," she said after Winsor called her in. "We're leaving in about five minutes."

Winsor was lying on her bed, though she'd already made it and gotten dressed. She had an arm flung over her eyes. "I don't know if I'm coming."

Josh walked across the dark room toward her. "Migraine?"

"Yeah. It's not awful yet, but the lights at school will make it worse."

"Want me to take you to the hospital?"

Winsor sighed and dragged herself into a sitting position. "No, that's okay. Thanks."

Some of the hostility that had been in her voice lately was gone. Josh ventured to sit down beside her on the bed.

"You should stay home and rest. Whim can take you to the ER if you need to go later."

"I know, I just . . ." Another sigh. "I don't want to spend all day at home with Haley. He's been acting like such a freak lately."

"Yeah," Josh echoed. "He's . . . have you noticed that he's started walking like Ian?"

"What, with that swagger?" Winsor actually smiled. "Yeah, and his posture, too. I swear he's two inches taller when he's standing up straight."

An easy moment passed between them, and Josh almost reached out to hug Winsor. Suddenly there were a thousand things Josh wanted to tell her, things she'd been thinking the last month and been unable to say, little fears and complicated emotions that couldn't be understood by one person alone.

"Do you ever . . ." Josh asked, "I don't know . . ." She was terrified of admitting how she felt, but at the same time, she wanted desperately to reconnect with Winsor. "Do you ever . . . . almost wish he *were* Ian?"

Winsor stopped smiling. "No. No, Josh. Nobody can replace Ian."

Suddenly Josh remembered pushing a tree branch out of the way and seeing Ian and Winsor lying on a gray plaid blanket at the bottom of the valley below, their bodies clothed only by the gloaming's deepening shadows. She remembered how she had stood there, as dumb as a deer staring patiently into the headlights of approaching death, until Haley took her hand and led her away. Now she felt a rage as fierce as her shock had been then.

Nobody can replace Ian, she heard Winsor say again.

Josh stood up from Winsor's bed. "You'd know, wouldn't you?" she said, and walked quickly out of the bedroom.

She ran up the stairs to her apartment, unexpected tears threatening. Too many emotions crowded her heart; she couldn't sort them out.

She heard Will's voice coming from Deloise's bedroom and followed it, feeling a sense of relief. Will was a safe place. She didn't have to think about any of this if she was with Will.

"Because your father wouldn't even let you wear that tank top the other day," he was saying. "There's no way he's going to let you go out in those bra straps."

"Spaghetti straps, Will. They're called spaghetti straps, and it's a dance, not a school day."

"What's a dance?" Josh asked, reaching the doorway. The apartment was dark and chilly, but Deloise had two lamps and a space heater on in her room.

At Josh's appearance, Deloise looked guilty. "Friday," she said. "There's a dance."

"Oh," Josh said. She'd forgotten all about the Valentine's Day dance. Suddenly her hot chocolate tasted too thick and too sweet. She set it on Deloise's dresser.

"What do you think?" Deloise asked, holding a dress up against her jeans and sweater.

"I think Will's right—Dad will never let you wear that."

"Then I guess we'll have to make sure he doesn't see it," Deloise replied, tucking the dress into the back of her closet. "Will thinks I look hot."

Josh shot him a glare that might have come from a manual on how to be an overprotective older sister. He lifted his hands. "I did *not* say that," he swore.

"No, but your pupils dilated," Deloise pointed out. "That's what pupils do when they see something they like."

"For crying out loud," Josh said while watching Will make protesting hand gestures.

"Like yours are doing now," Deloise told her.

Josh turned the glare on her sister. "Are you ready to go?" she asked.

Deloise shut the closet door while giving Josh a most innocent smile. "Ready."

Winsor was already in the kitchen, wearing sunglasses and chugging down a cup of coffee at a speed that even Whim couldn't match. Haley held out Josh's coat and, without speaking, lifted it for her to step into. His hands fell weightily on her shoulders for a moment before she jerked away.

"Don't push yourself too hard today," he told her as she grabbed her book bag off the floor.

She grimaced, knowing Winsor was watching. "Whatever," she told Haley.

"I'm going back to bed," Whim announced. "You each have a generous slice of apple kuchen in your backpack, so my work here is done."

"What, you just get up in the morning to hang out with us at breakfast and then go back to sleep?" Deloise asked. She fit a knit cap with the designer's name stitched on it over her carefully blowdried hair, and Whim reached out to tweak her nose while both her hands were occupied.

"Not *all* of you," he told her, and grinned as he headed out of the kitchen.

Deloise blushed when she realized that her sister, Winsor, Will, and Haley were all watching.

"Your pupils are dilated," Josh told her.

Deloise covered her cheeks with both hands and ducked out the back door. "Shut *up!*"

Through a Veil Darkly

I got a LOT of responses to my last post about the possibility of the trench-coat men being responsible for mystery disease CSAD. I got, like, an avalanche. I received e-mails calling me a nut, a lunatic, an idiot, and a dumbass, and more than a few threats. But I got ten times as many e-mails telling me to keep digging. The junta might not want to admit it, but there are a lot of dream walkers worried about the trench-coat men, and a lot of people scared of CSAD, and a lot of coincidences between the two. I get reports of new sightings of the TCM every day, and there are now twelve confirmed cases of CSAD in the Scott County area. Nine of those victims have been moved to long-term-care wards, and one is still in the ICU.

The other two victims are dead.

The junta is denying more vigorously than ever that the TCM are more than nightmares. The same with the idea that they might be related somehow to CSAD. But their denials are basically meaningless, because if they admit now that they know more than they've let on, and the information they held back could have saved victims, they're going to have a lot to answer for.

I never post information that I don't have some sort of evidence to back up, and as of an e-mail twenty minutes ago, I feel confident in reporting that several dream walkers have evidence of Feodor Kajażkołski's involvement with the TCM. That's right, the Madman of Maplefax is likely mixed up in all this somehow. My source for this information had already made their local government representative aware of this evidence, which had been fairly well received, and was stunned yesterday when they realized that the purpose of the meeting in Braxton was to solidify the junta's position of denial and to attempt to quell rumors.

This just smacks of a cover-up.

What Through a Veil Darkly is demanding is that the Gendarmerie conduct their own investigation. As many of your have likely forgotten (or just never learned) the Gendarmerie was established in the 1400s under the Rousellario monarchy as a constabulary force. It was inherited by the junta and is considered by many to be the closest thing we have to a junta oversight. The Gendarmerie is our best chance for a real investigation into who the TCM are, their connection to Feodor Kajażkołski, and how to stop CSAD.

Twenty-one

That afternoon, Josh gave Will a pile of reading to do and then prowled the library like an overcaffeinated librarian. And probably one who was used to a much bigger library. Will tried to focus on the reading—something about faking abilities to reassure dreamers—but he was distracted by Josh's grumbling and half-voiced mutterings.

She tossed a dozen volumes onto the table and sat down, flipped through the pages, stuck a marker in one volume, and then went back to the shelves. More books, more markers. Will watched her read and make comparisons and curse and then find more books. When she had pulled down half the library, he finally asked, "Josh, what are you doing?"

She gave him a guilty look over one shoulder. Then she slowly turned and sat down in the chair across from him. "I can't sit and do nothing," she began. "It's . . ."

"Not in your nature?" Will suggested, trying not to smile.

"Right. And I got to thinking, what if we could check on Feodor? See what he's up to in that universe of his?"

Will did not like where this was going.

"Just take a peek at him, you know? Whim said people visit him there. And then I thought, well, we use the looking stone to spy on the Dream before we enter it. What if we could look at Feodor's universe the same way?"

"You want to build an archway to his universe?" Will burst out, clapping shut the book in his own hands.

"Not an archway," Josh said. "Not exactly. It would be like a one-way mirror—we'd be able to see him, but he wouldn't even know we were there. Only, I'm not sure if that's possible."

Will considered. He wanted to please Josh—he always wanted to please her, to ease that pained look on her face—and she had grown more and more restless the past several days. But an archway went both ways, and he wasn't going to take any chance of letting Feodor into the World.

"You need . . . a window," he said. "Instead of an archway."

She nodded.

"A very strong window." He thought some more. "How do you build an archway?"

"You have to cut through the Veil with a blade of light."

"A what?"

"It's just a very narrow beam of light. You can use candles inside boxes with a hole in them, so they shoot out a single beam, or a lantern with a special kind of hood. You have to reflect the lights off a lot of mirrors, and when you have this whole reflective pattern set up just right, you use another laser to trace the pattern of the reflected beams of light, and that does it."

"So it's scientific. Huh." He leaned back in his chair. "I thought it was some sort of magic."

"Grandma always says there's more magic to it than people realize, but I couldn't tell you for sure how it works. This is as much as I understand."

She pushed an open book across the table. The pages showed a wildly complex arrangement of mirrors with beams of light bouncing between them. Will skimmed the surrounding text and then turned the page and continued reading. A few minutes later, just when he was starting to think the book offered no hints to their dilemma, he found something.

"Can you explain this to me?"

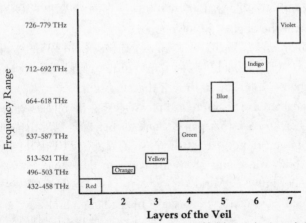

Figure 7.6: This chart demonstrates the frequency range of the light required to pierce each of the seven layers of the Veil. Application of full-spectrum light will pierce all seven layers simultaneously.

Josh studied the diagram he pointed to, then said, "Each layer of the Veil requires light of a different frequency to cut through it. Frequency corresponds to color."

"What are the layers of the Veil made of?"

"I don't know. Although one layer falls right out when you open an archway, and then you can use pieces of it as looking stones."

Will had wondered how looking stones were created. He supposed this explanation made as much sense as any, given that they were discussing something that might or might not be magic.

"I don't know what the other layers are made of," Josh admitted. "They turn into fairy dust as soon as you cut through them."

She slid the book back across the table to Will, and he sat and stared at it. He felt like some important idea hovered within his reach, and he could catch it if only he could see that it was there. He read another page, and then another, and finally the idea began to reveal itself in his mind.

"Listen to this," he said. "'Although candlelight has traditionally been used, automatically employing the entire spectrum of visible light, it has recently been discovered that application of specific, narrow-frequency light will fail to fully penetrate the Veil, as evidenced by looking stones, which can be cut using a light in the 432 to 458 THz range.'" He looked up at Josh. "Does that mean what I think it means?"

Her brows were drawn tight. "Do you think it means that full-spectrum light will cut through the Veil, but red light will cut through only one of the layers?"

"Yes! What if we did everything you normally do when you create an archway, but we used a light frequency that only partially penetrates the Veil? We'd pick a light color closer to the red end of the spectrum and just cut through the first few layers of the Veil, maybe up to the second or third. Wouldn't that create an archway we could see through but not walk through?"

Will wasn't sure if he was outlining a plan or just babbling like an idiot. His mouth had been running faster than his mind could follow, chasing that new idea even as it revealed itself.

"Did that make any sense at all?" he asked.

"I think," Josh said slowly, "that if we pull this off, we'll win the Nicastro Prize in Dream Theory for young dream walkers. It comes with a college scholarship."

"We're really doing something that groundbreaking?"

"No, we're doing something that *clever*."

She had never given him that look before, a look of admiration and excitement. The look clung between them like static electricity, and he wondered how big the spark would be if he touched her.

"But I see a major problem," she said, bringing him down from his high. "Like Whim said, we don't know how to find Feodor's universe. If we just build an archway, it will automatically open to the Dream. How do we get the archway to open to Feodor's universe instead?"

"Oh," Will said. "It could take a while to solve that."

It took them four days.

They waited until everyone had gone to bed. They'd taken the night shift so that they could be assured six hours alone in the archroom. First they built a second frame around the empty doorframe from the armoire they'd broken before. Then Josh and Will meticulously hot-glued the mirrors into the empty doorframes, tilting each one to the correct angle.

"Are we sure this is safe?" Will asked, squeezing hot glue onto the back of a two-by-two-inch mirror.

He was having a case of buyer's regret. Maybe because he and Josh had been up until two that morning figuring out how to arrange the mirrors; or maybe because they'd found the information in an article originally written in Swedish and he wasn't entirely confident of the Internet's translation; or maybe because he had just realized that pleasing Josh might not be a good enough reason to risk opening a porthole between universes. But he suspected he would gladly do stupid things to get her to look at him again the way she had the afternoon they'd come up with this plan.

"We can't be sure," Josh admitted. She was using an X-Acto knife to slice wine corks into wedges the exact right angle to prop up the mirrors. "But the book said that the further you get from the violet end of the spectrum, the fewer layers you cut through. We won't cut deeper than yellow, and that's pretty far from violet."

"What if other parts of the spectrum pierce other universes? What if red pierces hell?"

She stopped cutting to look up at him. "Do you even believe in hell?"

"Actually, no. But that's not the point. What if something comes out?"

"Then we'll shoot it."

Hoping for some sort of reassurance, he asked, "Have you ever done anything like this before?"

He expected Josh to say no and give him another excuse. Instead, she turned as white as full-spectrum light and dropped the cork in her hand. She might as well have fainted, the change in her demeanor was so sudden.

"Am I being arrogant?" she asked, her voice dazed. "Am I doing this for the wrong reasons?"

"What?" Will said, startled. "No. Of course not."

"You'd tell me if I were, wouldn't you?"

He didn't understand how questioning their process had led to Josh's questioning her motives and judgment. "Hey, I'm the apprentice, remember? I don't know anything. My whole job is to freak out when we do the scary stuff."

"You were right to tell me not to go in the Dream last time," she said in a numbed voice. "And you were right to come in after me. Sorry I shouted at you."

"It's okay." Will moved a pile of mirrors to one side so he could scoot across the floor and put his arm around her. She was always in so much pain, and he was always helpless to do anything about it. "I forgave you for all that a week ago, remember?"

She sat and stared at him, lips parted, breathing shallowly, and he felt her weighing something, arguing with herself. Finally, she said, in a confessional whisper, "I was arrogant once, and someone got hurt."

Ian. She means Ian.

He wondered what she had done. Had she knocked over a candle and started the fire that killed him? Had she asked him to run back inside the burning cabin and save something for her? Had she twisted an ankle and needed saving?

It never crossed his mind that she was truly responsible for Ian's death.

But looking at the tears in her pale, pale eyes, he knew that she believed she had killed Ian.

How terrible to believe such a thing, he thought, *to carry that knowledge around. No wonder she always looks sad.*

Will wished he knew better how to comfort her. He wanted to kiss her forehead, but her boundaries were so tall and so impassable; he was afraid the gesture would go awry. "Everybody makes mistakes, Josh." He gave her a squeeze instead of the kiss and added, "I'm sorry I'm giving you such a hard time. I'm just nervous. I get kind of cranky when I'm nervous."

Josh seized on the opportunity to lighten the conversation. "It's a defense mechanism?" she asked, and then she smiled, because they both knew she'd learned the term from him.

"It's a defense mechanism," he agreed. "Look, forget about worst-case scenarios and maybes. Just tell me this: do you believe, deep down, that we can do this?"

She was quiet for a long time, her eyes lingering on the doorframe in front of them. Then she looked back at Will, and there was a new certainty in her face. She nodded.

"Then we'll do it," he said.

When they had finished with the mirrors, they propped the doorframe up against the wall. They'd purchased four miniature lanterns and fitted each with a metal hood. By punching holes in the hoods and covering the holes with gel filters, they created lanterns that put out single beams of colored light. The gel filters had been hard to come by in the exact shades necessary, and they'd had to turn to Deloise, who talked to one of her drama-geek friends, who pointed them toward a theater-supply company.

Finally, they attached one of the lanterns to the top of the exterior doorframe, lit it, and sent a beam of red light shooting between the mirrors.

By that time, Will didn't really expect anything to happen. The mirrors, the corks, the gel filters, all that hot glue—what kind of magic was performed with hot glue? The longer they had worked and the more their creation resembled something from the set of a grade-school play, the less anxious he felt. All of this would turn out to be for nothing. He was sure of it.

Still, when it came time to open the window, he waited until Josh had gotten a 9mm SIG Sauer from the gun locker and loaded it before he actually opened the archway. Will had fired that gun exactly once before going back to Deloise's .22; the 9mm kicked all the way up his shoulder.

They dragged their doorframe and extra lanterns into the arch-room, and Josh said, "All right, key check."

Will pulled his lighter and compact out of his pocket and watched Josh do the same. She frowned at the blue plastic lighter. "I wish I hadn't lost my Zippo."

"It was nice," Will agreed.

She glanced at him. "It was a gift," she said shortly, and Will knew he had bumped one of her sore spots again. But she shook it off and said, "You set?"

"Set."

"Then let's do it."

This was the most tenuous part of the plan, and if it didn't work, the whole endeavor was kaput: Will was supposed to direct the look-ing stone to show them the part of the Dream Feodor's universe had been cut from. After a good fifteen different plans—most of them complicated and requiring much travel—they had come up with this simple idea. They were hoping that when Feodor's uni-verse was cut from the Dream, it had left a scar, like an amputated limb, and that if they opened an archway within the Dream right on top of the scar, it would lead to Feodor's universe instead of the World.

"What's wrong?" Josh asked when Will just stood and stared at the looking stone.

Will shrugged. "I don't know how to begin."

"Just do what you'd normally do."

Beginning turned out to be the easy part—he pressed his palm to the looking stone and closed his eyes, and suddenly the Dream was all around him. He felt the wind whipping by him as he stood on the crest of a mountain, heard car tires peel water off the surface of a highway, smelled the sunsetlike odor of fresh-baked bread. Then, almost as soon as he identified each sense, the input narrowed to a single dream in which a young girl gathered flowers in a field.

She had no idea what was slithering about in the high grass.

"We have to go in," Will said, opening his eyes as he spoke.

Josh grabbed his shoulders. "We can't go in, remember?"

Through the archway, Will watched the girl whip her head around at the sound of something moving through the grass. She wanted to believe it was just the breeze. . . .

"Will," Josh said. She grabbed his chin and forced him to face her. "Find Feodor."

Feodor. For a moment Will rebelled, certain that nothing could be more important than saving that little girl, but as hissing began on one side of the field, then the other, he knew that even if he hadn't had other priorities, he wouldn't have gone through. He had no defense against a plague of flesh-eating snake-worms.

The little girl shrieked once, then vanished beneath the high grass.

"Feodor," Josh said again, and Will closed his eyes.

The Dream bombarded him again: the crackle of burning wood, moldy garbage, bank deposit slips. Will tried to sort through the dreams, to pull back from them until he reached the edges of the Dream, but there were no edges, only a gentle curve that made him think he traveled over the inner surface of a sphere. It felt as slick as ice, and he spun across it, not sure what he was doing or if he was getting anywhere, if he covered miles or inches, if hours or minutes had passed.

Wait—what was that?

He'd passed over something, a place where two dreams fit together incorrectly. Will struggled to slow his sliding and turn around, and then it took a while of blind searching to find that spot again, the one that felt like a record needle jumping from one track to the next. "Here, I think," he told Josh.

"You found it?" She sounded surprised.

"Maybe. I found something."

Opening his eyes, he saw a dream parking lot located behind a strip mall, where several Dumpsters were piled high with trash. A few feet from the Dumpsters, a line ran through the scene from the sky to the ground, and on the other side of it, an angry nun in an elaborate wimple was walking up and down the aisles of a classroom, smacking her ruler against her palm and watching the children scribble on handheld blackboards. The two scenes looked like photographs cut down the middle and laid side by side.

"That's so weird," Josh said.

Will stood up, keeping his hand on the looking stone. Josh snapped her 9mm into a hip holster, then grabbed the mirror-laden armoire door and carried it through the archway into the parking lot. When the Dream allowed her easy entrance, Will followed with the extra lanterns.

On the strip-mall side, the sun was shining. Actually, several suns were shining. The labels on the Dumpsters were in what was clearly meant to be an alien script, and Will noticed that the trash bags appeared to be breathing.

"Ah, this nightmare might be picking up speed," Will said. "We should do this fast."

Josh grew still and thoughtful the way she often did before she had an insight about a nightmare. Will was beginning to develop a theory about what she was actually doing during these moments, and it wasn't thinking, but now wasn't the time to bring it up.

"Agreed," she said after a few seconds. "Where should I put this thing?"

They propped the armoire door against the rear wall of Bebe's Exotic Reptiles, then scooted it to the right until one half overlapped with the nun's classroom. By scooting it, they were also able to avoid detection from the cranky nun.

They'd agreed that Will would perform the actual opening so that Josh could aim the gun. Not that—if their plan worked— anything would come out of the archway, but they'd agreed to err far on the side of caution, and Josh was still a much better shot than Will. So he relit the lantern affixed to the top of the doorframe and watched as the ruby light bounced between the mirrors. Using a second lantern and starting at the top of the doorway, he traced the lattice of ruby-colored beams all the way around. He hadn't understood most of what he'd read, but what he had gotten was that the actual opening occurred because of how the lights intersected, and if the beam he directed lost contact with the network inside the doorway, even by a millimeter, the whole thing would fail.

Will worked very, very slowly.

By the time he reached the top of the doorway again, his arms were shaking and he had to grip the lantern with both hands. Just before he completed the pattern, Josh said, "Careful," and he stepped to the side of the door. As soon as he retraced the beginning of the pattern, the first layer of the Veil fell out of the doorframe.

Will only saw the first layer as a disturbance like heat in the air until it hit the blacktop, where the entire pane turned into red glass and shattered.

"Nice work," Josh said afterward.

Will rested his arms for a minute, then switched the red lanterns for the orange ones and repeated the entire process. The second layer felt like a piece of cloth made of light and warmth, and it broke over Will and turned to fairy dust that coated his arms and the red glass at his feet.

Josh walked up to the armoire door, stepping carefully through the glass shards, and reached out and tried to put her hand through the doorframe—a surface stopped her. She rapped her knuckles against it, but it made no sound.

"It worked," Josh said, her voice breathy. "I'll be damned."

"Where's Feodor's universe?" Will asked. At the moment all he could see through the doorframe was a misty gray haze. "Should I do the third layer?"

Josh frowned. They'd hoped that the second layer would look into Feodor's universe, but unless he'd imagined himself living in a very foggy place, they'd run into something else entirely. Neither Josh nor Will had wanted to risk cutting through the third layer. "Try a piece of looking stone."

The chunks of looking stone scattered across the concrete were an inch and a half thick. Will lifted one a little larger than his palm, being careful of the sharp edges; someone must have shaped the looking stone in the archroom. The surface wasn't as smooth as glass or as rough as stone but had a powdered texture like an un-polished gem. The deep-red color made Will think of rubies.

He held the piece between his hands and tried to do the same thing with it that he'd done with the looking stone at home. At first he thought nothing was happening—then a small black speck appeared out of the mist and grew larger at increasing speed. Fi-nally it seemed to fling itself at the window, and Will knew they'd made it.

Feodor's universe was a city, a dark, rain-filled city—or rather, what was left of a city. The remaining brick buildings sat amid piles of smoke-stained rubble that had once been their neighbors. Water splashed along the black cobblestone and formed rivers that ran down the cracked and crowded streets. There were no signs of life—no people, no animals—just row after row of debris and the wreckage of a war.

Will laughed aloud. "It's perfect," he said, and he heard Josh re-lease a long-held breath. She lowered the gun.

But it wasn't *perfect*.

Even as they exchanged grins, astonished by themselves and each other and their Nicastro Prize–worthy creation, their view through the doorframe changed. They had been looking out over the city before, but now they seemed to zoom forward and down, into the street, across a rooftop, through a mess of shingles and wallboard, and then the image stabilized in a single room.

Josh raised the 9mm.

Although it had been bombed, enough of the room remained to identify it as a parlor or sitting room. Two walls and part of the ceiling were missing, but the rest of the room had escaped largely untouched. The surviving walls bore an ashes-of-roses paper print, and two upholstered chairs sat on opposite sides of a cracked marble-top coffee table.

A man sat in one of the chairs. A sketchpad rested in his lap, and he ran a pencil over it in long, smooth strokes. Will recognized Feodor from the photo in his computer file. He had a small, focused face with crisp lips and wide gray eyes. His hair was cut close to his skull, and he wore an old-fashioned pair of black trousers, suspenders, and a gray shirt. But this man couldn't possibly have been Feodor, because he looked no older than thirty.

The man stopped sketching midstroke. He stared directly at the window.

The smile he gave them was both coy and cold.

We didn't figure out how to close this thing, Will realized suddenly.

That was bad. That was very bad, because the man was looking back through the doorway at them—and from the way he turned his gaze slowly from Will to Josh, Will knew he saw them.

"Hello, children. Are you looking for someone?" He spoke with a Polish accent that softened what otherwise might have been clipped words.

"He's too young," Will told Josh, turning away from the window for a moment.

She nodded, but Feodor had heard Will speak.

"What a kind compliment," Feodor replied. "Admittedly, my

body is not as young as I would wish. But I enjoy keeping up appearances." He placed the sketchpad on the coffee table—Will could just make out a drawing of the city's ruined skyline—and stood to face them. Although not a tall man, he filled the window. "You are very young yourselves, children. What is it you've come here for?"

"We just wanted to check on you," Josh said.

Feodor tilted his head skeptically. "Check on me? That is not why people come here."

Will glanced behind himself at Josh. "Why do people come here?" he asked.

"You might ask the one who sent you," Feodor suggested.

"No one sent us," Josh said.

"No?" Feodor tilted his head and a smile played across his lips. "Then perhaps you have outsmarted someone."

What does that mean? Will wondered, but he had no time to hold on to the thought, because Feodor lifted his hand and pressed it against the window.

"Stay back!" Josh barked, pointing her 9mm at him. Will backed away from the doorframe, but Feodor removed his hand with a dismissive wave, as if to say, *It is nothing.*

"Apologies," he said. "Apologies. I meant no alarm. Please forgive my curiosity."

Will swallowed. They needed to get this interview done quickly and then figure out a way to close this window. "Are you involved with the men in trench coats?"

"Trench coats? They sound like Nazis."

"They aren't—Hitler has been dead for seventy years," Will said, exasperated.

"Has it been so long?" Feodor brightened again. "In that case, my appearance *is* most impressive. Would you like to see how I maintain it?"

"That's not why we—" Will began, but the image beyond the window was moving, like a movie camera that started with a slow pan, then picked up speed until it was flying down streets so quickly that all Will could see were black, gray, and white lines. When it slowed again, it framed a dim room, perhaps a basement, where Feodor stood beside a metal table with a naked corpse lying on it.

"This is my real body," he said. The excitement of explanation animated his face. "Do you see this sheath that covers it?"

The "sheath" was a silver plastic shroud that had been wound around the body's limbs and torso, even its head. It looked to Will like Feodor had mummified himself with shrink-wrap. At the ends of the individually wrapped fingers and toes, nails had ripped through the shroud and grown so long they curled, and Feodor's face was obscured by white hair that—with no place to go—had grown down over his eyes and mouth.

"The sheath provides for all my needs—oxygen, nutrition, elimination—while maintaining my brain in a perpetual state of hibernation, which allows my dreaming mind to project an image of me that's much younger than I really am. But I'm not limited to my own image. I can project myself as anyone I want. Observe."

Instantly, Feodor was gone, and Hitler was standing in his place. Josh swore.

Hitler lifted his arm in a Nazi salute, goose-stepped in place a few times, and then laughed wildly.

"I can even be you," Hitler said in a thick German accent, and turned into Will.

To say that Will felt like he was looking in a mirror was an understatement. Rather, he was so convinced by the image before him that he felt suddenly afraid that he had left his own body and was looking at it from the outside.

"Or I can be a machine," the other Will said.

Huh? Will thought, but he thought too slowly, because a great silver funnel appeared, its tip pressed against the window. The funnel began to spin with a groan of gears, and then released a dazzling burst of white light, causing the window to shudder.

Josh fired.

The bullet hit not the window but the doorframe itself, which broke and splintered. The instant the pattern of lights went out, the window disappeared, the image of the funnel and Feodor's shrink-wrapped mummy vanishing as the entire doorway fell over. All the little mirrors broke and the lantern broke, and Will spun away, shielding his face with his arms as shards of glass and drops of burning kerosene flew through the air.

Afterward, the packing area behind the pet shop seemed quiet, despite the nun who was now using her ruler to slap the hands of a little girl wearing a dunce hat. Or maybe the gunshot had temporarily deafened Will's ears. Either way, he felt a strange calm as he looked around and saw nothing but him and Josh and a parking lot full of broken mirrors.

A garbage truck pulled up next to the Dumpster, and tentacles began slithering out from the trash. Will carefully beat out a few drops of kerosene burning on the ground near his feet.

Josh clicked the safety on the gun. She was breathing a little fast—they both were—but otherwise she looked as steady as Will had ever seen her.

"You all right?" she asked.

"Yes. Nice shooting."

"Thanks."

They stood there for a minute and looked at the bits of broken mirror and red glass on the concrete, while one of the garbage collectors got dragged into the Dumpster with a scream. "We probably should have figured out how to shut the window before we opened it," Will said.

"I thought I did a rather good job of shutting it," Josh said.

He couldn't argue with her there.

Twenty-two

"I say we write it up," Josh told Will the next day, sitting in the safe tranquility of the library again.

"If we write it up, everybody will know we did it."

Josh knew she was still a little giddy from their success the night before. They'd actually managed to do something no one else had ever attempted, and they'd done it without another trip to the hospital. Granted, Josh could have waited to see if the window would have survived Feodor's assault instead of just blowing the whole experiment to pieces, but she didn't regret doing so. For once, she'd taken the cautious route.

Besides, she was *proud* of what they'd done. Proud that they'd thought of it, figured it out, and made it work. Proud that they'd done it together. She was even proud that Will had stuck exactly to the plan. For the first time, his presence had felt like having a partner by her side instead of a student, and she'd liked having him for a partner.

"Besides which," Will said, "how are we going to explain how Feodor was able to see through the window? Dreamers never notice us looking through the archway."

This oddity had caught Josh's attention as well.

"I think he sensed we were there," Will said, not waiting for her opinion. "I think he's been in that universe for so long that he's tied into the fabric of it."

"Yeah, but if he has such great control over that universe, why did it look like a war zone?"

"Young Ben said he never got over World War II. People re-create the circumstances of their youth all the time. He might just have been more literal than most."

Josh made a face. She didn't get people most of the time; no way was she going to be able to understand Feodor. "I've been thinking about what he said, that someone sent us."

"Any idea what that means?"

"None. Who would have sent us? And why?"

Josh was about to mention Feodor's strange compliment—*Then perhaps you have outsmarted someone*—when Deloise popped into the library. "Hey," she said. "Davita just called. She wanted me to let you know that somebody found the origins of the trench-coat men—some British student film." Deloise smiled, obviously thinking that she was delivering good news. "They're just mass-media bogeymen after all."

"What?" Josh asked. She jumped out of her chair so fast Deloise backed up a step. "That's not possible."

Josh had told Davita how the men had changed the Dream. Davita, of all people, should know it wasn't possible for them to be imaginary.

Deloise continued retreating into the hallway as Josh advanced on her, looking confused and like she half expected Josh to kill the messenger. "Well . . . gosh, that's what she said."

Josh brushed past her sister and headed for the kitchen as fast as her knee would allow, a sense of panic driving her. She dug through her family's cluttered, ancient address book until she found Davita's phone number. While she dialed, Will watched her from the kitchen doorway.

"It's Josh," she said as soon as Davita answered. "What's going on?"

Davita got straight to the point. "Someone found a four-minute British student film featuring the two men. It got picked up by an American late-night comedy show, and since then it's been all over the Internet."

"So what? That just means more people have seen them in their nightmares. Did you tell my grandfather what Will and I saw?"

"I told him."

"And?"

"He said you were foolish and disobedient and you couldn't possibly have seen one of those men change the Dream and you must have misheard the name Feodor."

"I didn't mishear anything!" Josh felt her palms flush. She knew better than to take her grandfather's judgments personally, but his words stung all the same.

"Calm down," Davita said, infuriatingly calm herself. "Peregrine doesn't want to start a panic, and he's right that we don't have any hard evidence that these men are more than nightmares. We're suspicious, but we don't know with any certainty."

I know for certain, Josh's gut whispered. *I know, I know, I know. . . .*

"So now we all just go back into the Dream with no idea what we're up against," she said aloud. "Great."

"Josh, I'm working on it."

Josh looked at Will, who had come close enough to hear Davita's voice. For a moment she considered telling Davita what she and Will had done the night before; about Feodor's war-ravaged universe, his strange youth, that comment he'd made that they couldn't explain—*Then perhaps you have outsmarted someone.*

But what good would it do? She hadn't learned anything for certain that connected him to Gloves and Snitch. Davita was right: she needed hard evidence.

"Fine," she said to Davita, and then she turned to bang her forehead against a cupboard.

To celebrate the solved mystery of the trench-coat men, Kerstel made an enormous dinner that included game hens, corn bread, four vegetables, and pecan pie. It also included dry red wine, which got passed around the table like a pitcher of iced tea, and Josh drank far more of it than she should have.

Because she was really, *really* angry, and because she was supposedly an adult now and drinking was the only adult thing anyone would let her do, but all that she managed to accomplish was to get tipsy and trip while getting out of her chair. Haley caught her and the whole room cracked up.

Josh had never felt less like an adult in her life.

Despite her announcement the day before that she was going to move back into her bedroom, she barely made it to the office. Haley actually carried her part of the way, and when he kissed her cheek before he left, she would have thrown a punch if she could have figured out which one of him to hit.

She flopped onto the futon without bothering to open it. While she waited for the alcohol to wear off, she made a semilegible—but likely incomprehensible—entry in her diary. She was still ranting about the hypocrisy of the adults in her life when Will knocked on the open door.

"What?" she snapped, and he held up one hand to ward her off.

"Just thought you might want some water."

"Oh." She did, actually, want some water, and Will was holding a large glass of it with the hand that wasn't preparing to fend off blows. "Sorry. Come in."

He gave her the water, full of clinking ice cubes, and then sat down in the chair at the desk, after which he thought to ask, "May I sit?"

"Yeah, yeah. Sorry, I seem to be a cranky drunk."

"You do. Drink the water, it will help. My mom used to say, 'A gallon of water the night before will cure any hangover.'"

Suddenly Josh felt like a complete ass. She'd gotten drunk in front of a guy whose mother was an alcoholic. And she was supposed to be his *teacher*.

"Sorry," she said for the third time. "I forgot. About your mom. Sorry."

Will shrugged. "People get drunk, Josh. It happens." His expression was far away, and even though Josh felt like a jerk, she didn't see any judgment in his look. "I got drunk a few times, just to see what was so great about it."

"What happened?"

"It was fun at first. I usually hung out with some guys, playing poker, just goofing off. And then one night somebody offered me another beer, and I said, 'All aboard what's going aboard!' And I realized I was quoting my mother." He laughed, and although his voice hadn't been bitter, his laughter was. "After that, I don't know, the whole thing lost its charm." He shrugged again. "Doesn't matter. Just drink your water."

"I didn't mean to . . ."

"I know. You're pissed off at your grandfather because he doesn't believe us. Frankly, I'm kind of pissed off at him too. He's your flesh and blood. He should believe you. *I* believe you."

"You were there."

"Yeah. But I'd probably believe you even if I hadn't been."

The room was still spinning. Josh tried to drink the water, but her stomach hurt. "You shouldn't trust me so much, Will," she said, rubbing her face.

"Why not?"

Because the last guy who trusted me died.

She kept a hand over her eyes, to shield them from the lights in the hallway, to shield herself from Will. The more time she spent around Will, the more she wanted to confide in him, and the more she dreaded doing so.

He wouldn't trust her afterward. He wouldn't respect her. He probably wouldn't even like her, and that partnership they'd formed the night before would vanish.

"Josh," he said, and she felt him sit down beside her on the futon. He pried her hand away from her face. "Whatever you're saying to yourself, it's the booze talking, not you."

Not true, not true, she told herself. The voice in her head sounded like Ian's.

But at that moment she wanted to believe Will—believe in his kindness—so she did, and she put her head on his shoulder so she wouldn't have to look him in the eye.

At least, that's why she told herself she put her head on his shoulder, and then sighed and turned to press her forehead against his neck, and let him wrap his arm around her.

But then, that might have been the booze talking too.

Twenty-three

The next evening found Josh and Will tackling the Romanian training circuit again. By the third time through, Josh's knee was throbbing and Will had lost all his coloring.

"I can't do that again," he panted, bending over.

"Me neither. Let's go get some water."

They would have been late for dinner by a half hour if Kerstel had been home, but since she had dragged Lauren off to a post-humanist art exhibit, the only meal was the one Winsor and Whim were debating in the kitchen.

"We have eaten enough pizza from Roggey-Warren in the last year to fill a truck," Winsor was saying as Josh followed Will out of the pantry. Winsor glanced at Josh as she emerged, then very deliberately turned her eyes away.

Josh didn't care. She was limping again, badly. Her knee was engulfed in flames.

"What about Serena's Pizzeria?" Whim suggested.

"I don't think so." Josh sat down hard in a chair, trying not to wince. "Last time we ordered from there . . ."

"They delivered me instead," Will finished, going to open the fridge.

Whim lifted his thin eyebrows. "Obviously they have new coupons."

"That's when Will got designated as Josh's apprentice," Winsor explained. That nasty little note in her voice was back, the sliver-thin knife in her words. She must not have forgotten Josh's barb the other day. "Because Deloise ordered pizza. If she hadn't, Josh would have ended up teaching Schaffer Sounclouse."

Suddenly the pain in Josh's knee was of no consequence. "What?" she asked at the same moment Will spun around to look at Winsor.

Winsor's eyes moved playfully between the two of them. "Don't you remember? Less than a minute after you two went down to the archroom that night, Schaffer Sounclouse showed up at the front door. You probably saw him when you came upstairs again."

There had been so many people there that night that it was impossible for Josh to recall everyone in particular.

"Who's Schaffer Sounclouse?" Will asked.

"He's Young Ben's great-grandson," Winsor replied. "Didn't you realize he was here, Josh?"

"No, I . . ." Her voice was choked, tinny. "I didn't think anything of it."

"He came over to meet the apprentice," Winsor said. "He left pretty quickly, but I figured that if Will hadn't showed up . . ."

"If Deloise hadn't ordered pizza," Whim added, seeming to enjoy the unfolding puzzle.

"He would have *been* the apprentice," Will finished. "You would be training Schaffer."

"He's not terrible," Winsor put in, "but everybody says he needs a decent teacher."

Josh couldn't think clearly, couldn't decide what this new information meant. It had been one thing to believe that someone else might have arrived in Will's place, but to hear that the intended apprentice had actually arrived at the house . . .

Josh realized her mouth was hanging open. She closed it and looked at Will, who was standing with his back to the open refrigerator, staring at her.

He looked terrified.

Whim, who was either oblivious to what was happening or else creating a reason to leave the room, picked up the phone and carried it into the hallway, and Josh heard him place a carryout order for Thai food.

"Are you two okay?" Winsor asked. She added innocently, "You didn't have another training accident, did you?"

Something in Will's expression was pleading for Josh to speak, but she didn't know what to say. How could she reassure him when they now had proof positive that fate had intended someone else to be her apprentice?

Tell him that it doesn't matter how it happened. Tell him it doesn't matter if we screwed up fate—he's here now. Tell him that you don't wish he was someone else.

"I, um, we—" She coughed while trying to get the lie out. "We're fine. That's weird, with Schaffer. I didn't realize he'd come by." She stared at the floor for a while longer. She couldn't keep looking at Will; his desperation burned her like acid. "But, um, like Dad says, fate doesn't make mistakes."

"Deloise does," Winsor quipped, and Josh wanted to punch her. It was one thing to try to hurt Josh, but it was quite another to be cruel to Will.

"Stop it," Josh said, but all she could think to do was repeat herself. "If fate doesn't make mistakes, then Deloise calling for pizza is what was supposed to happen."

Winsor snorted. "Tell that to Schaffer Sounclouse."

Josh got up from her chair and, despite the pain in her knee, staged a pointed and dramatic walkout.

She was halfway down the hall before she realized that Will hadn't followed her. He probably thought she had walked out on him, too.

I should have said, "Then God bless Deloise for ordering pizza," she thought, letting herself into the office. *Or, "It's a good thing Will showed up first." Or just, "Schaffer Sounclouse sucks."*

The words had come to her too late. But it didn't matter—she had already lied.

She was fairly certain fate *could* make mistakes.

She didn't come out for dinner. Will felt sick to his stomach and didn't think Thai spice would help, but Deloise insisted he eat and the food did calm him. Distantly, he recalled Kerstel asking him to make sure Josh ate something.

He had known almost from the start that his arrival at the Weavers' home had been unexpected. But it was different now, knowing that not only should he not have been there but another dream walker should have had his place. Maybe working with Schaffer would have been less stressful for Josh, since he knew what it was she was struggling with. Maybe she would have taken his raw talent and molded him into someone skilled, instead of having to start from scratch with an outsider.

When Will had believed he had accidentally taken Louis's place in the scheme of things, it had bothered him. But comparing himself to Louis was far kinder to his self-esteem than comparing himself to the naturally inclined apprentice Josh could have had.

He felt guilty for taking that opportunity away from her—and hell, from Schaffer, too—and he knew she must be disappointed. Still, it stung how she had just walked away.

After dinner he found himself cleaning up the kitchen with Whim. Winsor and Deloise had gone downstairs to walk, and Haley was in the living room, watching television and writing endless notes. Earlier he'd given Will an itemized list of their delivery order.

"So you and Josh didn't realize Schaffer had come by like two minutes after you, huh?" Whim asked, bundling up the trash.

Will glanced at him from the sink as he scrubbed dishes. "No," he said. He hadn't meant to say it so quietly, but he barely heard himself.

"And since Josh bolted like a bank robber when she found out, you're thinking horrible things?" Whim grinned at him, not unkindly. "The thing with Josh is," he went on, opening the back door and pitching a bag of garbage in the general direction of the bins, "you can't ever assume she's saying what she's thinking."

"I've realized that."

"It's not that she'd rather have Schaffer as her apprentice—it's that she'd rather not have known she was going to have an apprentice at all."

Will considered that, shutting off the water in the sink. "Go on," he said.

"Josh doesn't want to know what her scroll says," Whim explained. Now that he had finished cleaning up dinner, he began making himself a snack. "It's because of Ian and all that. I think that after what happened to him, she'd just as soon let fate run its course in her life without her awareness. I don't blame her—and I say that as a guy who opened his scroll."

Will was sick of being polite. "What exactly happened to Ian?" he asked.

Whim stared at him incredulously, a cracker halfway to his mouth. "No one's told you?" he asked.

"Everyone seems reluctant to talk about it."

Whim rolled his eyes and let the cracker drop to the table. "*That's* why I hate this family," he said, bristling. "Too many things they don't want to talk about, or pretend not to notice, or act like never happened."

Will closed the dishwasher and turned it on. Kerstel had spent half an hour with him one evening, showing him how to use all the appliances that had always been broken during his childhood.

"So," he said, sitting down in a chair across the table from Whim's, "what happened?"

Whim considered, growing calm again. "Did Josh flat-out refuse to tell you?"

"No, but I never actually asked Josh. She avoids the subject."

"Yeah, that's not surprising." Whim tapped the cracker on the table as he thought. "She probably doesn't want me to tell you."

Frustrated but determined not to be a jerk, Will said, "I don't want to pressure you to break confidences."

"Hell, Ian was my best friend; I have every right to tell you how he died. The question is how much about Ian and Josh I should tell you, and how much of what happened before he died. How much do you know?"

"I know they were together for a very long time, but they broke up shortly before Ian died. I know he died in a fire at a cabin up in Charle."

Whim nodded slowly. "All correct. What else?"

Will hesitated before saying, "I know that Winsor was in love with Ian."

Whim broke into a slow smile. "You're sharp. That's half the story right there. But I may as well tell you the rest. So, keeping in mind that all truth is subjective, here's *my* version of what happened:

"I thought Ian and Josh would be together forever. I thought they were one of those couples who would have a seventy-fifth anniversary. It was weird, because they weren't exactly perfect people, and I didn't think they had the healthiest relationship. But it was the kind of relationship that usually lasts, you know?"

Will nodded, even though he didn't know. He couldn't imagine Josh with anyone.

"Ian's dad abandoned him and Haley when they were six. That's when Haley started to get weird, and Ian always had to stick up for him. It made Ian . . . prickly. He was a good guy—funny and full of ideas, sort of gallant in a way—but he had this temper that could get completely out of control. He acted real overconfident, but I always thought he was pretty insecure underneath."

"A lot of guys are like that," Will agreed.

"Yeah, well, Josh, on the other hand, had no confidence. No disrespect, but her mom was crazy hard on her. Jona was crazy about dream walking to begin with, and then when she found out that one of her kids was a dream-walking prodigy, she just drove Josh like a workhorse. And Josh is Josh, right? She's awkward. She never knows what to say. She doesn't really believe she's good at anything."

Will was glad he wasn't the only person who had experienced this side of Josh.

"When Jona pushed her, she didn't know how to push back. If Jona criticized her—even for something small—all Josh heard was, 'You're a failure.' And I think that's why Josh needed Ian. She'd get so upset by how much her mom was asking, and Ian would just say, 'Stop freaking out. You're fine. Get over it.' He didn't really make her believe in herself so much as tell her that she was stupid for *not* believing in herself." Whim paused. "I think that difference is important."

So do I, Will thought.

"Josh talked to him the same way. If Ian started to get into something with somebody at school, Josh would tell him, 'You're being an ass. Knock it off.' Sometimes, honestly, I didn't like the way they talked to each other. But like I said, there was also something really solid about them. They liked their relationship. They were happy with it.

"Ian and Haley's seventeenth birthday was last May. Seventeen is a big deal around here. Young Ben gave them their scrolls. I don't know what happened to Haley's, but Ian opened his. Opening your scroll is a toss-up—it might be full of great things, it might be full of terrible things, it's written in verse so you can't figure half of it out anyway, but if you don't open it you'll never know. I opened mine, and there were shocks. There were things I hadn't anticipated and things that upset me, but I didn't—and I don't know anyone who *did*—freak out the way Ian did.

"His scroll said he would fall in love with Josh. No big deal, right? It had already happened. But his interpretation of the scroll's prediction was that what he felt for Josh wasn't real. That somehow he only loved her because the scroll said he would. You know those movies about witches who cast love spells and then don't know whether the men love them because they love them or because of the spell? That's what Ian was afraid of, and from there he spiraled into this whole identity-crisis thing.

"He broke up with Josh. Just called it quits after . . . I don't even know how long. Even before they were old enough for it to be a romantic thing, they were together. They needed each other. And he just broke up with her.

"Josh went into total shock. It's one thing if a guy dumps you because he doesn't love you—it's another if he dumps you *because* he loves you. For about three weeks she walked around like she didn't know right from left. And then she just started working again. She worked twelve, sometimes fifteen-hour shifts, even if she had to miss school.

"But Ian was the one who really lost it. He got into some sort of shouting match with a teacher and ended up suspended for three days because he threw a staple remover at her. I started hearing things about him at school—that he was going to wild parties, hooking up with strange girls, drinking like a fish. I know for a fact that he beat the crap out of Elliot Meyers. When I pointed out that he was doing all the stupid things Josh used to stop him from doing, he told me he was making up for lost time.

"And then . . ." Whim winced. "This is where it gets weird. I don't want to present this the wrong way. Winsor is my little sister, and I love her. But she did some pretty sick stuff, and I don't want to present that the wrong way either. About a year before Ian died, Winsor started dating Haley.

"You're into psychology. Am I wrong that it was totally weird of her to date the identical twin of the guy she was in love with?"

"It's totally, completely, utterly weird," Will agreed.

"Thank you. I thought it was weird. I never understood why they were together. But it's not like Winsor could have pretended she was with Ian when she was with Haley. They were so different they were practically fraternal. And I don't know exactly when Winsor fell in love with Ian, because she kept that to herself. I don't think she wanted to hurt Josh. So maybe she fell in love with him and then gave up on ever being with him and then got interested in Haley, all on his own merits." Whim grimaced. "I doubt it, but I like to think that way.

"But then Ian dumped Josh, and Winsor got her chance."

He hung his head. Will had never seen sorrow or regret on Whim's face, but he saw it then. The emotions aged Whim and destroyed his easy manner.

"I wasn't as aware of what was going on as I should have been," Whim said. "I should have realized that Josh was completely obsessed with escaping into the Dream and Ian was a wreck without her. But when I tried to talk to him—all of his fears seemed so irrational to me that I didn't even know how to listen to him. He acted like he thought the scroll had seen through him, figured him out or something, and he was trying to prove it wrong. I don't know. It was all I could do not to say, 'What the hell is wrong with you, man?' and hearing that just would have pissed him off. But even so, I was his friend, and I should have stopped him from self-destructing.

"We went to Josh's mother's cabin in Charle for the Fourth of July, like we did every year. Lauren had to work, so it was just all us kids and Kerstel. I thought things were going well. Ian and Josh were at least being cordial. He wasn't bolting every time he saw her.

"Then Winsor and Ian disappeared on Saturday afternoon, and when it started to get dark, Josh and Haley went to look for them. And guess what state they found them in?"

Will winced.

"Exactly. Josh looked utterly shocked when she got back to the cabin. I think that, until then, she'd been hanging on to some hope that Ian would come to his senses. But not after that. Ian and Winsor got back after dark, and I still remember how Winsor blushed when she realized we all knew exactly what they'd been doing. She had all these leaves in her hair. It wasn't really my business, but I was pissed off at her anyway. She didn't need to get involved in Josh and Ian's mess.

"Del was like, 'Anybody want to play Monopoly?' and Kerstel and I pretty much just fled upstairs with her. None of us wanted to watch them duke it out. But I should have stayed. I realize that now. They were way too upset to be reasonable—they needed a chaperone. I mean, they were shouting so loud we could hear every word from upstairs with the door closed.

"Maybe three hours later—I wasn't really watching the clock—the smoke detector in the living room went off. Like, nine times out of ten a smoke detector goes off because it needs a battery or somebody overcooked a chicken, but for some reason, that night, Deloise and I just knew it was the real deal. We didn't even say it out loud, we just looked at each other and then started running. She ran to get Kerstel, 'cause she'd gone to bed, and I ran to call 911.

"There was nobody in the living room. I thought maybe they'd all left until I saw the basement door open. Smoke was pouring out of it. When I ran down there, the whole room was on fire, the walls, the ceiling, the furnace, and the air was so thick with smoke that everyone was choking, but Winsor and Haley and Josh were still down there. Winsor was screaming at Josh, 'What did you do?!' I'd never heard her scream like that before, and Josh just kept repeating, 'I didn't let go of his hand; I didn't let go of his hand.'

"Even after I pulled Winsor to the floor and Haley dragged Josh down, she and Winsor kept arguing. Finally, I grabbed Winsor by the shoulders and shook her, like in a movie, and I said, 'You're gonna die down here!' She sort of snapped out of it, but Josh just looked at me and fainted dead away. The three of us dragged her up the stairs and out the back door. Deloise and Kerstel were already outside, but nobody knew where Ian was—then, out of nowhere, Winsor said that Ian was dead. That was the first time anybody said anything about Ian being dead, but Win couldn't tell me how, or where his body was, and Deloise started demanding that if he wasn't in the house, where was he? And nobody could say.

"The firefighters arrived, but the cabin was a lost cause. It burned right to the ground. We all went to the hospital to get treated for smoke inhalation, and because Josh had turned blue from shock, and while we were there Kerstel called Davita and made Winsor tell her what had happened.

"Apparently the fight in the living room was pretty epic, and Josh got upset and went down to the basement. I asked, but I never could get out of Winsor how they went from fighting to deciding that they were going to open a new archway into the Dream.

"I suspect it was Josh's idea. She's the only one who would have gotten upset and tried to run to the Dream. Opening a new archway is dangerous, which is why it's only done by groups of older dream walkers. Josh's mother died doing it in that same basement, and the dream walker she was working with was lost in the Dream. I don't know why Josh thought she could do it, but maybe she thought she had something to prove. None of them know exactly what happened next, partly because they all took in a lot of Veil dust. All Josh could say was that something had gone wrong. Winsor thought the archway opened straight into Death, even though that isn't possible. Somehow Ian fell in, or Ian couldn't get out, or he'd been attacked. Nobody was sure of anything except that Ian was dead. Davita went over that point again and again with Josh until she was crying with frustration, because there was a possibility that if Ian hadn't died, then he might still be caught in the Dream. But Josh and Winsor and Haley were all absolutely certain that Ian was dead.

"Davita called the junta and they sent search parties into the Dream anyway. It's almost impossible to find anyone there, since it's constantly shifting, but they had to look. After a week, when it became clear that they weren't going to find Ian, they didn't have any choice but to give up. We never even had a memorial for him."

The kitchen was very quiet. The dishwasher had finished its cycle, and the only sound from the living room was the soft burble of the laugh track on television. Whim was hunched over the table with his forehead in one hand, his cracker smeared with peanut butter still uneaten.

Will swallowed very slowly and waited, hoping Whim would continue. There had to be something else to this story, some end, some clue as to what had happened in that basement. But when he couldn't wait any longer and started to speak, Whim shook his head.

"That's it," he said, holding out empty hands. "That's all I know. Maybe Josh could tell you more, if you could ever get her to talk. But I didn't open the archway with them, so I don't really know what happened. The Gendarmerie, which is like the dream-walker police, did a full inquiry, and even they couldn't figure out what happened."

Will sighed. Were the specifics so important? He'd wanted to know how Ian died, and now he knew as much as he was ever likely to. "Thank you for telling me all of this."

Whim nodded. "You're Josh's apprentice, you have a right to

know what happened that night. Or at least as much as I can tell you. Josh seems like she's doing pretty well, all things considered. There's a lot of guilt left, I think, and sometimes she looks . . . I don't know. Trapped. But she's better than I thought she'd be." Whim finally ate his cracker while Will got up from the table and opened the dishwasher. "Part of why I insisted that we come back now is that I wanted to be here for Valentine's Day."

Valentine's Day was less than a week away. Will glanced over at Whim as he began drying the dishes. "Why Valentine's Day?"

"It was Josh and Ian's anniversary. Not their real anniversary, but they'd been together so long they didn't know their real anniversary. I just wanted to be here for Josh."

Will decided that Whim was a good guy, even if he did torment his sister at times. "What about Haley?" Will asked. "Everyone seems to think he's changed since Ian died."

Whim's voice was soft. "Haley's sick," he replied, but he said it so delicately that Will recognized his frustration.

"Haley hasn't gotten over it?"

"Not even close." Whim sighed. Maybe it was just the light, but Will thought he saw deep shadows form under Whim's eyes. "I'm not sure Haley's ever going to get over it."

The back door opened and Kerstel and Lauren walked into the kitchen. Whim's manner changed instantly; the shadows beneath his eyes vanished, he stretched out his long legs and crossed his ankles, and he clasped his hands behind his head. Suddenly he was smiling and casual, and Will realized for the first time how much of Whim's easygoing demeanor was a front.

After an impromptu feast of cookies and milk with his adoptive parents and Whim, Will headed upstairs. The office door was open when he passed, and he paused in the hallway outside it. He could see Josh lying on the futon, her shoes and watch still on as if she hadn't meant to fall asleep. She'd probably gone down to the arch-room after she walked out on him earlier.

He wondered how many more nightmares she had forced herself to enter before she'd finally collapsed. She looked so tired, so drained, that Will's lingering anger for how she had treated him vanished. *She's doing the best she can,* he thought, stepping into the office and reaching down to gently brush a lock of hair away from her eyes. *She always does the best she can. I should know that by now.*

He covered her with an afghan and went upstairs to bed.

Twenty-four

Josh forgot all about the Valentine's Day dance until she saw Deloise's tickets on Friday night. She stood in the kitchen and stared at them until Deloise asked, "Do you want to come after all?"

Deloise looked stunning. Her light-filled brown eyes stood out even more than usual thanks to a fawn-colored suede dress that fell just below her knees. A cloth headband and low wedge sandals made it not just clothing but an outfit, and for once even Josh admired her style.

"No." Josh had never been a fan of dances, but she especially didn't want to go to one that would only remind her of Ian. "You look great, though."

"Thanks. Let's hope I can get out of here before Dad sees me and makes me wear something else." Deloise finished transferring her stuff from one purse to another and called into the living room, "Haley? You ready to go?"

Josh lifted her eyebrows. "You're going with Haley?"

"No, he's just driving me and Will."

Josh nearly choked on the soda she was drinking. "You're going with *Will*?"

Deloise chuckled. "Don't look so jealous, Josh. No, I'm not going with Will. I'm meeting Neil there and the photographer is paying Will to be his assistant."

"Will can't drive you?"

"Will can't *drive*. As he put it, 'No parents, no car, no drive.'"

Suddenly feeling guilty, Josh realized that this was something she should have known. The information would have come out in conversation if she'd ever actually spent any time talking to Will about something other than dream walking.

I'm such an awful teacher, she thought, sighing aloud. She hadn't thought the evening could get any more depressing.

Haley appeared in the doorway, and Josh dropped her soda can.

Haley had never looked more like Ian. He was wearing Ian's Brooks Brothers suit, black on black on black, with Ian's Roman-coin cuff links and tie tack. His black curls had been trimmed and soothed with a minimal amount of soft gel. He smiled the confident smile Ian always wore. Even from six feet away, Josh could smell Ian's amber-scented cologne. She stepped backward, and her heel crushed the aluminum can she had dropped. Soda pooled on the floor.

"Evening, J.D.," Haley said. He caught her eye and flashed a bold smile.

The hurt muscle in Josh's chest began tearing itself apart.

He's here, she thought. *Three steps and I'll be in his arms.*

But she knew that wasn't true.

"You look nice," Deloise told him slowly, and Josh could tell that it was taking every ounce of her good manners to overcome how creeped out she was.

"Thanks. I thought I'd go in with you for a little while, maybe say hi to some of the guys from last year."

But you don't have any "guys," Haley, Josh thought. *You didn't have any friends except us, remember?*

"Del," Haley said suddenly, "heads up." He grabbed Ian's leather jacket off the back of a chair and tossed it to her. Deloise barely had time to pull it on and cover her bare shoulders before her father entered the kitchen with Will.

The sight of Will was somehow a relief to Josh. As casual as the other two were formal, he had on navy-blue slacks and a thin black T-shirt. He was wearing Whim's sports coat, and it was too big and very rumpled, but at least he wasn't in costume. At least he was recognizable. "You'll be home by eleven?" Lauren asked Deloise.

"Absolutely," Haley said, and Lauren glanced at him, then did a double take.

"Um . . ." he started before trailing off, too startled to speak.

"We'll be home on time," Deloise promised. She grabbed the tickets off the kitchen table and opened the back door. Alex called from the living room that the news was starting. Before Lauren went to join him, he glanced at Josh and noted, "You've spilled your soda."

Alone together in the kitchen, Will helped Josh mop up the mess on the floor. "Are you sure you don't want to come?" he asked her.

"I'm sure," she said. She stopped him before he knelt down in the puddle. "Are those Whim's pants?"

"Not this time. Deloise ordered them out of a catalog. She says they're helping me define my ambitions and climb my inner mountain." He shrugged. "They're machine washable; I like that."

Josh felt like smiling for the first time that evening, so she did. "They look good."

"Thank you." They both stood up, and she carried the paper towels to the trash can. "Are you going to walk tonight?"

"Probably." When he didn't reply and didn't leave, she asked, "What?"

"You should come to the dance," he said. "You should get out in the real world."

She thought it was a strange thing for him to say, and she was a little afraid he was asking her to the dance. "Why?"

"Because . . ." He sighed, then shook his head. "Try to do something fun tonight," he said. "Try not to . . . let the season get you down."

The season? Josh wondered, and then she understood: Someone had told him that Valentine's Day was her and Ian's anniversary. She heard that he was worried about her, but his concern didn't take away her feeling of having been spied upon, gossiped about, maybe even judged.

No, almost certainly judged.

"I'll be fine," she told Will tartly.

"Oh," he replied with another sigh, "I know. Believe me, I know."

"You coming?" Haley asked, ducking his head through the doorway.

"Yes," Will told him quickly. He brushed his fingers against the back of Josh's hand as he passed her on his way out the door, and for a long moment afterward she stared at the place where he'd touched her, uncertain what to make of his action. She'd thought he was angry at her—or maybe she was angry at him—or maybe they were both just tired of the distance she was trying to keep between them. The more she tried to push him away, the more she wanted to be close to him.

Maybe she should tell him everything. Maybe his alienation would be easier to bear than this tension.

She wandered into the living room and sat down on the couch next to her father. He put his arm around her and she leaned her head against his shoulder.

"Are you doing okay?" Lauren asked her.

"Yeah, I'm fine," she said, which was a complete lie, but she didn't know what good telling the truth would do.

Winsor's dad, Alex, sitting in the armchair, said, "You know we're all here for you, Josh. I know Valentine's Day was your anniversary, but I don't want you to think you're going through this alone. We're all missing Ian, every one of us who knew him. Especially Haley, I think. Valentine's Day isn't just about romantic love, it's about . . ."

Josh tuned him out. The trick with Alex's soliloquies was to only listen to the first sentence: *We're all here for you, Josh.* And Josh did truly appreciate that.

She watched the news with her father—more about the people

in the strange comas that Whim's blog had been going on about, but no new information—and then decided that it really was time she moved out of the office and back into her bedroom. The last few days, she'd just been too tired to get around to it, and she had so much stuff scattered around the office now that gathering it all up would be a major undertaking.

After piling all her clothes into a laundry basket, she began the trek upstairs. She reached the second floor landing just as Winsor was attempting to embark it, and Winsor stepped back, crossed her arms, and waited for Josh to pass without bothering to hide her irritation.

Josh initially felt guilty, but all that anger she had been trying to swallow for months had grown beyond her ability to choke down. Before she'd made it up two more steps, she spun around, hurled the laundry basket onto the landing, and shouted, "Dammit, Winsor!"

Winsor jumped against the wall when the laundry basket hit the floor, and she stared up at Josh with astonishment and something close to either fear or derision. Maybe both.

"I can't do this anymore!" Josh told her. "All right? I just can't do it. If you want to fight, then let's fight, because I am sick to death of you walking around tossing your hair and rolling your eyes and acting like you're too good to be in the room with me. So just say whatever you need to say and let's get it out there already."

Winsor's blue eyes were wide, but a pitiless half smile played on her lips. "Okay," she agreed, walking back up the steps to the landing. "Let's have it out then. You go first."

Josh wasn't ready to go first. She looked at the laundry strewn all over the floor and ran her hand through her hair, and finally she managed to say, "You should have told me how you felt about Ian."

"You shouldn't have acted needy just to keep him."

The words felt much like the kidney shot she'd taken a few weeks before. Josh had had no idea that Winsor thought she "acted needy" so Ian would stay with her. "I didn't! And I know you made him even more paranoid about his scroll. You encouraged him to break up with me!"

"I told Ian to do what he wanted to do. You should have let him go when he broke up with you."

How could Winsor have possibly expected her to let go of Ian, then or ever? To this day, Josh didn't know who she was without his memory. "You shouldn't have dated the identical twin brother of the guy you were secretly in love with," Josh shot back. "You *used* Haley! How sick is that?"

"You shouldn't have opened an archway when you had no idea what you were doing! You think you're so special, that there's nothing you can't do!"

"Special?" Josh cried. "I'm the opposite of special! The only thing in my life that made me special was that Ian loved me, and you made sure to take that away, didn't you?"

"He broke up with you!"

"Yeah, and it was less than a month before you were seducing him in the forest! He just needed time to get his head on straight. He would have come back to me if you hadn't thrown yourself at him!"

"Yeah?" The smile was gone from Winsor's face. Instead, a dark flush spread across her chest and up her throat. "Well, he'll never come back to you now, because you got him killed!"

There. The words had finally been said. Josh and Winsor stared at each other across the landing, and the statement hung between them like the reverberations of a chime that had been struck very hard. Josh felt her chin begin to tremble, and then hot tears poured into her eyes, and she sat down on the stairs and sobbed.

All the guilt and anger and terrible sadness she had been trying to hold off for months finally overwhelmed her. She had lost Ian—for all of them.

"Josh," Winsor said, and then Josh heard her sigh. Her tone had changed from furious to defeated. "Josh. I shouldn't have said that."

"It's true," Josh told her between sobs. "You know it, I know it, everybody knows it! Just no one's saying it!"

"Nobody's thinking it but you," Winsor insisted. "And—me, and I—I'm only thinking it because—I'm so *angry* that he's dead." Josh looked up in time to see Winsor break into her own tears, and she flung herself down on the step next to Josh. "How *dare* he go and die and leave us with all this emotional crap we can't resolve. How dare he die and just not be here anymore! He's dead, so he's not here today and he won't be here tomorrow or the day after, and it's like he just dropped out, like he just quit the play and we're all still here trying to put the show on without him! I want to scream at him every moment of every day, and he's not here to yell at, so yeah, I get angry at you, because it *was* your idea to open the archway. But we both know nobody ever forced Ian to do a damn thing, and he could have walked away anytime if he hadn't been such a conceited, hardheaded prick, and if he hadn't been so hopelessly in love with you that he had to prove he didn't care about you by impressing you!"

Winsor put her face in her palms, and her tears ran in rivers between her fingers. She had described how Josh felt about Ian's loss more perfectly than Josh herself ever could, and Josh wished they had known months earlier that they were experiencing the same things. Still weeping, Josh put her arms around her friend, and they cried together for the first time.

The door to the Avisharas' apartment opened and Whim stepped out. He surveyed the two girls, sitting on the stairs, holding each other and bawling, and shook his head. "The dam finally broke, huh?"

"Shut up, Whim!" Josh and Winsor told him in unison.

"Women," Whim muttered, and went back into the apartment.

When they were alone again, Josh said, "I'm sorry."

"I know that!" Winsor snapped, sounding just as angry as she had before. She used splayed fingers to push dark, wet strands of hair out of her face. "Don't you think I know that, Josh? You are the most miserably sorry thing I've ever seen. You're punishing yourself like you shot him in the face, and that's driving me as crazy as anything, this martyr-for-your-sins bit, and how you're dream walking like you have a death wish, and poor Will tiptoeing around trying not to ask for anything from you."

Josh winced. She knew Winsor was right about how she had acted, and she hated it.

"Let me tell you, Josh, if I really wanted to punish you, I could have just seduced Will. The boy's so lonely here he's begging for it." She glanced at Josh and added, "Oh, don't look so shocked. You're the one who thinks I'm a whore."

"I never said that," Josh protested, trying to shake off the shock she felt.

"Yeah, but you thought it. Everybody's thinking it. I'm the girl who slept with identical twin brothers. For a while people at school were calling me Mrs. McKarr, can you believe that?"

Despite everything else between them, Josh felt bad for Winsor. "How did it even get out at school?"

"Oh, it was Whim, I know it was. He loves gossip more than he loves any of us."

Josh wanted to say she was sorry again, but she didn't know how Winsor would react. She put an arm around her friend's shoulders instead. "I wish you'd come and talked to me."

Winsor laughed grimly. "When?"

"Whenever. Through all of it. I know I'm not good at talking, but I could have at least listened."

Winsor's jaw relaxed a little. "Well, I'm talking to you now."

"Do you . . ." Josh began, and then started over. "Do you want to keep talking, and maybe eat a bunch of ice cream?"

"You and your sweets," Winsor said, but a ghost of a smile had crept onto her face. "Take your laundry upstairs. I'll go get the ice cream and meet you in your room."

"All right." Josh hesitated an instant, then hugged Winsor quickly before rising. "I'll see you upstairs."

Josh both smiled and sniffled as she carried the clothes basket up to the third floor. She knew that this was still going to be a hard night, that she and Winsor had a lot of difficult things to say to each other, but at least they were talking again.

As she crossed the empty apartment, she paused outside the

open door to Will's bedroom. *Is Winsor right?* she wondered, peering into the dark room. *Is he lonely here? Have I let him be lonely?*

She set down the laundry hamper and turned on the overhead light. Will's room was unnaturally tidy for a teenage guy's. He'd made his bed perfectly. The clothing in the hamper had been loosely folded. Stepping inside, Josh realized that he'd put all his self-help books back in the cardboard box with his name on the side that he'd brought from the county home.

He still thinks I'm going to send him back, she thought, and a fresh wave of regret washed over her. Absently, she ran her finger down the spines of the books. *I am the worst tea—*

Her body hardened as though iron had cooled in her veins.

On the spine of one book, written with a felt-tip permanent marker, was the name *Hianselian Ambrose Donovan Micharainosa.*

Josh yanked the book out of the box. She snapped the journal open and saw the note taped inside; for a moment, she didn't recognize her own handwriting.

How dare you, Will?

Journal in her arms, she flew out of his room and into her own, determined to drive to the high school right then and confront him. This was beyond a betrayal of trust; it was an insult; it was—

She flipped on the overhead light in her bedroom and stopped short on the threshold, faced with such a sight that she stopped thinking entirely.

The bedroom was strewn with clothes. They appeared to have exploded out of a duffel bag in the corner like lava from a volcano. Her dresser drawers were open, and her things had been taken out, rearranged, dug through. School papers that had been rotting in her desk for years were scattered across the floor.

From behind her, Winsor said, "I see Haley didn't inherit Ian's organizational skills."

Josh turned to see Winsor holding two pints of ice cream, two spoons, and a squeeze bottle of chocolate sauce. Her throat was dry, making it hard to speak. "What the hell happened in here?"

"Well, between your messiness and Haley's, your room is"—Winsor shrugged—"a mess."

"Why has Haley even *been* in my room?" Josh demanded, stepping over an open shoebox of loose photographs.

Winsor frowned. "Didn't Del tell you? He's been staying in here."

Josh was shaking so hard her voice trembled. "You let Haley stay in my room?"

"It wasn't my idea," Winsor told her. She set the ice cream on the dresser like a peace offering and then stepped back. "But there's no furniture in his apartment and you were staying downstairs."

"I don't care! Look at this, Winsor. He didn't just stay here—he tore the place apart like he had a search warrant. He even moved the furniture!"

Winsor looked around thoughtfully. "No, he moved it back to where it was before Ian died."

Josh gawked at the room. She reached out to steady herself against the dresser and then noted that it had been moved two feet farther from the window—to where it had sat a year before—and she wrenched her hand back. "God, Winsor—why is he acting like this?"

"He's gone mad." Winsor picked up a glass bottle from the desktop. "Here's what's left of Ian's cologne."

Reluctantly, Josh followed Winsor's lead and began putting the room back in order. Her belongings appeared to have been rearranged at random, as if Haley had tried to put them away but had forgotten where they went. She found a blouse in her nightstand and a deck of playing cards under her pillows.

"There's something really wrong with Haley," she said, wondering how her friend had become so out of touch with reality.

"Yeah," Winsor agreed. "He was always weird, but at least he was consistently weird. This is just crazy."

A few minutes later, Josh found the journal she'd discovered in Will's room. She'd forgotten all about it when she saw her bedroom and must have set it on the bedside table unconsciously. Now she picked it up again and rubbed her thumbs against the cover. The fabric felt like sandpaper against her skin.

"What's that?" Winsor asked.

Josh swallowed as she held it out. "I think it's Ian journal. I mean, it must be his. It has his name on it."

Winsor took the book hesitantly. She turned it over but didn't open the cover. "You read this?" she asked.

"No. I found it in Will's room a minute ago."

For a moment Winsor looked like she was going to smile again. "That boy's got guts," she said instead.

"Well, he's going to regret that once I get a hold of him." Josh glanced around again, debating whether she still wanted to go to the high school to find Will. In the end, she decided that she did. Haley would have to be dealt with, but she wanted to talk to him when she wasn't furious. He was a fragile guy, and she knew that if she started yelling, he would just shut down.

"I'm going to the dance," she said, taking the journal back from Winsor.

"To yell at Will? Tonight?"

"Yeah. Want to come?"

Winsor shook her head. Josh shrugged and started stepping back across the wreckage toward the door. Halfway there, her knees buckled, and she sat down hard on a sweatshirt and a latch-hook rug.

"Josh?" Winsor asked. "Is your knee okay?"

Josh's hand trembled as she reached out to push away another piece of clothing. Distantly, she noticed that it was the skirt she'd worn on her seventeenth birthday. Beneath was a piece of parchment weighted down at either end with a textbook to battle seventeen years of being rolled up.

"Josh?" Winsor asked again, leaning down next to her. When she saw the scroll, she immediately looked away. "Oh!"

"Win," Josh whispered, "I didn't open this."

"What?" Winsor's surprise overrode her manners, and she slid down next to Josh.

Josh couldn't stop her eyes from reading the words.

Joshlyn Dustine Hazel Weavaros

Eldest of her family's five,
she'll only live to see one die.
One mother lost to the Dream,
One lover lost in between.
Avishara and Weavaros:
two families' flags that still fly close
until sundered by betrayal
of each other and the Veil.
Half-past her birthday, seventeen,
an apprentice to spoon-feed.
Blessed with talent majuscule,
she'll earn a scholarship to school.
Among the dream-walking elite,
a love to gladden her heartbeat.
Flame and children, girl and boy,
a family that brings her joy.
A happy life, a good career,
only her grandfather to fear.
The falcon is e'er a threat,
but within her epithet
she'll read her fate desired:
"'Twas in the Dream that she expired."

"Josh," Winsor said, "did Haley open this?"

Josh shook her head, then nodded, then shrugged. "He must have. I didn't." Her mouth tasted like chalk dust. She ran her finger along one edge of the parchment. Anger was beginning to seep through the numbness again. "I have to go," she said, and stood up.

"Don't you want to . . . I don't know, absorb this for a minute?"

Josh stopped in the doorway to look back at her. "What's to absorb? I mean, I'm going to get into Kasari Academy; that's great."

"But he . . . Haley *read* it. He broke the seal on your birthright."

"Yeah, I know. I'm so angry at him I can't even feel it."

"He's sick," Winsor said. "He's really, really sick. Be angry, but don't be angry at him."

Josh swallowed. One rage at a time—she had Will to hate just then. "All right." She heard how numb her voice sounded.

Winsor reread the scroll as she rolled it up. "The wording in this is so odd. And the rhymes seem so . . . simplistic. I know each scroll is different, but this doesn't sound like Young Ben. Maybe someone else wrote it."

Josh barely heard her. What did she care who had written the scroll, or if the rhymes were lousy? Good or bad, she had never wanted to see them at all.

Winsor reverently held out the scroll. "Here."

Josh didn't want to touch it. She didn't even feel like it was hers anymore. "Just put it in the desk or something," she said as she left the room, and she pulled the door shut hard behind herself.

Twenty-five

Another night, the gym might have looked nice to Josh, but tonight, she found the streamers and stage lights cheesy and somehow deceptive. She didn't see either Haley or Deloise around. Louis noticed her and called her name, but she ignored him as she headed for the drink table, where Brianna Selts was slipping something acrid into the punch.

"Bri," she said, "is the guy taking pictures still here?"

Brianna pointed to the far corner, where an arbor decorated

with fake flowers had been erected for couples to stand beneath while being photographed. "I think he's packing up." She examined Josh's jeans and gray sweater with a critical eye. "Interesting fashion statement," she said, her voice laced with derision, but Josh was already cutting through the crowd.

She passed Jay Appleton, who was nursing a bump on the back of his head with a bag of ice, and Alece Vernon, who was breaking up with Evan Lovett right there on the dance floor. Somebody had spilled a drink, and the janitor was trying to rope off the mopped area. The latest boy-band release—coincidentally, from Josh's father's label—blared.

The photographer was just locking the case for his flashbulbs when Josh reached him. Will was rolling up a backdrop, but he stopped when he saw Josh.

For a moment words failed her. She almost punched him, but the photographer happened to walk in between them. Besides, it would have been irresponsible; she knew how to break his nose and drive it backward into his brain, killing him instantly.

"What's wrong?" Will asked.

She still had the journal. It had rested on her lap throughout the drive like a live coal. She held it up for Will to see in the colored carnival lights.

He swallowed, then set the backdrop on the floor. "Alan, I've got to go. Can you give me a call tomorrow?"

"Sure," the photographer said. "Good work tonight, Will."

"Thank you," he replied, already walking away.

He tried to take Josh's elbow and she shook him off, but she held him with her gaze as if with a clenched fist. Without a word, she followed his lead out the double doors to the lobby. He glanced nervously at her several times as they exited the gym, but even when he was looking away she stared at the back of his head. She wouldn't have been surprised to see little red sniper-rifle dots appear in his hair.

The doors swung shut behind them. The noise in the lobby was muted; only the music's bass line could still be heard. There were no streamers here, no harlequin masks or sweet scents of punch and soda. A few security night-lights splashed into the lobby, but mostly it was dark.

Josh took advantage of the lobby's emptiness by putting at least a dozen steps between herself and Will. She clenched Ian's journal in one hand.

Will exhaled slowly, waiting for her to speak. She said nothing, just let him stew while she ground her gaze into his eyes. When he took a step forward, she stepped back. He got the message.

"I know that—" he began, and before he could finish, Josh hurled the journal at him.

It hit him in the forehead, hard, and then fell to the floor in a rustling of pages. Will stumbled back, his expression shocked. Josh closed the space between them and darted down to pick the journal back up.

"How dare you," she hissed, poking one corner of the journal's cover into his chest like a finger. "This was *not* your business, and it was *not* your place to go into my family's private history and take it."

"It *was* my business," Will told her, and she didn't know whether to be surprised or infuriated that he had the guts to speak back to her.

"You wouldn't tell me," he went on, "what happened to Ian."

"And you wanted to hear the gossip," she snapped.

"No, Josh, I didn't. That's not what this is about."

"No," she agreed, "it's not. This is about respect."

"*Respect?*" he asked incredulously. "I have *nothing* but respect for you."

"Then why didn't you respect me when I made it perfectly clear that I didn't want to talk about Ian?"

"Did I bring it up with you? Did I push when you kept changing the subject? No. Never. I never asked for more than you wanted to give me. But I did wonder, and I did read Ian's diary."

"*Why?!*" She was shouting by then, her voice echoing off the walls. "Why did you think you had the right to do that?"

His face darkened with an anger Josh had not foreseen. "Because— like it or not—I am in this as deep as you are."

"In what? In Ian's death? You barely even knew him!"

"No, this has nothing to do with Ian, Josh. This is about you and me. I wanted to know what happened to Ian because it happened to you. It didn't have anything to do with gossip or disrespect. I wanted to know why you're afraid to talk about him and why you don't want to open your scroll and what had happened between you and Winsor that wrecked your friendship. And most of all, I wanted to know why you're so terrified of getting close to me."

"You don't have a right to know why! That's my business, not yours—"

"How can it not be mine?" he shouted back. "We work together for hours every day. When I go into a nightmare, all I have to defend myself with are the tricks you've taught me. I eat food your stepmother cooks, and I wear clothes your sister picks out, and I sleep in a room full of furniture your father paid for."

"And that's not enough?"

"*Not enough?*" he repeated in disbelief. "Do you have any understanding of what my life was like before this? Do you know how bad things have to get before a twelve-year-old kid will tell his mother that he'd rather be a ward of the state than live with her? I threw my family away, Josh. I didn't expect to be handed another one—especially not one as happy and perfect as yours. I know I don't have a right to any of it."

Will's words cut Josh. They were fighting about her privacy— she *wanted* to fight about her privacy—but she wasn't ready to talk about Will's place in her life, and she was nowhere near being ready to assure him of his own worth.

Will deflated, shaking his head. "I didn't ask Lauren and Kerstel to adopt me. I didn't ask Deloise to be so sweet and innocent that I start feeling protective every time I see a guy making eyes at her. I didn't ask for daily updates on my life from Haley, or for Dustine to look out for me, or for Whim to be my friend. I didn't ask for any of this, but I would be a fool to throw it away."

Josh turned her back on him, trembling, aware for the first time of how impossibly enmeshed his life was with hers, how close he was to her heritage, her family's secrets, her own secrets. They were all a hairsbreadth from being revealed to an outsider.

And he was right. He was right about all of it. That was the worst part.

Will spoke again, and she heard tears choking his voice.

Don't cry, Will. I don't know how to comfort you.

"I know it was a mistake that I ended up in your life," he told her. "I know I'm the last person you want near you, and that you resent me. But I see these things eating you up inside and I . . . I would do anything to help you, if you'd only tell me what to do."

She didn't move for fear that the world would shatter around her like cheap crystal, that one of those glass shards would split her down the middle and the half of her that wanted to turn and put her arms around Will would do so while the rest of her collapsed, broken and unwilling to let him in.

"Josh." He touched her arm and she couldn't control the shudder that ran through her body. She didn't want to look over her shoulder and let him see the damp lines running down her face.

She heard his steps retreat. "I'm going now," he told her hoarsely. The door to the gym opened and a slow song poured into the lobby. Below it, Josh could just hear Will's departing words, spoken almost to himself.

"I don't even know your full name."

Then the door closed, and she was alone again.

What did you just do, Josh?

She fled through the school's main doors and into the night.

Why did you let him go?

She splashed through a puddle, and the frigid water soaked her shoes and socks.

You've lost him.

By the time Josh reached the car, her lungs were rattling with the effort not to cry. She put Ian's diary on the hood—although she was loath to unfurl her hands and let go of it—and reached into her pockets.

They were empty. All four of them. She peered inside the car and saw her key ring hanging from the ignition. She tugged on the car door, but it was locked.

"Oh, shit, shit."

I can't go back in and face him, she thought, and the helplessness of her situation ruined her last bit of self-control. She pressed her forehead against the car's hood, her skin contracting against the touch of the icy metal, and cried.

"J.D.?"

She looked up and saw Ian—*no,* it was *Haley, goddammit*—striding toward her. He stood straight and tall and took her hands between his without the slightest hesitation.

"What are you doing out here?" he asked. "You're shivering."

Words failed her. She shook her head.

"Are you crying?" he asked, leaning down to peer into her face. "What happened?"

"I just . . ." Her shoulders twitched uncontrollably. "I had a fight with Will," she managed to tell him. "And now I've locked my keys in the car."

"You and Will fought? Over what?"

She wanted to blurt it all out, how she had rushed to school ready to behead him and, in trying to push him further away, had opened the door for him to say everything she didn't want to hear.

Oh, yes, she wanted to tell *Ian* all about it.

"It doesn't matter," he assured her. "So you fought. It happens. But your scroll says he's destined to be your apprentice—it'll work out."

"Oh my god, Haley," she murmured, suddenly remembering who was standing in front of her—that he was insane, that he'd read her scroll.

"No, it's okay," he told her. "The scrolls don't make mistakes."

"Forget the scroll!" she shouted at him, shocking herself.

He stepped back, all traces of laughter vanishing from his face.

"Forget the scroll," she told him again. "It doesn't make anything all right; it doesn't fix things. Just because the scroll predicted that I'd have an apprentice doesn't mean I'm a good teacher. It doesn't mean I know how to let anybody in. It doesn't mean that Will being here is the best thing for either one of us."

Her voice broke, and then she was crying again, sinking down the side of the car into a heap on the asphalt. She pressed her hands against her eyes, and the warm tears stung as they dripped between her frozen fingers.

Fix it for me, Ian. Just fix it all. Tell me what to do.

"Oh, J.D.," Haley said. No one else had dared to use that nickname since Ian died, but when she heard it, the last eight months might never have happened—Ian was there, with her, and whatever had fallen apart he would put back together. She felt him blocking the wind as he sat down next to her, and she didn't protest when he pulled her into his arms. "It's okay, love."

"Oh my god," she whispered again. She knew he wasn't Ian. She *knew*. But if he wanted to make believe, how could she stop him? She couldn't stand his touch but neither could she push him away. She needed Ian so much. She had tried to live without him, but she didn't know how.

"Stop crying," he told her. "We can fix this."

His words only made her cry harder, because they were exactly what she wanted to hear, and because it was so painful to hear Ian's voice and know he wasn't really with her. But Josh didn't move away from him. He was warm all around her, his inherited Brooks Brothers suit was soft against her cheek, and she smelled the amber cologne beneath his shirt.

"I still love you," he said, pressing his lips to her temple.

She hid her face in his shoulders, kept her eyes shut against his jacket. "Do you even know," she asked him, trying not to moan, "which one of you came out of the archway that night?"

He rocked her. "Not really," he admitted.

She didn't know either. Sitting in the freezing parking lot, lying against Haley's chest while he wrapped his jacket around her shoulders, she realized she didn't care. She needed his strength, needed him to distract her from thinking about Will and the pain of their argument, needed him to be decisive when she was so torn she didn't even know which decisions to make.

Forgive me, Ian, for missing you so much I'll settle for your ghost.

She nestled deeper into the comfort of his arms, finding peace in the scent of amber that clung to him. One of her hands crept up to touch his chest and feel the heart beating beneath his skin, and she smiled. Then her fingers crept, like the little legs of a spider, up his chest to trace his collarbone, as she had so many times, and she slipped her hand up to cup his neck, finding his pulse again.

His arms tightened around her. She looked up at him and his face was so close, the parking-lot lights reflected in his hazel eyes, and she could feel his shallow breaths move across her lips. He lowered his head at the same moment she tugged on his neck, and they leaned close to kiss.

Haley could have mimicked Ian's walk, cut his hair, worn Ian's clothes; but there was no way he could have guessed how Ian kissed—lips enclosing hers, his top teeth a hard line against her mouth, holding her so close that she couldn't see past him.

I'm home, Josh's heart said, and for one moment she felt true relief from the pain in her chest that had dogged her all these months. Ian was there in front of her, around her, touching her, so familiar, and her body lit up like a Christmas tree. For that moment, she didn't care that it was Haley's hand buried in her hair, Haley's strong mouth molding hers, Haley's arm pulling her tight against him. The relief that coursed through her was almost as intense as the desire that drove all vestiges of cold from her body.

That was when Whim arrived.

His car tore into the parking lot, rolled over the curb, and stalled. Josh and Haley pulled away from each other at the same moment to turn and watch as it rolled over a pair of shrubs. The sight of Whim's hideous baby-blue Lincoln Town Car shocked Josh back to reality.

What did I just do?

"Wait here," Haley ordered as he released Josh and stood up.

She unconsciously tucked her arms into his jacket as she followed him. "Whim!"

The car had stopped moving after destroying several rosebushes and tilting the flagpole. Whim climbed out, startled, and then ran to Josh and Haley. Raindrops like scattered light fell from the sky as the three of them dodged between parked cars to converge beneath a streetlight.

"Where's Del?" Whim asked.

"Inside," Haley told him. "What's wrong?"

Whim shook his head, looked away. He hardly appeared to be breathing. He moved constantly, turning away and then back, pushing at his hair, wetting his lips, as if he couldn't decide what to say.

Josh had never seen Whim at a loss for words.

"Whim, what happened?" she whispered.

He met her gaze with his blue eyes and shook his head. "The trench-coat men," he told her. "They came out of the Dream, right into the house."

No, no, that's not possible. . . .

"Did they . . . ?" she asked, and couldn't bring herself to finish.

"They attacked. Kerstel and Winsor are on the way to the hospital." He grabbed hold of Josh's hand. She could feel the shocked pulse in his palm. "Josh," he said, "they killed your grandmother."

Josh remembered her lighter—the one Ian had given her—and how Gloves had been reaching for it when she escaped from the Dream.

He used it to open an exit, she realized. *All of this is my fault.*

The light bathing them from the parking lamp flickered with black spots, and Josh knew she was about to pass out. She felt Haley catch her before she hit the pavement, but she passed through his arms and then through the pavement and down into a void of silent guilt that closed and trapped her inside.

Twenty-six

Will had been down this hall before. Light fell evenly from the ceiling fixtures, but unaccountable shadows clung to every corner and doorway. Slits, like sniper sights, were built into the doors.

"Mom?" he called.

He went to the first door. The bottle of vodka in his pocket banged against his hip as he walked, ready to quench his mother's thirst. Through the narrow window, he saw a woman lying on a rumpled cot. Her strawberry-blond hair was spread over the pillow, but she was curled up on her side and he couldn't see her face. Blood stained the sheets beneath her.

"Mom!" he called. The woman flinched, but she lifted her head.

Will was almost afraid to believe he'd finally found her. *It took so long,* he thought, watching her rise slowly off the cot. Her arms unwound from around a white teddy bear with a pale-green bow tie, which she placed gently on the bed before climbing unsteadily to her feet. Matted hair fell around her face as she walked to the door, hunched over with pain.

"Will?" she asked.

Something was wrong, he realized. Something wasn't right.

"I've been here before," he said aloud. His hand closed around the bottle of vodka in his pocket. "Mom isn't here. She's never here."

He turned back to the window. The woman on the other side wasn't his mother. It was Kerstel.

She opened the door and leaned wearily against the frame. Her bottom lip was split open in two places and had turned a plum color that lipstick could never match. "Hon, what's wrong?" she asked.

Will looked down and saw the blood pooling at her feet. "You're hurt."

She nodded. "They came out of the Dream."

"My mother . . ." He tried to fit the pieces together, to understand how Kerstel had taken his mother's place. "I think they might have my mother."

Kerstel considered for a moment and then shook her head. "Your mother isn't here, Will. Not anywhere."

"But if I find her . . ."

Kerstel took the bottle of vodka from him, her hands smearing blood across the glass. She showed him the label: *Pure Spring Water*.

"You'd give her this? It's just water, Will. She doesn't want water."

"Do you need it?" Suddenly his mother was of no concern. That responsibility was no longer his. He took the bottle back, twisted off the cap, and held the bottle to Kerstel's lips. She didn't push his hand away until she had drunk half the water.

"Thank you," she said. The color came back into her cheeks, but it made her look fevered instead of strong. "I wanted to be stable for you," she said, her voice breaking. "I wanted you to feel safe in our house, I wanted . . ."

She cried weakly, leaning against the doorjamb for support. Will could barely handle seeing her so injured and fragile; seeing tears roll from her eyes—and for him, no less—brought him to the edge of panic. He reached through the doorway and wiped the blood from her cheek.

"You were," he told her. "And I do."

"Just remember that I tried," she said. "And that we loved you—"

She cut her words off as she shut the door.

Will watched her through the window until she curled up on the bed again. She took the white teddy bear in her arms and held the bottle of spring water—now a baby bottle—to its lips. The teddy bear began to feed hungrily.

Someone should be there with them, Will thought, but when he tried the door it was locked.

Reluctantly, he stepped away from Kerstel's room and checked the others. They were all empty except the last, where Ian, wearing a black suit, was using a Sharpie to write the same phrase across the wall, over and over.

I SAW A GATE BEYOND THE ARCH I SAW A GATE BEYOND THE ARCH I SAW A GATE BEYOND THE ARCH I SAW A GATE BEYOND THE ARCH

He turned suddenly, his green-hazel eyes drilling into Will's.

Then he opened his mouth, and a horrible, reverberating eagle scream shattered the glass window in the door and filled the hallway.

"*TELL JOSH!*"

Will covered his ears with his hands but felt his palms sprayed with blood by his bursting eardrums. He fell to the floor as the scream continued, then—

He woke up on a hospital waiting-room couch.

Josh had given up trying to sleep. The waiting room was no place to rest, between the ringing phones and the television that never shut up. Whim couldn't stop moving; Deloise couldn't stop crying. The Avishes were in Winsor's hospital room, and Laurentius was pacing the hallway outside surgery. Only Will had fallen asleep, scrunched up on a waiting-room couch far too short for him, Whim's borrowed sports coat rolled up under his head.

Josh watched everyone with the detached feeling of sitting in the audience at a play. She had been to St. Dymphna's Hospital a dozen times, but tonight the whole building seemed like a movie set; everything looked just *too much* like a hospital. The furniture was all covered in pastel-colored polyester, and landscapes in the same color scheme hung on every wall. The nurses wore scrubs with cartoons or flowers or Valentine's Day hearts on them. The biohazards were all safely locked away in brightly marked containers.

Josh sat on a couch across from Will. Haley sat beside her; now fully himself again, he wrote one note after another on his stenographer's pad, and Josh knew he was upset because he wasn't writing on the lines. Whim went upstairs to be with his parents and Winsor, and Deloise wiped her eyes and blew her nose and headed for the bathrooms.

Josh understood now why Gloves had wanted her lighter. He had been looking for a way out of the Dream, and he must have gotten a hold of a mirror somewhere, because he'd succeeded in opening an exit. He and Snitch had burst in on Winsor in the arch-room, then attacked Dustine on their way down the hall, and taken on Kerstel, Alex, and Lauren in the living room. Kerstel had already been in surgery when Josh arrived at the hospital, but Josh had briefly seen Winsor, who was catatonic. When EMS had arrived at the house, Winsor's heart hadn't been beating, and it had stopped twice more in the hours since. She'd suffered a brief seizure in the ambulance. The pink outline of a gas mask marked her face.

Josh had been too late to see her grandmother; Dustine had died in the hallway. In her mind, Josh pictured the quilt Dustine had given Will, the dark circle of Death with people walking into it—but not out. Never out.

The image destroyed what was left of Josh's numbness. The sudden, stunning realization that her grandmother was dead—really and truly inaccessible, lost to her—fell over her like a shadow from which she could never emerge. She had left the play, just as Winsor had accused Ian of doing, leaving the rest of them to carry on the show without her.

Grandma Dustine is dead because of me, because I was brash and went into the Dream when everyone, even Will, said not to. Kerstel and Winsor are in the hospital because of me. I might as well have hurt them with my own hands.

Josh wished then that she believed in something, in a trustworthy guiding source like God or a saint or divine intelligence. But dream walkers came in all faiths, and saying "God bless so-and-so" was about as much religion as Josh had ever had. She didn't even really believe in the True Dream Walker; at that moment, she was rubbing his plumeria pendant between her thumb and forefinger but finding no comfort in it.

She wanted Ian.

"Haley," she said, her voice weakened to a whisper. Haley looked at her with wide eyes and damp lips. "I need you to help me," she told him. Her own eyes felt hot and raw. "Can you help me? Like . . . like you did in the parking lot?"

He shuddered. "Oh god." He knew what she meant.

"Please?" She felt like everything was sinking downward, toward the ground two stories below. "Please, Haley, just for a couple of minutes."

She held her hand out, begging him. He ignored her offer and took her in his arms instead. When she began to cry, he held her head against his chest as if to keep her from falling to pieces.

"Stop crying," he said, his voice strong. "Stop it, J.D. It won't help."

He said exactly what she needed to hear, but she only felt worse.

"My grandmother . . ." She tried to justify her tears by telling him how desperately she hurt, but her emotions were too vast to partition into words. "Kerstel . . . my father can't lose Kerstel, it will wreck him."

"She'll make it."

"If I hadn't let Gloves get my lighter, he could never have come out of the Dream."

"Stop blaming yourself for what they did."

He was saying all the right things, and yet, there was something wrong with his tone. She got the impression, as she tried to find comfort in arms as warm and yielding as tree branches, that he was patiently waiting for her to finish needing him.

Josh pulled away. Haley's gauntness was vibrantly apparent to her—the pale color of his lips, his shaking hands. He wasn't Ian—she knew that. And they were both under so much stress that neither one of them could pretend he was, even though they both needed Ian at that moment.

"Josh," Whim said from the waiting-room doorway. She didn't know how long he had been standing there, but she noticed at the same moment that Will was awake, sitting up on the couch across from her.

When she saw her own weakness through their eyes she realized how pathetic she was. Crimson with shame, she forced herself to completely release Haley. Without a word, he rose and left the room, ducking past Whim with hunched shoulders.

Whim sat down on the couch next to her. "Josh," he said. "He's sick."

She swallowed. "I know."

"No, you don't. We went to New York and Boston, we went to Switzerland, we went to China. We have seen doctors on three continents, and no one seems to be able to help."

Startled, she met his eyes. "What?"

"He's sick," Whim repeated. "Even medication only helps a little."

"Wait. You went away to . . ."

"I left home because Haley mailed me a note saying he thought he was losing his mind. Do you think I wanted to just walk away after Ian died? But when I got to Haley's house, and I saw him . . . I can't even explain. Sometimes he really does believe he's Ian for days at a time. Sometimes *I* almost believe he's Ian. He's confident and friendly and willing to take chances. While I tried to find better doctors, he partied in Europe. He went to dance clubs, Josh. He wasn't anything like Haley."

Josh shook her head. "No," she said, "he's just—it's a defense mechanism. Pretending he's Ian is just a defense mechanism for when he can't handle things."

Whim nodded. "Precisely. He can't handle the fact that Ian died, so he pretends to *be* Ian. The problem is, he can't stop. And he's never going to stop if you keep encouraging him. As hard as this is—as much as you need Ian right now—Haley has to learn to face things if he's going to get better."

Josh would have been angry at Whim for speaking to her like he would a child if she hadn't understood why it was so important for her to hear him clearly. Having Haley around, seeing him act like Ian, was a temptation she could barely resist. She had given in to it, but she wouldn't let that happen again. Haley had always been— albeit in his own strange way—her friend. She wasn't going to contribute to keeping him sick.

"I get it," she told Whim. But the truth was that she felt like she'd lost her last comfort. "Thank you for taking care of him," she added. And she meant it.

"Yeah, well . . . sometimes I wish I could have been home instead, taking care of you guys." Whim put his hand over hers.

"We managed," she said, but there must have been a bitter note in her voice, because Whim turned his face to the floor.

"I think you should go home," he said. He glanced at Will, who had sat in silence during Whim and Josh's conversation. "All of you. Get some sleep, eat."

"Is Winsor any better?" Josh asked.

"No. Worse. They're—" He grimaced. "They're talking about pacemakers and brain damage from oxygen deprivation. She still hasn't said a word."

No, please, not Winsor, too.

"Josh," Will said. "Go home."

Josh hadn't looked him in the face since she turned away from him at the dance, but now their eyes met briefly. She didn't expect to see so much pain in his face. Discomfort—yes. Disgust for how she had used Haley—probably. But not the unmasked sorrow that greeted her now. Not the compassion or the longing. She remembered what he'd told her in the school lobby.

I see these things eating you up inside and I . . . I would do anything to help you, if you'd only tell me what to do.

She'd fought so hard for the distance between them—but he was here, now, in the hospital with her family, waiting to see if the woman who had just adopted him would die in surgery or not. He was right—he was in this just as deep as she was, and he probably needed a hug just as much as she did.

But after pushing him away for so long, she didn't know how to stop, so she just said, "Would you go get Haley and Del?"

And he just nodded and left the room.

Twenty-seven

Will didn't know where Haley had gone. He tried the surgery waiting room first and then headed for Winsor's room.

The hospital was quiet so late at night. Many departments were closed, lights dimmed, and even the nurses spoke in whispers and moved softly in their sneakers. The serenity of it unnerved Will; people were, after all, still dying here.

He passed Winsor's parents asleep in another waiting room, Saidy's head resting on Alex's shoulder. Asleep, they hardly looked upset. They might have been here for their daughter's tonsillectomy, for all the fear on their faces, except that Alex had a blackening eye from his fight with the trench-coat men.

Will found Haley in Winsor's room. Winsor was awake, in a distant, trancelike sort of way. She wore a loose hospital gown that slid down to reveal one pale shoulder. The blankets drawn over her waist were smooth, as if she hadn't moved since the nurse had tucked her in. At least a dozen wires reached out from the neck of her gown, all attached to a silent computer screen in the wall above the bed. Not a foot from her pillows, a defibrillator waited in case her heart stopped again.

She blinked often, but her eyes never focused. She seemed to be looking at Haley's arm more than anything else. But the thing that upset Will the most was the pink outline of a gas mask around her mouth and nose.

Will stepped up to the side of the bed. "Hey, Winsor."

Her gaze drifted toward him. It stopped before reaching his face.

"Can you hear me?" he asked.

Winsor exhaled as if she had meant to speak and failed. Her eyes drifted.

Will pulled a chair to the side of the bed and sat down. Haley sat across from him, his arms wrapped around his shins. Josh had asked Will to bring Haley back to the waiting room, but he decided she could wait a few minutes. He wasn't quite ready to deal with her glares and silent accusations yet.

He felt like he'd ruined everything between them. If Whim hadn't arrived at the dance, he had no doubt he would have spent the night back in the county home instead of the hospital. Regardless, he was certain Josh hated him.

"How's Winsor doing?" Will asked Haley.

Haley's eyes darted toward him suspiciously. He shrugged. Will recognized Haley's notepad and pen on the bedside table, so he picked them up and tossed them across the bed. Startled, Haley flipped his chair in an attempt to scramble backward.

"Oh, damn," Will muttered. He got up and walked to where Haley was sprawled on the floor, disoriented. When he held out his hand, Haley flinched.

"Let me help you up," Will said.

Their fingers met, and Haley winced again, but he allowed Will to pull him back onto his feet. This time, Will set the notepad carefully on the edge of the mattress in front of Haley. "Want to talk?" he asked.

Haley extended a hand toward the pad, then drew back his trembling fingers. He said breathlessly, "Don't do that."

Will wasn't sure he'd heard him correctly. "Don't do what?"

"Encourage me," Haley told him, and then looked away, back at Winsor. "Don't lie."

"I'm sorry," Will said, stunned by the mettle in Haley's voice, "did I lie about something?"

"Whim told you about me, about the doctors and the hospitals."

Had Haley heard them talking downstairs?

"I'm not crazy," Haley said. "Whim wants to think that. The truth scares him."

"The truth?"

"That I . . . see things. That I know things."

"What things?" Will asked uneasily.

"*I would do anything to help you, if you'd only tell me what to do,*" Haley quoted.

Will had said that to Josh in the school lobby the night before, and he knew Josh would never have related his words to Haley. She was pathologically incapable of gossiping.

Haley must have overheard us, Will thought. *He must have been eavesdropping.*

Oblivious to Will's shock, Haley asked, "Did you mean that?"

It took Will a moment to realize that Haley was asking about what Will had said to Josh, what—in his own mind—he had considered a promise. "I meant it," he admitted.

"That's good. Josh needs someone to . . ." He shrugged. "Be nice to her. She's not very nice to herself. She won't admit it, but she's been thinking about you saying that."

"Haley—" Will said, his throat tight.

"Do you want more proof? I can tell you all sorts of things. I know that Dustine found you in the library and gave you Ian's journal. I know she told you that you'd be an outsider till the day you die. I know your mom liked vodka best, but if she was broke she'd drink mouthwash or hand sanitizer or vanilla extract. I know you accidentally drank cherry schnapps once, because you thought it was cherry syrup and you put it in a Coke."

Will felt sick and stunned. He had never, *ever* told anyone that he'd drunk cherry schnapps—not even the social workers. His twelve-year-old self had been afraid he'd get sent to Detox.

Whatever excitement Haley had found in proving himself faded, and his voice softened. "I know these things," he explained. "I saw them when I touched your hand. Ian used to tell me, 'Be careful when you talk, Haley. Don't let them know.' Now he says, 'Save them. Save Josh.'"

Will's brain continued to insist that Haley was delusional, but his body shivered. He didn't believe in psychic powers, and yet he couldn't disbelieve Haley. Something about the way Haley's face changed when he spoke—not with the eerie power of Ian's presence, but as if he felt more and more free—unsettled Will. "What do you see when you touch Winsor's hand?"

Haley's expression darkened. "I see the man with the canister putting the gas mask on her. And then . . . nothing. She's gone. I don't know where she is—I can't find her." He put his hand on Winsor's as if to see if she had returned. "I keep calling for her, but I think maybe she can't come back."

"Haley," Will said again. "How do you know these things?"

"Ian said no one would believe me, back when we were kids, right after Dad left. He said, 'If your own father won't believe you, no one else will.' But Ian always believed me. 'Can't tell Mom,' he said. 'Someday we'll tell Josh.'" Haley shook his head. "But she won't believe me now. It would hurt too much. She's the one who keeps calling him back." His tone was faintly resentful, but then he looked ashamed of himself and added, "Maybe I do too."

Either Haley was in the middle of a breakdown, Will decided, or else . . . had he spent his life writing notes because he was afraid of what he would reveal when he opened his mouth?

"I know all these things," Haley said again. "I used to tell Ian, but now there's no one. It scares Whim. It would hurt Josh. Winsor won't even speak to me."

Will watched Haley run his thumb over Winsor's knuckles, not with Ian's boldness but with the tenderness of a former lover. Whim had said he never understood Haley and Winsor's relationship— maybe it had been so simple as to confuse people. Maybe Haley had just loved her.

Haley sighed and set Winsor's hand gently on the bed. He looked at Will, and though he didn't ask aloud, his question was obvious.

"You can tell me," Will said, coming to a decision. "You need to tell me. You can't carry all that by yourself."

"Will . . ." Haley began, and then stopped, and Will wasn't sure if he was asking a question or speaking Will's name. Finally, he asked, "Will you believe me?"

Suspecting that Haley would know if he lied, Will thought the question through before he answered. He saw Haley looking him in the eye, speaking in complete sentences, expressing emotion, free of his notepad and pen . . . Haley had never appeared more sane.

Delusions make people act less sane, not more.

"I'll believe you," Will promised.

Haley smiled, and then, suddenly shy again, turned away. He leaned down to kiss Winsor's dark hair. "Come on," he said. "Let's go home."

Josh wasn't prepared for the scene. The clock had just struck four in the morning when they finally arrived home, but there was a Forward Cleaning Service van parked in the driveway. Two thick tubes ran from the van through the back door.

The kitchen lights were on, and coffee percolated on the counter. From the living room came the sounds of motion, traffic, industrial equipment. Josh stopped dead in the doorway.

She hadn't slept all night, but she hadn't felt it fully until then, when the world threatened to slip away. Two guys were cleaning the carpet, and her stomach turned at the sight of red froth bubbling out of the rug. A woman stripped bloodied drapes off the windows, and the furniture had been piled haphazardly on one side of the room.

Josh turned as Haley wandered past her into the pantry and, presumably, the archroom. "Whim," Josh said. "Take Del upstairs. Go through the hallway."

Neither one asked any questions. Whim just put his arm around Del's shoulders, and she leaned gratefully against him, and they left the kitchen through the doorway that led directly to the hall, bypassing the living room. Whim nodded to Davita Bach, who was hurrying toward Josh. Despite the odd hour, Davita was dressed in a royal-blue suit that set off her red hair and the rubies in her ears. She frowned as if displeased with herself when she saw Josh and Will.

"I'm sorry," she said, having to raise her voice above the clamor in the living room. "I thought you wouldn't be home until tomorrow and all of this would be finished."

Josh felt the blood rush to her hands when she saw Davita. She probably would have been angry at Davita regardless, but the fact that the woman looked so put together, so *untouched,* sent Josh into a fury.

"I warned you!" Josh said. "Grandma warned you—she believed me!"

"I know," Davita said, raising her hands in surrender. "I did what I could—"

"You did *nothing!*"

In that moment, Josh could have been moved to violence. She could have kicked in doors and thrown her fists through walls and shattered windows. But even as she lifted a hand to slap Davita's beautiful face, tears rushed her eyes, and she just stumbled down the hallway instead.

Davita called after her, but Josh didn't turn back. Will followed her, his footsteps a soft echo of hers on the stairs.

She was vividly aware of the emptiness in the third-floor apartment. From far below came the muted sounds of the cleaners. Only the end-table lamp warmed the room.

Will came in after her. He didn't speak, but she felt him behind her, and when she turned to face him, instead of the accusation she expected to find, she saw the same look she'd seen during their fight at the dance, the same longing to be let in, so she threw herself down on the couch and blurted out, "All of this is my fault."

Will considered a moment before stepping closer and sitting down on the coffee table in front of her. Very calmly, he asked, "How's that work?"

"They used my lighter to leave the Dream. Then they got a mirror somewhere and they came here and hurt everyone."

Will put his head in his hands as he said, "Josh, you need to go to bed."

"No, you're not listening to me—"

"No, Josh, I *am.* And now is not the time to talk about this."

"But it's my fault, don't you see—"

She stood up and brushed past him so that she could pace

around the living room. Her need to move was closely tied to her desire to escape her own skin.

"It doesn't matter," Will told her, rising. "It was an accident; you had no way of knowing what would happen."

"No, I *knew* they weren't just nightmares."

"And you told your grandmother and Young Ben and Davita. You warned them—they didn't listen, and that's on them, not you."

"Grandma listened! She listened and she died!"

The pattern of shadows Josh cast on the floor as she moved was making her dizzy. Will climbed over the coffee table to cut her off as she made another circuit. He grabbed her arm, stopping her pacing. When he spoke, his voice was laden with frustration. "You did what you could. You warned the right people. They didn't believe you, and there was an accident. That doesn't make it your fault. You are exhausted and you need to sleep."

She tried to shake him off and had to settle for shaking her head vigorously. "What are you doing, Will?" she nearly shouted. "Why are you defending me when this is obviously my fault?"

"Because," he replied, raising his voice for the first time, "because—*because*—"

And then he kissed her.

Josh was so surprised she barely had time to respond before Will pulled away.

"Because," he said, and only the lowering of his voice suggested anything had occurred between them, "you're hurting terribly and you want someone to blame, and since you can't get your hands on Snitch and Gloves, you're going to blame yourself."

Josh stared at him. *Will just kissed me,* she thought.

Then she was kissing him, and he had his hands in her hair and her fists were full of his T-shirt and her body was alive with an exhilaration strangely close to dreamfire. She felt like either one of them might fly apart at any moment, and she clutched him as a way to hold him together, hold herself together—

"Stop, wait," he said, pulling away. "We can't do this. This is crazy."

Josh forced herself to let go of him, but her hands ached with the emptiness.

"I can't handle this tonight," he said.

He looked as drained and weary as Josh felt. His black T-shirt had come untucked from his slacks and his auburn hair was tangled from moments of captured sleep on the hospital couch. His blue eyes were almost as bloodshot as Deloise's, as Josh knew her own must be, and he was shaking. She could tell him that he wasn't part of her life, her family, her problems, but he was going to hurt alongside her anyway.

And apparently he was going to kiss her too.

"Sorry," she said.

He shook his head. "There's nothing—"

"No, I mean, for last night. For attacking you like that."

He shrugged slowly, as if even that gesture were exhausting. "Maybe I deserved it. Right now I'm too tired to remember."

She wanted to reach out to him, pull him close for a minute, long enough to sort out what those kisses had meant. Had he kissed her to shut her up, or had he kissed her because he was too exhausted and broken-down to stop himself?

She didn't want to scare him. She had spent so long pushing him away that now the desire to be close to him terrified her. So instead of kissing him again, she only laid her palm against his cheek. Will turned his face into her touch and closed his eyes, resting there, and Josh let her fingertips stroke his skin. Why had she been so afraid of letting him in when he had never been anything except kind?

Will rolled his face against her hand and placed a very slow kiss on the inside of her wrist.

Oh, Josh thought, and she shivered.

When he opened his eyes, they had already found hers, as if he had seen her through his eyelids. He said, "Please go to bed, Josh."

She took a step back and stumbled on her bad knee. He wrapped an arm around her waist and she didn't fight him. "Come on," he said, leading her into her bedroom.

He didn't turn the light on, but slid her onto the bed. While he tugged off her shoes, she found her voice again and said, "Will?"

"Yeah?"

"I'm going to want to talk soon."

He dragged a comforter off the floor and covered her with it.

"You know where to find me," he told her. When he went back into the living room, he left her door open, just a crack.

Twenty-eight

The next morning, Josh woke Will to tell him that they had been summoned to testify before the junta. He had a bad feeling about it, but he started getting dressed.

He had just pulled on his pants when he remembered that he'd kissed Josh the night before.

"Oh, man," he muttered, rubbing his head. "What was I thinking?"

He'd been thinking that he was so tired, and so sad, and so sick of listening to Josh beat herself up, and that kissing her was as close as he could get to saying, "Shut up, I don't care what you've done, I think you're amazing." Then as soon as he started kissing her he panicked because maybe he'd gone too far, and he'd finished by babbling some sort of argument for why she was too hard on herself.

"Not smooth, Will," he told himself in the bathroom mirror. "Not smooth at all."

He supposed some sort of explanation was in order, but Josh didn't ask for one as they ate a quick breakfast. Whole-grain toast and eggs for Will, hot chocolate and cherry Pop Tarts for Josh. She didn't say anything except that Kerstel had made it through surgery.

The limo was chilly within, and rain threatened without. As

they rolled down the long driveway, Davita flipped open a laptop. She looked just as put together as she had the night before, but her fingers were sluggish on the keys. "What's your full name, Will?" she asked.

He looked at Josh. She shrugged. "I'm not sure yet," he said.

"Well, we have eighty minutes to figure it out. Name some of the men from your mother's side of the family."

"Paul, John, Ralph, Luke, Neal, Mark—"

"Isn't there anyone in your family with a name that isn't one syllable?" Davita interrupted.

Will had to think. "I have a distant cousin named Toly, which I think is short for Anatoly."

Davita nodded her approval. "It's close to Anatolijus, which is an old dream-walker name. Do you have a historical figure yet?"

"Sigmund."

She glanced up. "What the hell is Sigmund?"

Will explained and her brows furrowed in exasperation. "Fine, you're William Anatolijus Sigismondo Kansas. No, Kansisuvth."

He gave up. The atrocity she had just made of his name was one he should have expected. Glancing out the window, he reminded himself, *You aren't really one of them.*

"Josh," Davita said. "Does Will know what people will expect of him?"

Have you taught him any manners? Will translated.

A lock of light-brown hair fell onto Josh's forehead as she turned to look at the older woman. "He'll be fine." She had hardly spoken to Davita since they got in the limo.

Davita tilted her head skeptically. "Does he know how to greet elders? Does he know how the amphitheater will be set up and where to sit when he enters? Does he know whom he'll be meeting and what subjects can and cannot be discussed?"

"No," Will said. "He does not."

Josh sighed. "Let's go over some things."

Over the next hour, she attempted to explain how the junta worked and the protocol for speaking before it, but she obviously had little interest in politics and social niceties. Davita made frequent interjections. While Will felt uncomfortable at having been singled out, he was also relieved that someone had thought to tell him these things. Josh was an amazing teacher of how to be a dream walker *in*-Dream—less so out of it.

"And, naturally, my grandfather will be there," Josh added as they exited the highway and plunged into downtown Braxton. "Probably waving sparklers and drinking Champagne."

"Josh," Davita said, her voice full of disapproval.

"You know he hated Grandma. I'm telling you, if he makes one smart remark about—" Josh's voice caught in her throat and she had to clear it before she went on. "I'm gonna kick him, just like I did when I was six."

"You kicked him?" Will asked.

"Yeah." Josh broke into her lopsided smile. "He made Deloise cry, so I side-kicked him, right in the chest. Knocked him over, too." Her pleasure at the memory faded. "Every time I see him I want to do it again."

"There will be no kicking today," Davita said sternly. "This is a serious matter, Josh."

An hour later, they arrived at the junta's headquarters. Maybe it was just the rain, but the gray skyscraper seemed more sinister than Will remembered from his first visit.

On the ride up to the nineteenth floor, Will examined himself critically in the elevator's mirrored walls. Whim had loaned him a gray robe to wear, and Deloise had pinned it so that Will didn't trail a foot of fabric behind himself, but somehow he still looked like a little kid dressed as a priest for Halloween. The only thing he liked about the outfit was the pin he wore over his heart with the Weavaros family emblem—an arched foot wrought in silver, set against a field of peridot gems.

"We were having one made up for you, but . . ." Josh had said as she pinned it to Will's robe that morning.

She was almost finished before he realized what she meant. "This was Dustine's?"

Josh gave him a sad smile. "She'd want you to have it. She liked you, you know."

Will touched the pin and felt the cool stones and silver beneath his fingertips. "I was beginning to think that maybe she did. We had a lot in common."

Josh gave him a curious look, but he didn't explain. To her, Dustine had never been an outsider, and he decided not to change that.

The elevator opened onto a carpeted lobby where several dozen dream walkers made small talk and drank coffee. Josh led Will through it to the amphitheater.

The room was a circular ocean of seating with rows of chairs climbing the walls. But despite the hardwood stage, the golden velvet upholstery, and the chandeliers hanging from the ceiling, there was no mistaking the courtroom for a theater; armed guards hovered on either side of the door and heavy-duty steel rings for manacles protruded from the polished floor.

A row of regal, high-backed chairs cut through the first two rows of seating and dominated the room. "That's where the junta sits," Josh said. She gestured to several ottomans, covered in studded leather and standing on legs carved of black marble, set on the stage floor before the junta's thrones. "Those are for witnesses."

Josh and Will took seats in the second row near an aisle, and Davita sat in a reserved area to the side of the junta. "I wonder where Young Ben is," Josh murmured, scanning the room.

The members of the junta were elegant and smiling figures, wholly unremarkable in a way that unsettled Will. None of them looked particularly wise or enlightened or significantly different from anyone else in the crowd.

Except, of course, for Peregrine, who was moving from one cluster of people to the next, greeting everyone. His robe was the same as Will's except that it was red shot through with black and gold thread, and it shimmered when he walked.

"Your grandpa looks like a Vegas act," Will whispered to Josh, and he got her to laugh.

Once the junta was seated, the room quieted around them, finally falling completely silent. Will's nervousness turned to impatience as the junta spent the next hour dealing with unrelated matters. Finally, Josh and Will were called, and he followed her up to the row of ottomans arranged onstage and tried not to look like an idiot in a borrowed dress.

"Journeyer Weavaros." A female member of the junta rose, and Will was sitting close enough to the junta's thrones to read the large brass nameplates set on the table before them. Anivay la Grue was elderly, of Native American descent, and she had thick black hair cut short around her chin. She smiled with her greeting and then added, "I believe we have not yet met your apprentice."

Josh said, "Your Eminences, fellow dream walkers, may I present Will Anatoly Sigmund Kansas?"

For a moment, Will completely forgot that anyone else was in the room, although he could hear Minister la Grue saying, "Welcome to the fold, Apprentice Kansas. May you always walk safely."

He looked at Josh, and she gave him a tiny, private smile.

He could have kissed her right then.

"Thank you," Will said, speaking as much to Josh as to the junta minister.

They sat down, and the interrogation began.

"We have asked you here today," Minister la Grue said, "to discuss those known only as 'the men in trench coats,' whom many in this room have witnessed. Would you please describe your encounters with them?"

Will let Josh do the talking; she might hate social situations and feel uncomfortable in her own skin at times, but she knew dreams. She told the junta and the witnesses of her three encounters, beginning with a description of the nightmare she was in at the time. She relayed in detail each of the trench-coat men's actions, their gas masks, their canisters, Gloves's gloves. She even told them about the bitter smell of chemicals that clung to them.

When Josh finished, Peregrine Borgenitch rose from his seat. What might have been intended to be a stately motion looked more like a first-grader jumping at the recess bell. Will was sitting close enough to Josh to feel her tense as her grandfather walked around the table to Minister la Grue.

"Minister la Grue," he said, "if I may . . ."

She looked displeased, but she acquiesced and returned to her chair.

"Josh," Peregrine said, and then added, "my dear," in a strange, smarmy voice. "You were in-Dream when you saw this man—this man you call Snitch—*apparently* alter the Dream."

"There was no 'apparently' about it," Josh said. "He looked right at the exit Will had opened, and the doorway vanished."

"He didn't, I don't know, wave a wand at it?"

"No," Josh said through gritted teeth. "He didn't have a wand."

"Did he make any signs with his hands, any gestures?"

"No."

"So all he actually did was glance at the doorway?"

"He . . ." Josh struggled with her words. "He looked at it, intensely. His eyes narrowed."

"And did lightning bolts shoot out of them?"

"No, I told you—he didn't have to do anything. He just looked at the doorway and it vanished."

Will restrained himself from putting a hand on Josh's back. Her whole body was vibrating with anger. *What is this guy trying to prove?* Will wondered. *Aren't we here because Snitch and Gloves turned out to be real people? Why keep trying to disprove their abilities?*

"How far away from him were you at this point?" Peregrine asked Josh.

"Four feet."

"And after he glanced at the doorway, he went back to trying to put a gas mask on Haley Micharainosa?"

"Yes."

"And why was he doing that?"

"I have no idea."

"Because, as I recall, you said this man, Snitch, was *wearing* a gas mask. Was there gas in the nightmare?"

"Not that I noticed."

"Hmm." Peregrine paced a few idle steps, his hands clasped behind his back, before turning sharply—and somewhat melodramatically—back to Josh and Will and asking, "And he identified you?"

Josh nodded. "He said, 'You're Jona's daughter.'"

"Did he recognize Haley?"

"I don't know. He didn't speak to Haley."

Peregrine didn't ask about Will. Will hadn't expected him to.

"But he recognized you. Just *you,* Josh."

"Yes." Although Will doubted that Josh had any more idea than he did what Peregrine was trying to prove, she was upset enough to say, "So what? Lots of people know who I am."

Peregrine made an embarrassed expression, like Josh had just said something arrogant. "Well, they certainly do now."

One of Josh's hands clenched, and Will thought for a moment that he was going to have to stop her from jumping off her ottoman and attacking Peregrine. Luckily, her grandfather suddenly sat down.

Minister la Grue stood up again. "Thank you, Journeyer Weavaros, I think we've heard enough. Unless you have something else to add?"

Josh's voice sighed with relief. "No."

"Good day, then. May you walk safely."

Will stood up with her and was stepping down from the platform when Minister la Grue added, "Apprentice Kansas, please stay a moment."

"Wait—what?" Josh asked. One of her feet was already on the ground and the other was still on the platform, giving her a half-frozen appearance.

"The junta would like to speak to Apprentice Kansas alone for a moment."

Josh and Will looked at each other, equally surprised. "Is that necessary?" Josh asked.

Peregrine smiled. "Yes."

"As his teacher, I request permission to stay."

"Denied." Peregrine smiled wider.

Will saw the fury in Josh's eyes when she looked at her grandfather, but she forced it down as she turned back to Will. "I'll be right outside," she promised in a whisper.

The room was perfectly still except for Josh as she left. When the doors closed behind her, Will felt cold and hyperaware of everything—the patterns of light on the polished floor, the aftertaste of coffee in his mouth, the way the legs of his ottoman weren't quite even, causing it to rock when he shifted. The junta must have been fifteen feet away, but he could see their faces as if they were at arm's length.

"Apprentice Kansas," Peregrine said, and Will started. A few soft chuckles came from the crowd, and Peregrine grinned big. He liked catching Will off-guard.

"Apprentice Kansas, did you ever see the men in trench coats when Journeyer Weavaros wasn't with you?"

"No, but I've never dream walked without her."

Peregrine nodded. "Do you consider her a good teacher?"

"Excellent."

"What makes her an excellent teacher?"

"Her patience, her clarity, and her understanding of what she teaches."

"Would you elaborate on her understanding?"

Will didn't know exactly what the man was asking for. "She has a lot of experience dream walking. She's well trained, and she knows what to expect."

"She knows what to expect? How does she know?"

"Experience." He struggled to not sound . . . spooky. "Instinct," he told them.

"Instinct?" Peregrine looked delighted with Will's answer. "How exactly would you define 'instinct,' Apprentice Kansas?"

Will got the distinct impression that he was being danced into a corner, so he gave a textbook answer. "As the subconscious interpretation of subtle cues that the conscious mind misses."

"That must be fun to watch," Peregrine commented. There was a vicious glint in his eyes. "Sometimes you must think she's practically psychic."

"I've never thought that," Will told him honestly, thinking of Haley.

Peregrine abruptly changed tack. "How many dreams have you walked with Journeyer Weavaros?"

"I don't know."

"Estimate, if you would."

He considered for a moment. "Maybe seventy."

"How many nightmares would you say were successfully resolved?"

"Many."

"Many? Does that mean most of them?"

"Most of them," Will agreed.

"Three out of five? Four?"

"Nine out of ten." He remembered the study that had pegged Josh's resolution rate at 88 percent.

"So what you're telling us," Peregrine said, summarizing to suit his purposes, "is that not only does Journeyer Weavaros have an uncanny ability to anticipate what might occur in-Dream, she's also able to fully resolve almost every nightmare?"

I want to say no just to watch his face fall, Will thought. Reluctantly, he answered, "Yes."

"Apprentice Kansas." Another dramatic spin-turn. "When Journeyer Weavaros takes action within a nightmare, how quickly does the dreamer usually respond?"

"Very quickly."

"Faster than when you take action?"

"Yes, but my actions aren't as well chosen—"

"When Journeyer Weavaros takes action, would you say the dreamer responds quickly, or instantly?"

Instantly—at least, it often felt instant. Some days, it was as if the dreamer followed Josh's train of thought and didn't even need her to act. Other days, things moved slower, but often—

Will suddenly understood what Peregrine was trying to make him say, so he said the opposite. "Quickly."

But everyone had seen him hesitate. Peregrine pounced.

"When the man you call Snitch glanced at the exit you were holding open, did Journeyer Weavaros follow his gaze?"

"Of course she did—she was trying to see what he was looking at. So was I."

"So, at the moment that the doorway vanished, Snitch wasn't the only one looking at it."

Any other answer would have been ridiculous. "No, he wasn't."

The room was too quiet. Will couldn't quite believe Peregrine was going to ask what Will thought he was going to ask until the words were spoken.

"Have you ever seen Journeyer Weavaros, in any way, alter the Dream?"

Will was only distantly aware of the room's reaction: not just murmurs and whispers, but fully voiced expressions of disbelief. Will himself felt only cold fury.

He gave Peregrine a hard look. "*No.*"

Peregrine appeared undeterred by Will's answer. "After the doorway vanished, you opened a second exit, correct?"

"Yes."

"What was Journeyer Weavaros doing?"

"Beating Snitch with a microwave."

"But she didn't kill him. And she apparently didn't kill the man she called Gloves, either, did she?" He considered. "Why do you suppose she didn't kill them?"

It was a stupid question—these were all stupid, leading, preposterous questions. But when Will opened his mouth to declare that Josh wasn't a bloodthirsty killer, Peregrine held up his hand.

"You have been a great help, Apprentice Kansas. Thank you. You're free to leave."

But Will couldn't leave, not when Josh had been so inaccurately portrayed. Knowing he might be making an awful mistake, Will said desperately, "I believe that Josh's ability to act so effectively within the Dream comes from her habitual breaking of Stellanor's First Rule of dream walking."

The crowd murmured; someone actually laughed; someone else said, "What's Stellanor's Rule?"

Peregrine just appeared perplexed.

"Stellanor's First Rule of dream walking is never to let the dreamer's fear take you over," Will said.

"Yes, I think most of us here—"

"I believe that each time Josh goes into a nightmare, the first thing she does is consciously break Stellanor's First Rule in order to give herself a more complete picture of the situation and a better chance of anticipating what might occur."

Peregrine clearly hadn't appreciated being cut off. "And she's told you that she does this?"

"No."

"Then how do you know she's doing it?"

"I've . . . It's just something I've deduced by observation."

"Yes, well," Peregrine said dryly. "Thank you for your uneducated opinion. You may go."

Will stood up, but he made no move toward the door. He couldn't go, not with so much unsaid, not after he'd thrown Josh under the bus for nothing. Peregrine, halfway back to his chair, paused to look at his granddaughter's apprentice when he realized Will wasn't walking away.

"Now what?" he demanded.

"She warned you," Will said. "She warned you about those men, and you did nothing. Dustine—" He heard his voice crack as he recalled the day she had sought him out in the library. Instead of the argument he meant to make, he heard himself say, "She was kind to me."

Peregrine's face changed. The little smirk of pleasure he had worn throughout the interrogation faded and revealed something closer to despair. A tremor ran through his jaw.

Whatever else Will had been about to say, he forgot it then.

"Yes," Peregrine said softly, "I imagine she was."

Will turned away from the junta and strode toward the door so fast he almost slid on the marble floor in his ridiculous slippers.

Davita rushed toward him. "This is a sham," Will hissed before she even had time to speak. "You walked us right into a trap—and you knew, didn't you? You knew what he had planned!"

"Will, wait a minute—"

"How dare you drag us down here to perform in your kangaroo court!"

Davita grabbed his arm, but he shook her off. "Don't go out there and say that to Josh," Davita begged. "You're only going to make this worse."

"I don't think it can get any worse," he snapped, and flung the doors open.

Josh met Will in the anteroom. "What happened?"

"Will, *don't*," Davita said again.

Will glanced at her—at the makeup she used to conceal herself, at the flawless, unquestionable face she put on. He looked back at Josh. "Your grandfather is trying to pin you as an accomplice."

Josh stepped back, growing smaller, as though Will's words had weakened every part of her. She shook her head.

"Dammit, Will, stop!" Davita said.

"He wanted me to make it look like you're working with them. He wanted me to say that you can control the Dream, that you have their powers. Josh." Will leaned forward, trying to push through the stunned glaze over her eyes. "We have to leave now. We have to get out of here before they take this any further."

"You can't leave," Peregrine announced, appearing behind Will. A huge, gloating smile now dominated his face. "We need you to stick around for a while, Joshy."

"Let's just go," Will told her.

"I have a warrant," Peregrine pointed out. "You could join Ben Sounclouse in the jail."

"Young Ben—" Josh began, before repeating, "A *warrant*?"

"By order of the junta, if you try to leave the building, I am authorized to use whatever force is necessary to keep you here."

"On what grounds?" Will demanded.

"That you conspired to commit Dream crimes, including murder, intended murder, and anarchistic use of inter-universal gateways." He looked more pleased with himself than ever. "Same charges as Ben, the crafty old fool."

When Josh proved speechless, Will burst out, "You're a scapegoat, Josh. These ineffectual idiots can't catch Snitch and Gloves, so they're trying to pin everything on you."

"Peregrine," Davita broke in, "go back into the amphitheater for a minute. Let me talk to Josh."

Peregrine folded his hands across his bloated belly. "I don't think so, Davey. I don't know what you've been trying to hide from me— you and Ben Sounclouse—but I'm not going to politely leave the room while you conspire against me."

"Josh lives in my district," Davita shot back, "so until I sign your damn warrant, it's worthless."

"I don't trust these people," Will told Josh desperately, but she barely seemed to hear him.

"I think this young brat is the one you shouldn't trust," Peregrine snapped. "He just made you both look like fools in front of the entire community. And as for you, Davita—you've forgotten your place, and who put you there. You would have burned to the ground with the royal palace if I hadn't stood up for you." He drew himself up. "However, I'm a reasonable man, and I'm willing to be reasonable now. I'll make you a deal, Josh. I'll give you this warrant, and you can shred it or burn it or wipe your ass with it, but in return, I want your scroll."

The words were so unexpected that they took Will several seconds to process. He guessed that Josh had the same issue by the hollow way she repeated, "My scroll . . . ?" Even Davita stood mute, her open mouth revealing the lipstick on her front teeth.

"That's right," Peregrine said. "This warrant, for your scroll. Hell, I'll even release Young Ben."

"Why?" Josh asked.

"I've got my reasons."

Will didn't know what decision Josh would make. Apparently neither did Josh, because she just stood there, frozen, until Davita said, "This is ridiculous, Peregrine. She's not going to give you her scroll." Turning to Josh and Will, she said, "The limo is outside. Go back to the house and stay there, I'll call. This isn't what it looks like, Josh, believe me."

"I don't know what to believe," Josh said, finally finding her voice again. Her eyes had lost their glaze, and she looked sharply at Davita. "We warned you—we told you about Feodor and the men and that they weren't just a nightmare. We told you and Grandma that!"

"You told us," Davita agreed. "And we told your grandfather."

"No, you didn't," Peregrine said with a look so innocent it was almost a parody. Then he smiled at his own joke.

"Are you *happy*?" Josh shouted at him, her temper finally exploding. "You hated Grandma for all those years and now she's dead and you're *happy*?"

Josh lunged at him, and Will and Davita both threw themselves in front of her. Davita grabbed Josh's chin and made her look away from her grandfather's cruel smile. "Josh, I am trying to protect you. Will, take care of her."

He nodded as Peregrine said, "Yes, have the outsider look after her. That will work."

"Shut up," Josh said. Then she called her grandfather a name that made Davita wince. Will hadn't heard that kind of language since he'd left the county home.

Peregrine laughed. Will was more than a little desperate to leave, but as he took Josh's right hand, Peregrine wrapped his spindly fingers around her left arm. Will felt a surge of incredible anger that this twisted little man would grab Josh so tightly.

"You're not going anywhere," Peregrine told her, deadly serious.

Davita only groaned. "Pere—"

"Let go of me," Josh told her grandfather in a flat, cold voice. "That's the only warning I'm going to give you."

His other hand snaked toward the shoulder of her robe, and Josh twisted within his grasp. From under the folds of her wool and silk robe, her slippered foot shot out like a thrust sword and connected soundly with Peregrine's breastbone.

He went down without a sound, flat on his back. Josh and Will stumbled away while Davita swore and dropped to the floor beside him. Peregrine's eyes fluttered shut, then opened again. He tried to speak but his mouth moved as silently as a fish's.

Josh looked at Will. "I knew I'd end up kicking him," she said.

Will honestly couldn't decide whether he wanted to laugh or cry.

"Go!" Davita told them. "Just go!"

They turned and bolted for the elevator.

Twenty-nine

When they reached the sidewalk, Josh could still feel her grandfather's hand on her arm. He might still have been digging his fingernails into her flesh, the sensation was so strong.

Outside, rain fell so hard it blurred the lines of the buildings. Josh and Will ran toward the limo, parked a block south. The first puddle soaked Josh's slippers all the way through. Will ran beside her with his eyes wide and his auburn hair plastered to his neck, cringing when lightning struck less than half a mile away.

"In!" Will told her, throwing open the limo door. She tumbled into the vehicle, a chilly but safe harbor from the wind and rain. Will followed, slammed the door, and started hitting buttons randomly. "Where's the intercom?" he muttered as the dome lights flashed on and off. For a moment the moonroof opened, prompting both of them to swear as water poured inside.

"Here," Josh said, flicking a switch.

"Yes?" a voice prompted.

"Tanith, immediately."

"Yes, ma'am."

A moment later the limo rolled forward. Josh and Will both pulled off their soaked robes, and Will found two chenille blankets in a drawer beneath the seats. Josh didn't realize she was shivering in her yoga pants and T-shirt until he wrapped a blanket around her shoulders.

The thunder came again—three, four times, not so far in the distance. Between the tinted windows and the inky black clouds, the cabin of the limousine was as dim as a cave.

"Does any of this make sense to you?" Will asked. Josh could just make out the line of his head and shoulders sitting across from her.

"What, you mean why my grandfather is blackmailing me to get to my scroll? I have no idea!" She'd thought she felt angry, but the underlying note in her voice was hurt. *He's supposed to be family. . . .*

"He messed up when he didn't listen to us, and now he's trying to cover his ass," Will theorized.

"Do you know what 'anarchistic use of an inter-universal gateway' is? It's what happened when I let Gloves keep my lighter."

"Josh, that was an accident."

"Maybe," she agreed, "but it was still a crime. Maybe I should let Peregrine arrest me."

"If Snitch and Gloves hadn't gotten the lighter from you," Will told her, his voice hardening, "they would have gotten one from somebody else."

"But they didn't get it from someone else," she said. "They got it from me."

Exasperated, Will asked, "Why are you so determined to be at fault for this?"

Strangely, his anger made her laugh. "Because they always let me off."

Then, with a recklessness close to hysteria, she blurted out, "'Go ahead and fall in love even though you're too young, Josh, 'cause your mom died. Your grades are crap, but we won't worry about that because you're sharp in a nightmare. And never mind how you broke every rule in the book and opened an archway without permission and someone died. He was your ex, so you've probably suffered enough. We'll let that slide, too.'"

She felt Will listening, felt his presence in the dark. "I screwed up, I did. Just this once I want them to see me and see exactly what I've done, not some censored version. Kerstel nearly died, and it *was* my fault. Grandma *did* die, and that's my fault too. I wasn't supposed to dream walk, and I went in anyway. You even told me not to, but I did. If that makes me an accomplice, they *should* arrest me."

Then she was crying. Will could tell her that it hadn't been her fault, but that wasn't going to take the bloodstains out of the carpet or erase the sound of Kerstel's labored breath as it struggled down the phone lines.

Josh covered her eyes with her palms and the thunder clapped so hard her heart shook in her chest. She felt Will put his hands on her knees.

"Josh," Will said. He no longer sounded angry.

"Sorry."

"No, don't be sorry. Keep this in perspective. You chose to break a rule, you're guilty of that, but you had no idea that you might be putting others at risk. If you had thought for a moment that someone else might get hurt, I know you wouldn't have gone in. Everybody knows that."

"But my grandmother is still dead," she whispered.

He sighed. "I know," was all he said.

Her chest was tight, but she couldn't keep crying. The tears balked inside her as if they knew their own uselessness. All she wanted was a chance to say *I never meant to put you in danger.*

She wanted to say the same thing to Ian.

Lightning cracked like the dome of the sky was being shattered into pieces. Light flooded the limo and, for a moment, Josh found Will's eyes. She could see him across from her, touching her knees as if determined to hold on to what little she would give him and biting his tongue to keep from asking for things he knew she didn't want to share.

She was so tired of hiding from him.

"I know I've been pushing you away since you got here," she said tentatively. "Part of it *is*, 'Wait, wait, he's an outsider, don't show him that.' Part of it's just me. But everything you said outside the gym was true: you're in this as deep as the rest of us. When Snitch and Gloves came out of the Dream, it might just as easily have been you in the archroom as Winsor. I have to accept that."

She held her breath when she was done. The rain still pounded, as angry as she'd ever heard it, but a pocket of quiet filled the limo. Under the storm she heard her heartbeat and Will's breathing and the water peeling off the wheels.

Say something, Will.

"I appreciate that," he told her finally, but it didn't sound like a good thing. The tone of resignation in his voice set her immediately on edge. He leaned back in his seat, moving away from her. The warm places on her knees where his hands had rested turned cold.

"Will?" she asked. The darkness between them was deep. "Will?"

"I don't want to be an obligation," he told her. His voice was grim. "I don't want to be one of the burdens you're carrying around."

"You're not—" she began weakly.

"I am, that's what you just said. I know it looks like I got the good side of this deal—suddenly being adopted and offered things I only dreamed of—but it's hard for me, Josh, *hard* to know that I'm always going to be the outsider. I'm the guy who showed up instead of Schaffer. I'm the mistake Deloise made. I know that."

Oh god. She didn't want to hurt him. He was always so good to her.

"What do you want from me?" Josh asked, feeling stretched as thin as rice paper.

The terrible resignation came back to his voice. "So much more than you want to give me."

She heard what Will didn't say. She had heard it in the gym and not known how to reply, she had felt it in his kiss and tried to ignore it, but she recognized it now—recognized the question she still didn't know how to answer: *Are you going to let him love you?*

He deserved to know the truth; he was too good a guy for her to keep lying to him. Sooner or later he would find out what she'd done. Better to destroy his illusions now.

"You wouldn't want to be here if you knew what happened to Ian," she said.

Will's voice rose bitterly out of the dark. "Forget Ian, Josh. I don't want to wrestle your secrets out of you."

It's not fair that you feel this way when you don't know what you're getting into, Josh thought, *or what happened to the last guy.*

"I have to tell you," she said finally.

"Don't use him as currency."

Feeling cut, she said, "Will, that's not it. I just . . . I have to tell you."

A gust of wind rocked the limo. "I know more than you think I know," Will said.

"What do you mean?"

"Whim told me about you and Ian, and how he read his scroll and broke up with you. He told me about Winsor and Haley, and"—Will's voice dropped slightly—"Winsor and Ian. And how the cabin burned down when you tried to open an archway."

Stupefied, Josh said, "Whim told you all of that?"

"Yeah. He thought I should know."

Winsor's right—Whim is a huge gossip. Josh expected to feel invaded, but a sense of relief surprised her instead, the way her sadness at the mess with the junta had surprised her. "Did he tell you it was my idea to open the archway?"

"He guessed that it was. Does it matter?"

Will was giving her an out, she knew. All she had to say was no, and he'd let it drop. He'd let her off the hook, the way he always had, the way everyone else did.

Josh was done being let off the hook—too many people had gotten hurt. But she took a moment to breathe, to ready herself, to steady her ax before she brought it crashing through this wall.

"We had this fight, me and Ian and Winsor. After they got back from the—" She was already choked up, and she had hardly begun.

"The woods," Will said. "Whim mentioned that."

Josh felt relieved again, for a different reason. She went on. "Yeah, after that. Winsor started the fight, I guess. She wanted to talk about everything that had happened. She wanted Ian to talk too, and he couldn't talk without getting angry, so he got angry at me. Like it was my fault he broke up with me and then got naked with Winsor in the woods.

"Ian and I hadn't spoken in a month. We both blew up. We said awful things to each other. I called Ian words I'd never spoken out loud before. He called me worse. We'd been together so long, we knew exactly how to hurt each other.

"We went on for a couple of hours like that, just trying to destroy each other. I was crying, Winsor was crying. I think even Haley was crying. Finally, Ian went outside for a cigarette. He started smoking after he opened his scroll. I decided to be gone before he came back.

"There are only three bedrooms in the cabin, and Kerstel was in one. That left one for me and Del and Winsor, and one for the guys. So I could either share a room with Ian or Winsor. I went into the basement instead.

"I hadn't been down there since my mother died. Everything was exactly the way it had been when she died. There were mirrors glued to a frame where the new archway was supposed to be and a crate full of stones to build it with. I remember there was a bucket of cement for the arch, too, and it had hardened. I sat on it and looked around at the lanterns and the mirrors and the instruction books, and just being in that house felt like a huge double blow. It was where I'd lost Mom, and it was where I really lost Ian, too, because I guess part of me had always thought he was going through a phase and would get over it and come back to me. But if there was any chance, we killed it that night.

"This guy named Geoff helped my mother open the archway, but he got lost in the Dream and never came out. I imagined what that would be like. All I wanted was to get out of the house, and the Dream seemed like the perfect place to forget everything. I decided to open an archway myself and just get the hell away from everyone. I was setting up the mirrors before I even thought about what might happen.

"One of the mirrors slipped because my hands were shaking, and Winsor came downstairs when she heard it break. She could see what I was up to. When she couldn't talk me out of it, she got Ian, who yelled at me. And I was so stupid—first I called him a coward. Then I said he was talentless and that he'd made himself look good by walking with me all those years. Next thing I knew, he was grabbing the lantern out of my hands and saying he'd do it himself.

"Winsor said that if the two of us were going to open an archway, she was going to help. She knew it was dangerous. We all knew. Haley came down and hovered at the foot of the stairs just as we were really getting going. He kept shaking his head, like he had a bad feeling.

"The process for opening an archway is nearly the same as what we did for the window. The opening on this side went fine—we just turned on the lasers and traced the lights and, suddenly, there was a . . . a space.

"Ian went in first, then I followed. This is the dangerous part of opening a new archway. You have to climb into whatever part of the Dream you've opened and build a corresponding archway on that side while fending off nightmares at the same time, and you have to connect the two archways to seal off the edges of the Veil or else fairy dust will just keep pouring out and poison you.

"We were holding hands, because once we went into the Dream, there was no way back into the World until we finished the archway on the Dream side—unless we kept physical contact with someone in the World. So Ian held one of my hands and Winsor held the other, and I stood sort of right within the archway.

"I thought we'd gotten lucky. The archway from the World to the Dream opened into a dark room. Just a dark room. I saw a window, a high window—like a dormer, round, and a night sky beyond it. But the room was empty, as far as we could tell.

"Ian set up the archway on the Dream side and lit the lantern, and at first I thought we'd done it. I felt all the layers of the Veil fall out of the archway. But then . . . I don't know exactly what happened. Something landed on Ian. He hit the floor, and I had to get on my knees to keep hold of his hand. I couldn't see what was pinning him down. I could hardly even see Ian except that he was covered in Veil dust. Haley started shouting through the archway, 'Get out! Get out!'

"And then the dreamfire took us all over. I couldn't block it out. Everything was so dark, and Haley was yelling, and something made a horrible sound, like a chuckle, and Ian shouted my name.

"For a second, nothing that had happened the last month meant anything, not even the things we'd said to each other that night. When we got down to that kind of danger, nothing mattered but holding on to each other.

"Winsor was holding my hand with both of hers, and Haley grabbed my elbow, and they pulled me out. I was still holding one of Ian's hands, so I dragged him into the basement with me. Haley knocked over the wooden frame with the mirrors on that side, and it hit the lantern and knocked it into a pile of insulation.

"Then Winsor started screaming, 'What did you do, Josh, what did you do?' and I realized I hadn't brought Ian with me, but I didn't understand because I couldn't remember letting go of his hand. I kept looking at my palm, expecting his fingers to be there, and I looked back into the archway, but all I saw was darkness.

"And then . . . Ian screamed. Not like in the movies—it was a real scream. I couldn't see what was happening to him, but when he screamed I knew that whatever was in that dream was killing him. And then the screaming stopped. The nightmare killed him.

"Haley started screaming. I tried to go back through the archway, but Winsor grabbed me. I fought her, even after I realized that the lantern had caught the insulation on fire. I kept trying to get back through the archway until the smoke overwhelmed me.

"Whim came downstairs and dragged us all to the floor. But when he started crawling toward the stairs, I realized we were leaving the basement. We were giving up on Ian, and tomorrow Ian would be dead, and the day after, and the day after . . . I just passed out.

"Whim got us out. Winsor and Haley probably would have made it outside, but not me. He saved my life.

"The week after that is a blur. I was in the hospital for a while and then I was at home, but I don't remember much except listening to Winsor cry in the room below mine. And some Gendarmerie detectives asking me questions. The first time things came into focus, I was standing in the archroom downstairs with my hand on the looking stone. Nightmares were flying past so quickly I couldn't even register one before I lost it to the next. I've never been able to do it again, but I knew that I was looking for Ian, running some kind of search for him. Three hours later, I was sure he wasn't in the Dream. I gave up hoping right then and there. I knew Ian was gone.

"The next morning when I woke up, I thought I heard him say, 'I saw a gate beyond the arch.' And I've been hearing those words ever since, even though I can't imagine what they mean."

The rain had fallen off to a patter. Thunder growled sullenly in the distance, and the cabin of the limousine began to fill with light in an afternoon dawn.

Josh wiped at her cheeks with the edge of the chenille blanket. She had been crying freely as she spoke, amazed at how quickly the words came, how easy sharing all of this with Will was.

"And, see," she went on, when he didn't speak, "the horrible thing is how I've picked myself up again. When I realized I couldn't find Ian in the Dream, I jumped in, resolved six nightmares, and then went to bed. I miss him, every day, but I came out stronger. Do you see that? You didn't know me before—you saw me at school but you never knew how unsure I was. Ian showed me how strong I am. When we broke up, that was why I didn't freak out.

"I *used* Ian. I used him for years, and then when I didn't need him anymore . . ."

Will—who had perhaps seen before she had that she wasn't finished speaking and now saw that she was—said, "When you realized you didn't need him anymore, you let go of his hand. Is that what you think, Josh?"

There was enough light in the limo by then that she could see his face. His hair had dried in loose waves around his cheeks, and his jeans and gray shirt were damp. His expression was carefully neutral, but she saw a deep sadness in his eyes.

When she didn't answer, he went on, "When people rebound after a relationship ends, a lot of them do it like Ian did. He wanted to prove that he didn't need you, so he turned to Winsor. But other people might rebound differently. They might, say, delve into work and fill the holes in their lives very quickly. It's a different way of rebounding, but it doesn't make you a murderer."

His words surprised her into speechlessness. "I get the feeling," Will said, "that Ian gave you a lot. But Whim made it clear that you gave Ian a lot in return. His death was an accident, no two ways about it. I know you well enough to know that you wouldn't have let go of him by choice, no matter how much he had hurt you."

"You don't think I'm . . ." She struggled for the right word. "Cold?"

He gave her a small smile. "I think you're afraid of being vulnerable again. And also afraid of your own strength. Maybe you want to believe that you still need Ian because it helps you reassure yourself that you didn't kill him."

More tears filled her eyes. "You're going to be a great therapist," she told Will, laughing a little and wiping her face with the back of her hand. She should have realized weeks ago that he would respond to her story with calm psychological insight rather than judgment.

Josh hoped she wasn't too late to right things between them. "So where does that put . . . you and me?"

Will shook his head. "Don't ask me. This is why shrinks have shrinks."

Somehow, she knew he was holding back. "Don't deflect," she said, using another term she'd learned from him.

He scoffed at her, but with a smile. Then he grew sober again. "I completely understand why you didn't feel comfortable telling me, but if I had known this when I got here, I would have given you more room. I think it would have been better for you. Now that I know . . . it seems more obvious than ever that I'm in the wrong place."

"That's not—"

"Does Schaffer know?" Will interrupted. "About Ian? Would he have understood why you can't trust anyone right now? Would you have felt so completely responsible for his safety?"

Josh's back straightened, and her voice lost its gravelly crying sound. "Will, forget Schaffer Sounclouse. You want to look at all this from a psychological standpoint? Here you go: Schaffer represents all your insecurities now. You've never even asked me if I would have rather had him for an apprentice!"

The calmness left Will's face, revealing a desperate fear held beneath it. He leaned so far forward that his elbows touched his knees. "Would you?"

"No!" It wasn't even a question in her mind. "Schaffer's untrainable! He can't keep focused for more than thirty seconds, he misses obvious clues, and he still doesn't know right from left. Whereas you are so sharp, and so interested, and you remember everything I tell you. You never complain, and I've never met anyone with as much looking-stone talent as you. I couldn't have asked for a better apprentice."

He gave her that small smile again, the one full of fondness but lacking any hope. "What about in your life?" he asked in a calmer voice. "Because the way this works, I'm not just a pupil—I'm the guy living in the room next to yours who you have to see at every meal."

"Who kisses me in the middle of a sentence for no apparent reason?" Josh couldn't resist adding.

Will looked down, but he was laughing a little. "Yeah. I guess I might want to be that guy too."

Josh didn't know what to say next. She dug her fingernails into the knees of her jeans.

Don't hurt him, Josh. Don't you dare hurt him.

She wetted her lips. "Maybe it's just been bad timing. You're a . . . great. It's not your fault I'm in a messed-up place. But I don't know that I can—I don't know if I can even be a decent friend to you right now."

Will reached across the limo and touched her clenched hand. This time his smile was genuine, as worn-out as her own but affectionate. "Let's just give this a rest for a while, okay?" he asked. "We'll figure out later whether or not we can keep working together."

She hadn't realized that the stakes were so high, and she knew as soon as the words were out of his mouth that she didn't want him to leave, that he meant more to her than she had admitted to either one of them. But until she could offer him something more, what could she say?

"All right," she agreed.

Thirty

Davita had ordered them to go straight home, but Josh told the limo driver to take them to the hospital first. If she was going to get arrested, she wanted to see Winsor and Kerstel first.

They visited Winsor, but her friend's silence and sightless eyes unnerved Josh. Kerstel was hooked up to machines and covered in bruises, but at least her face changed when she saw her stepdaughter enter her room. At least her fingers squeezed when Josh took her hand. Winsor's hand had lain as limp as a dead kitten.

To Josh's surprise, Will brushed the wires and tubes aside so he could kiss Kerstel's cheek.

"I had a dream about you," Kerstel told him.

"I know," Will said.

Josh wasn't sure what he meant, only that he and Kerstel were smiling at each other in a way that made her faintly jealous. Kerstel and Lauren had only taken Will in because he was Josh's apprentice, but now Josh saw that Will had won his own place in Kerstel's affection.

She wondered if Louis Poston would have managed that.

When she and Will got home from the hospital, he collapsed on the apartment couch in front of a soccer game. The house below them was unusually quiet, Josh thought, lingering in the apartment doorway. It felt empty—she sensed Dustine's absence from the first floor, Winsor's from the second, Kerstel's from the third.

"You okay?" Will asked her.

"Yeah. I just need a nap."

Will, stretched over the length of the couch, closed his eyes. "I might do the same."

Josh went to her bedroom, opened the door, and hit the switch on the wall, which caused the overhead light to come on, which caused Haley—who had been sleeping soundly in Josh's bed—to fly upright as if he were rising from a tank of ice-cold water. Anyone else would have shouted, but Haley just gaped at her with an expression of astonished betrayal, as if she'd woken him by kicking him in the gut.

She had forgotten that Haley had taken over her bedroom recently. "You can't—" she began, and then she saw her scroll spread out on the floor just as it had been two days before, a textbook at each end to keep the parchment from rolling. If Winsor had put it away, Haley had gotten it out again.

"What are you *doing* with this?" Josh hissed, and shut the door behind her to keep from waking Will.

She darted toward the scroll, but Haley was closer and faster and ended up holding it over his head like a trophy. He climbed onto her bed, feet mired in her comforter.

"Give me that," Josh said, the anger from her initial discovery returning. "You never should have opened it!"

Haley changed his grip on the scroll, holding the top edge in both fists. He bit his lip as if thinking, and then his mouth hardened resolutely.

He tore the scroll in half.

"What are you *doing*?!" Josh asked again, and she struggled to keep from shouting. She grabbed at his hands but only came away with a corner of parchment. Haley began ripping the rest into strips. "Haley! Stop it!"

He tore the strips in half and then, much to Josh's astonishment, threw them at her like confetti. As bits floated down around her, he said, "It's a fake."

Josh stopped trying to catch the flakes of parchment and stared at him. "What?"

He sank back against the wall behind her bed. Josh looked at the pieces in her hand and then at him, and finally she just shook her head.

"It's a fake," Haley repeated.

"How do you know?"

"I . . . know."

"How?"

He shrugged helplessly. "I touched it. And I just . . . knew. I . . . know lots of things."

That had probably been the longest statement Josh had heard Haley make—when he wasn't acting like Ian—since he'd returned to town. That fact alone made her uncertain.

"Young Ben wrote it to protect you," Haley continued. "He's trying to protect you. We . . ." And here his voice faltered and faded. "We all are."

Maybe. Something in his expression looked genuine. Josh had a hard time disbelieving him. And although she couldn't make the pieces fit together—literally or figuratively—somehow the idea of a fake scroll seemed in keeping with her grandfather's strange desire to possess it. Winsor had said that the writing style seemed off, too.

Except that the idea of a fake scroll was so preposterous that Josh couldn't even conceive of it. The whole idea of a scroll was to tell truths. It served no other purpose.

"Protect me from what?"

Haley considered the bits of scroll scattered on the ground. Finally, he said, "From yourself."

He spoke as though the words hurt him. Josh didn't know why, or even what his answer meant, but she saw a clarity in Haley that was rare.

None of that, of course, meant that he wasn't crazy.

"All right," she said, shrugging. She began collecting the shreds of parchment. "Whatever. Can you please find somewhere else to sleep?"

His face sharpened with anger, and for a moment he looked so much like Ian that Josh's breath caught. Then he darted past her, slamming the door on his way out.

A moment later, the door burst open again, and this time Haley was dragging Will—who was blinking rapidly at the sudden onslaught of light—by the wrist. "Tell her!" Haley demanded.

Josh had just gotten an envelope and was putting the torn-up pieces of scroll in it. She paused to watch Will say, "Tell her what?"

Haley had gone from looking like Ian to looking like a very angry Haley, which was an expression Josh had never seen before. It involved pursed lips and drawn brows and, after Will's question, an actual foot stomp. Then he whispered in Will's ear.

Will ran a hand through his curls, which were even more unruly than usual from his brief nap on the couch. "Oh, yeah. He did ask me to tell you that he's psychic."

Josh didn't know which was more ridiculous. "He's *psychic*? And *you,* the guy who wants to be a psychiatrist, believe him?"

"Haley, maybe you could give Josh some sort of demonstration."

Haley looked uncomfortable, like a little kid being teased by adults, but he took Josh's hand. Josh was still too stunned to protest.

"You told Will about the fight at the cabin on the drive home from Braxton," Haley said. "But you didn't tell him how Ian threw the mug at the wall and it broke, or how Winsor slapped you, or how when you went into the basement you threw up behind the radiator."

Josh pulled her hand out of Haley's grasp. Not because she didn't believe him—because in one brutal, revelatory instant she did—but because she was afraid of what else he would see. "Why didn't you tell me?" she asked, more stunned by his silence than the news. "I've known you my whole life."

"Ian said we could, someday. But then he died. . . ."

Ian had been intensely protective of Haley. When he and Josh had dreamed about the future, getting married, having their own home, Ian had always insisted on a little guesthouse for Haley to live in. She didn't doubt that his protectiveness had gone far enough to exclude her from information that might put Haley in danger.

If he's really psychic, then my scroll's really fake, Josh thought. *Which is good, because it means no one's opened the real one. Anything could be written in it. . . .*

Suddenly, she felt panicked, like a restless child who had been sick for days and could endure it no longer. It must have shown on her face, because Will said, "Josh?"

"Can I talk to Haley alone?" she asked.

"Ah, I guess. I mean, yes, of course. I'll be in my room."

Josh waited until he had left, closing the door behind himself, to sink onto her bed.

"Is Will in my real scroll?" she asked, her voice hardly above a whisper. "Is there an apprentice in the real scroll?"

Haley's face softened. He shook his head.

"Oh my god," she whispered with each breath. "Oh my god. Shit. *Oh my god.*"

"Young Ben made the apprentice up," Haley whispered back. "Then he sent Schaffer over here that night. Only Schaffer was late, 'cause he got lost."

"*Why?* Why would Ben do that?"

Haley shrugged. "Schaffer's not a very good dream walker. Ben thought you could help."

"That's crazy. That's ridiculous. Ben can't just make things up! And now Will is my apprentice because Schaffer doesn't know right from left?"

Haley tilted his head and asked, "Do you mind?"

It was such a bizarre question that Josh almost laughed. She had been a stressed-out mess for the last six weeks—of course she minded!

And yet . . . she kept thinking of the talk she'd had with Will in the limo. It had never felt so good to pour her heart out to anyone. And she couldn't deny that they'd had fun opening the window together, or that she might have gone on kissing him all night if he hadn't stopped her. And God bless Deloise for ordering pizza, because Schaffer would have been an infuriating student, but Will was amazing, and she actually felt really proud of how far he'd come.

She imagined what would happen if she got up, marched into the bedroom next door, and told Will the truth. His belief that he didn't belong in her life, that he wasn't wanted in the dream-walker world—it would only get worse. Josh knew he'd insist on going back to the county home. Her father would continue to send him money—which Will would refuse. All the trust he and Josh had worked for and fought for and built together would be destroyed. Every time they'd bump into each other at school, the combination of tension, guilt, and resentment on both sides would be unbearable. Josh would go into the Dream and he wouldn't be around to give her brilliant psychological insights and nervous backup. She would be lonely. She hadn't realized how lonely she had been until Will arrived.

All her thoughts fell silent in the face of a single, overwhelming truth:

I don't want him to leave.

She finally had a reason to send him away. It was a perfect, irrefutable reason—the sort that she had longed for six weeks ago— and she wasn't going to use it. Whether or not fate had planned their relationship, she was grateful for it.

Josh nodded resolutely. This was one secret she would gladly keep from him forever.

"I don't mind at all," she said, and laughed. "But what about everything else in the scroll?"

"Do you really want to know?"

Part of her did. Part of her felt that, now that she'd read the fake one, she might as well at least know how much of it was true. But in the end, that would be the same as opening the real scroll, even if she only read part of it. So she just shook her head.

"That's what I thought," Haley said.

He was talking more, she noticed. *He must know so many secrets,* she thought. *It must be hard not to blurt them all out. No wonder he stays so quiet.*

"You could have told me about being psychic," she said. "I would have helped, if I could."

"I know."

Haley didn't give her a reason why he hadn't told her, but Josh already knew. Ian had once told her that—no matter how much he loved her—he would always be loyal to Haley first, because Haley needed Ian more than Josh did. Ian hadn't hidden Haley's secret because he didn't trust Josh; he'd done it because, when it came to his brother, he didn't take chances.

"Ian loved you a lot," Josh told Haley.

Haley smiled sadly, but he looked far away. "He thought I was weak."

Josh tried not to let Haley see her wince; Ian *had* thought Haley was weak. "He thought I was weak too. He was always trying to toughen me up."

"You're tough now," Haley offered.

"Am I?"

He nodded. "You're brave. You're strong. You're a good teacher." He smiled again, less sadly. "You're a good friend."

"I want to be." She couldn't remember the last time she had sat and just talked with Haley. The last time they had been alone together, they'd found Ian and Winsor in the woods, their clothing hanging from tree branches. Josh had frozen, unable to look away, unable to inhale, until Haley had taken her hand and drawn her away.

Josh shook the image from her mind. "If you ever need to talk, about the psychic stuff," she told Haley, "I'm here."

Haley reached out and hugged Josh, astonishing her. She couldn't recall Haley ever spontaneously hugging her. "He loved you a lot too," Haley said. "Even at the end."

Josh was still trying to make sense of his words when Haley stood up and walked toward the door. If he understood that Ian was dead, if he could reflect on it, why . . .

"Wait a sec," Josh said.

Haley hesitated before turning back, as if he knew what she would ask.

"Why do you pretend to be Ian?"

His expression was unreadable; too many emotions like too many beams of colored light shining on a single spot. "I don't," he said finally. He voice had dropped to a soft, broken halt. "It's just that—sometimes—Ian gets confused—*he thinks this is his body.*"

Thirty-one

The next day, Snitch got caught.

News of the arrest shot through the house, and within moments everyone was crammed into the first-floor living room watching the world's most exclusive cable channel, DWTV.

Even with her eyes fixed on the television, Josh was aware that the room looked strange—the carpet had been replaced that morning, but it was not quite the same shade as it had been before, and an old living-room set from the basement had been dragged upstairs.

The drapes on the windows were missing, which reminded her that Kerstel and her father—who had spent a good six months trying to pick out those curtains due to Lauren's complete indifference—probably didn't know about Snitch's arrest.

Laurentius had come home for a few hours of sleep and then returned to the hospital, where Kerstel continued to improve. During that time, he had thoroughly berated his elder daughter for kicking her elderly grandfather in the chest. But Josh had told her side of the story convincingly enough that she got the initial punishment—a month's grounding—knocked down to being made responsible for making sure everyone ate breakfast while Kerstel was in the hospital.

"No way!" Will said when she told him. "They really do let you off for everything."

"Seriously," muttered Deloise, who'd lost a week's allowance after Lauren saw the outfit she'd worn to the dance.

Winsor's parents were taking turns staying with her; when news of Snitch's capture reached the house, Saidy was at the hospital and Alex was home, leaning forward out of the big armchair to get a better look at the TV.

The hospital televisions certainly didn't get DWTV. It only aired on televisions that had been carefully modified to pick up what even SETI would think was pure static, and it was run entirely by dream walkers. Josh had always been disappointed that the programming resembled C-SPAN more than the Discovery Channel, but for news from the dream-walker world, it was the only place to go.

After all, what other station would have reported the arrest of a tall man in a green-black trench coat on charges of anarchistic use of an inter-universal gateway?

The TV screen showed Snitch in steel shackles being dragged down a hallway by two men in Gendarmerie uniforms who strained to force him forward. His gas mask had been removed—curiously, it had been replaced by a white cloth face mask—but he still wore his trench coat, and it looked slick, as if he had just come in from the rain. His glassy black eyes stared vacantly into the camera.

"Is he contagious or something?" Will asked. He was sitting on the couch with Whim and Haley, and Josh was sitting on the floor in front of him, sandwiched between his ankles. She let her hands rest lightly on his shoes, and every so often he gave her shoulders a little squeeze with his knees.

"What's wrong with his eyes?" Alex asked, still watching the TV.

"I don't know," Whim told his father, "but they creep me the hell out."

"Whim," Alex said with a tired sigh that suggested he didn't expect to be heeded, "try to watch the language."

Josh tried to focus on the reporter's words as he began the story from the top. "For those of you just joining us, one of the elusive criminals known only as the trench-coat men has been caught. He was apprehended at seven thirty-five this evening by Rhianwen Girstelul in Victoria Town."

"That's right near Charle," Josh said.

"Near your mom's cabin?" Will asked.

"Yeah," Josh said, startled by the reminder that Will knew the whole story.

The reporter continued. "Requests for a statement from the man have been denied by the junta until after he's been questioned by the Gendarmerie. When asked why the man's gas mask has been replaced with a sterile mask, junta spokesman Elio Haviera-tyoti declined to comment."

"Remind me what the Gendarmerie is?" Will asked, pronouncing the word uncertainly.

"Dream-walker police," Josh said.

"And our only hope if we ever need to revolt against the junta," Whim added.

"Whim," Alex said with another sigh, "try to watch the treason talk."

"We do know," the reporter said, "that Ms. Girstelul apprehended the man while he was trying to gas her mother in the backyard of their home."

The camera zoomed in on a canister with carrying straps sitting on a metal table. Josh heard Haley inhale sharply, and he slid down from the couch to sit next to her on the floor. "Josh," he whispered. "Josh, look."

"Yeah," she agreed, distracted by one of Will's hands weighing on her shoulder. They had been finding little reasons to touch each other all afternoon while pretending that wasn't what they were doing.

Haley tugged the sleeve of her shirt. "No, *look*."

The camera had panned back to Snitch. "What?" Josh asked, tearing her eyes away to look at Haley.

His breathing was fast and shallow. "That's . . . that's . . ." he began. Then his chest heaved as if he might throw up, and he fumbled for his pad and pen.

A second later Josh had the note in her hand. The lack of date and address alone would have told her how important Haley considered the content.

Winsor is in the canister.

She looked at him, speechless. Haley, of course, couldn't bring himself to say anything. He dashed off another note.

GET HER!

Josh climbed to her feet, the notes still in her hand. "Will, you want to help me and Haley make some sandwiches?"

"Sandwiches?" Will asked, but when he looked at her, she widened her eyes at him and he added, "Yeah, let's make everybody sandwiches."

When the three of them were alone in the kitchen, Josh put the slips of paper into Will's hand. "Read these," she said, keeping her voice low.

Will's face grew pale as he read the notes. Haley's eyes were wild. His chest throbbed on the verge of hyperventilation. He stood in the kitchen doorway until Will gestured him closer.

"Okay," Will said to Haley, "it's good that you told us this. Can you breathe a little slower? Josh, would you get him something to drink?"

Josh was willing to accept that Haley had psychic powers, but she didn't feel like she had any idea how to help him deal with them. That was Will's department. She just went to the fridge and poured a cup of the cran-raspberry juice Haley liked.

The glass rattled against Haley's teeth while he gulped. "You're going to help her, right?" he asked. "She's trapped in there. In the canister. It's like a cage."

"Yes," Will told him. "Josh and I are going to help."

Haley nodded. His eyes never left Will's face, and Josh was startled to realize that Haley trusted Will. Something had changed dramatically between them.

"So you're saying that the man in the trench coat, Snitch, put Winsor in the canister?"

"Her *soul*. Her *soul*'s in the canister."

Josh frowned, alarmed by the idea—incredible as it was—of someone messing with Winsor's soul. "Why did they put her soul in the canister?" Will asked.

Haley struggled, more with understanding than with words, it seemed. "She's . . . fuel? Or . . . power? I don't know."

Josh met Will's eyes. "Having her soul in a canister might explain Winsor's coma."

"It might explain all the CSAD patients' comas," Will agreed. To Haley, he said, "What do we need to do to help?"

"Get them out," Haley said without hesitation.

"Out of the canister. Good. By just opening it?"

"I . . . don't know." Haley's voice rose with panic. "I'm not sure!"

"That's okay," Will said soothingly. "We can figure that out once we get a hold of the canister. Do you think you can put the souls back in their bodies?"

Haley shrugged helplessly. "I don't know if it works like that."

Will squeezed Haley's upper arms in one of those guy not-hugs. "It's gonna be okay. Josh and I are going to help you, right Josh?"

"Definitely," Josh said. "I'll call Davita and see if we can get a hold of this canister." She opened the family address book and shuffled through the mess of business cards, looking for Davita's.

"Thank you," Haley said, and he heaved a great sigh. "I need to get a—get ready." He turned and fled the room.

"Well," Will said. "That was unexpected."

"Yeah."

Josh set down the address book without finding Davita's card. She turned to face Will. "I need to say something."

Will's eyes widened with alarm.

Rather than reassuring him, Josh launched in. "Thank you. For whatever you did that made Haley feel like he can trust you, and he could tell you about the"—she glanced at the kitchen door to make sure they weren't overheard—"psychic thing, and made him realize he can talk instead of writing notes: thank you."

Will's lips were parted and speechless.

"You're a good friend," Josh said. "To both of us."

She hesitated for a moment, then stepped forward and hugged him. His flannel shirt was soft against her cheek.

He tightened his arms around her. "I try to be."

And he was good—not just to Haley but to her. Since she'd found out that his apprenticeship wasn't predicted in her scroll, she had begun to realize how much she had held that prediction against him. Her fear had blinded her to the fact that, however he had come into her life, they were learning to be a good team. The way he always saw the best in her made her feel like she didn't have to be strong and hard and perfect. Maybe, despite her mistakes, she was good enough as she was.

She tilted her head back to smile at him, and he smiled in return, but neither of them made any move to let go of each other. Josh remembered the time she had impulsively hugged him after they'd finished fixing up his bedroom. He hadn't been sure how to respond then, but this time it was different. This time he knew her secrets and her faults, and when she let her head fall back the way she had before, this time he kissed her.

A good friend indeed.

He kissed her with careful tenderness at first, cupping her face between his palms like she was a sweet, wild bird he was afraid to spook. Josh felt the fine trembling in the muscles in his hands and knew he was restraining himself the way he had for weeks now.

Well, she'd had enough of that. They both had. Josh pushed his hands away from her face so that she could wrap her arms around his neck, holding him close and deepening the kiss. That was all the permission Will needed; he scooped her up and set her on the counter next to the stove so that they were the same height. Josh locked her ankles behind his knees and he slid one hand under the hem of her sweater and splayed his palm out against the small of her back. Josh shivered, a flush breaking out all over her body, and Will paused just long enough to smile at her reaction. Then they were kissing again, in a thrilling panic, and he—

"Oh—heavens to Betsy!" Deloise cried, and Will jumped back three feet, managing to break out of the circle of Josh's legs.

"Hey!" Whim protested from the doorway. "You aren't making us sandwiches!"

"We're sorry," Deloise said, regaining her composure. She started backing herself and Whim—both of them grinning—into the living room.

"It's all right," Josh told her, although she felt her flush becoming an outright blush.

"Yeah, we'll go now," Deloise said, but before she left she couldn't resist adding, "Looks like you guys are doing some heavy training." Whim cackled with laughter.

Alone, neither Josh nor Will said anything, but he walked back to the counter, where she sat with her head down. She couldn't bring herself to look at him. He grazed her hot cheek with the backs of his fingers, then ran the tip of his thumb over her lips, and when she smiled he let his forehead fall against hers.

"Was that out of line?" he asked in a voice just above a whisper.

"No." She put her hands on his shoulders, then slid them onto his neck, feeling the warmth of his skin. She didn't know how she could feel so shy and so bold at the same time.

"Good. But maybe I should go, because if I don't . . ."

"I won't get around to calling Davita?" Josh asked, daring to look up at him. He smiled at her, and the happiness in his expression caught her off guard. Had *she* made him that happy?

"Yeah. So maybe I'll go wait for you."

"I'll find you," she promised, remembering what he'd said the night they met, and they both laughed a little unsteadily. She couldn't resist laying a kiss on the corner of his mouth.

Still wearing that look of happiness—and what else? Contentment?—Will left her to go wait in the living room. Josh pressed her palms to her burning cheeks.

I hope I'm ready for this, she thought.

Oh, but she'd felt ready in the moment. She'd had no doubts when they were holding each other. Only now did she begin to second-guess herself.

Her heart was still beating quickly when she looked up and saw Haley standing in the other doorway, trying to scramble back into the hallway before Josh noticed him.

His expression was crushed.

"Haley—" she said. Josh dashed after him, but he made it to the stairwell before she caught up.

"Wait a sec." She grabbed his sleeve, and he shook her off. "Haley, wait."

She jumped up two stairs and managed to trap him by putting her hands against the wall on either side of his shoulders.

He wouldn't even look at her. He tried to duck under one of her arms, and she twisted to block him. "Haley, please."

Still refusing to meet her eyes, he said, "Ian saw you in the kitchen with Will."

Oh my god.

Her heart couldn't beat fast enough to keep pace with her panic.

But Haley didn't go on, and she had to say something. "That wasn't how it looked."

Although, of course, it had been.

A transformation ran over Haley. He tilted his head forward and looked at her from beneath his brows. A sardonic smile twisted his mouth. "I suppose you were using him, too?" he asked in a low, dangerous voice.

"No, that's not . . ."

Sometimes—Ian gets confused—he thinks this is his body.

Josh had tried to block out Haley's revelation from the night before. The idea frightened her too much to contemplate it for more than an instant. But now she had to accept that if Haley wasn't delusional—if he was truly psychic—then these moments when he acted like Ian weren't the result of a defense mechanism. He really was . . .

Josh couldn't deal with the thought. She pushed it away.

"Ian's dead," she said. "He died last summer."

The green flecks in his hazel eyes lit up like mica in firelight. "Is that what you tell yourself when you play the slut?" he hissed.

Josh was too stunned to reply, but when he tried to kiss her, she instinctively ducked. He lost his footing and stumbled down the stairs to the landing; she could almost feel the life rushing out of him as he passed her.

Haley hunched over, breathing hard. A combination of panic, pain, and helplessness made up his expression. Josh was almost afraid to approach him, but she made herself walk down the steps and place her hand on his shoulder.

He was refusing to look at her again. "Sorry."

Josh wanted to cry. "Can you stop him from doing that?" she asked.

Haley shook his head. "He doesn't mean to," he whispered. "He gets confused."

She stopped doubting Haley right then and there, because however painful losing Ian had been, having him here—like this—was worse. Haley would never have faked, or even subconsciously chosen, such a cruel tease.

"How did this happen?" Josh wondered aloud, and she was surprised when he answered.

"You," he said.

"Me?"

"You held on to him; you brought him back to the World. But he stays with me because we're twins. He thinks this is his body." Haley pressed his lips together and then added, "Sometimes I do too."

Josh, afraid of what—or whom—a hug might wake up in him, squeezed his shoulder.

"Josh?" Whim called from the kitchen.

After giving Haley one more squeeze, Josh ran down the steps to meet Whim. "I'm here."

Whim's cell phone was in his hand. "I just got a call from somebody inside the Gendarmerie who claims he knows Snitch's real identity."

Josh struggled to switch from Haley's paranormal phenomenon to Whim's conspiracy theories. "Do you believe him?"

"No way to know yet. But I want you to come with me to meet him."

Josh's brow furrowed. "Me? Why?"

"Because if he's telling the truth, you're going to want to hear what he has to say."

Thirty-two

Rain shook the sheet-glass windows of the all-night doughnut shop, and the temperature dropped ten degrees near the windows, but Whim had insisted that they sit in the darkest corner.

"He's going to be freaked out enough that I brought people with me," Whim had said, referring to his informant.

Will sat next to Josh with his hands wrapped around a giant cup of coffee, which was surprisingly good considering that the doughnut shop was located off a highway exit that also hosted a gas station, an abandoned diner, and exactly nothing else. The doughnuts were so good that they'd torn through six of them and then ordered a dozen more.

Josh was sitting next to Will and drinking a glass of milk so big it had come in a souvenir cup. She was in sugar heaven.

Something big had changed between them, as though once Josh's defenses had started to crack, they had crumbled completely. She sat close enough to Will that their arms brushed, and every so often she'd given him a private little smile. She was giving him one now as she asked if he wanted to split a Long John.

"Sure," Will said, even though he was fairly close to throwing up. He smiled back at her. He couldn't stop smiling at her.

"You two disgust me," Whim said. "Why don't you each start eating one end of the thing, and you can meet in the middle like in that movie with the dogs?"

Will looked at Josh and said, "Okay," and she gave an acquiescing shrug and stuck one end of the Long John in her mouth.

As Will leaned forward to capture the other end, Whim burst out, "Stop it! What the hell is wrong with you two tonight? If this guy comes in here and sees two people choking to death on the same doughnut, he's gonna bolt!"

Josh bit off her end of the Long John and, still chewing, said, "You need to chill out, Whim."

The end of her sentence was punctuated by jangling of the harness of bells attached to the door. "I think that's him," Whim hissed.

They waited while the young man who entered bought a cup of coffee and a bagel. "Who comes to Doughnut Heaven and buys a bagel?" Josh whispered. Will ignored the temptation to suck the frosting off her lower lip. Whim used a compact he usually carried into the Dream to covertly watch the man select a table and sit down.

"Okay," Whim said, snapping the compact shut. "I'm going in."

While he was at the man's table, Josh said, "He's so wound up. He thinks he's going to break some huge story. I'm sure this guy doesn't actually know anything."

Several minutes passed before Whim and the stranger came over to the table in the corner. "Josh, Will," Whim said, "this is, ah, Serpico."

Serpico was a short goth kid who couldn't have been more than twenty. He wore a long black duster, weighty black boots with soles three inches thick, and eyeliner that might actually have been Sharpie. He had a lot of piercings. A *lot*. Will figured that if somebody had run thread through all the holes in that guy's face, they probably could have made a dream catcher.

"Hi, Serpico," Josh said, with no trace of mockery; Will thought that maybe she didn't get the reference. "Want a bear claw?"

"Hell yes," he said, sitting down across from her. "This bagel blows."

"So," Whim said, "you said you work for the Gendarmerie. What rank do you hold?"

Serpico shook his head. "I don't have a rank, man. I'm an assistant janitor."

Josh looked like she was about to bust out laughing.

"So where is your information coming from?" Whim asked. "Are you reading official documents out of the trash?"

"Naw, naw, man, they shred all that stuff. But one of the other guys heard two bigwigs talking about it. He said the guy in the trench coat's real name was Geoffardus Simbarticolsi."

The name meant nothing to Will. He only realized it was significant because Whim looked at Josh for a reaction, and when Will did the same, he saw that the huge glass of milk was about to slide out of her hand. He caught it just in time.

"Geoff?" Josh repeated weakly. "You're certain they said it was Geoff?"

"Yeah. They went back and forth on telling his old lady, Mary."

"Marni," Josh corrected in an empty voice. "Her name's Marni."

When the table fell silent, Will asked, "Who's Geoff?"

"Everyone thought he was dead," Josh said. "He opened the archway at the cabin with my mother. But only Mom's body was found, so we thought Geoff was lost in the Dream."

"Yeah," said Serpico, "I heard some stuff about a cabin. The Gendarme cap wants to storm it, but some old guy on the junta's blocking her."

The light came back into Josh's eyes, but it was fueled by anger. "There's more than one old guy on the junta," Whim warned.

"More than one who would stop the captain of the guard from storming the cabin?" Josh asked. "Don't you see what happened? Somehow Mom and Geoff cut two archways, one to the Dream and one to Feodor's universe. Geoff got trapped inside Feodor's universe, and Feodor did something to Geoff to turn him into . . . whatever he is now."

"Then why didn't Feodor just come walking out?" Whim asked.

"They might not have finished that archway. It might only open in one direction."

"But Geoff made it into the Dream," Will pointed out.

"That's true," Josh admitted, thinking. "But not for years. Not until—"

"Oh, damn," Whim said. Will had never heard his voice full of dread before.

"That night at the cabin," Josh said, her voice growing increasingly monotone, "what if we opened the archway to Feodor's universe instead of the Dream? And then, when Ian went inside, we thought he was marking the other side of the archway, but he could have been opening an archway to the Dream. . . ."

And then, breathlessly: "They never found Ian's body."

This can't be happening, Will thought. *Everything she's gone through . . . there can't be another blow waiting for her. I have to stop this.*

He watched helplessly as Josh's face changed, as all the guilt and self-blame she'd released in the limo came back into her expression.

Whim coughed, then gagged, then got himself under control. "No, no way," he said.

He looked almost as freaked out as Josh, and Will remembered that Whim had been Ian's best friend. "The guy we call Gloves," Will said, "is he Ian's height?"

Josh nodded.

"What about eyes—we haven't see his eyes. Or his face. What about how he walks?"

"He fights like Ian," Josh said. "Like he's had training." She stared at the tabletop and the plate of doughnuts. "I have to get out of here," she said, and then she ran out of Doughnut Heaven.

In the car, Josh shot back down the highway at breakneck speed and with a ferocious attitude. Will tried to look at her and not at the road; it was harder to block out the honks of outraged drivers.

"Josh," he said, "you can't go after Feodor."

She didn't reply.

"I'm dead serious. This is when we call Davita and tell her to send in the troops."

"Will's right," Whim said from the backseat.

"No." Josh swung the car around with such speed that Will's stomach didn't know which way to lurch. "What has Davita managed so far? She couldn't even get Peregrine to listen to us. I can't trust her."

I *can't trust her. Not* we *can't trust her.*

"Are you listening to yourself?" Whim cried. "You're a seventeen-year-old kid who just got off crutches, and your grandma just died, and you'll probably totally freak out when you see Ian. You can't do this."

The highway lights caught her pale eyes, giving them a yellow, wolfish glow. "I can. I have to—"

"*No,*" Will said, and he said it in a tone he remembered his father using before his parents divorced.

Josh turned to stare at him, and he shouted, "Look at the road!"

She looked back at the road just in time to avoid rear-ending a truck full of horses, but the line of her mouth remained hard and stubborn.

"You don't *have to,* Josh," Will said, sounding like his father again. "I don't care if you opened that archway knowing exactly where it led and shoved Ian inside—you're not the person to fix this. You're exhausted, and you've had one shock after another today, and you're going home to bed. *Ian is dead.* Gloves isn't the Ian you knew; he's a zombie."

The volume of his voice made the car's interior feel all the more silent when he stopped. Will felt ashamed of himself as soon as he finished. He was her apprentice, not her father.

But if Lauren had been there, he probably would have been cheering Will on.

"That's just terrific," Josh said finally. Her tone burned like acid. "Thanks for your loyalty, Will. I suppose you'll physically restrain me?"

He didn't want to hurt her. But he wanted even less to see Gloves and Feodor hurt her.

Josh must have taken his silence for the answer it was, because she said, spitting venom, "Never mind. An outsider wouldn't understand."

Will gritted his teeth to keep from arguing with her.

"Whim, what about you?"

Whim's voice was firm. "You know I love you like my own little sister, Josh, but this is freaking suicide and I'm not letting you do it, even if I have to tie you to a chair."

"God, you were his *best friend*, Whim. Who lets their best friend live as a zombie puppet?"

"It's not Ian!" Whim shouted. "That thing isn't Ian anymore!"

Josh and Whim fought the rest of the ride home, but Will sat in silence. He thought of a dozen more good reasons why Josh shouldn't go into Feodor's universe and didn't voice any of them, because he knew his reasoning was logical and that Josh wasn't acting according to logic just then. She was a hurt animal—a tiger willing to destroy the jungle to get a thorn out of its paw.

And he knew she would destroy him, too, if he got in her way.

At the house, Josh vanished into her bedroom. No slammed door, no shouting. Whim found Deloise and Haley, and he and Will told them what they'd learned. Deloise cried. Haley just closed his eyes. The four of them sat vigil in the living room between Josh's bedroom and the apartment door.

"I still don't understand how all of this works," Deloise said. "There are three archways at the cabin?"

"No, there are only two," Whim said. "But there's a third between Feodor's universe and the Dream."

"Hang on," Will said. "I have something that might help."

He retrieved the diagram of the three universes that Josh had drawn for him during their first lesson and laid it out on the coffee table.

With a pencil, he added another circle. "So, Jona and Geoff built an archway between the cabin and the Dream. That one goes both ways, but they also accidentally built an archway to Feodor's universe, which is this fourth circle. That archway only opens one way, so you can only enter Feodor's universe through it. You can't come back into the World using it."

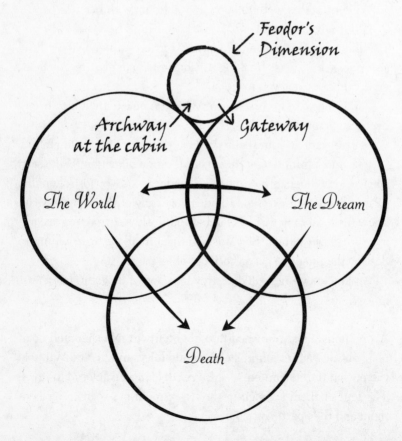

"But Josh said that Ian cut an archway on that side," Deloise pointed out. "When he was in Feodor's universe."

"Right," Will said. He added an arrow to the diagram. "He cut a one-way archway between Feodor's universe and the Dream."

"So the only way into Feodor's universe is through the cabin," Whim said, "and the only way out is through the Dream."

"Also right."

"And Ian's . . . some sort of zombie?" Deloise asked miserably, wiping her eyes again.

"Ian stays with me," Haley said quietly. "Feodor only got his body."

Ian's scroll makes perfect sense now, Will thought. He was contemplating the last two lines—*Death has her own tales to tell / but those I do not know so well*—when Josh's bedroom door opened.

She'd been crying; tears still glistened along her jawline. "I'm going downstairs to walk," she said. "You can follow me down there if you want, but please leave me alone while I'm dream walking."

They all trooped down the stairs after her. At the archroom door, she said, "All right, that's far enough."

Whim and Deloise looked at each other and shrugged.

Josh shut the vault door.

"Something's wrong," Haley said.

Will had the same feeling. He glanced at the archroom door, wondering what he'd missed. "Maybe she really is just going to walk a couple of nightmares. I mean, that's how she usually works off stress."

"I can't imagine her giving up that easily," Whim said.

"Impossible," Deloise added.

They stood together in silence for almost a minute. Will kept thinking about the nightmare in which she'd turned a beer cooler into an exit. She'd taken the cases of beer out, then climbed inside. . . . But what did that have to do with their current situation?

Once she'd made the beer cooler door lead somewhere, she and Will had been able to use it to create an exit from the Dream. But they'd already triggered Chyman's Dilemma, so they didn't come out of the Dream in the basement. . . .

"She's going to the cabin," Will said with sudden conviction. "Josh is going to trigger Chyman's Dilemma and try to exit through the archway in the cabin."

"What?" Whim said. "That's not possible."

What could Will do but shrug? "She's Josh. And we did it once before by accident. She could do it again."

Haley turned and tapped his code into the keypad on the door. But when they entered the white room, the archway was empty. Josh had already gone into a nightmare and triggered Chyman's Dilemma, breaking the archway's *ligamus* hold on her. She had allowed the Dream to swallow her up.

"No!" Deloise cried. She checked her watch. "The cabin is an hour's drive away."

Will had a better idea. "I can use the looking stone to find her in the Dream."

"No way," Whim said. "That's insanely hard."

"I'm Josh's apprentice," Will said shortly. "I can do this. Do you have a lighter and mirror?"

Haley touched his pants pockets. "Yes. I'm coming with you."

"So am I," Whim said.

"We can't all go," Will pointed out. "Somebody has to stay here and get in touch with Davita. We need her to send the Gendarmerie into Feodor's universe as backup."

"I'll stay," Deloise said, though she looked ashamed of herself. "I want to come, but . . . I don't think I can handle seeing Ian like that."

"It's okay," Whim said, putting his arm around her shoulders. "You'll make an excellent ground person."

Deloise hugged each of them and said, "You guys bring her back, okay?"

Haley nodded. Whim promised. Will just hugged Deloise again and whispered, "You know I'm not ready to lose her yet."

"I know," she whispered back. "And I always knew I'd have a brother someday."

Will blinked back the tears in his eyes.

Minutes later, standing in front of the archway, he pressed his hand to the looking stone and felt it warm to his touch. The milky red glass grew soft and melted into another palm pressing back against his.

The Dream shimmered into view, and Will had to close his eyes to avoid seasickness. He ignored the images it was sending him—the terrors and the fears and the darkness. He blocked out everything it was trying to say. Instead, he sent himself into the stone with a message:

Find Josh.

He gathered around himself his sense of her, his memories. Her voice, her focus, her nervous tics. Her unflinching protection of those she loved. The scent of hot chocolate in the morning. Her pale, gossamer-green eyes. The feel of her forehead buried in his shoulder. Her unexpected—and unexpectedly sweet—kiss.

I'll find you, Josh.

He sent his heart into the void, searching for hers.

Thirty-three

Josh hit the Dream hard and fast. She barely knew where she was going before she jumped in, which proved to be a mistake.

A bedroom decorated for a child. A grown woman cowered in the corner, her tearstained face lit by the lights of a rotating star map. Pink block letters on the open door spelled out the name Tanessa.

The woman took no notice of Josh. Downstairs, a plate shattered. People shouted.

Josh didn't want to be there. She'd chosen this particular nightmare because she sensed it was nearing its end, and she needed to sit through the end of a nightmare to trigger Chyman's Dilemma and break *ligamus*. For the first time in her life, she walked into a nightmare and completely ignored the dreamer's fear. She was here on a mission other than resolution.

Will didn't understand. She had opened the archway to Feodor's universe, she had let Ian go in first, and if Ian's body was trapped doing Feodor's business, it was her fault. If his spirit was haunting Haley, it might still be possible to reunite him with his body, but even if not, she couldn't leave Ian like this—hurting, roaming, soulless. He wouldn't have wanted to be a puppet.

Sobbing, the woman Tanessa crawled under the bed. Josh fought the urge to hurry her. Will might be a coldhearted traitor, but he wasn't stupid. He was going to figure out what she was doing quickly enough.

From the floor below, a shot rang out. Instinctively, Josh dropped to the floor. Tanessa screamed, her voice muffled by the bed skirt.

Footsteps pounded up the stairs.

Josh realized she had made a serious mistake. She hadn't thought this dream had a villain—she'd thought the woman was dreaming of her parents fighting. But apparently the situation was much worse. Josh could only hope that whoever was coming upstairs didn't enter the bedroom.

Dozens of dolls and stuffed animals filled the shelves on the walls. As the footsteps approached the bedroom door, a baby doll in a sparkly dress called out in a whisper, "She's here!"

The other toys echoed—and within seconds, a chorus of "She's under the bed! Here she is!" sang through the room.

Oh, shit! Josh's eyes searched the room for a hiding place. The closet—too far away. The desk—not big enough to hide beneath. The door—

Not a good option either, but her only one. She ducked behind the bedroom door and pulled it in front of herself just in time to hear a revolver being cocked. Through the crack between the door and wall, she saw a fleeting dark shadow as a man entered the room.

Josh shut her eyes, but she couldn't block out the fear flooding the Dream. It made her heartsick.

Save her! Josh's instinct screamed, as loud as she'd ever heard it. *Save her! Save her!*

The fear swelled up around her, filling the room to the ceiling like a red haze. Josh clenched her hands around her plumeria pendant to keep from flinging the door away.

This was actually quite close to how the dream-walker royals had proven their worthiness to rule: by sitting through nightmare after nightmare, doing nothing, for one day and one night. Supposedly, enduring the pain and fear of so many dreamers would make them compassionate.

Josh didn't buy that any monarch had ever passed that test. No one could stand this agony for very long. It was unbearable.

You were meant to save her, Josh's instinct whispered. *You must save her.*

The man lifted one corner of the footboard and threw the whole bed across the room.

"Daddy!" Tanessa wailed.

The revolver went off. The wailing stopped, replaced by a gurgling sound.

Something sick and sharp cut through Josh, and she accidentally let her forehead fall against the back of the bedroom door, sending the door swinging.

Tanessa's father spun around, aiming the gun at Josh's chest. Behind him, she saw Tanessa lying on the floor, blood pouring from her mouth.

Wake up, Josh thought. *Wakeupwakeupwakeup!*

But Tanessa didn't wake up, and her father shot Josh in the chest.

She felt her breastbone crushed against her heart and lungs, making it impossible to inhale. Her knees buckled and she sank toward the floor.

Then the nightmare ended, and Josh went tumbling, legs scooped out from under her.

She landed on her back on the ground, a sharp stick poking into her back. Above her, tree branches encroached on a dreamy blue-and-white sky. The Dream had shifted, and she'd landed in a forest. Her chest hurt worse than ever, but she managed to lift her hand and find the bullet, still hot . . . caught in the center of the Kevlar vest Davita had given her for her birthday.

Best birthday present ever, Josh decided. The vest wasn't more than a quarter of an inch thick and felt like nothing more than several dozen sheets of thin plastic tarp stuck together; Josh couldn't imagine how it had stopped a bullet. But she was grateful that it had. Very, very grateful.

If she hadn't been lying on the ground just then, she might not have heard the hoofbeats soon enough. As it happened, she rolled out of the way just in time for a cavalry unit in Confederate uniforms to trample the grass where she'd been lying. The dreamer, a shirtless young man riding a slow-trotting donkey, followed behind them. He was trying to pull on his uniform while keeping hold of his rifle and forcing the donkey to run faster.

Josh, safely crouched in the bushes, touched the Dream's fear just enough to test it—a simple old "running late" dream.

Winsor would have stopped to resolve this one, she thought, recalling her friend's odd compassion for humiliation nightmares. Dejected, she got to her feet and began trudging after the cavalry.

"Josh!" a familiar voice shouted behind her.

Impossible, she thought. There was no way Will could have reached her once she'd broken *ligamus.*

But she turned to look, and he had. Not only that, but he had brought Haley and Whim along. They were trekking through the woods toward her.

"What the hell are you doing?" she demanded, more frustrated than angry. But a small part of her was glad to see them, especially Will. She'd gotten used to having him around in-Dream.

But she was still planning to knock him unconscious at the first opportunity.

"I found you!" Will said, looking pleased with himself.

"How?" Josh asked.

He held up his left hand.

It took Josh a moment to understand. "You used the looking stone?" she asked. "That's not even possible."

"That's what I said," Whim replied.

They met in a small clearing. Josh crossed her arms.

"You're not going to stop me," she told them all. Whim and Will exchanged glances.

"Here's the thing," Whim said. "Haley and I have spent the last seven months drinking piña coladas on the beach, gorging on French pastries, and avoiding physical exercise; and Will's still in training—"

"We aren't sure we can take you," Will summarized. "And we don't want to tire you out before you face Feodor. So we agreed that the best chance of keeping you alive is to back you up."

Josh softened. She had already begun to feel ashamed of how she had spoken to her friends in the car, and now she felt like a royal jerk. She couldn't deny that some of Will's concerns had merit, but she still felt honor bound to save Ian.

"Do you understand why I have to do this?" she asked.

"Because every second Ian's body is walking around doing Feodor's work is an insult to the person he once was?" Will suggested lightly.

She blinked, astonished to realize that Will did, in fact, understand.

"I get it, Josh," he told her. "But I still think it's a bad idea."

"That's why you're the apprentice," she said, and started walking deeper into the woods.

Thirty-four

They worked their way across the Dream, waiting for a nightmare to resolve and drop them into another, creating a porthole there to see if it opened to the cabin in Charle, finding that it did not, and waiting out another nightmare. After an hour, Josh finally poked her head through the Veil and saw the fire-gutted basement of the cabin.

"Go," she ordered, and they all went.

Josh climbed through and landed on a concrete floor. Around her stood the half-demolished remains of her mother's burned cabin—everything black and smelling faintly of woodsmoke even now, the stairs to the second floor impassable, the ceiling burned away to reveal a half-moon.

"Do you have a plan?" Whim asked. "Because truthfully, I was sort of hoping the Gendarmerie would get here before we did."

"Find Feodor. If he'll give himself up to the Gendarmerie, we take him to the house and call Peregrine." She wasn't thrilled by the idea of involving her grandfather, but she doubted Feodor would give himself up anyway. "If he won't give up, we kill him."

"Do you think you're capable of killing a real person?" Will asked.

"If I have to," she said, although she wasn't certain. She'd killed nightmares before; she hoped that would serve as enough experience to give her the nerve to kill a real person.

"What about Ian?" Whim asked.

"You mean Ian's *body*," Will corrected.

Josh thought hard, avoiding Will's gaze. "Haley?" she asked. "Can we save him?"

In a small voice, Haley said, "I don't know."

"We'll deal with Ian when we find him," Josh said with forced nonchalance. "The first thing we have to do is make sure that Feodor can't keep creating . . . whatever he's creating."

"Zombies," Will said pointedly.

Josh's palms flushed and she gritted her teeth to keep from telling Will that she would be fine; that whatever Feodor threw at her, she could handle; that she knew the difference between Ian's body and his soul. But she couldn't say that for certain. Whim had been right in the car when he said that she didn't really know what she would do when she saw Ian.

But she wanted to find out.

She pulled out her lighter and compact and sent a beam of light toward the air she had stepped through moments before. The archways here had no stone frames, no edge markings, but she knew approximately where they should be.

The Dream opened back onto the nightmare they'd come out of. "Haley, try your keys while I keep this archway open," Josh said. Haley shone another light in the same direction, and a second archway appeared.

Twin images floated side by side—one for each eye, a soundtrack for each ear. Josh saw the Dream through one Veil, and through the other, she saw Feodor's universe and the same dark room she had walked into eight months before, where one high dormer window let in a few rays of light.

"Last time, Feodor attacked as soon as we entered," she said. "So stay close to—"

She broke off as the scene through the archway changed. The view slid, like a camera zooming and panning, then stopped high above a narrow, rubble-filled street with crumbling concrete buildings on either side and chimneys shooting into the smoky sky. Burning wreckage reflected orange light off the dark clouds and the glittering, diamondlike raindrops falling on the city.

Close to them, only a few feet below the archway, Feodor stood on a rooftop. He wore a white shirt with brown pinstripe slacks and a matching vest, all drenched with water, and he held a golden watch attached by a chain to his pocket.

"Every nine seconds," he declared, his eyes on the city below. A squadron of planes flew overhead. Josh couldn't see them against the utterly black sky, but she heard them. Feodor raised his voice. "That is how often a bomb hits Warsaw during these air raids. Every nine seconds."

Though he must have already been aware of them, he slid his watch back into his pocket and looked up at the archway as if surprised.

"Hello again, children. Ah, you've brought friends—oh!" Feodor smiled, suddenly near laughter. "How much one of your friends looks like a friend of mine!"

His amusement stole some of Josh's confidence. She'd expected to fight with him, but she'd hoped to do it with her fists. Feodor's joke reminded her that he was mad in addition to being dangerous. In fact, his insanity almost certainly made him more dangerous. Josh met Will's eyes, and he gave a little shake of his head. *We don't have to go in,* he seemed to say.

"Are you going to come and visit this time?" Feodor asked. "Or just stare through my window like vagrants again?"

He backed up a few feet to give them room to climb onto the roof, bowing his head graciously as he moved. Josh placed herself in front of the ragged archway and then gave a little jump the way she usually did at home, and her cross-trainers landed solidly on the rooftop.

Once inside, she heard far-off sounds that had previously been masked by the rain: bombs exploding, buildings crumbling, an air-raid siren. The rain stank of stomach bile and each drop bit her skin where it landed, like a mosquito. Josh drew her arms close to her body and ducked her head down.

Feodor smiled, his gray eyes large and round, his eyelashes sparkling with rainwater. He made her a little bow. "Welcome to Warsaw," he said. "Of course, your friend is welcome also, since we are already acquaintances. And your other friend, he must come as well, to meet his doppelgänger. But who is this stranger you have brought with you?"

"His name is Whim," Josh said flatly as Will and then Haley joined her on the rooftop. "You sucked his sister's soul out."

Feodor took the accusation in stride, merely giving an admissive nod. "Even so, I think that perhaps our party is large enough." He called toward the archway, "It was a pleasure to meet you! Please give my regards to your sister!"

"Wha—?" Whim cried, but the archway closed and cut him off.

That's not good, Josh thought. Feodor could control who entered his universe, which meant he could probably also control who left it. Before she could figure out what to do about that, Feodor turned and called, *"Kapuścisko!"*

Josh didn't know what that meant—he might have been calling out "Abracadabra!" in Polish for all she knew.

But then she saw the man she had called Gloves. He walked across the roof to Feodor, who threw an arm jocularly around Gloves's shoulder. Rainwater shone on his green-black trench coat, and mud he hadn't bothered to scrape off clung to his boots.

Now that Josh knew who he was, she could see Ian in him—the right height, the right build, even a black curl sneaking out from under the brim of his black-banded fedora.

"I call him Kapuścisko," Feodor said, "since he never told me his name. It means 'little cabbage.' The French use it as a term of endearment."

Josh didn't care what the French did. She knew from Feodor's smile exactly why he'd chosen the name.

Because cabbage was all Feodor had left of Ian.

Ian was a vegetable.

Josh walked straight over to Gloves. He didn't move; she wasn't even certain he was looking at her. She stood helplessly before him, trying to reconcile Ian's hazel eyes with the black ones she saw now—endless void eyes, literally soulless. His eyes held nothing when he looked at Josh.

"Take off your mask," Josh said.

"And your gloves," Feodor added.

Gloves obeyed. He loosened the mask and let it swing from a strap around his neck, then pulled off his gloves and put them in his pocket.

Ian's face—so like Haley's, and yet so different—no longer

resembled either one of them. The features were slack, disinterested, and so pale that Josh wondered if the sun ever rose in Warsaw. A rough pink outline of the gas mask ran from under his chin to the bridge of his nose and back again.

Feodor reached out and lifted Gloves's left hand—Josh still could not think of him as Ian—to show her his palm. An oval-shaped scar, like a burn, marked his skin.

"Are you the one who pulled him back?" Feodor asked Josh in a low, intimate tone. "An astonishing act, to hold so tightly to another that you tear him from his skin. Your passion quite inspired me."

Josh wanted to touch Ian's hand, but her own hands refused to move. She recognized his fingers; the shape of his thumb; his nails, though they had grown strangely long; the tiny scar on his inner wrist where his watch buckle had cut him.

Earlier, she'd thought that there was no way to predict how she would react when she saw Ian. If asked, she might have listed any number of possibilities.

Disappointment would not have been among them.

She'd come here to save Ian, but Ian wasn't here. The trench-coat-clad boy wore Ian's face beneath strands of Ian's curling black hair and held out Ian's hand to her, but he wasn't Ian. He might have recognized her intellectually, but he didn't look at her with love.

Feodor had done this to Ian. Anger flooded Josh like a torrent of black fire running through her body.

"What did you do to him?" she asked Feodor.

Feodor shrugged. "Very little. You were the one who tore out his soul. Such things are possible, in the moment one moves between universes. But you left me his body, which has been most obedient and helpful. I hope that seeing him this way doesn't make you sad." He circled her, his steps even and graceful.

Haley hesitantly approached Gloves, looking at his twin brother as if afraid of what he would see. Gloves's eyes flicked toward Haley.

Feodor spoke to Gloves. "Kapuścisko, meet Kapuścisko." Then to Haley: "Kapuś—"

Haley exploded.

"Don't call him that!" he shouted at Feodor. "Don't you *ever* call him that! His name is Hianselian Micharainosa! He is not your little cabbage!"

Will and Josh both grabbed Haley's arms to keep him from a full-on assault.

Feodor laughed and leaned his head on Gloves's shoulder, which only made Josh and Will's job harder. Then he slowly straightened, examining Haley with the first sign of seriousness Josh had seen in him.

"Or was it *you* who held on to little Hianselian's soul?" Feodor asked. "For I see his *duch,* his spirit, all around you."

Haley inched behind Will, as if he could hide Ian's spirit from Feodor's sight.

"But he has changed, I think," Feodor continued. "I think he is your *anioł stróż* now, your . . ."

"My guardian angel," Haley whispered, and Feodor smiled, delighted.

"Just so. Who says American children are stupid?" He gave Gloves a slap on the back and said, "Come, smart American children, let me show you my work."

"We aren't here to see your work," Josh snapped. "We're here to bring Ian home, and arrest you and take you back to the World to stand trial."

"You cannot remove me from this universe without causing its collapse," Feodor told her. He smiled with just one corner of his mouth. "And I suspect there are things here that you would like to see preserved."

With that, he took off across the rooftop, skirting piles of soot-stained rubble and collapsed chimneys. Gloves followed.

Josh watched them with frustration for a moment. She'd had some idea that she could beat the location of the gate to the Dream out of Feodor, but now she realized how ridiculous that plan had been. Feodor would gladly die without telling her what she needed to know for the sake of his own amusement. Right now, they had no choice but to play his game.

"Are you all right?" Josh asked Haley, concerned by his outburst. But Haley didn't even look at her, just took off after his brother.

"Okay, new plan?" Will asked as they followed.

"We'll have to take them both at once. But not yet. We need to find out where the gate to the Dream is first."

"It could be anywhere," Will pointed out. "Warsaw is a big city."

Josh let her gaze drift across the blocks of rubble, where the fires of burning buildings illuminated columns of smoke, wrecked structures, overturned cars, and objects so thoroughly ruined that Josh couldn't even identify them. Yes, it could take a very long time to find a single gate in all of that.

Feodor led them across the rooftop to a rickety iron fire escape that, against all odds, had survived the every-nine-second bombings. Despite her misgivings, Josh climbed down the wet, rusty stairs, holding the railing at all times. Finally, they reached the street level of the stone-fronted building, and Feodor held open the door while ushering them inside.

"Kapu—I'm sorry, Hianselian, the lights, if you please. Welcome to my laboratory, children."

Feodor's laboratory looked like a cross between Josh's high school chem lab and a Victorian parlor. The ashes-of-roses wallpaper clashed with the metal tables, and the Tiffany lamps shed colored light on glass beakers and broken mirrors. In one corner, Josh recognized the shrouded form of Feodor's physical body resting on a table.

The far wall of the laboratory was made of clear glass and looked into a room that reminded Josh of the archroom at home—white floors and walls. But it was empty inside.

"Apologies for the mess," Feodor said, ever the pleasant host. "When my experiments fail, I can't bring myself to bother cleaning them up. It's so . . . unjust." He waved a hand. "Please, look around. It's so rare I have the opportunity to share my work."

Despite the numerous experiments laid out, Josh felt drawn toward the room with the glass wall. Beside the glass wall stood a doorframe fitted with a giant funnel, as though a person could step through the doorway and be squeezed out the funnel's tip. Josh recognized the material the funnel was made of—it was the same silver-white of the canisters Snitch and Gloves wore.

On the wall behind the doorway, canisters were mounted from floor to ceiling, like trophies or deer heads. Tubes running from the valves at the top of each canister connected them directly to the surface of the funnel.

"What is this?" Josh asked.

"A way out," Feodor said. "I'm going to free myself from this universe. The gateway to the Dream will not admit me—I must burn through the boundaries of this world."

Josh wasn't surprised by his goal. He had tried to use the machine to break through the window she and Will had built. "What does the funnel do?"

"It is not a funnel," Feodor replied. "It is a drill. Watch."

He flipped a switch on the wall. A mechanical whir filled the room, although nothing appeared to be moving. Then, gradually, each canister lit up with a different-colored light: some bright and strong, others weak and pale. Josh saw dark oranges and bright purples and soft blues; the longer she looked, the more colors she saw. She felt drawn to the wall of canisters, and as she walked toward it, the soul lights grew larger and brighter. She heard sparkly sounds—music or laughter—but just as she reached out to touch a particularly beautiful peacock-green light, Feodor put his arm around her.

"I know," he said, guiding her away, "they're quite hypnotic, aren't they? But they'll only bore you with stories of their lives, and you mustn't encourage them. Besides, this is the truly interesting part."

He placed her so that she could see through the freestanding doorway and into the funnel, which shuddered as if immense power were running through it. A fog filled the funnel and then coalesced into images—a house, grass, a woman running after a child, a restaurant, the ocean, a nest full of robins' eggs. In short, the World.

Feodor threw the switch back the other way, and in seconds, the fog and the images dispersed. Josh glanced back at the canisters just as their lights faded completely.

"As you can see," he said, "the machine is incomplete. I have almost pierced the universal barrier into the World, but not quite. I need a few more souls for that."

Josh remembered what Haley had said when she'd asked why Feodor wanted souls: *Fuel?*

He'd been exactly right.

"You made a machine powered by souls," Will said, coming to stand next to Josh.

"Yes. Nothing here in Warsaw can power an escape—the architects saw to that. Souls were the only things I could acquire that weren't made from the fabric of this universe."

Josh guessed the wall held close to sixty canisters. "But how do you get the souls into the canisters?" she asked, hoping he would tell her something that would help Winsor.

Feodor responded with a condescending smile, as if he doubted her ability to understand his explanation. "Magnets," he said simply. "Manipulations of the body's subtle electromagnetic energy field which render the flesh inhospitable to the spirit. Or, if that's too sophisticated for you, think of it this way: the gas tank is a vacuum, the mask is a hose, and the spirit gets sucked out of the lungs like biscuit crumbs from a carpet." He chuckled. "I think of it as a modern interpretation of the Egyptian 'opening of the mouth' ceremony."

Josh didn't know what that meant, and she didn't care. "What does it do to the bodies?"

"The effect is similar to that of being struck by lightning. Without a soul to generate spiritual energy and the will to live, the body is directionless and will eventually wilt."

"Can the souls be returned to the bodies?"

Feodor made a funny face, as if she were entertainingly queer. "It is possible, should one desire such a thing. The empty bodies are quite useful, however, quite . . . malleable."

"What does that mean?" Will asked.

"It means he did something to the bodies he got his hands on," Josh said, glancing at Gloves. "Something that allows him to control them and allows them to alter the Dream." She looked back at

Feodor; he was smiling at her, pleased by her assessment. "More magnets?" she asked.

"Magnets," he said, as if making her a promise, "are only the beginning."

Sickened, Josh turned away from him. Looking back at the wall of canisters, she felt glad that Winsor's soul was not trapped among them.

She hadn't noticed before because she had been so absorbed by the lights, but each canister had a label attached to it near the bottom. Some labels held numbers, others names.

"Do all of those canisters have souls in them?" Will asked. His voice sounded as stricken as Josh felt.

"All but one."

Feodor reached out and tapped a canister. Josh and Will both leaned close to read the label.

Joshlyn Weavaros.

Josh released a shocked little cry. "What the hell is that?" Will demanded.

"I would have made one for you," Feodor promised him, "but I didn't know you were coming. Or Hianselian the Second." He gestured to Haley, who stood by the window to the white room.

Josh went to stand with Haley, wanting to get as far as possible from the canister that bore her name. "How did you know *I* was coming?" she asked Feodor.

Feodor smirked. "Your grandfather told me that you would."

Too stunned to reply, Josh watched Feodor fiddle with the tubing where it connected to the funnel. "That is why people come here, of course. They bring me their sons, their husbands, their boyfriends, a child once or twice. Some even bring themselves, the arrogant snots." He glanced back at Josh. "But Peregrine was the first to bring me a granddaughter."

"Peregrine doesn't even know I'm here," Josh said. "He didn't send me."

"No? You came after your Hianselian. I imagine you rushed to action as soon as you learned he was here. How did you come by that information? An anonymous letter? A carelessly spoken word? A document you should not have seen left out by accident?"

Josh's eyes whipped to meet Will's. "Serpico?"

He shook his head, but a line had appeared between his eyebrows. "I don't know. Even if Peregrine did put him up to telling you about Geoff, how could he have known that you would figure out Ian was here?"

"It wasn't that big a leap. It hardly took two minutes."

Josh felt blood rush to her palms with the desire to grab a weapon. "Okay, but why set you up to come here?" Will asked.

"Oh," Feodor said, and laughed again. "He didn't tell you, did he? Sometimes they don't tell them, especially the young ones. After all, you might not have come if you'd known."

Satisfied that his funnel's valves were sealed, he brushed his hands on a nearby rag and then said matter-of-factly, "Your grandfather believes that you, little Joshlyn, are the True Dream Walker. And he believes a very old rumor that I will initiate the True Dream Walker."

It was Josh's turn to laugh.

Maybe Will was right and she'd had too many shocks in one day, but she simply could not believe Feodor. Her grandfather didn't think she was a creature of legend. He didn't even like her; he just wanted to control her because she was . . . talented.

Haley slipped his hand into hers. Josh stopped laughing, startled that he had touched her.

"He's right," Haley said in a hushed voice. "You *are* the True Dream Walker."

Dumbfounded, she gaped at him.

It was Will who burst out, *"What?"*

Haley shrugged, and then he laughed as if relieved. He had a sort of half-hysterical glee on his face. "I've been waiting so long to tell you that. You can't imagine."

You're right, Haley: I can't imagine.

"You're insane," Josh told him. His face froze and then fell, but Josh didn't feel even a glimmer of sympathy. They were in a madman's re-creation of WWII Poland trying to dismantle a machine powered by souls, and she didn't have time to listen to nonsense. "I'm not the True Dream Walker, Haley. That's absurd. Every mention of the True Dream Walker in scrolls over the years has talked about *him* and *his* return, and how *he'll* be able to alter the Dream at will. None of that stuff applies to me."

"No," Will said. "Everybody's a *him* in old documents."

"It's ridiculous."

Haley looked at Feodor, as if he expected the man to yield backup. When Feodor only yawned indifferently, Haley's next try was Will, who joined them near the window-wall. Josh watched them communicate silently, remembering the strange bond they had formed, and she wanted to protest, to stop this absurd discussion, to keep them from ganging up on her.

"Listen," Will said to her. "Maybe when your grandfather kept asking me if I had ever seen you alter the Dream, he wasn't implying that you were working with the trench-coat men. Maybe what he wanted to know was whether or not it was possible that you're the True Dream Walker."

Josh just shook her head. She couldn't believe they were having this conversation, and now of all times. Feodor wanted to put her soul in a canister on his wall, and she was arguing about mythology.

Haley looked at her hopefully again. "I don't believe it," she told him.

"You have to believe it."

"I don't."

Will threw his hands up in the air and laughed. "Why the hell not? This explains why your grandfather was so weird, why you're so good at dream walking, why you have such great instincts. I just thought you were breaking Stellanor's First Rule all the time—"

"I *do* break Stellanor's First Rule all the time!" Josh shouted.

They stared at each other. "You do?" Will asked.

"Pretty much every time I walk into a nightmare I break Stellanor. And how the hell did you figure that out?"

"I don't know. Maybe because I watch every single thing you do in-Dream, and every time we go in, you stand there with your eyes shut for a second, and afterward you know all this stuff I don't know. Which is something no one else seems to be capable of, by the way, and only makes me more certain that you're the True Dream Walker. Maybe that's why your grandfather tried to blackmail you for your scroll, because it's written in there."

"It's not in my scroll," Josh told him.

"It's in your real scroll," Haley said.

Oh, no.

"The *real* one?" Will asked, in a voice higher and tighter than before. "What about the one you have?"

His eyes flashed to hers, and she felt whatever ground had been recaptured between them in the last hour roll out from under her feet. "It doesn't matter," she told him. "Just forget about the scroll. It doesn't matter what it says."

But her words were too little too late, because Will stared at her as if she had knifed him in the belly. "Tell me, Josh."

But what could she say? If she lied, he would know, and she couldn't bring herself to speak the truth.

Will stared at her, a deep line between his eyebrows. He kept waiting for her to speak, and when she didn't—couldn't—he slowly lifted his hands and turned the palms up helplessly. She'd seen that look on his face once before, in a nightmare where the dream-fire had swallowed him, and she realized for the first time that this rejection from her and her world wasn't just a fear for him, but a fear so deep it threatened his sense of self.

You finally did it, Josh. You broke his heart.

"Now that we've established that you have believers," Feodor said impatiently, "let's move on to the testing, shall we?"

No, Josh thought. She kept grabbing at Will's eyes with her own, but he'd lowered his face to the floor. But Feodor continued his lecture, indifferent to his guests' drama.

"Do you know what a Tempering is? It is how the monarchy used to prove the worth of kings and queens to rule. Someone told me not long ago that the monarchy had been overthrown. I certainly hope that's not true."

He looked at Josh as if she might inform him further, but she said nothing. She didn't care about Feodor's desire for news, and she didn't give a rat's ass about the monarchy. After the damage she had just done to Will, she didn't care about much except revenge.

Anger was replacing the pain she felt, and that was good.

"But yes, you're right, no time for history lessons. Back to the Tempering. I will put you in that room"—Feodor gestured to the other side of the glass wall—"and then, using this little device"—he pointed with one finger to a piece of quartz crystal wrapped in silver wire that stuck out of the wall—"I will bombard you with every awful memory I possess and every negative emotion I've ever felt. And believe me, there are quite a few. Eventually—perhaps in minutes, perhaps in an hour or two—your soul will flee from your body and from that room through a pipe in the ceiling, coming out here"—he ran his hand along a rubber tube that connected to the canister with Josh's name on it—"and providing the final burst of energy necessary for my drill to dig out of this prison of mine."

"That's never going to work," Josh said. The evening was only becoming more surreal.

"If you're the True Dream Walker," Feodor agreed with a condescending smile, "I suppose it won't. But you aren't the True Dream Walker, are you? And you should keep in mind that it has worked on dozens of other people, so it won't do for you to doubt my methods."

He had a point there.

Josh tightened her grip on Haley's hand. "And then what about my soul?" she asked, mocking Feodor with her tone. "I'll sit in a canister for the rest of eternity? That sounds like fun."

"Oh, I don't think it's so unpleasant," Feodor said, his voice softening. He looked at her with gray eyes that, under other circumstances, she might have found beautiful. "I imagine it's much like being held. We all want to be held, no? Held up, held together, held close." He walked toward her with slow steps. "How would you like to be held, Joshlyn? And by whom?"

He lifted his eyebrows as he spoke the last word, which made Josh's stomach clench.

"Not you," she said.

"Ah, too bad. Of course, once your soul flees, your body—now freed from the limitations of a mind imbued with consciousness—will be able to alter the Dream at will, and at that time I will go about making the arrangements we discussed earlier, involving magnets, that will allow me to give you commands. So I suppose that, in a sense, I will be able to hold both your soul and your body, and we will set forth into the World at large, I the master, and you and Hianselian the servants." He smiled again, pleased with himself. "Rather incredible, the things I discovered in this laboratory, no? A pity so few people have ever heard of them. But they will, after I leave this place. Someday the entire world will know my name."

Will, who had been standing bent at the waist, his hands on his knees, straightened slowly. Josh thought that maybe he was angry too, because he asked Feodor coldly, "Is the rumor true?"

Feodor glanced at him. "Which one?"

"The one Peregrine believes, that you'll initiate the True Dream Walker."

Feodor considered. He'd lost his smile, and Josh wondered if anyone had ever asked him that question before.

"I don't know. I can only tell you what my mother told me: that my scroll said I would Temper the True Dream Walker. But she said that just before she died of blood loss. *In my arms,* as you Americans would say. Seeing as both of her legs had just been blown off, she may not have been thinking clearly."

His humor was gone, replaced by a chill bitterness. He still looked at Will, but his eyes were unfocused by memory.

Will took a few steps toward him. "Someone told me that you tried to summon the True Dream Walker, that you destabilized the Dream to do it."

"Yes, yes," Feodor murmured, "I did that."

"You must have wanted the True Dream Walker back very, very badly to do such a thing."

Feodor's gaze sharpened. "If you had seen Europe crumble like a dry cracker, you might have done the same." Then he clapped his hands together, creating a sound like a gunshot. "Enough reminiscing. On to the test."

He lifted a hand, and Josh's body rose off the ground. She looked down at her feet, scrabbling to find the floor again, but Feodor flung his arm, and she spun through the air. Haley tried to keep hold of her hand, rushing after her like a child chasing a balloon, but Josh was moving too fast.

She flew through the doorway to the white room beyond the glass wall, where Feodor let her fall to the floor. She felt a strange jerk and saw her lighter and compact float out of her pants pocket and back into the laboratory. Then the door slammed shut.

She had known that Feodor might be able to alter his universe, and she had seen him change his projection of himself, but Josh hadn't expected him to be able to hurl people about like badminton birdies.

We should never have come here, she realized.

White tile covered the walls and floor, even the ceiling, and now that she was inside the room, Josh realized that silver wire ran in a grid between the tiles. Tiny crystals hung from the wire. They looked like Christmas lights, but Josh knew they served a more sinister purpose. Somehow, they allowed Feodor to channel his emotion into the room.

In several places around the room, Josh saw flaking brown smears of blood and puddles of what might once have been vomit. She looked up, into the pipe through which Feodor had promised her soul would flee. Right now, it offered no escape, being far too small to climb through.

Josh knew she needed to use these precious moments to come up with a plan, but she was so terrified that her mind darted from one idea to another, never staying with one long enough to develop it. She tried the obvious things: yanking on the locked doorknob, throwing herself at the window. Catching the bottom of the pipe, she used it to swing herself up high enough to kick the ceiling, but the tile there felt just as sturdy as the walls and floor.

She watched through the window as two chairs slid across the floor to face her through the window. She couldn't hear them, but she knew they must have made an awful racket. Feodor deposited Will and Haley in them, and with a dance of his fingers, made ropes bind their wrists to the chairs' armrests. Will thrashed like a tiger; Haley just grew pale. Invisible hands gathered the compacts and lighters from their pockets and dropped them on a far-off table.

For a moment, her eyes met Will's. *I'm sorry,* she mouthed, and he shook his head. Josh didn't know what that meant, and she didn't have time to find out because Feodor went to stand by the window-wall. Meeting Josh's eyes, he smiled and gave her a mock salute. Then he put his hand on the crystal protruding from the wall.

She'd thought he would need to warm up or gather his memories, but the pain hit her instantly, like a ten-foot ocean wave knocking her across the room and onto her back. When she reached out to push it away, her hands met nothing, and the pain turned into a sound, a high-pitched wail that made her wrap her arms around her head.

Then she smelled the pain. At first she thought she'd found a moment of relief, because she smelled woodsmoke and thought of a campfire, but the woodsmoke carried odors of less pleasant things with it. The scent of burning gasoline clawed at her throat; cooking flesh made her gag; and then the smoke turned chemical, its own weapon of war, and Josh lay on the floor coughing until the scents turned to tastes and she rolled onto her side to add her vomit to the collection on the white tile.

Then Feodor hit her everywhere at once, all her senses, and she was blind and deaf, caught in her own head where her mind tried to make sense of the feelings of agony and anguish by imagining terrible events: the deaths of everyone she loved, eternity spent alone, the end of all life; but the emotions themselves were what suffocated her. Despair, helplessness, hatred.

I have to hang on, she thought—but what was there to hang on to? Her memories of her life slipped away, forced out of her head by Feodor's own, and she saw Warsaw as he remembered it, everything on fire, constant shouting, panic without end. She heard his sister, Bryga, so small, screaming until her throat bled. She saw his mother die just as he had described, and felt Feodor's raging misery as, one by one, he lost every single person who mattered to him. She saw the world transformed until he could recognize nothing good in it, and she saw him walk for days and only find more of the same.

You have to believe, Haley had said, but what was there to believe in now? That she was the True Dream Walker? Such a pretty fiction. She wished she believed it, but she didn't.

Despair crushed her, as endless as the universe itself. There was nothing else, and it grew deeper and heavier and louder. Josh squirmed inside it, trying to find some relief, but the bonds of suffering only tightened. Finally, she gave in to the despair, not once but again and again; she stopped trying to prove that she was not helpless, weak, or faulted—even to herself. She surrendered over and over.

And over and over, the pain only grew worse.

Thirty-five

Feodor was going to kill Josh. That much was clear to Will.

He sat in a chair with his wrists tied to the armrests and watched as Feodor sank every ounce of his misery and insanity into the white room. Josh thrashed on the floor, but Will doubted she was conscious of her body because no one who could feel pain would crack her head against the wall and beat her arms and legs on the floor so hard that Will feared her bones would break. Or maybe the physical pain was just all the relief she could find from Feodor's poison.

Feodor stood with his eyes half-closed, wearing that dreamy

look he'd worn earlier when he spoke of the True Dream Walker's return. He murmured to himself, running his tongue over his lips every so often. "Yes, yes, *there*. Remember my sister? Everyone said she was the bright one. Here is where she met her end. Oh, *yes*."

Josh's mouth opened in a scream Will couldn't hear. He felt like crying.

He wasn't meant to be here. He knew that now, knew that his place in Josh's life was unequivocally illegitimate. When Haley had revealed that Josh's scroll was a fake, Will had felt so devastated that he'd promised himself he would leave the Weavers' house and never come back.

None of that mattered anymore. When Feodor's memories had hurled Josh to the ground, Will had struggled so hard against his bonds that he'd thought he would tear out of his own body in order to help her.

Beside him, Haley watched Josh with an expression of mixed hope and horror. Will had believed him when Haley said that Josh was the True Dream Walker, but he began to doubt it now as he watched her suffer so helplessly. If she had been able to stop that pain, she would have. Anyone would have.

"She has to believe," Haley repeated.

"Go into the forest," Feodor told Josh. "You see what they did to my teacher, what they did to all the teachers? Look at that crater where his face used to be."

Josh threw up again.

"Hey!" Haley said, but he said it in a sharp, demanding voice, and when Will turned to look, he found a stranger sitting beside him.

Ian tossed his head to get Haley's hair out of his eyes and said, "She's not gonna make it."

Will, already shaken, was too shocked to reply.

"This isn't a Tempering ritual," Ian went on. "It's just torture. He'll kill her once he has her soul."

"Ah," Will got out, "I don't know what to do."

Ian's tone was blistering. "Well, figure it out. You're supposed to be a smart guy."

Then he was gone, leaving Haley deathly pale and doused with sweat.

As bizarre as Ian's sudden appearance had been, he was right. Will was the only one who could stop this now. But with his hands tied, none of the things Josh had taught him were any use.

What would I have done before I met Josh? he wondered. And then he knew.

"Feodor," he said. The man's half-closed eyes flickered toward him. "You've got to push her harder."

Feodor nodded. "Yes, yes, past her limitations."

"When were you at your lowest? Show her that."

"My lowest. Hmm." He frowned as if faced with too many choices.

"Show her the moment when you wanted the True Dream Walker to return the most, when you needed the True Dream Walker to come and save you."

"Ah!" Feodor smiled. "That night, I remember."

In the white room, Josh began convulsing.

"You thought of the True Dream Walker then, didn't you?" Will asked quickly. He tried to keep his voice from shaking, but he was terrified that he had just pushed Josh past her breaking point. If he had killed her . . .

"You imagined the True Dream Walker coming to save you."

"Yes," Feodor agreed.

"What would the True Dream Walker do? How would he save you?"

"Fire! He would incinerate the Nazis, and the Italians, and the damned Russian turncoats! And he will! He will burn them like stick dolls!"

This wasn't going in the right direction. Josh rolled on the floor and slapped her skin as if she were on fire. "But after that," Will rushed on, "would the True Dream Walker free Poland? Would he bring the dead back to life?"

"Yes!" Feodor's face lit with a crazed light. "Yes! He'll give my mother back her legs!"

In the white room, Josh stopped thrashing. For a terrible instant, Will thought she had died, but then he saw her chest sink in a long sigh.

He couldn't believe he had been angry at her a few hours ago.

"Who else will he heal?" Will asked Feodor, before whispering to Haley, "I have to talk to Ian."

Haley bit his lip.

"Now!" Will hissed, and Haley swallowed and shut his eyes.

"He'll give my teacher back his face!" Feodor cried. "The dead will walk out of Palmiry Forest together, singing 'Poland Has Not Yet Perished'!"

"Not bad," Ian commented, appraising Feodor's state.

"You see that guy behind us, in the trench coat?" Will asked, knowing he had no time for niceties. Ian glanced over his shoulder and grimaced at the sight of Gloves, who stood guard over them as unmoving and lifeless as a mausoleum angel. "That's *your* body, Ian. It's yours, and Feodor stole it from you. Can you get back into it?"

Ian inclined his head toward Gloves, and Haley's features went slack for a brief moment, during which Gloves stumbled and coughed. Then Gloves resumed his statue act, and Ian again animated Haley's face.

"Almost, but I can't get in. There's something blocking me—he did something to keep me out. I can feel it, though. I'm so close."

Will thought. Feodor burst into song, waving his free hand and singing robustly in Polish. He stomped a beat with one foot.

"Could you give it a command?" Will asked Ian. "A single command?"

Ian considered, then nodded. "I can try. What's the order?"

"Tell him to kill Feodor's body. His real body, back in the corner, in the shroud."

Ian cocked a little smile and rushed out of Haley.

All things aside, Will was beginning to like Ian.

"And you?" Will asked Feodor, raising his voice. "Will they give you medals?"

"So many that I will walk stooped like an old man!"

On the floor in the white room, Josh smiled, her eyes still closed.

"We will enslave the Axis, and our enemies will fall to their knees when I pass by. I will take not one wife but one from every country we defeat, and they will cower and never meet my eyes for fear I will cause them to burst into flame!"

Feodor was too lost in his fantasy to notice Gloves approaching his mummified body. He began singing again: *"Jeszcze Polska nie umarła, kiedy my żyjemy!"*

Will watched, hardly breathing, as Gloves climbed on top of Feodor and wrapped his hands around the man's neck.

Feodor's projected image never noticed. He continued to sing, even as his image began to fade. Gloves bent over his body, crushing his master's throat.

Feodor lifted his arms, but not to fight for his life. He waved his hands gracefully through the air, dipping them rhythmically as he conducted an imaginary orchestra. His gray eyes, though they had begun to bulge, glistened with the joy of a faraway paradise, then slowly grew dull, and his hands floated down to rest on his chest as he lost consciousness. His singing voice grew distant before trailing off. He flickered out and then back one more time, but in the last instant before he faded forever, his face was full of joy. He died smiling.

It was not, Will thought, a fitting death for such an evil man.

But it would do.

Gloves sat on the floor next to his master's body. His face registered no expression, but he sat like a loyal dog, waiting for instructions.

The lights in the laboratory flickered off, but only for a moment. When they came on again, Will saw Josh sit up on the other side of the window. She examined her arms and hands, which she had beaten red from thrashing, and then she rose uncertainly to her feet and tried the doorknob. It remained locked.

"Damn," Will muttered. Still tied to his chair, he walked hunched over to the door and opened it with his teeth.

Josh didn't come out, just stood in the white room and stared at him. Her arms were covered in rising bruises, and Will saw more all over her face. He didn't doubt she had a concussion.

"What happened?" she asked. Her voice drifted with soft confusion. "Am I dead?"

"No, you're going to be fine. Untie me."

She frowned but reached out to work on the ropes that bound his wrists. "I had the most wonderful dream," she said, sounding more like Feodor than Will liked. "I dreamt the True Dream Walker returned and saved the world."

She freed one of Will's arms. "Go untie Haley," he said. "I can get the other one."

She wandered unsteadily toward Haley, then turned back to Will. Her dreamy peacefulness faded, replaced by confusion and weakness. "I failed, didn't I? I failed the test."

Her vulnerability in that moment made Will want to hold her. "Of course not."

"I did, though," she said, and she turned away with sadness. "I'm sure I did."

The lights flickered again.

Everyone looked at the ceiling, even Gloves. In the distance, the sound of constant bombs exploding and air-raid sirens stopped, only to be replaced by a rushing sound, like white noise growing louder and louder.

"It's collapsing," Haley whispered. "It can't exist without Feodor."

This seemed to wake Josh from her trance. "Oh, shit," she said.

Will yanked at the rope on his wrist and loosened it enough to pull his hand through. He ran over to Haley and freed one of his arms while Josh got the other.

Gloves suddenly rose and headed for the door to the street. Something about the action reminded Will of a dog who—hearing a signal for danger too high-pitched for humans to register—gets up and runs away.

"Follow him," Haley said, leaping out of the chair. He grabbed both his and Will's lighters and compacts off the table and handed one set to Will. "He knows where the gate is!"

Haley ran toward the door, but Josh gazed around the room as if trying to place it. "We have to go," Will told her.

She shook her head. "I know I failed. Hundreds of times. Thousands."

"We have to go *now*," Will repeated, and he grabbed her hand and dragged her toward the door. After a few zombielike steps, she began to run with him.

By the time they reached the street, the whole world was shaking. Half-collapsed buildings collapsed the rest of the way, creating avalanchelike slides of rubble. Will struggled to follow Haley in the fading light, but he held tight to Josh's hand. When she tripped on a charred wooden beam, he pulled so hard on her arm that he lifted her back onto her feet.

Gloves darted through the streets like he was running a familiar obstacle course. Haley managed to match his pace, but Josh's steps were slower than usual, her reflexes hesitant. Keeping a firm grip on her hand, Will kicked pieces of wreckage out of their way as he ran, clearing the path for her as much as possible.

The shaking grew worse until the street was rising and falling beneath their feet. He felt like he was trying to run on a trampoline. Gloves and Haley safely crossed a street ahead, but as soon as Josh and Will started to follow, a four-story building beside them began to collapse.

"Run!" Will shouted, but he didn't wait for Josh to speed up before breaking into a sprint. He clenched her hand—he'd get her across that street safely or else he'd get there with her torn-off arm.

In his haste, he didn't look down in time to avoid a fallen street sign. As he fell forward, the ground dropped out from under him, and he rolled into empty air. Josh's hand slid from his grasp, and when the ground rose up again to slam him, he landed as hard as if he'd fallen ten feet. Joints all over his body cracked.

The building on the corner failed neatly from the top floor down, like boxes falling into each other, and only the air blowing out and shattering the windows let Will know that the building protested its demise. For a moment he watched it, unable to get up from the jolting street. He thought he might have hit his head. The building they'd been running toward came down—not neatly but in a meteor shower of detritus, pelting Will with debris.

Something landed between his shoulder blades and flattened him to the pavement. Something big.

Will had always been analytical about pain. He'd thought that if he could choose not to fight it—to accept it as a product of nerve conduction and ignore the alarm it caused—he could free himself of physical pain forever. It had worked well enough for small cuts and dentist visits, but this pain was something else entirely. There was no ignoring it, no allowing it. He made a choking sound and wondered if his airways were blocked, but no, it was just that inhaling made the pain follow the arch of his ribs from his back into his sides.

"Will," Josh said, her voice so drowned out by the cacophony of collapse that his name sounded like a whisper. She knelt beside him, and he knew it was bad—even worse than it felt—by the way she began saying, "Shit, shit," over and over, like a benediction against panic.

Her words almost made Will smile. In spite of the pain, he felt fond and tender toward her. If this was the end, he was glad she was with him.

Then again, maybe all he felt was the euphoria of the dying.

"Haley!" Josh shouted. *She must be waking up again,* Will thought as he recognized the look on her face. She'd worn the same tough, unflinching expression when they entered Feodor's universe, and Will was relieved to see it again. "Help me!"

The pain changed as Josh and Haley dragged the heavy thing off of Will's back. The pressure moved from his spine to his left shoulder, and then he saw a giant hunk of concrete hit the street beside him with a crack. The size of it shocked him—no wonder Josh had cursed. After a moment of relief, the pain returned, not as loud but still too loud. But at least he could breathe.

Will managed to climb to his knees. Moving made him want to throw up, and he was afraid that if he made one wrong turn, his spinal cord would snap—but if they stayed much longer, it wouldn't matter if he could move below the waist or not. Behind them, Warsaw was on its last legs. Block by block, the streetlights and building fires blinked out, and a sound like a ferocious waterfall grew nearer and louder, white noise turning black.

"Where's Gloves?" Josh shouted. Their guide was nowhere in sight.

Haley pointed to a corner. "He turned left there."

"Shit!" Josh shouted again. "Get Will's other side!"

Taking Will by the arms, they lifted him to his feet. The pain shifted and resettled like a jostled pile of bone fragments; Will hoped that wasn't really what he was feeling.

Before he could adjust to the pain, they were running again, and Will stumbled along, aware that he couldn't feel the fingers on his right hand. That had to be a bad sign.

Then they turned where Gloves had, and they saw the gate.

At the end of a wide boulevard, the world ended with a two-story iron gate painted dark green. Beyond it, the city simply stopped, as though a black canvas had been erected behind the bars. Gloves was trying to drag the enormous gate open, but it weighed too much for even his strength.

Will slumped against the bars a few feet away from Gloves and watched Josh and Haley throw their weight behind his. If Gloves was surprised by their help, he didn't show it.

We came all the way here for this guy, Will thought, trying to rub feeling into his hand again. *All this, and he's not even a person anymore.*

The three of them managed to create an eighteen-inch opening. Strangely, no light or mirror was required for the space to fill with glittering Veil. Gloves vanished through it, then Haley, but when Josh turned to help Will, her eyes lingered in the direction from which they had come.

In the distance, blackness swallowed Warsaw. Even the fires couldn't stand up to the rising tide of nothingness.

"Feodor would have loved to see this," Josh said.

The nostalgia in her voice freaked Will out.

But then she looped one of Will's arms around her neck and helped him stand, and they followed Haley through the gate and into the Dream, leaving Warsaw to meet its final destruction alone.

Through a Veil Darkly

Emergency! Help Needed NOW!

At this very moment, three dream walkers have entered the pocket universe where Feodor Kajażkołski has been housed since 1962 and are facing off with the madman over the issues of the TCM and CSAD. Just before they entered his universe, they told me that they'd found evidence that the TCM are not nightmares, but are actually two dream walkers: Geoff Simbarticolsi and Ian Micharainosa. Both were believed to have been lost in the Dream, when in fact, they had been taken hostage in Feodor's dimension and either brainwashed or otherwise compelled to do his will. He has been sending them into the Dream in order to attack dreamers, and it is these attacks that have resulted in CSAD.

The junta knows all of this, but so far nothing has been done. The three dream walkers who are confronting Kajażkołski are only teenagers, and if no one steps up to help them, they could easily wind up in trench coats themselves.

Please, call your local representative or a member of the junta (phone numbers below) and demand that action be taken to save our young people! Time is short! Spread the word!

Thirty-six

They stepped out of Feodor's universe and into a quiet hallway in the Dream. The change disoriented Josh. No more soot in the air, no more bombs lighting the sky, no more rumbling streets. Just silence and pile carpeting. The hallway looked familiar to Josh, but maybe everything would look familiar after the foreignness of Feodor's Warsaw.

Josh turned to Will and said, "Let me see how bad it is." All three of them were banged up. Josh wasn't sure why, but bruises rose all over her arms and her entire body hurt terribly. Blood dripped from a cut on the side of Haley's neck, but Will was the one she was worried about.

He stood hunched over, leaning on his left shoulder against the wall, but he twisted a bit to show her his back. His white-and-blue flannel shirt bore a red wash of blood down the back. Josh used her fingertips to carefully pull the torn fabric away.

She cursed again. No wonder he couldn't stand up straight—his whole back was turning purple. A ragged wound ran between his shoulder blades; not an incision but a wound the size of two palms where so much flesh had been rubbed away that she could see muscle and bone.

From the time since she'd woken up in the white room until she saw the boulder land on Will, she hadn't felt afraid. She'd known Warsaw was collapsing, but she'd known it through a numb haze. She hadn't needed to feel afraid to know that she had to run.

But seeing that chunk of concrete fall out of the sky and slam Will to the ground, and now—seeing him hurt so badly—scared her. There was a real chance that Will wouldn't be all right.

"Josh," Haley said.

This was her fault. She should never have let them follow her.

She should never have gone herself—Will and Whim had been right.

"Josh," Haley repeated.

"What?" she snapped, and Haley shrank back. "Sorry."

"We're at the cabin," he said.

Before she could ask what he meant, she understood. That flowery wallpaper—she did recognize it.

Thanks to Feodor's experiments, Gloves had the power to alter the Dream at will, and for reasons Josh couldn't fathom, he'd chosen to re-create her mother's cabin. The last time she'd seen this wallpaper and this hallway had been the night Ian died and the cabin burned.

"Why are we here?" Haley whispered, as if afraid the walls would overhear.

Cautiously, Josh broke Stellanor's First Rule and felt . . . nothing. "There's no dreamer here."

"I thought that wasn't possible," Will said.

"It shouldn't be possible. Gloves must be manipulating the Dream somehow." Josh shook herself. "It doesn't matter. We have to get you out of here." She dug in her pockets before remembering that Feodor had taken her compact and lighter. "Who else has keys?"

Haley produced his compact but had lost his lighter. Will's pocket produced nothing but greasy shards of mirror and plastic. "I must have fallen on it."

"So we have no lighter," Josh said. Now a new, different sort of fear filled her.

She cursed again. She had no idea how many times she had cursed that day. It was beginning to feel like a normal addendum to any sentence.

"Gloves might have a lighter," Will said. "He and Snitch opened an exit. One of them must have been carrying."

Josh's hope flared and then died out completely as she realized that there was no way to get Will on his way to a hospital before she faced Gloves. And she knew she wouldn't be fighting her best if she was worrying about Will at the same time.

They had only one option. So she took it.

"Here's the plan," she said. "We go after Gloves. We get his keys. Will, you hang on to Haley's compact in case you get a lighter first. Haley, help Will open an exit and get him out. It doesn't matter if the archway opens to China, just get him out. Toss me the keys before you go. I'm going to stay and . . ."

She didn't know how to finish the sentence. Was there still any hope of reuniting Ian's soul with his body, or had that possibility died with Feodor?

"Maybe I can knock him out . . ." she began, and then that statement, too, fizzled. Whatever Feodor had done to Ian's body, Gloves had a fierce survival instinct.

"I'll help," Haley offered. He took her hand the way he had in Feodor's laboratory. "I'm with you," he said, and she realized he was looking at her with an expression of purest trust. "We can bring him home."

"I hope so," she said.

"Gloves is afraid of you. He knows who you are."

Why did Haley feel the need to bring up this delusion about her being the True Dream Walker again? "Haley, no—"

"*You* know who you are."

She remembered the hours and hours of training she had gone through, days filled with combat lessons and mud runs, nights filled with every terror imaginable. She thought of the sore muscles and the broken bones and the chipped teeth. She had sweated and burned and cried and bled through the last seventeen years. She was no magical creature—just a girl who had made a thousand mistakes and kept going.

"I'm not," she told Haley. "The True Dream Walker wouldn't have screwed things up the way I have."

Haley gave her a kind half smile and stepped closer to her. "It's okay if you can't believe it yet. But you know I'm not crazy. I'm not mean. I wouldn't lie to you about this. So, if you can't believe it yet, believe me, okay? Believe me when I say that you are the True Dream Walker."

Josh didn't even recognize him in that moment. He wasn't a

bizarre impersonation of Ian and he wasn't the shy, trembling boy she had grown up with. The fragility in him had hardened.

"I failed Feodor's test," she said, making one more weak protest.

"Maybe not," Will said.

His face was pale and wet, and he was leaning wearily against the wall again. If Josh had never seen Haley so confident, she had never seen Will so defeated.

Seeing him in so much pain, she wished she could just take him and go. She wanted to peel that shredded shirt away and bandage his wounds, do something to help repair the damage she'd caused. She wanted to kiss his hands and beg his forgiveness.

"It wasn't a true Tempering," Will went on, his voice somehow both weak and gruff. "It was just an excuse for Feodor to torture you. You might succeed in a real Tempering."

She remembered having similar thoughts during the woman's nightmare just a few hours before. "No, I'd fail that, too. I know I would."

Why did Will believe in her? Hadn't he watched her fail, not just in the white room but again and again over the last six weeks? She had been cold and careless and rash. Why did Will have this irrational faith in her? It was the only irrational thing about him.

"We need to move," she said, tired of fighting. "Remember, our first priority is to get Will out of the Dream."

The hallway extended in two directions. One led to the living room, the other to the basement stairwell. Josh didn't question where Gloves had intended for them to go.

Everything in the basement was just as she remembered it from eight months before. At one end of the unfinished room stood the stairs, and at the other were the furnace and fuse box. Between them, a bucket of hardened cement rested next to a pile of smooth stones for outlining the Veil and holding it open. Mirrors sent arcs of light shooting all over the room like colorless rainbows.

Gloves stood at the far end of the basement with his eyes closed. He had taken off his trench coat and gloves, and underneath he wore the same outfit he'd had on the last time Josh had seen him: black jeans and a forest-green polo shirt. He didn't look the least bit bedraggled. His clothing was tidy. His hair was dry and combed off his face.

Perhaps he had altered his appearance to confuse her, or maybe it was another facet of this bizarre reenactment. Josh stopped at the bottom of the steps and waited for Haley and Will to fall into place behind her.

Ian opened his eyes.

They were hazel and arranged into white, iris, and pupil.

Josh gasped.

Ian said, "Evening, J.D."

His voice had inflection. It was casual and fond and a little bit nervous but determined not to let it show. His face was animated, his mouth curved in a knowing smile.

He was *Ian* again.

"Haley?" Josh said uncertainly.

"I don't know," Haley whispered, a frantic edge to his voice. "I can't feel anything."

"It could be a trick," Will put in. Josh had the same fear—that Gloves still possessed Ian's memories and was putting on a grand performance.

Ian lifted his eyebrows. "I'm not trying to trick anybody," he announced. "I . . ." He shook his head as if overwhelmed. "This is as much a surprise to me as it is to you."

He shrugged, and the force of déjà vu caused the ache in Josh's chest—that wound she had carried for eight months—to open up again. He was Ian, and she needed him tonight. She had never stopped needing him.

"What happened?" she asked, already walking toward him.

"I don't know." He took a step in her direction. "Somehow Feodor kept me—my spirit or whatever—from being able to get back into my body. But when he died, it was like my body opened up again, only I . . . I couldn't find my way back for a couple of minutes." He shrugged. "I don't know how to say it."

She almost smiled. How many times had he told her that he didn't know how to say it?

"I knew you'd find me," he said. "I always knew." He grinned and turned to Haley. "Hey, little brother."

Josh realized that Haley was standing next to her. She looked over her shoulder and saw Will leaning against the wall, one arm wrapped tightly around his torso. Blood dripped from the hem of his shirt.

Ian and Haley stared at each other. "Little brother" had been a joke between them, because despite having been born first, Haley had always seemed younger.

Josh touched Haley's hand, and he dragged his gaze back to her. "What do you think?" she asked.

He shrugged nervously. "I . . . just don't know."

"Look," Ian said. "I don't know what's going on here any more than you do. All of my memories are mixed up with these dreams I had, that I was back in the World. . . ."

"You were," Haley told him. His voice grew halting again, as if whatever confidence he had gained was lost in his twin's presence, and he reverted to being the Haley he had been when Ian was alive. "You stayed with me there, sometimes you . . ."

"Used you," Ian finished, and he ground his teeth. "God, I did, didn't I?"

He sounded so disgusted with himself, so honestly affected that Josh marveled. Every tiny detail, imperfection, trademark, was right there. And yet she was afraid to believe.

"Josh," Will said from behind her. "Sorry to interrupt, but I really do need a doctor."

He sounded irritated, and Josh felt bad for forgetting him, even for a moment. His face was so pale she could see freckles she hadn't known he had, and blood dripped steadily from his shirt hem.

"Yeah," Ian agreed, walking toward him. "You definitely do." He paused a few feet from Will. "I know you. You're Will—you're Josh's apprentice."

He glanced over his shoulder at Josh. His eyes were slightly tilted, questioning and accusing at the same time.

And Josh knew he was back.

Only Ian could produce that particular jealous and yet conspiratorial look. Only Ian would think he had the right. Josh felt as if a light had come on inside her; something warm and bright was filling her up with joy.

She smiled at him, and he lifted his eyebrows again.

"I never let go of your hand," she said.

He took her hand then and held it tightly. "I know. Now, let's get out of here. I have . . ." He dug in his pockets. "I have Josh's lighter. Why do I have your lighter?"

He held out the rose-gold lighter he had given her years before. Josh hadn't seen it since she dropped it in the Dream.

"I'll explain later," she said. "Will has a compact."

Will didn't move. He was studying Ian with the same intensity he had often turned on Josh.

"Will?" she asked.

Slowly, he shook his head. "No." He took a step back, straightening up with a wince. Keeping his eyes squarely on Ian, he said, "This is why he didn't kill us flat-out, Josh. He has a lighter but no mirror, so he can't leave the Dream without our compact."

Josh felt her heartbeat quicken like a car engine revving up. Will was right—Ian couldn't use the mirrors in the basement because they were all part of the Dream. He needed a World mirror.

Ian swore and then said, "This is ridiculous."

So quick to anger, so Ian-like.

"You don't trust me?" he asked. "Fine. You open the archway—I won't even touch anything. I'll just follow you through. Here." He handed Josh the lighter.

"No," Will said again. "I'm not letting you out."

Ian's lips parted in outrage. "Josh?"

She put the lighter in her pocket, as if having it out of sight would calm the argument it had started. "Will's just being careful."

"He's being paranoid."

Ian walked back to where she stood and took both of her hands.

Josh jumped when she felt his fingers against her palms and his thumbs on her knuckles. She had forgotten how firm his touch was.

"J.D.," he said, lowering his voice, "look, this is nuts. I know you're probably pissed off about the whole thing with Winsor, but now is a lousy time to get into it. Somebody beat you to a pulp, and Haley looks like he's going to pass out, and this guy"—he pointed to Will—"is standing there bleeding to death."

Over his shoulder, she could see Haley and Will. They were both moving slowly toward the stairs and exchanging silent glances.

What do you see that I don't? she wondered. *What's got you so scared? It's just Ian being Ian.*

She didn't understand why there were tears in her eyes. Ian was still speaking, still trying to convince her that he was who she wanted so badly for him to be, and she barely heard him until he said, "Josh, look at me."

She did. His hazel-green eyes were filled with concern.

"I just don't want us all to die in here. *I* don't want to die in here. I want to go home, and take a hot shower, and get my life back. And I want to be with you, Josh, okay? All this time floating around without a body, I got a lot of thinking done, and the thing I thought most was, *Wow, I can't believe I blew it with Josh.* But this is our second chance, J.D., I see it so clearly now."

She nodded, even though a numbness had begun creeping over her. She really hadn't thought the night could get any worse.

"Let's go home," he said, and hugged her.

His arms lifted her right off the floor. She let her chin fall onto his shoulder and wrapped her arms around his shoulders. Will, watching them, shook his head.

Ian's hand touched her hip. His fingers moved gently, searching.

"Haley?" she asked, still holding on.

She wasn't the only one crying. Haley, already near the top of the stairs, sniffled helplessly.

"He just doesn't feel right," Haley said.

Ian's fingers found Josh's lighter and began drawing it out of her pocket.

She closed her eyes long enough to clear them of tears, letting go of one more beautiful, brief-lived dream. Then she steeled herself.

One hand grabbed his, the other grabbed his hair and jerked his head back.

No tense shock ran through his body. No surprise registered on his face.

He took a quick step forward and threw her up against the cement wall.

His eyes were a glossy black wasteland, his face vacant.

The charade was over.

Thirty-seven

"Run!" Josh shouted. Gloves smacked her against the wall again, but she kept hold of his hair as she fell, ripping out a fistful on her way down.

He lost his balance and crashed backward into the arrangement of mirrors and candles in the center of the room. Glass shattered into long, triangular slivers that spun across the floor as if across ice. Blood streamed from a patch of his scalp.

Josh scrambled to her feet just in time to block a punch aimed at her face, but he countered it with a kick to her stomach. The impact knocked her into the wall again. While she was gasping from the pain in her gut, Gloves turned to look at the stairs where Will and Haley still stood.

"Go . . . go!" Josh told them, unable to say it louder than a hiss. But she was too late.

Gloves inclined his head and narrowed his eyes. The stairs and door vanished, replaced by another cement wall. There was no way to escape from the Dream version of the basement now.

Will jumped off the stairs before they vanished, but Haley was standing on the top step when it dissolved. The sudden, ten-foot fall caught him off guard, and he cracked the back of his head on the wall, then fell in a heap on the floor, unconscious.

At least, Josh hoped he was just unconscious.

But before she could even fear for him, Will hit Gloves from behind—an unschooled, openhanded, girly slap that did as much as blowing on him would have. Will knew Gloves was out of his league and jumped away as soon as the slap was delivered.

"He has to concentrate to change anything," Will told her, ducking to avoid being crushed by Gloves's fist. "Keep him distracted."

Josh struggled to get back on her feet. The pain in her stomach was retreating to a dull ache, but she felt how weak Feodor's torture had left her. Her remaining strength wouldn't last long.

Gloves came at her and they wrestled. A hundred memories of training with Ian came back to Josh. She used everything she had against him, but this wasn't the Ian she had grown up with. Gloves barely registered pain and never gave her an instant to breathe, not even a split second to rest between attacks. He fought entirely without reserve. Josh would have expected that losing his soul would diminish his motivation to live, but it seemed just the opposite—that only an animal desire to survive remained.

When Josh began to flag, Will jumped in to distract Gloves. But he swayed on his feet, and Gloves didn't waste any time in hand-to-hand combat. Head down, he rushed Will, not to hit him but to drive him into the wall and crush his wounded back against the concrete. Josh, on her knees a few yards away, saw Will's eyes roll back in his head and heard him make a sound—possibly a scream—muffled by a gurgle. He collapsed.

Not a good sign.

Gloves leaned down and pulled the compact from Will's pocket.

The sight of Will crumpled on the floor enraged Josh, and she sprang to her feet with newfound energy, but her rage only made her sloppy. When she sent a roundhouse kick toward Gloves's head, he caught her foot and twisted it so that she sprawled facedown with her hands on the floor. Then Gloves kicked her in the gut again, forced her onto her back, and climbed on top of her.

When she tried to hit him, his fingers caught her arm with inhuman speed. He brought her elbow down on the floor, and then again, and again, until the joint shattered.

Josh felt her fingers relax almost before she felt the pain. Not just a physical pain, but a deep sense of brokenness, a crack in her foundation. Gloves's hands closed around her throat, and she would have gasped at the fire that shot from her fingers to her shoulder, but he had cut off her airway.

Time slowed while he choked her. With her left hand she cut deep scratches in his arms, the blood growing sticky under her nails, but he didn't respond. He was sitting on her thighs, immobilizing her legs, and because his arms were longer than hers, she couldn't reach far enough to gouge out his eyes.

So this is how it's going to end, Josh thought. The fact that it really was going to end shocked her, despite all the evening's close calls. She stared into Ian's face, Ian's lovely face with the barren black eyes and no expression, too stunned to truly hate him.

No triumph showed on Gloves's face.

She could hardly believe what she saw behind him: Will was climbing to his feet. After that second injury to his back, she'd been sure he wasn't getting up, but here he was, gaining one foot and then the other. The maniacal smile on his face was one she'd never seen before, though, and it scared her. He didn't look like himself.

He staggered as he came up behind Gloves, his chest heaving as he struggled to lift one arm above his head. In his hand, he held an icicle-shaped shard of mirror. But with a burst of strength, he reached Gloves in two long, smooth steps and brought the mirror down into Gloves's back, the jagged, broken end cutting into his own skin as he forced the mirror between Gloves's ribs.

"Hands off the girl, asshole!" Will shouted and, like the smile, his voice wasn't his.

Ian? Josh thought.

Gloves grew still with shock. Then his hands actually tightened further around Josh's neck, and he lifted her head, then slammed her down so hard that when her skull hit the floor she heard a sound like an eggshell breaking.

For a moment her mind shut down. She couldn't hear, or see, or feel her throbbing arm or the air rushing back into her lungs as Gloves released her. For just that moment, she knew perfect inner silence, and then a thunderstorm erupted at the back of her head, and she opened her eyes.

"Oh god, J.D., I'm sorry, I'm so sorry, oh god—"

Will's eyes rolled back in his head, and he passed out on the floor next to Josh.

Gloves was on his knees a few feet away. He twitched, twisting and arching his torso as if he were trying to force the mirror out. The way he jerked and the lack of expression on his face made Josh think of an android. When twisting didn't work, he searched blindly with his left hand and finally pulled the mirror out, slicing his hand and fingers. Josh couldn't see the wound, but through his legs she saw blood begin running onto the floor in a steady stream.

Gasping like a fish on the floor, she watched him toss the mirror away and inhale deeply. If he had been capable of emotion, she would have said that he was frightened, but maybe she only thought that because his whole body was trembling violently. He crawled to one wall, sat painfully back on his heels, and stared at the wall for a long, long time while blood ran down his back and pooled around his knees. Finally, he lifted the compact and lighter, and a blue door appeared in the middle of the wall, the sort of door one might find on the front of a home.

He's going to leave us, Josh thought, *and the Dream will shift, and whatever nightmare we fall into, we won't be able to fight it.*

But Gloves didn't leave. He started to rise, and then he swayed like a charmed snake and collapsed sideways, making no movement to soften his landing against the concrete floor. So much blood had collected around him on the floor that it splashed when he fell into it; Josh felt the spray on the side of her face.

Oh my god, she thought. *I think he's dead.*

Ian had killed himself. He'd had to borrow Will's body to do it, but he'd managed.

He saved my life. Her heart sang with a strange, astonished joy. *Ian saved my life.*

If that wasn't forgiveness, she didn't know what was.

Then she thought, *I have to get us out of here.*

But try as she might, she couldn't rise. She couldn't even roll over. Each time she moved her head more than an inch, the vertigo was so intense that her stomach rose in her throat, and she knew that if she vomited now, she would choke to death.

"Josh," Will whispered. She turned her head that one inch to look at him, and the pain shifted toward her temples, easing a little near the back of her neck. His cornflower-blue eyes were dark, and the skin around one was swelling.

My apprentice. Look what I let happen to you. I tried to tell them I wasn't ready, that I'd be a terrible teacher, but no one listened, and now look what I've done.

"You can change this," he told her. His voice was weak, but she felt comforted to hear it, even if his words were absurd.

He had never gotten what he deserved from life: not from his parents, not from the county, and certainly not from her. She hated herself for not having been strong enough to be the teacher and friend he needed. She hated herself for hurting him again and again.

"You have the power, Josh," he said. "Please, *please* believe it."

She didn't have any power. She had fallen for Feodor's tricks, and for Gloves's, too.

Around them, the walls and ceiling began to slowly fade, becoming pale and misty.

"Josh," Will whispered. He was pleading now, tears in his eyes. "Just this once, don't be afraid of your power."

She felt his hand close around hers and realized how cold her skin was. The ceiling above her looked like a cloud, and she imagined that behind it she'd find a beautiful spring sky, not another nightmare.

"In the limo, you said that no one ever sees you, that they let you get away with everything because you're special. You said they would let you off the hook no matter what you did. Well, *I* see you, Josh. I don't know all your secrets and I haven't been around all your life, but I saw you when you were mad at me in the school lobby, and when you were scared and falling into Haley's arms, and when you were kissing me in the kitchen. I *know* you, and I know what kind of power you have because I've seen you in the Dream, too. And I am the one person who is not going to let you off the hook."

He stopped speaking for a moment to catch his breath, which rasped each time he inhaled. Then he said, "I don't want to die tonight. Neither do you, but you'll give up this fight because you're too afraid to trust yourself. You'd rather believe you're a screwup who always gets let off the hook than admit how amazing you are and take responsibility for being so strong. If we die tonight, I'll know the truth—that we died because you were afraid of being special. That's *your* dreamfire, Josh, admitting how strong and smart and great you are. It's easier for you to stay small. But I know you, Josh, and I don't think you're small, not a bit, so don't you dare just lay there while the Dream shifts and drops us into God knows what nightmare to die."

His hand tightened around hers, and she realized she was crying again. Her eyes were so sore, she thought she must have been crying for days now. Behind Will, the blurry white walls looked like feathered wings extending from his busted back.

"Go on," Will whispered. "The Dream is shifting, but you can stop it. Hurry."

Haley believed. Young Ben believed.

But if Will believed . . .

"How do I . . . ?" she asked, the words half-formed.

"You *know* how," Will whispered, so fervently that in that instant she did know.

Her eyes closed, and she let the Dream come to her, this Dream that had been her second home, her escape, her playground. She broke Stellanor's First Rule like she'd never broken it before, allowing not just the fear within the Dream to come to her, but the joy, the sweetness, the sorrows and delights and memories and wicked fun. She opened herself to secrets and dark corners and swore to set the twisted roads straight and turn the sky right-side up again. She reached out to the edges of this universe, this reflection of the World rippling on the surface of a pond, and gave herself up to the voices of the dreaming.

Her father had always told her not to give in to the dreamer's fear, but tonight the dreamfire was her own and greater than that in any nightmare, greater than the terror Feodor had forced into her. This fear swirled around her like dark, icy water, and she knew that the Dream felt it. Tonight the Dream quit speaking and listened to her, to what she needed to tell it.

My name is Joshlyn Dustine Hazel Weavaros. I have walked your lands all my life and calmed as many storms as I was able. I have risked my life and the lives of those I love to heal you. Now I am seventeen years old, I am claiming my own, and it's time to return the favor.

A ripple moved through the Dream, as if it had been waiting generations to hear her voice and was amused by her unnecessary forcefulness. Josh's hands filled with sand and cloud and someone, maybe Will, said, "Go on, then. You know what to do."

She was the floor, she was the walls, she was the shards of broken mirror. Her arms stretched across the ceiling and beyond into other dreams. Her heartbeats were the seconds of time; her breath was change.

She held out her hands, and the Dream stilled. She, Will, and Haley were suspended in a melting white room, but she made the walls and floors hard again, put everything back in place.

"Josh," Will whispered, but he used a different voice this time, a voice that was awe and pleading combined.

She opened an archway to the familiar archroom in her basement at home, but no one was there, so she opened another archway—a new one, which took only a thought—to the living room, where Deloise was sitting on the couch with a cup of tea in her hands, her beautiful face aged by worry.

When the archway opened three feet in front of her, she jumped up so fast she forgot about her teacup and let it roll off her thigh, spilling tea down the leg of her lavender jeans. For three seconds she stared through the archway, her mouth agape, and then she shouted, "Saidy! Whim! Get in here! Hurry!"

Josh's mind drifted, only half-conscious of what was happening, until she felt the night air on her skin. Out in the World, rain was falling, and the stretcher Josh rode bounced up and down as Saidy rushed her toward an ambulance. Cold water splashed her face, reminding her of the rain in Warsaw—but this was only World rain, only the ocean running in circles. Josh saw her bloodied arms sparkling with fairy dust.

The metal bars of the stretcher clanged as they loaded her into the ambulance. The doors closed and the vehicle tore onto the road with its siren wailing. The pain in Josh's head and her elbow came back, along with the overwhelming sense of weakness, but she opened her eyes and saw Will looking at her from the stretcher beside hers.

She reached out with her good hand and found his under the white sheet that had been thrown over him. His gaze was detached and serene, and Josh hid nothing from him when she gazed back. She felt his pulse slowing under the skin of his palm and squeezed tighter.

"Stay," she whispered. Her throat burned, but she said it again. "Stay."

A sort of smile came onto Will's face and his fingers closed around hers, but his heart skipped one beat, then another. Josh remembered holding on to Ian's hand when they went through the archway into Feodor's universe for the first time, remembered how hard she had held on, so hard she had dragged his spirit back into the World.

She thought she would hold on to Will twice as hard.

Through a Veil Darkly

Feodor Kajażkołski Is Dead (No Thanks to the Junta)

By now many of you have heard the news—news that even the junta couldn't cover up. Three teenagers—Josh Weavaros, Haley Micharainosa, and Will Kansas—faced off with legendary madman Feodor Kajażkołski in the pocket universe to which he was exiled in 1962.

And they won.

At the time of this writing, Josh Weavaros is currently in a medically induced coma after suffering a depressed fracture to her skull and exhibiting unusual brain-wave patterns. She is so covered in bruises that she's unrecognizable. Will Kansas required a skin graft to cover a massive wound on his back. Only Haley Micharainosa, who suffered a concussion and minor contusions, has been released from the hospital.

And where, you might ask, where were our leaders when these three teenagers were in such dire need? Nowhere to be found. Josh's own grandfather, Peregrine Borgenitch, dismissed an eyewitness who had WATCHED the three enter Kajażkołski's universe, and continued to insist that doing so was impossible. He was holding a press conference and was in the middle of a sentence expressing just that sentiment when Anivay la Grue received word that Josh, Haley, and Will had returned. Even if the eyewitness

had been wrong, the possibility of him being right should
have warranted an immediate response from the
Gendarmerie.

Less than six months from now, the Accordance Conclave
will be held and proposals accepted for what form the
permanent North America dream-walker government should
take. A lot of people have said they'd just as soon keep the
current arrangement. I hope that the gravity of this incident
causes them to reconsider.

Thirty–eight

Josh regained consciousness several
times before truly waking up. Once to the sound of kind women's
voices telling her, "Open your eyes, honey," and a whiny mechanical
beep; a second time when she was moved from one bed to another;
a third time just long enough to hear her father say, "She's falling
asleep again. Is that safe?"

In between, she returned to jagged nightmares where Feodor
led her through ruined cities, through forests burned to cinders
beneath smoking gray skies, to the black shores of oceans of blood
where red waves rose to douse her in stinking pink froth.

When she finally roused herself from the chemical bog of seda-
tives and pain medications, Haley was sitting at her bedside. Everything around her—the sea-foam-green walls, waffle-knit white
blankets, and rock-hard pillows—confirmed her suspicion that she
was at St. Dymphna's Hospital. *Home away from home,* she thought.

After the chaos of her dreams, the sound of nurses' chatter in the hallway and the hum of televisions in other rooms reassured her that she was safe and sound.

She groaned, and Haley looked up from the notebook in which he was writing. He smiled at her, a sweet little Haley smile. For the first time since he'd come back to town, he wasn't wearing a single article of Ian's clothing; now he'd dressed himself in very grubby jeans and a yellow turtleneck with a red-and-green Christmas sweatshirt over it.

"Hi," Josh said, half choking on the word. Her throat felt like it had been scratched by a cat. She tried to move, but her body had turned to stone and a frumpy cast encased her arm all the way up to her shoulder. Light from a large window drilled into her eyes. "What day is it?"

"Thursday."

Thursday? "What day did I get here?"

Haley smiled again. Aside from the purplish remainder of a bruise on his temple and a bandaged wound on his neck, he looked fine. Better than fine, in fact. Peaceful.

"Sunday."

She had never managed to knock herself unconscious for four days before.

"Is Will all right?" she asked, trying to sit up. She noticed that purple and green bruises covered her arm that wasn't in a cast. "What happened to me?"

Haley rose and found the controls on the side of the bed. Sitting was much easier with mechanical assistance. "Will's okay, and the bruises are from thrashing around on the floor while Feodor tortured you. You have a lot of them."

Josh winced. She never wanted to relive those memories.

"How okay is Will?" she asked.

"He went home yesterday. But he needed surgery and lots of stitches and a skin graft."

Either all the blood was rushing from her head or else she was passing out from relief. She closed her eyes and relaxed the muscles that she had tensed upon waking.

"Your dad is mad at you, though, for going into Feodor's universe. Will says he's really just relieved that you're not dead, and he's using anger to avoid the fear he felt."

Josh smiled, opening her eyes again. "And you're talking."

He blushed. "Kinda."

"No, it's very cool."

Haley hesitated and then said, "When we got to the hospital, I was the first to wake up, so I had to make up a story for the doctors."

He was so adorably pleased with himself. "Really?" Josh asked.

"I told them we were abducted by aliens. They made me talk to a psychiatrist."

Josh laughed. "You'll have to fill me in on all the details so I can back you up."

Haley smiled at his feet.

"Oh," she asked, "have you seen Winsor? How's she doing?"

Haley lifted his head, no longer smiling. "She's the same."

"You couldn't get the canister?"

"Davita brought it. But . . . I couldn't . . ." His face twisted with frustration, his lips pursing the way they did when he was angry. "It's like a puzzle box."

Josh nodded, disappointed but unsurprised.

"I think the canisters are meant to be long-term cages," she told Haley. "We might need, I don't know, a physicist or somebody to take it apart before we can get her out. Maybe someone at Willis-Audretch would know how." Haley looked relieved at the idea of bringing in expert help.

"What about all the other souls, the ones hooked up to Feodor's machine?"

The relief in Haley's face vanished. "I don't know. I think . . . they're probably lost in the Dream. Even if they could find their bodies, I don't know if they could get back in."

Josh blew out a long breath. *This is bad,* she thought. *I don't know how to fix this.*

She wondered if her newfound abilities as the True Dream Walker would help, and hoped so.

Haley touched her cheek, and she looked at him. He opened the fingers of her left hand and pressed something cool and heavy into her palm. "Ian asked me to give you this."

Josh lifted her hand and saw her lighter, the one Gloves had tried to kill her for. The words *To J.D. Love Always, Ian* were still engraved in the rose-gold plating, but now there was a new dent—a dent that underscored *"Always."* Josh ran her thumbnail along the groove.

"Thanks." She turned the lighter over in her hand, feeling the metal warm from her touch. "Is he still hanging around?"

"He died," Haley said without sadness. "He's gone."

That ache in her chest—oh, she would have thought it would be gone now, but it throbbed the same as ever. Maybe it always would.

"You get to just be you now, huh?" she said.

"Yeah." Haley smiled, but he put his hand over hers as if he knew how much she was hurting.

Her eyes were wet. She'd come so close to getting Ian back. For a moment, she'd looked into his eyes and—just like before—hadn't realized it was her last chance to say good-bye. Voice breaking, she asked, "Will he be all right?"

Haley tilted his head as if the answer were obvious. "Of course."

Josh went home two days later, woozy with pain meds and anti-seizure meds and anti-inflammatories. Deloise made her hot chocolate, and they sat around the kitchen table with Haley and Whim; Will—who was probably on a similar drug regimen—was taking a nap. In response to the multiple tragedies that the Weaver-Avish family had experienced, dream-walker communities around the world had sent flowers and, more locally, food. The kitchen reeked of pollen and casserole.

"You are never allowed to scare me like that again," Deloise informed Josh. "I was nearly out of my mind."

"She was," Whim agreed. "I had to make out with her for half an hour to calm her down."

"Whim!" Deloise cried, and she turned and smacked him with a kitchen towel. "That never happened," she told Josh, but she had flushed bright pink.

It totally happened, Whim mouthed to Josh.

If it did, Josh mouthed back, *I'm going to kick your ass.*

It never happened, Whim agreed.

Deloise wasn't the only one upset with her. Haley had somewhat understated the situation when he'd said Josh's father was mad at her.

"I am sick to death of visiting people in hospitals!" he'd told her. "Especially you! Do you know how serious a depressed skull fracture is? It's a miracle you can still walk and talk!"

He'd put her on maximum-security grounding for two months, and this time she thought he might stick with it for at least a couple of weeks.

She didn't mind. Now that the adrenaline and panic were gone, she could see just how foolish and shortsighted she had been. Besides, she was having surgery on her elbow in a week and was expecting to log a lot of hours on the couch.

"Is Young Ben out of jail?" she asked her sister.

"Yeah. Peregrine dropped the charges after he heard Feodor was dead. It's not like anybody in their right mind would believe Young Ben had anything to do with him. Ben sent the tulips."

"I thought Ben sent the poppies."

"No," Deloise said slowly, "the poppies are from . . . well, you'd better read the card."

She carried over to the table a stunning arrangement of several dozen red poppies in a white porcelain vase. "Bet this cost a pretty penny," she said.

"I thought it was illegal to send people poppies," Whim remarked, "because you can extract opium from them."

"I don't think they came from a flower shop," Deloise said as Josh opened the card.

Dear Miss Weavaros, Mr. Micharainosa, and Mr. Kansas:

You are hereby formally invited to a banquet celebrating the life and accomplishments of the recently departed Feodorik Kajaźkolskiocsi. As honored guests, you will be seated at the head table and invited to share your recollections of this brilliant, visionary man.

Yours sincerely,

The Grey Circle

The invitation was embossed in gold leaf on heavy card stock—very expensive.

"What the hell is the Grey Circle," Josh asked, "and why are they celebrating Feodor's life?"

"And why did they invite *us*?" Haley added.

"The Grey Circle is a group of people who basically worship Feodor," Whim explained. "They think he's a genius, and they meet to talk about his ideas and try to take them to the next level. They probably want to pick your brain about what his universe was like and what sorts of things he was building."

"But we more or less killed him," Josh said.

Whim shrugged. "They're nuts. They'll twist whatever you say to make it sound like he had a glorious death."

Josh thought about that. Feodor hadn't had a glorious death, but he had died believing he was living a glorious life. As much as she hated Feodor and as relieved as she was that he was dead, she couldn't help feeling a little glad that, in a way, he'd gotten what he always wanted. She'd been in his head, she knew what torment he'd lived in, and she couldn't bring herself to begrudge him his victory. She couldn't even resent his idyllic death, because he'd had a supremely miserable life. Josh probably knew that better than anyone.

But she doubted the Grey Circle would understand.

"Who sent that?" she asked, pointing to a potted plant she couldn't name. "It's beautiful."

"Davita, and it's an orchid." Deloise stood up and plucked a card from between the flower stems. "It's addressed to you."

"I had to stop her from opening it," Whim added.

Josh tore the envelope open.

Dear Josh,

    I'm terribly busy, but I'll be by to see you soon. In the meantime, know
that I'm furious with you, very proud, quite amazed, and in deep trouble with your
grandfather. Say hello to Will for me,

    Davita

PS: The royal family sends their regards.

"Wow," Deloise said. She sighed happily. "Let's dismantle the junta and restore the monarchy."

Josh thought that royalty would probably just be another group trying to control her, but she didn't say anything. Let Deloise have her dreams the way everyone did.

"Royal family," Whim scoffed. "There's no one left but a few distant cousins." He took the card from Josh and put it back in its envelope. "What did you end up telling the Gendarmerie?"

"More or less the truth," Josh said. "Minus the whole True Dream Walker part."

She'd admitted her new secret identity to her sister and Whim. It just felt easier.

"Was Peregrine suspicious?" Whim asked.

"Oh yeah. I don't know how he knows, but he does. I'm going to have to watch out for him."

Haley reached out and put his hand over hers. "*We're* going to have to watch out."

And he smiled at her.

It seems like it's been a lot longer than a week since the last time I wrote. It will probably be a lot longer than a week before I write again, too, because it's killing my elbow, but I want to record this.

It's past midnight now, and I'm still awake. I guess I should be resting, but I've been flat on my back for days and tonight I just can't sleep. Too much on my mind.

I am really, really going to miss Grandma. I wish so much that I could say good-bye. Good-bye, and that I'm sorry. My disobedience did contribute to her death, and there's no use in pretending. It contributed to Kerstel's injuries and Winsor's coma. As usual, my family thinks I'm a hero and not guilty of anything, but the truth is I'm seventeen, I'm an adult in the world of dream walkers, and I've done what I've done. All I can say is that I think I've atoned. I've lost, too.

This whole stepping-up-to-adulthood thing includes being honest about my abilities, too. I am the True Dream Walker, I have that power, and I have an obligation to the Dream to keep it balanced. No more being afraid of responsibility. No more being small. No more telling myself that

"God, you look terrible," Will said.

Josh stopped writing and looked up. Her pen bit into the diary's page and made a large black blot.

She was sitting in the living room in her family's apartment, curled up on the couch under a down comforter. The television was on, but she'd turned the sound down. Except for the bluish light of the screen, the room was dark.

But not dark enough that she couldn't see Will standing at the end of the couch. He wore a pair of his old sweatpants and a loose black T-shirt. Stitches crossed his left eyebrow, a magenta bruise ran down half his face, his right hand was bandaged, and lumps of medical gauze and bandages under his shirt made him look like a hunchback. Josh knew she looked just as bad, but the sight of him all battered upset her.

"Is there an inch of you that isn't black and blue?" he asked.

"I haven't found one yet." She had no idea what else to say. "I just got home. You'd already gone to bed."

"Yeah, these meds knock me out. I've been sleeping weird hours since I got back."

Since you got home. She wanted to correct him, but didn't.

They were both quiet, and the television emitted a dim laugh track. "Do you mind if I sit down?" Will asked.

"No," she said quickly.

He sat down sideways, facing her and with one leg folded in front of him. "I can't lean my back against the couch," he explained, pressing his side against the cushions instead, "or I might mess up the skin graft."

"How bad is it?"

"The meds help with the pain, but nothing seems to stop the itching. I heard you fractured your skull."

Josh shrugged. "My elbow hurts more."

"Lauren says it's going to need surgery. That's no fun."

"Yeah."

They ran out of conversation. Josh finally capped her pen and closed her journal, then set them on the coffee table, which she discovered was worse because she no longer had anything to do with her hands.

"So," Will said, with forced casualness.

"So," she agreed.

He glanced at the television, glanced away.

"Look," Josh said, unable to deal with the tension any longer, "I don't care whether you're in my scroll or not. You're here and . . . you're *my* apprentice and I'm keeping you."

Will lifted his eyebrows and almost smiled. "You're keeping me?"

She laughed at herself. "I guess I'm asking you to stay."

The seriousness crept back into his face. "I don't want you to ask me out of pity. Or a misplaced sense of obligation. Or because you'll feel like a jerk if you don't."

"I'm asking because I want you to stay," she told him. "Because I like having you in-Dream with me, and because I need someone like you around, someone who won't cut me any slack."

The light of the television made his auburn hair seem more brown than usual. Josh had a nice view of it when he lowered his head.

She heard the same resigned, sad tone in his voice that she'd heard in the limo just after they'd seen the junta. "You're asking because you need me."

Don't, Josh. This time, don't screw it up.

Just say it.

"And because I'm in love with you," she blurted out, and Will's head snapped up.

They stared at each other for a moment, and then Josh felt herself go pink and tried to cover her face with her good hand. "I can't believe I just said that."

"No, it's—"

"Completely inappropriate—"

"It's not—"

"Because you're my apprentice, and I think you might legally be my brother now and—"

"Josh, stop," he finally said, and dragged her hand away from her face.

She was afraid to look at him. She didn't want to look. She squinted at him so hard she could only see part of his face. But the part she could see showed that he was smiling at her, and all the defeat and fear and exhaustion had vanished from his expression.

"After all we've been through," he said gently, "I think that was the bravest thing I've seen you do yet."

He kept hold of her wrist to stop her from covering her face again and, careful of her bruises, leaned forward and kissed her. One perfect, lingering kiss, after which he asked in a whisper, "Do you think I don't feel exactly the same way about you? Because I swear I do."

Josh released a small laugh, but she was crying a little too, and all she could think of to say was, "Come here," whereupon she tried to climb into his lap before realizing how painful that would be for both of them. They spent a moment figuring out how to get closer without further injuring one another, and then Will pulled the comforter around them while dropping kisses onto Josh's forehead.

She used the remote to turn off the television. In the silence afterward she heard his heart beating under her palm and remembered the moment in the ambulance when his pulse had slowed and she'd feared it would stop. Now she was shaky with relief that he was still here, that she had said the right thing to tell him how she felt, that he wanted as much from her as she wanted from him.

"So," he said, "I guess this means I get to stay your apprentice."

Josh smiled to herself, closing her eyes. "Actually, I was thinking maybe you could become my partner."

"Really? That would be cool." He kissed the top edge of her bruised ear, so lightly, and she remembered one other thing she had to tell him.

"Will?"

"Yeah?"

"My full name is Joshlyn Dustine Hazel Weavaros."

He kissed her forehead again, and she lifted her face for more.

Epilogue

They fell asleep on the couch that night, and despite the shelter of Will's arms, Josh dreamt of Warsaw.

She dreamt that she stood on the rooftop of a building staring out over the glory of the city before the war. Only the arms wrapped around her were not Will's but Feodor's, and he stood behind her and whispered of the destruction to come. As he spoke, bombs began to fall, buildings caught fire like oil-headed torches, screams from far below drifted up to them on the wafting smoke.

"We can't be here," Josh said, coughing. "We destroyed this place."

"So you did," Feodor whispered in her ear, his breath flicking her skin like the tongue of a snake. "But you *remember* it."

A bomb landed in a busy intersection, flinging nearby people through the air in every direction. The planes few so close overhead that Josh could see the empty, black eyes of the pilots.

"And you know what they say," Feodor said. "No one is ever really dead—as long as someone remembers them."

His arms tightened around her as the sirens rose to a desperate scream.

Dreamfever

For Gosha,

my favorite

List of Characters

Family

Josh Weaver (Joshlyn Dustine Hazel Weavaros)
Will Kansas: Josh's apprentice
Deloise Weaver: Josh's younger sister
Lauren (Laurentius Weavaros): Josh and Deloise's father
Kerstel Weaver: Lauren's wife, Josh and Deloise's stepmother
Peregrine Borgenicht: Josh and Deloise's grandfather, Dustine's estranged husband
Dustine Borgenicht: Josh and Deloise's grandmother, Peregrine's estranged wife (deceased)

Friends

Winsor Avish: Josh's best friend
Whim Avish: Winsor's older brother
Saidy and Alex Avish: Whim and Winsor's parents
Haley McKarr (Micharainosa): Ian's twin brother
Ian McKarr (Hianselian Micharainosa): Haley's twin brother (deceased)
Bayla Sakrov: Whim's ex-girlfriend
Bash Mirrettsio: a dream theorist, Bayla's boyfriend
Mirren Rousellario: heir to the deposed Rousellario monarchy
Katia: Mirren's cousin
Fel and Collena: Mirren's aunt and uncle
Young Ben Sounclouse: the local seer

The Junta

Peregrine Borgenicht: a member of the junta, and leader of the Lodestone Party

Anivay la Grue: a member of the junta and leader of the Troth Party

Davita Bach: the local government representative

Ithay Innay: a member of the junta

Gor Speggra: a member of the junta

First Prologue

This is my last entry: I'm going into the Dream tonight.

I didn't know I was going to do it until this morning. I woke up to the usual pitiful celebration—coffee and pastries on the good china and everyone dressed as if we were going to visit a restaurant. Aunt Collena gave me yet another robe, mostly, I think, out of the subverted hope that I'll give her my silk one with the peacocks on it. Uncle Fel gave me a computer mapping program, which now holds top honor as the single most ironic gift I've ever received; how long does he think it will take me to map our little universe? Katia was the only one who actually took my preferences into consideration and gifted me with Vampire Nazi Hunter 4: Mars.

A pity I won't live to play it.

At the end of the meal, Uncle Fel said to me, "So, how does it feel to be nineteen?"

At that moment, I knew I was going through the archway, because being nineteen felt like nothing. It meant nothing, just like my life has thus far and may forever if I don't do something to give it meaning. I will live and die here, in my perfectly mapped cell, having wasted my mind and extensive education playing video games and drawing comic books no one will ever read, a girl who never had cause to wear anything besides luxurious robes and will likely demand to be buried in the silk one with the peacocks on it just to spite her aunt.

Aunt Collena may be right that the dream walkers don't need me and that the people of the World—overcrowded as it is—don't need another rich white girl, but I know for certain that _I_ need them.

I must go now, before I lose my nerve.

~~Amiryschka Heloysia Solei Rousellario~~
Mirren

Second Prologue

Josh gazed out the windows at Warsaw. Far below ran a wide, tree-lined boulevard set with ornate five- and six-story buildings. Streetcars rushed up and down the boulevard, but on either side, horses drew carriages loaded with crates and burlap sacks. Hundreds of people moved below, swarming and seething, climbing up and down from trams, dodging carriages, migrating in and out of buildings, the men in trench coats and fedoras, the women in calf-length skirts. From four stories up, Josh watched them, astonished at their multitude and how all of them seemed to have a destination to which they could not be late.

A sound—laughter?—made her turn, and she took in the sunny apartment. Here in the parlor, art predominated. Lamp shades boasted stained glass in shades of green and yellow; on the fireplace screen, three young women in Empire ball gowns dined on a green lawn; and above the mantel, an ornately carved wooden clock ticked away the time with generous lassitude. Someone had left a cloth-bound book open on the striped sofa, and a half-full teacup cooled on the marble-topped coffee table.

Feeling happy and at peace, Josh sat down at the spinet piano, opened the keyboard cover, and began to play. She couldn't have named the tune, but she liked how the slow notes resonated in the air above the din from the street below.

A girl with long blond sausage curls dashed through the room wearing a green velvet dress and white tights. Her skirt's pleats were in disarray, and the white satin sash meant to tie around the dress's drop-waist had come undone. A pure white puppy followed on the girl's heels, barking, and the girl laughed in the breathless, drunken way of children as she ran into the hallway.

"Bryga, stop!" a young man called, but he had more or less given up by the time he reached the parlor. Seeing Josh, he smiled. He was a handsome youth, perhaps fifteen years old, not tall but nicely proportioned, and very neat in his gray pants and white shirt. With his gray eyes and blond hair, he could have been a charcoal sketch come to life.

Josh's fingers missed a note when she saw him, and she fumbled the next few measures. She recognized the young man, she even remembered that his name was Feodor, but she felt uncertain about him. Despite his trim appearance, she sensed that he was dangerous.

Someday, his eyes would be shadowed by painful memories, hardened by horror like steel thrust into an ice bath, his glance turned strange and clever, his lips thinned by an ironic, grimacelike smile. Josh knew this. Someday, he would be unable to speak a single sentence without disgust or mockery or manic glee clipping his words.

But not yet. Now he was still a young man, a bit overconfident but full of wit and exuberance and, yes, even goodness.

"We'll never get her trained, will we?" he said.

"The dog, or the girl?" Josh asked.

Feodor sat down beside Josh on the piano bench. "Preferably the girl—she'll live longer."

He began to play a gentle counterpoint. Bach himself could not have written a sweeter harmony, and for a time, they sat companionably and drew song from the instrument before them.

But Josh's eyes lingered on Feodor's hands. A scrape marred the skin on his left index finger, and she couldn't help thinking that soon there would be more scrapes, and cuts, and burns, and blood dried beneath the nails, and someday his scarred hands would build things, terrible things. . . .

"Josh?" Feodor said, so softly that her name blended with the notes of the piano.

"Yes?"

Without warning, he wrenched his hands from the keyboard and slammed the cover shut.

Josh jumped, and she would have run except that Feodor's eyes clenched her. He no longer smiled, no longer joked, and she had been wrong—he was not innocent—they had not gone back far enough—perhaps they never could—

"What are you doing here?" he asked in a low hiss. "And why did you bring those?"

He cut his head to the left, and when Josh looked behind them, she saw two devices sitting on the marble coffee table. Their curved metal panels and wire-wrapped crystals stood in contrast with the soft elegance of the room. Josh turned and moved from the piano bench to kneel beside the coffee table, and she reached out to touch one of the devices.

She explored the wire-wrapped circlet first. She knew it was meant to be worn on the head like a crown, even though it bore little resemblance to one. A bundle of wires and metal bands formed nearly a complete circle, with a jagged crystal on each side situated to rest above her temples and another cluster meant to press against the base of her skull.

The metal felt oddly warm, and she detected a faint vibration running through it. "What did you do to these crystals?" she asked Feodor.

She no longer felt afraid of him. In fact, seeing the two devices, she felt excitement stir inside her. She didn't know what these things were, but she knew they were powerful.

Feodor reluctantly knelt beside her. All his bravado had abandoned him. When a siren began to wail beyond the open windows, he sat up very straight and looked toward the street with alarm.

"Feodor," Josh said. The siren held no interest for her; she knew what it meant. She touched his arm. "What did you do to these crystals?"

Frowning, he returned his attention to the circlet. "I reversed their polarity."

Outside, an explosion. The apartment building shook and the

windows rattled. On the coffee table, cold tea sloshed over the rim of its teacup. Feodor clapped his hand to Josh's back as if he meant to force her to the floor, but Josh didn't feel concerned.

"It's just the war starting up," she said.

The second device was meant to be worn on the forearm like a vambrace. Inside a metal sheath, more crystals—some of them flecked with ash—were connected by a network of fused wires made of a variety of metals: copper, selenium, chromium, molybdenum.

Above the street, air fire filled the sky like a cosmic snare drum. The collapse of a nearby building began as the shattering of stone and evolved into deafening white noise.

"Feodor!" the little girl called from the other room. Her voice was high with fear.

"I'm coming, Bryga! Stay where you are!"

The apartment building shook again. A painted landscape behind the couch crashed to the floor, and in the other room, the puppy barked.

Feodor tried to leave the parlor, but Josh grabbed his arm. "Show me how to put these on," she ordered.

"Bryga—" he began.

"Can wait. Show me."

He obeyed, but with angry speed.

"The wires have to run along the cephalic, basilic, and median veins." When he lifted her right arm, Josh saw all of her veins pulsating just beneath the surface of her skin, as if they were fighting to escape her flesh and join with the device.

The firing of cannons continued outside. Human and mechanical screams wove together in a single wail. The apartment darkened as smoke blocked out the sun.

"Feodor!" Bryga called again.

Feodor snapped the vambrace closed around Josh's forearm. The ends of the wires dug into her skin, and she sensed that she had just hurt herself but couldn't feel it yet. Then she forgot her concern as warmth flowed down her arm and into her hand. Feodor placed the headband around her skull, and when he used a leather cord to close the open ends, he tightened the headband so that the crystals cut into Josh's scalp. For a moment, she had a dire headache; then the same warmth began to fill her head.

Yes, she thought. Yes. She felt as though she were expanding, extending outside her body, into the devices, past them, into the world around her, spreading, unstoppable.

A bomb exploded in the street outside, shattering not just the windows but the stained glass lamp shades as well. Feodor dropped to the floor, covering his eyes, but Josh stood up while the building still shook, shaking her head and flinging glass from her hair.

"Feodor!" Bryga screamed.

"I'm coming!" Feodor called to her, and he crawled toward the hallway.

"Stop!" Josh commanded, and he did stop, though his expression was furious. "Watch."

She held out her equipped arm. Spreading her fingers wide, she extended her hand toward the window and reached.

She didn't imagine what she wanted to happen—that would have been degrading. She didn't have to justify herself by explaining. All she had to do was reach. The warmth crawled down her forearm into her hand and then flooded her fingers. When heat burst out of her fingertips, the world outside the empty windows froze, then repaired itself in fast motion. Shards of glass pieced back into the window frames, the fires sucked up their smoke, the fallen buildings righted like people rising and brushing themselves off after an earthquake. The painting slid up the wall and resettled on its nail. The screams and sirens fell silent and were replaced by the idyllic ding ding of the tram and the hollow knocking of horseshoes on cobblestone streets.

Calm, steady sunshine again filled the parlor. Josh, stunned by her own strength, slowly retreated to the piano bench and—after a moment of staring at her hands and thinking, They aren't even shaking—resumed playing. After a few measures she recognized Poland's national anthem rising around her. She played it with a decisive, valiant hand, and though she did not know the lyrics, she remembered the first line.

Poland has not yet perished!

This time, when Feodor sat down beside her, he didn't try to play along. He only turned her face with gentle fingers on her chin and kissed her.

Josh hummed as she kissed him back.

She woke, shuddering and aroused, and went into the bathroom to splash cold water on her face. When her blood had stopped pounding, she tiptoed to Will's bedroom and crawled into bed with him. Lying beside him helped her remember who she was with.

And who she was.

One

Josh Weaver shaded her eyes as she mounted a low dune, her heels digging deep into the hot sand with each step. Above her, an oversize sun the color of goldenrods roasted the landscape, and around her the desert stretched endlessly in all directions, like a dusty orange carpet that just kept unrolling.

"I'm getting sand in my shoes," Will Kansas, walking beside her, complained.

Josh glanced at his torn-up sneakers, one with a ripped heel and the other burdened with black tar, and smiled. Will could destroy a pair of shoes faster than anyone she knew.

Along with the shoes, he wore jeans—also in bad shape—and a navy-blue T-shirt with a Serena's Pizzeria logo on it. Unruly clumps of auburn hair stuck to his damp forehead, his blue eyes were screwed up against the light, and a pink streak was swelling across his cheek where he'd been hit by a shutter in an earlier nightmare, but he looked good to Josh. He always looked good to Josh.

Out of the corner of her eye, she saw him glance at his watch.

"You too tired for this?" she asked. Since they'd gotten the crap kicked out of them by a zombie and a deranged scientist four months earlier, they both wore out faster.

Will shrugged. "Nah, I'm okay."

"I could help with this one," she offered.

"No," he said firmly. "Stay here. Practice your merging."

Josh heard the anxiety in his voice but didn't know how to soothe him. His skin graft had healed, his stitches had come out, and he had the feeling back in his fingers, but emotionally he was far from recovered.

She put a hand on his arm. "If you need me, just give a shout."

"Don't worry," he said, checking his shoulder holster. "I won't."

Josh sighed.

The structure atop the dune didn't look quite like anything else Josh had ever seen. Long adobe walls stretched toward the open sky, reminding her of the Southwest, but the lack of roof meant the building offered little protection from the sun.

Closing her eyes, she carefully broke Stellanor's First Rule of dream walking: *Never let the dreamer's fear become your own.* She'd been breaking it for so many years that she didn't even pause to consider the wisdom of her action.

She allowed the dreamer's fear to touch her, just one fingertip, then two, and the taste of panic she felt wasn't the connection with the Dream that she wanted, but it told her what she needed to know.

"It's not a building," she said, her eyes flying open. "It's a labyrinth."

She and Will reached an opening into the structure and stopped walking.

"I was pretty sure this is a monster dream," Will told her. He had been the one who had chosen the nightmare back in the archroom. "And you know what monster lives in a labyrinth, right?"

"The Minotaur. Half bull, half man."

Will's blue eyes widened in surprise. "Yeah."

Josh frequently napped during world lit, which Will knew. Six months ago she might not have known the word "labyrinth," let alone been able to identify the Minotaur. But that had been before a madman with an extensive classical education had downloaded his memories into her brain. Now she not only knew the Minotaur, she could quote lines about him from both Ovid and Dante.

But Will didn't know that, and Josh had been biting her tongue pretty hard the last four months to make sure he didn't find out.

From inside the labyrinth came a deafening bellow. The ground shook so hard, Josh had to grab Will's shoulder to keep from falling over. She wasn't certain, but she thought she heard a word in the cry.

"Did it say 'spheres'?" she asked Will in a whisper.

"I thought it said 'deers.' Are you sure you want to try this *now*?"

Josh nodded. "Just keep it distracted."

Will unbuckled his shoulder holster and removed a .22 semiautomatic. "I should have brought a bigger gun."

Today was the first time Josh had let him bring any sort of gun into the Dream. He was not actually much good with them, despite having practiced more than most Olympic shooters. She tried to figure out a polite way of taking the .22 away from him and couldn't come up with one.

"Love you," was all she said.

He grinned, kissed her quickly, and headed into the labyrinth. "Love you back!" he called over his shoulder.

Josh sank to the ground until she could sit against the labyrinth wall. The heat captured in the adobe felt good against her back and shoulder blades, and she took a few long, deep breaths to settle her heart rate.

She was already losing interest in the nightmare—what she wanted was to merge with the Dream itself. She felt hungry for its ease and expansive freedom. She had felt it once, felt her mind blown open to contain all the World's dreams and nightmares at once, and she had been trying to recapture that sense of unity and connection ever since.

So far, she had been unsuccessful.

Inhale, exhale. Inhale, exhale.

She closed her eyes and focused on the air moving in and out of her lungs.

Inhale, exhale. Inhale . . .

She stopped thinking, as much as she could. Instead she felt her body's weight on the sand, the relentless heat of the sun tightening her skin, and the dull ache in her right elbow that never fully went away. She focused completely on her physical self.

An image flashed in her mind. With a phantom's eyes, she saw the labyrinth as if from above. The walls were moving on tracks hidden beneath the sand, sliding from side to side, blocking off and opening up routes at random. Staying lost forever in such a maze would be easy.

Then the flash was over, and she was back in her body.

The night she and Will and Haley had almost died, she had felt the entirety of the Dream inside her, the whole universe filling her skin. This comparatively meager merger felt like being teased, but it was as close as Josh had been able to come.

More deep breaths, more focus . . .

The next flash showed her Will, jumping out of the way just in time to avoid being crushed between the ends of two walls, and the dreamer, a little old Middle Eastern man in jean cutoffs and a red tank top that hardly covered his pot belly.

Finally she saw the Minotaur, and she understood for the first time why the Greeks had considered it a terrible monster. It stood taller and overall larger than she had ever expected, so large that its bull's head looked proportional, and its swarthy body rippled with muscle. It didn't even have a neck—its jaw just expanded into its shoulders, and its whole upper body twisted when it turned to look at something. Its horns were chiseled to needle points, each pointing forward and slightly out to the side.

But none of that made the Minotaur anything more than intimidating. What scared Josh was what the monster had done to itself: it was trying to become human, one body part at a time. Swaths of human skin in varying shades of pink and brown had been sewn over its fur. Its cow's eyes had been torn out and replaced with human eyes, one blue and one green, and they were too small to fully fill the Minotaur's cavernous eye sockets. Strangest of all, it had pulled out all its teeth and was wearing a pair of human dentures that filled only the front third of its bull's snout.

It released a roar, half bull's bellow and half human shout, and the word it shouted was neither "spheres" nor "deers" but *"EARS!"*

Gross, Josh thought.

Just before the flash ended, she caught a glimpse of someone else: a young woman, her face hidden by a curtain of dark red hair, collapsed at the end of one corridor. She appeared to be fast asleep.

Who is that? Josh wondered, the surprise jerking her back into her body. *And how can she be sleeping?*

From somewhere nearby came the sound of adobe being crushed. It sounded like the Minotaur had gotten tired of searching the maze and started tearing walls down instead.

Josh tried to settle back into her breathing, but she was distracted by the flash of the young woman sleeping in the sand. She didn't seem to fit in this nightmare, which meant she was probably a second dreamer.

More than one dreamer could participate in the same nightmare; sometimes people really *did* meet in their dreams. But multi-dreamer nightmares were usually more chaotic than this one thanks to the manifestations of multiple subconsciousnesses appearing simultaneously.

But a dreamer was what the redhead had to be, and since Will hadn't found her, that made her Josh's responsibility.

For the hundredth time since she'd woken up from her coma in February, she felt overcome by frustration. The power of the True Dream Walker that she had used to save Will, Haley, and herself had abandoned her. She had retained only one ability, and it was a small one.

It wouldn't help her now. She was going to have to do this the hard way.

As she jumped to her feet, gunshots echoed through the labyrinth. Josh counted three, and then she heard the Minotaur's inhuman roar: *"SKIN!"*

Sounds like a hit, she thought.

As Josh ran into the labyrinth, Will fired again, and the bullet must have hit home, because the Minotaur released a bellow more terrible than any he'd emitted before.

"EST!"

She ran toward the Minotaur, whose location was easy to identify because it stood taller than any of the walls around it.

Sooner than she'd expected, she saw the redhead collapsed at the far end of a corridor. She loped down the corridor while calling, "Come on! Let's get you out of here!"

The redhead didn't stir until Josh shook her. Then she opened bleary gray eyes, examined Josh briefly, and went back to sleep.

"You've got to come with me," Josh said.

"Go away please," the girl said.

For an instant, Josh considered opening an archway and waking the girl up. But two-dreamer nightmares didn't always play by the rules; if Josh woke the girl up, the nightmare might end, causing the Dream to shift and tossing Josh and Will into different nightmares. He'd never been in-Dream alone before.

"You can either run or I can drag you," Josh told the redhead, and when she got no immediate response, she grabbed the young woman's ankles.

"No, no!" the redhead protested. "I can walk. Just help me up."

Moments later, Josh began questioning whether or not she should have carried the redhead after all. The young woman could hardly stumble along at a fast walk, never mind run.

They made it to a clearing where the rubble of shattered walls covered the desert floor. "Stay here," Josh told the redhead, and helped her sit down behind a partially demolished wall. Two more shots went off.

From deeper within the labyrinth, the Minotaur bellowed, *"UUUMMMS!"*

Gums? Josh wondered, beginning to run again.

She headed for the bellow, into the passage of fallen walls it had created. She hadn't gone far when she caught sight of the Minotaur. It crashed through walls, head-butting one and punching through another, and the skin on its hands had been peeled back to reveal raw bone and muscle. Its thumbs were missing.

Oh, Josh thought, pulling the .32 from the holster at the small of her back. *Not "Gums!" It meant "Thumbs!"*

How Will had managed to shoot off both its thumbs was a mystery to her.

"Will!" she shouted, taking aim, and then she shot the Minotuar twice in the back of the head.

One bullet stuck in his flesh, but the other actually bounced off his scalp and fell onto the sand. Even before the creature turned and fixed a look of gross hatred on her, Josh was pretty sure that neither shot had penetrated the creature's skull.

"Josh?" Will called out incredulously. He peeked around a corner and—seeing that the Minotaur's back was turned—ducked into the corridor. His expression startled Josh: he looked almost as mad as the Minotaur. "What are you *doing*?"

"Come this way!" Josh called. "I'll cover you!"

He protested, and she fired three shots, this time into the beast's chest. Its breastbone was covered in a patchwork quilt of pieces of skin, each a different hue, but they all bled the same dark blood where the bullets pierced them.

"Go back!" Will called. Behind him, the little Middle Eastern dreamer peeked out at the Minotaur, which had dipped a finger in one of its wounds and was now sniffing its own blood.

"No, come this way. There's another dreamer."

"CHESSST!" it roared, throwing its head back.

Josh fired again. Will's expression grew even darker, but he grabbed the dreamer's hand and dragged him down the corridor toward Josh.

Clearly, the bullets were doing little to slow the Minotaur down. *I should have brought an ax,* Josh thought. *Axes are always more useful than guns.*

Suddenly she flashed back on the nightmare she'd had the night before. Feodor, and the war, and the strange devices. What would she have given at this moment to have the circlet and vambrace, to be able to reach out and change the Dream, to have whatever she needed to protect Will?

She would have given almost anything.

But she didn't have the circlet and vambrace, or even an ax, so she tried something new. Instead of aiming for vital organs, Josh shot at the Minotaur's knees. One shot went between its legs, but the other two hit their mark and blew the creature's kneecaps off like corks exploding from wine bottles full of blood and bone fragments.

Unfortunately, the shot that had gone wild had hit the dreamer's foot as he and Will tried to scramble past the Minotaur. "I'm hit! I'm hit!" the little old man cried out. Then, rather comically, he added, "Good-bye, cruel world!"

Josh and Will both rolled their eyes. Will dragged the dreamer toward Josh, who shot the Minotaur a few more times to distract it as they passed by. Then she slung one of the dreamer's arms around her neck, and she and Will carried him at a run back to the clearing.

Behind the partially demolished wall, she found the redhead asleep on the sand. Stunned, Josh stood with her mouth hanging open for a moment. Dreamers could dream that they were sleeping, but when they did, they inevitably began dreaming that they were having another dream.

"Wake up," Josh said, kneeling down. She shook the girl's shoulder through her windbreaker. "Come on, you have to wake up."

"Just leave me," the redhead murmured without opening her eyes.

"Nope, you're coming with me."

As Josh helped/forced her to her feet, the Minotaur emerged from the labyrinth. It appeared to have torn its lower legs off completely and was now walking on the ends of its thighbones. The method proved surprisingly speedy.

Josh didn't have time to open an archway to the World in the traditional fashion, by reflecting light into a doorway, so she closed her eyes and imagined an archway right in front of them, standing in the open air with no need for a doorframe to hold it up. With that image in mind, she opened her eyes and thrust her left arm out. A burst of dense air flew from her palm, shot ten feet forward, and then expanded with a ripple into a freestanding archway. Its surface glittered like a gossamer fabric, but when Josh and Will shoved the redhead through, no material held her back. Josh cast one more glance at the Minotaur—now only a dozen paces away— and she grabbed the other dreamer's hand and jumped.

Creating archways was the only True Dream Walker power Josh had retained. If not for that, she would have questioned her destiny entirely.

The burst of air conditioning that greeted her in the sterile white archroom was both soothing and refreshing. She inhaled, feeling satisfied, until she saw Will glaring at her.

"What the hell were you thinking back there?" he demanded.

His anger caught her off guard. "What?" she asked, more out of surprise than defiance.

"I could have dealt with that by myself. But what did you do? You—*you,* who was perfectly safe—decided to jump into the middle of danger for no reason at all!"

"I had to get the girl out," Josh protested, finding her voice again.

"No, you didn't! Who cares about the girl? She was just one dreamer!" And he must have known what Josh was thinking, because he added, "She sure as hell wasn't *your* responsibility!"

"And I'm not *your* responsibility!"

Josh didn't like the tone she was using. She knew it meant she had already lost her temper and all she could hope for now was that she wouldn't kick anybody or say anything she couldn't take back.

Will must have recognized her tone, too. He got that condescending look in his eye that meant he was retreating into psychoanalyst mode. Josh hated that look.

Both her tone and his look had become all too familiar recently.

"I told you that I don't want you to be reckless anymore, remember?" he said hotly. "I told you after that *Titanic* nightmare that it freaks me out when you take stupid risks."

"And you get to decide which risks are stupid? I'm supposed to check in with you before I do anything? *You're* the apprentice, Will, remem—"

A whimper interrupted Josh's rant. She and Will looked in the direction from which the sound had come.

The redheaded girl was huddled against the far wall of the arch-room, her blue-green windbreaker sparkling with fairy dust.

Josh saw movement out of the corner of her eye and realized Will was pointing his gun at the girl's head.

"Will!" she cried, and at the same moment, the girl fainted.

Two

Shoot her.

That was the only thought in Will's mind. The girl had come out of the Dream, just like two others once had, and if somebody had been around to shoot them the moment they arrived, a lot of people wouldn't have gotten hurt.

Shoot her in the head.

His finger twitched against the trigger. Only the sound of Josh shouting his name stopped him from firing.

Josh rushed forward in a valiant effort to catch the young woman as she fainted. She failed, but the stranger collapsed in a rather neat pile, with her head resting on one forearm. Will kept his sights on her as she fell, like a hunter following the flight of a bird.

"Crap," Josh said. She got down on her knees next to the girl's inert form, then glanced at Will. "Could you *not* point the gun at me?" she demanded.

Her words broke through the dark tunnel in which Will's mind was caught; still, he lowered the gun with reluctance. "I'm out of bullets," he said, realizing the truth of the statement as he spoke.

"Do I care?" Josh asked. "What was the first thing I taught you about guns?"

It had been *Never point a gun at a person unless you're going to kill them.*

But I was going to kill her, Will protested silently. *I think that maybe I still should.*

He aimed the gun at the floor with one hand and rubbed the back of his neck with the other. He had to stop thinking that way.

Feodor was dead. He hadn't sent the girl.

"Go get me some smelling salts, would you?" Josh asked.

"Yeah, sure." Will heard how hollow his voice sounded.

"And Will? Don't bring the gun when you come back."

"Sure," he said again.

He exited the archroom into the basement, a long, concrete room with small windows near the ceiling. In the center of the room sat the training mats and equipment: heavy bag, kettlebells, cardio machines, a rack of weights. At the far end of the room, where storage bins of holiday décor were piled to the ceiling and out-of-style furniture kept house for ghosts, Will had set up a research center with his files organized in the drawers of a gray metal desk and a timeline of Feodor Kajażkołski's life strung across mismatched corkboards.

Will's friend Whim Avish called the timeline Will's "stalker wall."

Ostensibly, Will was investigating Feodor in hopes of learning something that would help Whim's sister, Winsor, who had remained comatose since one of Feodor's goons had attacked her. But Will was self-aware enough to know that his real motivation was more personal and less reasonable: Will was afraid of the man. And he was irrationally afraid that Feodor was coming back.

Pulling his eyes away from the stalker wall, he locked the .22 back in the gun safe. Then he opened the giant emergency first-aid kit and found a few packages of smelling salts. Plastic tubes in hand, he typed in the code to open the vault door to the archroom.

The arch to which the room's name referred stood in the center of curved white walls. Two pillars of gray stone rose out of the ground beneath and up through the floor to create an archway overhead. Nearby, a slab of frosted red glass the size of a textbook stood suspended at waist height on top of a metal pole. At the moment, the archway appeared empty, but Will knew that if he pressed his hand to the red stone—the looking stone—the archway would become a portal leading to the Dream universe.

Josh was sitting on the floor with the redhead's feet in her lap.

"I'm sorry about that," Will said. "With the gun."

"It's all right," Josh replied. "Her coming out of the Dream like that was . . . well, unexpected."

Josh didn't say, *Freakishly similar to last time, when my grandmother got killed and my best friend got her soul sucked out and my stepmother got beaten into the ICU and almost lost a baby she didn't even know she was carrying.*

Josh didn't say that, because she didn't talk about Feodor. Not ever.

As Will broke open a plastic tube of salts and held them close to the girl's nose, he got his first good look at her face. He had never seen a beauty quite like hers. Delicate, feminine features were laid over a heavy—almost masculine—bone structure, and the combination made her appear both winsome and strong. Her dark red hair hung all the way to her waist, even tangled into early-stage dreadlocks as it was.

She was beautiful in spite of her current state, which included shadows beneath her eyes so dark and deep that they looked like Halloween makeup, a scratched and swollen chin, dirt lines discoloring her broken nails, and chapped white lips.

Almost immediately, the girl woke with a grimace and began trying to rise.

"Wait a sec," Josh said. "Take it easy. You fainted."

The girl looked around the room with large gray eyes and an expression of distress that suggested she thought she might not have woken up at all.

"What's your name?" Josh asked.

The girl stared at her, panic-stricken. "Am I dead?"

"Definitely not," Josh said.

The answer relieved some of the anxiety in the redhead's face. "Are we still in the Dream?"

"No," Josh repeated.

"It's a miracle," the girl murmured.

She closed her eyes, slowly this time, and released a long sigh. Josh and Will waited for her to open her eyes again, but she didn't, and when her breath began to deepen, Josh said, "Did she pass out again?"

"I think she just went to sleep." Will touched the young woman's shoulder. "Miss? Can you wake up?"

He gave her a little shake, then a less little shake, and finally her eyes opened again.

"You need to stay awake," Josh said. "You might have a head injury."

Will assumed Josh was making this suggestion based on the fact that the redhead had visible injuries to her hands, neck, and face, and blood stained her ripped turquoise jacket.

The young woman's eyes fluttered shut and then dragged open again. "May I sit up?"

"Slowly."

Once sitting, she insisted on climbing to her feet, and she took a few slow steps toward the archway. Josh stayed close by, as if worried the redhead would try to leap back into the Dream.

"I didn't catch your name," Josh said.

The redhead made no reply. She touched the stone archway with one hand, then passed her fingers through the empty space between the pillars. Will noticed that her right pant leg was torn vertically and something dark had seeped through the back of her jacket. A patch of hair had been torn out of her scalp.

"I'm sorry," she said, turning back to them. "You'll have to forgive me. I can't recall my name. It's on the tip of my tongue, but I can't quite catch it."

"You don't remember your name?" Josh asked. "What about where you're from, or how you ended up in the Dream?"

The redhead shook her head. "Nothing."

"You don't remember *anything*?" Josh asked. Her tone had gone from skeptical to incredulous. "You have . . ." She hesitated before using the word, as if embarrassed to put forth such a silly idea. *"Amnesia?"*

"Yes. Yes, I think I do."

Josh looked at Will, and that was all she needed to say, *Do you believe this?!*

Will held a hand up for her to be patient. Not that he believed the redhead—her downcast eyes and the speed with which she'd spoken had broadcast her lie. He was just hoping to figure out *why* she had lied.

"Does your head hurt?" he asked.

The redhead looked at him beneath eyelids that kept threatening to close. "Yes," she said. "It hurts. I need to sleep."

"Take off your windbreaker," Josh said, "so I can check you for injuries."

She fumbled with the zipper on her jacket and finally tugged it open.

"Damn," Will said when he saw her.

Bruises, cuts, scrapes, a serious bite, puncture wounds, and even what appeared to be burns covered her skin.

Josh's animosity vanished. "What hurts?" she asked briskly.

The redhead gave a long list of pains, and Will believed her about every one. Joints were swollen, scrapes ran in every direction, bruises spread far and wide. She had a three-inch gash on her back that was clearly infected and another bite on her leg beneath the tear in her pants.

While Josh inspected the visible injuries, Will did a quick and dirty evaluation of her mental state. She knew who was president, how many continents were on the Earth, and that Schwarzenegger had played the Terminator, but she was two days off the date and claimed not to remember anything about herself except the name Nan.

"Is that *your* name?" Will asked.

"I don't know."

When they were finished, Josh and Will conferred on the other side of the room.

"She needs stitches, antibiotics, and probably a rabies shot," Josh whispered. "Obviously she's been in the Dream. How else did she get burned *and* bitten by an animal *and* hit in the head *and* shot with an arrow? But the weird thing is some of those bruises are fresh, but some of them are a few days old."

"What does that mean?"

"Maybe she's just been dream walking nonstop for the last week—and doing a terrible job—or maybe she's been lost in the Dream for *days*."

If she had been in the Dream for days, fighting off monsters and running from disasters and enduring the fear of so many dreamers, that would explain why she was so exhausted and possibly even her bizarre lie. People could easily become delirious after several days without sleep.

"There's no way to be sure without a CT, but I don't think she has a concussion," he told Josh. "Or at least, if she did have one, she's recovered enough that she's able to go to sleep without falling into a coma. The best treatment might be to just let her sleep, at least until Saidy's off work."

Saidy was Whim and Winsor's mother, and she lived on the second floor. She was also a paramedic, and over the years she had cleaned a lot of wounds, stitched a lot of cuts, and driven a lot of people to the ER.

Josh nodded. "She can take Grandma Dustine's old room. She probably needs food, too. Let's get her upstairs."

Watching Josh gather the redhead's discarded jacket, Will felt the muscles around his rib cage contract and press painfully on his lungs. *It's so easy for you to feel responsible for people*, he thought. *If they're in the Dream and in danger, their well-being is instantly more important than yours.*

She'd told Will once that she felt ashamed of the fact that she sometimes had difficulty caring about other people's problems, that she worried she wasn't as compassionate as she should be. But Will thought that this sense of absolute responsibility was its own kind of compassion and astonishing in its own right.

He just hoped it didn't get her killed someday.

Josh explained about Saidy and that they'd get the girl medical attention as soon as possible. "You said you remembered a name? Nan? Is that what we should call you?"

"I suppose . . . Nan will do as well as any other name."

"All right. Are you a dream walker, Nan?"

Oddly uncertain, Nan said, "I believe I am, Josh."

"Well then, you can stay here until we figure all this out," Josh said. "Salt among oceans, right?"

Will didn't know what that meant, but it made Nan smile for the first time. She had a beautiful smile; it conferred a sense of wise benevolence and, at the same time, vigor. She didn't look tired when she smiled. "Salt among oceans," she repeated, as if in agreement. "I am very grateful for your hospitality." She added ruefully, "Although I doubt I'll be able to sleep in someone else's bed."

"Why not?" Will asked, opening the archroom's heavy door. "You don't remember your own, right?"

Nan almost tripped over her feet as she followed. "Right," she agreed.

As they crossed the basement, Will noticed Nan's eyes fall on his stalker wall. "Is that . . ." she muttered, and then shook herself, as if she had started to fall asleep again. Will put a hand on her elbow to nudge her up the stairs.

Josh and Will lived in a large Greek Revival–style mansion that had been converted into a triplex. Josh's family lived on the third floor, and Saidy and Alex Avish lived in one of the second-floor apartments. Will had recently been booted from his third-floor bedroom to make room for his adoptive parents' new baby, but he didn't mind. He and Haley and Whim were living in the other second-floor apartment, where they had created a teenage dude paradise.

As they crossed the first-floor landing, Will caught a glimpse of a hideous lime-green-and-butter-yellow-striped cardigan walking into the library farther down the hallway. "Haley!" Josh called. "Come here for a minute!"

Will hoped Josh wasn't about to do what he thought she was about to do.

Haelipto McKarr, most often addressed as Haley, was best known for not saying very much. When Will had first met him, Haley was being haunted by his brother Ian's disembodied soul, which had occasionally possessed Haley's body. It had taken a while for Will to suss out who Haley was apart from his brother, but when he finally had, he'd discovered an observant, infinitely kind guy whose subtle sense of humor was easy to miss. Will liked him tremendously.

Hell, by the time they freed Ian's soul—no easy task—Will had come to like Ian, too.

Will understood immediately what Josh intended. Haley's psychic powers operated partly through touch; a handshake or kiss on the cheek could tell him all kinds of things. Will didn't like the idea of Josh using Haley's abilities to get information from people against their will, but he didn't argue, because as long as Nan kept up the amnesia act, he still considered her an unknown. And unknowns had a way of becoming dangers in his experience.

"Nan, this is Haley," Josh said, careful to set the introduction up properly. "Haley, Nan."

Nan pushed herself upright from the wall she had been leaning against and held out her hand. "How do you do?" she asked.

Haley took her hand slowly, hardly touching her with more than his fingertips.

Then, just when Will thought he would let go, Haley grabbed Nan's hand like a drowning man clutching at the side of a boat. Nan released a cry and pulled away.

Haley sucked in a wet, sick-sounding breath and ran for the stairs.

"Oh, my," Nan said in a dreamy, drowsy voice. "I should have washed my hands first."

Her eyes closed and she fell against the wall. Josh, grabbing Nan to keep her upright, gave Will a look.

"I'll go," Will said. As Josh revived Nan, Will jogged up the stairs to the second floor.

The guys' apartment looked exactly as one would expect an apartment occupied by three teenage boys to look. Nothing on the walls except a flat-screen TV and a poster for *Alien*, carpet that hadn't been vacuumed in months, a bag of chips spilled on the grubby old couch, and a trash-rescued bookcase packed with movies and video games.

Haley had taken the master bedroom when he moved back in— this was, in fact, *his* apartment—but his bedroom looked just as bad as the living room did.

"Hey," Will said when Haley let him in. He brushed some clothes off the desk chair and sat down. "What happened back there?"

Haley didn't look good. He looked like he'd just realized he had food poisoning and would inevitably begin vomiting soon. He'd even opened the window, in spite of the June heat.

At Will's question, he started to pull a steno pad and pen out of the pocket of his awful green-and-yellow cardigan, then stopped himself. He and Will had begun their friendship on the premise that Haley could tell Will things—even crazy things—and Will would believe him, but sometimes Haley still fought the urge to censor himself, and sometimes Will still found the things Haley told him hard to swallow.

"I saw . . . a lot," Haley managed to say. "She's in danger."

"Okay. What kind of danger?"

Haley cracked his knuckles. "I can't . . ."

Will hadn't seen him reduced to sentence fragments in a long time, and that worried him. "You can tell me, Haley. You know I only want to help her."

He realized he sounded patronizing at the same moment Haley sent him a sharp glance. The days when he had to talk to Haley like he was a five-year-old were over. Will shrugged apologetically, and Haley shrugged back in forgiveness.

"I can't tell you," he said, as if forcing the words out. "The more people who know who she is, the more danger she's in."

Well, that explains why she's lying about having amnesia, Will thought, but otherwise, he hated this news. He needed to know who Nan really was, what sort of trouble she was in, and whether or not her troubles could expand to encompass those around her.

But he saw a rare determination in Haley's eyes. *I can trust Haley's judgment,* he told himself, even as he remembered how Haley had eaten that cheddar with the mold growing on it two weeks before.

Cheese and people are not the same.

Will sighed. "What do we do?"

"Hide her. Call Davita."

"Davita?"

Davita Bach was the local representative of the dream-walker government. Although she had stuck her neck out to protect Josh and Will on more than one occasion, Will had never felt entirely confident that he could trust the woman. Anyone who worked for one government while wearing the symbol of another hidden beneath her blouse made him doubt her capacity for loyalty.

"Call her," Haley repeated. "Tell her to come here. Don't tell her why until she's here."

"You're worried about the phone?" Will asked, half-disbelieving.

Haley looked him square in the eyes then. "No one can know she's here. She can hide in my room. I'll sleep on the couch."

"*Your* room? *Where?*" Will cast his hand about the room.

"I can clean up," Haley protested. "Please, Will."

Will felt too frustrated to smile back. Six months ago he would have respectfully let the subject drop, but today he wanted to make demands. He wasn't just curious—he *needed* to know what was going on. If they were in danger—if Josh was in danger—and he didn't see it coming, something terrible could happen and he'd be helpless to stop it.

He knew that Gloves—Feodor's zombie henchman—trying to kill them had changed Will. These days, he wanted to know everything going on: who was where, and with whom, and when they would be back. He wanted to do everything himself to make sure it got done properly, so he could know with certainty that things were taken care of.

He knew he wasn't okay. But he also knew that he should trust Haley in this, that he had no reason not to. Besides, letting Nan stay in their apartment would allow Will to keep a close eye on her.

"Can you promise she isn't a danger to us?" he asked.

Haley looked perplexed. "She just needs a place to hide."

"Okay," Will said. "I'll call Davita."

Haley sank back against the bedroom wall, relieved. "Tell her . . ." He thought. "Tell her that the tragedy isn't a tragedy yet."

"Will she know what that means?" Will couldn't help asking.

Haley frowned again, uncertain. "I hope so," he said.

Will went downstairs to tell Josh the new plan, and by the time they got Nan up to the second floor—she swayed on each step—Haley had cleaned 90 percent of the mess in his room. He'd accomplished this by dragging the mess into the living room, rendering it a minefield of dirty clothes, sci-fi novels, steno pads, and Sharpies.

While Haley put clean sheets on his bed, Will tried to coax Nan into eating a peanut-butter-and-blueberry-preserves sandwich. She made it through about half, but Will could tell she was out of energy—she couldn't even remember how to open a soda can and just kept spinning the tab like the hand on a clock. Finally, Josh took her into the bedroom and helped her out of her filthy clothes and into a T-shirt and pajama pants. Nan was asleep before Josh closed the bedroom door.

Hours later, Saidy confirmed Josh's earlier suspicions: Nan had a sprained wrist, two broken fingers, one twisted ankle, a ruptured eardrum, three infected wounds, and a toenail that had to come off immediately. Since Nan was able to remain awake long enough for Saidy to evaluate and treat her, they decided it was safe to let her go back to sleep afterward.

The story they had agreed on and told Saidy was that Nan was a dream walker who had gotten lost in the Dream for a number of days and that they wanted to let her rest before putting her on a plane home. The only part of the story Nan got wrong was that instead of saying she was from Chicago, she named Geneva as her hometown. Frantic glances were exchanged until they discovered that Nan knew an inordinate amount about Switzerland and was able to converse easily in French.

"Maybe she's really Swiss," Josh whispered to Will.

Saidy left, and Nan slumped over on the bed, mumbling, *"Au revoir,"* as she fell back to sleep.

Late that night, Will woke to the sound of his bedroom door opening. No light came from the living room, but he knew that the figure darting into his room was Josh. He rolled to the far side of his twin bed and held up the blanket for her to climb under.

He didn't have to ask what was wrong; he knew from the way she trembled that she'd woken up from a nightmare. Ever since Feodor had tried to kill her with his memories—and Feodor had lived through the worst parts of World War II—she'd been having nightmares. He suspected that some of those memories had simply stayed in her subconscious.

"Sorry," Josh whispered.

"For what?" Will whispered back, tucking her in beside him. "Letting me sleep next to my girl?"

He kept his words light to hide his rage. He had never hated anyone the way he hated Feodor Kajażkołski. Feeling Josh hide her face in his shoulder and hold him with her fists clenched against his back made Will want to go buy a bigger gun. It made him regret the peaceful death he had allowed Feodor. The man should have suffered the way Josh was suffering now.

But Will knew that anger was only ever a shield against hurt or fear, and he didn't want to burden Josh with either of those, so he just tightened his arms around her. Her neck was sweaty, but he kissed it anyway. "You're safe. Go to sleep, Josh. You're safe here."

He didn't know what she'd dreamed of, and he didn't ask because he didn't think he could bear to know.

He was right.

Three

Waking was difficult. Mirren struggled up into

her mind, which was as gray as early morning, but her body kept calling out to her like a foghorn: *Sleeeeep. Sleeeeep. Sleeeeep.*

She opened her eyes, despite the pain, and saw that the foreign bedroom was dark and empty. She didn't understand why she had woken up until she realized how full her bladder was. Since entering the Dream, she had peed in a lot of weird places, and she wondered what new dreamscape she would mark as her territory this time.

Then she remembered: She had left the Dream. She was in the World.

Her heart thumped, causing an echoing throb in her bladder. The *World*. She had finally escaped and reached the World.

She recognized the bedroom she'd fallen asleep in. Someone had closed the window, and the room had grown cool. Mirren wished she had asked where the bathroom was before she'd fallen asleep, but perhaps this way was better. She'd have an excuse to walk around without an escort.

Suddenly the stranger's bed felt safe and familiar, the house beyond it a vast and dangerous vista.

You're in a house, she told herself. *No doubt it's similar to the houses on TV. There will be a kitchen, and a bathroom, and bedrooms.*

She hoped there weren't any dogs.

Summoning strength against the numerous pains and stiff muscles that protested her movement, she climbed out of the bed and approached the window. The anticipation she felt at looking through the glass was so intense, it felt almost like fear. After a minute spent wrestling with the lock, she knelt in front of the open window to press her face against the screen.

She closed her eyes and breathed deep.

The warm air that entered her lungs smelled faintly sweet, but also ruddy. She didn't have names for the scents—one note was grainy and rich like velvet, another carried a sour smell like spinach. Ripe, gaudy florals; a faint chemical odor she imagined to be smog; even the metallic burn of the window screen. The air felt damp in her throat, and every time she inhaled she tasted something new. Crickets chirped charmingly—she recognized them from films—and tree leaves rustled one another as a slow breeze blew. Mirren opened her eyes and stared out at the branches and the moon passing behind them.

She felt dizzy from the wonder of it all.

But her bladder ached. She made herself stand up and go to the door; the window would still be open when she returned.

Although she didn't remember changing her clothes, she now wore a T-shirt and too-short flannel pants. She hesitated at the door, unsure if this was an appropriate outfit to wear outside of the bedroom or if she should attempt to locate a robe.

The thought made her laugh. All those beautiful robes she had left behind, only to find herself in need of one here.

Her hand closed around the cold metal doorknob. *Just a house,* she reminded herself, but she had never been in any house besides her own.

Her mind was waking up, and it was full of warnings. It reminded her that she was trapped in the World with no way to get home, that her family likely thought she was dead, and that if anyone here found out who she was, they might very well have her executed. She had done a terrible job of blending in so far—she knew she had. She should have figured out how to open the Coke on her own, and her amnesia story was ludicrous, not to mention whatever had gone wrong with the handshake.

But she was pinching her thighs together as though trying to carry a dime between her knees, and she realized she couldn't put off finding a bathroom any longer. With a resolute motion, she turned the knob and opened the door.

She'd thought everyone would be asleep, but someone was sitting on the living room couch watching television. When he heard the door open, he turned his head, and she recognized him as the guy who had squeezed her hand and then run. *Haley,* she remembered. Mirren hadn't realized it was a unisex name.

The people on television were dancing in a club, and the colored lights wavered over the living room walls like aquarium lights. Mirren had always wanted to visit an aquarium. So many romantic scenes in films took place in them.

But Haley stood up and turned on a lamp missing its shade. Then he picked up a remote control and shut off the television, and after that they were just two people standing in a brightly lit room amid piles of dirty laundry.

Haley appeared younger than the teenage boys on television, less muscular, still a little gangly. His hairstyle looked less like sculpted bedhead than just bedhead, and she couldn't tell if his green-and-yellow cardigan was fashionable or some sort of security blanket he wore at night. As she watched him, wishing she had something witty to say, he reached into his pocket and pulled out a small pad of paper and a Sharpie.

Should she walk away? Was their earlier mishap his way of telling her that he didn't care to know her? He flipped pages on the pad as if looking for notes, but after reaching a blank page and staring at it for several seconds, he put the pad and pen down on the couch.

"Hey," he said to Mirren. The word seemed to require a great deal of effort to pronounce.

Mirren smiled, because she knew the socially appropriate response to his greeting. "Hey," she replied.

He thought some more. Then he said, "I know who you are."

Her breath caught in her throat.

I must have given myself away the moment I opened my mouth. I have to get out of here.

"Is there a ladies' room nearby?" she asked.

Haley wet his lips, looking confused. He pointed at a door next to an open laundry closet.

The bathroom was small and not very clean. It smelled of something both sour and musky that Mirren couldn't identify. Throwing back the soap-streaked shower curtain, she saw what she was hoping for: a window.

A very small window.

I won't fit through that, she admitted to herself. Her rapid breath grew frantic as she sat on the closed toilet lid. She was so scared, she couldn't imagine removing a single article of clothing, let alone urinating.

I just got here; this can't be my end already. What sort of destiny is that? They told me so many times that I wasn't ready—why didn't I listen? What was I thinking when I left home?

She had been thinking that she had been a prisoner all her life and that she didn't intend to die a prisoner. She had been thinking that she was nineteen, the age of royal majority, and she needed to prove—to herself and her family—that she was worthy of being her parents' daughter. She had been thinking that she couldn't stand one more day in the Hidden Kingdom.

In retrospect, her behavior appeared very foolish and very immature.

Haley knocked softly on the bathroom door. "Mir—Nan? I—I don't know what to call you. Are you okay?"

He didn't sound like he was going to kill her. That was some comfort.

"Just a moment, please," she called back.

Still shaking, she rose and faced herself in the mirror. Her red hair hadn't been washed in days and hung in strands of rat's nest. Her gray eyes were bloodshot, her lips nearly colorless, high spots of color dominated both cheeks, and various bruises, braces, and bandages covered her appendages.

What would Aunt Collena say if she could see me now?

The thought made her smile, and the sight of her own smile made her realize that she had not lost all of her dignity.

"Heed these words," she whispered to her reflection. "You are the last member of a deposed monarchy, and you may never become queen of so much as a prom, and you have no idea how to act or speak or even shake hands. But you were raised to be a dream-walker queen and you are going to conduct yourself like one, even in the face of appalling circumstance. Now empty your bladder before you piss yourself with fear."

Then she washed her face, combed her hair, brushed her teeth with someone else's toothbrush, and forced herself to use the toilet.

Haley was sitting on the couch, knees pulled up to his chest, when she exited the bathroom. Mirren squared her shoulders beneath her borrowed T-shirt and sat at the other end of the couch.

"I apologize for making you wait," she said. "I had to attend to a personal matter. But my attention is entirely yours now."

Haley stared at her with hazel eyes as helpless and uncertain as a child's. Despite his rumpled and—what was the word, "grungy"?—apparel, he had an attractive face with well-balanced features and fair skin that his sisters or girlfriends must have envied.

"If I may ask, how did you recognize me?"

He wet his lips again, said nothing.

Either I am terrible at making conversation, Mirren thought, *or else he's even worse.*

"You said you didn't know what to call me. Mirren will be fine, when we're alone. Naturally, I'd rather you didn't disclose my identity to anyone else, but that's your decision. In the meantime, I'd like to hear your demands."

Haley blinked in alarm, then picked up his pad of paper and his Sharpie and began to write. As she waited, she recalled having once heard something about the odor of Sharpies. She wondered if it would be inappropriate to ask to smell his pen.

He tore the page out of the pad and held it out to her.

I just want to help you get home.

"Oh," Mirren said. "Oh." She closed her eyes briefly because there wasn't a wall nearby for her to bang her head against.

"I'm so sorry," she said, the words tumbling out. She felt trapped and stupid and rude. "I assumed that because you're a dream walker—well, I shouldn't have assumed that . . . I'm sorry. I assumed incorrectly." She felt breathless. "May I open that window?"

Before he could reply, she stood up and pushed a floor-length curtain aside, only to discover that the glint of glass she had seen had come from a door and not a window.

A sliding glass door, she recalled. She pushed the handle sideways and one layer of glass slid alongside another, making a soft *swish.*

What an aptly named architectural element, she thought.

Then she inhaled, and all the scents she had tasted through the bedroom window returned—stronger, richer. She tilted her head back to lift her nose and stepped onto a porch that ran the length of the house. Until the warm air hit her bare arms, she hadn't realized how cold she was.

Tilting her head back farther, she could see the stars. Real stars—living, burning stars that had reached across the galaxy to show themselves to her. They looked the same as the fake stars at home, and yet something made them indefinably beautiful and filled her with wonder.

"Dear God," she whispered.

The door made its *swoosh* sound, and she turned to see Haley closing it behind him. For an instant she felt fearful again, but he gave her a very small, very meek smile, and she remembered his note.

She wanted so much to trust him, to have an ally in this huge World, to have a friend to . . . just to have a *friend*.

"I've never been outside before," she admitted. "It's . . ."

She wanted to say *magical,* but she was afraid of sounding stupid and childish. Instead, she turned her face back up to the brilliant sky. She almost thought she could feel the moonlight on her skin, light and lively and cool.

"There's no sky where you live?" Haley asked.

"There is. I mean, there's an imagined sky. An excellent likeness, I'll admit. But when I look up at it, I don't feel anything except that I'm looking at a very high ceiling. This feels . . . vast. Open." Touching the wooden railing, she added, "Like I might even fall off the planet if I don't hold on."

Haley smiled, but when she caught him, he ducked his head.

"I've always been a little obsessed with gravity," she admitted. "I used to spend hours dropping stones off a bridge where I live. When I was little, I thought that the reason the stones fell so fast was that the creek was where they belonged, that things meant to be together would draw each other. Birds got drawn up into the sky, plants reached for the sun, bodies fell to the ground when they died. It was all part of my distorted childhood theory of physics." She laughed. "Actually, I sort of feel like that's how I ended up here, that I was so meant to be here that I . . . attracted a path."

Haley leaned against one of the columns that lined the porch. "The place you live . . ." His mouth twisted in a little frown. "It's not in the World, is it?"

Mirren stared at him, confused as much by what he didn't know as by what he did. "Should I know who you are?"

He smiled more easily this time. "No. I'm nobody. I just—sometimes when I touch someone, I see things. About them. I guess it's . . . like a, a psychic thing."

A *psychic* thing?

"Oh," she said. She had no idea what an appropriate response to such a declaration might be. Nor was she entirely certain whether or not to think him crazy.

"S'okay," Haley told her in a tiny voice, his smile fled. "You don't have to believe me."

"No, no, I don't mean to—I mean, I—I'm sure you're telling the truth."

According to your own distorted version of reality.

She felt guilty as soon as the thought crossed her mind. How was Haley's belief that he was psychic any less reasonable than her own belief that she had somehow manifested a way to join the World because it was where she belonged?

Bewildered, she fought the urge to tug on her right earlobe, a gesture her aunt Collena had often said made her look ten years old. "I'm so sorry—apparently I'm awful at conversation."

Haley chuckled. "I'm the one who writes notes."

"Is that what you do when you're nervous? I should try it."

"Here." He extracted his steno pad and Sharpie and held them out to her.

Mirren laughed. "I'll let you know when I need them." She looked up at the moon again, taking another deep breath. "So, what did you see when you shook my hand?" she asked.

"I saw . . . You were holding a jewelry box. It had a fancy star on the lid, and inside was all this jewelry, with like red-orange stones. You and a younger girl put them on, and then you danced around in long nightgowns. Like you were at a party, or a . . ."

"A ball," Mirren finished, her voice flat. "Dear God, you *are* psychic."

Haley shrugged.

"I remember that night. Katia and I—Katia, she's my cousin, but we were raised like sisters—we got all the royal jewels out and put them on, and we listened to the waltz from *Eugene Onegin* over and over and acted out the ball scene from *Anna Karenina*." Mirren peered at Haley as if she might find the explanation of his ability somewhere on his face. "My aunt and uncle told exactly one person besides me about Katia. No one else knows she was ever born."

Haley shrugged again.

"You're right, too, that we've never lived in the World. We call the place the Hidden Kingdom, but it's really just a pocket universe, which is sort of like—"

"I know what they are."

A pocket universe was a section of the Dream cut off from the rest and formed into its own miniature universe.

"Really?"

He nodded but didn't explain, so Mirren continued. "After my parents were killed, my aunt and uncle took me to the Hidden Kingdom to keep me safe. I've lived there my whole life." She tried not to sound bitter. "They thought they were protecting me by keeping me there. They wouldn't even tell me *how* to leave; I had to find my own way. Truthfully, I'm not sure if they ever would have let me go."

Despite the heat, chill bumps rose on her arms.

"So," Haley said carefully, "you don't need my help getting home?"

They looked at each other and smiled. "No, I don't need help getting home. I've been dreaming of the World for so many years; now that I'm here, nobody's sending me back. I can just be me here—nobody's niece, no queen-in-training. I can go to college and swim in the ocean and eat fast food. And I can dance at a real ball. This is where I'm meant to be."

"Gravity," Haley agreed.

"Exactly! And . . ." She swallowed. "I could have real friends."

She didn't know if she was being presumptuous or not. To her relief, Haley turned so that he stood beside her, facing the lawn, and said in a timid voice, "You can have all the friends you want."

Filled with impetuous delight, she said, "My name is Amyrischka Heloysia Solei Rousellario. But please call me Mirren."

He ducked his head, but this time Mirren knew that meant he was smiling. "Haelipto Krismon Mozeiush Micharainosa. But everyone just calls me Haley."

Mirren wondered if the gravity that had drawn her to the World had drawn her to Haley as well. If so, she was grateful to gravity. She was so happy, in fact, that she turned and hugged Haley.

The hug seemed to catch him off guard, and Mirren immediately realized her mistake.

"Oh, I shouldn't have done that," Mirren said. "Did I make you see things again?"

"No," Haley said softly. He managed to raise his face long enough to emphasize the point. "No."

"I'm just so excited," she said by way of apology.

Haley nodded. With his hand, he gestured to the World beyond the balcony. "You should be."

Four

Josh loved waking up next to Will, but less so when the thing that woke her up was Haley letting himself into Will's bedroom unannounced.

"Um, hi," Josh said. She rubbed her eyes and poked at Will, who was sprawled out in bed beside her. "Will, wake up. Haley brought us doughnuts."

"Huh?" Will's eyes flipped open, then scanned the room. "Wait—there are no doughnuts! You little liar!"

Josh laughed and inserted herself between his arm and side. She supposed she should be more polite or demure or whatever—dream-walker culture was painfully prudish—but instead she nestled her head against Will's chest and closed her eyes again.

"What time is it?" he asked.

"Quarter of still-too-early," Josh told him. "Haley, what's up?"

"I need to tell you something," Haley said. "It's bad."

Skippy, Josh thought. "It's too early to hear bad news."

"No, it's not," Will said. He propped a pillow against the headboard and sat up, causing Josh to slump awkwardly against his side. "Go ahead, Haley."

Josh grumbled to no avail. She knew that in the future, Will would be one of those psychiatrists who was available to his patients no matter the hour.

"It's about the girl," Haley said. "Her name isn't Nan. It's Amyrischka Rousellario." To Will, he added, "She's the lost dream-walker princess."

"What?!" Josh nearly shouted. "Are you serious?"

Haley nodded.

"Wait, the princess from the old monarchy?" Will asked.

"Yeah," Josh said. "The one my grandfather overthrew. The king and queen had a baby daughter who either died or went into hiding after the revolution, and no one's seen her since. Until now, apparently."

Josh—who had never cared about princesses—knew this only because Deloise had several books on the monarchy. As the years had passed, a certain romantic nostalgia for the old regime had developed, as is wont to happen with royals who die tragically—and leave behind princesses who may or may not have died.

"What was the princess doing wandering around in the Dream?" Will asked.

Haley explained the situation—that Mirren lived in a pocket dimension for her own "safety" but had eventually found an archway leading to the Dream and jumped through it, only to get lost in the Dream.

"You're telling us she ran away from home?" Josh summarized.

Haley considered. "Yes."

"Great. So her aunt and uncle are probably going to be pissed at us. Please tell me she's not here because of the Accordance Conclave."

After twenty years in power, the dream-walker junta was finally going to hand over power to a permanent government. At the Accordance Conclave, the dream-walker population of North America would be allowed to vote for the form of government they wanted.

Josh was a conservative, a member of the Troth Party. Her grandfather, on the other hand, was the head of the Lodestone Party and was running on a platform of dream-walking reform. *Radical* reform.

"I don't think she knows about the Conclave," Haley said, answering Josh's question. "I think . . . she was very sheltered."

"So you didn't want to tell us who she was because you think she'll be in danger if people find out she's a member of the old monarchy?" Will asked. "Does anyone still care?"

"Yes," Haley and Josh said in unison.

"There's still a party trying to have the monarchy restored," Josh explained. "It's led by some distant cousin. My grandfather tolerates them because they don't have much real power, but technically what they're advocating is illegal under the junta. Part of why they have so little power is that the cousin was twenty-sixth from the throne or something, but if they actually had the legitimate Rousellario heir, they might come up in the ranks real quickly, and I'm pretty sure Peregrine would have them all arrested. But you said Mirren's not here about the Conclave, right, Haley?"

"Right."

"So, she just has the worst timing in the world. And apparently the worst luck, too, since she's now her worst enemy's granddaughter's houseguest." Josh ran a hand through her hair, feeling how tangled and dirty it was. She wanted a shower. "If she's not here for the Conclave, then what's her plan?"

Haley shrugged. "She said she wants to go to college, swim in the ocean, and eat fast food."

None of those things sounded very princessy to Josh. "There wasn't a McDonald's in her pocket dimension?"

"No. Her aunt is a health nut."

"That would explain why she didn't know how to open a can of Coke," Will remarked.

"Wait a sec," Josh said. "Couldn't she have just imagined a McDonald's and her pocket universe would have created it?"

"Feodor could only do that because he was lucid dreaming," Will reminded Josh. "His physical body was asleep, remember?"

"Oh, yeah. I had forgotten that."

But as soon as Will brought it up, her mind filled with the image of Feodor's time-ravaged body, each limb and digit wrapped in a cobweblike sheath. Only his toenails and fingernails, grown hideously long and curved, had protruded from the shroud. Even worse, she remembered what it had been like to be *inside* the sheath, an uncomfortably hot, stiff cocoon.

"If nobody in Mirren's pocket universe could lucid dream, then the place where they lived probably never changed from what Feodor created it to be," Will said.

"What?" Josh asked, looking at Will and wondering if she had heard Feodor's name only because she'd been thinking of him.

"Come on," Will said, "who else would have built a pocket universe where the royal family could hide out? Who else *could*? In the 1950s, everybody knew that Feodor was secretly working for the king and queen. Half the stuff he invented ended up in the royal family's hands before his bosses at Willis-Audretch could even get a patent on it."

"Oh," Josh said hollowly. She'd known all of that before, of course, she just hadn't realized that Will knew.

Will's eyes were alight with an anger that had become all too familiar recently. Josh always saw it when he talked about Feodor, which was part of why she avoided the topic. She was afraid of his anger, especially afraid of what would happen if he turned his rage on her.

Will didn't know it, but he had so many reasons to be angry at her.

Josh knew that things between her and Will weren't right, but she didn't know how to fix them. Since Feodor and Gloves had tried to kill them, a tension had grown inside Will, and it never really went away. He always seemed to be on high alert, and the smallest things startled him. He'd begun trying to train again so soon after he got released from the hospital that he'd torn the stitches out of his hand. And there was his obsession with guns, too.

Not that Josh felt she was in a position to judge him. On a good week, she slept through the night twice. But the problem with the nightmares wasn't just that they terrified her; far worse was how she had become Feodor's unconscious conspirator.

She had a theory that when Feodor had tried to kill her with his memories, the bad memories weren't all that got through. Somehow, everything that Feodor had ever known or experienced had been planted deep in her subconscious. At night, all sorts of memories played themselves out in her head, twisted and warped, yes, but she believed they were based on true events. How else had she known what his sister, Bryga, looked like long before Will pinned a photo of her on his stalker wall? How had she aced a chemistry quiz even after she daydreamed through all her classes? How had she understood two women in a sporting goods store when they were speaking Russian?

She couldn't have. But Feodor had spoken Russian almost as well as he had Polish, he'd mastered chemistry before puberty, and his sister's face had haunted him until the day he died.

Josh certainly wouldn't have minded a free education obtained without studying, or even memories of Bryga, who had been a beautiful, brilliant child, if she hadn't felt like a part of Feodor was living on inside her. He had died, but not before he'd downloaded himself into Josh. Almost every night, she found herself in his world, often standing beside him in the lab as he broke new ground in quantum physics and dream theory.

Upon waking, she'd scramble for a pencil and write so quickly that she didn't know what she was recording until she examined it later. Formulas, algorithms, diagrams, explanatory notes in Polish or French that she might or might not remember how to translate the next morning, exquisite three-dimensional sketches—and she wrote everything down while switching the pencil from her right hand to her left and back again, as Feodor would have.

And that was why she hadn't told anyone about the nightmares. Deloise might have understood, and sometimes Haley looked at Josh in a way that made her think he recognized the demon inside her, but Will would have shot her on sight.

One morning in late March, she'd realized that among her growing collection of sketchbooks were the complete plans for a wristwatch that Feodor had built when he was nine. The wristwatch performed one delightful function: it kept accurate time within the Dream.

Such an innocuous invention. Feodor had built it when he was a mere child, before the war, before he went mad. Surely it was harmless.

That was what Josh told herself when she started building the watch—that she wasn't crossing any line, wasn't falling prey to Feodor's strange charisma, that just because she had to hide her actions from everyone she cared about didn't mean she was doing anything wrong.

The wristwatch worked as perfectly as the plans had promised it would. Just told the time, and it was always right. Josh felt reassured after she took it into the Dream for the first time. *See,* she thought. *It's no big deal. Just because Feodor went crazy later doesn't mean that every single thing he invented was dangerous.*

The successful completion of the wristwatch had been thrilling. In some ways, it had actually reassured Josh that she was in control, and for a few days, she had contemplated telling Will. *We can turn what he created into something good,* she would have said. *We don't have to be afraid of him anymore.*

But the fear that Will would reject her, be horrified and sickened by what she had become, and the unsettling romantic developments in the nightmares held her back. The first time Feodor had kissed her, she'd woken up choking on her own vomit. Her waking self didn't want that, but her sleeping self grew more and more infatuated, and eventually even her conscious mind grew sympathetic. She was reminded of something Winsor had once theorized: that no one could know another person fully and not fall in love with them, at least a little bit.

Maybe so much of Feodor's mind lived on inside her that she couldn't help seeing the best in him.

But she'd be damned before she fell in love with him.

That evening, when Will was out with Whim, Josh put on the wristwatch and went into the Dream alone.

The nightmare she chose belonged to a man in his forties, corporate type: clean-cut, boring hair, the kind of body that came from doing lots of cardio but no weight lifting. She stood on an elevated platform beside him. Before them stretched a mechanical gauntlet. The path over nine more platforms was obstructed by swinging axes, bursts of boiling steam, wooden logs that closed together from either side, and huge metal teeth that shut so hard, sparks flew from the incisors.

No way was Josh going in there. But she could try to help the dreamer.

"I'm going in," he said. "I'm just going to go as fast as I can."

"Wait a sec," Josh told him. "We can figure out a pattern to get you through safely."

"No, I don't think that will work. I just have to be fast."

Josh put her hand on his shoulder to keep him from leaping to the next platform, and he was lucky she did, because a flamethrower overhead filled the space between platforms with fire just the instant he would have been jumping through.

He cursed.

"It's all right," Josh told him. "There's a pattern. We can count it out. The next time the flames appear, we'll start counting."

They spent the next five minutes working out the pattern. Josh had chosen this nightmare because it presented an opportunity for her to try out the wristwatch, which allowed her to accurately time the sequences. The pattern wasn't nearly as complex as it first appeared, and Josh was almost tempted to try the gauntlet herself. If only the course had been slightly less fatal and any attempt to leave it wouldn't have resulted in an endless plunge into darkness.

"You ready?" she asked the dreamer.

He was jogging in place. "Put me in, coach!"

"We go on four. Wait for the fire burst . . . One, two, three, four!"

The dreamer jumped to the second platform. Josh kept calling out numbers as the seconds passed. He waited for the ax to pass overhead twice before leaping to the third platform. From there he had less than a second to get to the fourth platform before a burst of hot steam scoured his skin. . . .

He made it, but just barely. Josh knew his timing was already off, and she shouted the numbers as loudly as she could, but he missed his cue.

The fifth platform broke in half every nine seconds, dumping anyone standing on it into the abyss below. The sequence shouldn't have been a problem, but the dreamer was still standing there, looking confused.

"Above you!" Josh shouted. "Jump!"

The dreamer leapt straight up just as the platform broke apart beneath him. He grabbed the metal bar overhead and hung there, squirming, as the platform came back together.

"Drop!" Josh yelled, but she'd lost the count. Between the fifth and sixth platforms were the chompers—a five-foot-wide metal jaw that snapped shut every two or three seconds. Josh knew the sequence, and she told the dreamer to wait while she sorted out what part of it the chompers were currently in, but he either couldn't hear her or was too panicked to listen. He saw the chompers close, then reopen, and he dove headfirst through them.

The metal jaw closed.

"No!" Josh screamed as the teeth bit into the dreamer's chest. Over the bursts of fire and steam, she heard his ribs crack. The jaw opened, but not far enough for him to escape, and then a tongue appeared, and a hollow metal throat, and the teeth were chewing the dreamer up and swallowing him.

Josh stood alone on the platform, cursing wildly. She knew that she could jump through the chompers and follow the dreamer into whatever horror his subconscious had in store for him next, but instead she furiously thrust her hand out and opened an archway back to her basement.

Back in the archroom, she grabbed a white towel off the table and wiped the Veil dust from her face. "Stupid, stupid, stupid," she muttered. If she'd been able to access her power, she could have saved the dreamer. He would be sleeping peacefully right now; instead he was probably being digested.

She pulled off the wristwatch and hurled it across the room. "What use were you?" she yelled at it.

No use, she thought. *It was no use. I was no use.*

Her nightmare came back to her—the war, the devices, the comfort of being able to put everything to rights.

She wanted that power.

Five

Whim drove a monstrous 1981 baby-blue Lincoln Town Car with matching leather interior that he called Liberace. It was the only car Will had ever felt embarrassed to be seen in. He didn't care much for Whim's driving, either. Josh drove too fast and with too much confidence; Whim just drove *badly*—he'd once clipped a city bus.

The Grey Circle—or Feodor Fan Club, as Josh called it—met once a month, and members rotated hosting duties. Tonight the front door of the Fosperaida mansion had been propped open with a geode the size of a basketball, so Will and Whim let themselves inside. They crossed the foyer's parquet floor into a living room so large that it contained three different seating areas.

Will was still getting his bearings when a feminine voice as smooth and slick as hot oil said, "Well, if it isn't the Pied Piper of conspiracy rats. Hello, Whimarian."

The young woman stood taller than Will, almost as tall as Whim, but she walked with the stealthy sway of a panther, gouging the carpet with her stiletto heels. Although Will couldn't say why, he thought her short blue-and-white kimono looked expensive, and she wore a silver bracelet with diamonds running all the way around it, too.

Will noticed her beauty at the same moment he noticed her expression, which was somehow both seductive and mocking. She looked up at Whim from beneath long brown lashes, like she was peeking at him through a hedge, but the corners of her painted lips pulled back in the faintest of smiles, as though someone had gently pricked her there with the end of a dagger. "Here for the free food?" she asked.

Whim's eyes were so large, his eyelids had vanished into his brow. His voice shook as he hissed, "What the *hell* are *you* doing here?"

The girl shrugged, holding her shoulders at the top of their range of motion as if she were posing briefly. "I could ask you the same thing," she said. She sounded unfazed by Whim's anger. "I've been coming here for two years. Then I go away to college for a couple of months and when I come back they're letting anyone in."

"I was invited," Whim said sharply, which wasn't technically true. Will and Josh had been invited, and Will had brought Whim.

The girl released a puff of air with a *pffff* sound. "Whatever you say, Whim."

Whim gritted his teeth, but when he spoke this time, his voice carried a determined casualness. "Will, this is Ozbeilia Sokkravo-taine."

She held out a cool, fine-boned hand and Will shook it. "Call me Bayla."

"This is Will Kansas," Whim said. "Josh's apprentice."

"Oh," Bayla said, and she laughed. "You've cleaned up very nicely, I'm sure."

Will didn't know how to respond to that. "So have you," was all he could think to say.

Bayla laughed again. She lifted two glasses from a nearby table and held them out. "The wine is superb. Have a glass."

"No, thank you," Will said, but Whim accepted one of the glasses she held out.

According to dream-walker tradition, seventeen years of age made one an adult, and it was more or less the dream-walker drinking age as well. But Will had a genetic predisposition for alcoholism that ran back at least three generations.

"Oh, come on," Bayla said, nudging him with a sharp elbow. "We're all dream walkers here. No one's going to yell at you for having a glass of wine."

"Seriously, no," Will said. "Stop asking." The words came out more firmly than he'd meant them to, and a little too loudly as well.

Bayla laughed and looked to Whim, as if she thought he would join her in her bemusement. Instead, he set his own glass of wine pointedly back down.

Bayla rolled her eyes. "Have a nice evening, children."

Just as she turned to walk away, a young man joined them. He slipped an arm around Bayla's waist and smiled. Straight-nosed and bespectacled, he carried an air of aristocratic intelligence at odds with his friendly smile and wrinkled clothing.

"Friends of yours?" he asked.

Bayla leaned against him and said dryly, "I suppose. Bash, this is Whim Avishara and Will . . ."

"Kansas," Will supplied.

"Kansas," Bayla repeated, as if the name tasted sour.

Bash enthusiastically shook Whim's hand, but he dropped it when he heard Will's name. "Will Kansas! Well, this is quite a thrill!"

He shook Will's hand like he wanted to take it home as a souvenir. "I'm Bashuriel Mirrettsio. Call me Bash. You're a nominee for the Nicastro Prize this year, aren't you? I won six years ago. My own experiment never went anywhere, I'm afraid."

"Oh," Will said, relaxing. "Congratulations. Yeah, Josh and I are nominated."

"You're a shoo-in," Bash said. "I read your paper. I read all the Nicastro finalist papers. I'm hoping that one day they'll put me on the selection committee." He was so excited that he was completely ignoring the glares Whim and Bayla were exchanging. "I think your experiment could have terrific applications for making archway creation safer. I'd love to talk to you about your paper. Both of you, I mean."

That was the first time a dream walker had ever remembered Will in an invitation while forgetting Josh, instead of the other way around. Will felt vaguely charmed in spite of himself.

"Sure," he said. "That would be fun."

"Darling," Bayla said, "I think we should go find seats before the presentation starts."

"Oh." Bash looked at her as if he'd forgotten she was there and wasn't thrilled to have been reminded. "Yes, of course." He pulled a business card out of his pocket. "Please, feel free to give me a call anytime. And give my compliments to Josh."

Will accepted the card and said, "I will."

Bayla was practically dragging Bash away by then. Will glanced at the business card.

Bash Mirrettsio
Associate in Applied Physics
Willis-Audretch

Willis-Audretch, Will thought, recognizing the name of the shady dream-walker think tank and invention corporation. *I should have known.*

"What a loser," Whim said. "I can't believe she's with such a dork."

Will gave him a withering look until he said, "What?"

Will sighed.

He tried to pay attention to the presentation, but he had too much on his mind. Partly Whim and Bayla, but mostly the way he'd responded to Bayla's offer of wine. He knew he'd overreacted, and although he could justify himself by saying that no one should ever have to turn a drink down twice, he knew exactly why he'd gotten upset: he'd been scared he would accept the glass Bayla had held out to him.

Before he'd become Josh's apprentice, he'd gotten drunk a few times. The anxiety he'd felt had outweighed the fun, though; he'd found himself constantly evaluating his behavior for signs of addiction. Finally he'd decided that drinking wasn't worth the stress or the risk that it would get out of control.

But since that night spent in Feodor's nightmare Warsaw, he'd found himself thinking about alcohol. About how it made everything lighter, how it made pleasure easy and trust easier. He never drank it, just thought about it.

But he thought about it a lot.

Finally, the lecture caught Will's attention. He'd found that the content of the presentations fell into two categories—romantic re-hashes of Feodor's troubled life and hard-core scientific lectures. Tonight's presentation was the latter, with a hint of the former thrown in: Feodor's last book.

Sometime after Feodor had vanished from public life, he had apparently mailed to his editor a partial copy of a manuscript for a new book. The editor, although well versed in dream theory, had been unable to make sense of the manuscript, and he wrote back to Feodor saying that his work was the incomprehensible excrement of a troubled mind and that he should consider check-ing himself into a hospital. Shortly afterward, Feodor had been arrested for dream staging, and the editor had burned the man-uscript.

Or, at least, he had claimed to. But for half a century, supposed fragments of the manuscript had floated around the dream-walker underground.

The presenter that night had gathered the pieces of the manu-script available and was attempting to put them together into some sort of cohesive idea.

The word that had grabbed Will's attention was "magnets."

"Magnets are a vital part of Kajażkołski's theory of light har-monics," the presenter was saying when Will turned his attention completely to the lecture. "He understood the relationship be-tween energy and magnets and that there is more than one energy field surrounding the human body. According to him, the first energy field is esoteric, the so-called spiritual body. The second energy field is the body itself, and its energy is made up of the subatomic particles from which matter is formed.

"Some attempts have been made to manipulate the physical

body with magnets. For example, ultrasound therapy or transcranial magnetic stimulation. Even knee braces with magnets in them. But Feodor believed that magnets could be used to manipulate the subtle body as well."

Will grabbed Whim's arm. "That's it!" he whispered. "That's what he did to Winsor!"

Unfortunately, the proposal seemed to be as far as Feodor had taken the idea before his exile, and the rest of the lecture dealt with other, more complex issues of light harmonics theory that Will could hardly follow. He made a point, though, of taking the handouts the lecturer offered, which contained copies of all the known manuscript fragments.

Afterward, during the coffee hour, Will noticed a number of people drifting upstairs in twos and threes.

"Where do you suppose they're going?" he asked Whim.

Bayla's voice came from behind them, causing Whim to jump theatrically.

"They're doing Veil dust," Bayla said, sidling up next to Will. She turned her lower lip down in a pout and ran the tip of her finger along it, as if to indicate something.

"*Doing* Veil dust?" Will repeated. "Doesn't Veil dust drive people insane?"

Veil dust was a substance emitted when a person crossed between the World and the Dream. It was literally made up of atomic bits of the Veil.

"Only in large doses, and only if you breathe it," Bayla said. "If you take small doses through a mucus membrane, you don't get high. You get *deep*."

"Deep into trouble," Whim muttered.

"*No*," Bayla said irritably. "Deep into everything. Veil dust helps you make connections you couldn't see before. Scientists have amazing breakthroughs on Veil dust. Artists find inspiration. If your heart is broken, Veil dust can help you heal it."

"It sounds like a drug," Will said, thinking that someone had once told him similar things about ecstasy. That guy had ended up hospitalized for depression because he'd burned through all the serotonin in his brain.

"It's not a drug, it's a mystical substance," Bayla said. "It shows you the truth." She lifted a plucked eyebrow at Will. "And if you want to understand the mind of a madman, Veil dust might just help you see through his eyes." She stepped closer and said softly, "I can get you upstairs. If I vouch for you, they'll let you in."

Her breath—or maybe her lip gloss?—smelled like chocolate cherries. The scent was enticing, as was how close she stood and the sly promise in her eyes.

"Hey, I'm right here," Whim pointed out, but Bayla ignored him.

For a moment, Will was tempted—by the Veil dust, not by Bayla. He was pretty sure she was only flirting with him to make Whim jealous. But the chance for a scientific breakthrough was hard to pass up, and he could admit to himself that Veil dust—regardless of whether or not it was a drug—intrigued him.

He forced himself to say, "Thank you, but I think I'll pass."

"Too bad," Bayla said, batting her dark eyes. "That's where the real meeting begins." As she walked away, she added, "If you ever change your mind, give me a call. I'll hold your hand."

On the drive home, Will asked about Veil dust.

"Yeah, I've tried it," Whim said. "Ian and I used to do it once in a while."

"What's it like?"

"It's like . . . things look different. You hallucinate a lot, but you feel like what you're seeing is everything revealing itself, like you're seeing everything's true form. And sometimes you're like, *Man, the World is so beautiful.* And other times, you just freak out because everything you're afraid of is true."

"So it's all just hallucinations," Will tried to clarify.

"Yeah . . ." Whim didn't sound certain. "The thing is, sometimes

I would come out of it and know things I hadn't known before. Crazy stuff people would never have told me. But it was like I could see inside them."

Will pondered this. Veil dust was a drug, but it wasn't a drug. It made a person hallucinate, but it also showed them the truth, or it showed them what they were afraid of.

"Why would the Grey Circle be using it?"

"I don't know. But one thing I do know: we can *not* tell Josh and Del that they're doing Veil dust here, or they're never going to let us come back."

Will glanced at him across the front seat. "I don't want to keep secrets from Josh."

"You don't have to keep it a secret, but don't bring it up."

"That's the same thing, Whim."

"Not in my book. I'm telling you, Josh will flip out. She *hated* it when Ian did Veil dust. She considered it a violation of the Dream's sacredness or something."

Will groaned. That did sound like Josh. And he did want to keep coming to these meetings, even if "the real meeting" was upstairs. He'd just started making progress figuring out what was wrong with Winsor.

"I won't bring it up," he agreed.

"Thanks," Whim said. "One other thing. Could we maybe not mention that we bumped into Bayla?"

"Okay, who *is* Bayla?" Will demanded. "What is the story with you two?"

Whim, pulling off the interstate, grimaced. "So, this is embarrassing, but when I was fifteen, Bayla and I tried to elope. We bought a car for four hundred dollars and we tried to drive it to Mexico because we thought we could get married there without our parents' consent—which is not true, by the way—but the car broke down in Louisiana. I wanted to hop a bus, but . . . Bayla bailed. She'd pretty much been losing patience since the A/C went on the fritz outside Mobile. She called her parents and told them to come get her."

A shade of sadness tinted Whim's voice, which surprised Will. Whim wasn't much for regrets, but four years had passed and he was still hurt that Bayla had given up on him. "Wow," Will said. "That sucks, man."

"Yeah, well, I don't know what I was thinking in the first place. Bayla's a treacherous bitch. I should have seen that from the start."

Apparently he's still angry, too, Will thought.

"She did look good, though," Whim added. He smiled at the memory. "She looked amazing, actually."

Uh-oh.

"I won't mention that part to Deloise, either," Will said.

Six

The French toast tasted like happiness.

After every bite Mirren took, she closed her eyes to savor the sweet, eggy goodness. The flavors made her want to write an overblown ode stuffed with words like "sultry" and "delirious" and "profane."

Now I understand why people get fat, she thought.

Whim had woken her that morning with the announcement that they were going to brunch at Fat Mac's Flapjacks. "They" turned out to be Whim, Deloise, Josh, Will, Haley—and Mirren. She couldn't tell him that she'd never been to a restaurant before, but she was relieved when he and Josh ordered the breakfast bonanza for the entire table. Shortly afterward, platters of pancakes, waffles, biscuits, eggs, sausage and bacon, and six different types of syrup had arrived. Mirren was determined to try every single thing.

Katia would love this, she thought, and for the first time since she'd left the Hidden Kingdom, she felt a little homesick. But the emotion was largely drowned out by her excitement at being out in the World. She'd ridden to the restaurant in Josh's car, which had been utterly terrifying, but during the parts when she hadn't been screaming, she had stared out the window in awe at the buildings, the people, just the size of the World, and the space of the sky. Now she couldn't help gazing around the restaurant's dining room at the people assembled with their different hairstyles and clothing and constant cell phone use.

The people at her own table fascinated her as well. Haley sat to her right and had rolled up sausages in a pancake, which Mirren recognized as the classic pioneer dish "pigs in a blanket." Josh had drenched her waffles in syrup and powdered sugar, while Will preferred bacon and eggs. Deloise was neglecting her own plate so she could hand-feed Whim strawberries with whipped cream and chocolate sauce. Mirren found that endearing, although everyone else seemed to find it nauseating.

"Whim," Josh said, "if you don't get my little sister's finger out of your mouth, I'm going to break your legs with a hammer."

Whim rolled his eyes, but he did quit sucking the whipped cream off Deloise's finger. She remained sitting in his lap, however.

"Nan," Whim said. "What's that short for?"

"Gertrananette," Mirren improvised.

"Wow," Whim said. His eyebrows shot up, but he looked down at his plate as if trying to hide his reaction. "Is that, uh . . . German?"

"German and French. We speak both in Switzerland."

"I think it's pretty," Deloise offered.

"Thank you." Mirren personally thought it was hideous, but she liked Deloise.

She wasn't finding it hard to lie about being from Switzerland. Her ridiculously thorough education was finally paying off.

Whim, while carefully angling a forkful of blueberry pancake into Deloise's mouth, asked, "What do they think about staging over in Switzerland?"

Staging? Mirren wondered, and felt uneasy.

Staging was the practice of creating dreams in order to manipulate dreamers. It was banned in North America because—all too easily—it could be used to control people's minds. The example Mirren always remembered was a first mate on a naval ship who staged dreams for the other crew members until they joined him in a mutiny.

"Much of Europe is divided into hectorates," Mirren said. When she got blank stares, she explained, "Small, self-governing regions that are loosely affiliated. Most have agreed not to stage in hectorates other than their own, and most hectorates are either too small or too oddly shaped to allow for well-targeted staging, so it's largely a nonissue."

Thank heaven, she added silently.

"Staging is a big issue here," Whim said, "what with the Accordance Conclave coming up. Looks like it will finally pass."

Halfway through his sentence, Mirren bit into something hard in her sausage. She took care to be polite as she spit it into her napkin, but she couldn't resist glancing down; a fragment of bone stared back at her.

Staging is a big issue here, Mirren repeated silently, and she tasted blood and realized she must have cut her gum. *No wonder Collena worked so hard to keep me in the Hidden Kingdom,* she thought. *Out here, there are bones hidden in food and staging is about to become policy.*

Haley leaned close to Mirren, his shoulder brushing hers, and whispered, "Are you okay?"

"What is the Accordance Conclave?" she asked him. Then, seeing that they had the table's attention, she repeated the question to no one in particular, "What is the Accordance Conclave?"

"Nobody in Switzerland has heard of the AC?" Whim asked Mirren. "That's bizarre."

"Don't be so American," Deloise told him. "None of us know

anything about the European hectorates. Why should they know anything about us?"

Will and Haley exchanged a glance Mirren couldn't read.

"The Accordance Conclave is a continent-wide vote on what type of government to replace the junta with," Will explained. "The group with the most support is the Lodestone Party, which is—"

"I know the Lodestone Party," Mirren interjected. "They—"

They killed my parents.

She folded the napkin so she wouldn't have to look at the bone any longer.

"You probably should know them," Whim said with a laugh. "You're eating breakfast with the party leader's granddaughters."

The happy bubble Mirren had spent the last hour inside of popped and left her feeling very full and very sick.

"Please excuse me," she said, rising. Her napkin unfolded as it floated to the floor; the bit of bloodied bone mocked her.

You think this hurt? Just wait for what comes next.

She knew what was coming next. She could see the thought on the horizon like approaching storm clouds, and she knew she had to get out of the restaurant before the rain fell. She headed for the front door. Behind her, exclamations of Whim's confusion and Deloise's concern filled the air.

"Do you want me to come?" Will asked.

"No," Haley said. "I've got it."

Mirren hit the door with both hands, causing a harness of bells to ring, and ran straight into the parking lot. Tires squealed, a horn blared, and Mirren shrieked as a hulking red vehicle stopped less than two feet from her. The driver screamed obscenities at her.

"I'm sorry, I'm sorry," Mirren cried, and dashed toward the only thing she saw that looked comforting: a large grassy area with a small creek running through it.

She didn't slow down until she reached a place where the creek ran through a channel beneath the road. A concrete slab buried next to the water protruded enough to create a little bench where she could sit without ruining her borrowed clothes.

Although she had closed her eyes, she felt Haley sit down beside her. Maybe her skin picked up his body warmth, or maybe she just sensed his presence, but she knew he was there even when he didn't speak.

Some people don't speak with words, she thought, and she felt grateful not to be alone at that moment.

Wasn't it silly of me to think I could come here and not confront Peregrine? she wondered bitterly. *We have been circling each other from afar, drawing slowly closer, since the day he killed my parents. We've swung around our orbits, but gravity has always been moving us toward the moment our paths would cross.*

When she opened her eyes, she saw that Haley had picked a few long blades of grass and was twisting them together. "My family didn't tell me about the Accordance Conclave," she said.

Haley nodded as if he'd already known. Maybe he had.

"Now that I look back on it, they must have been hiding things from me for years. Newspapers kept getting lost on their way to us, or a page or two would be missing. Our liaison to the World started having"—she made air quotes with her fingers—"'computer problems' and couldn't print the blogs I was reading. There's no Internet in the Hidden Kingdom, of course." She rubbed her eyes. "They must not have wanted me to know that support for staging was gaining so much traction."

"Why not?" Haley asked.

"Because they knew I'd be obligated to try to stop it."

Haley ran a blade of grass between his thumb and forefinger. "It's . . . Staging is very dangerous, isn't it? More dangerous than people know."

Mirren realized then how much Haley might have seen. She'd brushed his hand while reaching for the butter in the restaurant—or perhaps before that, the time she'd hugged him, the handshake . . . any contact could have revealed her secrets.

"Mirren," he said, and he touched her again then, so hesitantly, just his hand on her back. He struggled for a moment before saying, "Everyone has secrets. I don't . . . I don't share what isn't mine. It's like . . . a responsibility." He blushed prettily and added, "It's a duty."

Mirren knew then that gravity had brought her to Haley just as it had brought her to Peregrine. She had arrived alone in a strange land, and she could not believe that by mere chance, she could have met someone who so perfectly understood her responsibilities.

"Thank you," she said.

Haley shrugged as if to say, *Of course.*

"No," she said. "For being my friend."

And he smiled.

"There's something about you," he said, his voice even quieter than usual but his words more certain. "I can't look away."

Her heart beat hard, twice. She wanted him to keep looking, yet she felt obligated to say, "You should get as far away from me as you can. It's entirely possible that Peregrine Borgenicht will have me assassinated as soon as he finds out I'm alive."

Haley shook his head. He took a deep breath and straightened his back, and Mirren saw that it was hard for him to sit up straight, to take up so much room in the World. "I'll keep you alive—I mean, I'll help. If you want, I mean."

Then he ducked down a little, as if afraid of being such a tall target, and Mirren felt inspired by his tiny act of courage.

"I feel so betrayed," she admitted. Her voice cracked with tears, but she didn't care. "Now I have to forget about living my normal, peaceful life, because I have to stop the Lodestone Party from taking power." She glanced around the park, which was spotted with dandelions she'd never had the chance to smell. "It would be such a shame to die now."

"We won't let you die," Haley promised. "The others will help. They all hate him."

"I just want . . ." She reached out to touch Haley's face and then stopped herself. "I want everything, I suppose."

She *did* want everything. She wanted to kill Peregrine and take over the government and go to college and eat sugar and kiss Haley.

But somehow her life in the World was already becoming as pre-determined as her life in the Hidden Kingdom had been. *Gravity,* she thought again, with less gratitude this time.

"Come inside," Haley said. "We'll find a way."

"All right." Mirren climbed to her feet. "But we should come back to this park sometime."

"Park?" he asked.

"Yeah. This is a park, right?"

He smiled like he was trying not to laugh at her. "It's an unde-veloped lot with a storm drain."

Mirren burst out laughing. "It *is*? But it's so pretty!"

Haley held out his hand, and she took it. As they walked back toward the restaurant, he said, "I'll take you to a real park."

"Can we have a picnic?"

"Yes."

Mirren squeezed his hand, even as she thought, *We'd better go soon.*

Seven

Feodor's laboratory—all scorched ashes of *roses wallpaper and metal autopsy tables covered with dirty crystals and shattered beakers. Josh sat in the window seat and looked out at the ruins of Warsaw, admiring how the different columns of smoke wove together like strands of silk thread, each its own subtle shade of gray.*

"You can see so much more of the sky now that the buildings have been knocked down," she told Feodor. "They should never have been put up in the first place."

He laughed, a sharp sound that cut her ears. Josh winced and looked back out the window just in time to see the worsening rain bring down one of the few remaining chimneys. It made a sound like the rush of a creek as it fell.

Josh loved the city. She could sit in the window seat and stare out all day, or wander through the wreckage, admiring the poetry of shattered pottery, the tenderness of one-eyed dollies, the poignancy of discolored photographs. Sometimes she liked to try on stained clothing or broken jewelry that she found, modeling ripped silk stockings and blackened wedding dresses for Feodor.

But the city just as often infuriated her. Each time she tripped on rubble, coughed on the filthy air, felt a wall she was leaning against collapse, she thought, Something must be done about all this.

Leaving the window seat, she went to stand beside Feodor at one of the long tables where he had laid out his experiments. She recognized the circlet and vambrace immediately.

"Show me how these work," she said, thinking of what their power could do to rebuild the city.

"I already showed you."

"You showed me, but I want to understand. To know them the way I know you."

He smiled at her, and when he spoke again, his tone was intimate, so soft that she had to lean forward to hear. "And how do you know me?"

She pressed the side of her leg against his, winding her foot around his shin like a snake. "Completely."

"Is that so?"

"Yes." He continued to fiddle with the devices, and Josh insinuated herself between him and the table until she stood in the circle of his arms. "I know you better than I know myself."

"Benefit of hindsight, I suppose," he murmured, before kissing her lightly. His eyes were so many shades of gray, but each of them glowed with their own light, as if they still carried a bit of the fire that had turned them to smoke.

*"Very well," Feodor said, and he cupped her face in his hands. "I'll
help you understand. . . ."*

*He squeezed her head between his palms and began to lift. Josh
scrambled to catch hold of his wrists, but her heels were already leaving the floor. A terrible pain spread from the base of her skull down
into her neck as Feodor continued to lift her up. She clutched at his
wrists, his arms, scratching, digging, then reached for his face, but
her arms were too short. When her toes lost contact with the ground,
the pain in her neck grew fearsome, the pain of a body's weight hanging on sinews that simply could not support it.*

*Feodor's eyes glowed white. "Now you know," he said, and he
shook her once, up and down, hard.*

Her body fell to the floor.

Her head did not.

Josh actually screamed as she woke up. She had never done that
before, but she did it now, and her hands came up around her neck
to make sure it was still connected to her head. She tried to run
from the nightmare but succeeded only in cracking her cheek on
the bedroom wall, because for some reason she had woken standing on her bed.

I'm going to die, she thought. *I'm dying. No, I'm awake. It's a trick.
Where's my head?*

Strangely, it was her head she felt she had lost, not her body.
She choked on her own breath, ran into the bathroom to retch, and
ending up only coughing into the toilet. The invasive scent of the
toilet bowl cleaner nauseated her even more.

She couldn't calm down. She couldn't stop touching her throat,
her neck, digging with her fingers to make out each tiny vertebra.

*Damn you, Feodor. Damn you, damn you, damn you. I should
have killed you myself. I should have kept you alive and made you
reverse what you did to me. I should bring you back to life and make
you fix this.*

The door at the other end of the bathroom opened, and

Deloise—wearing a matching floral tank top and lace-edged shorts—rushed to Josh's side.

"What's wrong? Are you sick? I heard you scream." She hugged her sister close. "It's okay, Josh. It's okay. You just had a bad dream."

Josh hugged Deloise back, letting some of the hysteria work it-self out in the embrace. Slowly, though, her breath did calm, and finally she was able to release her sister and sit back against the vanity.

Deloise poured her a glass of water and sat beside her as Josh drank it. "Want to tell me about it?"

Josh shook her head. She was aware that Deloise was worried about her, that she knew enough about Josh's nightmares to be rightly concerned, but telling Deloise the details would have felt like deliberately exposing her to a deadly virus.

"Maybe you should go talk to a therapist," Deloise ventured hes-itantly. "I mean, it seems like the nightmares are getting worse instead of better."

Josh stared into her water glass. She didn't need a therapist—she needed an exorcist.

"I thought I was dating a therapist," she joked. Deloise didn't laugh.

"He's not a therapist yet, and he's in even worse shape than you."

"I know, I know," Josh said. She would have had a hard time not noticing. "I'll be all right, Del."

She spent a few minutes reassuring her sister, then Deloise hugged her again and went back to bed. Josh washed her face and returned to her own room.

She stopped dead in the doorway.

In her blind panic, she had not noticed the walls. Josh, who had never cared much for interior decorating, hadn't painted or papered or hung posters, so until tonight the walls had been quite blank. But her subconscious—or perhaps Feodor's subconscious—had thought them too blank, blank canvases, even, and she must have climbed on the mattress in her sleep, and that was why she'd woken standing, because the walls that formed a corner around her bed were covered in writing.

Mostly the writing appeared to be mathematical formulas. Some chemical. A large number of annotated diagrams showing how wires should be arranged, where magnets and crystals should be placed. An astonishingly detailed anatomical diagram of the circulatory system in the right arm.

He did this, she thought.

Six months before, she might have been able to grudgingly recognize $E=mc^2$ as something Einstein had discovered. Tonight she knew it meant that an object's mass multiplied by the square of the speed of light described how much energy the object could emit.

No, she didn't *know.* She *remembered.*

Because Feodor had known.

She climbed onto the bed on her knees and traced the diagrams with a fingertip. There was the circlet, there was the vambrace. The drawings on the wall showed her how to treat the crystals, how to connect them to the wires, which wires to use, where the magnets should go, the direction of polarization.

Show me how these work. I want to understand.

Well, he had showed her all right.

She glanced at the clock—3:27. There was still time.

Sitting down with a large sketch pad, she transferred the writing on the wall onto paper. She did this almost entirely from memory, only occasionally checking the walls.

Exactly how much of Feodor's memory she had was unclear to her. She suspected that all of it was in her mind somewhere, but information recall often had to be triggered by a dream or situational necessity. She hadn't remembered that a Minotaur lived in a labyrinth until she'd needed to know.

Except that . . . As she copied, she realized that the plans were incomplete. The vambrace and circlet worked by using a signaling network built across the Dream, like cell phones communicating via cell phone towers, but the walls contained no instructions on how to build this network. Without it, the equipment was useless.

Josh felt disappointed and, at the same time, relieved. The vambrace and circlet were incredibly powerful. If she put them on, she'd be able to forget about connecting with the Dream mentally, forget her breathing exercises, forget struggling and fighting. The Dream would open to her like a flower blossoming. The vambrace and circlet would give her exactly the power she had been trying so hard to attain.

But since she didn't have the complete plans, that was one moral argument she wouldn't have to have with herself.

She worked until almost seven and then went down to the basement. A search of the numerous half-empty paint cans turned up no white paint, but she did find half a gallon of white primer, which was even better.

As Feodor's diagrams and formulas vanished beneath the primer like rubble hidden beneath snow, Josh wondered if she should have copied the plans at all. Maybe they were somehow as morally corrupt as Feodor had been, as fundamentally dangerous. . . .

But she remembered the nightmare from a few nights before, how he had tried to save his little sister and her puppy, how angry he had been when Josh stopped him, and Josh thought of her own sister. If he had loved Bryga the way Josh loved Deloise, there had to have been something good in him, right? He had to have had a good heart beneath all the madness.

Was that even possible?

When the walls were again innocence white, Josh opened the window and turned on a fan, then tiptoed down to Will's room to sleep. She managed not to wake him up this time as she slipped into bed. His back was turned to her, but she put her arm over his side and tucked her hand inside his. He was endearingly responsive when he slept: If she snuggled up against him, he would hug her close; if she put her hand in his, he would hold it.

But that morning, for some reason, he didn't. His fingers fell heavy and lax against the back of her hand, and a sense of loneliness washed over her. Lately they were always off doing their own thing—he was in the basement with his laptop and his stalker wall, she was in the attic with her secret projects. She had begun to miss the days after their encounter with Feodor, when the medications kept the nightmares away and they were both too banged up and loopy on painkillers to do anything besides sit on the apartment couch together, watching movies, occasionally either making out or ordering pizza. For a few nights they'd even slept on the pull-out couch together, their proximity sanctioned by the celibacy of their injuries and the public nature of the living room, and during the days they'd found time for what they'd never done previously: hanging out. They'd told each other crazy stories and jokes and made fun of television. Will had taught her card games. Josh had taught him knife tricks. She'd thought then that she was so lucky to have him, lucky to be with someone so genuine, who believed she was good enough just as she was, who always looked in her eyes when he said that he loved her.

She'd felt like she could tell him anything then, but the memories had come between them—his *and* Feodor's. Now she had a whole new world of secrets she hadn't shared with him and *couldn't* share. He hated Feodor, and if he found out that the man's memories were living in Josh's subconscious, she was afraid he might start to hate her.

Or at least break up with her.

Someday we'll both get over it, she told herself, watching dawn break over Will's sleeping form. *We'll figure out how to live with it. Someday I'll be able to tell him about the nightmares without him freaking out.*

Yeah, and he'd take down his stalker wall then, too.

Sure.

Eight

"So," Will said, "maybe we should talk about what happened yesterday."

Josh, who was sitting at the kitchen table and sharpening a knife with a whetstone, looked at Will with confusion.

"I mean at the restaurant," Will clarified.

They were getting ready to meet with Davita, each in his or her own way. Mirren was arranging the tea set and trying to keep Josh from getting metal shavings all over the lace tablecloth. Haley was writing on his steno pad. Will was trying to prepare everyone emotionally. Out of all of them, Will felt he had the hardest job.

"The restaurant?" Josh asked.

"Yes. When Mirren went running out of it."

Mirren's face was as composed and distant as it had been the day before, her eyes politely cast toward the floor. After she'd returned from the parking lot with Haley, she'd claimed to have vomited into the bushes outside, blaming all the sugar and refined flour she'd eaten. Will hadn't believed her for a moment.

Apparently Josh had. "She needed to puke."

Will sighed. "Right. She needed to puke because Whim had just dropped it on her that your grandfather is the one responsible for killing her parents."

"Oh, that." Josh began sharpening her knife again, the blade grating loudly against the stone. "Whim didn't know that would freak her out."

"Josh." Will felt himself quicken with anger, the way he did so often and so easily these days, and he briefly made his hands into fists in an attempt to release the energy. He couldn't blame Josh for being Josh. "I think Mirren would feel more comfortable if she understood a little more about your relationship with Peregrine. Specifically the part where you aren't fond of each other."

"Oh," Josh said again. "All right." She spoke to Mirren but didn't stop sharpening her knife. "I hate my grandfather. Like, a lot. He's a terrible person, he treated my grandmother like crap, and he tried to get me, Haley, and Will tortured to death last February. I figure that makes you and me allies." She used a towel to wipe the grit from her blade. "So we're good?"

Will would have given a very different explanation, but Mirren was smiling with her lips pressed tight together, as if trying not to laugh. "We're good," she said. "And I would be happy to have you as an ally."

She put the kettle on for tea, and shortly afterward, the doorbell rang. Will got up to answer it, but Kerstel beat him to the door.

Will loved his adoptive mother like he'd loved his alcoholic birth mother, who had given him up to the state when he was twelve. Sometimes he thought he loved Kerstel more. She hadn't just gone out of her way to make him part of their family, she'd taken the time to build a real friendship with him, even reading his favorite self-help books and teaching him about her own passions, philosophy and posthumanism. But every time he looked at her since the attack, a blind black hatred for the man who had hurt her filled him like black smoke, working its way from his gut to his limbs, his fingers and toes, his eyelashes.

He immediately felt bad for having made her get up and answer the door. In addition to the terrible injuries she had sustained when Feodor's zombies had come out of the archway and attacked the household, Kerstel had learned in the ICU that she was six weeks pregnant, and the combined toll had worn her thin and weak. She still had nerve damage in her right arm, and she couldn't stand for more than ten minutes.

"You should have let someone else get it," Will told her.

"I need the practice," Kerstel said as she held the door open so Davita could enter. "You think Lauren's going to get up with the baby in the middle of the night?"

"No," Will said sincerely. "I think Deloise will."

They all laughed, even Davita. Deloise was so excited about a baby joining the family that she had learned to knit baby booties.

Davita Bach stood five feet ten, knew fifteen different ways to French-twist her titian-red hair, and wore a power suit like she'd been born in one. That afternoon she had on a cream-colored suit with dark brown pinstripes. Usually the small gold Rousellario family crest she wore on a chain around her neck was hidden beneath her clothes, but today it hung in full view against a light brown silk blouse.

"Have you picked out a name?" Davita asked.

"Lauren and I are at war over the name," Kerstel admitted. "He wants Bramko, I want Popolomus."

Will secretly thought both names were hideous, but Davita expressed admiration for the choices. Finally, they left Kerstel to her protein shake and a book called *A Child's Understanding of the World* and headed for the kitchen.

Although Josh and Will believed Davita would feel the same loyalty to Mirren that she had to Mirren's parents, they'd agreed not to take chances. When they entered the kitchen, Josh was sitting beside Mirren with her knife hidden in her lap. She remained sitting when Mirren stood.

Davita looked to Will in the silence that followed, and he realized she was waiting for him to make introductions. Dream walkers loved formal introductions. "Davita, this is Mirren Rousellario. Mirren, Davita Bakareilionne."

Mirren extended a hand across the kitchen table, but Davita laughed uncomfortably at the sight of it and instead dropped to one knee. The unexpected motion caused Josh to spring out of her chair, knife in hand. Dismayed, Mirren touched her lips with two fingers.

"Please get up," she said to Davita, pushing Josh's knife arm down. "There's no need for that."

Davita straightened, but she said, "I want you to know that I'm here only to serve you, Your Majesty."

The title made Mirren wince. "Please, just call me Mirren."

"You are the daughter of my king and queen," Davita insisted.

"The king and queen are dead and the kingdom destroyed," Mirren said flatly. "Please call me Mirren or nothing at all. Let's sit down."

The kettle whistled, and Haley got up to fill the teapot.

"I'm relieved to see that you're well," Davita said, taking a seat. "Your family has been very worried."

Mirren smiled, but her anxiety was evident in the lines around her mouth. "My new friends have taken excellent care of me."

We're her friends? Will wondered, and snuck a glance at Josh out of the corner of his eye. He could see her trying to hide how taken aback she was.

But Will noticed that when Haley returned to the table with the teapot, he scooted his chair very close to Mirren's, and he remembered how he had offered to go after Mirren with Haley the day before and how quick Haley had been to say no.

Five months ago he was in love with Josh on Ian's behalf, Will thought. *Now he's putting the moves on a princess.*

He wondered how Haley had come out of their encounter with Feodor so much stronger when Josh and Will had come out so damaged.

The sudden intensity in Mirren's voice drew him out of his thoughts.

"I am sorry that Katia has been worried," she was saying. "I'm truly sorry for frightening her." Her voice hardened. "But as for my aunt and uncle, it serves them right—for what they've hidden from me, for how they've lied to me, and especially for keeping me trapped in that universe for nineteen years."

Whoa, Will said. The tone of the conversation had changed abruptly, and he saw Josh's right arm tense, no doubt tightening her grip on the knife beneath the table.

"Who's Katia?" Will asked as Haley poured him a cup of tea.

"Katia is my cousin," Mirren explained. "She was born in the Hidden Kingdom fifteen years ago and she's never once been allowed to leave it."

"Miss Mirren," Davita said, her tone distressed, "even I didn't know you have a cousin, and I'm sure your aunt and uncle would be very upset if you let the word get out. They're trying to—"

"Protect her?" Mirren finished as though she'd heard it a hundred times before. "Like they protected me by imprisoning me? By lying to me?"

"I'm sure they did what they thought was best for you."

Haley said, "Mirren is an adult. She has the right to make her own decisions now."

Davita stared at him as if he were a talking toaster, but Mirren smiled her beautiful, wise smile and softened.

"My family and I have very different priorities," she said. "Their priority is to see me live out my life trapped in a medieval castle, married to a man of their choice, and breeding like a rabbit, and my priority is to stop staging from becoming government policy."

Josh and Will exchanged glances. This was the first Will had heard of Mirren's intentions, but it put her panic in the restaurant the day before in perspective.

"I see," Davita said, her painted mouth slack with surprise.

"I have to make sure that the Lodestone Party does not win the vote at the Accordance Conclave and make staging permanent policy," Mirren said. "I know unequivocally that this is what my parents would want me to do. But I don't know how best to do it. And that's why I need you, if you're willing to help me."

Davita smiled faintly. "I've been waiting eighteen years to help you, Miss Mirren. But I'm concerned that you don't know how dangerous Peregrine Borgenicht is."

Mirren laughed. "I don't know how dangerous the man who killed my parents is?"

"I'm sorry." Davita blanched, her blush standing out against her pale cheeks. "That's not what I meant to say."

"I know it wasn't. And it doesn't matter. What I need, and what I would ask you to do, is to assess the political situation and figure out the best way for me to get involved. Should I run against Peregrine or try to sabotage him? Who else has a chance of winning and how can I support them? Do I need to come out publicly as the former princess, and will I get arrested and executed if I do?" Mirren tugged her earlobe. "And, if there's any way to convince Aunt Collena to let Katia join me in the World, I would like that. I hate thinking of her stuck back in the Hidden Kingdom. And I miss her."

Davita gazed down into her teacup, tapping one red fingernail against the gold rim. When she lifted her face, its color had returned, and she nodded resolutely. "If this is what my sovereign intends, it will be my honor to help her achieve it."

Mirren gritted her teeth, but they spoke a while longer, Davita taking notes on her tablet before departing. When she left, she took the tension in the kitchen with her, and everyone else began breathing easier.

Josh set her knife on the table and put four sugar cubes in her cold tea. "So, that went about as well as it could have."

"Yes." Mirren's shoulders slumped, and she pretended to sag with relief against Haley's side, which made him smile shyly.

Okay, Will admitted to himself. *They're kind of cute together.*

"Thank you all again for your help. I had no idea how nervous I was." Mirren threw back the rest of her tea like it was a much stronger drink, and Haley refilled her cup. "I realized, as I was making demands, that I've taken your support for granted, and I shouldn't have. I can't fully predict how much trouble my actions could stir up for you, and I don't want to make your relationship with your grandfather any worse, Josh."

Josh released a sharp laugh. "I thought I explained this earlier. My relationship with Peregrine is *over.* We aren't going to end up on *Dr. Phil* crying and hugging each other. I think he's a power-hungry monster who wants to control me—and," she added, catching herself, "everyone else. So if you need support with keeping him from grabbing even more power, I'm on board."

Mirren's reply was, as usual, diplomatic. "Regardless, I'm grateful."

Since Haley was obviously now on Team Mirren, Will supposed that meant it was his turn to decide where he would throw his hat. "Let me ask you a question," he said. "Josh told me that the monarchy shot down staging proposals for hundreds of years before the issue came to a head with Peregrine and your parents. She also told me that your family refused to give an explanation for why they wouldn't allow staging."

Mirren nodded, giving away nothing.

"I guess . . ." He wet his lips. "I guess my question is, are you sure you're doing what's in the best interest of the World and not just following in your parents' footsteps?"

Instead of taking offense, Mirren chuckled. "Allow me to explain as much as I can. Something most people don't know is that the earliest dream-walker kings and queens weren't heads of government, but of religion. They oversaw the seers, and since religion and science were tightly tied together back then, they controlled the knowledge of both dream mysteries—the spiritual elements—and what we call dream theory.

"One of their functions was the keeping of dangerous knowledge—because there *is* dangerous knowledge in the World, and in the Dream. Some knowledge must be protected."

Will remembered the terrible discoveries Feodor had made, the soul-destroying inventions, and he understood what Mirren was saying.

"With staging, the situation is such that if I explain to you *why* staging is so dangerous, I will be giving you the knowledge to make it far, far more dangerous. So I can't tell you why I have to keep staging from becoming standard practice. But I can tell you that—based on what I know—staging is one of the most serious threats to the balance of the three universes ever discovered. And that's more than I've ever told anyone, even my family, so I would appreciate it if you wouldn't repeat it."

Will believed her. She hadn't lived long enough in the World to be a great liar.

"Okay," he said. "I can live with that. But since I'm sticking my neck out for you, I need a favor."

Mirren tilted her head as if intrigued. Josh just looked confused.

"Four months ago, Josh and Haley and I had an encounter with Feodor Kajażkołski. It ended with him dead and a lot of people hurt."

Her gray eyes widened. "Yes, of course, I read about it. That was you three?"

"Yeah," Josh said. "And in case you're wondering, it sucked."

Mirren's lips parted with something like awe. "I had no idea I had recruited such powerful allies." She gazed at Haley, and it was apparent that she was as drawn to him as he was to her.

"What we need," Will said, trying to regain her attention, "is your help to save a friend of ours. One of Feodor's minions sucked her soul into a canister, and we need to put it back in her body."

That got Mirren's attention. "How did he suck out her soul?"

"Violently," Josh put in.

Haley, who had kept his eyes on Mirren throughout most of their discussion, stared at the floor then. Will wondered if courting a girl was harder when one's ex was wasting away in a coma.

"We don't know how Feodor did it," Will said. "From what I've discovered, he began developing the technique he used before he was exiled. The Gendarmerie probably confiscated his notes as evidence, then turned them over to your grandparents. Is there any chance his papers might have survived the fire at the palace?"

Mirren tugged her earlobe. "Feodor's house burned to the ground with his papers inside it the night before his arrest. However . . . he was the one who built the pocket universe where I grew up. It was meant to be a safe haven my grandparents could retreat to—I think they sensed that the tides were turning against them. Please don't spread this around, but they filed thousands of documents in an underground vault in the Hidden Kingdom for safekeeping."

"That must be a lot of paper," Josh said.

"It's massive," Mirren agreed. "I can't guarantee that any of Feodor's things from Maplefax are down there, and I don't know how we'd convince my aunt to let me leave once I set foot inside the Hidden Kingdom, but I would be glad to see if there's anything filed away that might be of use to you."

Josh crossed her arms over her chest.

"Then I'll do what I can for you," Will told Mirren. He raised his teacup. "Long live Queen Mirren."

"I've gotta go work out," Josh said, and stood up. "Let me know what you need when you need it, Mirren."

"Thank you," Mirren said, but Josh was already striding away. Mirren looked at Haley with a raised eyebrow.

"Not you," he said, shaking his head.

"No, it was definitely me," Will agreed, and he got up to go after her.

By the time Will caught up to Josh, she was already in the basement throwing punches at a rubber boxing dummy.

"Josh," he said. "I'm sorry."

She ignored him; sometimes she tried to avoid confrontation by literally refusing to acknowledge what was happening.

"Come on, talk to me."

"I'm busy," she said, and landed a spin kick so hard that the dummy rocked on its stand.

Before she could throw another punch, Will stepped between her and the dummy. "This will go easier on both of us if you just tell me how you feel."

Reluctantly, she dropped her arms and released her fists. "I just wish you would stop obsessing over him," she said. "It's . . . it's creepy! I mean, you have all these pictures of him and news articles about him and you spend hours every day thinking about him and you go to those meetings. And now you want to dig through Mirren's archives for *more* stuff about him? I think you need to . . . try to let go or something."

I can't, Will thought. *I have to . . .*

"We have to help Winsor," he said. "We have to undo what he did."

"Yeah, I know. And I'm completely on board for that. I just wonder if, once she's better, you'll stop."

"Of course I will."

But he was already imagining the future differently, and he knew he wouldn't stop until he had collected every known piece of information about Feodor and built them up around himself like armor, so that when Feodor came back—

"I just want things to go back to normal," Josh said.

Did she still think of the first six weeks of his apprenticeship as "normal" time? To him, the four months that had passed since their encounter with Feodor had redefined "normal," shaped the time before it into something naïve and full of unseen dangers. Sometimes he felt like he'd been living in the Dream since February.

"It doesn't work like that," he told Josh. "Things don't get undone. All we can do is try to learn from what happened so that we'll be better prepared the next time."

Josh hugged him tightly. "Will," she whispered. "Don't you get it? Feodor is *dead*. There isn't going to *be* a next time."

Nine

The next day, Mirren met Winsor.

Josh could count the number of times she had visited Winsor on one hand. She hated going. She hated the perfume of piss that permeated the nursing home, the false cheer of the nurses' scrubs, and, most of all, the silence of the patients.

Winsor's room was a little less depressing than the rest of the place. There, the scent of urine was somewhat mitigated by a vase of lilies and irises, and silver-framed photographs lined the windowsill. A rocking chair sat on a rag rug, and a patchwork quilt in blue and white covered the bed . . . and the patient within it.

Not only had Winsor lost a great deal of weight in the last four months, but her very skeleton seemed to have shrunk, giving her the appearance of a twelve-year-old. She lay on her left side, propped in place with foam bolsters, but her right arm hung awkwardly behind her, the fingers on her hand curled into a half fist. Her hair—cut short for ease of maintenance—was dull and lank, and her pale skin sagged. Although her eyes were open, they didn't register her guests, only gazed at the wall in front of her.

The sight of her made Josh sick. It made Will angry. But strangely, it brought out the best in Haley.

"Hi, Winsor," he said, and he walked into her line of sight. Gently, he rearranged her arm and straightened the sleeve of her flannel pajama top. "I'm happy to see you."

Winsor said nothing and gave no indication that she had heard Haley. Mirren glanced at Will and Josh, as if she expected them to follow Haley's lead, but Josh couldn't imagine talking to Winsor any more than she could imagine striking up a conversation with a department store mannequin. She went to sit in the rocking chair, as far from her friend as she could get. Will just stood at the foot of the bed, frowning.

"Josh and Will are here," Haley said, "and we brought someone new. Her name is Mirren."

"Hello," Mirren said, only a little awkwardly. "It's a pleasure to meet you."

Haley crouched down to look Winsor in the face. He knelt there for several seconds before rummaging around in the nightstand drawer and removing a tube of lip balm.

"Winsor is Whim's sister," Will said. "She's in a stage three coma; she goes through cycles of waking and sleeping, but she's never fully conscious."

"That's so sad," Mirren said.

"Her brain can hear us, though," Haley said as he carefully applied balm to Winsor's lips.

Will shrugged. "There's no proof of that, but if Haley says it, I believe it."

All Josh could think was how Haley had said "her brain" instead of "she." Because Winsor's soul didn't occupy her body; *that* was trapped in a canister at Willis-Audretch.

"She's been like this for four months?" Mirren asked. "I read about the attacks in the papers, but the reports were vague. They didn't say anything about what happened to the victims later on."

"They're all like this, or worse," Will said. "Except the three who died."

"Four," Josh muttered from her seat at the window.

"What?" Will asked.

"The little girl died last week," she said, casting a guilty glance at Will.

Will ground his teeth.

"What is their diagnosis?" Mirren asked.

Still angry, Will said, "Persistent vegetative states due to frontal lobe damage. The CDC called it catatonic sinoatrial dysfunction, but they've stopped investigating since new cases stopped appearing. But most vegetative patients make sounds, some even scream or cry. Some of them will follow objects with their eyes. CSAD patients never do. They never move on their own, either, not even in response to pain."

"Do we know why not?"

Will shrugged. "Ask Haley."

Josh shut her eyes. She didn't know if she was upset because they were talking about Winsor like she was an interesting species of fish or because Josh didn't want to talk about her at all.

"She's not really here," Haley explained. "Her soul is still in the canister. Without her soul, her body . . . it doesn't care."

"We have the canister," Will said. "It's at Willis-Audretch being studied, but they haven't raised any hope that they can free Winsor's soul from it."

"It's wired to explode if they mess with it," Josh added, staring out the window again.

"Even if they could open it," Will continued, "we don't know if her soul could just fly back into her body or if we'd need to do something to help it. But Winsor is lucky in some ways—the majority of the other victims' souls were in Feodor's universe when it collapsed."

"What happened to them?" Mirren asked.

"They're lost in the Dream," Haley said.

Josh twisted her fingers together, bending her joints in uncomfortable ways. If all those souls really were lost in the Dream—probably sixty or more—then Josh and Will and Haley were to blame. They were the ones who had killed Feodor, collapsing his universe and forcing the souls into the Dream.

"You want to see something really creepy, though?" Will asked. "Look at Winsor's eyes."

The tone of Will's voice disturbed Josh. He sounded bitter, but a sort of pleasure underlined his rage, as if it felt good to him to be angry.

He turned on the bedside lamp. "Look," he repeated to Mirren, but Josh couldn't stop herself from obeying as well. Will turned Winsor's face—gently, but not as gently as Haley would have. Haley himself stood pressed up against the bedside table, as if unwilling to leave Winsor's side.

"What am I looking at?" Mirren asked.

"Her eyes used to be blue," Will said.

A bold, bright blue, Josh remembered. Like lapis lazuli.

Now they were a charcoal color, a single shade away from black. A fine black web, as thin and sharp as iron shavings, stretched across the surface of Winsor's eyes. The whites were tinted gray, as though a fine layer of ash had settled over them.

"Feodor's zombies had eyes that were completely black," Will said. "It seems to be slowly happening to all their victims. The doctors don't know what it is."

Her eyes were so beautiful, Josh thought. Now they were damaged, just like the rest of her—the frail, thin limbs; the skeletal face; the shiny luster gone from her black hair.

"I'm very sorry for your friend," Mirren said. "I understand now why knowing as much as you can about Kajażkołski is important."

Josh stopped herself from laughing. No matter how much they learned about Feodor, they would never be able to fix Winsor. Josh had half his memories, and even she couldn't figure out what he'd done.

"There are seventeen—sixteen, I mean, other people just like her," Will said.

"Sixteen," Mirren repeated. She shook her head. "Kajażkołski was working at the cutting edge of dream theory, and scientists are still trying to analyze his theories. My understanding of dream theory is good, but if no one at Willis-Audretch can help you, then what you're fighting against may be something only Feodor could comprehend."

"All I'm asking is that you help however you can," Will said in a way that made Josh think he had just ignored every word Mirren had spoken.

"I will," she promised. She placed a comforting hand on one of Winsor's fists. "How old is she?"

"She just turned eighteen," Haley said. He'd insisted that the whole household go to the hospital and sing to her and eat cake.

Mirren marveled. "I never would have guessed."

They left a few minutes later. Haley kissed Winsor's forehead and promised he'd be back in a day or two; Mirren said a polite good-bye; Will ignored the girl in the bed and started down the hallway. As she followed them out, Josh heard Haley admit to Mirren, "Winsor and I used to date."

"Oh," Mirren said.

Josh had no idea why Haley had told Mirren that. Now that she thought about it, she had no idea why they'd brought Mirren here in the first place. Will had said it was to show her how much Winsor needed her help, but Mirren hadn't met Winsor before this happened. She couldn't know that the small, shrunken body in the bed had once been vibrant and beautiful, that the mind that barely registered on an EKG had been clever and sharp-witted, that those eyes clouded by the veil of Death had been capable of seeing through everyone around her.

All Mirren saw was a sick child in a bed. She couldn't know the friend Winsor had been to Josh or understand all that Winsor had lost.

The guilt Josh felt after seeing Winsor led her to begin work constructing the vambrace and circlet. Not because the devices could help Winsor, but because Josh kept recalling how the devices had filled her with complete confidence and power in her dreams. She wanted to feel like that. She *needed* to feel like that. She needed to save the next Winsor.

Sitting in the first-floor office a few days later, she was clicking through the online database of dream-walking-related articles for anything that might help her build the network the devices required, when her eyes caught upon "Possibilities for Continual Dream Monitoring" by Bashuriel Mirrettsio.

The name looked familiar, but it took her a minute to connect it to the man Will had told her about from the Grey Circle meeting.

Will said he won the Nicastro Prize, she recalled. *Let's just see what he won it for.*

She printed the paper out.

Although today the trimidion is considered the gold standard in Dream monitoring, at the time of its invention, many considered it a mere first step toward observation of turbulence within the Dream, the paper began. *Inventors of the trimidion lamented its inability to pinpoint specific areas of turbulence and its vulnerability to cosmological events. It is the author's purpose to propose a next step in the evolution of turbulence monitoring through the creation of an in-Dream trimidion broadcaster.*

Josh read on with interest. The trimidion was a very old dream-walker tool—so old that she was surprised a record of its invention existed. A scale with three corners, it measured the amount of emotional turmoil with the Dream, the World, and Death at any given moment. Dream walkers used it as an early alert system that would inform them before the negativity in the Dream reached the point where it could rip the Veil between universes and cause nightmares to come pouring into the World.

Bash's paper proposed that trimidions be placed *within* the Dream. Each one would be monitored by a small computer that would broadcast—via radio waves—the degrees of balance or imbalance to a central computer near an archway. All a dream walker had to do was consult the central computer to determine which areas of the Dream contained the most emotional turbulence, then follow the radio signal toward the trimidion in the area where the most dream walking was needed.

The idea contained the hallmark of a Nicastro paper: innovation. Instead of expecting young dream walkers to be on the cutting edge of dream theory, the prize committee looked for ideas using available technology—often even technology considered out-of-date. Josh had never read anything that suggested using radio waves; she wasn't even certain they would act normally within the Dream.

The problem with the idea was that Bash lacked a method for anchoring the trimidion stations within with Dream. In fact, it was the same problem Josh had run into—

"Holy shit," Josh whispered.

Bash's trimidion station problem and Josh's cell network problem were nearly the same. She wondered if, in the years since he'd written this paper, he had come up with a solution.

She needed to talk to Bash.

Ten

Ten days after Mirren's arrival in the World, Davita called her and said to plan for a dinner meeting that night. Davita discouraged her from letting Haley join them, but since Davita was bringing a mystery guest, Mirren felt justified in bringing a familiar one.

Besides, she was all awash in adoration for Haley. She supposed she should have felt threatened by seeing how tender he was with his ex-girlfriend—and she did plan to ask him his feelings about Winsor at some point—but mostly what she felt was admiration. When Winsor's own friends had treated her like a plague victim, Haley hadn't hesitated to touch her or talk to her, which Mirren found endearing.

The restaurant was cozy, everything covered in green velvet and gold trim, and the maître d' led them to a private horseshoe booth near the back, hidden from the view of other patrons by two curtains.

Davita and another woman were already seated when Haley and Mirren arrived. They couldn't easily get out of the booth to say hello, but the stranger offered her hand for Mirren to shake.

"I'm Anivay la Grue," she said. Mirren realized she should have recognized Minister La Grue as the leader of the Troth Party and a member of the junta, but the woman no longer looked like she had in the photographs Mirren had seen. She appeared frail and desperately thin, yet at the same time her face was puffy. Her copper skin had darkened, and when Mirren shook her hand, that also felt swollen.

"How do you do?" Mirren asked as she sat down, careful not to show her surprise at the minister's condition.

They made small talk for a while. Minister la Grue—who insisted that Mirren and Haley call her Anivay—asked Mirren a bit about her life, which made her realize that Davita hadn't revealed her other-universe origins. Then they discussed the Accordance Conclave and staging and Peregrine Borgenicht. Anivay was still a sharp mind, and she had a warm, easy laugh. She criticized Peregrine's politics but not him personally, which Mirren liked.

The third time Anivay had to stop speaking to catch her breath, though, Mirren felt she needed to say something. "Are you unwell?" she asked gently, putting her hand over Anivay's.

While the older woman struggled to breathe, Davita said, "Anivay suffers from polycystic kidney disease. In the last several years, it has rapidly worsened into end-stage renal failure. She has difficulty breathing due to the buildup of fluid around her lungs."

"I'm so sorry," Mirren said, genuinely saddened.

Anivay held up a hand, as if to block Mirren's pity. "I'm seventy-two," she said. "I've lived longer than expected already."

"Anivay asked for this meeting," Davita said, "because she feels that her declining health has reduced support for the Troth Party. No one wants to elect a president who might—" Davita stopped short.

"*Die*," Anivay said firmly, finishing Davita's thought. "That's why I want you, Mirren, to take over for me."

"Me?" Mirren asked, astonished.

Anivay took a few shallow breaths before explaining. "You're young and beautiful. Davita says you're well-spoken, well-educated. And you're against staging."

"But I've never been involved in the Troth Party."

"We believe you can win them over," Davita said. "And we believe that we'll lose fewer people than we'll gain when the Monarchist Party joins us."

"The Monarchist Party wants a monarchy," Mirren pointed out, "not a republic."

"We'll change our proposal to a constitutional monarchy," Anivay said. "That way, the Troth Party will still get its republic and the monarchists will still get their queen."

Mirren glanced at Haley, but he appeared to be thinking.

"So I'd be a figurehead," Mirren said. "Would I have any real power?"

"Enough. You would have the right to propose legislation and to veto any legislation that you didn't feel was in the best interest of the North American dream walkers," Davita said. "Granted, the latter power is one I would recommend you use sparingly, but it would allow you to keep staging from becoming policy no matter what anyone else wanted."

Anivay took a long drink of water and then said, "Miss Mirren, I don't know you. But I knew your parents, briefly, and your grandparents before them. They were good people, the best sort of people. They never forgot that, whatever their titles, they were servants. They did what was best for their people, not themselves. Even dream walkers who disagreed with them never would have risen up and killed them without Peregrine Borgenicht. The spin he put on their assassinations afterward made it sound like the monarchy's downfall was inevitable, but remember: It was a coup, not a revolution. It only took one man to set fire to the palace. I'm telling you this because I want you to know that Peregrine is your enemy, not the dream walkers."

Mirren had to look away because of the tears in her eyes. She wanted so much to be accepted, to have a people. . . . She wanted to believe that Anivay was right and that the dream walkers had never lost faith in her parents. She wanted to believe even more that her inevitable confrontation with Peregrine could be as easy and civilized as running a campaign against him. But an uneasy feeling inside warned her even as it urged her forward.

"What are her other options?" Haley asked.

"The issue is time," Davita said. "She can join the dream-walker community and go into politics from the ground up, but that will take years. She can join the Monarchist Party, but they don't have enough votes to win the Accordance Conclave. This is the only way I could find of putting her into power immediately."

"What if I fail?" Mirren asked.

"Then Peregrine wins," Anivay said, "and we're no worse off

than we were before. Mark my words, if nothing changes, the Troth Party will lose this election."

"Do you think he'll try to kill me?"

"Depending on how well you're received, quite possibly," Anivay admitted.

Mirren liked Anivay, and liked her even more for not mincing words. But she didn't want to die.

"We each have our own reasons for wanting staging stopped," Anivay added. "You don't know mine, and I don't know yours. But we want the same thing. Let's work together to get it."

She had beautiful brown eyes, dark as just-tilled earth. When Mirren looked only at her eyes, she never would have guessed the woman was ill.

This is her last chance, Mirren thought. *And maybe my only chance.*

"Yes," she said.

When they left the restaurant, the clouds that had caught the sunlight earlier had turned dark blue, not with night but with rain. Mirren's breath caught in her throat, and she walked slowly toward Haley's truck with her palms turned up to the sky. She jumped when the first drops hit her skin, giggling at the same time, and only when the lightning cracked above her head and lit up the parking lot as if gilding it with silver did she run for the truck.

"It's amazing!" she cried, jumping into the front seat. "It rains where I live, but there's no lightning, no—*ahh!*" The rumbling, grinding thunder hit her body with the pressure of a shock wave. "No thunder!"

Haley grinned at her from across the bench.

She fumbled with the controls on the car door but quickly discovered how to roll her window down. She laughed, giddy with the excitement of the air pressure, the sight of tree branches being lashed by wind, the abandon with which the raindrops dashed themselves against the windshield.

She stuck her arms out the window the whole ride home, letting the cold rain pour down on her and the wind whip her arms until her skin burned. Only then did she realize how much the conversation with Davita and Anivay had frightened her.

They know Peregrine will kill me, she admitted to herself. *They don't care if I'm a queen or a martyr.*

The rain was still pouring when Haley pulled into the driveway. Instead of going into the house, Mirren took off into the yard and the shelter of a large willow tree, and Haley ran after her.

Beneath the tree's spreading branches, the world was as beautiful as she had imagined. Darkness and water had turned the tree leaves a rich olive green, and she flung off her shoes so she could feel the rainwater squishing between her toes in the grass. Rain far colder than the kind that fell at home drenched her purple dress, and she threw her arms around the tree trunk like she'd seen hippies do in movies. The willow didn't speak to her, but she did find comfort in its unyielding steadiness, especially when the lightning and thunder shook her.

"Isn't this beautiful?" she asked Haley as he ducked under the shelter of the branches. "I love nature. I love being outside. And . . . I'll do what they ask, because it's my duty. But I don't know how long I have—to live, or maybe just to do things like this and not have any consequences. And there are so many things I want to do. . . ."

He smiled like he knew. He was shivering, too, arms wrapped around himself, even in today's pink-and-brown cardigan, so she felt justified in inserting herself between the sweater and his chest. To her relief, he wrapped his arms and the wet fabric around her.

"I want to help you," he told her. "Tell me how to help."

She hugged him tight. He felt steady, almost as steady as the tree trunk had. "Don't let me lose myself."

Somehow, she knew he smiled. "I can do that," he said.

She looked up at him. He trembled harder against her, but his fingers moved in small circles against her back, so timid and yet so bold.

This is a perfect moment for a first kiss, she thought, but instead of kissing Haley, she said, "Are you still in love with Winsor?"

He tilted his head. "No."

"If we put her soul back in her body, is she going to wake up and feel like I stole her boyfriend while she was in a coma?"

"No," he said. "We broke up almost a year ago."

"You broke up with her?"

He swallowed. "She slept with my twin brother."

"Oh," Mirren said. "Is that why he doesn't live with you?"

"He's dead."

"I should stop asking questions." She felt like she had tried to kill one hornet and instead woken an entire nest. "I think I should have just kissed you when the moment presented itself."

Haley actually laughed aloud. "We can wait until it comes around again."

"Thanks."

So they stood there, nestled in Haley's cardigan, his face turned so that he could rest his cheek on the top of her head, and slowly, they both stopped shivering. Mirren didn't know how long they stood that way or how long they might have gone on, but eventually the rain stopped and the sun reemerged, turning the dampness around them to glowing orange mist.

The next day, Mirren announced that Davita had given her the go-ahead to admit her real identity to the household. She asked Josh to break the news because she felt that Josh had the highest status of the three people who knew her secret, but almost as soon as she began speaking, Mirren realized she should have asked Will instead.

"So," Josh said without preamble, "Nan's really the lost dream-walker princess. Her name's Mirren Rousellario, and she's going to try to beat the Lodestones at the Accordance Conclave." Josh stopped to think before adding, "Deal with it."

Laurentius and Kerstel exchanged glances. Deloise's jaw dropped, then her mouth slowly formed an *O*. Whim gave Mirren a skeptical look and squinted, as if trying to recognize her. His father, Alex, slid off the couch so he could fall to his knees.

"No, no, please," Mirren said. "Not this again."

"The Avisharas have always been loyal to the monarchy," Alex proclaimed. "The safety and protection of our home is yours, my queen."

"Thank you," Mirren said, because she honestly didn't know what else to say.

"Get off the floor," Alex's wife told him. "You look like an idiot."

"I should have figured it out," Deloise said. "You look so much like your parents! I have all these books about them, I used to read them all the time."

"Wait, we're taking her word on this?" Whim asked. "Remember that chick who spent her whole life claiming she was a Russian grand duchess, and after she died it turned out the real grand duchess was rotting in a mine shaft?"

"No, no." Josh waved at the words in the air. "Davita's doing a DNA test, but we've already pretty much confirmed it."

"Wasn't she convicted of treason?" asked Saidy, Whim's mother.

"Um," Josh said.

"Yes," Mirren admitted. "And even though the conviction was largely symbolic, helping me could be considered treason. I don't want to mislead you on that point."

"Oh my," Kerstel said.

Whim reached for the phone with exaggerated slowness, and Deloise shoved him.

"You're not calling anyone," Deloise said. "She was a baby!"

"So? It sounds like she's going to try to bring your grandfather down."

"Do *you* want to see him stay in power?" Deloise demanded. "Because if you're rooting for the guy who tried to kill my sister to lead our government, I need to seriously rethink this relationship."

Whim released an aggravated "*Aarrggg*. You know I don't like your grandfather. You know I don't want anybody snuffing Josh out. But he's not the only person in the Lodestone Party, and I *do* support staging."

"So go vote for him," Will told him irritably. "Mirren running isn't going to change the fact that you'll still have a ballot. Just remember not to check her name."

"How about a deal?" Deloise suggested. "You keep Mirren's secret, and in return, she gives you a scoop here and there for your website?"

"Website?" Mirren asked. She hadn't had a chance yet to explore the Internet, but it was near the top of her list of things to experience in the World.

"Hell, yes!" Whim exclaimed, and then he explained about his blog, *Through a Veil Darkly*. "If I break the story that the lost dream-walker princess is alive, I'll be a legend in the underground blog movement."

"Oh, for God's sake," Saidy said.

"So you want me to . . ." Mirren said.

"Just give me a call before you go public. Give me a good twelve hours' notice so I can post an announcement. I'll run it all past you before it goes live."

Mirren shrugged, but she'd have to check with Davita. "All right."

And that was the end of Whim's issues with Mirren.

Whim's mother was less interested in the political implications of Mirren's joining the race than she was concerned about bringing Peregrine's wrath down upon them, which was Lauren and Kerstel's major fear as well.

"Personally," Lauren said, holding his pregnant wife's shaky right hand, "my only concern is for the safety of my family. You're welcome to stay here, Mirren, until such time as your presence endangers my family, and at that time I'll have to ask you to leave. And, as long as I'm making speeches, I might as well add that I'm sorry for what happened to your family and for my former father-in-law's part in it."

"The same goes for me," Kerstel added.

"Thank you," Mirren said. "I would never want to endanger your family, and I'll do everything in my power to avoid doing so."

The household agreed on a code of silence regarding Mirren's presence there, but Mirren didn't know how long it would last. Davita was anticipating bringing her before the junta in just a day or two. With the Accordance Conclave so soon, they didn't have any time to lose.

Somehow they still made it to Young Ben's barbecue that evening, though.

Eleven

Young Ben lived in a crazy cabin on stilts at the edge of a swamp. He'd built onto the cabin several times, with the result that each addition had made the building more ramshackle and sprawling, like an aboveground bunker.

When the Weaver-Avish caravan pulled up the mud-and-gravel drive, Young Ben was standing on the porch beneath the light of orange bulbs—the better to keep the West Nile mosquitoes away. "Welcome, friends!" he called.

Everyone tumbled out of the car, grabbing packs of soda and sacks of groceries. Will took a bag of buns away from Kerstel, who protested that they weighed less than her purse, and told her to be careful on the steps. Josh hiked a microwave-sized watermelon up on her shoulder, and they followed everyone else up the rickety staircase to the porch.

"Will, good to see you," Young Ben said as Will passed him, and clapped him on the back.

Young Ben, who was somewhere between ninety and a hundred

years old, had only recently begun to stoop. Always plump, he'd put on a significant amount of weight in the past few months, and now a line of hairy, pale stomach protruded from what Will was pretty sure was an original *Ghostbusters* T-shirt.

"Get the groceries into the kitchen," Saidy called. "You can say hello afterward."

Everyone ignored her and clustered on the porch.

"Abendirk Sounclouse," Deloise said, her voice excited and a little formal, "allow me to present Mirren Rousellario."

Mirren held out her hand. "How do you do?"

Ben clasped her hand between his instead of shaking. "Ah, Princess Mirren. What a genuine joy it is to meet you."

Mirren smiled, but stiffly. Will knew she was about to tell Ben not to call her princess when he went on.

"I had the honor of knowing both your parents and your grand-parents. In fact, when I was born, your great-grandparents were on the throne."

Ben kept hold of Mirren's hand and beamed reverently at her. Will felt an unexpected pang of jealousy; over the last week he'd realized that, in many ways, Mirren was as much an outsider as he was. But here Ben was fawning over her, having only met her two minutes before, when after six months he still told people that it was "Josh's paper" up for the Nicastro Prize.

Will slipped past Deloise and into the house.

They ate an hour later, sitting around a grill built into the back deck so that it doubled as a fire pit. The food was abundant: hamburgers and hot dogs, potato and pasta salads, BBQ beans, ambrosia, chess pie, and Kerstel's own carrot soufflé, which Will thought he could probably live off of for six months or more.

"You can count on my vote," Young Ben promised Mirren. "Staging is an amoral plague upon the earth."

"What? That's a wild exaggeration," Whim told him, "and I say that as someone who's accused of wild exaggeration on a near daily basis. Ninety-nine percent of people who are in favor of staging want it because it could do a lot of good for a lot of people."

"And the one percent who don't?" Ben asked. "What about that fellow in France last year, the one who staged nightmares for his wife until she killed herself so he could collect the insurance money?"

"Obviously, that guy was just an asshole," Whim said.

"How did he find his wife in the Dream?" Will asked, curious in spite of himself.

"He built an archway in their bedroom closet," Josh explained. "After his wife went to bed, he'd sit there with the looking stone and wait until one of her nightmares came up. Then he'd jump in, dressed up like Death with the cloak and a sickle, and tell her she was getting sick, that she was going to die soon. Her doctors couldn't find anything wrong with her, but eventually the nightmares wore her down until she killed herself."

"That's awful," Deloise said. "How could he do that to his own wife?"

People are capable of terrible things, Will thought, thinking of Feodor, and suddenly he wanted to be away from this conversation. *Ben's right—staging is a plague upon the earth.*

Will went for a second serving of the soufflé and came back from the kitchen with that and a glass of punch. He didn't usually drink punch, but the liquid smelled unusually appealing tonight. As he sat down beside Josh on the cooler they were sharing, Kerstel said with surprising urgency, "*Will.* Which pitcher did that come out of?"

Will realized she was asking about his drink. "Ah, the pink plastic one. The glass one was empty."

"The plastic one has sangria in it," Kerstel told him.

"Oh," Will said. Sangria—fruit punch and wine. His brain flatlined; he didn't know what to do, so he just held the glass away from him as if it were an angry cat trying to scratch him. "Ah . . ."

The conversations around the fire died down for a moment.

"I've got it," Josh said, and took the glass from Will's hand. She jumped up and headed inside, and everyone started talking again.

Will didn't embarrass too easily, but he was glad his face was hard to see in the firelight. "I'm sorry," he said to Kerstel.

She reached out from her chair and touched his shoulder. "I wasn't criticizing. I just wanted to make sure you knew what you were drinking."

"I didn't," he said firmly.

But of course he had, hadn't he? He'd smelled the contents of the pitcher, but instead of telling him, *Booze,* his brain had just said, *Good. Drink that.*

He didn't doubt for a second that, subconsciously, he'd known what he was doing. And that scared the hell out of him.

His first instinct was to pretend nothing had happened, to go off by himself and find a distraction, to go home and work on his stalker wall. Yes, that's exactly what he wanted: to open his files and dig through the articles Feodor had written until he understood what the madman had been doing, how he could be outwitted, outsmarted, outfoxed.

Instead, he left his plate of soufflé on the cooler and went into the house to find Josh.

This is what girlfriends are for, he reminded himself. *Isolating myself right now is the worst thing I can do.*

In the kitchen, Josh was pouring the sugar water from a bottle of maraschino cherries into a glass of soda. "Hey," she said. "I'm making you a special drink."

"That's okay," Will told her.

"It'll be like sangria without the wine," she insisted, and he watched her mix cream of coconut into the glass. He was pretty sure she didn't know what was in sangria.

"It's fine. I'm not even thirsty. I . . . I'm kind of freaking out."

"It's no big deal. You just mixed up the pitchers."

"No, Josh, Saidy made sure to tell me which one had the sangria in it. I think I . . . I didn't realize it, but I poured the sangria on purpose."

Josh opened the refrigerator and hunted around, finally surfacing with a plastic lime full of juice. "You wouldn't do that. Besides, so what if you did drink it? You can have a sip of sangria. You *aren't* an alcoholic."

The room began to tilt, and Will grabbed on to the countertop. No, technically he wasn't an alcoholic. *Yet.* But hearing Josh brush off his fears frightened him more than pouring the sangria had. She didn't understand—he had to stay ahead of himself. One wrong step—one wrong *sip*—and it could all fall apart. *He* could fall apart.

Josh finished peeling a banana and stuck it in the glass. "Here. Drink this." She gave him a kiss on the cheek. "It's all good," she said. "Come on, let's go make s'mores."

She didn't notice when Will failed to follow her back outside. In the glass she'd shoved into his hand, one end of the banana rested surrounded by clots of unmixed coconut. Feeling at once panicked and numb, he carried the drink to the sink and poured it down the drain.

Josh had left the glass of sangria sitting on the counter.

Will poured that out, too.

He didn't want to go back outside afterward. He'd reached out for support and hadn't found it; now he wanted to be alone.

One reason Young Ben kept building onto the house, Will reflected as he wandered into the living room, might have had to do with his tendency toward hoarding. He had two complete sets of *Encyclopaedia Britannica,* a laundry basket full of wire hangers, a book called *Social Media for Grandparents*—although he had no computer—a cardboard box labeled "Blankets," and a display stand for pipes with only one pipe in it.

Will sat down on the couch. The clutter itself was sort of comforting, in a weird way, and he browsed through the mess on the coffee table. Beneath several stained pairs of pants, he found a photo album that must have been fifty years old. The black-and-white photos were glued to black pages, each picture smaller than Will's palm. The book was open to a photo of a beautiful young woman with a man who was a few years older than her, posed together on the porch of a house. She wore a plaid shirt and close-cut shorts, and the man wore high-waisted pants that showed off an infant beer belly. They were both grinning, and the woman had her face turned toward her lifted shoulder.

The pose struck Will. It seemed familiar, as did the woman's figure—

"Oh, my God!" he said aloud. "It's Dustine!"

The woman reminded him of Deloise because she was Deloise's grandmother. Will had known her for only a few months before her death, but now that he had identified her, he couldn't see anyone else. She even had Josh's chin.

If the woman was Dustine, that meant the man with her was probably Young Ben. This was, after all, his photo album. Will recognized him now, too—the height, the square face, the emerging gut.

I didn't realize they had known each other for so long, Will thought.

He peered more closely at the photo. Behind Ben and Dustine, a blurred figure moved inside the house, crossing the doorway at the moment the photo was snapped. The blurring was bad and the figure's face was turned away so that only part of his profile appeared, but if Will hadn't known better, he would have sworn the man was Feodor.

Ridiculous, of course. But he felt as if Feodor had somehow inserted himself in the photo just for Will's benefit, as though his ghost were infiltrating the edges of everything.

Will shivered, then chastened himself. As he forced his hand to turn the page, Whim, cell phone pressed to his ear, walked hurriedly from the kitchen to the hallway, cutting through one corner of the living room without noticing Will.

Whim loved that phone. He used it so much, he had to charge it twice a day. But something about the speed in his step aroused Will's suspicion that this was not a normal call from one of Whim's legion of friends.

It's none of my business, Will told himself, but he was already rising from the couch. *I'll just make sure nothing's wrong. . . .*

He followed Whim down the hall and stopped outside the door to Ben's office.

"I have fifteen people waiting on me," Whim was saying inside, "so this had better be pressing. . . . Maybe. . . . Is that what you think of me? . . . Charming. . . . Maybe. . . . If you want to see me, just come out and say it. . . . See, was that so hard? . . . Maybe."

The conversation went on in the same vein for several minutes. Whim seemed to be setting up a meeting, but he did a lot of arguing—the sort of arguing that's flirting at the same time—in the process. By the time he finally hung up, Will had a pretty good idea who had been on the other end of the line.

He was waiting in the hall when Whim emerged.

"Jesus," Whim said, stopping just short of walking into Will. "Where did you come from?"

"Was that Bayla?" Will demanded.

Whim continued to act startled. "Were you standing here eavesdropping?"

"Yes, I was," Will said. "And it's a good thing, because you seem to have lost your mind."

Whim stepped carefully around him, looking less amused. "She just wants to catch up."

"I thought that's what you two did at the Grey Circle meeting."

"I have a girlfriend. Bayla has a boyfriend. Remember any of this?"

"I remember that your girlfriend is more than capable of kicking your ass."

Whim waved the idea away. "Del couldn't kick my ass."

"You live on salami and Chex Mix," Will told him. "You're a paper doll."

Whim laughed and started back down the hall. "Well, this paper doll can dress himself. Worry about your own outfit, Will."

There was nowhere else for the conversation to go, Will realized. Whim was going to do what he was going to do, and there was nothing Will could do to stop him short of telling Deloise, and he really didn't want to do that.

So he went back outside and sat next to Josh, who held his hand. He watched Deloise and Haley teach Mirren how to make s'mores; Deloise's technique was refined, while Haley preferred to just immolate his marshmallows. He took Kerstel's side in the Kerstel-versus-Lauren baby-name debate.

He hadn't felt so alone since he'd left the county home.

Twelve

Davita called Mirren the morning of her presentation to the junta. She'd called the day before as well, twice in the afternoon, once after brunch and once before, and several times the day before that. So when the clock in Mirren's hotel suite in the Dashiel Winters Building struck 12:30—the presentation began at one o'clock—and Davita had not yet appeared, Mirren's concern became grave.

"She's probably dead," Josh said.

"Josh!" Will, Deloise, and Haley all cried.

Josh, pacing the floor-to-ceiling windows, said, "It's a logical conclusion."

"Even I wouldn't go that far," Whim said. He was sprawled out on the ultramodern couch, eating peanuts from the minibar.

"She's not dead," Haley told Mirren.

"She hasn't called," Josh reasoned. "If Davita can't operate her cell phone, she's either unconscious or dead."

"Or she's stuck on the side of the highway with a flat tire and no bars," Will said. "There's no reason to assume she's *dead*."

"Peregrine knows he'll be blamed if anything happened to Mirren, so he's taking out a key element of her support."

"I can't listen to this," Mirren muttered, fleeing to the adjoining bedroom. She dropped onto the end of the giant bed and flattened her palms against the skirt of her blue taffeta gown to keep herself from tearing the fabric to shreds.

She loathed the gown, but Davita had insisted that she dress both traditionally and conservatively, and for dream-walker ladies, that meant floor-length dresses with long sleeves. Worse still, Deloise had fluffed and pinned Mirren's hair into a style that made her look like Anne of Green Gables.

Haley appeared in the doorway and leaned against it.

"What do I do if she doesn't show up?" Mirren asked.

Haley didn't hesitate. "Go anyway. You'll do great."

Mirren didn't know if she wanted to hug him or slug him.

A hard knock on the suite door made them both turn their heads. As Mirren rushed, skirts rustling, into the living room, Josh opened the door and said, "Oh. I guess you aren't dead."

"Where have you been?" Mirren demanded, and she heard in her voice that she wasn't just anxious but angry.

Davita ignored them both. "I need everyone to leave except Mirren."

"Why?" Josh asked.

"Leave," Davita repeated.

"Where are we supposed to go?" Whim complained, but he followed Deloise into the hallway. The hotel suite was located on one of the upper levels of the Dashiel Winters skyscraper in downtown Braxton. A dozen floors below was the junta's amphitheater.

Haley hung back, and Mirren told Davita, "It's fine, he can stay," but Davita was firm.

"Everyone leaves."

When they were alone in the suite, Davita threw the dead bolt and fastened the chain on the door. "What's going on?" Mirren asked. "Where have you been?"

Davita sat down on the couch and motioned Mirren to sit beside her.

"I'm sorry I didn't call this morning to tell you I'd be late. I couldn't, because I went to see your aunt and uncle."

Mirren straightened with surprise, then leaned close again. "You went *into* the Hidden Kingdom?"

"Yes. I received a package from your aunt with a summons and instructions for getting there. As you anticipated, your aunt and uncle are vehemently opposed to your plan. They gave me this, to give to you, in the hope that it will convince you to abandon your ambitions."

From inside the jacket of her suit, Davita withdrew a bulky linen envelope. She handed it to Mirren, who couldn't prevent a heartbeat of homesickness when she saw the royal seal stamped in orange wax on the back.

"They told me what it is, but not what it says," Davita explained. "They said there's also something inside to prove that it came from them."

Mirren began to open the envelope, but Davita grabbed her hands to still them. "No! Wait until I'm gone. If you still want to go through with this after you read the—what's inside, call my cell phone. If not . . ." Davita paused, and she squeezed Mirren's hands again, not in a forceful way, but as if out of sympathy or even pity. "I'll understand."

Then she flew out of the room.

Careless of the linen paper, Mirren tore open the envelope. Her family's seal cracked, ruining the imprint of a star tetrahedron.

A flashing piece of sparkle and a torn piece of parchment, folded once in half, fell into her lap.

The sparkle came from a brooch the size of a silver dollar, with a platinum star tetrahedron set against a gold field. The edges were encrusted with her family's gem, the fire opal, deep blood-orange stones outlining the circle. Except near the bottom, where one opal had fallen out.

Someone could have faked the piece, but they couldn't have known that—over the course of years of being treated as a plaything by two little girls—one of the stones had fallen out. Mirren knew for certain now that this envelope had come from her family.

She clutched the pin in one hand, glad for this small relic of home, and used the other hand to unfold the parchment.

If a queen she would become,
one of two things have begun:
a martyr's death to seal her ruse,
or lead to Death Dream Walker True.

Mirren read the parchment three times before balling it up in her fist and hurling it across the room. Then she stormed into the bathroom and yanked the pins out of her hair.

If a queen she would become . . .

"Absurd," she muttered.

The pins fell into the sink. *Plink, plink, plink.*

. . . one of two things have begun . . .

"An absurd, appalling scare tactic dreamed up by *pathetic* control freaks."

The last of the pins fell into the sink, and she briefly tried to brush her snarled hair before slamming down the brush so hard that the handle snapped off.

. . . a martyr's death to seal her ruse . . .

"Who has ever heard of a clause in a scroll?" she shouted, stomping into the bedroom and kicking off her shoes. "*If* I try to become queen, then I'll either die a martyr—"

She grabbed at the zipper of her dress, catching it on the second try and yanking it to her shoulder blades, where it stuck.

. . . or lead to Death Dream Walker True.

"Or what? Magically summon the True Dream Walker, and then kill him? It's *absurd*! It's a forgery! It's Aunt Collena trying to ensnare me again. If she can't control me physically, she'll control me mentally!"

Mirren jumped up and down, grabbing at the dress's zipper,

which had stuck in the most awkward, unreachable spot. After cursing aloud at it, she gave up, ran back into the living room, and retrieved the ball of parchment from under the desk.

She knew it wasn't a forgery. She recognized the handwriting of the seer who had written it; his name was Freigh Vescomballetti, and she had studied a number of other scrolls he'd composed. Her aunt might have torn it from a scroll other than hers, but how many other people had tried to become queen *and* had scrolls written by Freigh? The odds were too high to seriously consider.

At the sound of a knock on the door, Mirren folded the parchment and hid it in her sleeve. Through the peephole, she saw Haley standing alone in the hallway.

"Something feels wrong," he said when she opened the door. "I got worried."

Mirren stepped back to let him inside.

"Will you unzip this?" she asked, turning her back to Haley.

"Um . . ." he said, and only then did she realize she was asking him to undress her.

"Please. I would rather be immodest than spend another minute in this taffeta tar pit." She gained a small measure of relief when she felt the dress come loose around her. "I'm going to change."

She went into the bedroom and closed the door partially. After removing the dress, she changed into the outfit *she'd* wanted to wear to the presentation: straight gray slacks and a white silk blouse with sheer sleeves. Feeling calmer, she fished the scrap of parchment out of the dress and stuck it in her pocket.

When she returned to the living room, Haley was examining the brooch. "The *Anna Karenina* jewels," he said.

"Yes." Mirren smiled faintly as she took the brooch from him. It was one of the jewelry pieces she and Katia had worn while acting out scenes from *Anna Karenina*.

She ran her thumb over the brooch's face. How many times had she pinned this brooch to a nightgown and had "afternoon tea" with Katia, both of them sticking their pinkies out as they raised their cups, discussing princes who didn't exist and—inexplicably—

speaking in English accents? They had pretended to be princesses then. How cruel that the same brooch that had inspired so many royal fantasies was now being used to crush Mirren's royal ambitions.

Mirren held out her arms and Haley wrapped her up in his. She closed her eyes and just felt how alive and real he was—his body warm and moving, a field like energy rising off him to surround her. None of those tea party princes had ever been so real.

If she died, he would hurt. Maybe his heart wouldn't break to pieces, but it would at least ache. Mirren wondered if she had the right to risk his emotions that way. And Davita—Davita would be devastated. Mirren *knew* she didn't have the right to take chances with someone's feelings like that. And her cousin Katia—her heart's sister—would lose her only friend.

"What do you want to do?" Haley asked.

Truthfully, she wanted to spend the afternoon letting him hold her. But that wasn't the direction her life was pushing her.

"I want to tell the junta I'm here," she said.

"Do you need to change?" Haley asked.

"No." Mirren picked up the brooch from the coffee table and affixed it to her blouse. "This is what I'm wearing."

Realizing that her bid for queen was likely a kamikaze mission filled Mirren with a strange fearlessness. She had to slow her stride as she entered the amphitheater in order to keep from barreling into Josh, who was walking in front of her. Will and Haley flanked her sides, with Whim and Deloise behind them, and Davita brought up the rear, all of them wearing hastily donned robes in various colors.

Sound rose in a flutter of whispers and then stopped short, silent as Mirren passed by. Whim's blog had posted the news of her return the day before, but even he hadn't expected it to be taken seriously. Mirren allowed herself to meet people's eyes as she passed, giving them a serene smile no matter how hostile their looks. Most of them, though, appeared curious rather than angry.

Except for one man who spit on the floor near Mirren's feet, causing those nearby to admonish him and Will to unsheathe his machete. Mirren just laughed as she sidestepped the wet spot and continued toward the stage.

I'm going to get killed doing this, she told the man silently. *Your spittle does not frighten me.*

The amphitheater stretched endlessly upward like a dovecote, with rows upon rows of balconies and mezzanines. At the bottom, the ocean of audience broke around a raised circular platform. Josh stepped to the side of the stairs leading to the platform, allowing Mirren to ascend alone.

The platform's polished wooden boards shimmered like gold. Mirren kept her chin up as she took a seat on a single ottoman placed before the junta's seven thrones, and she folded her hands loosely in her lap.

She recognized all seven members of the junta from her studies. Of course, identifying Peregrine Borgenicht was easy, even before he leapt out of his throne in a sparkling green robe. Mirren had looked at hundreds of photos of him, starting the day her uncle pointed Peregrine out as the man who had set fire to her parents' palace. She had memorized the jumble of oversize features that made up his face: the giant, rheumy eyes; the red ears with lobes like hanging fruit; the thick, perpetually wet lips—all of them mounted on an undersized, bald head.

He looks like he's going to do magic, Mirren thought, taking in his sequined robe, and she had to stop herself from laughing. He was, after all, a dangerous man.

"Before we begin," Peregrine said, giddy with excitement, "I want to clarify what you want us to call you. Should I call you Lady, or Princess, or Your Royal Highness?"

Mirren didn't flinch. "Miss will be fine."

"Miss? That's odd. It is the understanding of this court," Peregrine said, striding toward her, "that you are claiming to be Amyrischka Rousellario."

"The court is misinformed." Mirren locked her eyes on Peregrine's and ignored the surprised murmurs of the onlookers.

"Is it?" Peregrine asked.

"Yes. To say that I am claiming to be Amyrischka Rousellario implies that I am asserting something that may or may not be true. Since I am, in fact, Amyrischka Rousellario, and have already proven such with DNA, my claim has already been verified. Furthermore, since I am not a princess of any existing monarchy, the most appropriate form of address is *miss*."

Be calm. Be polite. Be brief.

Davita's advice rang in Mirren's ears, but she couldn't follow it—not with the rage and the carelessness that were running through her veins.

"Well then, *Miss* Amyrischka, would you like to tell us why you're here?"

"To submit a proposal for a constitutional monarchy to the Accordance Conclave."

Shocked rumbling came from the crowd. Even Peregrine's eyebrows darted up—for an instant.

"A noble intention. But why would you think the dream walkers would elect someone who has been convicted of abdication of duties, betrayal of moral duty, and treason?"

Peregrine moved continuously. Mirren would have thought he was pacing except his expression was one of exhilaration and not anxiety. He looked more like he was an actor making use of every inch of the stage.

"Because I was convicted," Mirren said as amiably as she could, "in absentia, of crimes I supposedly committed as an infant."

"You're still a criminal," Peregrine replied curtly. "As of this moment, I am taking you back into custody in order to fulfill your original sentence."

The crowd filled with voices, but Mirren—who had anticipated something similar—said, "Beheading, wasn't it?"

"Yes." Peregrine's mouth twitched, and then he shuddered as if with repressed pleasure.

"Wait a moment," one of the other junta ministers interjected. Mirren was pleased, but not surprised, to see that the speaker was a middle-aged, dark-skinned man with glasses. His name was Ithay Innay, and he was one of Mirren's favorite ministers of all time. Although his deep thoughtfulness sometimes led to indecision, the stands he took were well reasoned and rooted in compassion.

Minister Innay stood up from his throne and motioned the audience to quiet down. "We aren't going to impose a death sentence on someone whose convictions were clearly symbolic. At the very least, she should be retried."

Peregrine smiled smugly. "I have no issue with that," he said. "Let's put it on the books."

Dammit, Mirren thought.

He'd danced her right into a corner.

Having pending criminal charges would make Mirren ineligible to submit a proposal to the Accordance Conclave.

"No," said Minister Speggra, a giant bearded man who looked like a cross between a biker and a Viking. Mirren held her breath despite her desire to appear calm; Speggra was one of the ministers Davita had anticipated would be against Mirren.

"We aren't going to waste time retrying her," Minister Speggra declared. "She was an infant, for God's sake! If she weren't a Rousellario, we'd laugh at the idea of charging a baby with treason."

As little as Mirren had been expecting Speggra to come to her aid, she got the feeling Peregrine had anticipated it even less. "But," he began with an actual sputter, "we brought those charges to ensure that no one could reestablish the monarchy—"

"*You* brought those charges against her," Speggra replied, "back when this council really was a fascist junta. I want a vote. All in favor of vacating the previous conviction against Amyrischka Rousellario, rise."

Five judges rose from their seats while Peregrine scampered to sit back down in his.

I can't believe this, Mirren thought.

"Then that's that," Speggra said. He settled back into his throne;

despite its size, the wood still creaked beneath him. "Ithay, tell them what we decided yesterday, when Peregrine conveniently failed to mention he was going to pull this stunt."

Mirren had forgotten how much Speggra hated "malarkey."

Minister Ithay rose.

"To clarify," he said, "no one is doubting Miss Rousellario's identity. However, because she has no experience in our current form of government and has been raised in hiding, outside the bosom of the dream-walker community, she will be required to pass Agastoff's Trials before her proposal will be accepted."

Agastoff's Trials, Mirren repeated in her mind. *I should have thought of that.*

Agastoff's Trials had been created to prove the worthiness of rulers who were either not of royal blood or only distantly related to royalty.

"For those of you who haven't read your dream-walker history, there are three trials. The first is the Learning, an exhaustive interview intended to test the knowledge of the applicant regarding our history, laws, culture, and traditions. The second is the Tempering. However, because no one has ever seen Miss Rousellario dream walking, we will instead ask her to prove her ability to dream walk by resolving three nightmares that the junta will select for her. The third is the Proving, a terrible task that will test the applicant's cleverness and loyalty. Miss Rousellario, do you accept Agastoff's Trials as a means for determining your worthiness?"

What could she say? Historically, she had little room for argument. Agastoff's Trials had been the accepted course for more than a thousand years. She could have argued over the modifications, but she wasn't certain she'd win.

Davita met her eyes from the crowd and shook her head.

Mirren knew that Davita would tell her to go on the defensive and demand to know what evidence they had that she wasn't loyal, well trained, and well educated. But Davita's main goal was to protect Mirren, even more than to see her succeed. She'd proven that an hour ago when she'd given Mirren the envelope from home. And what Mirren realized was that enough of this audience was against her that she needed to win their affection. If they needed to see her triumph over impossible odds, she'd show them that.

Or die a martyr trying.

"I agree," Mirren said.

Through a Veil Darkly

Interview with Princess Mirren

Princess Mirren was presented to the junta yesterday, amid gasps of surprise and the awed faces of those in attendance. She demonstrated phenomenal poise as Peregrine Borgenicht hammered at her and tried to reinstate her original sentence of beheading. (Good for Minister Speggra for calling Borgenicht out on attempting to use the legal systems to enact personal vendettas.) When the junta demanded that she pass Agastoff's Trials, not only did she know what those are, she agreed without complaint. No one else running in the AC is being forced to pass weird trials. When is the last time Peregrine Borgenicht even went into the Dream?

Today, she took a break from preparing for her trials to chat with me. Click **here** to listen to the audio of this interview, or read the transcript below.

Me: So, Princess Mirren, how are your preparations going?

Mirren: Really well. I'm excited.

Me: You have the Learning in just a couple of days. Are you ready for it?

Mirren: Absolutely. The Learning is the trial I feel most confident in, actually. My aunt and uncle were a little obsessive about my education, so I've spent a lot of time studying.

Me: How do you feel about the other two trials?

Mirren: I have to admit I'm nervous about those, because I don't know what to expect.

Me: The dream-walking trial seems pretty straightforward, but what about this Proving? What sort of terrible task do you think the junta is likely to assign you?

Mirren: I haven't the slightest idea. Historically, it could be anything. A lot of people think that Agastoff included the Proving in his trials as a way to veto truly unsuitable candidates. The basic idea is to test the candidate in whatever arena he—or she—is weakest.

Me: What are some previous Provings?

Mirren: Well, they've run the gamut from riddles to feats of strength. One man was asked to bring the head of his newborn daughter in a box.

Me: Ew!

Mirren: Luckily, he was a very clever man. He cut a hole in the bottom of the box and stuck his daughter's head through it. He actually ruled for some years.

Me: Is it true that legendary dream-walker wunderkind Josh Weaver has agreed to help you prepare for your dream-walking trial?

Mirren: Yes, and I'm deeply grateful. She's an amazing teacher. I'm learning a lot from Will Kansas, too.

Me: Has Josh made you do that Romanian circuit-training video?

Mirren: No. . . .

Me: Good. Don't let her, or you might never walk again. Well, that's all I have right now, Princess. We'll be rooting for you. Good luck at the Learning.

Mirren: Thanks, Whim.

Comments:

jlouston says: She forgot to tell him not to call her princess.

> BParKw2 says: That's because she secretly loves it.

>> Mari_Onette says: She told everyone not to call her princess when she was presented to the junta. She shouldn't have to remind each individual person.

sWord says: Rock on, Princess!

Byzantine_m993 says: In 1492, Agastoff's Proving for Paijenno Barikna was to sentence his own father to life in prison for selling DW secrets. I hope she gets something like that.

> Trewbador says: Make her admit to everything her parents did.

> Mari_Onette says: She's not her parents. Why can't people figure that out? She didn't even know them.

amynewhousen2415 says: She's so beautiful!

knight_of_darkness says: Shame on Borgenicht and the rest of the junta for laying the sins of her parents on her. She didn't even know them.

pratto391 says: Let's not go royal-crazy. This isn't Britain. Sure, she's hot, Borgenicht's not, but she hasn't proven herself in any way yet. Hold off on the unadulterated worship.

Thirteen

It was a beehive.

At least, Will thought it was a beehive. Wax hexagons formed the walls, floor, and ceiling, and they were thin enough to diffuse the light passing through them. In the center of the six-sided chamber, in an even larger wax cell in the floor, the light outlined a body curled into the fetal position.

"Assessment," Josh said to Mirren.

"Ah . . ." Mirren glanced around. "We're in a beehive, obviously."

"What are common associations with beehives? What do they represent?"

"Honey?"

"What's the source of danger?" Josh asked.

Mirren winced. "Unclear?"

"Where's the dreamer?"

"In the big wax cell in the floor? I don't know." Mirren tugged on her earlobe. "She's the only person here. Shouldn't we be *doing* something?"

"No," Josh said. Will—who had been her pupil for much longer than Mirren had—knew that unless Josh saw something requiring immediate action, she was more than capable of standing around dissecting the situation with no more anxiety than an audience member lingering in a theater complex hallway discussing a film. Will also knew how infuriating her calm could be.

Will was fairly certain that Mirren was dealing with some post-traumatic stress from having spent four days in the Dream. Josh had been training her for a week already, but every time they brought her into the Dream, her usual poise gave way to stuttering and shaky hands. Will was hoping that enough trips back into the Dream would act as a sort of exposure therapy to help her work through her anxiety.

Assuming none of the nightmares retraumatized her, of course.

As Mirren struggled to answer Josh's questions, Will noticed that within the cells that made up the walls, black shapes were moving against the light.

"What's that?" he asked.

"Bees!" Mirren cried. "We should go."

"They don't look like bees," Josh said, and that was when the first finger burst through the wax and toward them.

A field of fingers followed, popping through the walls like dandelions. They shot out of the wax in ones and twos, not just pointing fingers but digging fingers, fingers eager to escape their enclosures.

"What's happening?" Mirren cried.

Before another word could be uttered, the fingers freed themselves, and they were not only fingers but *hands,* hands that ended before they could become wrists. Some of the hands sprang from the walls to the floor, but many launched themselves directly at the three dream walkers in their midst, an avalanche of appendages.

Even Josh screamed.

The first hand that landed on Will grabbed his elbow and crawled toward his shoulder. He shouted and swatted it, but it held tight to his arm.

Then a dozen hands were clinging to him, climbing up his pants like spiders, grabbing hold of his hair, weighing down his shirt, digging nails into his skin. With his own hands, he tore at the vermin, but for each one he pulled off, another half dozen jumped onto him. Somehow one got a thumb inside his mouth at the same moment a pinky slithered into his ear canal.

He bit frantically at the thumb, but its fingers were joining it, forcing Will's mouth open and climbing inside. Another hand jammed two fingers into his nose.

They're suffocating me! They're going to choke me to death!

Josh shouted something unintelligible. Will stomped his feet and felt small bones crunch beneath his sneakers. Fingernails scraped the back of his throat, and he stuffed his own fingers into his mouth, forcing his jaw open to an unnatural degree, as he tried to get a grip on the spit-slick intruder.

Josh shouted again, and this time Will heard her: *"Lighters!"*

Only when he heard her voice so clearly did he realize that Mirren had stopped screaming.

He yanked his lighter out of his pocket and lit it on the first spin of the wheel. He held the flame so close to his face that he smelled his hair burning. One hand and then another dropped to the floor, skin singed pink, and Will stomped the life out of each one. He paused only to hook his finger around the thumb in his mouth and yank the hand out of his throat. He stomped that one really, really hard.

"Cough, Mirren!" Josh was shouting. "You have to cough!"

The hands—*They must have some kind of group consciousness,* Will thought—realized he was winning the battle thanks to his lighter, and they fled his body in an exodus of extremities. Together, they began digging open the cell in the middle of the floor where the dreamer lay trapped.

"Will!" Josh said. "Mirren needs the Heimlich! I'm too short!"

Mirren was in serious trouble, Will realized. A hand had managed to get all the way into her throat, and it was now too far down and too wet for either Josh or Will to extract. Mirren was swaying on her feet, her lips a dusky violet shade getting bluer by the second.

"I've got her," Will told Josh, wrapping his arms around Mirren from behind. Josh had taught him the Heimlich maneuver months ago, and it wasn't very complicated, but he'd never performed it on someone actually choking.

He made a fist and wrapped his other hand around it. Then he jammed his fists into Mirren's diaphragm and forced them upward—hard. So hard that he felt bad.

But Mirren coughed.

"Bend over!" Josh ordered, and Will released Mirren so that she could bend at the waist while Josh dug around in her mouth and finally tore out a squirming hand.

A buzzing sound made Will look away from Mirren, and he finally got a glimpse of the person in the floor. Mirren had been right that she was the dreamer. She was also a giant bee.

Her woman's body had sprouted thick black-and-yellow fur from head to hip, and instead of legs, she had a stinger with multiple razor-sharp barbs. Her eight-foot wings beat so hard that not only did they fill the room with a buzzing as loud as an airplane engine, they kicked up a gale.

She had domelike bee's eyes, too. And barbed antennae. And for some reason, a mouth full of dagger-shaped fangs. Will pulled the plastic compact out of his pocket and ran to the only doorway—a six-sided opening that led to an identical chamber.

"Josh, we need to go," he said, watching the dreamer rise through the air to hover near the ceiling. He used the mirror to reflect his lighter's flame into the doorway, and a rainbow shimmer filled the opening.

Mirren was still coughing.

"She just needs a minute—" Josh said.

The bee-woman turned toward them, and her buzzing intensified. Her stinger dripped a substance that looked like honey but sizzled where it hit the wax floor.

"Josh!" Will shouted. *"Now!"*

He'd never told her what to do in-Dream, let alone shouted at her, but it got her to look up.

"Holy shit!" she yelled, and she grabbed Mirren's arm and yanked her through the glittering Veil.

Will followed, and an instant later he tumbled onto the archroom floor. Beside him, Mirren coughed and cried simultaneously.

"Well," Will said, "I think we've succeeded in retraumatizing her."

They took Mirren to the kitchen to calm down. Josh made her hot chocolate, and then Deloise wandered through, and when she heard what had happened, she insisted on making Mirren a batch of her famous gingerdoodle cookies.

As Deloise was beating the butter and sugar together—and swatting at Josh's hand to keep it out of the bowl—the back door opened and Whim walked in. He looked at Mirren's white face and hunched posture and asked, "Do I even want to know?"

"Where have you been?" Deloise asked, turning off the hand mixer. "I couldn't find you."

Whim balked just long enough that Will knew the answer.

"I went down to the minimart for a KitKat," Whim said.

Sure you did, Will thought.

While the girls argued over the safety of eating raw eggs, Will said, "Hey, Whim, did you notice that scratch on the Lincoln's bumper?"

"Scratch?!" Whim cried.

"It's not long, but it looks deep. Come outside and I'll show it to you."

Will led him out the back door and down the steps to the Lincoln.

"I don't see it," Whim said.

"Forget the scratch. I made it up."

"What? Why would you do that to me?"

Will opened the driver's-side door and stuck his head inside the car.

"Do you know what that smell is?" he asked.

"Vintage luxury?" Whim suggested.

"Perfume. Which Deloise doesn't wear, because she has allergies." Will opened the backseat door and examined it. "Right here, we have dirt on the inside of the door."

"I'll get some leather cleaner," Whim said, but Will went around the car to the other side and opened that rear door. After a few seconds of looking . . .

"Hah!" He raised his arm triumphantly. "And here we have the smoking gun."

"I can't even see what you're holding," Whim said. His expression was decidedly unamused, and he'd put the uneaten half of his candy bar in his pocket.

"It's a hair. It's a very long, very dark brown hair. I found it on the seat on this side, which is where Bayla was lying while you two made out in the backseat, your shoes rubbing against the inside of the door and leaving that dirt because you're too tall to fool around in the backseat of a car, but you had to do it in a car so that no one would see because you're *cheating on Deloise*!

"And then you stopped at the mini-mart to buy a KitKat on your way home so you'd have evidence to back your story up, right?" Will slammed the car door shut.

Whim rubbed his mouth and chin with his hand. "Okay, all right, just . . . hold your horses for a minute. Stop freaking out."

"I'm not freaking out," Will said indignantly. "And if you think I am, then that tells me exactly how little you care about Deloise, because you ought to be freaking out over what you've done to her."

"Oh, my God, Will, calm down. Can you hold off your next nervous breakdown for five minutes so we can talk about this like reasonable people?"

"What the hell does that mean?" Will shouted, even as his mind said, *It means you're shouting.*

Whim threw his hands up in the air. "It means you've been so high-strung and judgmental lately that there's no point in trying to have a rational conversation with you!"

Whim turned and strode away across the back lawn, which stretched for several acres. Will was too stunned and hurt to even think of following him.

I haven't been judgmental, he told himself.

Yes, I have. But I've had to be, because everyone else is being so careless!

No, that's a ridiculous thought. Whim's right—I'm becoming really high-strung. I can't even think clearly.

He rubbed the back of his neck, suddenly aware of how tight and painful it was.

Everything needs to stop, if it would just stop for a couple of min-utes, if I could just catch up . . .

The thoughts were coming too fast for him to keep up, and he realized he was actually holding his head in both hands, digging his fingertips into his scalp the way the disembodied hands in the nightmare had. He let go, cursing himself.

I can't think, I can't think.

"Will."

Will opened his eyes and saw Whim was standing in front of him, and the concern in Whim's expression far outweighed the anger.

"Will, man, what is going on with you?" Whim shook his head. "Let's talk for a minute."

Will silently followed him across the lawn to the run-down gazebo, where they sat on wooden benches with peeling white paint.

"Spill," Whim said.

Will shrugged. "I don't know."

"You can do better than that, psychology boy."

Will knew he'd meant it as a joke, that his friend was trying to lighten the mood, so he forced a tiny smile.

"I just . . . I used to feel like people needed to make their own mistakes and learn from them. And now I feel like I have to stop them, at least from making terrible mistakes, because they don't understand that— I don't know. There are repercussions for things, right? I'm just trying to keep it all together."

Whim listened to this shoddy explanation and then said, "But it isn't all falling apart."

"I don't know how you can say that. You're cheating on Deloise. Mirren's probably going to be assassinated. Josh can't even sleep through the night without waking up screaming. I mean, *somebody's* got to step in and fix things."

"No, they don't," Whim told him. "You're blowing all this out of proportion. Peregrine won't kill Mirren because everyone would know it was him. Josh needs to go see a doctor and get some sleeping pills or a massage or something. And I'm not cheating on Deloise."

Will gave him a look that he hoped conveyed a skeptical-bordering-on-scornful question. "Really?"

"I'm *not*," Whim insisted. "Bayla and I are just working through some emotional stuff from the past."

"With your hands?" Will asked.

"Don't talk about it that way," Whim said sharply, surprising Will. "Bayla and I went through a lot. We're still going through a lot. So, no, we shouldn't have fooled around today. But if I don't get her out of my system, I'm never really going to be able to *be* with Deloise. She'll never have all of me, you know? I want her to have all of me."

That's not how love works, Will thought, but he managed not to say it.

"Besides, even if I was cheating on Del with a dozen girls, it still wouldn't be *your* problem, Will. You aren't responsible for me."

"I know that."

"Are you sure? Because during that little demonstration back at the car, you looked a lot like my mom."

Will laughed ruefully. Saidy was known for her temper.

Whim grinned. "You feel a little better?"

"Yeah. I'm sorry I went off on you."

"It's okay."

"Really?"

"Yeah. I grew up with my mom *and* Winsor *and* Ian. I'm not afraid of the strap."

"You're so nuts, Whim."

"I know it. Look, about Bayla . . . If you feel like you have to tell Del, I can't stop you. And I'll try not to get pissed off at you. But all I'm asking for is time. You don't have to cover for me, you don't have to lie for me, I'm just asking you not to say anything, and I promise, a month from now I'll have Bayla out of my system for good."

I'm going to regret this, Will thought.

But Whim was such a good friend to him, and it wasn't like he was trying to make a fool out of Deloise.

"Okay," Will said.

Whim clapped him on the shoulder. "You're a good man, Will Kansas."

Will sighed. "I hope so."

Fourteen

Mirren's kamikaze attitude vanished after she nearly choked to death on the hand. Somewhere in the back of her mind she had assumed that hers would be a swift death carried by an unseen bullet. One second she'd be talking, or eating, or laughing, and the next . . . nothing.

Her near murder by the hand had been the opposite: visceral, messy, agonizing. She didn't want to die like that.

The next day, instead of going into the Dream again, Mirren let Haley take her to the pool to teach her to swim.

Josh had been appalled when she'd learned that Mirren couldn't swim, even after Mirren explained that the only body of water in the Hidden Kingdom was a foot-deep creek. Mirren thought that the swimming lessons were a waste of time—what were the chances she'd need to swim in one of the nightmares the junta chose for her trial?—but she was glad to be with Haley and away from the Dream.

Tanith's outdoor swimming pool was packed with vacationing children, but the indoor pool was nearly deserted except for lap swimmers. Haley led Mirren to the shallow end, where she forced herself into the cold water. "I'm freezing," she said.

She was also very nervous about being in a swimsuit, although the one-piece she had picked out had come from what Deloise referred to as "the old-lady bathing dress" section. So far, though, Haley had politely refused to look at anything except her face.

Despite her attraction to Haley, he was not a good teacher. His patience seemed to be infinite, but he couldn't explain worth a damn. While teaching her to float, he kept telling her to "just lie back," but every time she did she went under. They'd been in the water less than fifteen minutes when she began to miss Josh's ordering her around.

Finally, Haley put his hands under her back while she stretched out, and she managed to rest comfortably on the water's surface—although she was fairly certain Haley was holding her up.

"Relax," he told her.

She tried, but it caused her to sink down, and only Haley's hands kept her from going under. "S'okay," he assured her. "You're okay."

After that, Mirren tried to keep her body rigid. The effort threatened to exhaust her.

All of this is exhausting, she thought. *Why am I putting myself through this when I'm going to die anyway?*

"Haley, have you seen my scroll?" she asked. She assumed that, at some point, he might have seen it when he touched her.

He hesitated, then nodded.

"So you know I'm going to die."

He looked away, and Mirren felt herself sink into both despair and the water. So he *had* seen it.

Then Haley turned back to her, and his face had changed. He looked older, more awake, and he straightened his perpetually slumped shoulders. "No future is certain," he told Mirren. "I know that better than anyone. And I'm tired of being afraid of what will come."

"Have you been afraid?" Mirren asked. "I never knew."

"I have been afraid every day of my life," he admitted, still moving her gently through the water. "I've been afraid of what I know, what I don't know, of trying to change things."

"How do you live like that?" She didn't mean to challenge him, but she had gotten her first real taste of fear these last few weeks, and she couldn't imagine living a whole life that way.

"I haven't. I mean, I've done nothing. I've been so passive. I've hidden. And people have gotten hurt."

She'd never heard him say so much or express himself so intimately. With a little thrill, she whispered, "Tell me about it."

His hazel eyes turned distant with memory. "I sat back and watched my brother fall apart. Maybe I could have saved him from himself, but I was so afraid he'd turn on me. And instead he hurt Josh, and he hurt Winsor, and then he got himself . . . Maybe I could have done something. I never felt like I had the right."

"And now?" Mirren asked, in awe of the ease with which he spoke and the strength that had come over him.

"And now there's you." He smiled, without ducking his head. "You're so strong. My friends—my family—it's easier for them if I'm weak, if I'm just backup. But you make it okay for me to be strong, too."

"Oh, Haley," Mirren said. She didn't try to hold back her tears; she wanted him to see how much she admired and adored him, and she was about to hug him when he held up his hands for her to see.

She was floating all on her own.

"I'm doing it!" she cried, and Haley laughed, and then she did hug him, hard.

Thank you, gravity, she thought, *for drawing me to someone who can both help me and be helped by me.*

Gravity had known what it was doing.

Three weeks after she left it, Mirren returned to the Hidden Kingdom.

Returning involved none of the difficulty or trauma that leaving had required. Mirren's family had two faithful servants who functioned on their behalf in the World; their primary duty was to procure supplies—food, medicine, complete DVD sets—and deliver them to the Hidden Kingdom, which they accessed through a special archway secreted in a furnace room. Mirren had never been allowed to know to where in the Hidden Kingdom the archway opened, and she was surprised to pass through and find herself in the stables. She had checked for archways there a dozen times.

"So, if you came through this archway," Josh said, "why didn't you come out in the furnace room? Why did you end up in the Dream?"

"Because," Mirren explained, brushing hay off her skirt, "this isn't the archway I found. There's a second one under a bridge in the woods, and it leads to the Dream. That's the only one I could find, so that's the one I went through."

"Wait," Will said. "Your family didn't tell you where either of the archways were? What if something terrible happened to your aunt and uncle?"

Mirren shrugged and petted the nose of her horse, Natasha. The animal sniffed suspiciously at Haley's hand but finally decided to lick it.

"Then Katia and I would have been stuck here forever," Mirren said.

She rubbed her nose against Natasha's so she didn't have to see the looks being exchanged behind her back. "I missed you," she whispered, and Natasha licked her hand.

"That was insanely brave of you," Josh told her as they left the barn. "I mean, to jump into the Dream for the first time by yourself?"

Mirren smiled and accepted the compliment. She decided not to bother adding that she'd had no way out of the Dream, since her aunt and uncle had never allowed mirrors or fire-starters in the Hidden Kingdom.

Walking with Haley behind Mirren and Josh, Will said, "I have to admit, I wasn't expecting a universe Feodor designed to look quite so much like Disney World."

Mirren followed his line of sight to the castle, and her time away allowed her to see it with new eyes, all peaked red roofs and white stone walls, guarded on all sides by evergreen trees and the steep face of the hill it had decapitated. They'd arrived just before dawn, hoping to slip in and out before Mirren's family woke. Beyond the castle, orange light encroached on the horizon like dust kicked up by the horses of an approaching army.

"It's huge," Josh said. "I didn't know it would be so huge."

"According to Aunt Collena, Feodor based it on Moszna Castle in Poland," Mirren said. With a grin, she added, "Except this castle has one hundred turrets, and Moszna Castle only has ninety-nine."

She had been the one to suggest they visit the Hidden Kingdom and look for Feodor's papers. She knew Will had been biting his tongue to keep from bugging her about it, and besides, if she was really going to die, she wanted to go home one last time.

She'd forgotten how steep and long the steps to the castle door were. Her legs were used to the discipline, and Josh seemed unfazed, but Will and Haley were panting by the time they got to the top.

"From here," Mirren warned, "we need to be very quiet." She wondered if she should make them take their shoes off—Aunt Collena was very strict about shoes in the house—and decided not to bother.

As she led them through the dark castle, noting how the gold and silver in each room caught the early light, she found herself wanting to stop and tell stories—the year they'd celebrated Christmas in the library, how Katia had once gotten stuck under a claw-foot tub while playing hide-and-seek, Uncle Fel's obsession with Post-it notes. How could she have had such a wonderful childhood and been a prisoner at the same time?

Too soon, they had to descend to the basement.

"This place is massive," Will said in a low voice when they were deep enough underground that Mirren felt comfortable turning on a light.

"It starts to seem small if you spend enough years here," Mirren assured him.

She led them into a vast carpeted room filled with row after row of red filing cabinets that matched the red-and-gold carpet and the pale gold wallpaper.

"Whoa," Will said. "How much do you have down here?"

"This isn't everything," Mirren said. "There are other rooms like this. But the files on Feodor will be in here." She took a basketball-sized ring of keys off a brass hook on the wall. "Remind me what we're looking for precisely?"

"Feodor's last manuscript."

Josh and Haley went to examine some of the gilt-framed portraits hanging on the wall, but Will followed Mirren into the stacks and stayed glued to her side.

"Do you mind stepping back?" she asked. "There might be things in this drawer that—that I shouldn't share."

Will frowned as he took two small steps back. "I need to know—"

"I brought you here, didn't I?" Mirren asked. "I think I've earned a little trust."

Will looked abashed. He took two much larger steps back. "You're right."

Mirren spent the next ten minutes digging through files, looking for anything relevant to Winsor's condition. "This is just Feodor's history," she told Will, feeling guilty for making him wait. "Do you want a transcript of his trial?"

"I already have one," Will said.

They moved on to other drawers and other disappointments, but finally Mirren saw a note tucked in a file on Feodor's translations: *For light harmonics, see file #8938007.*

Rising through the file numbers, Will and Mirren ventured deeper into the maze of cabinets and to the far end of the room.

One of the chandeliers had burned out above them, giving that row a darkened, ominous feel. Mirren hesitated before unlocking the drawer.

"Step back, Will."

When he had backed up a full yard, she turned the third key.

Compared with the other files in the drawer, the one labeled "Kajażkołski—Theory of Greater Evolution" seemed out of place. As she flipped through the first ten pages, she saw nothing on the same scale as in the other files. She was noticing mathematical errors while just leafing through.

"I think this is a manuscript, or at least part of it."

Will took the file as if she were handing him a premature infant and immediately carried it to an area with enough light to read.

Alone with the drawer, Mirren glanced through the files again. At the back was a thick collection of papers labeled "Staging."

She knew what the pages inside said. She knew that she was risking her life to keep those pages' secrets.

With a sigh, she began to close the drawer. Then her eyes caught on another file.

"Death," was all the label said.

Death? Mirren thought. *I don't remember a file on— Oh, wait.*

The key ring slipped from her hand.

Inside the file was the oldest known copy of a ritual, held safe in protective plastic. Beside it was an Italian translation from the sixteenth century, also enclosed, and beside that, a slightly fragile English translation from the early 1900s.

Would I? she wondered.

After reading the page through, she glanced at Haley. He and Josh were examining a jeweled trimidion in a display case, and he was wearing his little Haley smile.

What wouldn't I do? she asked herself. *If it means staying in the World, living my life, being with Haley, what wouldn't I do?*

Mirren removed the English translation, folded it into eighths, and tucked it in her bra.

Through a Veil Darkly

Princess Passes the Learning with Flying Colors

Princess Mirren appeared before the junta today and gave a phenomenal performance. Over four hours of questioning, she answered questions regarding dream-walker history, government, culture, and mission and proved that she knows everything there is to know about being a dream walker. Even Emfyte Kresskadonna couldn't stump her.

The princess again demonstrated remarkable poise, despite her voice becoming more and more hoarse as the interview went on. She even sang a few bars from *Opan Omgritte,* the only dream-walker opera ever written. (Who listens to that? I never have.) And who isn't impressed by a young woman who can actually understand dream theory? She even speaks fluent Hilathic! The junta didn't even bother taking a vote before declaring that she had passed the trial.

Comments:

Byzantine_m993 says: No one speaks "fluent" Hilathic. We only know the meaning of a thousand words in Hilathic, so anyone can memorize them and then call themselves fluent, when in reality they probably don't know enough words to have a conversation.

2400jokes says: She sounds stuck up. Just like Byzantine_m993.

amynewhousen says: She's not stuck up. She's just a nerd.

tetracycline says: I had this dream last night that I was a priest and she came to confession and told me she helped Webishinu fake his own death and she knew all along that he didn't die in the Dream.

babykim says: She probably DID know. Didn't Webishinu work in dream theory? Maybe she wanted to keep him quiet.

tetracycline says: I'm pretty sure she was in preschool when that happened.

Worchester_RWatson says: The Learning is the easiest trial, hands down. We'll see how much all her book-smarts do for her when she has to go into the Dream.

pouter40242 says: She wouldn't shut up! Shut up! SHUT UP!!!!!!!

lochtess says: You all shouldn't be laughing. The Dream is a dangerous place, and the smallest mistake can be fatal.

jshg_hammer says: Go back to your loch, Tess.

Fifteen

Against the black-and-gray ruins of Warsaw, *the brightly lit house stood out like a blazing beacon of hope. Both the exterior and interior walls were made of glass, so Josh and Feodor could stand outside and see straight into the cozy yellow kitchen, where a plump woman in a ruffled apron was trying to force her son's hands into a cauldron of acid.*

"No!" the boy was screaming. "You can't make me do this!"

"Stop fighting!" his mother admonished.

At the kitchen table sat on older man, smoking a pipe and perusing a newspaper. "Listen to your mother, Caleb," he said.

Outside the glass house, Feodor chuckled. "The unquestionable wisdom of parents," he mused.

The acid in the cauldron bubbled and spit, and its droplets burned tiny wormholes into the white granite countertop.

Caleb's mother had bound his wrists with cooking string and was pushing him closer to the cauldron. "Afterward you can have a big bowl of ice cream," she promised.

Caleb's fear hit Josh like a chaotic crash of musical notes played all at once—too loud, too fast, too urgent.

"I have to save him," she said. She attacked the exterior wall of the house with a sharp side kick, but the glass barely reverberated.

"Do you?" Feodor asked.

His placid, amused expression confused her. "Of course I do."

"You're certain?"

She couldn't figure out what he was asking. How could she not save this boy from having his hands burned off? How was that even an option?

"But how will I play the piano with no hands?" Caleb wailed.

"You won't," his mother replied. "Won't that be a relief? No more arpeggios."

"No more paying for lessons," Caleb's father added. "No more paying to get the damn thing tuned every six weeks. No more Bach."

"Amen to that," Caleb's mother agreed.

Feodor continued to look at Josh as if waiting for an answer. Holding her eyes, he gestured silently to a wooden table sitting outside the house. A black velvet cloth had been spread over the tabletop, showcasing the harsh metal forms of the circlet and vambrace.

"I thought you said I shouldn't use them," Josh told him.

"Did I?" Feodor pondered.

Caleb's mother had succeeded in forcing him close enough to the cauldron that splashes of acid were nipping at his skin. "It burns!" he wailed.

Josh stroked the circlet. The metal felt unnaturally cold to her, and the idea of pressing such frigidity against her skin made her hesitate to put on the devices.

But Caleb screamed as the acid burned his fingertips, and the terror in his voice gave Josh the courage she needed to clamp the vambrace around her forearm. Immediately, the metal warmed against her skin. When she slipped the circlet around her head, a sensation of relief ran down her scalp. She aimed her arm at the glass house, and the power streamed into her hand like molten pleasure. Her mind expanded, beyond her skull, beyond the Dream, beyond space and time. From there, from God's point of view, she knew everything.

"It feels good, no?" Feodor asked, tracing the metal hinges with his fingertips. "So very, very good."

Josh couldn't deny that it did. With a thought, she slammed a lid over the cauldron, sealing it tight against the acid.

"No!" cried Caleb's mother, staring at Josh through the glass wall. "You don't understand!"

But Josh knew everything. She felt everything. Her wisdom swept through her, unimpeachable. She would sit in judgment of the whole world.

With dancing fingers, she manifested a long strip of duct tape over the mother's mouth.

Caleb tore away from the woman with a gleeful shout and ran to the piano in the living room as the strings that bound his wrists fell away.

"You know what is best for them," Feodor assured Josh. "Your field of vision is so much wider than theirs."

"Yes," Josh whispered as her thoughts bound Caleb's parents in splendid, weblike shrouds.

Caleb flung open the piano cover and began playing even before he sat down. "Poland has not yet perished!" he sang.

Josh barely recognized the tune. Caleb had rearranged it, changed its pace and key so that instead of the strident, honorable anthem Josh knew so well, what emerged from the piano was a mocking two-step fit only for a honky-tonk bar.

Feodor hissed through his teeth, and the piano lid slammed down on Caleb's wrists. Josh heard bones break beneath Caleb's rending scream, and she shook her vambraced arm at the house, but nothing happened. She thrust again, slamming her hand against the glass wall, directing her thoughts . . . nothing.

The devices had abandoned her.

The piano lid flew back up and sucked in Caleb's arms up to the elbows, the black and white keys chomping at his flesh.

With a desperate cry, Josh resorted to beating on the glass exterior of the house. Caleb screamed as the piano pulled him in, rivulets of blood running down the keyboard, and from the kitchen, his bound and helpless parents watched as the instrument devoured their child.

And Feodor laughed and laughed.

Josh turned on him, but before she could summon the power of her thoughts, he kissed the tip of her nose.

"Your wisdom," he said. "All yours."

In the morning, Josh called Bash Mirrettsio. She was anxious—anxious and hiding in the garage, where no one was likely to overhear her—but Bash sounded delighted to hear from her and not at all surprised. When she said she was hoping to discuss his Nicastro paper, he was even more delighted and invited her to his office the next day.

Josh had only been planning a phone call, but his office at Willis-Audretch was in downtown Braxton, and coincidentally, Mirren would be in Braxton at the same time, meeting with Anivay la Grue. The only difficulty lay in finding an excuse to go without taking Will. Finally, she told him that the elbow she had broken in February had been bothering her recently, and she was going to Braxton to see her orthopedist. Will offered to come along anyway—him being a good boyfriend—but she assured him that the trip would be boring and not worth his time.

It was easily the biggest lie she had ever told him.

When Josh walked into the lobby of Willis-Audretch, the World's only dream-walker think tank and research center, her knees weakened.

Feodor's memories bloomed in her mind, like a gray tint coloring everything she saw. Yes, the décor had changed, the reception desk was in a different place, and a metal detector had been installed, but she *recognized* this place and the bones of the building.

Not me, Josh thought. *Feodor.*

"Ma'am?" the man at the receptionist's desk asked. "May I help you?"

She gave her name at the desk, then paced the waiting area, and only a few minutes later, Bash appeared. He was both nerdier and better-looking than Josh had expected. His blue pants clashed with his red-and-brown shirt, and they all clashed with his orange tie, which he'd obviously yanked on a few times, but none of that distracted from his crow-black hair or the bright smile that revealed tidy square teeth. Despite his classic good looks, Josh couldn't get past his white Velcro sneakers.

As they headed up to his office, Bash made small talk without Josh's help, which worked well since she was too overwhelmed to carry on a conversation. Everywhere she looked, she saw not only the modern reality, but the past superimposed over it: doors painted two colors, floors with two different carpets, even two different series of creaks in the elevator.

Josh began to feel a sort of dread as they passed through the door labeled "Applied Physics Department." Her shoulders sagged when they entered Bash's office without disturbing the door to room 327, which Feodor had unlocked every morning when he came into work. Josh didn't know if she felt relieved or disappointed.

"Help yourself," Bash said. "I'm sure there's a pot in the break room."

Josh blinked at him. "What?"

"You said you wanted coffee, right?"

No, she had turned over her shoulder and barked, "Cree, where's my coffee?" just like Feodor had done every single time he'd come in to work.

This confusion resulted in Josh ending up sitting in front of Bash's desk with a large mug of coffee, which she didn't drink and had doctored into a warm milkshake.

"So, as I mentioned, I loved your paper," Bash told her. "Particularly the part where you performed your experiment without any sort of supervision or permission. Sometimes I think that the Nicastro encourages young people to get into trouble."

Bash laughed. Josh made herself smile again.

"I'll be frank," he said. "You look anxious. What did you want to talk about?"

Josh swallowed; the drink did nothing to relieve the bitter taste in her mouth. Reluctantly, she opened the manila envelope she'd brought along and drew out a handful of pages. "I was reading your paper, and you talked about using trimidions to monitor the state of the Dream at various points, then sending radio signals back to a central location."

Bash nodded, apparently unsurprised that she had followed the paper.

"I've—" She struggled with the first word, since it wasn't quite a truthful one. "I've been working on sort of the opposite idea, that a central device could broadcast signals to various points within the Dream."

His aristocratic brow furrowed. "To what purpose?"

"Well," Josh stumbled again. Somehow she had been hoping to avoid telling him *why* she wanted to do this. "I've been . . . I mean, it might be possible to . . . The central problem is how to create fixed broadcasting points on the surface of the Dream, since it's constantly expanding and contracting."

Bash didn't protest the leap in topics. "Which is exactly why nothing in my original paper has proven applicable. We'd need to place trimidions throughout the Dream at fixed locations, so that we'd be able to know exactly where the signals were coming from. But the Dream is always changing shape, like . . ."

"The sea," Josh suggested.

"A sea without a bottom. How can you fix something to the surface of the sea?"

Josh fiddled with the papers, not sure which ones to show him.

"What if . . . we could change the polarization of Dream particles to prevent them from shifting?"

For the first time, Bash seemed surprised.

"That would be quite an accomplishment. That isn't actually what you're working on, is it?"

Josh pushed forward one of the pages she'd torn from her sketchbook. Bash immediately drew it toward himself.

"What is this?" he asked, but then he began reading and stopped asking questions. Josh anxiously checked over the calculations again, once grabbing a pen to scratch out a couple of words in Polish, hopefully before Bash noticed them.

"Where's the rest of this?" Bash asked, the lighthearted tone in his voice gone.

Josh showed him the next page.

For the next forty minutes, he read, sometimes tapping the equations with a capped pen as he worked through them in his mind. Finally, he sat back in his chair and blew out a long, marathon-runner breath.

"This is mind-blowing," he said. His voice was very serious. "You wrote this?"

Josh hesitated before nodding.

"How? I mean no offense, but your Nicastro paper wasn't anywhere near this. Who have you been studying with?"

Josh squirmed in her chair. "I haven't been studying with anyone. I've just been reading a lot."

Bash wasn't buying it. "I find that impossible to believe."

She was going to have to tell him *something*. "You probably heard that I had a run-in with Feodor Kajażkołski a few months ago."

"Yes, I did hear that. You're telling me that this is his work?"

That would make more sense, wouldn't it? Josh thought.

She'd considered telling Bash at least part of the truth. The problem was, if she admitted she had gotten her ideas from Feodor, how would she explain when she kept coming up with new ones?

"No, the work is mine. But I hit my head while I was in his

universe. I fractured my skull really badly, and since then . . . I've been thinking differently. Dream theory just sort of makes sense to me now." She tried to give Bash a light smile, like it was no big deal. "My dad's really confused about why my grades have improved so much."

That part, at least, was true. She'd been accused of cheating twice in the last months of her junior year, and she'd resorted to taking proctored Saturday exams to prove herself.

"I bet," Bash said. He flipped through the sketchbook again. "I would have been surprised if you had said this was Feodor's work. It's too orderly, too much hard science."

She smiled for real then, even as she wondered what Bash's comment might imply. Were Feodor's ideas being filtered in some way as they passed through her brain, altered and made more orderly, possibly even less dangerous?

"I didn't get the impression he was a super orderly person," she said.

"What *was* your impression of him?" Bash asked, looking up at her.

No one had asked Josh the question that way, but the answer poured out of her mouth before she could give it a thought. "I think he was a luminary whose light was distorted by the shadow of evil."

Where had *that* come from? Was that how Feodor saw himself? Josh had never said anything so poetic. She added, to break the strange tension she'd created, "What did the monarchy say before they exiled him? That his genius was matched only by his madness?"

"I hadn't heard that one." Bash gave himself a little shake. "Unfortunately, if we come back to this brilliant work you've written, we're faced with a problem that perhaps only Feodor could have solved. How are you going to stabilize the Dream particles in their new polarity?"

"I was hoping that was where you could come in."

"Flattering." He tapped the pages with his capped pen and thought. "Give me a while to work on it."

"I would be grateful if you would."

"I'm excited, honestly. I haven't seen anything like this since— I don't think I've ever seen anything like this. May I keep these pages?"

Josh nodded after a pause. "I'd appreciate it if you wouldn't show them to anyone else, though."

Reluctantly, he said, "It's a temptation, but I'll respect your wishes. I wouldn't want anyone showing my work around before it was ready."

"Thanks."

As she stood up, though, he added, "Josh. You must realize the implications of what you've created."

Suddenly she felt his excitement, not just at the ideas she had given him, but at the thrill of this secret.

"If you could build this machine and find a way to anchor transmitters in the Dream, you could transform Dream particles in any way you wanted. You could alter the Dream."

Josh swallowed. She knew only too well.

"Let's not get ahead of ourselves," she said. "One step at a time."

By the time she reached the elevator, she was trembling.

Sixteen

Long after everyone else had gone to bed, Will remained sitting at the desk in front of his stalker wall, trying to put together the pieces of Feodor's last manuscript.

Combining the copies from Mirren's archive with the four copies of the manuscript the presenter at the Grey Circle meeting had given Will, he had seven total copies. None of them were complete individually, but put together they appeared to make a whole manuscript.

Except . . . When Will went to check a page number on the last page of one manuscript to see how much it overlaped with another, he noticed that the last words were different on what should have been identical pages.

Maybe one is a revised copy, he thought, but he lacked the knowledge of dream theory to make heads or tails of either version. Instead, he reexamined all the copies he had, page by page, to make a list of places where they diverged.

The longer the list became, the more certain Will felt that the discrepancies had nothing to do with revision. He was still poring over the pages, trying to make sense of the words, when Mirren came downstairs in a green silk pajama set.

"Oh, hello," she said. "I thought everyone had gone to bed."

"So did I. Trouble sleeping?"

"I'm nervous about tomorrow."

The next day was her dream-walking trial.

She perched on the corner of Will's desk. "I'd never been nervous before I came to the World. I had nothing to be nervous about. Now I'm finding that I don't like it very much."

"No one does," Will agreed.

"I keep wondering what nightmares the junta will pick, and if I'll have any idea what to do when I face them. I know that if I can just get over the hump of figuring out an approach . . ."

Will decided not to tell her that after six months of training with Josh, he was still learning the same thing. Instead, he said, "Why don't we go pull up some nightmares in the archway, and we can toss ideas around about how to approach them? We can't go into the Dream, of course, but—"

"I would be extremely grateful," Mirren said. "Would you mind?"

"Not at all. Playing the teacher instead of the apprentice is sort of fun." He started to rise and then realized the opportunity he was passing up. "Oh, wait, before we do that, could you take a look at these copies of Feodor's last manuscript?"

He explained to her about the numerous versions of the text, and she pulled up a chair beside his so that she could examine the pages more closely.

"How much dream theory do you know?" Will asked.

"Quite a bit. Of course, that in no way means I'll be able to read this. I've read some of Kajażkołski's earlier work, and it always took me hours to parse it out." She read over a page of which they had four copies. "This doesn't even sound like his other work. And the first paragraphs on these two versions are the same, but the equation that follows them is radically different."

"Are either of them right?" Will asked.

Mirren required a calculator and scrap paper to figure it out. "I don't think so. This one is pure nonsense. But . . ." She tapped some more. "The second equation is much better, but it only fits with the explanation given on this Xeroxed copy over here."

"So you're saying that none of these pages make sense by themselves, but if you take parts of each one and fit them together, they start to make sense?"

"They might," Mirren said. She copied out the explanation and the equation it referenced onto a new sheet of paper, then two more paragraphs—from different copies—and another equation from yet another source. "Now *this* makes sense. This I could believe Kajażkołski wrote."

"What does it say?"

"It talks about evidence of the subtle body in our DNA. The subtle body is what he called—"

"The soul, I know. The part of us that enters the Dream universe when we sleep."

"Some people prefer to think of it as our consciousness. He says that our consciousness is present in our DNA, and he's written an equation to measure the subtle body's vibration based on DNA content. He compares how our souls function to our ability to see stars. When the sun sets, you can see the stars, but the stars are always there regardless of whether or not they're visible. He thought that when the body dies, part of the soul remains in the DNA."

She frowned. "I shouldn't have said this made sense. 'Reads coherently' would have been a better description."

"You don't believe in souls?"

"I do, but what does he mean by saying that our souls can be found in our DNA? There's a passage here about how if your arm gets cut off, your consciousness is still attached to your arm. This equation at the bottom of the page appears internally consistent, but I have no idea what it does." She shuffled through the pages, seeming to grow more frustrated. "Sorting all this out will take days."

Will felt reluctant to let the subject drop, but he knew Mirren needed to focus on her dream-walking trial.

"Well, we aren't going to manage it tonight," Will said. "Let's go watch some nightmares."

Mirren nodded, the relief plain in her face.

The archroom was cold this late at night. Whim and his father were on nightmare duty, and Will fetched a second chair so that he and Mirren could sit comfortably and watch through the arch as a kitchen tried to eat their friend and his dad. Will attempted to provide some educational commentary, but most of the time he was pretty sure Whim had no sort of plan at all.

When the nightmare ended, Whim and his father left Will and Mirren alone to work the looking stone. "Less than an hour, we promise," Will said, knowing that the middle of the night wasn't a great time for dream walkers to go on break.

"No rush—I'm famished," Whim said as he left.

Will pressed his hand to the looking stone and enjoyed the eerie sensation that the powdered red glass was pushing back against his palm. Touching the looking stone activated the archway and caused a section of the Dream to appear within the archway's confines. The first nightmare to pop up within the archway involved a gunfight on a small fishing boat.

"So I guess the first thing I'd do," Will said, "is make sure I know who the dreamer is. And then I'd try to distract the dreamer away from the guns. I'd say, 'I found it!' or, 'This way!' so they'd think I had something they needed or I'd found an escape route. But Josh says I try to influence dreamers too often."

"That's because you're better at it than she is," Mirren said, making Will glance at her.

"Am I? I guess I am." Even though he knew Mirren was right, the comment unsettled him. "It's not that Josh doesn't want me to be good at things—"

"I didn't mean to imply that."

"It's just, she gets anxious when I use tools she's not sure will work."

Perhaps because he was thinking about Josh while he had a hand on the looking stone, or perhaps just by chance, Josh appeared through the archway.

"Will," Mirren said, her voice somehow different from before.

Josh stood on a battleground, surrounded by half-creature soldiers, and black smoke streaked the poppy-red sky above her. She wore a smoldering, blackened ball gown, something she never would have donned in real life, and she looked on as the goblin-men around her fought one another. They were not so much two armies against each other as just a sea of writhing enemies fighting only for themselves.

Feodor stood beside Josh. He was younger than he had been in his universe, but Will still recognized him. His brown pants and white shirt were the only tidy things in sight. He stood next to Josh with his hands by his side, a smile playing over his lips like sunlight.

"Is that . . ?" Mirren asked.

Feodor stepped up behind Josh, and he slipped those small, clean hands around her waist. As he slid them up her sides, she raised her arms, and Will saw some sort of contraption on her left arm from wrist to elbow, a strange metal brace or piece of armor. It reflected the red sky, and a similar reflection made him notice that she wore a metal crown, hanging down low over the back of her neck.

She raised her arms above her head, and Will stumbled out of his chair, revolted at the sight of Feodor sliding his hands up Josh's body. She opened her mouth; her jaws were full of gnashing fangs, and she released a roar that could have been in either Polish or Demonic.

No, Will thought.

Josh flung out her machined arm, and black fire erupted from her palm. The bolt reached for miles, burning the warring creatures to cinders and charring the earth. She cast her fire as far as Will could see, releasing a triumphant roar, and as she scorched life from the earth, Feodor brushed her hair away so that he could trace the back of her neck with his tongue, his arms clutching her close, his hands cupping—

The Veil popped.

In the silence afterward, Will realized that the dream hadn't ended, he had just broken contact with the looking stone long enough that the archway had let go of that particular nightmare.

"Will," Mirren said, but he couldn't look at her. She touched his shoulder. "I'm sorry," she told him, and then she just stood there, the weight and heat of her hand growing on his shoulder.

Will waited for himself to react. He knew there were any number of psychologically legitimate responses, and he waited to see which one he would experience, but oddly what he thought was that he finally understood why Haley was so enamored with Mirren. She didn't obfuscate or distract, she didn't avoid or pretend, she just told the truth and faced what was ahead of her. And for a guy like Haley, who couldn't help seeing the truth when he touched someone, that must have been a very great relief.

Will nodded to himself, filing the information away, and then noted that the psychological reaction his brain had chosen was avoidance.

"I'm sorry," he told Mirren. "I think that's all we have time for. I'm sure you'll do great tomorrow. Good night."

Then he even managed to smile.

"Remember," she said, ignoring his words. "It was a nightmare, not a fantasy."

He nodded and walked upstairs to the Weavers' apartment. For a moment he paused outside Josh's bedroom door, wondering what he would see if he went and sat in the armchair by her bed. Would she lie trembling, the pillowcase torn by her clenched hands, body rank with sweat? Would she be moaning—

He went back down to the second floor and his own apartment. For the first time, he depressed the lock on his bedroom doorknob.

He climbed into bed, but every time he closed his eyes, he saw Feodor's hands sliding up Josh's small body and her mouth full of teeth and the way the pale green of her eyes had vanished beneath a reflection of the poppy-red sky.

So he didn't close his eyes, and he didn't sleep.

Seventeen

Mirren knew she was squeezing Haley's hand so hard that she must have been hurting him, but she couldn't let go.

I can't do this, she wanted to say. *I'm not ready. Take me home.*

Braxton was a large enough city that the main archways were located in a central hub known as the Arches. Aboveground stood a public park with beautiful Gothic arches decorating the walking paths. Belowground, a nine-archway hub provided an organized area where the local dream walkers could put in their hours.

The archways—all marked by much tidier and more recent stonework than the one in Josh's basement—stood in a wide circle in an underground room. Two archways were in use by dream walkers, but the others stood empty, and one had several rows of chairs set before it. The junta, out of their robes but still imposing in business attire, spoke in a huddle, no doubt arguing some final issue of protocol. Josh had insisted that Will test the archway's looking stone; Mirren didn't know if she was more surprised that Josh thought the looking stone might have been tampered with or that Josh trusted Will more to test it out than she did herself.

Photographers and reporters made up a large percentage of the people in the archroom as well. Mirren counted Whim among them; he hadn't stopped typing on his tablet since they'd arrived. She had been startled by the presence of so much media. How many reporters did one secret society need?

Even though they'd come inside through the janitor's entrance, a crowd had been waiting for Mirren when she'd climbed out of the limo. A lightning storm of camera flashes had blinded her when she'd tried to enter the building. People had shouted questions, and a group of protesters had held up signs and hollered, "Off with her head!" Someone had hurled a tomato at her, and even though Josh had caught it in midair, the animosity had still frightened Mirren.

"Everyone here is rooting for me to fail," she told Haley as they waited for the junta to pick a nightmare.

"Not everyone," he said. She could tell by the way he was ducking his head that being around so many people was making him nervous, but he hadn't hesitated to agree when she'd asked him to come.

The rules of the trial were simple. The junta would pick three nightmares for Mirren to enter, and she had to resolve each one, meaning she had to guide the dreamer to face his fears, or confront her demons, or escape from the nightmare's danger. If Mirren woke the dreamer or exited the Dream without resolving the nightmare, she'd fail.

"Remember Gilcrest's Warning," Josh said. *"An archway reveals no more of a nightmare than a mirror unmasks a soul."*

"Didn't Gilcrest's wife kill him by feeding him bonbons full of arsenic?" Mirren asked, which made Will burst into tremulous laughter and Josh look at him with confusion.

Mirren was worried about Will. He obviously hadn't slept and he'd been wearing a sort of deranged smile all morning.

Mirren promised herself that once this trial was over, she'd reach out to him.

"The point is," Josh said, "the junta will only be able to see so much through the archway. They might send you into a nightmare that's a lot more dangerous or a lot less dangerous than they expect."

"Is that supposed to make me feel better?" Mirren asked.

"No, it's supposed to remind you to stay alert and make no assumptions." Josh ran a hand through her hair. "I could try to think of something encouraging to say, but at this point, either you're ready or you aren't."

Mirren didn't feel ready.

The junta broke their huddle, and Peregrine Borgenicht came over to wish Mirren luck.

Mirren smiled as sweetly as she could and said truthfully, "I wouldn't be here without you."

He laughed and took his seat, but Mirren felt an unexpected fury. She squared her shoulders. "I bet he won't be smiling when I resolve the third nightmare," she muttered.

Josh smiled at her then. "*Now* you're ready."

Mirren soared through the first nightmare. On a cruise ship transporting prison inmates, she avoided being killed by rioting prisoners and coaxed the dreamer—the onboard massage therapist—into saying what she'd always needed to say to her father. The Dream resolved just in time for Mirren to avoid going down with the ship.

The second nightmare was harder. Mirren followed a preteen diver up to the top of a ten-meter platform and tried to talk her out of her performance anxiety. The little girl wasn't afraid of diving as much as she was of letting people watch her dive.

But nothing Mirren said seemed to help. The girl continued to tremble and hyperventilate, and Mirren began to fear that the

Dream would shift before she resolved the nightmare, and finally she just said, "Come on, we're going right now!" She grabbed the girl's hand and yanked it as she ran off the end of the platform.

The fall was two seconds of mindless terror as the air tore at her flailing limbs. The girl fell with her, but they separated half-way down, and while Mirren managed to get her body mostly into the pencil position Josh had taught her, nothing she did could prevent the girl from landing on top of her.

Mirren heard her neck pop against the underwater silence, and her left arm went numb. Time stretched as she struggled to surface. The girl kicked her in the face, knocking Mirren back, and her numb arm was slow to respond, but she finally got her head above water and sucked in a grateful breath.

Beside her, the girl was treading water, a giant grin on her small face. The crowd was on their feet, cheering.

The nightmare dissolved.

"If there was a time limit," Davita told Peregrine, "you should have brought it up when we agreed to terms. But since you didn't, I'm informing you that Miss Mirren is taking a one-hour break to receive medical treatment and recover."

"The fatigue of back-to-back nightmares is part of the trial!" Peregrine argued.

They kept arguing. Minister Speggra got involved, too. Mirren turned the chair she was sitting in away from them, causing Saidy—Whim's mother, who was a paramedic—to admonish her to hold still.

"You need a cervical collar," she added.

"She can't dream walk in a neck brace," Josh said.

"She's sprained her neck badly enough to involve the nerves in her arm. I can tape the hell out of it, but what she really needs is to sit still."

"There aren't too many nightmares we get to fight by sitting still," Josh said.

"She doesn't have to go back in," Haley said, and everyone looked at him, even Saidy.

"Meaning what?" Josh asked finally. Mirren saw Haley flinch a little at her tone, but he pulled himself up and spoke again.

"Mirren," he said, "do *you* want to keep going?"

For a moment, her neck stopped hurting. All she felt was happy. *Out of everybody here, he's the one who thinks to ask me.*

"Of course she wants to keep going," Josh said. "This was all her idea. None of us would be here if she didn't want to do this."

On the one hand, Josh was right. Everything had been put into motion by Mirren herself. On the other hand, such endeavors had a way of taking on a life of their own, and Mirren knew that if she gave up, a small chorus of people would try to convince her to keep going.

Haley wouldn't be one of them. He didn't care if she was a princess or a queen or a nobody. And he didn't care if she got something started and realized halfway through that it wasn't what she thought it would be and needed to back out. She didn't have to prove anything to him.

Strangely, that made her want to be brave.

"Mirren?" Davita was asking.

Mirren made herself look away from Haley. "I just need an Advil and a cup of coffee, and I'm good to go."

The sound of the rain beating on the car's roof startled Mirren with its volume. She'd been in a car during the rain only once, and she couldn't remember if it had been this loud. She didn't think so.

She sat in the passenger's seat, and hot air from the defroster bounced off the windshield and onto her, carrying a dry, staticky scent. In the driver's seat was a teenage boy, black, maybe three or four years younger than her. He hardly looked old enough to drive, but he was scrawny to begin with—thin wrists, knobby elbows, a hairless chin he needed to lift to see over the dashboard.

He didn't react to Mirren's presence in the car, prompting her to ask, "Where are we going?"

He glanced over then, smiled. His smile turned down at the corners, sad or maybe wistful. "Green Lake."

"This is poor weather for a day at the shore."

The boy nodded, giving another empty smile.

They drove past a wooden sign announcing the entrance to the marina. The road wove between stands of maple and birch, passing turns toward various campsites. Mirren didn't know if she should try to pump the dreamer for information or let the nightmare unfold, but when they entered the marina she felt safe saying, "So, we're getting on a boat?"

The boy didn't answer, and Mirren realized the marina was empty at the same moment he slammed down on the gas pedal and sent the car flying toward the water.

"No!" Mirren shouted, grabbing for the wheel.

The dreamer pushed her away, grimacing. The sound of the rain on the car roof was drowned out by the rhythmic *thwack* of the car tires bouncing over wooden boards.

The dreamer had managed to drive the car right up onto the pier, which was barely wide enough for the car. They were still a third of the way from the end when the vehicle's left tires slipped off the edge, and their inertia sent them careening straight into the lake.

What Mirren felt was not fear but fury.

"What the *hell* is the matter with you?" she shouted at the boy.

The car began to sink, and the sound of the rain hitting the roof grew fainter as more and more of the vehicle sank underwater. Mirren frantically pushed the button to roll down her window, but it must have shorted out.

"I want to die," the boy said with surprising calm and dignity. He tightened his seat belt.

Mirren didn't know what to say to that.

Josh had briefly covered how to escape from a sinking car. Very briefly. In fact, the only thing Mirren could remember was that unless they got out before the car was submerged, their chances of surviving were, as Josh had put it, "complete shit."

The car was nearly completely underwater already, sinking fast, and the weight of the water against the car door was enough that Mirren couldn't open it. Water lapped at her ankles.

She realized she was breathing too rapidly. She would need to hold her breath if they were going to reach the surface. But the way the light inside the car faded as they sank deeper, and the knowledge that they were going to have to wait until the car was completely full of water before escaping, was freaking her out.

She closed her eyes for a moment. She'd been to the pool half a dozen times, three times with Josh and three with Haley. She knew how to kick, to stroke, to float. . . .

We must be fifteen feet under by now.

The water reached her waist, so she unhooked her seat belt. "Get ready to swim," she told the dreamer, but he'd closed his eyes and was holding out his arms like he was inviting the water to take him.

"Stop that!" she said, and when he didn't react, she slapped him. He started, lips parting with surprise.

"I'm getting out of here, and I'm taking you with me."

"No, I want to die." He held out his arms again. "I'm at peace."

How can he be sitting there like Buddha under the tree while he's drowning? Mirren wondered furiously. *This is a nightmare—*

A nightmare.

She slapped him again. "Hey!"

"Ow!"

"If you're at peace, why are you so scared?"

The boy's lips parted, and then his fear rose to the surface, even as they sank deeper into the water.

"I just don't know what to do!" he told Mirren, blurting out his problems like she was his best friend. "Mom is always mad at me, but she'll never forgive me if I go live with Dad, and I *hate* Leann and the way she nags me about my grades."

He went on and on while the water level inside the car rose.

Mirren kept hoping that the emotional disclosure would be enough to resolve the nightmare, but when the water reached her chest, she felt she had to interrupt him.

"That's a lot to deal with," she said as calmly as she could. "Why don't we talk more once we're back on dry land?"

The dreamer surveyed the car's dim interior. "I think what's done is done."

"No, it isn't!" she cried, panic overwhelming her. "I'm going to the surface, and I'm taking you with me!" She grabbed his shoulders. "The water pressure against the car doors is too strong for us to open them yet. We have to wait until the car fills. Then the water pressure will equalize, and we can open the doors and swim to the surface. You have to take a deep breath and hold it right before the water fills the car, okay?"

The water was already lapping at their chins.

"This is never gonna work," the dreamer said. For the first time, he looked upset.

Mirren wished she could slap him again, but her arms were underwater. "Yes, it is! It *is*! Ready? Now!"

She took in a deep breath, but she had waited too long, and a gulp of water entered her lungs along with the air. Immediately, she coughed, and she'd lost half of her air before she was able to overpower the spasms in her chest. Still, she felt her lungs seizing up, trying to expel the water, and beneath that, despair.

I can't make it.

The car was nearly pitch-dark. She groped along the door, feeling for the handle. Every second she didn't find it was a second wasted, and by the time she wrapped her hand around it, she didn't know if she was seeing black spots because light no longer reached the car or because she was already passing out.

The door opened grudgingly, but the meager breath in her chest wasn't enough to draw her toward the surface. She kicked, meaning to kick off the side of the car but instead just smacking the door with her foot.

The surface was a misty green light far above, and her legs were heavy. The terrific shoes Deloise had helped her find weighed so much. She paused to take them off, but afterward, her legs felt no lighter. Was the surface getting dimmer instead of brighter? Mirren realized she was forgetting to use her arms.

I'm going to die, she thought very calmly. *I'm just . . . going to die.*

She began to understand how the dreamer had faced his death so peacefully. Or at least pretended to. Like him, deep inside she was terrified. But the water was so cold, and each time she moved she lost what little heat she had accumulated, and finally she could no longer hold off the need to cough and watched those bubbles of air she had fought so hard for drift away.

Like tiny moons, she thought, and closed her eyes.

And then something jerked her, hard, and she was cold again, very cold, and she struggled against a tight, warm noose around her neck, pulling her, pulling her, and then her head burst above water and she heard herself gasping and the dreamer laughing.

She opened her eyes. He *was* laughing.

She tried to speak and ended up coughing, and the dreamer caught her when she threatened to slip under again.

"I thought you were a goner," he said. His eyes were bright, elated. "When I got up here and realized you weren't with me, I was sure you were dead."

He looped an arm around her waist and helped her to the pier, where she clung to a wooden piling slick with moss.

"You went back down for me?" she asked between coughs.

"Yeah." Somehow he managed to shrug sheepishly while still treading water. "I'm actually captain of the swim team."

They both began laughing, and Mirren was coughing again when she splashed onto the archroom floor in a puddle of green water.

"How can you say she resolved the nightmare when the dreamer had to save *her*?" Peregrine demanded.

Mirren wasn't even on her feet before the politicians began arguing.

"Haley, Haley," she said between coughs, turning her head from side to side. "Get me out of here. Haley, get me out of here."

She caught sight of Will, and Haley was beside him, and the two of them lifted her bodily off the floor. They didn't even discuss a plan, just linked their arms behind her back and under her knees, and they had her out of the archroom before anyone could protest.

"I'm freezing," she said, clinging to Haley. She just wanted everything quiet, to sit down, to get warm.

They guided Mirren into the empty men's room. "Set me down, set me down," she begged.

They set her on unsteady feet, and her knees dipped dangerously before steadying. Haley drew Mirren into the communal shower and turned warm water on over her, not bothering to fuss with their clothes before wrapping his arms around her and stepping into the spray.

Standing between the hot water and Haley's warmth, she realized she was going to live.

At least, one more day.

Eighteen

 stood guard at the men's locker-room door while Mirren changed. Deloise, who was not biologically related to Kerstel but had nonetheless inherited her practicality, had packed not only dry clothes for Mirren, but also dry shoes, a few toiletries, a protein bar, and vitaminwater.

Whim wasn't helping much with the guarding; he only had eyes for his tablet. "Which is better? 'Mirren inspired the dreamer to heroism' or 'By playing the damsel in distress, Mirren tricked the dreamer into affirming the importance of life'?"

"Which one means she drowned?" Will asked.

Will needed to be done for the day. He hadn't slept the night before, and he'd spent most of Mirren's trial watching Josh instead of the archway. She seemed no different today from any other day in the last four months, and she hadn't knocked on his door the night before.

"Maybe I can combine them," Whim mused.

When they reentered the large archroom behind a mostly dry Mirren, a few people began clapping. A few others booed—one woman started hissing like a cat. Mostly, though, people were silent.

Minister Innay made the announcement. "By a vote of four to three, the junta has determined that Amyrischka Rousellario has passed the second trial." Afterward both the clapping and the booing were louder.

"Because she has successfully passed the first two of Agastoff's Trials," Minister Innay continued, "we now charge Miss Rousellario with her third and final trial, a terrible task, known as the Proving. The junta charges you to locate the Karawar, also known as the gathering whistle, and present it to the junta. You have nine days to complete this task."

Immediately, reporters showered Mirren with questions. Davita rushed her out of the room before she could answer, Haley on their heels, and Will and Whim followed, with Josh and Deloise bringing up the tail.

They left through the front entrance this time and exited the building into the park above. Among the park's decorated arches, the protesters had doubled in number, and whatever semblance of order had existed before Mirren's trial was gone. Before she got halfway to the curb and the waiting limo, one of the protesters hurled an egg at her. The shell fragmented into a hundred pieces when it smashed against the side of her face, and yolk dripped onto her dry T-shirt.

Will was still frozen with surprise when the protesters let loose, eggs flying from all directions. Josh twisted one fist up in a protester's shirt collar and pulled the other back for a punch, but she stumbled after the woman ground an egg into her eye.

Despite Will's confused feelings toward Josh, a sense of protectiveness spurred him to hit the protester as hard as he could. He'd never hit a woman outside of the Dream, but he didn't hesitate to do so then, or to raise a threatening fist when she straightened up with a sneer.

"You want anoth—" Will began, and then half a dozen eggs riddled his body. Some of them, he discovered, were frozen solid and felt like paperweights. He fell to his knees.

"Run!" Josh shouted, covering her dripping eye with one hand.

Davita hustled Mirren into the limo parked at the curb, but Haley was on the ground wrestling with a guy twice his size. As Will tried to rise from the pavement to help his friend, the woman he'd hit earlier slugged him in the gut. Josh reached his side in an instant, her eye squished up against further attack, spinning like a whirling dervish of pain as she cleared away the protesters who had gathered around Will. She even head-butted a man.

When the protesters had backed off enough, Josh grabbed Will's hand and dragged him toward the limo. Will saw Deloise break a man's nose with the heel of her palm while Whim pulled Haley up from the ground, and then they were all diving through the car doorway.

Someone grabbed Deloise's ankle as she tried to pull it inside the vehicle, and she used her other foot to kick him in the face.

"Go!" Josh yelled at the driver, and he tore away from the curb with the back door still hanging open. Whim wrapped his arms around Deloise's waist to anchor her. More eggs pelted the vehicle, each shell bursting like a firecracker.

"He took my shoe!" Deloise protested.

"You're lucky that's all he got," Whim told her, and he dragged her deeper into the limo.

After hours of ice packs, ultrasounds, and waiting for an ophthalmologist to come pick the eggshell out of Josh's eye, they were released from the ER into Davita's care. Mirren was wearing a neck brace and had her arm strapped to her side, Josh looked like a very short pirate in her eye patch, Haley's ear was bandaged beside his black eye, and Deloise was wearing a paper surgical shoe over her bare foot.

All in all, Will suspected they'd gotten off easy.

Despite attempting to land anywhere else, he ended up sitting next to Josh on the ride home. He felt awkward, but he doubted she could tell because he was sitting by the eye she couldn't see out of. The doctor had said she had to wear the patch for a couple of days, but he didn't expect any damage to her vision.

Will's relief confused him. He'd been up all night, obsessing over her betrayal, yet he couldn't stomach the thought of anyone hurting her. Neither of them had hesitated to defend the other, but he still didn't want to be anywhere near her.

"I don't mean to be indelicate," Davita said as they got on the highway headed back toward Tanith, "but I'd like to talk about the Karawar for a moment. Only if you feel up to it, Mirren."

Mirren had been unable to stop crying in the ER, and the doctor had given her a sedative—a strong sedative. Will suspected that if she hadn't been wearing a cervical collar, she wouldn't have been able to sit up.

"I don't care," she whispered.

"I care," Josh said. "Forget the next trial—why did we get attacked back there?"

"Apparently the crowd didn't agree with the junta's decision to pass Mirren," Davita said.

"Most of the protesters were there before we arrived," Whim

pointed out. "And some of those eggs were frozen, which means they planned this at least a day ago."

"How did they know we were going to use the janitor's entrance?" Josh asked. "Davita, did you tip them off?"

"Of course not," Davita said, but Will could tell Josh didn't trust the answer. He didn't either.

"I thought I'd win them over," Mirren whispered. "If I did well."

"There weren't any protesters when Mirren came into Braxton for the Learning last week," Josh said. "What happened between now and then?"

None of them knew. Like Mirren, Will would have expected her success to bring people over to her side, not alienate them.

"I've been monitoring DWTV and *The Daily Walker*," Davita said, "and they haven't posted anything overly critical. A few editorials that were, perhaps . . . unkind."

"What about online?" Josh asked. "What about *Through a Veil Darkly*, Whim?"

"I'm practically running a Mirren fan club," Whim told her. "Which you'd know if you bothered reading it."

Josh opened her mouth to retort, but Deloise said quickly, "What about the comments you said were weird?"

"What comments?" Mirren asked.

Whim shrugged uneasily. "Just, you know, a few conspiracy nuts have basically blamed her for every single political screwup and scandal since the beginning of time. Including the St. Edward's Island Massacre."

"That was more than a hundred years ago," Deloise pointed out. "Accusing Mirren of being involved doesn't make any sense."

"Yeah, I tried to explain that, but nobody really wants to hear it. I think some people are getting a kick out of being over-the-top. I mean, who would actually believe that Mirren's going to lead the Gendarmerie in a coup? It's the Internet, you know? It's all just hyperbole."

"Hyperbole?" Davita asked, her voice rising within the limousine. "Two gendarmes were beaten by a crowd in Braxton last night."

"Oh," Whim said with a wince. "I did not know that."

"I can't have someone Mirren is associated with fomenting rebellion," Davita told him.

"I'm not fomenting anything!" Whim replied. "I wasn't even part of that conversation!"

"Why not?" Will asked. "You're the moderator, aren't you?"

Even Deloise was angry at Whim. She smacked the back of his head and said, "Did you at least ban those people from the site?"

"Yeah, of course," he said. "I mean, I will."

"Oh, my God," Josh said. "What else are they saying?"

"Everybody loves her," Whim protested. "Everybody except the people who don't want a queen and the people who . . . think she's Adolf Hitler. But it's really a very small group of people who have flipped out. I assume they're the ones who showed up with eggs today."

Will remembered the twisted expression of the woman who'd smashed the egg in Josh's eye. Her rage had billowed around her.

Isn't all of this somehow disproportionate? Will wondered. *What is it about Mirren that makes people act like idiots? Is there really that much animosity toward her parents, all these years later?*

Or is it something else?

Mirren was crying again. "Can we talk about this later?" Haley asked pointedly.

"Yeah, of course," Whim said, straightening up. He put a hand on Mirren's shoulder, which made her jump. "Don't worry, friend. We won't let anything happen to you. That pretty head's gonna stay right where it is."

Mirren cried harder.

"Whim!" Deloise cried, and smacked the back of his head again.

"This is all very disturbing," Davita said. "I think we should arrange professional security for you, Mirren."

"The Accordance Conclave is less than two weeks away,"

Deloise said, pulling a package of tissues from her purse. "You just have to hang on a little longer."

Mirren dried her face slowly, taking deep breaths as she did so. "I'm sorry," she said. "I'm being childish."

"No, you aren't," Haley told her.

"You really aren't," Josh said.

Mirren wiped her nose. Somehow she managed to look elegant even when crying. "Maybe I should quit. Maybe the dream-walker community is trying to tell me that they don't want me to lead them. Maybe we don't need to wait until the AC to hear them."

Everyone protested—except for Haley, Will noted. He kissed her hair and said nothing.

"But you're so close," Josh said. "All you have to do is give the junta that thing, that—what's it called?"

"The Karawar," Mirren said.

"Yeah," Josh said. Then she added, "What is that?"

"It's an ancient horn," Mirren said tiredly. "When blown, it emits a sound that only dream walkers can hear. The archaeological evidence suggests it called dream walkers to an annual meeting, before the advent of quick communication."

"Why would Peregrine want it?" Josh asked.

Mirren and Davita looked at each other with identical expressions of bewilderment. "I don't know," Mirren admitted. "Everyone stopped using the Karawar after the Industrial Revolution. My family only held on to it so it wouldn't be lost."

"So you have it?" Deloise said. "What would happen if you gave it to Peregrine and he used it?"

"My understanding is that all the dream walkers in the area— up to three or four hundred square miles—would hear a whistling sound and feel a strong urge to walk toward Peregrine. But the urge wouldn't be undeniable, and since almost no one knows what the sound means, most of them would probably fight off the urge and stay home."

"Like a dog whistle for dream walkers," Whim said. "That's awesome."

"My only thought," Mirren said, "is that Peregrine's trying to prove I'm as secretive as the monarchy used to be. Admittedly, they never would have turned the Karawar over to anyone. Maybe Peregrine thinks I won't, either, and that he'll be able to point at me and say I'm nothing new. But I have no issue with giving the Karawar to the junta, or to whatever government the dream walkers elect. If that's the trap Peregrine is trying to set for me, why would he have chosen the Karawar? He must guess I have access to far more powerful instruments, ones I *would* resist giving up."

"Maybe the other ministers chose the task," Davita suggested.

"Or maybe," Josh said, "Peregrine is planning to use the Karawar in a way we haven't thought of."

Mirren sank down into her neck brace, like a turtle withdrawing. "Let's hope not."

Exhausted, they lapsed into silence during the second half of the trip. Josh let her head fall back and took Will's hand in hers, but her touch made his skin crawl. *Does she let Feodor hold her hand in her dreams?* he wondered, pulling away.

Josh lifted her head. She turned halfway in her seat so she could see him and whispered, "Is everything okay?"

If he'd caught her dreaming about Ian, her ex-boyfriend, he wouldn't have been nearly as upset. He didn't expect her never to think about anyone else or to control the content of her dreams. What bothered him wasn't that she'd dreamed of someone besides him; it was that she'd dreamed of *Feodor.*

Feodor had hurt Will. He'd hurt Josh, too, and Haley, and Ian, and Winsor, and dozens of other people whose souls he had trapped. That Josh dreamed of him touching her, kissing her, was perverse. It suggested that something was deeply wrong in Josh's mind, and as much as anything, Will felt like a fool for not having seen that in her sooner. She'd tricked him, just as Feodor had.

"Did you have a nightmare last night?" he asked her.

Did she hesitate before shaking her head? In the dim light, he couldn't tell.

We had one of our most important talks in a limo, he thought, recalling how a thunderstorm had darkened the car's interior that day; today the summer sun had set and left them in a purple gloaming. That day she had told him the truth, and today she'd lied.

"Will?" she asked.

He couldn't deal with it all just yet.

"Tomorrow," he whispered. "Let's talk tomorrow."

Through a Veil Darkly

A Royal Romance?

We here at *TaVD* have obtained the first confirmation of a romance blossoming between Princess Mirren and Haelipto McKarr. Some of you will remember Haelipto as one of the three teens who confronted and defeated Feodor Kajażkołski back in February, although he is the lowest-profile member of the trio. Humble, thoughtful, and good-natured, he's also able to turn heroic at a moment's notice, as he demonstrated when he and Will Kansas rushed the freezing and half-drowned princess into a hot shower (photo below).

Princess Mirren seems to have fallen hard for young Mr. McKarr, whom she calls Haley, as do his close friends. Although they met only a few short weeks ago, rumor has it they not only spend every waking moment together, but the princess even sleeps in his room! Will he prove to be the steady support she needs as she works her way through the trials, or will their royal romance crumble under the stresses of life in a world that long ago gave up on a dream-walker monarchy?

Comments:

scorpio_666 says: What a slut.

    JMallShopper says: Seriously. Three weeks and she's already living with him!

    FemmeFatal says: I'm shocked to hear you slut-shaming someone you don't even know. Young women need to support each other in building self-esteem. Maybe if Mirren had friends who helped her do that, she wouldn't need to throw herself at a guy to feel confident and beautiful.

pouter40242 says: I thought that guy was a deaf-mute.

MCampbell_TarkenElectric says: I had this dream that she told me she was secretly behind the Silty incident.

    fgh243l says: Of course she was!

    MCampbell_TarkenElectric says: She said she faked Silty's death, that he's really been living with her in Switzerland.

        FemmeFatal: What? That's crazy. I knew Silty. He never would have abandoned his wife and kids to live in Switzerland.

Nineteen

When Josh entered the living room, the first thing she noticed was that someone had spray-painted the word "tulz" across the windows at the front of the house.

"What is that?" she asked Deloise.

"Oh, my gosh!" Deloise cried. "That's awful! Who did that?"

Deloise had already returned to the kitchen to warn Mirren by the time Josh figured out that she was looking at the word "slut" reversed. Someone had graffitied the living room windows.

Haley didn't let Mirren see the slur and instead took her straight upstairs to rest. Whim and Will followed them, leaving Josh and Deloise in the kitchen with Lauren, Kerstel, and Whim's father, Alex.

"I'll clean the windows tomorrow," Josh promised, disturbed by this further sign of acrimony toward Mirren. "Do I need to find her somewhere else to stay?"

"I don't know," Lauren said. "But I'd be lying if I said I wasn't concerned about her being here."

"Where would she go?" Alex asked. "We're the closest thing she has to family."

Everyone except Josh, Will, Haley, and Davita believed that Mirren's family was back in Switzerland and didn't approve of her political ambitions. Even Deloise didn't know about the Hidden Kingdom.

"Davita said the security team should be here before midnight," Kerstel said.

"I don't know that two men will be able to hold off a mob," Lauren told his wife. "But I have to admit that I can't imagine turning her out now."

"And she and Haley are so fond of each other," Kerstel said.

"As my son has so carelessly informed the world," Alex added.

"What does that mean?" Josh asked.

"I think I'm the only person in this house who actually reads Whim's blog," Alex reflected. "A few hours ago he posted a picture of Haley and Mirren in the shower together after the trial."

Can't people just lay off Mirren for a day or two? Josh thought, even as she got up from the table. "I better go warn Haley. Maybe he can make sure she doesn't see it."

She went upstairs to the guys' apartment. Haley was watching TV in his raggedy old flannel bathrobe, looking tired and like he didn't want to interact anymore that day. But when Josh relayed the news, he grabbed his tablet and pulled up *Through a Veil Darkly*. Josh stood near him so they could read the latest entry together.

Haley finished before she did, but not before she'd read the brunt of the post and caught a glimpse of the photograph of Haley and Mirren in the shower. "Whim!" Haley shouted, and Josh jumped at the volume of his voice.

Haley banged on Whim's door, then let himself in. His eyebrows were drawn together in anger, making his features sharper and his face older. "What is *this*?" he demanded.

Josh followed him into Whim's room, which was outfitted with a minifridge, a hot plate, and a microwave stationed among the mess. Whim was lounging on his bed—just a twin mattress on the floor—and typing on his laptop.

He sat up when Haley stormed into the room. "Okay, dude, don't freak out. I'm trying to do Mirren a favor."

Haley waved the tablet at him. "You said she's sleeping in my room!"

"Technically, that's true," Whim said, but under the heat of Haley's glare, he admitted, "Okay, so I juiced it up a little. Everybody loves a royal romance."

"They're calling her a slut," Haley said.

"I was trying to bring in some of the good press you got after the Feodor thing. You know, unpopular girl dates a popular boy, and then she's popular, too?"

Through his teeth, Haley said, *"I'm not popular."* He held up the tablet. *"Pouter40242* thinks I'm a deaf-mute!"

Josh struggled not to crack up. She felt terrible for Haley and Mirren, and she was proud of Haley for laying into Whim, but that deaf-mute rumor had been going around since they were in middle school.

"Well, now he knows you're not," Whim said. "Look, somebody was going to write this article eventually. People have noticed that you're glued to Mirren's side. Better that I choose the tone for the story."

Haley's lips were pursed so tightly, they were almost white. "You didn't do this for Mirren. You did it for yourself."

"Haley," Whim said, clutching the hilt of an imaginary knife in his chest, "you wound me."

"Stop writing about her!" Haley demanded.

"I can't do that," Whim said. He turned faintly green. "Do you know how much traffic I'm getting these days? The website is finally paying for itself."

Haley turned and stormed out of the room.

"At least close the comments section," Josh told Whim before following Haley.

She found him on the balcony off the living room, leaning against the railing and glaring at the lawn. "I'm sorry about Whim," she said. "He's—"

"I know who Whim is," Haley said curtly. "He's a fundamentally selfish person."

Josh gawked at him, and he ducked his head, his momentary confidence fled.

"Sorry," he muttered.

"No apology necessary. I mean, you aren't wrong. Just . . . you reminded me of Ian for a second. In a good way."

For a moment, Josh wondered what Ian would have thought of Haley and Mirren together, then decided she didn't want to know. But Haley's thoughts must have taken a similar course, because he said, "Next week is the Fourth of July."

The holiday would mark one year since Ian's death. Or rather, one year since they'd thought he had died. One year since Feodor had turned Ian's body into his puppet. Josh had been trying not to think about the approaching anniversary, but the flags and holiday sales had made it impossible.

"We could go put flowers on his grave or something," Josh said.

"I'm not—" Haley stuttered, and then in a familiar half whisper finished, "I might not be around."

Before Josh could ask what he meant, he retreated into the house, his shoulders drawn up to his ears.

That was weird, she thought. She hadn't seen Haley panic like that in a long time. And his phrasing had been so ominous. . . .

She set aside the urge to question him further—he'd tell her when he was ready—and went upstairs, unsure what else to do.

Will had said they'd talk the next day; did that mean he didn't want to see her tonight? It wasn't even eight yet.

She sat on her bed, digging her big toe into the carpet and trying to figure out what she could have done to upset him. Had he found her notes or her workshop in the attic? He couldn't have been too angry, or he wouldn't have punched that lady who crushed the egg in Josh's eye.

The apartment phone rang, and since no one else was around, Josh answered it.

"Hello?"

"Hello. Is this Josh, please?"

"It is."

"Hi, Josh, this is Bash Mirrettsio calling."

Suddenly she was glad she had been the one to answer.

"I hope it's all right, me calling you at home like this," he said. "I realized after you left that I'd forgotten to get your phone number."

"I don't have one. But it's all right." She closed her bedroom door firmly.

"Good. Well, I won't beat around the bush. I was inspired by our meeting the other day, and I've done nothing since except try to figure out how we could make your inventions work. Honestly, Bayla is going to kill me if I don't pay her some attention, but I simply can't focus on anything else. And I think—I *think*—I may have found a way to attach our cell phone towers to the sea."

Josh sat quietly for the next ten minutes and listened to Bash describe what he had done. He'd taken her idea of reversing the polarity of the particles and run with it, and he talked so fast that Josh had a hard time following the science behind his explanation.

"Wait a sec," Josh burst out. "How did you do this without a particle accelerator?"

"Willis-Audretch has a particle accelerator."

He went on, but Josh couldn't keep up with all his jargon and his peculiar use of analogies. She'd have to ask Bash to explain everything again when they had a pad and pen in front of them.

"I suppose there is one other question," Bash continued, "which is simply this: Do we want to keep moving forward? Up until now, this conversation has been purely theoretical. But if we place these towers in the Dream, we'll have taken a very large step into the actual."

Did I spend all these months writing on sketch pads and walls and my own body parts just to stop now? Josh wondered. She recalled last night's dream again, not the red sky, but the feeling of quiet peace that had filled her when all the monsters were dead and the fighting was over. She wanted that peace.

She wanted that power.

"Let's do it," she said.

"I was hoping you'd say that. Excellent. Do you want to come see the particle accelerator?"

Of *course* she wanted to see the particle accelerator. But how would she explain another trip to Braxton without Will?

"I'd love to, but things are kind of a mess around here at the moment. I might not be able to get away."

"Oh, yes, I saw the news reports. They said your princess made a poor mermaid, despite the long red hair."

Josh laughed, even though the joke was a little lighthearted for a near-death experience.

"I'm just glad they passed her."

"Any chance she'll turn over the Karawar?"

"A pretty good one, I think," Josh admitted, and she knew she probably shouldn't be telling Bash any such thing, but it felt nice to talk lightheartedly with someone, and he was sort of a friend. "Listen, can you come by tomorrow night around eight? I'm scheduled to dream walk. We could try attaching the towers then."

Bash's voice brightened. "Splendid!"

"Come to the back door, all right? Don't ring the bell out front."

"Are we playing cloak-and-dagger?"

More than I'd like, Josh thought, but she told Bash, "Just a bit. I'll see you tomorrow—have fun with your particle accelerator."

By the time she woke up the next day—well after noon—Will had already left the house. He'd taken off to the mall with Whim and Deloise, which left Josh confused because he hated the mall.

Is he just trying to get away from me? she wondered. For the first time ever, she wished he had a cell phone she could call.

Since he didn't, she spent a couple of hours scrubbing the spray paint off the house and the rest of the afternoon training. The doctor had told her to leave the eye patch on until the next day, but she thought she'd be safer training with it off. Her eye didn't hurt unless she rubbed it.

When Will, Deloise, and Whim didn't return for dinner, she helped Kerstel cook and then put herself through three rounds of a Romanian circuit-training video that left her gasping for air.

Afterward, she sat on the back porch and waited for Bash, watching the security guards wander around the yard. One of them was texting. While Josh glared at him, Haley and Mirren walked out the back door. They were holding hands.

"You guys going out?" Josh asked, concerned about their safety.

"We're going back to the Hidden Kingdom," Mirren said. "I've decided to give the Karawar to the junta."

"Oh," Josh said, and then realized how unsupportive she sounded.

"I just want all this to be over," Mirren admitted.

"Do you want me to come? We could wait until early morning, like last time."

"Thank you, but I think we'll be fine. My aunt and uncle are usually in bed by ten, and if we bump into my cousin, she'll likely just ask to come back with us."

"Be safe," Josh told them as they climbed into Haley's truck.

Alone, listening to the security guard argue with his son's mother on his phone, Josh wondered if Haley's cryptic comment the night before might have meant he would be in the Hidden Kingdom on the Fourth of July. That was a less frightening thought than others she'd had.

The security guard was threatening to sue for custody by the time Bash drove up the driveway and around the back. He parked and exited his car, at which point the security guard called from twenty yards away, "Is he okay?"

"Who's that?" Bash asked, squinting into the darkness.

Josh raised her hand and gave the okay. "He's the world's worst security guard. He might be tied, though, with the guard in the front yard, who I'm guessing didn't stop you."

"No one stopped me. I did notice a man taking a smoke on your porch swing, though."

Josh swore to call the security company and give them hell. *After* she and Bash tried out his invention.

"Are you wearing an eye patch?" Bash asked.

"Yeah. It's a long story."

"I heard you were in a fight."

"All right, it's not that long a story. Do you need help with these boxes?"

"Sure," Bash said, smiling, and they each grabbed a large cardboard box from the backseat of his car.

Luckily, Saidy was at work, Alex had retired to his apartment for the evening, and Haley and Mirren were out, so no one saw Bash as Josh led him down to the basement.

"Nice setup," Bash said, watching Josh type her code into the bank-vault door that protected the archway.

"It works," Josh agreed. Only then did she realize that he had likely memorized her code, and she made a mental note to change it after he left. Not that she didn't trust Bash, she just . . . Well, it seemed prudent.

"What's in the boxes?"

Bash grinned and opened one up. "Your towers."

Josh picked up one of the metal devices. Once they'd started calling them "towers," she had begun mentally picturing a tiny cell phone tower, but what Bash had created looked more like an aerosol can with a glass button on top.

The idea was to plant towers at intervals within the Dream. The circlet and vambrace would relay Josh's thought to the towers, and the towers would broadcast a signal to the Dream, telling it what Josh wanted it to do.

"I still don't completely understand how you stabilized the polarity of the Dream particles," she told Bash as she examined one of the towers.

"Like I said on the phone, I took them down to nearly absolute zero . . ."

His explanation made even less sense to Josh than it had on the phone the day before, partly because he kept using unfamiliar acronyms like "ARN" and "UH" and then throwing in abbreviations like "Z-tat" and "fro." For the first time, Josh became aware of how much progress dream theory had made after Feodor's exile. Except for his own research, he'd been out of touch with the field for fifty years, and Josh felt like an idiot when she had to stop Bash over and over to ask him to explain.

When she asked him to explain why the type of radiation he'd used wouldn't fry her brain as soon as she put the circlet on, a fleeting expression crossed Bash's face, so quickly that Josh wasn't able to fully grasp it. Anger? Irritation?

But the expression was gone when he said, "No one has to worry about that since the invention of simo pulsation."

"Simo pulsation?" Josh repeated.

"Yes, but that led to a larger issue with the polarity of Z-tat in relation to the ARN . . ."

And he was off again.

Bash does this for a living, she told herself. *And he isn't half a century behind. I'm sure all of this makes sense if you know the lingo.*

"Let's give it a try," she said.

Bash grinned again. "Excellent."

Josh had hidden the circlet and vambrace under a pile of towels in the archroom. When she produced them, Bash admired the construction.

"This is a hell of a job," Bash said, running his fingers over the wires in the vambrace. "Show me how it goes on."

"These three wire bundles have to align precisely with the veins in my arm, especially the tips here." Josh winced as she clamped the vambrace shut around her left forearm. This was the first time she'd had the nerve to do so. "They actually cut into my skin at the wrist."

The pain was curiously momentary. After the initial bite of the wire tips, Josh's arm began to feel warm and relaxed—just as it had in her nightmares. She experienced the same thing when she put on the circlet, only the pain occurred at the base of her skull.

"How do they feel?" Bash asked. This time she recognized his expression—envy. He wanted to be the one wearing the devices. Josh didn't blame him.

"They feel good. I think I'm ready."

She placed her free hand on the looking stone and watched the Veil come to life inside the archway. After several minutes of flipping through nightmares, she found one with kids playing basketball. "This one might work."

Bash pushed his glasses up his nose and peered at the archway. "Yes, that's good."

He picked up one of the boxes and jumped through the archway, and Josh grabbed the other and followed him. To her surprise, the box felt much less heavy than it had earlier, and she wondered if the vambrace provided increased strength in her left arm.

The nightmare they jumped into featured a nighttime basketball court lit by streetlamps so bright that they turned the sky beyond them pitch-black. A number of races were represented on the team, but there was only one Korean kid, and Josh touched his fear just long enough to know that he considered this chance to impress his friends a matter of life and death.

Josh was carrying the box with one arm by then—no question that the vambrace increased her strength.

Standing near the corner of the court, Bash pulled a tower from one of the boxes. "Attaching them is straightforward. Decide where you want to put it. Set it down, and then push the button on the top as firmly as you can. It takes a little force. You'll hear a snap when it attaches." He demonstrated, pressing the button down until Josh heard a sound like a pencil snapping, and the glass button glowed white.

"If the button is glowing, it's attached," Bash said, sounding pleased with himself. "But we can double-check by trying to pull it up."

He grabbed the tower and tugged, and although Josh couldn't see anything that would be holding it in place, the object refused to move. She even tried digging away some of the earth around the can's base, but the tower seemed to be attached to space itself.

A cell phone tower on the sea, she thought.

Bash grinned at her, and she smiled back.

"How many towers do we need to attach before the circlet and vambrace will work?" she asked.

"Just one, I assume. But they probably only have a range of about fifty feet. Maybe we should try putting one at each corner of the court?"

Josh nodded and took two towers from the box. She walked to the nearest corner of the court, where the teenagers were attempting a Globetrotters-style ball-passing display. The demonstration wasn't going well; the dreamer, especially, seemed to be letting his nerves get the best of him.

She knelt at the corner where the court ended and the lawn began and set the tower on the ground. With her unencumbered hand, she pressed down on the button, hard, then harder, then so hard that she thought the can would collapse, and finally it made a snapping sound. The button on top lit up.

"My eye!" one of the players screamed, and the guy's teammates all turned slowly to stare at the dreamer.

"You popped his eye!" a player accused.

"I'm sorry! I was just throwing him the ball. I didn't mean to—"

"I'm blind!" the bloodied guy cried.

A strange sensation filled Josh then, as if something had shifted subtly inside her head. In her mind, she felt a growing awareness of the towers she and Bash had just placed, and as she walked toward the kids on the court, her awareness changed based on her proximity to each tower. They had become her spatial reference points, her cardinal directions, and the warmth in her arm and head grew hotter.

The basketball players had gathered in a circle around the dreamer. They were badgering him, calling him names, and darting forward to shove him. Josh felt the impending violence fill the air like a low-pressure front before a thunderstorm, and her heartbeat sped up to match her step as she broke into a run.

No, wait, you don't have to run.

She stopped running and raised her left arm instead. Just like in her nightmares, she spread her fingers and *reached,* past the air, past the substance of reality, and heat shot down her arm and out her fingertips like matterless beams.

The dreamer rose into the air and out of the reach of the bullies. He started screaming—he didn't know what was happening, even his *subconscious* didn't know what was happening—but Josh smiled as she watched the kids below jump up and down, futilely attempting to grab his feet. She caught hold of the fabric of the Dream as though it were a bedsheet, and she gave it a hard shake. The bullies fell like bowling pins.

As Josh reveled in her power, she caught a glimpse of her own outstretched hand, with the fingers spread unnaturally far apart and the sinews beneath her skin rising, and saw how much they resembled the hands of Feodor's zombies. At the same instant, she felt the dreamer's fear evolve into true dreamfire, the deepest and most primordial of fears. He believed then that he was going to die.

Unease filled Josh. Didn't he understand that she was protecting him?

Maybe not. Maybe he couldn't see the situation from her point of view, from such a wide field of vision, but she was doing this for him. She knew what was best. . . .

No, Josh thought. Memories of the nightmare in which the piano had eaten Caleb flooded back to her. *I don't have the right to do this,* she thought. *I don't have the wisdom.*

Josh let her arm drop, let the power retreat into her arm, and released her hold on the Dream. The dreamer, dangling in the air, fell and landed on two players, who began cursing him.

I thought I wanted this. Even as the words formed in her mind, a dozen arguments against the admission were rising. She just didn't know how to use the power yet—the dreamer didn't appreciate her help—next time she'd make sure the dreamer knew she was on his side—

What we're all afraid of is having no control, she realized, in a voice louder and calmer than the others. *And I can't help someone by taking even more control away from them.*

"Josh?" Bash asked, coming to stand beside her.

Josh tried to rub her temple, but the circlet was in the way. "Let's get out of here."

"Wait, are you done?"

"Yeah."

With a thrust of her hand, she opened an archway in the middle of the court.

"How did you do that?" Bash asked, his eyes wide, and only then did Josh remember the exact balance of how much and how little he knew. The circlet—she wasn't thinking clearly.

"The vambrace did it," she lied, and walked through the archway.

The moment she landed in the archroom, she began unlatching the vambrace. Bash landed behind her as she pulled the device from her arm, and she gasped at the sight of the damage the vambrace had done. Not only had the wires that bit into her skin created bloody marks like leech bites, but the magnets had left quarter-sized burns.

"Shit," she said, and let the vambrace fall to the floor. Her arm looked shriveled, too, like a salted snail, and her veins pulsed bright blue beneath her skin. Quickly, she pulled the circlet off, taking more than a few strands of hair with it.

She touched her temple and her fingers came away bloody. "I need—" she began, and then the back of her head exploded.

She was on the floor before she realized what had happened—that Bash had hit her with the folding chair. Even then, her primary concern wasn't to fight back but to avoid passing out. Because she'd fractured her skull and had a serious concussion four months before, she had to be especially careful about not hitting her head again, and she felt somehow that if she could remain conscious, that would lessen the damage done to her brain.

The archroom door opened and closed. She heard it; she couldn't open her eyes.

I'm awake, she thought. *I'm awake. As long as I'm thinking, I'm awake.*

The door opened and closed again. She felt Bash roll her onto her stomach, and she tried to ask him not to hit her head again, but the words just came out, "Ddddaaaaa."

He didn't hit her head. Instead he tied her up with a rope, ankles and wrists together so that she was unable to stand.

Josh heard him gather up the vambrace and circlet and realized for the first time what he had been after. *That's probably not good,* she thought.

"Nice working with you," Bash said.

The archway door opened and closed one last time.

Through a Veil Darkly

Message board: Princess Mirren: She's just like all the other Roussellarios

Trashprotractor says: Didn't her mom start out the same way? Everyone thought she was so lovely and elegant, and she told us all that she would be open in a way the Rousellarios had never been, and then she turned out to be just as elitist as the rest of them.

> scorpio_666 says: Uh, her mom was not lovely and elegant. Have you forgotten those satin dresses she always wore? I don't think the woman even owned pants.

>> JillKramer says: Oh my God! I DID forget those dresses! They were so hideous.

> wingnut24the says: I had a nightmare about her where she was wearing one of those dresses, and she had a crown on. She told me that the Gendarmerie is planning to overthrow the junta.

>> jshg_hammer says: Dude, I had the same dream! Sort of. I mean, she was wearing the dress and the crown, but she was showing me around her secret hiding place. It was like the Bat Cave, and it was full of weapons and armored tanks and stuff.

> Worchester_RWatson says: I had a dream she was my French teacher, and she wouldn't stop giving us more homework.

copenite says: Trashprotractor is right. Maybe she wasn't raised by her parents, but she still has their money and their priorities. For every single thing she said at the Learning, I bet there are five secrets she knows but won't tell.

> markamBCGI says: That would be a ridiculous number of secrets.

pashtofrank says: Being educated and being elitist are not the same thing.

gilandsons says: I hope she dies in the next trial. I want to see blood in that red hair.

> JillKramer says: That's so sick!

> prancingpony says: HAIR BLOOD! HAIR BLOOD! HAIR BLOOD!

Twenty

When Will had woken up that morning, he'd known one thing: he couldn't face Josh.

So he went to the mall.

He usually relished emotional disclosure; Josh was the one who was afraid of expressing her feelings. But today the thought of telling Josh what he'd seen made him want to cut out his tongue. As he followed Whim and Deloise from store to store, he wondered if he wasn't less afraid of asking Josh about her nightmare than he was of hearing her answer. Maybe he just didn't want to know.

So he stayed at the mall. He bought Deloise a pair of shoes to replace the ones she'd lost the day before. He choked down a plateful of greasy bourbon chicken in the food court. He helped Whim pick out a new cell phone case.

When his friends were done shopping, he convinced them to go to the movies. He swore that a new action flick was awesome, when in fact he had heard the exact opposite. Then he sat in the theater, hands clenched around the armrests, revolted by the scent of popcorn butter.

Unbelievably, the movie contained a scene in which the hero's girlfriend tried to seduce the villain.

I can't stay here, Will thought. *I can't watch this. I'm going to lose my mind.*

"Can I borrow your phone?" he whispered to Whim.

Whim looked surprised but offered up the phone.

Will carried the phone into the mall. He figured out Whim's contact list but didn't find the name he was looking for. Then he opened up the call log and saw a lot of recent calls to and from someone named Mike. He dialed the number.

"Hello, sexy," a female voice said.

"This is Will Kansas."

After an instant of silence, Bayla gushed, "Will! What a nice surprise!"

"Remember what you and I talked about after the last Grey Circle meeting?"

"Mmm, of course. Have you changed your mind?"

"Yeah. Yeah, I guess so. How soon do you think we could do that?"

"Whenever you want, love."

"How about tonight? You, me, and Whim?"

"Sounds heavenly. I'll come by around nine?"

"Fine. And, ah, thanks."

"See you in a few."

Whim was startled but not displeased by Will's arrangements. "Haley and Mirren are going to go get the Karawar, so we don't even have to get them out of the apartment," he mused. Then he set about manically cleaning up the living room. He even changed the sheets on his mattress, which Will tried not to think about.

At eight thirty, Bayla texted that she was on her way, but the news seemed to worry Whim. He began rubbing his mouth and chin like a contemplative villain, and maybe the reference was subconsciously intentional because Will had noticed he did it only when feeling guilty.

"Suddenly I'm worried this isn't a good idea," Whim said.

"Why not?"

"Don't you have trouble with drugs?"

"Not exactly, and according to Bayla, Veil dust isn't a drug; it's a mystical substance."

"True. But it can still be misused." He clapped Will's shoulder. "What the hell, right? If you say you're cool, that's enough for me."

Will felt strangely disappointed that Whim hadn't pushed him harder to find a different solution to his anxiety problems. Maybe with a little help, he could have found one; instead, he was using Veil dust as a stopgap to keep himself from drinking. Even if he wasn't technically an alcoholic and wasn't technically working at staying sober, he felt like he would still be giving something up by using Veil dust.

Just pride and the future opportunity to feel self-righteous, he told himself. *What do I need pride for, anyway?*

What made the decision for him was the fact that he had no idea how else to go on. Something had to change, and quickly, some pressure had to be relieved, and if this was what it took to un-clench his stomach and calm his mind, so be it.

Bayla arrived half an hour later dressed in very tight gray jeans and a wispy purple top. She'd painted her eyes a smoky purple, but she must not have been wearing any lipstick, because Will was pretty sure that if she had been, it would have been all over Whim's face after their ardent kiss hello.

Oh, man, Will thought. *I don't know if I can watch this all evening.*

He closed the apartment door behind her, even though the house was basically deserted—only Whim's dad and Josh were around; Alex was watching his game shows, Josh had taken a dou-ble shift in the archroom, and Deloise had gone to her school friend Nate's birthday party. Still, Will couldn't shake the feeling that they could get caught at any moment.

"So," Bayla said, plopping onto the couch. "Whim, what have you got to crush this up with?"

"Give me a minute."

Bayla pulled a ring box from her purse. Inside was a tiny plastic bag.

Will held out his hand. "Do you mind?"

She passed him the bag and he held it up to the light. Inside sat about a tablespoon of sparkling, iridescent dust. When he shook it, he caught glimpses of rainbows.

Josh is right, he thought. *There's something magical about this.*

Despite the feeling that he was violating something sacred, he handed the bag over without comment when Whim returned with a mortar and pestle. "How much Veil dust have you been doing?" Bayla asked at the sight of the tools.

"They were Ian's," Whim said.

"Oh, Ian." She sighed. "I miss that guy." She poured the Veil dust into the mortar and began crushing it up. To Will, she said, "How's his widow?"

She meant Josh. "Bayla," Whim said sternly.

"She's not his widow," Will told her.

Bayla smiled, both bashful and coy. "Sorry, I forgot she's yours now." She took a bottle of water out of her purse and poured a few drops into the mortar. "This is just sugar water, to bind it. Also, some people don't like the taste." She kept grinding away until the dust and water had been mashed into an elementary school–style superthick white paste. "All systems are go."

"What do I do?" Will asked.

"Just scoop some up on your fingertip and rub it inside your lower lip."

"Then what?"

She pulled a battered pack of tarot cards out of her purse. "Then I'll tell your fortune while we wait to get deep."

They each scooped up a bit of paste about the size of a die— Will took less than the others—and rubbed it inside their lower lips. Aside from sugary, the Veil dust tasted of something Will couldn't identify—smoke? maple syrup? He rubbed his tongue against his lip, trying to catch enough of the flavor to identify it, but it kept getting away from him.

Bayla pushed aside the mortar and pestle and the bag of Fritos Whim was working on to make room on the coffee table for her cards. "How long does this take to kick in?" Will asked as she shuffled.

"Not long."

Whim stretched out on the couch with a smile and closed his eyes. Will couldn't stop sucking on his lip, the way he'd always chewed on his cheeks when the dentist numbed them to fill a cavity.

Bayla let him cut the deck and then she dealt. As she laid out the first card, Will realized that she was using not a tarot deck but some sort of dream-walker oracle system. "Two of Spirals, reversed," she said, naming the card as she turned it over. "The Two of Spirals is a relationship card, but when reversed it suggests a relationship based more on fantasy than reality. It suggests that you care about Josh more in your head than your heart."

"What?" Will asked. "I think you're reading that wrong."

"Well," she admitted, "the card might mean that Josh cares more about *you* in her head than her heart."

"I'm not the one in her head, either," Will said, thinking of Josh's nightmares, but he found himself picking up the card to look more closely at it. Two black spirals were set against a fuchsia background, connected by their tails. Will grew dizzy as he looked at them and tried to follow the lines with his eyes. The spirals appeared to be turning, not in a steady motion but in a pulsating one.

Will put the card down, but the room looked wrong. Or else the room looked fine, but Will felt that he remembered it differently. He expected to see a green sofa on the wall where the TV sat, though he couldn't imagine why.

"Who's in her head, then?" Bayla asked.

"What?" Will asked.

"Who's in Josh's head if not you?" Her eyebrows twitched suggestively.

Feodor, Will thought, looking back at the card. He had an idea for a painting then—a painting of Josh, Feodor's face visible within a spiral drawn over her head, Will's own face cast in the spiral above her heart.

She's not in love with him, Will thought, afraid to hope the idea might be true. *He's just in her head.*

"The Archway," Bayla said, turning over another card on the coffee table, "means an arrival or departure."

"That's not at all vague," Whim cracked. He leaned over to sniff Will's shirt, which was weird. "Why do you smell like vodka?"

"Because you're high. I haven't had any vodka." To Bayla, he said, "What kind of arrival or departure?"

"Well, it came right after the Two of Spirals, so it could mean you and Josh splitting up."

"Are you at all serious," Will asked, "or just trying to make me feel bad?"

Bayla giggled. Her pupils were the size of shirt buttons. "Sorry, that's what the cards say."

Her response only made Will more confident that she was screwing with his head. "Let me see the cards. Don't you have a book with explanations for these?"

"Let's turn on some music," Bayla said, ignoring his question even as she handed him the deck.

Whim turned on the television and fiddled with the remote. "Everybody fond of George G?" he asked. Apparently he was referring to Gershwin, since "Let's Call the Whole Thing Off" began playing.

Will examined the Archway card. It depicted a stone archway, not unlike the one downstairs, built in a grassy meadow. The archway appeared empty, but when Will looked closely at a pond in the background, he realized the water's surface didn't reflect the archway. The longer he looked, the less certain he was which universe the card depicted.

Deception, he thought. *Trickery. That's what the card really means.*

He glanced up at Bayla and Whim, who were dancing in imitation of Ginger Rogers and Fred Astaire. *The card's about them, about the people they're lying to.*

Or maybe not. He didn't believe in this sort of thing, not usually. But his thoughts had started to move in strange directions, making connections he might not have seen otherwise: how Josh had deceived him about her nightmares, how he had deceived her by hiding how much he knew, how Whim deceived Deloise and Bayla deceived Bash, even how Mirren deceived everyone by hiding why she wanted to stop staging.

How Feodor had deceived them all by pretending to die.

No, no, Will thought. *He really did die. I saw it.*

His gaze had fallen on the green couch, only there was no green couch in the room. If there had been, it would have been sharing the same space as the TV.

Children's nightmares, he thought. *The most unstable of dreams.*

He couldn't exactly see the green couch in front of him, but he could picture it so strongly that it might as well have been in the room. In fact, as he stared at the place where it should have been, two figures appeared, lying with their limbs entwined, their mouths sealed together.

It's Haley, Will thought, but as the boy's polo shirt and slacks grew more solid, he realized his mistake. *No, it's Ian. And the girl is Josh.*

Her hair was longer—Will had never seen it long, and that, along with a certain softness in her features, made her look younger.

"When's your mom coming home?" Josh asked.

"Hopefully never," Ian said, and they laughed between kisses.

Will sat mesmerized by the two ghosts.

"What about Haley?" Josh asked.

"Who cares if he walks in? Let him. He might learn a thing or two to show Winsor."

Josh frowned in admonishment and Ian grinned.

"I think this really happened," Will said, not to them but to himself. "The room remembers."

"You're starting to get deep," Bayla told him as Whim dipped her. "Let the dreamfever take you."

Will brushed his hand through the air, expecting the images to ripple, but his fingers touched the back of Josh's head, ruffling her silky hair. She and Ian both looked at Will.

"Excuse me, this is a private party," Ian said, but Josh tried to straighten her clothing.

Will didn't think she recognized him. Why would she? Until he'd become her apprentice, they had barely spoken two words to each other at school.

He held out the deck of cards, and Josh drew one.

"I can't protect you from this," Josh whispered as she stared at the card, and her features aged. The playful smile disappeared and her green eyes appeared paler than ever.

"The thing about Josh," Ian said, reaching up to wrap his arms around her waist, "is that she doesn't need a friend, or a therapist, or an apprentice. She needs a *man*."

He yanked her down on top of him and the card floated from her hand.

Will picked it up. The label at the bottom of the card read, "Walker of Stones." It depicted a man with his pockets turned out, holding a brass scale in one hand. The card had landed upside down, so that the tiny people standing on the scales seemed about to plunge into open air. When Will turned it right-side up, he couldn't shake the idea that the people were going to be thrown from the scales and that the man holding the beam above them was a puppet master.

Peregrine, Will thought. *The Walker of Stones is Peregrine.*

He didn't know if that made sense. Organizing his thoughts was growing more difficult. *Feodor is in Josh's head. Deception. Peregrine.*

He tried to sit down, but the chair he lowered himself onto turned out not to exist, and he tumbled onto the carpet. Bayla laughed at him. *The chair is from the past,* he thought. *There used to be a chair here. Or there will be. It's a future chair.*

Instead, he got up and sat on the couch—not the green one, which had disappeared along with its occupants—the regular grayish-brown one he sat on every day. He watched Bayla and Whim dance to "The Man I Love."

Feodor. Josh's head. Deception. Peregrine. They all go together somehow.

Whim was a good dancer, and Bayla knew how to let him lead. A cloud of violet smoke enveloped them, like a fairy-charmed cloud, and the tender expression in Whim's eyes when he looked at Bayla made Will feel like he shouldn't be watching them.

In her head. Deception. Peregrine.

Bayla smiled, and Whim kissed her briefly, gently, before she turned her face to rest her cheek against his shoulder. As they turned, the light shone on her silver bracelet, creating the illusion that she was holding a silver blade against his neck.

Will sat up. They kept turning, and Whim's eyes closed, a peaceful expression on his usually animated face.

Bayla drew the Two of Spirals, Will thought. *It's about her and Whim—not me and Josh.*

He scrambled to lay the three cards out in order on the coffee table.

Bayla is in Whim's head. Deception. Peregrine.

He didn't know if he was hallucinating or not when Bayla lifted a finger to her lips as she rotated past him.

Aretha Franklin came on, singing "It Ain't Necessarily So."

Bayla is a spy for Peregrine. All this with Whim has been an act. I can't protect you from this, Josh had said.

Bayla grinned at him as she and Whim twirled around the room. Her lips pulled back to reveal bloodstained teeth.

"Will!"

Ian was standing in the doorway to Whim's room—no, it had been Ian's room once. He beckoned Will with a finger.

Uncertainly, Will gathered up the cards and followed Ian into Whim's bedroom. Everything inside it was different. All Whim's crap was gone, replaced by a queen-sized bed that was much too big for the room, a pile of sports equipment, and a shoe rack full of expensive sneakers.

"Check it out," Ian said, crouching at the foot of the bed. With a fingernail, he pried the metal heat duct cover away from the wall. "Reach inside."

I'm going to regret this, Will thought, but he couldn't resist sticking his hand into the wall. A few inches past his wrist, he felt something cold and smooth.

He pulled out a pint of vodka.

"That's for you," Ian told him. "I saved it all this time for you."

Will gazed at the bottle, at an incomprehensible label written in Russian. His hand shook. "I don't want this," he told Ian, and he dropped it on the floor before running out of the apartment.

Down he went, past the first floor and straight into the basement, but Ian followed him. Will had been certain Ian couldn't leave the apartment, yet he could hear the taller boy's footsteps behind him on the stairs, hear him calling, "It's cool, man, it's cool!"

Will fled across the basement, heading for the gun safe, but he tripped on a stray free weight and fell to the floor in front of his desk. When he stood up, Ian was sitting in the chair beside the desk, sipping from the bottle and looking at the timeline of Feodor's life.

"That's a pretty sweet stalker wall," he told Will.

"You can't be here," Will said. "You're dead!"

"That's the great thing about Veil dust. The past—the present—it all comes together. Maybe I'm dead—maybe you're dead—maybe we're alive together in a new life." Ian held out the bottle. "To Veil dust!"

Only when Will reached for the vodka did he realize he was still holding Bayla's card deck in his hand. As he set it down on the desk, the top card stuck to his sweaty hand and flipped itself over onto the desk.

The Nine of Moons. A woman climbed a twisting rope ladder into the sky, collecting moons. Four were already tucked in her bag, and another five hung waiting.

Will stared at the card, but all he could think was that the ladder looked like a DNA double helix. It offered no insight to his dilemma. He waited, hoping something would click in his mind, but all he felt was a fine tremble in his bones and increasing anxiety.

Finally, he picked up the Nine of Moons to put it back in the deck, and his eyes fell on the paper beneath it: Mirren's re-creation of the page from Feodor's last manuscript.

Will read, "A tangential link between body and consciousness, manipulated by influential magnets, creates the possibility of using fragmentary physical specimens to locate specific souls within the Dream."

"Fragmentary physical specimens," Will murmured.

"That means small," Ian told him.

Will looked at the card, still in his hand.

DNA. It means that anyone with a sample of my DNA can locate my soul within the Dream.

"Who's got your blood, Mr. Kansas?" a softly accented voice asked.

Ian was gone, and Feodor was sitting in the chair by the desk, the bottle of vodka in his hand. He wore the same neat white shirt and gray vest in which Will had seen him last, and he greeted Will with the same innocuous smile.

Will was so caught off guard by the sight of him that he simply said, "No one has my blood."

Feodor reached out and picked up the deck of cards, causing Will to stumble backward into a chair. Its metal legs shrieked against the cement floor as it slid across the room.

Feodor didn't react. He shuffled through the deck and then laid out the three cards Will had drawn earlier: the Two of Spirals, the Archway, the Walker of Stones. At the end of the line, he placed the Nine of Moons.

"Look," he said, and Will looked, but the only thing he saw were the bloody fingerprints left on each card where Feodor had touched them.

"Oh God," Will said, backing away even farther.

Blood began to slowly seep out of Feodor's pores, tiny pinpricks of red expanding and merging until a crimson sheen covered his face and hands. In seconds, the fabric of his shirt went from white to red.

"Stop!" Feodor commanded. "It's only blood! Pay attention!"

He pointed to the Nine of Moons, and the swift motion of his hand flung blood flying across the desk in thin ropes.

"We have work to do!" Feodor said. "Death is a mere inconvenience!"

Will turned and ran across the basement, knocking over the free-weight rack and nearly getting tangled up in a jump rope along the way. He reached the archroom door and frantically punched in his code, only to see the light turn red instead of green.

"And you wonder why she comes to me at night!" Feodor taunted. "I can give her the World, the Dream, the Death—all of it!"

Will punched his code again, and the light turned green as internal gears unlocked the door. Before it had finished opening fully, Will was through and yanking the door shut again.

"You are a child—"

Will could still hear Feodor screaming on the other side of the door. As he backed away, he heard a different voice: Josh's.

"Will?" she asked.

He turned around and saw her tied up on the archroom floor.

"You're not real," he said.

"What? Of course I am."

"No," Will told her, sinking to the floor. "You're just inside my head."

He curled up in a ball and ground his face against his knees until his brow bones hurt. "Will," Josh kept saying. "It's really me. Are you all right? Can you untie me? I promise I'm real."

His head hurt. His eyes ached deep within every time he tried to open them. He needed to sleep, but Josh kept talking to him.

"Will, look at me. Please."

He forced his eyes open against the daggers of light. "What?"

Her face was only a few feet away, a black patch over one eye, but he thought he saw something foreign in her expression, and he wondered if she had come from the future or the past.

"What's wrong?"

Will closed his eyes again. "I'm deep on Veil dust," he told her.

Then he took a long swig of vodka from the bottle in his hand and went to sleep.

Twenty-one

Haley found Josh sometime after midnight. By then she had been bound for hours, watching Will sleep and wondering if he'd been serious about the Veil dust. She hoped not.

While she slowly coaxed her stiffened muscles out of the positions to which they had become accustomed, Haley sat on the floor beside Will's unconscious form and explained how he and Mirren had come home to find Deloise standing on the second-floor balcony and emptying Bayla's purse onto the lawn below.

"I guess Bayla brought over some Veil dust," Haley concluded. "And then Deloise got home and found her with Whim. . . ."

He winced.

"How bad was it?" Josh asked, remembering how she and Haley had once caught their respective loves naked in the forest. Together.

"Bad," Haley said.

"That's just skippy," Josh said, thinking about which punch she'd use on Whim.

They woke Will, but he was too disoriented to make any sense. "The seeker of blood," he mumbled as Josh helped him to his feet. "The two of blood. The nine of—"

"Blood," Josh finished in unison with him. "Yeah, we get it."

Haley was examining the bottle of vodka curiously. "This is the brand Ian used to drink."

Josh hated the idea that Ian had been a heavy enough drinker to have a favorite brand.

"Ex-boyfriend," Will slurred, "of blood."

"Should we take him to the hospital?" Josh asked.

"The bottle's nearly full. He's probably still just coming down from the Veil dust."

As they prodded Will up the stairs, Josh asked Haley, "Have you done Veil dust?"

"No. I'm— It would be bad for me."

"It's bad for everyone," Josh said. "It never did Ian any good."

Haley frowned. To her surprise, he said, "It has its uses. But not for Will."

As they crossed the first-floor landing, Josh said, "You never asked why I was tied up on the archroom floor."

Haley pursed his lips. "I . . . try not to see other people's business. But sometimes I can't help it."

"So you already know?" Josh was still getting used to having this side of Haley out in the open, and the idea that he could spy on her—whether or not he did so deliberately—freaked her out. She'd had a lot to hide lately.

"I know that you're going to explain it to all of us in the morning," Haley said. "I can wait."

He gave her a smile then and guided Will into their apartment. Josh forced her throbbing muscles to carry her up to the third floor, and she found Deloise in her bedroom, sitting on her bed amid a sea of tissues.

"What happened?" Deloise asked at the sight of her sister's burned and bloody arms.

Josh gave her a very short version of the evening's events and promised to tell the whole story in the morning, but Deloise heard that Josh had gotten hit on the head and insisted they go to the ER that moment.

"I'm all right," Josh insisted. "I just had a CT yesterday."

"Either you can come with me to the ER," Deloise said flatly, "or I can wake Dad up."

They went to the ER.

"Haley told me what happened earlier to night," Josh said as they sat in a curtained room waiting for the scan. "Do you want to talk about it?"

Deloise removed a packet of tissues from her purse. "I got home from Nate's party, I went upstairs to say hi to Whim, and the living room was empty but music was playing. Then I saw light coming through the slats in the door to a laundry closet, so I opened the door, and there they were making out on top of the washer and dryer. They were even doing laundry at the same time, and Bayla had dryer lint in her hair."

For a fleeting moment, Josh was tempted to laugh. Nobody was better at making a complete fool of himself than Whim.

"Were they naked?" she asked instead.

"No, but they had every single button undone. Bayla was—Oh, I can't even say it."

Josh took Deloise's hand. "I'm really sorry they did that. And I'm sorry you had to see them doing it. I know how that feels."

"Yeah." Deloise picked at an imaginary pill on her skirt. "Is there something wrong with us Weaver girls, something genetic, that makes guys cheat on us?"

"No!" Josh said. "There's nothing wrong with you, Del. This wasn't your fault."

"I don't know. I've never done what Bayla was doing to him in the closet."

"Deloise!" Josh cried. "Don't even think that! If Whim has been putting pressure on you to do things . . ."

Deloise gave her a look Josh couldn't read. "You're too young!" Josh said.

"I'm sixteen. You were sixteen."

"That was completely different. Ian and I had been together for years. We were committed to each other."

"Well," Deloise said angrily, "obviously Whim isn't committed to me." She folded her arms across her chest. "Oh, stop looking at me like that, Josh. I haven't had sex with Whim. And after tonight, there's a pretty good chance I never will!"

Then she burst into tears. Josh had never felt that she was the world's greatest big sister, but she at least felt confident that the right thing to do was coax Deloise to sit beside her on the bed so Josh could hold her while she cried.

"Sorry, Del," she said, smoothing her sister's blond hair.

"I just can't believe he screwed this up!"

I can, Josh thought.

The sun was rising by the time they left the hospital, Josh with a clean bill of health. Haley was already up—or maybe he'd never gone to sleep—and made them cheesy eggs with bacon for breakfast.

"I think we should have a meeting," he said afterward. "All of us."

Josh reluctantly agreed. She went upstairs to pull on clean clothes, but as she brushed her hair in the mirror, she wondered if Haley had been right that she was going to confess her secrets at this meeting. The thought filled her with panic, and she rubbed the plumeria charm she wore on a chain around her neck as she walked down to the guys' apartment.

In addition to the bright red burns where the magnets had touched her skin, the points where the wires had cut her flesh were inflamed, both on her arm and on her forehead and neck. She'd managed to hide the burns from the ER doctor using her bangs and a sweatshirt, but when she entered the guys' apartment, Mirren looked up from Haley's tablet and immediately said, "Josh, what happened to your arm?"

"Um, I'll explain in a few minutes," Josh said. "Let me wait until everyone's here."

Will appeared in his bedroom doorway; maybe he had heard her voice. He had changed clothes, but he still looked haggard, his cheeks shadowed with stubble, his eyes blinking often as if they wouldn't clear. Anger and defeat warred in his expression.

He fell onto the couch next to Deloise, so Josh sat beside Haley on the floor, glad for his silent support. "Who are we missing?" she asked.

"Whim," Will said. "He's in his room."

All eyes turned to Deloise, who said, "Somebody else call him."

After a moment of silence, during which no one made any move toward Whim's room, Will hollered, *"Whim! Get in here!"*

Whim emerged, looking like he'd slept well and awoken refreshed, and except for an underlying sheepishness in his expression, he appeared no different from the way he had the day before. "Did I hear someone ever so sweetly call my name?"

He dropped onto an oversize beanbag chair that—because of his height—looked proportionally normal in size. "What's up, friends? Why the official summons?"

"Why do you think, Whim?" Deloise asked.

Whim made an exaggerated wince while shrugging his shoulders. "I guess it might *possibly* be because Will and I got a little carried away last night."

"A little carried away?" Deloise repeated at the same time Haley said: "We're here to talk about a lot of things."

But Deloise was going to have her say. "You used a sacred substance to get high and then got your freak on with Bayla in the laundry closet!"

Genuine alarm flashed on Whim's face. "I don't actually remember that last part. Although it would explain why I woke up reeking of fabric softener."

"This is not a joke!" Deloise snapped. "I'm angry at you, and I have every right to be!"

Mirren was looking everywhere except at Whim and Deloise. Haley was staring at the floor. Josh wondered if she should suggest her sister take her conversation somewhere private, but she couldn't get a word in edgewise.

"I'm not saying that you don't," Whim told Deloise. "Obviously, I screwed up last night. I don't know what Bayla was doing here or why I didn't shut the front door in her face—"

"Stop," Will said suddenly. "Just stop it." He took a deep breath, and the weariness of the movement almost made Josh get up and go to him.

"He's been seeing her for weeks, Del," Will said. "Ever since the last Grey Circle meeting. I've known almost the whole time, and I should have told you, but he kept saying he was going to break it off, and I didn't want to hurt you. I'm sorry. It was my fault she was here last night, though. I called her and asked her to bring over some Veil dust."

"Weeks?" Deloise cried. *"Weeks?"*

Whim cast a pleading glance Josh's way, but she had no intention of helping him, not after seeing Deloise break down in the ER earlier. The only reason she wasn't breaking his nose right now was that she didn't want to take the opportunity away from her sister.

Or maybe not the only reason. She also felt stunned that Will had known and not told her, and that he had initiated the Veil dust party the night before.

I thought I was the one keeping secrets.

"Thanks, bro," Whim told Will, his usual lightheartedness gone. To Deloise, he said, "Okay, so, I've been seeing her for a few weeks. At first we were just sorting through some emotional stuff from the past, and then I guess we got sort of caught up in memories—"

"Oh, shove it," Deloise said. "Unless some part of this story involves you taking a blow to the head and forgetting I exist for the past month, I don't want to hear it." She crossed her arms. "Next topic, please."

"We aren't done with this one," Will said grimly. "Bayla is a spy for Peregrine."

"What?" Josh cried, and she wasn't the only one.

"That's ridiculous," Whim said, though the defensiveness in his voice had been replaced with surprise.

"Think about it," Will said. "How did the junta know that a dream-walking trial would be harder for Mirren than a Tempering? Someone told them she'd already passed an informal Tempering, but didn't have much dream-walking experience. Is it coincidence that the junta picked *three* water nightmares for her to resolve, or did someone clue them in that she just learned to swim? Who told the protesters we were going in through the side entrance? Whim called them, or else he called Bayla, who called Peregrine."

"Whim," Deloise said, "how could you?"

"I didn't!" Whim told her. "Will's making all of this up!"

Josh wanted to believe that Will was making it up, that he was seeing things that weren't there, but . . . *If Whim's been cheating on Deloise,* she thought, *who knows what else he might have been up to?*

"Why?" Mirren asked Whim, her voice trembling. "Why would you do that? What have I done to you?"

"Nothing, you're awesome," Whim told her. "I'd never screw you over like that."

"Not on purpose," Will said, his tone sour. "That much is true. Our Whim doesn't have a malicious bone in his body. But he does have lots and lots of vain bones; I'm sure he told Bayla those things to impress her. He didn't know she was a spy."

"She's not a spy," Whim said, but he sounded less sure than he had before. "That's crazy talk. Why would she be a spy for Peregrine?"

Because Peregrine has always suspected I'm the True Dream Walker, Josh realized. *That's why he tricked me into entering Feodor's universe, so Feodor could test me. And that's why he sent Bayla to spy on Whim—because he thought Whim knew about me.*

"Maybe I'm wrong," Will conceded, and he shrugged. "I've only met Bayla twice. And I'll be the first to admit that I came up with this theory while on Veil dust. So I'll put it to those of you who've known Bayla for years. Do you think she's capable of something like this?"

There was a long silence, and then Josh said, "Shit."

"I second that," Haley said.

"You told me you hadn't heard from her in years!" Deloise raved at Whim. "She's a—a bad person! I remember what she was like!"

"Del, you were twelve years old the last time you hung out with her," Whim protested.

"That's right, and she laughed at me when I wouldn't smoke with her."

"That doesn't make her a spy for Peregrine!" Whim argued. "That just means she's a terrible babysitter!"

"She wasn't *baby*sitting me!"

"Stop!" Josh ordered. She sighed. "Whim, get out of here."

"What?" Whim said, nonplussed. "What does that mean?"

"It means we need to talk about some sensitive things and we can't risk you relating them to Bayla."

Whim threw his hands up in the air. "Okay, so I bragged a little to Bayla. I didn't know she was working for Peregrine!"

"Nobody's accusing you of being a traitor," Josh said, to which Will added, "Just a patsy."

Whim glared at him. "You have been a lousy friend to me today."

"So? I've been a lousier friend to Del," Will snapped.

As Whim reluctantly made his way toward the hall, Deloise added, "Oh, and in case you weren't sure, we are officially broken up."

He gave her one look—angry and desperate and frightened all at once—and then left. He didn't quite slam the apartment door, but he shut it hard.

Josh ran a hand through her hair and tried to think of what to say next. She wasn't ready to admit her own misdoings yet, so she said to Will, "Can I ask you about the Veil dust?"

He shrugged again. "Yeah."

"It was your idea?"

"Yeah," he said flatly.

"Was last night the first time you'd done it?"

"Yeah. And last."

"And the vodka? Did Bayla bring that, too?"

"No." He frowned and rubbed the back of his neck. "This is going to sound crazy, but . . . what I remember is Ian giving it to me."

Josh and Haley looked at each other, and Josh knew they were both recalling what he had said about the vodka being Ian's brand.

"I thought he pulled it out of a heat vent in Whim's room," Will added. He dared a glance at Josh. "How much did I drink?"

"A little more than two shots," Josh told him. She'd actually measured out how much was missing from the bottle before deciding whether or not to take him with her to the ER.

"That's something, I guess," he said.

Josh tugged on strands of carpet. "Why did you do it?" she asked.

Will released a deep breath, but it wasn't so much a sigh as the beginning of anxious breathing. "Ironically, I thought the Veil dust would keep me from drinking."

Will, Josh thought, taken aback. Had he been struggling not to drink? When had that started?

Then she remembered how upset he'd gotten at Young Ben's barbecue and realized that Will had tried to tell her how much he was struggling. She'd been too caught up in her own secrets to hear him.

"Why did you want to drink?" Deloise asked, her voice gentle and sympathetic.

Will's lower lip trembled for half a second; Josh had never seen it do so before.

"Because," he said, "Mirren and I saw one of Josh's nightmares through the archway downstairs. She was dreaming she was killing people and . . . kissing Feodor."

Josh didn't mean to move—her body just did. Like a violent, squirming attempt to escape Will's words, she jerked back against the TV stand, uncrossed her legs and pulled them to her chest, and grabbed her forehead with both hands as if she would have torn it off.

"It was a nightmare," she heard Mirren say firmly. "It wasn't a daydream about something she wanted."

Josh had thought she was going to come clean about everything that morning, but now she knew that she never would have admitted to the strange romantic component of her nightmares. She ground the heels of her hands into her eyes.

No wonder Will had been avoiding her.

"Why didn't you tell me you knew?" she asked.

"Why didn't *you* tell *me*?" His voice quivered.

Josh hid her face against her knees again briefly before forcing herself to push forward. "I don't know why the nightmares are like that, and I was afraid you'd think they mean . . . you know."

"That you're in love with the man who tried to kill us both?"

"But I'm *not*. I'm sure I'm not!"

"She wakes up every night crying from those dreams," Deloise said. "Whatever she and Feodor are doing in them, I don't think she's enjoying it."

"Every night?" Mirren asked. "Why haven't you seen a doctor?"

"Because it isn't a medical problem!" Josh burst out. "It's not a psychiatric problem! It's—" She stopped on the precipice of admitting how deeply her encounter with Feodor had changed her. She had known she might never go back to the way she was before, but only then did she realize how afraid she was of letting other people know.

"When he sent all his bad memories into my mind," she admitted, "somehow the bad memories weren't the only ones that I got. I got his happy memories, too, and his ideas, and his education. . . ."

"You remember his whole life?" Deloise asked.

"No, not nearly all of it. But I think that all of it might be in my mind somewhere."

"You said you have his ideas," Will said. "Which ideas?"

This is the last moment he's going to love me, Josh thought, and whatever words she might have said dried up in her throat.

"Yeah," was all that came out.

Haley put his arm around her shoulders.

"Yeah?" Will asked.

She ducked her head beneath Haley's arm and pinched her eyes shut.

"Yes, she remembers his inventions," Haley said. "Yes, she remembers how to build them."

"*Did* you build them?" Will asked.

Josh, eyes still closed, nodded.

Will cursed, and she heard the floor squeak as he got up from the couch. "Josh!" Deloise cried with a gasp.

"What were you thinking?" Will asked.

Josh wanted to hide beneath Haley's arm and behind her closed eyelids forever. Her shame burned like a snakebite.

"Why, Josh? *Why?*" Will shouted.

Haley nudged Josh to face her friends. "S'okay," he told her. "Tell them."

When Josh forced her eyes open, black lines flickered across the room. She blinked a few times, and when her vision cleared all she could see was Will, standing behind the couch and clenching the back edge as if he would hurl the sectional across the room.

"Mostly I just wrote down the things I learned in the nightmares," she admitted. "But I did build three of Feodor's inventions. Partly I did it because I thought that eventually I'd dream of something to help Winsor. And partly, I . . . I just got so frustrated trying to connect with the Dream. I don't know what the point of being the True Dream Walker is if I can't help anyone, and I thought Feodor's inventions could help me. I just want to do my job, I just want to make the Dream safe!"

Will released a bitter half laugh. "Dear God," he said. "You're not in love with Feodor—you're in love with his power!"

And that, Josh realized, was true.

Will shook his head, releasing the couch back to cross his arms over his chest. "You're such a fool, Josh."

"What else was I supposed to do?" she asked. "What would you have done?"

"I would have trusted that whatever fate had decided to make me the True Dream Walker would teach me how to use that power when it was good and ready."

The answer was so stupid that Josh stopped feeling guilty and started feeling angry. "Bullshit!" she told Will. "You don't trust anyone to do anything—you're a complete control freak! You won't even let Kerstel cook by herself! And if you hadn't been panicking over every tiny thing, maybe I could have come to you and told you what was going on months ago!"

"You want to blame *me* for this?" Will said, a hard look coming over his face. "I'm out of here."

"I'm not done!" Josh shouted.

"Yeah? I am!" he shouted back as he headed for the door.

"Last night," she told him, "while you were getting high and helping Whim cheat on my sister, Bash Mirrettsio tied me up and stole two of Feodor's inventions that will allow him to control the Dream."

More gasps from Deloise, a little cry of dismay from Mirren, but Josh looked only at Will. "If Bayla is working for Peregrine," she said, "I guess it's reasonable to assume that her boyfriend is, too."

Will leaned against the apartment door and slid slowly to the floor, his face empty with shock.

"Bash Mirrettsio the dream theorist?" Mirren asked.

"Yeah," Josh said.

"What do you mean by the inventions can control the Dream?"

Josh swallowed. "When you go into the Dream wearing the devices, you think a thought and it happens."

"This isn't . . ." Will murmured. "This can't be . . ."

"And now Peregrine has it?" Deloise asked.

"Possibly. Probably." Josh wanted to hide in Haley's arm again, but he'd gone to sit in the recliner beside Mirren. "I'm sorry, everyone. Will, I'm sorry. I— You were right. I wanted the power that I'm supposed to have."

"How do you even know you're supposed to have it?" Deloise asked. "Maybe Will is right and that part of being the True Dream Walker will come when it's supposed to."

"Maybe he is right," Josh admitted.

"Who's got your blood?" Will whispered.

Josh didn't know if she had heard him wrong or if he was cracking up, but the words made her shiver.

"I'm sorry," Mirren said. "I don't wish to disrupt the conversation, but Josh has mentioned several times that she believes she's the True Dream Walker. Does anyone have evidence of this?"

Josh had been so busy fighting, and had grown so accustomed to Mirren's presence, that she had entirely forgotten to watch what she said. They all had.

"She's definitely the True Dream Walker," Deloise said. "But we don't tell people that usually." She managed a weak smile. "We like you."

"Haley?" Mirren asked. Her eyes swam with tears, which Josh didn't understand.

"It's true," he said, and his smile was much bigger.

Mirren began to cry. She also began to laugh, and one or the other action led her to develop the hiccups. "I'm so—*hiccup*—relieved!"

Deloise smiled again, but she looked as confused as Josh felt.

"Were you afraid it was you?" Josh asked.

"No. But according to my scroll, there's now a—*hiccup*—much greater chance I'll live through all this."

Before Josh could ask what that meant, Will said sharply, "Why are you all celebrating? Don't you see what's going on here?"

He'd gotten up from the floor, but his body was visibly shaking. Josh had never seen his cornflower-blue eyes so large. "What's going on here?" Deloise repeated.

"Peregrine has the devices to control the Dream," Will said. "He's always been obsessed with staging, right? Now instead of going into the Dream and having to bring props and costumes and whatever else, he can just put on these devices and instantly create whatever nightmare he wants."

"So it's a lot easier for him to stage nightmares now," Deloise said.

"And the nightmares can be much more elaborate," Mirren added.

"No, no!" Will said. "That's just the beginning! Now he has the Karawar, too!"

Josh wasn't certain how the Karawar would help her grandfather, but Mirren caught on immediately.

"He can use the Karawar to call the souls of dream walkers to the part of the Dream he controls," she said, "and then stage dreams specifically for them."

"It's not just that!" Will continued. "Feodor tried to tell me last night. *Who's got your blood?* he kept saying. It's Peregrine! He has all our blood, because we all gave blood samples to the junta's DNA database!"

Oh, my God, Josh thought. *He's right.* And at the same time, she couldn't help wondering, *Will saw Feodor when he was high?*

"That means Peregrine has tiny pieces of our souls!" Will ranted. "Evidence of the subtle body is present even in the tiniest fragment of DNA! He's going to use the blood samples and the Karawar together somehow, and then he'll be able to stage nightmares for specific people!"

No, Josh thought. *No, that can't be right. That can't be possible.*

She looked at Mirren, even though Feodor's memories were stirring, each realization flicking on like a ceiling light, and the more memories illuminated her mind, the clearer the picture became.

Yes, Feodor's voice whispered to her.

"I . . . I think it could work," Mirren said, and she touched her fingertips to her forehead, as if she too, couldn't believe her own thoughts.

"Wait," Deloise said. "Are you saying that he could go get the sample of my blood from the junta's database, and use the Karawar to call my soul into the part of the Dream he controls, and then stage terrible nightmares for me?"

"Yes," Will said. "Yes."

"And he's doing all this just to rig the election?" Deloise asked.

"Forget the election!" Will cried. "With this, he can rig anything he wants! He can make you *kill* Mirren!"

"Oh, my God," Josh said again. "What if he's already been staging dreams telling people to kill Mirren? What if that's why everyone's turning on her?"

"But I thought Peregrine needed the Karawar to stage nightmares for dream walkers," Deloise said.

"Yeah, if he wants to target *specific* dream walkers," Josh explained. "But he could have been staging dreams the old-fashioned way, by using the looking stone to find dream walkers' nightmares and then jumping into them."

"Who's got your blood?" Will whispered again.

Josh recalled the day she had taken him to the Dashiel Winters Building to officially become a dream walker. He'd been uncertain about giving a DNA sample, and she'd urged him to do so.

Better safe than sorry, right? she'd said.

Oh, how wrong she had been, just like she'd been wrong about building the devices, and hiding her nightmares from Will, and trusting Bash.

I have to fix this, she thought. *Will's still my responsibility.*

"All right," she said. "What are we going to do?"

Twenty-two

They more or less panicked.

Josh began listing all the awful things Peregrine could induce them to do to one another. Deloise alternated between shushing her and repeating that somehow Whim had to be at fault for all of this. Will just sat on the couch with his bloodless face hidden between his knees.

Mirren didn't know whether to laugh or cry. She had just discovered that she might very well live through this—and that they might very well all die. The only thing she knew for certain was that if she had a chance of surviving, she wanted to fight for it.

She called Davita and impressed upon her the importance of locating and detaining Peregrine immediately.

"Do whatever it takes, even if you have to . . ." She tugged her earlobe. "I don't know—even if you have to personally assault him. Bind him to a heavy chair and then call me. Oh, and do the same thing with Bayla Sakrov and Bash Mirrettsio."

"You want me to assault your main competition in the election?" Davita repeated. "Mirren, do you have any idea what this will do to your reputation? This is career suicide."

"I have bigger concerns than my reputation right now, Davita."

Haley, who had resorted to scribbling notes on a nearby notepad, thrust one into her hand.

protect the cradle he wants our belly button

"Haley, I don't know what this means," Mirren told him. "This doesn't make any sense." To Davita, who was still barking in her ear about explaining herself, she said, "I have to go."

Haley crumpled up the next note and tossed it into a growing pile on the floor, but the note after that he gave to Mirren.

"'Open the Royal Trimidion'?" she read. "They tore down the Royal Trimidion during the overthrow."

After briefly choking on the words, he croaked, "Build another."

"I don't know what to do," Josh said to no one in particular. "Maybe we should break into the Dashiel Winters Building and try to destroy the DNA database."

Mirren had spent enough time at the junta's headquarters to know that the chances they would be able to break in were zero.

"Josh," Will said desperately, lifting his head, "we aren't marines."

"Maybe if we cut the power to the building for long enough, the blood samples will rot. They're probably refrigerated, right?" Josh suggested.

"I'm sure they have a backup generator," Will said, his voice rising with what Mirren suspected was hysteria. "They have a bomb shelter—they must have a generator!"

Although Mirren appreciated that Josh had moved so quickly to problem solving, so far her anxiety seemed to be short-circuiting her brain.

Josh ran her hand through her hair like she meant to rip each strand from her scalp. "We could go to the Gendarmerie and just report the devices stolen. Then we'd have a whole bunch of people looking for them."

The Gendarmerie were the rough equivalent of dream-walker police.

"Now that makes sense," Deloise said. "They can put out an APB for Bash and Bayla, or whatever the Gendarmerie equivalent is."

"Yes," Will said. "Adults. Let adults deal with it."

"What if the gendarmes catch Bash with the devices?" Mirren asked. "Won't they just turn the devices over to the junta? And no one will believe us if we say Peregrine's involved. We have no proof except Will's hallucinations."

"You're probably right," Josh muttered. She sighed with frustration. "At least I can go into the Dream and pull down the towers Bash and I put up."

"How will that help?" Mirren asked.

"If Bash has more of them, he could be putting them in the Dream right now, and making the area he controls bigger and bigger. At least I can dismantle this section."

"But couldn't Peregrine or Bash be in the Dream, using the devices to control that section of the Dream, while you try to take it apart?" Mirren asked. "They'd be able to control you then, too, right?"

"Maybe," Josh admitted, and from her expression, it was clear the possibility hadn't occurred to her previously.

On the couch, Will was so pale and sweaty that Mirren thought he was likely to pass out, which worried her for multiple reasons. Aside from her concern for Will, she knew Josh wouldn't be focused on the issue at hand if she was trying to take care of him.

To Mirren's relief, Deloise was the one who wrapped Will in a blanket and hugged him to her side.

"We'll figure this out," she told him. "It'll be okay."

Will just kept watching Josh pace.

Mirren put her hand over Haley's to make him stop scribbling. "Just let me think for a moment," she said, and he exhaled as if relieved and then capped his pen.

Mirren blocked out the room as much as she could and tried to concentrate on what she knew:

Josh believed she was the True Dream Walker but was unable to access her power for some reason.

Josh had Feodor's memories—if not all, then many of them.

Josh was desperate enough to wield the True Dream Walker's power that she had made a serious lapse in judgment and created dangerously powerful devices, which Bash—and likely Peregrine—now controlled.

Now that Peregrine had the Karawar, he could stage dreams to influence everyone whose DNA was stored in the junta's database. This included everyone Mirren knew in the World, with the exception of herself.

Interestingly, even though Peregrine was now much more powerful, Mirren believed her chances of surviving had increased. The passage torn from her scroll came back to her:

If a queen she would become,
one of two things have begun:
a martyr's death to seal her ruse,
or lead to Death Dream Walker True.

She'd already chosen to try to become queen, which meant she was on her way either to being murdered as a martyr or to killing Josh.

There was one other possibility.

"May I speak to you alone?" she whispered to Haley.

A minute later, they were alone in his bedroom. Mirren went to the drawer Haley had emptied for her and from beneath the linen drawer liner withdrew the sheet of paper she had brought back with her from the Hidden Kingdom. After reading through the secret ritual it described one last time, she held it out to Haley, who took the brittle page from her with light fingers. As he read the handwritten words, he sank onto his bed.

Without looking at Mirren, he gave the page back to her.

"Do you understand what it says?" she asked.

He removed his steno pad from the pocket of his gray cardigan and rubbed his thumb over the glossy cover like it was a talisman. "I can't help you with that," he said.

Mirren glanced at the page, half expecting its contents to have changed since she had last read it. "I don't understand."

"I can't . . . I can't tell you if you should use that."

She had experienced Haley when he was anxious and when he was shy, but she didn't know how to read him now. Gently, she lifted his chin with the edge of her finger.

"Haley?"

His hazel eyes were pained. "I know too much," he whispered. "I see too far. I can't . . . influence what you do."

"Oh." Mirren turned to drop the paper back into her drawer. *The disadvantages of loving a psychic,* she thought, and wondered if she did, in fact, love him.

She had always assumed that love grew from knowing another person deeply, from learning to see all the wonderful things in him or her. She'd expected to have to study her lovers the way she had studied books and physics and languages, to tease out every nuance of personality.

But as she slipped onto the bed beside Haley, she wondered if love couldn't grow from seeing a single profound beauty in someone. If it could, she knew that seeing Haley try so hard to grow was enough for her.

"Don't tell me," she whispered, hugging him. "You don't have to tell me."

"I want to tell you everything," he admitted. He rested his chin on top of her head. "I feel like you're the first person I've met who wouldn't run screaming."

"I wouldn't run," she told him. "Not from you."

He pulled back to look into her eyes, as if he needed to witness the truth in them, and whatever he found there made him smile. Mirren tilted her head and ever so slowly kissed him, not on the mouth, but on the hinge of his jaw. Her own boldness astonished her, and the heady taste of his skin made her open her mouth.

"Mirren," he whispered, but the end of her name turned to a groan that told her he would not always be so quiet or so gentle.

He slid his hand into her hair, and she knew he was going to turn her head and kiss her full on the mouth, and she was going to let him, and at that exact moment Josh opened the bedroom door and said, "All right, the plan goes like this: First, I go into the Dream. If I stand outside the basketball court, I can reach into it and pull out the towers, and that way I won't risk my whole body. Then I start building another vambrace and circlet, although it might take me a few days to build a whole new set since I'm out of beryllium copper."

Only then did she appear to realize what she had interrupted.

"Oh," she said. "Uh, sorry."

She ducked back into the living room, but the reminder of the danger they faced had ruined the moment. "I suppose I should call Davita again," Mirren said, rising reluctantly from the bed.

"I suppose," Haley echoed, smiling.

Mirren caught his hand. "You owe me a kiss," she said.

He stood and placed a soft kiss on the top of her head.

"Now you owe me two," she told him.

Haley and Will accompanied Josh down to the archroom, while Mirren called Davita again. Davita had said that no one could find Peregrine, which was unusual for a Tuesday. He was known for being obsessively punctual and scheduling down to five-minute intervals.

"Where are you?" Davita asked.

"Where am I?" Mirren repeated, surprised by the question.

"Yes. Where are you?"

Something in Davita's voice unsettled Mirren.

"What do you mean—where am I?" she asked, knowing full well that her aunt would have called Mirren rude.

"Are you at Josh and Deloise's house?"

Again, something . . . was Davita's tone too intense? Mirren couldn't shake the feeling that something was off.

"No," she lied. "We're on our way to brunch someplace downtown. Fat Mac's, I think Josh said? And then Deloise is going to take me makeup shopping."

"That's fine, then," Davita said. "Call me when you get back to the house."

"I will," Mirren promised, but she frowned at the phone as she ended the call.

Why does Davita want to know where I am?

What if Peregrine had already gotten to her?

Josh, Haley, and Will returned from the basement much sooner than Mirren had expected, and from their faces, she knew they had brought bad news.

Josh dropped like a stone onto the couch. "Bash lied to me," she said in a voice so quiet and flat that Mirren drew closer to hear. "He told me he had come up with a way to fix the towers to the fabric of the Dream. Something about simo pulsations . . . I thought he knew more than me, that I just wasn't following, and that's why it didn't make sense. But what he really did was burn holes in the Veil and jam the towers in like corks."

"What does that mean?" asked Deloise, who had rejoined them to hear the news.

"It means I can't remove them," Josh told her. "At least, not without tearing the Veil. I can't even disable them, because I'm not sure how they work." She shook her head. "This is all my fault."

Mirren sat down beside Josh. She wanted to say something comforting, but the truth was she agreed that much of their current situation was Josh's fault. So she just patted Josh's shoulder and said, "If we can't remove the towers, then we're going to have to fight Peregrine on the battlefield he's chosen: the Dream. The question is, can you make a new set of devices stronger than the set Bash has?"

"Possibly," Josh said, and she looked at Mirren with a respect that was new. "Although, given what this set did to me, a stronger set might kill me."

We're not so different, Mirren thought, *Josh and I.*

"I'll start working," Josh said, rising.

"No," Will said, speaking for the first time since they had returned, and they all looked at him.

"If Bash can alter the Dream at will," Josh said, "then I'll need something even more powerful to stop him."

"No," Will repeated, and then his voice, which had been so weak and frightened, exploded like a piñata full of gunpowder. "This is an awful, absurd plan," he said. "I don't want to be part of this. The *only* thing we're going to do is go to the Gendarmerie, and we're going to tell them everything, Josh, including what the devices do and that Feodor invented them, because when they hear that, they're going to have a fit and send a small army to find them. They'll have Bash in custody by sundown."

Josh stood frozen, her lips parted, as if Will had never criticized her before or as if she had suddenly realized he was right, and Mirren felt she had to step between them, to break whatever hold Will had over Josh.

"What if the Gendarmerie doesn't catch Bash?" Mirren asked. "What if they do catch him and he's already given the devices to Peregrine? We don't have any evidence that Peregrine is involved. All he has to do is hide the devices and play innocent. What if Josh is detained or even arrested and can't build a new set of devices, and Peregrine starts staging dreams? How are we going to stop him then? The first thing I would do, in Peregrine's position, is stage dreams for the gendarmes themselves to make them unfailingly loyal to me. What if Peregrine builds dozens more devices, and starts handing them out to those loyal guards?"

Will looked at Mirren with something like hate in his eyes.

Whatever is between him and Josh, she thought, *it is very complicated.*

"Fine," he muttered. "Fine. I'm hungry." He barked, "Is anybody else hungry?"

Then he stormed out of the apartment.

"Oh, my God," Josh said—mostly, it seemed, to herself—and went after him.

Mirren felt an emotion she hadn't experienced in a long time and realized it was embarrassment. "I handled that badly," she said.

Deloise gave her a sympathetic smile. "Will is hungover and emotionally exhausted. Don't take him too seriously." She sighed. "But I *am* hungry. Let's go find something to eat."

Mirren let Haley wrap his arm around her waist and lead her toward the stairs. Deloise followed them.

Mirren was still lost in thoughts about the difficulty of navigating other people's issues when she followed Will and Josh into the kitchen. She saw only a flash of movement beside her and heard Deloise cry, "Knife!" before Haley used the arm he had wrapped around her waist to yank her backward into the hallway.

Whim's father, Alex, lunged toward her with a large, serrated knife. As Haley yanked Mirren out of the way, Josh pushed Alex's arm to the side so that the blade missed Mirren's torso and instead pierced the refrigerator door.

Mirren couldn't help screaming as she scrambled across the hallway carpeting. She lost sight of the kitchen, but she heard something big hit the floor, and then Will cried, "Stay down or I'll break your arm!"

Silence filled the hallway. Deloise and Haley stood between Mirren and the kitchen door, both of them in fighting stances as if ready for another attacker.

"What—*the shit*—was that?" Mirren heard Josh demand.

Mirren's heartbeat sounded like a roulette wheel in her ears, but she made herself climb to her feet. She was determined to meet the first attack on her life with dignity.

"She has to die!" Alex cried from the kitchen.

When Mirren entered the kitchen, Will had Alex on the floor and was kneeling on the older man's back, keeping both his arms in a lock.

"Three weeks ago you were professing your family's undying loyalty to the monarchy," Josh was saying. "What happened?"

"I was duped!" Alex cried. "She's lying to you! She's lying to all of us!"

"About what?" Will asked skeptically.

In a hushed, creepy voice, Alex said, "There's sorcery in her eyes."

"Ah, right," Josh said. "Del, we're gonna need some rope in here."

"You're under her spell," Alex warned Will, trying to crane his neck to look behind him. "She'll lead all of you to Death."

"Why do you think that?" Will asked.

"I had a vision. I saw the royal crown upon the skull of Death, I saw the wine she drank spill from her bare ribs, I saw emerald rings slip from her finger bones. Her woman form rotted away and revealed the soul-carcass beneath."

Mirren's family had been accused of many things: greed, secrecy, pride. But this was the first time Mirren could recall "undead" being thrown into the mix.

"*What?*" Josh finally asked.

"Hold on," Will said. "Alex, when did you have this vision?"

"Last night."

"You mean your vision was a dream?"

"A foretelling!"

Mirren took a quick step back as she realized what had happened. Will must have realized it at the same moment, because he said, "Peregrine got to him."

"No," Josh swore, but it sounded more like an emotional denial than a logical one. "But then why not one of us? You or me—or Haley?"

"I slept like the dead last night," Will said. "Maybe the Veil dust knocked me out too deeply to dream. Whim, too."

"And Del and I were at the hospital all night," Josh said, "so we didn't sleep at all. Mirren doesn't have a DNA sample on file."

That left only Haley to account for. "I'm immune," he said, tapping the center of his forehead. "And I never gave the junta my blood."

"Why not?" Josh asked.

He shrugged. "Ian said not to bother."

Will squinted at him like he didn't understand, and Josh rolled her eyes. Mirren still didn't know enough about Ian to understand what either reaction meant, and she was distracted from wondering when the back door opened and Whim walked in, carrying a bouquet of two dozen pale pink calla lilies. He stopped short on the kitchen's threshold and took the scene in with wide eyes.

"Free me, son!" Alex cried.

"So," Whim said slowly, "if this is some sort of payback, I'm gonna say it's already gone too far."

"Where's your mom?" Josh asked.

"Seriously, Josh, do what you want to me, but leave my family out of this." Only then did he stiffen with alarm. "Oh God, what happened to the fridge?"

They secured Alex to a chair, and after a long debate over Whim's trustworthiness, they realized they had little choice but to explain the situation to him.

"So, not only did I cheat on my girlfriend and force Will to lie about it for me and leak some info about Mirren, I actually made Peregrine aware that Josh had built a very dangerous device and more or less helped him steal it and brainwash my father to commit murder?" Whim clarified at the end.

"That's about the square of it," Josh said. "Now, back to my original question: Where's your mom? And where are Dad and Kerstel?"

If Peregrine had gotten to Alex, he could have gotten to Saidy or to Lauren and Kerstel. And convincing them that Mirren was a threat wasn't even the worst he could do; Mirren felt sick at the thought that he might hurt Kerstel's baby.

Lauren was apparently at work, and thankfully, Kerstel was asleep in bed. After a long, tense search, they found Saidy hiding under a tarp in the back of Haley's truck with a syringe containing enough morphine to ensure that Mirren never felt pain again.

"You aren't safe here," Josh told Mirren flatly after wrestling Saidy to the ground.

Mirren's chest hurt at the idea of leaving the house, and only then did she realize how comfortable she had become there. The old Greek Revival had been her home since she'd left the Hidden Kingdom. The world outside it still felt big and scary.

But she knew Josh was right. "Where should I go?" she asked.

At that moment, Whim's cell phone rang. He held it out to Deloise so that she could see the caller's name, but she turned away.

Watching them, Josh said, "I think you should go camping."

Through a Veil Darkly

Message board: Is everybody dreaming about Princess Mirren?

Jacobean says: Maybe all these dreams about her are a sign. Like, the True Dream Walker is trying to let us know what will happen if we vote for her.

dirtybird says: If she is planning an overthrow with the Gendarmerie, why bother with the AC?

> **spoooore says:** Maybe the overthrow is a backup plan in case she loses.

> > **dirtybird says:** Um, it's kind of obvious she's going to lose. If she has a backup plan, she should have used it already.

YashaGottleib says: You're all just making this up to make her look bad.

> **jshg_hammer says:** I'm not making it up! I totally dreamed about her.

> **WMRyna47 says:** She already looks bad.

JillKramer says: You're all just dreaming about her because she's on DWTV every night. Media influences nightmares. Dream Walking 101, bozos.

> **Jacobean says:** It's possible. I read this page before I had the first nightmare.

> **WMRyna47 says:** Nightmares aside, she's still completely corrupt.

prancingpony says: HAIR BLOOD! HAIR BLOOD! HAIR BLOOD!

YashaGottleib says: I agree with Jill. This is all just media influence. She isn't planning a secret overthrow and she doesn't have a secret army.

WMRyna47 says: She turned Josh Weaver against us!

gilandsons says: Yeah! Josh is ours!

JillKramer says: What does that even mean? Turned against who?

brigby9j9j9 says: We gotta save Josh! The princess will use her as a hostage!

WMRyna47 says: Where's she live?

SmokeythePear says: Tanith. Message me for the address.

JillKramer says: Has everybody on this board just gone totally crazy?! I'm calling the Gendarmerie.

gilandsons says: You're aiding the enemy!

prancingpony says: I want in. HAIR BLOOD!!!!!!!!

Jacobean says: I just called Josh's house, Jill. No answer.

JillKramer says: I hope we aren't too late.

Twenty-three

While everyone else frantically packed, Will risked waking Kerstel up and explaining what was happening. Josh had explicitly told him not to because she wasn't certain that Peregrine hadn't brainwashed her stepmother, but after the morning's revelations, Will had decided he didn't have to listen to Josh anymore.

"I was up and down all night peeing," she admitted when he asked how she'd slept. "I think the hormones are giving me insomnia."

"Well, you might thank the baby for that once you've heard what's going on," Will said, and he filled her in on as much as he thought he safely could. He didn't say where they were going, but at least she knew enough to be able to protect herself, Lauren, and her unborn son.

Before he left, she pulled him into a tight hug. "Come back safe."

"I'll try. I mean, we will."

As he headed downstairs to pack, she added, "And Will? Take care of each other."

"I'll try," he said again, but he knew she could tell he was hurting.

Just as the sun began to set over Iph Lake, Josh pulled into a camping space at the campground's far end. Although Iph Lake was overrun with people enjoying the summer fishing and the opportunity to cool off in blue waters, Josh had picked a site so far from a bathroom that they had the block to themselves.

Haley pulled in behind them, and Whim parked in the next spot over. They set up two tents with a speed that surprised Will; he'd never been camping before, but it was a favorite activity of the Weaver-Avish-McKarr household. After raiding the basement for equipment, they'd hardly had to buy anything besides food and soda.

Josh's idea was simple: They had to disconnect. If no one could find Mirren, no one could kill her. Their camping trip would be free from cell phones, computers, and communication with the dream-walker world, and they'd stay off radar until they came up with a better plan.

There had been some debate over who would travel with Mirren. Josh had insisted on going along to protect Mirren, and she'd wanted Will to go with her. Will had been relieved by the idea of getting away—he wanted Josh as far from an archway as possible. Deloise was coming, but she hadn't wanted Whim to come, and when he'd insisted, Deloise had responded by running the calla lilies through the garbage disposal.

Thanks to his psychic powers, Haley was the only one who was entirely safe from Peregrine's influence, but he believed he could protect the others. To that end, he and Mirren had made a detour to buy semiprecious stones, tiny mirrors, five pounds of Himalayan pink salt, and a lot of string. Once Whim got the fire going and Deloise began mixing up a big pot of Velveeta Shells & Cheese, Haley used the string to hang dozens of crystals and quarter-sized mirrors from the tree branches arching over their tents.

"These will help?" Josh asked, peering up at the rocks as they spun slowly in the breeze. "What are they?"

"Moonstone, malachite, black tourmaline, and amethyst. They'll help."

Before bed, Haley gave them each a dose of over-the-counter sleeping pills. "So you'll sleep too deeply to dream," he explained. "And wear these. If the bone breaks in the night, we'll know Peregrine got to you."

He then handed out greasy chicken bones with pieces of string tied to them.

"Are they necklaces?" Deloise asked, putting hers on.

"Are they *lunch*?" Whim asked. They'd stopped at a fast-food chicken place during the drive.

Haley just smiled.

They set up a girls' tent and a boys' tent. Will was happy to turn in early and climbed into his sleeping bag as soon as he began feeling the effects of the sleeping pills.

"Um, Haley?" Whim said, lying down beside Will. "I understand that salt circles are supposed to protect people from evil and all that, but why the hell did you draw one *inside* the tent?"

Haley giggled. "I didn't want to kill the plants outside. This is a forest."

"Dude, there is so much salt in my sleeping bag. Wait . . . chicken bones, salt . . . It's a stew! Run, Will, run!"

Will didn't laugh, but he couldn't hold back a smile. "Why is it so hard to stay mad at you?"

"Because God knew that if he made me any other way, I would have very little chance of survival," Whim quipped.

Will chuckled, but he couldn't resist saying, "For a guy who just got dumped, you're awfully chipper."

"Have no fear, my friend. No woman can resist the charms of the Whimarian. By this time next week, Deloise will be back in my arms and all will be right with the World."

That's a nice thought, Will reflected as he sank into sleep.

But it will never happen.

The next three days were strangely calm for Will. He gave up on the idea that he might be able to help the others sort out their problems and instead began exploring the campground. Leaving Josh and Mirren to pore over a sketchbook full of equations and fret about the devices Josh had built, he pretended he was as carefree as the rest of the campers. He swam with Haley; he kayaked with Deloise; he fished with Whim. If tensions ever arose at the campsite, he just wandered off on his own to hike through the forest and enjoy the quiet. He even bought a cheap digital camera from the camp store and used it to take photographs of the water, the trees, the birds that soared overhead.

He tried to ignore the fact that Josh's and Mirren's stress levels were obviously increasing. The first night, he woke briefly to the sound of Josh thrashing around in the girls' tent, calling out for help, but he was so tired that he fell back to sleep as soon as he heard Deloise calming her. The second night, Josh woke them all up with shrill, animal-like screams that caused Whim to try to leap to his feet. He ended up with his legs mired in his sleeping bag and fell over on top of Haley.

By the third night, Will had grown attuned to the desperate whimpers that preceded Josh's full-blown panic. Deloise must have as well, because Will heard her voice through the walls of the nylon tents as she shook her sister awake.

"You're okay, you're okay, you're awake now. It wasn't real."

Then he heard Josh crying, not just whimpering but full-on crying, and Deloise shushing her.

From the other side of the tent, Whim whispered, "Isn't there something you can do for her, Haley? Different stones or more salt or a tinfoil hat?"

"It isn't coming from outside her," Haley whispered. "It's in her mind. That's Will's arena, not mine."

Will didn't know if Haley meant Will should be the one to comfort Josh because he was her boyfriend or because he'd read a lot of self-help books.

Pick one, he told himself.

Josh was still crying. Will sat up, unzipped the tent door, and brushed the salt off the bottoms of his feet before stepping into his sandals.

"Knock knock," he said outside the girls' tent.

Josh unzipped the door and fell into his arms while trying to climb out. "Sorry," she moaned. "I can stop. I'll figure out how."

The sight of moonlit tears on her face broke him. He'd only seen her cry, really cry with tears—what, twice? She hadn't even cried when Gloves shattered her elbow.

I'm an idiot, he thought, and hugged her.

"Mirren was right—they're nightmares," he said. "They aren't fantasies. I'm not mad at you."

For some reason, that made her cry harder.

They sat down on the cooler together, far enough from the tents that they could whisper to each other in private. Will found such comfort in holding Josh that for a moment he couldn't remember why he'd stopped.

"Why didn't you tell me about the nightmares when they started?" he asked.

"I did," she insisted. "Every time I slept in your room, I was telling you."

She felt so small to him tonight. She always felt small—she *was* small—but usually Will could feel the strength coiled inside her, the power ready to explode the instant she called on it. Tonight she felt small and so fragile, like a hummingbird.

"But why didn't you tell me about the devices and . . . the other stuff?"

"For the same reason you can't say it! Because it's twisted. And it's almost, sort of like cheating on you." She hid her face against his shoulder. "And, honestly, I think I didn't tell you because I knew it was wrong to build the circlet and vambrace and I knew you'd call me out."

"I would have!" he agreed. "I mean, damn, Josh, what were you thinking?" She shrank back, but he kept his grip around her tight. He had no intention of letting either of them pull away tonight. "People need other people, Josh. None of us is complete alone. And one reason you need other people is because sometimes your judgment isn't that great."

She laughed. "Yeah, that's true. Every time I do something stupid and reckless, I do it in spite of somebody telling me not to." He felt her relax against him again. "Do you need me?"

"Of course. I need you to get me out of my head, because when I spend too much time there, I go a little crazy. I'll always need you."

The night was warm, but Will felt her shiver.

"But—but—now you're going to hate me forever."

"What?" he asked. "Why would I hate you?"

But she must have passed him her shiver, because he felt it slide through him like the warning whisper of a ghost. *Don't tell me,* he thought. *Let's just stay at this lake forever. We can be happy here. We can survive.*

"Because," she whispered, "I have to go find Feodor."

"What does that mean? Like, in your dreams?"

"No." Her voice caught in her throat. "I have to break into Death and find him. He's the only one besides Bash who can figure out how to remove the towers."

Will was confused; whatever he had feared or expected, this wasn't it.

"But if you go into Death, you'll die. Besides, even if you went to the afterlife or whatever and found Feodor's . . . soul, and it told you how to remove the towers, you wouldn't be able to tell anyone who was still alive."

Josh gently detached herself from him and stood up so she could pace around the coals of the campfire. "That's not quite how it works. I might be able to—" She turned and called toward the tents, "Mirren? You want to come out here?"

A flashlight came on in the girls' tent, and Mirren emerged a few moments later, pulling a light sweater on over her pajamas.

"Tell him," Josh said.

Mirren sat down in a chair and said, very quietly, "Will, I'm going to tell you something that I never thought I would tell anyone, let alone three people. It's one of the secrets my family keeps, one of the things we know that are the most important to keep secret. You will understand why as soon as I tell you. I need your promise that you will never tell anyone, for any reason."

Will hated every word. More secrets—hadn't he and Josh been trying to get rid of their secrets? Nothing good had ever come of one, and here he was being asked to keep another.

"I'm done keeping secrets," he said. "I'm sorry if that's inconvenient."

He rose from the cooler, but Josh grabbed his arm. "Mirren, tell him."

"If he won't—"

"He doesn't have to promise," Josh insisted. "Will would never tell people things that would hurt them. He's a dream walker; he understands responsibility."

Mirren gave Josh a long, level look and said, "It's on you, then."

"Fine."

Will almost protested that he didn't want to know, but Mirren was already speaking in a low, quick voice that carried only a few feet through the darkness. "My family knows a ritual to break into Death. That is the correct term—'to break in.' It would allow us to enter Death, hopefully to find Feodor and ask him how to remove the towers, and then return to the World, without us dying."

Will waited to see how he would react, but the information was lost on him. What Mirren was suggesting was so unbelievable that he simply didn't believe it.

"And you've done this ritual before?" he asked.

"No," Mirren admitted.

"But you know someone who has."

"No."

"But you have some sort of evidence that this is actually possible."

Mirren glanced at Josh. "The ritual hasn't been performed—or, at least, recorded as performed—in recent memory. But I believe it will work."

"Yeah. That's about what I thought."

Will started toward his tent.

"I don't even know what I got out of bed for," he muttered to himself.

The girls chased after him, but he blocked out their protests and arguments. The plan was crap. The plan wasn't going to work. They were going to have to keep thinking while he went hiking and fishing and photographed ducks.

Finally, Josh jumped in front of him and cut off his path. "All right," she said. "Maybe it won't work. Probably it won't work. But at this point we don't have any other ideas, so I don't see why we shouldn't at least try it."

Will felt boxed in—Josh in front of him, Mirren behind him—and trapped most of all by this terrible thing they were suggesting.

"You don't see why we shouldn't try it?" he repeated slowly. "You don't see why going into the Death universe and calling out one of the craziest people there to ask his advice, which you would apparently then consider following, is a bad idea?"

"He's dead," Josh said. "He can't hurt us anymore."

"You don't know that!" Will felt his pulse speed up. The easy dismissal was wearing off and the realization that Josh was actually talking about going to find Feodor was sinking in. "Do you think being dead made him less crazy? 'Cause I think it probably just pissed him off, and in case you've forgotten, we're the ones who killed him!"

"Mirren says he's a shade, he won't be able to hurt us."

"Mirren doesn't even know if her ritual has ever worked or if it will work for us. For all she knows, Feodor could take over your body as soon as you get there."

"No, I *know* that can't happen," Mirren said.

Haley emerged from their tent, wrapped in his disgusting old robe. "Your girlfriend's insane," Will told him. "You need to— She's trying to find him!"

"Please," Josh pleaded, "listen to us. This is a long shot, but it might work."

"I don't want it to work!" he burst out. "Are you listening to yourself? You're talking about going to find Feodor! The evil sociopath who nearly killed us!"

"We just need to ask him a few questions—"

"What makes you think he'd tell you anything? Why would he help you?"

"Mirren says Death changes people—"

Will began laughing. "Yeah, I'm sure it does." He tilted his head back and the stars above—or Haley's crystals—spun crazily.

He couldn't see Josh clearly, but he heard how helpless she felt when she spoke. "Will . . . we just don't know what else to do at this point."

"Pretty much anything else would be okay with me."

"Will," Josh said, and he saw her turn her head to glance at Mirren before going on.

"Don't look at Mirren!" Will barked, and his control snapped like the chicken bone he wore around his neck. "Mirren doesn't know what happened last time! She didn't see the look on your face when you realized Feodor had Ian, she wasn't the one you called an outsider when she tried to make you think rationally, and she didn't have to watch you vomiting and beating your head against the floor to try to escape Feodor's memories! So don't tell me that *Mirren* is any sort of authority on letting you risk your life!"

He was furious, but for some reason he was laughing, too, a creepy, high-pitched laugh, and he let Haley coax him to sit down at the picnic table.

This isn't happening, he tried to tell Haley with his mind. *This can't happen.*

Josh knelt in front of him and wrapped her small hands around his fists. "Relax," she said. "Relax."

Slowly, he was able to release his clenched fingers, and Josh slipped her hands into his.

"You were right," she said in a soft voice, "about going after Ian. It was lunacy, and I shouldn't have done it. It was exactly what you said—you told me I was being reckless and I didn't listen. I know that every scar you and Haley have is because of me. I know that you're shaking right now because you haven't gotten over what happened in Warsaw, and I know that's my fault, too, because I haven't been here for you since we got back." She swallowed. "I'm sorry, Will, that you're hurting because of me. I'm so sorry."

Will fought tears. He didn't want to break down now, he wanted—he *needed* to stay angry. Seeing Josh wipe her own eyes didn't help.

"I know I've screwed up again. Probably even worse this time than last. And I wish I could go tell my dad what I've done and trust that he and the Gendarmerie would sort it out, but by now Peregrine has probably gotten to all of them. I'm not trying to be a hero this time. But there's no one besides the six of us we can be sure aren't compromised. And there isn't anyone else who can build another set of devices, if it comes to that."

Will slid his hand up her wrist to gently touch the skin near one of the quarter-sized burns on her arm. "But look what they're doing to you."

"I know, I know," she said, choking on tears. "But if you're right about the power my grandfather has now, I don't think these burns will be anything compared to what he'll do to me."

The thought was too much for Will. "Oh, God—" he said, his voice breaking. He leaned forward until his forehead pressed against hers, and he put his hand on the back of her neck, only to find more sores and burns there.

"I don't want to lose you," she said. "Please. I can't go through with this knowing it will mean losing you. I need you now more than ever."

"I can't do this again, Josh. I can't handle it."

"Please, please. Just hang in there while we figure this out. We will, I swear, and then we'll go away. Anywhere you want, for as long as you want. I don't care if we miss senior year. We can go to Tahiti, or Ireland, or Greece."

"Therapy," he said, opening his eyes. "I want to go to therapy with you."

"We can do that," she promised. "We can go to therapy every day if you want."

He was hanging all his hopes on the possibility that they would survive this, and that if they did, whatever new wounds they had acquired would be healable. And he knew those odds were slim, that he should get up and walk away with what he had left of his sanity, but her words kept echoing through his mind: *I need you now more than ever.*

"Okay," he said.

Twenty-four

Gravity, Mirren thought. *It's pulling every-thing together.*

What were the chances that she would read a piece of her scroll that spoke of leading the True Dream Walker into Death, then stumble upon the ritual to do so, and finally discover that she had been walking side by side with the True Dream Walker all along?

These things could not have happened by chance. In all of it, she saw the hand of gravity, drawing her and Peregrine toward their final confrontation, drawing her scroll toward fruition, even drawing Will toward his obsession. She felt herself being pulled along. But she reminded herself, as she followed a weary flashlight beam deep into Iph National Forest, that astronomical odds could only be made more remote by adding one more unlikely scenario to the equation: reason to use the ritual.

This has to be what we're meant to do, Mirren assured herself again. *For all of these circumstances to have come together . . . how could gravity not be leading us to this conclusion?*

Josh had proposed alternatives. They could bomb the Dashiel Winters Building and hope the blast both killed Peregrine and destroyed the DNA database. Of course, they would kill scores of innocents in the process. They could change their names, dye their hair, and begin new lives somewhere else, but that saved only the six of them, leaving the rest of the World in Peregrine's bloody hands. They could, theoretically, wait until Peregrine surfaced, then stalk and kill him. This was the only practical plan they had. But Peregrine might not surface for weeks or even months, during which time he would be free to stage nightmares for anyone he liked.

So they were going to break into Death, find Feodor, and pray that he could provide a solution. And was willing to tell them what it was.

"This is far enough," Josh said, and the bobbing flashlights formed a rough circle as the six teenagers came together in a small clearing. "Will, you and Whim mark the doorway. Deloise, can you hold flashlights for them? Mirren and Haley, start setting up the singing bowls."

From weighty duffel bags, Mirren and Haley unloaded eleven hand-hammered brass bowls. Each sang a different note when a wooden mallet was run around the lip of the bowls. The instructions for the ritual scientifically specified which notes the bowls should produce, and because a number of frequencies weren't part of the Western world's musical scale, Josh and Haley had meticulously hammered the bowls' bellies until they produced the desired, off-key notes.

Will marked out a rough doorway on the ground in salt, and then he dug a firebreak around it with a trowel while Whim filled the doorway with an even layer of gunpowder. Deloise placed extinguishers on each side of the doorway.

She and Whim were staying behind. They had decided this during what should have been a brief, logic-based discussion of who was needed on the trip and had instead turned into an emotionally draining scene complete with tears and threats. Mirren and Josh were going without question. Josh wanted Will to come because she didn't feel she could trust her own judgment; Mirren didn't know how much help Will would be when he couldn't stop trembling. Deloise broke down at the thought of Josh going, claiming that Josh had sworn never to do anything dangerous again after her first encounter with Feodor, and Will backed her up. Mirren still didn't trust Whim and didn't want him to come along, to which Whim had taken offense. He'd finally relented but made the mistake of trying to comfort Deloise, who threw a cup of fruit punch in his face when he put his arm around her.

In the end, Josh, Will, and Haley had agreed to go with Mirren.

Whim and Deloise were staying behind to make sure they didn't burn down the forest.

"What time is it?" Josh asked, wiping her hands on her jeans.

"Seven to midnight," Whim said.

Will pulled on a backpack he'd loaded with protein bars, water, and weapons. The ritual provided almost no information on what they'd encounter once they reached Death, only a few warnings.

"Remember," Mirren said, "don't eat or drink anything except what comes from Will's pack. Don't accept any gifts. Don't take off your shoes. And *don't* tell anyone your name."

Haley nodded. Mirren wasn't sure why he was putting on a violet-and-yellow cardigan, since the temperature hovered in the mid-eighties, but she still thought his sweaters were as much sources of comfort as of warmth.

"What do we do after you go?" Whim asked.

Josh glanced at Mirren, who shrugged. "Wait," Josh said.

"What if you don't come back?" Deloise asked, her voice still gritty from crying.

Josh bent over to check that her knife was secured in its shin strap, but Mirren thought she did it just to avoid meeting her little sister's eyes. "Keep waiting," Mirren told Deloise.

Mirren didn't doubt that Josh understood the danger of what they were about to do. Mythology was full of stories about heroes who descended to the underworld and never resurfaced. *Beware the tricks of the dead,* read the last line of the ritual. Will understood—he couldn't stop understanding long enough to pull himself together. And Haley was a born seer, who accepted the danger and the inevitability of these risks with his usual grace and gravitas.

The real reason Mirren hadn't wanted Whim to come along was that she wasn't sure he understood the danger. He was having too much fun.

"Let's get started," Josh said.

Ritual in hand, Mirren took her place at the bottom of the doorway. Gently, she struck the wooden mallet against the rim of the smallest singing bowl, and while it was still ringing out a clear, high A, she began running the mallet around the lip of the bowl. The note continued, coalescing into a golden ribbon of sound, bright and strong.

Three breaths, Mirren thought, counting as she inhaled and exhaled. After the third release of breath, she nodded to Deloise, who struck another singing bowl, this one an F just lower than the A, and added its voice. Every three breaths, another note joined the chorus, a D, then a G, then a slightly off-key B. Not only did the volume increase, but Mirren felt the vibration of the instruments moving through her body, creating a stir like currents in water. The sensation was not unpleasant, yet it raised an alarm in her, a primordial warning that she was playing with powerful forces.

Another F, a C, a note between D and E-flat. Each successive singing bowl was larger, its voice lower and deeper. When Josh struck the ninth note, the birds roosting in the trees around them took flight. When Will played the tenth note, the ground began to shake. Mirren struggled to keep her mallet in contact with her singing bowl. Almost reluctantly, afraid of what would happen, she nodded to Haley, who struck the last note from a bowl the size of a kitchen sink. It bellowed with the voice of an ancient leviathan, and Mirren felt her bones shake within her.

It's too much, she thought. *We have to stop—*

A sonic boom burst through the clearing. Mirren dropped her mallets and clapped her hands over her ears, and she saw everyone else do the same as a shock wave centered on the doorway sent them all tumbling onto their backs. The gunpowder—which they had assumed they would have to light—exploded into three-foot-high flames.

Holy shit, Mirren saw Josh mouth, but she didn't hear the words because her ears were stuffy and blocked.

What do we do? Deloise asked silently.

I can't hear you, Whim told her.

Josh helped Will up. *Come on!* she mouthed.

Even the orange flames couldn't give Will's face any color. He let Josh take his hand, but he backed away from the burning doorway as she pulled him toward it.

Mirren clutched Haley with one hand and Josh with another, and they descended on the doorway. Will was shaking his head and trying to wrench his hand out of Josh's, and Haley was the one who grabbed him, not by the hand but by the belt, and dragged him forward.

The flames in the doorway vanished as suddenly as they had appeared. Where the earth beneath them had been, now a black hole stretched into the ground. Whim shone a flashlight into it, but the space devoured the light, revealing nothing.

"Ready?" Josh cried, and Mirren could just make her voice out, a buoy of sound in an ocean of white noise. "On three!"

Haley and Mirren counted with her. "One, two—"

Will shook his head desperately. "We can't!"

"Three!"

They jumped, pulling Will with them. Mirren felt herself stretched and compressed at the same time, much as she imagined going through a black hole would feel, a crushing sensation that she escaped only through the distortion of her physical form, and finally a *pop* that restored her to herself.

And then blackness, and the sound of lapping waves.

She didn't know how long she might have been sitting in the boat before she came back to herself. Perhaps the shock of passage had disoriented her. When she became aware of what was going on again, she found that her companions were in a similar state.

She was sitting on a bench in a wooden rowboat beside Josh. Haley and Will sat on a second bench, facing them. At the boat's stern, an old man in gray robes stood beneath a lantern suspended on a hook. He pushed the boat with a long wooden pole.

"Fair," he said to them.

Mirren blinked at him.

"You're fair," the old man said, but he sounded irritated.

"Uh," Josh said.

"The *fare*," Will told her. His lips were drawn tight and pale with anger, and only when he pulled off his backpack and began digging in one of the pockets did Mirren gather his meaning.

"He wants the boat fare," Mirren said. "For the passage."

"Oh." They all dug into their pockets and offered what they could find. The boat driver chose two nickels from Will's hand, a dime from Josh's, and Haley's quarter, and the forty-five cents must have satisfied him, because he planted his pole in the water and pushed the boat forward.

"Where are we?" Josh whispered, leaning forward. "This doesn't seem right."

"What, Feodor's education didn't include Greek mythology?" Will muttered. "We're on the river Styx."

Josh straightened up and looked around as if surprised—whether by the information or Will's tone, Mirren couldn't say.

Haley had his eyes pinched shut. Mirren took his ice-cold hand. "Are you all right?" she asked.

He opened his eyes and gave her a weak smile. "It's so quiet here."

It *was* quiet. The old man's pole hardly caused a ripple in the water, and not a breath of wind stirred the air. Mirren couldn't even tell where they were—everything beyond the water stretched into blackness, and they might have been crossing a starless ocean or traveling an underground tunnel.

"Excuse me, sir," Josh said to the old man. "Where are we going?"

The old man frowned at her. "Boat only goes one place," he mumbled.

They fell into silence. The darkness and the quiet seemed to encourage it, and Mirren listened to the lapping of the water against the boat, a sound as soft as kisses. She held Haley's hand until she felt his skin warm.

"Is that a light?" Josh asked. "Up ahead."

Mirren squinted into the abyss until she, too, could see a light, and as they drew closer the light expanded and took on a golden tone. Soon she made out a large templelike building set on a shore of yellow sand. The temple was round with a domed roof, surrounded by a circle of pillars. Though vaguely Greek, the dome was set with clear skylights, and colored stones created geometric patterns on the pillars.

The old man guided their boat up to the dock and tied it.

"Where are we?" Josh asked him.

"End of line," was all he said.

"You're telling me," Will muttered.

They climbed off the boat onto a dock made of white stone. The dock led directly into the temple, and sharp rocks covered the beach below. A wall on either side of the temple blocked Mirren's view of the rest of the land, but the intent was clear: anyone who arrived by boat would have to pass through the temple.

"Remember," Josh said as they walked up the dock, "don't eat anything, don't drink anything, accept—"

"Accept any gifts, walk barefoot, or tell our names," Will said. "We remember."

Josh shut her eyes briefly, as if to hold herself back, but she kept walking.

Mirren took Haley's hand again. He squeezed her fingers absently, staring down the coastline. The sand beyond the rocks wasn't just yellow, Mirren noticed as she followed his gaze. It shone, like gold.

They entered the temple through an empty double doorway. Inside, white marble reflected the sunlight that came in from skylights high above and bathed the chamber in warm light—or so Mirren thought initially. When her eyes adjusted, she realized that the yellow glow came not from the sun, but from three figures seated on heavy marble thrones.

"The living!" one of them cried in a voice that came from everywhere at once. "Who has brought the living among us?"

The figures were indistinct, three golden human forms swallowed up by their own luminescence. Mirren could make out the shadows of their eyes and mouths, but nothing else, no ears, no hair, no evidence of their sex. Their voices carried no gender markers, only an echo that clouded any accent they might have had. Mirren had heard them called many things: gods, judges, demons; now that she saw them for herself, the title that came to mind was the lords of Death.

"We came on our own," Josh said to the figures. Two of them rose from their thrones and walked toward their visitors, revealing astonishing height. As they came closer, Mirren found their luster painful to behold.

"Name yourself," commanded the figure that had remained seated, "you who have broken into Death."

"We aren't going to tell you our names," Josh said, and Mirren felt a flutter of panic inside, like the birds that had rushed from the trees.

She touched Josh's shoulder while stepping out in front of her friends. "Please forgive us," she said, and then stumbled for an instant while trying to decide what term of address would be appropriate. "Your Highnesses," she added, choosing the first nongendered term that came to mind. "We are four weary travelers who have come to beg your mercy. Our names are not fit for such glory as yours."

Then she curtsied. With her head down, she was able to glance behind her and see the others follow suit with awkward bows—even Josh.

Rising, she discovered that one of the figures was standing so close that she could feel its heat on her skin. She had to close her eyes as it brushed a hand along the side of her face, touching her hair.

"Nonsense," it said. "What are your names?"

"Begging your pardon," Mirren said, "we cannot say."

Now the other figure, which had been examining Haley with some interest, turned toward Mirren, and she felt its touch follow her spine from the back of her neck to the top of her hips, as if its radiant fingers could pass through her clothes.

"All beings have names," it whispered in a voice lower than that of the others. "Give us yours."

"I cann—"

"*Tell us!!!*" the figure bellowed, and it must have had breath, because it blew strands of hair across Mirren's face as she hid behind clamped eyelids.

In the quiet afterward, Josh said, "No." Her voice was calm but firm.

"Very well," the seated figure said, and Mirren felt the two beside her move away.

When she opened her eyes again, all three figures had returned to their thrones. Between Mirren and Josh, they had refused to give their names four times; maybe the lords of Death were allowed to ask only a certain number of times. The center figure, in a voice that betrayed none of its companion's rage, asked simply, "Why have you come, travelers?"

Mirren took a deep breath to steady herself before answering. "We have come to speak with a soul that resides here."

"And what is this soul's name?"

"Feodorik Kajażkołski."

The figure made a sound Mirren couldn't have reproduced or interpreted. "The *inumen*," it said. "Why do you wish to speak with him?"

She didn't know the term "*inumen*," but she could afford only an instant to wonder if it was part of the secret language of the dead.

Briefly, Mirren explained that someone in the World was going to use two devices Feodor had invented to upset the balance between the universes and that they needed to ask Feodor how to destroy the devices.

"The balance between the universes must be maintained," the figure on the right said, and the figure on the left—the one that had shouted at Mirren—abruptly rose and left the temple through an empty side door.

"You may wait," the center figure said. "We will bring the *inumen*."

"Thank you," Mirren said.

The figure that had walked outside walked back in just as abruptly, and Feodor Kajażkołski walked beside him. He arrived so quickly that Mirren found herself completely unprepared to face him.

She had seen him only in photographs, and she realized now that he photographed very poorly. Whereas his pictures always showed a simple man, someone who could be anyone, in person the intensity of his gaze and promising hint of a smile made him not just charismatic but hypnotic. He wore a white button-down shirt and gray slacks with a black belt and black shoes that looked somehow old-fashioned. He appeared perhaps twenty-eight; the edges of his thin lips still made a crisp line against his face, and a keen light burned in his gray eyes. Despite not being very tall, he filled the room.

Mirren heard Will's breathing speed up, and she saw Josh grab his hand. Josh didn't look too good herself.

"American children!" Feodor cried, a smile lighting up his face. "What a wonderful surprise! Always, you find me in the unlikeliest of places!"

Although he spoke with a Polish accent that softened the ends of his words, his tone was still somehow mocking.

"And you have brought me another friend," he added. "Please, an introduction."

"No," Josh said sharply, and this time Mirren didn't interrupt her. She'd thought that giving her name to the lords of Death would be bad; she sensed that telling Feodor would be far worse.

"Her name doesn't matter," Josh continued. "She's a friend of ours."

Feodor walked toward Mirren, a smile playing across his lips. "Perhaps you are correct." He tilted his head. "And yet, how familiar you look. . . ."

He can't recognize me, Mirren assured herself. She knew she resembled her grandmother, whom Feodor had known, but not to the degree that people could guess who she was. *He's just toying with us.*

"That red hair," he mused.

From the corner of her eye, Mirren saw Josh yank the knife from her shin sheath, but Feodor made no attempt to attack, only laughed.

"Get away from her," Haley said, stepping in front of Mirren.

"Oh," Feodor said. "Kapuścisko is in love!"

He pinched one of Haley's cheeks, then stepped away before Josh could attack him.

This is crazy, Mirren thought. Feodor had been in the room for only thirty seconds and he was already pulling their strings.

"Will, no!" Josh yelled as Will pulled a pistol from his backpack. Josh lunged toward him, but not in time to stop him from firing madly at Feodor.

The shots echoed in the cavernous temple, making it impossible for Mirren to count them. She and Haley grabbed each other at the same time, both of them trying to push the other out of harm's way, and they landed hard together on the floor. As Josh knocked him over, Will screamed and fired two or three more rounds, but when the noise of the gunshots and fracturing marble died down, the only sound left was Feodor laughing.

"The dead cannot be killed," he pointed out as Josh wrestled the gun from Will's hands. He held up his arm, which Will had shot a hole clear through, and Mirren watched the flesh close back up. Even the shirt healed.

"What is the meaning of this?" the golden figure on the left demanded, rising from its throne. "You have deceived us!"

"No," Mirren said, scrambling to her feet. "No, Your Highness. Please forgive my friend. He has been wronged by the *inumen.*"

Feodor shrugged indulgently. "My queen speaks the truth. I forgive the boy."

He does *recognize me!* Mirren thought, and she felt cold inside and out.

Josh unloaded the gun, jammed it in her waistband, and pointed to one wall. "Go and sit," she ordered Will, and he reluctantly obeyed.

"Very well," the center figure said. "Ask your questions."

Josh, keeping one eye on Will, walked just close enough to Feodor to speak to him. "Peregrine Borgenicht has gotten hold of two devices you invented, a circlet and vambrace set that can control the Dream. We need to know how to destroy them."

Feodor tilted his head again. "I never built such devices."

"But you wrote the plans to build them."

"My plans were destroyed."

Mirren waited, uncertain as to how Josh would handle him or even if he could be handled.

"One copy wasn't destroyed. That's what Peregrine used."

Feodor studied her and then slowly shook his head. "Tell me the truth, and I will tell you how to destroy the devices."

Josh ran a frustrated hand through her hair. "All right. You recognized us—that must mean you remember what you did to me."

"Yes." If Feodor felt any guilt, it didn't show.

"When you sent your memories into my mind, you didn't just send the negative ones. You sent *all* of them, and since you died, your memories have been coming back to me. I remembered your plans for the devices, and I built them, and Peregrine stole them from me."

For the first time, Feodor appeared serious. "How unexpected," he said, and crossed his arms over his chest. "You remember *everything*? All my experiences, all my thoughts?"

"Not all of them. They're coming back to me slowly."

Feodor spoke to her in a language Mirren assumed was Polish, and Josh's face fell. *"Nie pamiętam,"* she said.

"Ciekawe," Feodor replied, and he wandered slowly away from them, thinking.

"This isn't good," Josh told Mirren.

Mirren agreed, but she waited without speaking until Feodor wandered back in their direction. "What do you think Peregrine will do with my devices?" he asked.

Josh explained their suspicions about the Karawar and the DNA database. "Clever," Feodor said. "How did you create an interface with the Dream?"

Josh told him about Bash and the towers and the risk of tearing the Veil. Feodor nodded and went back to wandering. He avoided going near Will, who sat against the wall with his arms crossed, glaring.

Finally Feodor spoke, but not to Josh or Mirren. Facing the three thrones, he said, "I ask that you forget my name and allow me to return to the World."

"No!" Will and Josh shouted at the same time. Will sprang to his feet.

Haley reached out and captured Mirren's hand. When she glanced at him, she saw something desperate in his face, not fear but dread.

"Your Highness," she began, but the center figure held up a hand as if to quiet her.

"Explain," it said to Feodor.

"Peregrine Borgenicht, the man who controls my devices," Feodor explained, "will use them to stage dreams and to wield power over the World. If he uses them long enough, they will destabilize the Dream on a large scale. These children will not stop him without my help."

"Then tell us what to do," Mirren said, "and we'll return and do it."

"The solution is not so simple. I must examine these towers the girl spoke of to know how to defeat him."

"No," Will said. "He's lying!"

"What assurance do you offer that you will return to Death?" the figure on the right asked.

Feodor smiled, just faintly, and Mirren feared the figures couldn't see it. "I will leave a hostage," he said.

"*What?!*" Josh asked. She actually outshouted Will. "No way! *Not* going to happen!"

Feodor shrugged innocently and said, "Then I wish you luck."

He began walking toward a side door.

"Wait," Haley said.

Feodor stopped walking and turned back to face them. Mirren's heart skipped a beat.

"I'll stay," Haley said.

Her knees dipped, and it was Haley who caught her and held her up.

"You can't," she whispered.

"You need him," Haley told her. "You won't defeat Peregrine without him."

"That's crazy," Will said, coming to stand at Haley's side. "We aren't leaving you here."

"No way," Josh repeated.

"You have to," Haley said. His face was calm, and Mirren couldn't understand why until she realized—

She gasped. "You *knew*! You knew that if we used the ritual, you would have to stay here. Oh, dear God, why didn't you tell me?"

He smiled sadly at her. "Because if I had, you might not have used it. And without Feodor, you don't have a chance of stopping Peregrine."

"This isn't happening," Will said. "J—don't let him do this."

"I'm not going to," Josh assured him. "It's not an option. We'll think of something else."

Mirren heard her, but she knew that Josh's protests were useless. She could see on Haley's face that he had already made up his mind, not just a moment ago or even a day ago, but long before that.

"I decided the night I met you," he told her.

Hot tears pooled in her eyes. "Will I ever see you again?" she asked.

He took off his cardigan and wrapped it around her shoulders. "I don't know," he admitted. "But I hope so."

"Kiss me."

He smiled and kissed her, and it was the kiss she had been waiting for since she'd met him. Knowing she might never get another made it all the more bittersweet, and when it was over she wiped the tears from his cheeks—his or hers, she didn't know.

"Stop," Josh said. "You can't do this."

"I love you," Mirren told Haley.

He smiled again. "I love you, too."

He kissed her again, briefly, before turning away. Will grabbed his arm, and Haley said to him gently, "You can't stop me. It's my choice."

"It's a crazy choice!" Josh said.

"It's still mine." He spoke to the lords of Death. "I will stay here as a hostage for Feodor."

"Very well," the center figure said.

"No!" Josh shouted. "No! We don't agree!"

"Take care of her," Haley told Josh.

Mirren saw Will grab at the gun in Josh's waistband, but she closed her eyes, knowing he was too late. They were all too late; they had been from the start.

"It is done," the figure said, and the air pressure in the temple changed.

Mirren was still crying when she opened her eyes and found herself sitting on a patch of charred earth.

Twenty-five

Chaos broke out in the forest.

"How could you let this happen?" Will shouted at Josh.

"*I* didn't!" she shouted back.

Josh could hardly believe her eyes—Feodor Kajażkołski, getting up from the forest floor and brushing the dirt from his gray pants, then tilting his head back to gaze at the starry sky above them.

"Where's Haley?" Whim asked. "Wait—is that—?"

"Who are you?" Deloise cried.

Feodor smiled at her, made a little bow, and then held out his hand.

"Feodor Kajażkołski," he said. "Delighted."

Deloise, who was too polite to do anything else, shook his hand, which caused Will to lunge forward while shouting, "Don't touch her!"

Deloise jerked her hand back as if from a hot teapot.

"Josh!" Will barked, as if there were something she was supposed to do.

Josh was at a loss. Feodor might steal Deloise's soul, but he wouldn't bite.

"What the hell is going on?" Whim asked. "Where's Haley?"

"He's gone," Mirren said, still sitting on the ground. The earth beneath her had been scorched by the door into Death, and soot covered her hands and skirt, but she didn't make any move to get up.

"Gone?" Whim repeated.

"Haley stayed behind," Josh said. "As a hostage. Until we return Feodor."

"They *kept* him?" Deloise asked.

"He said he wanted to stay—"

"You *let* him!" Will told her.

"I couldn't stop him!" Josh burst out, using a forceful voice as much to convince herself as Will. "You heard what he said—he knew he was going to have to stay! He decided weeks ago! I told the golden people or whatever not to let him. What else could I have done?"

"How are we going to get him back?" Deloise asked.

"He's not coming back," Mirren said in a soft, broken voice.

"He *is* coming back," Josh insisted. "He's just staying there as collateral to make sure we return Feodor when we're done with him."

"I thought you were just going to ask him what to do," Whim said.

Josh pushed her hands into her tangled hair. "Look, things didn't go as planned. Feodor said he needed to get back to the World to help us, and Haley offered to stay behind."

"How long can you leave Haley there?" Whim wanted to know. "Can he even survive there?"

"I don't know!" Josh shouted. "Stop yelling at me! I don't know! I'm doing the goddamn best I can!"

That shut everybody up. Will retreated to a fallen tree, and Josh was horrified to see tears on his cheeks. Deloise was crying, too. Will motioned her to sit on the tree beside him, and he wrapped his arm around her. Mirren, Haley's cardigan wrapped tightly around her, remained on the ground, rocking slowly back and forth.

"It seems I have arrived at an awkward moment," Feodor said.

Josh couldn't look at him. All her nightmares had come to life and were standing in front of her in the form of this small man, and he was giving her this polite little smile, this awkward, forgiving little smile.

When he'd walked into the temple, her first thought had been that she was so happy to see him. He'd been an old friend with whom she had waited years to reunite, and in that moment the years and miles between them had meant nothing, and just as she'd shifted her weight to run into his arms she'd remembered who she was and the impossible situation between them.

And now they'd lost Haley.

Josh pulled on fistfuls of her hair.

"Okay, okay," Whim said, seeing how she was yanking. "Stop before you end up bald. Come here."

He hugged her and she forced her hands to relax, but somehow neither Whim's bony chest nor his wiry arms were reassuring. The moon appeared from behind a cloud, bathing the clearing in an

artificial silver dawn, and Josh remembered how the morning after the fire at her mother's cabin had been the first in an endless
string of days without Ian. She feared this morning, feared it would
be the dawn of days without Haley, and she wondered how she
would tell his mother that Josh was responsible for the loss of both
of her sons.

"We'll get him back," Whim assured her.

"I'm sorry," was all Josh could say.

When Whim released her, she saw Deloise and Will helping
Mirren to her feet. Mirren had gotten soot on her face, which only
added to her shell-shocked appearance.

"I'm sorry," Josh told her.

Mirren blinked at her and then said, "Why? If I couldn't convince him to stay, you couldn't have."

Somehow, knowing she was right hurt.

Mirren picked up one of the singing bowls and then placed it
back in its suitcase, and her purposeful action seemed to wake
everyone else.

Even Feodor tried to help, which resulted in Whim snatching a
box of gunpowder out of his hands.

"No explosives for you," he said.

Feodor made a little smile. "Apologies, apologies. I only meant
to assist."

Whim leaned close and said, "You sucked my little sister's soul
out. She's lying in a hospital right now, wasting away, while her
soul rots in a canister. When all this is over, I'll be the one sending
you back to Death, and it won't be through any magic door in the
forest."

Rather than appearing offended or upset, Feodor gave an
acquiescing nod. "As you like."

He caught Josh's eye as they departed the clearing. Caught it,
and held it, and all she could think as she stared into his gray eyes
was, *He knows, he knows, he knows.*

What he knew, she couldn't have said, only that she felt he
knew a truth about her that she would never have chosen to re-

veal, not to Feodor, not to Will, not to anyone, and she heard his voice as if he had whispered in her ear, *We are the same, you and I.*

She remembered how gently he had held her in her dreams, how tenderly, how sweetly he had kissed her.

She remembered the smug smile he'd worn when Haley said he would stay.

How he could be both of those people, she didn't know.

Josh turned her whole head away to break eye contact. "Go," she told him, but when she forced her feet onto the forest path, she caught sight of Will.

She didn't know what he'd seen or how much he knew—that her heart was a traitor, that she was powerless against Feodor, that everything was already lost—but she said quickly, to cover her tracks, "Keep your eye on him."

Will nodded and said nothing.

Though Josh felt that the trip to Death had taken at least an hour, Whim said that less than a minute had passed in the World. "Del didn't even have time to freak out," he said.

When they arrived back at their campsite before one in the morning, no one was tired, least of all Feodor, who kept gazing around in much the same way Mirren often did. He looked at his hands often, too, as if their solidity surprised him.

Whim was hungry, so he built up the fire and cooked a big pot of franks and beans. Initially, he dished out only five bowls, but Deloise pointedly passed hers to Feodor and he got the message. Feodor ate the beans slowly, with a peculiar look on his face, and he pushed the franks to the side.

"Let's get started," Josh said when he was finished, but Deloise said, "You barely ate, Josh."

"I'm fine."

"Nope," Whim said, and dumped another ladle of franks and beans in her bowl. "Now you get twice as much."

Josh gave him a look, but she ate. She'd gone through a thing after her mother died where she more or less stopped eating, and no one in her family had ever forgotten it. Tonight, though, it wasn't sorrow but impatience that made her reluctant; there were so many more important things than food right now.

So she ate, stealing glances at Feodor as she did. She wanted to be alone with him, where she could sort out the situation without Will watching her every second. Or she wanted to be alone with Feodor so she could confess everything to someone who wouldn't judge her.

He tortured you, she reminded herself. *He's not an old friend.*

But he *was.* He was the voice in her head, her inspiration, her terror. She had changed, she was not the girl who had nervously walked across the front lawn the night of her birthday, and he was the only one who could understand. He would forgive her bad judgment and her lust for power because they had come *from him.*

"May I ask where we are?" Feodor asked. "And also the date?"

Josh told him, despite the look Will gave her. What did it matter if Feodor knew when and where they were?

He made no visible response to the information.

"Please describe in detail the devices you built," he said to Josh.

She thought it was a strange request, but she outlined the circlet and vambrace, the configuration of wires, the placement of various crystals and magnets. Afterward he asked her to explain the towers Bash had built, and she did so as best she could, given that Bash had lied to her about how they worked.

Strangely, Feodor then returned to questions about the devices, particularly the vambrace. "And the polarization of the cephalic magnets?"

"South."

"How did you diminish the current sufficiently to avoid burning the skin?"

"I didn't, not completely. But I mitigated it by—" Josh stopped. "Why are you asking me this?"

Feodor lifted one pale eyebrow. "You brought me to the World to assist you. I am doing my best to comprehend the situation."

"But you designed the vambrace. Why are you asking me how it works?"

He begged her indulgence with a smile. "You must forgive me. Perhaps my recent resurrection has confused my memory, but I do not believe I created the devices you have described."

Nonplussed, Josh said, "What?"

"Of course you did," Will told him.

"What do you mean?" Josh asked.

"The headpiece you describe resembles an invention of mine, I believe, although mine was intended to produce a different effect. The armpiece—or vambrace, did you call it?—I do not recognize at all."

"Oh God," Whim said. "They sent him back stupid."

"But I drew it in my sleep," Josh argued.

Feodor made a little shrug. "Then I believe it would be most properly considered *your* invention."

She had wondered, while explaining the devices to Bash, how channeling Feodor's ideas through her mind might change them. Now she knew.

Josh saw herself then as she imagined Will had since he'd found out about her nightmares—as a stranger, a foreigner, even a monster. All those times she had criticized Feodor for the horrors he had created with his intellect; had she done any better when it was her turn to use his intelligence? Was her craving for control any less dangerous than his?

"Holey moley!" Whim said. "Josh, you're a genius now!"

Will got up from the table and walked away.

Feodor only stared at her queerly, waiting.

Josh remembered what Feodor had asked her when they were still in Death, what he had said in Polish so that the others wouldn't hear.

Why didn't I build the devices?

I don't remember, she'd told him.

And he'd said, *How interesting.*

But she remembered now. He had designed only the circlet, and it had been meant not to control the Dream, but to protect the wearer from dreaming.

And he hadn't built it because he'd believed it would drive the wearer mad.

"Teraz sobie przypomniałam," she told him.

I remember now.

She was afraid to look at Will. Instead she looked down at her hands, which rested on her sketchbook, full of what she had believed were Feodor's ideas.

"What's going on?" Whim asked.

"So, if Josh designed the devices, can you still figure out how to destroy them?" Deloise asked.

Feodor brightened. "I believe so. I believe that if you built a second set of devices, replacing the southern magnet on the cephalic vein with a diamagnetic substance—perhaps antimony—and coating it with copper, you would, ah . . . *boost* the power of the devices to such a degree that Peregrine's devices would be no match for yours."

It could work, Josh thought. Using a diamagnetic substance had never occurred to her, but of course Feodor was exactly right.

"It might even diminish the current enough to keep my skin from burning," she said.

"Precisely! The devices, as you have designed them, will eventually break down the integrity of the subtle body, killing the operator, but this change will weaken the effect so that you will far outlast your enemy."

And the power would be immense. Josh wasn't even sure she'd have to think of something before it happened—the Dream would conform as fast as her impulses. Peregrine's brain wouldn't have time to register that she was there before she captured him, and then she would finally be able to bring peace to the Dream the way she'd dreamed of for so long—

"Hell no," Will said.

Josh blinked at him. "What?"

He was standing at the far end of the campsite, next to Josh's car, as if he had been on the verge of driving away and stopped only when he realized what they were planning behind his back.

"You want *more* power?" he asked. "All along, you've been obsessed with controlling the Dream. You built two devices that could basically brainwash everyone in the World, and now your answer to dismantling them is to give yourself *more* power?"

Josh swallowed. *Yes,* she thought. *I just need a little more.*

"If that's what she needs to beat Peregrine," Whim said, "then that's what she needs."

"It would just be for a little while," Deloise began, and Will cut her off.

"Would it? Would it *just be for a little while,* Josh?" He began walking toward her, breaking a s'more stick into smaller and smaller pieces as he approached. "Would you stop Peregrine and then take the devices off forever? Would you throw them in the fire? Would you dismantle the towers? Or would you tell yourself that you know what's best for everyone and march into the Dream to fix everything the way you've been obsessing about ever since you found out—"

"Will!" Deloise cried, and only then did Josh realize that he was so far gone, he would have blurted out her secret to Feodor.

Will stopped and shook himself. "Find another way," he said curtly, and went back to breaking up the s'more stick.

Josh looked down at the sketch pad beneath her hands. She'd always felt it was full of dirty secrets. "He's right," she said. "I have to stop."

She rubbed at her tired eyes, longing to rub at her soul the same way, to shrug off this moral confusion. Did she want to build Feodor's better weapon because she wanted to protect the Dream or control it?

It didn't matter. She couldn't trust herself, not after all she'd done.

Yes, you can, a little voice inside her whispered.

She hadn't heard that voice in a long, long time, maybe not since the moment she'd rescued herself, Will, and Haley from death in the Dream so many months before.

Of course you could put the devices down afterward, the voice told her. *You would be disappointed, but you'd do it. Will is just afraid because Will is always afraid.*

She glanced at him, where he stood throwing bits of stick into the fire.

Maybe the voice was right. Maybe she would be able to use the devices one last time to defeat her grandfather and then let them go. But she knew one thing for certain: she would lose Will if she did.

"Think of something else," she told Feodor.

His earlier glee had cooled into something akin to distrust. "The best solutions are simple," he said. "I have given you a simple solution."

"It doesn't matter," Josh told him. "Building a bigger gun isn't the answer."

"You desire a moral weapon to point at an amoral enemy," Feodor warned. "Peregrine Borgenicht is not a stranger to me. You will not defeat him with your conscience."

"It's my choice," Josh said.

Feodor shook his head slowly. Josh recognized the emotion hidden deep in his expression—he didn't just think she was making a mistake, he was actually angered by her moral qualms. Feodor didn't believe in the limitations of conscience.

That Josh did reassured her.

"You can either come up with a different plan, or we can hike back into the forest and end your vacation right now," she told him.

He sighed. Then he smiled irritably and said, "Tell me again about the towers."

As Josh talked, Will came back to the picnic table and sat beside her.

By dawn, they had agreed on a new plan. It was a terrible plan, and Josh knew it. She suspected Will knew it, too, and Feodor actually laughed at them when they agreed to it, but it was the second-best plan they had, so they took it.

Afterward, they got ready for bed. "Ah," Feodor said, and then asked Josh, *"Gdzie tu jest toaleta?"*

She thought about telling him to piss in the woods and then shrugged. "I'll take you."

Whim refused to let them go alone, so the three of them walked the half mile down the road to the latrines. Whim went inside with Feodor, and Josh went to wash her hands at a nearby spigot, but when she straightened, Feodor was standing in front of her.

"This will not work," he said plainly.

Josh wiped her wet hands on her jeans, said nothing.

"I know you have not told me everything. I understand that you do not trust me, and that your friends would like to kill me, but if you wish to survive this encounter, you must confide in me."

The plan was not quite as bad as Feodor believed, but only because he didn't know that Josh was the True Dream Walker. And that was the last thing she would ever tell him.

She started to walk past him, but he touched her arm. He didn't grab her, he merely laid the cold tips of his fingers on her wrist.

"You said you have my memories. You must know something of who I am. I will stand beside you against Peregrine."

She didn't remember how Feodor knew Peregrine, if they had known each other. She did remember that he used to touch her like this in her nightmares, so lightly, such fleeting promises to draw her closer.

Right before he tore her to pieces.

Josh smiled at the sight of his skin against hers.

"I know exactly who you are," she told him, and she walked away.

After they had tied Feodor up and locked him in the trunk of Josh's car, and everyone else had gone to bed, Will found Josh sitting on the cooler beside the cooling fire.

He sat down beside her and took her hand.

"Promise me," she said, "that when this is all over, you'll still love me."

He kissed the side of her face, but she wouldn't look at him.

"I'll always love you," he said.

But she knew it wasn't true.

Twenty-six

Because they didn't know what they might encounter at the Weaver-Avish-Mckarr house—brainwashed parents, surveillance cameras, a torch-bearing mob—they decided to enter the Dream through the archway in the basement of Josh's mother's cabin.

Will hadn't been to the cabin since before their first encounter with Feodor; he didn't think any of them had. As they walked down the gravel drive toward the charred mess of rubble, Whim suddenly said, "Oh, my God! Is today the day?"

"No," Josh said tightly. "It's still two days away."

Will knew what she meant, but Mirren asked. "What's two days away?"

"One year since the cabin burned," Josh said.

"And Ian died," Deloise added, shooting Feodor an ugly look.

Will didn't think Feodor noticed. For the first time since his resurrection, he seemed confused, alarmed even. As they reached the remains of the cabin, he asked, "Where are we?"

"Just outside of Charle," Josh told him absently, her eyes searching for a way through the rubble.

But Will saw Feodor's face stiffen, not so much with anger as . . . fear?

"Whose home was this?" he all but whispered.

"What does it matter?" Whim asked, at the same time Josh said, "It was my mother's."

Will took a couple of steps toward them, uncomfortable with the direction of the conversation.

"You are Dustine Borgenicht's granddaughter," Feodor said. "I had forgotten."

He and Josh gazed at each other in a way that unnerved Will. Bad enough that they could communicate privately in Polish; could they read each other's thoughts now?

"Josh," Will said, but he had to shake her shoulder before she could look at him.

"What?" she asked.

"The plan?" Whim said. "Remember? Stopping your grandfather?"

"Right." This time she shook herself. "Right. Uh, I think we can use that beam to make a bridge to the basement stairs."

Ten minutes later, they were all jammed into one clear area on the basement floor. Will helped Whim push partially burned wood and the remnants of furniture and the scorched water heater out of the way while Josh located the archway to the Dream. Because this archway—which Josh's mother had died creating—had never been properly finished, no arch framed its edges and any bits of looking stone it had produced had long ago been swept away.

"Let's do a final equipment check," Josh said. They each had a roll of duct tape and a fanny pack stuffed with electronic signal transmitters.

Josh and Feodor had spent the day before building the transmitters. About the size of a sandwich cookie, each would emit a radio transmission when Josh pushed a separate activator. The idea was too far rooted in dream theory for Will to understand; all he knew was that once they had attached a transmitter to each tower—or as many as they could find—Josh would activate them and the entire network of towers would stop working without tearing the Veil. It had to do with signals—or waves, maybe?—and Dream particles and ionization.

Their first major hurdle turned out to have solved itself. When Josh shone reflected light onto the archway hanging in midair, the basketball court they had been so worried about locating appeared in front of them. But instead of the dozen basketball players who had been present when Josh first placed the towers, now several hundred people were crammed onto the court.

"This isn't right," Josh said. "This nightmare formed an hour and a half's drive from here."

"Maybe it shifted closer," Deloise said.

"If it had shifted," Josh pointed out, "it wouldn't still exist at all. Somehow the towers are preventing this part of the Dream from changing."

Feodor stepped closer to the archway. "I wonder if perhaps we are observing Kristiking's dreamspace."

"Which is what?" Will asked.

"Kristiking theorized that because the Dream does not occupy physical space, it is possible that all nightmares share space-time dimensions and occur simultaneously—"

"And I'm out," Whim declared. "Josh, give it to me straight."

"It means," Josh said, "that since the towers are preventing this part of the Dream from shifting, everyone who should be having their own nightmares in this area is having a big shared nightmare on the basketball court. It's not a good thing, but in this case it works in our favor, since we don't have to wander around in the Dream looking for the spot where Bash and I placed the towers."

"See how much simpler that was?" Whim asked Feodor.

Feodor eyed him dryly. "Kristiking would not think so."

Something was different about Feodor. Will had noticed it in the temple, and he noticed it again now. Although the man seemed just as dangerous as the first time they'd met, he struck Will as slightly less outright crazy. The manic glee in his eyes had dimmed, and . . . he was almost more attentive to the people around him, more aware of them as real people.

One by one, they jumped through the Veil; Will knew they each went for their own reasons. Deloise, because she wouldn't abandon her sister; Whim, because he wanted to kill Feodor at the earliest opportunity; Feodor, because this was the only way to extend his vacation; Mirren, because she was determined to save Haley; Josh, because this was her mess to clean; and Will, because he needed this to end. He needed all of it to end.

He just couldn't let Josh build even more powerful devices. The cycle would never end. More powerful devices would create more powerful enemies, which would require more powerful weapons, and so on, and so on. . . . No one solved problems by escalating the behavior that had created them. At least, not in psychology.

They landed in the center of the basketball court, where at least a hundred nightmares were occurring simultaneously. The court was jammed with people like right after a big tournament, and many of them were shouting at one another, some were tussling on the ground, one group was building a human pyramid.

"Try to stay together!" Josh called over the din. She led them along the edge of the court until they reached a corner, where she crouched down beside what appeared to be an aerosol can on the ground. "This is one of the towers."

"That?" Whim asked. "When you said towers, I thought you meant *towers,* not a can of hair spray."

"We called them towers because they work like cell phone towers," Josh told him. "Watch."

She pulled a transmitter out of her fanny pack and duct-taped it to the side of the tower. "Done."

"That's it?" Deloise asked.

"That's it."

Although Feodor claimed their plan was a terrible one, Will actually thought it was sort of clever. Once they had a dozen or so of the towers fitted with them, Josh would press that activator and send a signal that would deactivate not only the towers that were fitted with transmitters, but all of the towers.

Assuming, of course, that Peregrine and Bash hadn't increased the grid to include forty or more towers, in which case the signal would be too weak to destroy them all. And assuming Peregrine wasn't wearing the devices and didn't catch them installing the transmitters.

Will had been gung ho about the plan when they were back at the campsite. Now that they were in the Dream, he felt less certain. Especially because Josh knew the location of only the four towers that marked the corners of the basketball court, and the number of people around would make it difficult to find small cans.

As they crossed the basketball court, they discovered that the frozen area of the Dream extended into a formal garden. They began searching for more towers hidden beneath the ornamental shrubs and within flower beds. Unfortunately, the garden was as densely populated as the basketball court had been, and they struggled just to stay within sight of one another.

"I found one!" Deloise cried triumphantly.

We've been wandering around for at least twenty minutes, Will thought, *and we've only found five towers, and four of them were the ones Josh placed.*

Slowly, they made their way through the crowds. Will got jostled, elbowed, and even shoved, and more people stepped on his feet than he could count. The nightmares around him seemed to share a theme: interpersonal conflict. With the Dream unable to shift to accommodate the specifics of nightmares, everyone was just dreaming that they were in a mob full of strangers they didn't like.

Will estimated they'd been in the Dream for an hour by the time they found a sixth tower. Over the commotion of the dreamers, Josh called everyone to her. They huddled beside a fountain with a statue of an angry old man vomiting water into the pool.

"This isn't working," Josh said.

"Maybe we should split up," Deloise suggested. "We could cover more ground if we weren't trying to stay together."

"I'll stay with Feodor," Whim offered.

Will didn't like the idea of splitting up. He wanted to be able to keep an eye on everyone, to warn them if Bash or Peregrine showed up.

But it was already too late for that.

The first thing that caught his attention was the quieting of the mob. Rising on his toes, he saw that an entire section of the garden had not only fallen quiet, but gone motionless. The silence and stillness were moving toward him with the speed of an ocean wave, and he had just opened his mouth to warn the others when Josh screamed, "Abort!"

By then, the inertia was already overcoming them. Will watched in slow motion as Josh thrust her hand out, her movement growing slower the farther out she reached, and he waited for the archway to burst forth from her palm, and waited . . . and waited . . .

He felt himself still. He didn't so much go numb as terribly heavy, so heavy that he could no longer move, not even to breathe, and it was only by chance that his field of vision at that moment included Bash standing by the gazing pool.

"Look who I found," he said.

And then Will knew that this had been a very poor plan indeed.

Twenty-seven

Bash looked crazy.

From where Josh stood frozen, her arm thrust uselessly forward, she could see Bash almost directly ahead of her. He stood with his hands on his hips, wearing a button-down and khakis so wrinkled that he must have slept in them. He'd torn one sleeve off to make room for the vambrace, and above the circlet his black hair stuck up in greasy clumps.

What worried Josh most, though, was the crazy look in his eyes. They were bloodshot and overly wide, and they moved constantly, as if they were bouncing around in his head. Against Bash's pallor, his wet, red lips were parted as if with wonder.

Josh recalled Feodor saying that the devices would eventually kill the wearer. From the look of him, Bash had been wearing those devices since the moment he'd stolen them almost a week before.

"Josh," he said with a little giggle, and he stepped closer. He sniffed, then wiped his nose with the back of his hand, and Josh saw red smears on his skin. Now that he was only two feet away, she noticed blood crusted around the edges of the vambrace. "Wow, you brought the whole gang."

No one answered. They were all as frozen as Josh was, Will with his mouth half-open, Whim scratching the back of his neck, Deloise's mouth a perfect O.

Bash walked over to Whim and raised his fists. "She never loved you, you tool." He took a few quick steps on the balls of his feet before jabbing Whim in the face. Whim didn't move, didn't even rock back like a dummy would have. Bash might as well have been punching a marble statue.

"Ow!" he cried, and rubbed his knuckles. "Stupid, stupid."

As he flexed his fingers, he caught sight of Feodor, who had flung his arm protectively in front of Mirren. "Who is this?" Bash pondered. "A friend, or just a dreamer who wandered by? Tell me your name."

"Feodor Kajażkołski," Feodor said, only his mouth moving.

"What?" Bash cried. He released a hysterical laugh, high-pitched and wavering. "He's dead. Tell me your real name."

"Feodorik Jambulira Bronisławorin Kajażkołskiosci," Feodor repeated.

Bash stepped closer. "You do look just like him." He giggled, blinking his bloodshot eyes. "I guess I'll take you to Peregrine and let him sort it out."

Then he lifted his metal-clad arm and wafted his fingers through the air. An archway appeared a few feet before him, complete with a gray brick frame. Josh felt herself rise from the ground and shoot through the archway. As soon as she passed through the

Veil, her paralysis lifted, and she stumbled out of midair and into . . .

A very fancy living room.

Bash deposited the rest of her party around her, and their feet had hardly touched the marble floor before he was walking out of the room.

"Welcome home, Princess," he called over his shoulder with another quivering giggle.

"Where is my family?" Mirren asked.

He didn't answer, and as soon as he was out of sight, Josh turned to Mirren. "Where are we?"

Mirren swallowed. "This is the formal living room in my house."

"Why would he bring us to the Hidden Kingdom?" Josh asked.

"I don't know. He shouldn't even know this universe exists."

Before Josh could ask another question, Will grabbed her shoulder and spun her to face him. "Why didn't you open an archway?" he demanded.

She couldn't believe he was asking her such a stupid question, and her palms grew hot with anger. Shoving his hand off of her, she said, "Because I was frozen just like you were! This is why I told you this plan sucked. I warned you that this exact thing could happen!"

"We were all immobilized," Feodor pointed out. "She could not have opened an archway."

His head was tilted as if in confusion, which reminded Josh that he didn't know she was the True Dream Walker.

We aren't going to be able to hide that from him if we want to get out of here, she thought.

She dismissed the thought. What did it matter if Feodor knew her secret? Hopefully he'd be dead again in a couple of days. Assuming they could get out of here.

Even so, she waited until Feodor turned away to peer out the window before extending her arm and trying to open another archway. A handful of Veil dust glimmered in the air, then vanished.

"Bash must be stopping you," Mirren said quietly. "Maybe we can reach the archway to the World. It's in the stables."

"We should move now, before Bash comes back," Josh said. "Which way, Mirren?"

"Left at the door."

But the living room door was as far as they got. Josh tried to walk through and cracked her face so hard on an invisible barrier that she was knocked back. If Whim hadn't grabbed her shoulder, she would have fallen to the floor.

"Easy now," he said.

"There's something there," Josh told him.

They took turns banging on the invisible obstruction in the doorway. Their blows didn't even make a sound.

"Try another archway," Will said.

With no choice but to ignore Feodor's presence, Josh threw another archway. This time a shimmer like sunlit mist burst from her palm, but it faded away almost instantly.

"I am unclea—" Feodor began to say, but he was interrupted by Bayla's appearance at the doorway.

"That won't work," she said, and she giggled.

Bayla looked as bad as Bash, and all the worse because she normally appeared so put-together. Her designer jeans were stained with grease and soot, and she wore a dress on top of them, a color-block day dress that she'd zipped up only partway. Papery skin revealed bulging veins crisscrossing her face, and all her fingernails had turned purple. Her former beauty was almost unfathomable now.

"What happened to you?" Deloise asked, as though her shock had overcome her animosity.

"This is Peregrine's castle now," Bayla said. "He's going to make me a princess!"

Then she tried to do a little spin, but she lost her balance and careened into the hallway wall.

"What's wrong with her?" Mirren asked.

"I'm the star of the play!" Bayla told them. "I play Princess Mirren."

"She was fine last week," Whim said, swallowing.

"We traded, but not anymore. No more trades," Bayla said, frowning at him.

"Trades?" Whim sounded baffled.

"Secrets," she said, swaying from side to side like a little kid who couldn't stay still. "Secrets for kisses."

She made a loud smacking sound as she kissed the air.

"You were just using me to find out about Mirren?" Whim demanded. "You were spying on us for Peregrine?"

Bayla smiled as though he'd complimented her. "He wanted to know about Josh. But then I told him about Mirren and he got all . . . *excited*." She shivered at the word.

Josh cringed. Her grandfather had always wanted to know for certain that Josh was the True Dream Walker. He must have sent Bayla to seduce Whim, knowing that Whim was close to Josh and incapable of keeping a secret. But instead of dishing about Josh—or perhaps *in addition* to dishing about Josh—Whim had told Bayla everything about Mirren.

"But why are you helping Peregrine?" Whim asked. "It doesn't make sense!"

Bayla shrugged. "I had a dream. . . ." She picked at a scab on her arm. "I had so many dreams. . . ."

Will laughed queerly. "He staged nightmares for her."

"Who? Peregrine?" Deloise asked.

"Yes. He staged nightmares until he had control of her, and then he told her to seduce Whim and get him to talk about Josh."

Bayla stage-whispered, "He's my real father!"

"Your father!" Whim burst out. "He's not your father! I've met your father! He yelled at me for forty-five minutes once! You know who your father is, Bayla!"

"Shh," Deloise said, putting her hand on Whim's arm. "Calm down. She's not rational right now."

Deloise coaxed him to sit down on one of the white brocade

couches. He was trembling, and his face and neck had flushed the way they did when he was really upset. Josh could count on one hand the number of times she'd seen him flush like that.

"She was fine a week ago," he repeated.

"Staging would have allowed Peregrine to control her," Feodor said, "but it would not have led to this level of mental confusion. Obviously she has been wearing the devices."

Josh had already guessed as much. The burns down Bayla's forearm, the wounds that resembled leech bites, the black-and-red skin at her temples—they had all been inflicted by the devices. Josh touched one of her own burns in recognition.

"It's my turn next," Bayla said proudly. "After Bash."

"Those things are going to kill her," Whim said. "We have to do something."

"We'll be lucky to get out of here alive—" Will told him, and then broke off at the sound of footsteps in the hall.

Bash and Peregrine strode through the doorway as if the barrier didn't exist, and Bayla followed in her bare feet.

Peregrine smiled broadly at the sight of his guests. Although Josh had seen him only two weeks before, she was always startled anew by the painful imbalance of his features—the oversize lips and bulbous nose, the frighteningly large eyes. His face lit up when he saw Feodor.

"Kajażkołski!" he cried. "I didn't believe it when Bash said you were here!"

He offered his hand, but Feodor ignored it and opened his arms.

"It has been too long for a handshake, old friend," he said.

Josh watched in disbelief as they embraced.

"*What?*" Will burst out.

Feodor smiled coyly. "'Don't praise the day before sunset,'" he said, quoting an old Polish proverb.

"I knew we couldn't trust him!" Will cried.

He turned to Josh, his gaze blazing with fury, and she shook her head helplessly.

I thought I knew Feodor so well. I thought that since I had his memories, I had the upper hand.

But she hadn't remembered his friendship with Peregrine.

Greater than the shock she felt was the fear that she had once more incurred Will's wrath by making a bad decision. She had agreed to this plan for *him,* not for Feodor or for herself, but she knew that all Will would see was another example of her doing the wrong thing.

"How is this possible?" Peregrine asked Feodor.

"You may thank your granddaughters. They went so far as to fetch me from Death."

Peregrine released a laugh like the bark of a hyena. "My granddaughters," he repeated. "They're as impertinent and cocky as Dustine."

Feodor shrugged. He had an elegant shrug, as small and tidy as everything else about him, and Josh hated him for it. "How is Dustine?" he asked.

The question stunned Josh. She stepped backward again, bumping the backs of her knees on a coffee table, and she sat down on it.

Peregrine's spare eyebrows drew together. "You should know," he told Feodor. "Your man killed her, you bastard."

Feodor's smile faltered. "Pardon me?" he asked, his voice weakened.

"When your friends with the canisters attacked my family, the old bird's heart popped."

Josh watched the news register on Feodor's face. His breath quickened. "I am truly sorry, old friend."

She didn't know if she could trust his regret or not. Was every word he spoke, every flash of expression, every gesture, a lie?

Peregrine shrugged off the apology. "She had it coming."

"Don't talk about her like that!" Deloise shouted, at the same moment Josh sprang from the coffee table and rushed Peregrine. She didn't make it two steps before she hit another invisible barrier.

Her grandfather looked at her and laughed. "Haven't you figured it out yet? Bash controls everything here. And I control Bash."

"I hate you," Josh said.

Peregrine smiled. "I don't care."

But Josh watched as a fresh drop of blood appeared at Bash's temple and rolled down his cheek, leaving a wet, red trail. An idea began to form in her mind.

Peregrine clapped Feodor's shoulder. "This jewelry Bash is wearing—you built that, didn't you?"

Feodor responded with a modest nod, which only confused Josh more. *She'd* built the devices, not Feodor. If he and Peregrine were such great friends, why would he lie?

Whose side is he on? Josh wondered, but the answer came to her almost immediately. *His own. Always his own.*

"I knew it!" Peregrine cried. "The whole thing stinks of your piss."

"What is it you want, Peregrine?" Mirren asked, her voice as calm as ever.

Josh inched behind Will, whispering as she did, "Stay there."

Peregrine smiled at Mirren. Unlike Feodor, with his small, calculated amusements, Peregrine had a sloppy, slovenly grin. "I want your secrets."

Josh maneuvered herself far enough behind Will that her left arm was hidden from Peregrine's and Feodor's sight.

"What secrets?" Mirren asked.

"*All of them,*" Peregrine hissed, and his face darkened with long-held rage. "I want every secret your parents and your grandparents and your great-grandparents wouldn't give us because we weren't worthy, we weren't smart enough, or wise enough, or *good* enough."

Moving her arm as little as possible, Josh tried to open an archway. Nothing. She tried again. Nothing. But over Will's shoulder, she saw another drop of blood forming at Bash's temple.

"You think you're so goddamn special!" Peregrine ranted at Mirren, his crazed brown eyes swelling. "You could have changed the World a hundred times over, but all you did was sit on your secrets. You're a coward, just like your parents!"

Archway, archway, archway. The drop of blood rolled down the side of Bash's face, leaving a trail of pink on his ghostly skin.

"Do you truly think we should have molded the World to our liking?" Mirren asked. "What right did we have to make decisions for all of humanity?"

"What right did you have to deny them the choice? And you!" Peregrine snapped at Josh. "I know you're trying to open archways where you think I can't see. But it won't work. Bash!"

Josh went numb. She froze with her arm stretched out before her, a measly half breath left in her lungs.

Feodor leaned sideways, trying to see around Will. "How is she opening archways?"

Deloise, who must have caught on to Josh's plan, ran to the doorway and began kicking the invisible barrier. Bash froze her, too.

"Supposedly she's the True Dream Walker," Peregrine told Feodor.

Feodor looked back at Peregrine with an expression halfway between ridicule and wonder. "Is that so?" he mused.

Archway, archway . . . Josh closed her eyes and tried to open an archway with only her mind, but like in the Dream earlier, she was helpless as long as Bash had her immobilized.

"Didn't you Temper her?" she heard Peregrine ask. "She's alive, so she must have passed."

"Passing is not how I would describe it," Feodor said. "If she is the True Dream Walker, I would enjoy a demonstration."

Glass shattered. Out of the corner of her eye, Josh saw that Will had used a stone-topped end table to break one of the windows, forcing Bash to freeze him as well. Mirren rushed at Peregrine at the same moment, holding a peacock-colored vase over her head, and Whim tried to clobber Feodor with a porcelain ballerina.

Bash froze them all, and the room went still.

"Get Whim and Deloise out of here," Peregrine told Bayla. "Put them with the others."

Blood began to pool in Bash's eyes. Bayla picked up Whim's stiff form as if he weighed nothing and tossed him toward the hall. He bounced along the floor like a balloon filled with day-old helium, and Deloise followed.

"Leave the others," Peregrine ordered Bash. To Feodor, he said, "You want a demo? Let's give him a demo. Bash, unfreeze Josh. Come on, Josh, show us what you can do."

With air moving through her lungs again, Josh said, "I don't have to prove anything to you."

Peregrine smirked. "Don't you?" he asked. "Bash, why don't you provide a little incentive? I hear she's *very* fond of her apprentice."

Bash took in a deep breath, so deep that Josh expected him to shout or scream, but Will was the one who responded, releasing a choking sound and grabbing at his own neck.

"Will?" Josh asked.

He grabbed at his neck and shook his head.

He can't breathe, Josh realized.

"All right!" she said. "I'll do it. Watch."

"Bash, let her try."

She thrust her hand out again, this time in full view of her grandfather, and an archway exploded in front of her. Josh fought the temptation to go running through it. "Tell Bash to let Will go," she said.

Will's face reddened. Indents from invisible fingers marked his throat. But Bash closed the archway almost before Josh finished speaking.

Peregrine shifted from one foot to the other as if bored. "Do something else," he told Josh. "Alter the Dream."

Josh opened another archway, and then a third.

"Will, go through!" she shouted, but his knees buckled at the first step and he fell to the floor. His face had darkened to the color of a raspberry. Bash closed those archways, too.

"Something else!" Peregrine repeated.

"I can't!" Josh shouted, panic making her voice tight and high. "I can't do anything but open archways!"

"Bullshit!" her grandfather shouted back.

"Let him go, Bash!" Josh pleaded, and she heard the tears in her own voice.

But she also saw Bash put a hand on a china cabinet to steady himself. Blood ran from his ears. Every time he had to close an archway, the effort required chipped away at him.

"Come on!" Peregrine shouted at Josh. "Save your little boyfriend!"

Josh swung her hands out again, throwing archways like she was throwing punches, and Bash counterpunched by closing each one. She felt her energy begin to wane, her strength weakening. "I can't!" she repeated. "This is all I can do."

"Then you aren't the True Dream Walker, are you?"

"I don't know!" Josh admitted, as much to herself as to her grandfather. "I'm sorry. Maybe I'm not the True Dream Walker. I'll do whatever you want. Please let Will go."

She threw another archway even as she felt something within herself beginning to break down. Throughout the room, archways shimmered, the Veil revealing a dozen different nightmares. When Josh lifted her head, she saw that Bash's face was ghastly white, with stark red rivers of blood running down it.

He's going to die, she thought. *Maybe before Will dies.*

The realization of what she had to do hit her so hard that she stopped breathing.

I have to wear Bash out until he dies, and I have to do it before Will suffocates.

"What an interesting standoff," Feodor said conversationally, and Peregrine laughed.

Josh didn't know if killing Bash was fair or reasonable or moral, or even if Will still truly loved her, or if he would be able to love her once she became a murderer, and she didn't have time to find out. She just knew that she would never forgive herself if she didn't do everything in her power to save him.

Closing her hand around the plumeria pendant she wore, she said a silent prayer to the Dream. *I've tried so hard to be a good dream walker,* she thought. *Please don't fail me now.*

She was already exhausted—from opening archways, from the drama, from the guilt. She had very little energy left, but she gathered up what she could, a meager harvest of what was left of her. *Take everything I've got,* she told the Dream. *Just save him.*

She thrust her palms out to either side, releasing a cry as she did so, and dozens upon dozens of archways appeared throughout the room. They overlapped one another, stood within one another, crisscrossed the room like mirror images of one another in a fun house. Josh felt archways beyond archways open up—into the Dream, into the World, into the World beyond the Dream. Briefly, images of her basement archroom appeared, but they faded after an instant, and the arches collapsed, leaving behind a fine layer of fairy dust across the room.

Josh couldn't hold them open. She'd felt the power leave her, but something else as well, something important. Something vital. Something she shouldn't have given up. She fell to her knees, hollow and dizzy. As she did, she watched Bash mirror her fall on the other side of the room, heard his knees crack when they hit the floor. He reached out with his unencumbered arm toward the doorway, where Bayla stood watching with a confused smile on her face. For an instant he swayed as if praying, and then blood began to pour from his every orifice, and Josh knew he was dead before he landed on the marble because he made no attempt to soften his own fall.

Someone gasped, a sound like mud sucking at a boot, but Josh didn't know if it came from Will or Mirren.

Peregrine calmly removed a gun from the back of his waistband and pointed it at Mirren. Josh tried to stand, but she felt like she was trying to rise beneath a heavy blanket, and she didn't even have the strength to look behind her and see if Will was breathing.

"Bayla," Peregrine said, "it's your turn to wear the devices."

Bayla smiled brightly. She walked barefoot through the pool of her boyfriend's blood and wrestled his corpse for the vambrace and circlet. As she did so, she turned his head so that Josh could see his bloodstained teeth and slack jaw. All the capillaries in his eyes had burst, turning the whites of his eyes a solid, bright red.

Josh was too weak to gag.

Feodor walked past Josh so that he could check on Will. "Dead," he pronounced, and Josh felt useless tears gush from her eyes.

He can't be dead, he can't be, I'm so sorry, Will.

Bayla put on the circlet and vambrace, not even wincing when the wires bit into her skin, and presented herself proudly to Peregrine. He patted her on the head.

"Put Josh with the others," he said, and Josh felt herself lifted from the floor as if by magic. Desperately, she tried to turn her head so that she could see Will and prove Feodor wrong, but Bayla prevented her.

He can't be dead. As long as I don't see him, he's still alive.

As Josh floated out of the room, she heard Peregrine say to Mirren, "Now, about those secrets."

Bayla used the devices to fly Josh into a large bedroom, where five people were chained to a massive block of concrete.

"Josh!" Deloise cried. "Are you okay?"

Another set of manacles appeared and closed themselves around Josh's wrists and ankles, as if she could have tried to escape. Just breathing was difficult. Josh slumped to the floor between Deloise and Whim.

Nearby, a man, a woman, and a girl around Deloise's age sat on a couch. They all looked the worse for wear: the woman had clearly been beaten in the face.

"Who?" Josh managed to ask.

"This is Mirren's family," Deloise told her.

"Is Mirren all right?" the teenage girl asked.

Josh didn't even have the strength to nod.

"Where's Will?" Whim asked.

She closed her eyes. *He's not dead. He can't be dead. I killed for him, he can't be dead.*

Time might have passed; she wasn't sure. Her body was screaming at her, but she didn't know what it wanted or needed, only that she couldn't hold it up any longer.

Then suddenly someone was shaking her shoulders, and Feodor's face swam before her eyes.

"Open an archway," he ordered.

The mere thought caused a throb of pain between her temples. Josh's weakness pinned her to the ground.

"Give me the activator," Feodor said, but she looked at him skeptically. Her anger at his betrayal restored a measure of her strength.

"'Whom you befriend, you become,'" she told him, citing a Polish proverb, as he had done.

Feodor answered with another. "'Sometimes even innocence needs a mask.'"

Josh nearly responded in kind—she was favoring "'Your face and my ass are twins'"—when Whim said, "Speak English!"

"Who are you?" Mirren's aunt demanded.

In English, Feodor replied, "I am your only chance of escaping alive. Give me the activator, Josh."

"You betrayed us!" Whim said. He put his arm around Josh's shoulders. "We aren't giving you anything!"

Feodor's mouth tightened with irritation. "Stop being ridiculous. You claim to know me as well as I know myself—"

"No, I don't!" Josh hissed with the very last of her strength. "I don't even know who I'm talking to right now! Are you the Feodor who brushed his little sister's hair every night, or the Feodor who dumped his brothers in an orphanage? Are you the Feodor who invented modern methods of Veil repair, or the Feodor who created a drill powered by souls? Are you the Feodor who fought in the Battle of Warsaw, or the Feodor who helped the Nazis build—"

She ran out of breath, but it didn't matter anyway. What else could she say? She wanted Feodor to prove himself, even though she knew that was impossible, that there could be no redemption for the things he had done.

Bash's blood-filled eyes flashed in her mind. Perhaps there was no redemption for her, either.

Strangely, Feodor reached for her hand. His smile was small and sad. "I am all of those things," he said.

She wanted to turn away but couldn't, and even if she could have, there was no way to turn away from the truth. He had given her the answer to the paradox with which she had struggled for months: Was he a monster or a victim?

He was both.

Wasn't she the same? Hadn't she lied to her boyfriend and everyone else, and craved power, and built the devices when she knew how dangerous they were? And hadn't she done it all with the best of intentions?

"'Wherever you go, you can't get rid of yourself,'" Josh told Feodor, and she slipped the activator into his hand.

He smiled then, before turning away.

Twenty-eight

Will woke up in pain. His pulse rushed, a flash flood in his ears, making his eardrums throb, and every time he inhaled, he felt like he was breathing in crushed glass.

His eyes hurt, too, although he didn't know why. When he opened them, he saw Feodor crouching beside him with an impatient expression.

Then Will saw Bash.

He tried to sit up and had to settle for crawling away across the marble floor until he could prop himself up against the fancy curtains. Bash's back was arched, his burn-spotted arm stretched out as if he were reaching for help, for hope, for something that would have saved him from dying in agony.

The last Will remembered, he had been praying for the same thing.

"Don't be afraid; he is dead," Feodor said, as if that were some comfort. "Do you have a watch?"

Will stared at him.

"A timepiece?" Feodor asked urgently.

Will usually wore a watch, but he'd worn it into Iph Lake and it had stopped working.

"Do you have three brain cells left, or shall we use you as a coat-rack?" Feodor asked, losing patience.

"You're evil," Will managed to say.

"No one who knows me would disagree," Feodor said matter-of-factly. "Here." He removed his pocket watch and unhooked the chain from his belt loop. "I have modified this watch to keep time within the Dream, so you may rely upon its accuracy. I told Peregrine that I could alter these devices to keep them from killing him; however, I intend to fit them instead with two of the transmitters. Exactly fifteen minutes from now, I will ask him to test them. You have until then to find the towers Peregrine placed in this universe and fit them with the transmitters. At the fifteen-minute mark, I will activate the transmitters. Do you understand?"

Will heard about half of Feodor's second sentence before his brain lost track completely.

Seeing his blank stare, Feodor sighed angrily. "Perhaps Josh will take pity and keep you as a pet," he said, rising.

"Wait," Will said, the words scraping his throat as he spoke them. "Why should I trust you?"

Feodor rolled his gray eyes. "Your girlfriend wanted to know the same thing."

"I'm glad to hear that," Will replied, climbing to his feet. "You did try to kill us four months ago, after all."

"Four months?" Feodor asked, lifting his eyebrows. "I thought less time had passed."

Will didn't share Feodor's interest in time. "I should kill you right now," he said.

Coolly, Feodor said, "Try."

They both knew that Will was in no shape for hand-to-hand combat.

"You want me to believe that you've gone from wanting to kill us to wanting to save us?" Will asked.

Feodor smiled with just the corner of his mouth. "I never wanted to kill any of you. Your lives meant nothing to me. I wanted to escape that prison universe, and to do that, I had to kill you. Today, I want to escape *this* universe, but to do that, I need your help."

"Why? Peregrine would let you walk out of here if you asked him."

"No." Feodor shook his head. "We are playing a game, Peregrine and I, and we both know the other is playing. Eventually he will tire of testing how far I will go in order to keep playing." He straightened his shoulders as he prepared to leave. "If you do not wish to help me, I will do what I can on my own."

Will said, "Wait. How did you get the activator?"

"Josh gave it to me." Feodor produced it from his pocket.

Why did Josh give him the activator? Will thought. A bitter taste filled his mouth, ammonia and green onions.

She betrayed me. She betrayed all of us.

For him.

"I believe this plan is our best chance at survival," Feodor said.

Then I'm not going to let you be in charge of it, Will thought.

"I'll help you," he said, "but I want to be the one with the activator."

"If you aren't in the room with us, how will you know when Peregrine has put on the devices?"

"I'll go outside and put the transmitters on the towers, then come back inside and find you."

He held out his hand, but Feodor said, "You are being unreasonable. I will be in a better position to decide when to activate the transmitters."

"I don't care," Will said, his voice rising. "This is the only way I'm going to help you."

Feodor stared at him for a few seconds, his eyes as dark as thunderheads, and then smiled. He dropped the activator into Will's open hand.

"You'll find us in the file room," he said.

Twenty-nine

Mirren would have expected herself to be hysterical after watching Bash—and perhaps Will—die. Instead, she grew increasingly cold and matter-of-fact.

Life is a kamikaze mission, she reminded herself. *We're all going to die in the end, so we might as well do something important before we go.*

She stood in the file room, only ten feet from where Peregrine stood fiddling with the key chain he'd taken off the wall.

Three big steps, Mirren thought, *and I could grab him.*

Three steps was too far a distance; he'd shoot her by then. He had the gun tucked between his elbow and his side so he could examine the keys with both hands, and Mirren didn't doubt he was itching for a reason to shoot her.

She heard Bayla singing in the stairwell, but the person who floated into the file room wasn't Bayla.

It was Katia.

Mirren's cousin collapsed onto the floor as Bayla released her, and Mirren rushed to her side. "Are you hurt? Did she hurt you?"

Katia's silvery hair was in snarls and her clothes were stained, but otherwise she looked only a little the worse for wear. Her hug was reassuringly strong. "We thought you were dead," she admitted.

Mirren hugged her back tightly. "I'm okay. What about Fel and Collena?"

"They're all right. Peregrine's been holding us prisoner."

Reluctantly, Mirren released Katia and then rose. She could think of only one reason why Peregrine would have had Katia brought to the file room.

"I won't have her harmed," Mirren told Peregrine.

He smiled evilly. "Show me how to open the files, and I won't hurt her. You have my word."

Your word? Mirren thought. *And what is that worth?*

Before she could respond, Feodor entered the room carrying a chef's knife. "I'm afraid this was all I could find," he said.

Mirren had refused to tell him where her family's toolbox was. He'd told Peregrine that he could alter the devices so that they wouldn't kill the wearer, and Mirren hadn't wanted to assist him in any way. He had been gone a long time; she wondered how many rooms he had searched before giving up.

"Miss Bayla," Feodor said, "I will need to borrow the devices for a few minutes."

Petulantly, Bayla looked at Peregrine, who was holding the gun in his hand again. "But my turn just started!" she wailed.

"Don't be a brat," Peregrine said. "Take 'em off."

Bayla reluctantly removed the circlet and vambrace.

"Don't try anything," Peregrine told Mirren. To Feodor, he said, "How long will this take?"

"Ten, perhaps fifteen minutes," Feodor assured him. He set the devices down on top of one of the file cabinets.

"Make it ten," Peregrine said.

"Then can I put them back on?" Bayla asked.

"Stop whining." He made as if to hit her with the gun, and Bayla shrank back. "Now then, Princess, you were about to open the files."

Mirren glanced at Katia, even though she knew that the sight of her cousin would only make her feel worse. "Don't give him anything," Katia said.

She had always been the brave one: the one who talked back to her parents, climbed the castle walls, pulled out her own splinters. Mirren knew that Katia would endure whatever she could to protect the family secrets—and she didn't even know what those secrets were.

"I guess we'll have to do this the old-fashioned way," Peregrine said, striding over to Katia. He grabbed her by the hair.

"Don't kill her!" Mirren cried. "Please!"

"Oh, I'm not going to kill her. See, if I kill her, then I won't be able to torture her anymore." He grinned. "My father taught me that."

Katia's eyes were wide, but Mirren could see her trying not to show any fear. She allowed Peregrine to jerk her to her feet, one hand fisted in her hair, the other holding the gun to her face.

"You have to start small," he said. "I was going to start with ripping out her hair, but since I only have two hands—"

"I'll do it!" Bayla screamed.

Before Peregrine could even make a demand of Mirren, Bayla had sprung to Katia's side and wrestled a chunk of hair away from Peregrine's hold. She pulled, but all she managed was to yank Katia's head to the side. Katia winced but didn't make a sound.

"No, no, you're pulling too much," Peregrine told her. "Use half that much."

"Like, this much?" Bayla asked.

Mirren began to feel like she was floating. *This can't be happening,* she thought. *I can't—I don't know—how can I—*

Bayla, now clutching a smaller lock of hair, braced one foot against Katia's hip and yanked. Katia yelped as she swung her hips to the side, and Bayla came away with only a few strands.

Haley, Mirren thought desperately, *I wish you were here.*

"Let's brace her up against the file cabinets," Peregrine said.

Tears filled Katia's eyes as Peregrine forced her to stand next to one of the file cabinets. It came up to her chin. Bayla ran around the other side, so that she could brace herself against the cabinets when she pulled.

I'm such a coward, Mirren thought, but she closed her eyes. She couldn't watch.

She couldn't watch, and she couldn't stop them.

"Open your eyes!" Peregrine yelled at her. "This is the last time you'll see your cousin with a full head of hair! By the end of the night, she'll look like me!"

Katia gave Mirren a tiny, weak smile. Mirren tried to collect herself, to think, but she couldn't stop trembling. After all these weeks of threats and fears, and now seeing her cousin tormented, she was finally losing her composure.

Bayla yanked, and at the last second, Mirren shut her eyes. She heard Katia cry out through gritted teeth and something slam against the file cabinet, and when she looked, she saw Bayla holding a fistful of silver strands of hair.

"I thought her scalp would come off," Bayla said, examining the hairs.

"She's bleeding," Peregrine said. "That's enough."

Katia sneezed, then sneezed again. Blood oozed down the side of her face, the way it had Bash's.

He's going to kill her slowly, like he did Bash, Mirren thought, and then she heard Haley's voice.

Don't lose yourself, he whispered.

And for an instant, she felt him there with her, his hand squeezing hers.

She marched up to Peregrine, grabbed the hand with which he held the gun, and pointed the barrel at her cousin's temple. Peregrine realized what she was going to do just in time to jerk the gun to the side, and the shot Mirren fired went into the file cabinet next to Katia's head instead of into her skull.

Peregrine smiled, and Bayla began to giggle.

"Thought you were going to screw me out of my fun, didn't you?" Peregrine asked.

"I would rather see her dead than tortured," Mirren told him.

"We'd just start again with your aunt," he replied.

Then he shot Katia in the leg.

Katia screamed, not just out of pain, but from surprise, Mirren could tell.

"Missed the bone," Peregrine complained. "I'll get it with the next one. There's nothing quite like bone pain."

He glanced at Feodor as he spoke, and Feodor glanced back and shrugged coyly. Mirren didn't know what that meant, but she went to her knees beside Katia, who was trying to put pressure on her shin. The bullet had torn through her calf muscles, and she was bleeding from both entrance and exit wounds.

Mirren pulled her shirt over her head. With the long sleeves, she tied a tourniquet below Katia's knee and then used the rest of the material to put pressure on the wounds. "I'm sorry," she whispered. "I'm so sorry."

"Let me bleed out," Katia was whispering back, trying to remove the knot from the sleeves. "It'll be faster."

Peregrine laughed again, and Mirren didn't realize she was moving until her bloody fist connected with his face. She hit him hard enough that he fell backward onto his ass, and then Bayla tackled her, and they fell to the floor in a painful pile of elbows and knees.

Everything Mirren knew about fighting, she'd learned from Josh in a two-week period, and the knowledge wasn't enough to help her much. Bayla fought like a wild animal, with her nails and her teeth, growling and slobbering. Within no more than a minute, Mirren was bleeding from multiple bite wounds and her own patch of torn scalp, and one of her bra straps had been snapped.

"Stop it!" Peregrine shouted. "Stop it!"

He kicked Bayla, who reluctantly rolled off Mirren. Peregrine's eye was already beginning to swell, but he had no trouble aiming the gun at Mirren's face.

He trembled with rage. "I'll kill you!"

Mirren smiled a weak, bitter smile.

"Go ahead and shoot," she said. "I'm not afraid. I've got someone waiting for me on the other side."

"You think I won't do it?" Peregrine screamed, pointing the gun at her again.

"I think you will," Mirren said. "I think you're depraved enough to kill me. But I've known that from the start, and I swore to myself when I began this that I would do what my parents would want. You took their lives, and you might take mine and my family's, but that's all you're going to get from us."

The gun shook. "You stupid bitch," Peregrine swore.

Mirren's smile sweetened. "The file cabinets are reinforced tungsten steel, by the way. It'll take you years to cut them open."

Peregrine's whole body quivered. "You," he said, his voice trembling violently. "You . . . you . . ."

"Me, me, me," Mirren agreed.

Silence filled the room.

A martyr's death to seal her ruse, Mirren recalled, thinking of her scroll. From the way Peregrine held the gun, she could see straight into the barrel, and the dark void reminded her not of Death, but of deep space, and of gravity. *What's the ruse?* she wondered. *That I'm a martyr? That I'm a princess?*

Or is Death itself the ruse?

Katia grabbed Mirren's hand, and they waited.

"I believe the devices are ready," Feodor said calmly.

Peregrine's hand shook, and Mirren watched his finger tighten on the trigger.

"Of course," Feodor continued in the same casual tone, "you can shoot the girl before you test the devices. But I thought you might wish to use them to force her to unlock the cabinets. Or you might tear her body to pieces, rather than just shooting her."

The idea made Peregrine crack a smile. He was panting.

Slowly, he lowered the gun. Mirren released a breath she hadn't known she was holding.

"Fine," Peregrine said. "Give them to me."

When he looked away from Mirren, she felt as though she'd stepped out of a very hot spotlight.

I guess gravity isn't ready for me yet, she thought, and almost laughed. Instead, she hugged Katia. "Tighten the tourniquet," she whispered, and her cousin nodded.

Feodor carried the devices over to Peregrine, and as Mirren turned to watch him, she caught sight of a tiny movement in the file room doorway.

"Have you worn them before?" Feodor asked Peregrine.

"No."

Who is that? Mirren wondered. All she could see was a slice of blue fabric floating at the edge of the doorframe, perhaps a shirt. . . .

"Roll up your sleeve, please." Feodor turned Peregrine's arm in order to locate his veins.

Will ducked his head into the room for the briefest of instants.

He's alive! Mirren's heart jumped. She honestly hadn't been sure whether or not Peregrine and Bash had killed Will earlier—or Josh, for that matter—but when they'd left, he'd been lying motionless on the living room floor.

"Ow!"

Feodor had just clamped the vambrace shut around Peregrine's arm. "Apologies, apologies."

"Is it supposed to hurt like that?"

"I'm afraid so. The current requires access to the central nervous system in order to transmit electrical signals."

But something sour had entered Peregrine's expression, and he stopped Feodor from putting the circlet on his head.

Will peeked into the room again. He had something in his hand— the activator?

"Wait," Peregrine said. "Try them on her first."

He nodded toward Bayla.

"Yes, yes!" Bayla cried, rushing forward. "It's my turn!"

Feodor looked between them, and something in his face made Mirren think that this was not a good idea. "The devices have already damaged her system greatly. It will be impossible to prove that their new configuration won't hurt the wearer if we demonstrate it on someone already so injured."

He's up to something, Mirren realized as Will snuck another look at the room. *And Will—are they working together?*

Of everything that had happened to her in the last month, Will and Feodor working together seemed the most improbable.

"I want to wear them!" Bayla cried, and Feodor had to lift his arm to keep the circlet out of her hands.

"Then you test them," Peregrine told him.

This time when Will ducked around the door, he saw Mirren watching for him. He gave her the fleetest of smiles, and she felt a surge of hope.

But Feodor and Peregrine were staring at each other with such fire in their eyes that she was surprised the space between them didn't burst into flame.

"Do you think I'm stupid?" Peregrine hissed. With his unencumbered arm, he pushed the barrel of the gun into Feodor's gut. "Do you think I forgot what you did to me, *old friend*?"

"I think you've forgotten what I did *for* you," Feodor replied. He smiled, but his jaw tensed.

"I loved her—"

"Do not speak to me of love," Feodor snapped, and all the civil tidiness Mirren had admired before was gone from his expression. Now she saw the Feodor that Will was so afraid of, the man with the crazed rage in his eyes and the snarl that destroyed the crisp line of his lips.

Feodor lowered the arm with which he held the circlet, as if he had forgotten it. Bayla, who had been standing beside him, jumping up and down to reach it, grabbed the device out of the air.

"It's mine!" she cried, and jammed it onto her own head.

Feodor shouted, "Now, Will!"

For a heartbeat, nothing happened.

Then Peregrine's arm exploded.

Bayla's head blew apart like a dropped watermelon.

Peregrine, his face emptied by shock, stared at Feodor and then shot him in the gut before fainting.

The room shook, and Feodor fell to the floor beside Peregrine.

"Will!" Mirren screamed, throwing herself over her cousin.

Upstairs, something heavy crashed. Glass shattered, and the walls creaked. Plaster floated down like snow.

Mirren tried to put pressure on Katia's wound again, but Katia said, "I'm okay—help that guy!"

She meant Feodor. *She doesn't know who he is,* Mirren thought, and she didn't know if she should help him or not. If he died, would they still get Haley back? No one had told them.

Mirren didn't know what to do for Feodor except to put pressure on his wound, so she clapped her hands over the hole in his abdomen. Blood poured between her fingers, slick and hot.

Feodor groaned, his eyelids fluttering.

"What's happening?" Will shouted at him.

Mirren took off one of her shoes and used it to beat at the flames coming from Peregrine's arm. The vambrace had been blown to bits, and she couldn't bring herself to look at what was left of his arm for more than a second; the skin had blistered and burst like a microwaved hot dog, and his hand was gone entirely.

"We may have . . ." Feodor said, and his eyes fluttered again. "Activating the transmitters . . . destabilized this universe."

The floor began to vibrate, and the sound of crashing upstairs morphed into a crush of white noise.

"You must leave," Feodor told them. "Go."

"We can carry you," Mirren said.

"No! Save yourself, Your Majesty." His face had gone as white as the moon, his lips nearly colorless, but he smiled faintly.

Will grabbed one of Katia's arms and Mirren grabbed the other, but as they rose Mirren saw a crack in the ceiling running from both ends. It widened like a great maw diving down to devour them, and only when the ceiling collapsed did Mirren remember how much she had wanted to live.

Thirty

Josh was dying.

She could feel it in every bit of her body, a sense of shutting down, of one cell after another being turned off, of tiny fires burning out. The weakness that had suffused her limbs was fading to numbness, then to nothingness. Over the dragging of her own breath, she heard Deloise crying and begging her to wake up; she didn't even have the energy to squeeze her sister's hand.

But as the sensation of closure slowly shut her out of her body, she became aware of another place, somewhere deep inside her, that she could go, a place she remembered.

Death, she thought, and suddenly she wanted to go there, to escape the pressure of being forced from her own skin and instead run free on the golden shores of the river.

Something stopped her.

I'm not done, she thought.

I can't leave yet.

There's still so much I have to do.

She didn't think of her life or how she wanted to spend it. She didn't even think of the people she loved.

She thought of the Dream.

I was supposed to balance the universes.

She had failed. Why? Hadn't she had the power? She could feel it closer than ever before, but the tighter she held it, the farther away it moved.

You can't force it, Josh realized.

Somewhere, Deloise screamed. Furniture crashed, and a sound like a dozen trains approaching filled the air.

You can't force it, Josh thought again, remembering how hard she had tried to open an archway and save Will.

You have to follow it instead.

What did that mean? Now Whim was screaming, too, and other voices she didn't recognize.

You have to follow it—

Suddenly, she was surrounded by silence. She opened her eyes and found herself standing on a shapeless gray plain. Three strong lights shone away from her, illuminating three different paths.

On the left, she saw the gods of Death, radiating golden light, their arms outstretched for her.

In the center, she saw the Dream, the ocean of colored lights that were the souls of the dreamers.

On the right, she saw the World, all blue and green and bursting with energy.

But she didn't walk toward them.

You have to follow it, she thought, and she turned around to see where the lights originated.

Behind her, the gray brightened to white—white stone floor, white walls, an indistinct ceiling of white light. A few feet away, a rough-cut black pillar rose to waist height, water pouring down from it. Sitting atop the pillar was a pale stone shaped like an egg, small enough to fit in her hand, but just barely. The water burbled out from beneath the egg, and the reflection of the light on the moving water made the egg sparkle.

Follow it, she thought, and she put her hand on the egg. The shell was not completely smooth, but bumpy and a little rough, and it was warm, even though the water pouring down around it was chilly. Josh picked it up, liking the warmth in her hand.

And then she understood that some things were meant to be.

The knowledge hit her in a flash, a bright light turned on right before her eyes. *There is a plan for each of us,* she thought, and she saw the three universes as three stages where different parts of a single great play were being performed. They moved together like cogs in a clock, souls spilling from one to the next in a choreographed dance too complex for Josh to follow.

And her own part? She tried to focus on herself, on the line of light representing her path, but it was short and too bright. Her soul hadn't emerged from the Dream, as all the others had. Instead, hers simply appeared the moment she was born, an unexpected entrance in the play.

Because I'm the True Dream Walker? she wondered. *Is that why?*

She didn't even know if she was the True Dream Walker, but she followed the idea as it led her into memory. She remembered being in the Dream, watching Ian's body bleed out while she lay, helpless, on the floor. She remembered Will whispering to her, telling her that she had to admit she was the True Dream Walker and save them. She remembered giving her life up to whatever was meant to be, and how in that moment she had merged with the Dream so completely as to almost lose herself.

It's my ego, she realized. *I can't access the power with my ego in the way. I can't decide what should be.*

She was a servant to a greater power, and only when she was facilitating that power's intentions could she act as the True Dream Walker. It wasn't a god she served, or even a consciousness. It was the way of things, an inevitability, a current guiding souls.

Except mine, she thought. No path lay before her soul; she was forging it herself, every day, every moment.

She stared at the egg, feeling its heat in her palm, and within it she saw her own body, splayed on the floor with manacles attached to every limb. She saw Whim and Deloise cowering beside her with drawers over their heads to protect themselves from falling debris, and Mirren's aunt and uncle crouched beneath a mattress torn off the bed.

Stop, Josh thought, and the warmth within the egg increased. *Go back.*

She watched the bedroom walls straighten, the ceiling flatten itself out, and the plaster dust rise from the floor.

Get rid of those, she added, and the manacles vanished, along with the chains and the cement block to which they had been attached.

She felt the castle rise upright, like a pop-up tent opening. The Hidden Kingdom reordered itself neatly.

Josh's attention turned to the file room, floors below. Will, Mirren, and Katia lay curled in balls beside Feodor's bleeding body. Near the first row of files, Bayla's headless body was sprawled lifeless on the floor, and Josh passed her by without interest. There was nothing she could do for Bayla now.

Instead, she went to Feodor's limp form. He lay like a child, his small limbs heavy with the sleep of impending death. Josh touched him and waited, listening in a way she never had before.

Not yet, she thought. *Not yet.*

This wasn't Feodor's time. Not quite.

In his ear, she whispered, "All things grow toward the light. Even you."

His eyes flicked open, and he sucked in a great breath of air as the wound in his abdomen closed and blood rushed to his cheeks.

Josh ran her fingertips over Katia's leg, and those wounds, too, were healed.

There was one more person in the room, and even unconscious, pain and rage radiated from him. He'd lost his left hand, and the skin on his arm had burned away, leaving charred muscle visible, raw bones exposed to the air. But even more horrifying was the tangled mess of his mind. It was as twisted and thorny as an overgrown thicket from which no berries grew, and Josh knew she could heal him with a word.

Not yet, she thought again, this time with a different meaning. *He has to play out his purpose.*

But for the first time she felt something other than peaceful acceptance of the way things were meant to be. She didn't want to let Peregrine go on hurting people, and she struggled against the knowledge that she wasn't meant to change him. Maybe the wisdom was wrong—

In that instant, she lost the confidence and comfort that had come with holding the egg.

And she woke up standing in the bedroom.

Every cell in her body was alive, almost too alive, vibrating with energy.

"Josh?" Deloise asked. She was still crouched on the floor with a dresser drawer held over her head. "Wait—where are your chains?"

"Where are *all* the chains?" Whim asked. He gazed up at the perfect, smooth ceiling.

"What happened?" Mirren's aunt asked, peeking out from beneath the mattress.

Collena, Josh thought. She'd seen her in the vision and known her name. Also beneath the mattress was Mirren's uncle, Fel.

Josh didn't wonder how she knew these things or how the manacles had disappeared. When she had held the egg, all knowledge had been available.

"Peregrine's in the file room," she said. "We have to decide what to do with him."

She started for the door, ignoring Whim's and Deloise's protests of confusion. "Josh, what happened?" Deloise asked as she followed her sister down the hallway. "You were barely alive, and then the house started coming down."

"I'm alive now," was all Josh said.

How could she explain? For a brief moment, the way of all things had been clear to her, and she had been part of the stream of time, her own current helping to move it forward. But what could she tell Deloise except that she had left her body and held an egg? That she had somehow healed Feodor and Katia?

Except Josh was fairly certain she hadn't been the one to heal either of them. She had been the tool, but not the power.

She ran down the hallway and then down the stairs. She had

no trouble finding her way, despite having been to the Hidden Kingdom only once. The house's layout seemed to be part of the knowledge she now had.

"Josh," Will said when she burst into the file room, and the relief in his face was so real that Josh felt she could wrap it around her hand.

She threw herself into his arms, but he hugged her for only an instant before pushing her away by the shoulders.

"You gave Feodor the activator," he said.

Somehow she couldn't quite believe he was going to complain about that when Feodor's plan had likely saved both their lives. *I killed Bash for* you, Josh thought, but Will's expression contained no gratitude, only more accusations waiting to be voiced. There was no love in the look he gave her, and Josh wondered what direction their path took and whether they would walk it together or alone.

"I'm sorry," she said, and he shook his head, as if he couldn't believe how weak her answer was.

She turned away to escape his anger, and Mirren hugged her. Katia hugged her, too, even though they hadn't yet been introduced. Josh barely felt their embraces.

"Did you heal my leg?" Katia asked.

"Sort of," Josh admitted.

Feodor was standing with his blood-soaked shirt pulled up so he could examine his unblemished torso. Josh didn't hug him, of course, and he certainly made no move to hug her. In fact, he looked irritated.

"Thanks for your help," Josh told him. She knew exactly what he'd done.

"I demand an explanation," he said.

"Maybe later. Right now, we have to decide what to do with Peregrine before he wakes up."

Behind her, Whim was throwing up at the sight of Bayla's corpse. Feodor was pulling a bullet from his belly button, where his body had spit it out while healing. Mirren was examining her cousin's leg with gentle fingers, but she ran to her aunt and uncle when they entered the file room.

Josh ignored them all and sat down on the floor next to her unconscious grandfather. She had hoped that being near him would help her decide what to do, but if anything, it made the sense of peace she had brought back with her fade faster. Instead of seeing the path he was meant to take, all she could feel was her own fear that he would come after her again.

Will stood on Peregrine's other side. He used the toe of his shoe to nudge the gun across the floor and toward Josh. "Shoot him."

Deloise gasped.

Killing Peregrine was an option, Josh knew. Maybe the best option.

"He's insane," Will said. "If we don't kill him, he'll keep coming after us."

"I'm siding with this guy," Katia said. Will glanced at her and then did a double take, as if he hadn't realized she was in the room.

"You can't kill him!" Deloise cried.

Recalling the thicket that was Peregrine's mind, Josh said, "He's going to keep staging nightmares. We don't even know what World we're going back to, what he might have done to it. He could have turned Dad and Kerstel against us or convinced them to kill each other or to burn the house down."

Safety, that was all Josh had ever wanted. Safety for the dreamers, safety for her family. Safety for herself.

The same uncertainty that had snapped her out of her vision filled her now, and she wished she had been able to control her anger and fear long enough to see the path intended for Peregrine.

"So we'll put him in jail," Deloise said. "There are dream-walker jails!"

"Yeah, minimum security jails," Whim said, wiping his mouth with the back of his hand. "He'll break out the first day."

"Will is right," Feodor added. "This incident will only strengthen his ambitions."

"I agree," Mirren said, but then her eyes widened, and she grabbed the giant key ring off its hook and dashed into the maze of file cabinets. "Wait—maybe—"

"You can't kill him!" Deloise repeated, shouting it this time.

Josh tightened her hand around the gun, but she couldn't bring herself to point it at Peregrine. "He was going to kill us all, or turn us into slaves like Bash and Bayla."

"Josh, he's our grandfather," Deloise said, her eyes full of tears.

"I know," Josh said. She glanced at Mirren's aunt and uncle, who were standing near the doorway holding their daughter. "He hurt you, too. What do you think we should do?"

"Kill him," Katia said.

Fel and Collena exchanged a long look. Finally, Collena said, "The monarchy has never practiced capital punishment. Neither do we."

"Not even for him," Fel added, although the look on his face suggested he thought that maybe it was time to break with tradition.

They all want him dead, Josh thought. Carefully, she opened Peregrine's mouth and stuck the barrel of the gun between his teeth. The surest way to kill him was to shoot into the base of his brain. He was deep in shock, sweaty and pale. He'd never know what had happened; he'd never even wake up.

But the egg's wisdom tugged at her. *Not yet,* she kept thinking. *Not yet.*

"Josh!" Deloise shouted.

Will said, "Whim, take her upstairs so we can do this."

When Whim tried to grab Deloise, she hit him with a left punch so fast and sure that it would have made Muhammad Ali proud. Whim stumbled backward and careened into a row of file cabinets.

"Touch me again!" Deloise dared him. "Josh, don't do this!"

"I don't know what else to do," Josh told her sister. "How are we going to defend ourselves from him?"

She didn't know what else to do, but she didn't know if she

could do it, either. Why couldn't she have seen his path? The weight of the gun was making her hand tremble, and she was afraid she'd shoot by accident.

"Josh, you have to stop him while you have the chance," Will said, a frantic note entering his voice.

"Wait," Mirren said. She emerged from the stacks holding up a photocopy of a clay tablet with what appeared to be orderly chicken scratches on it. "We can banish him from the Dream forever."

"What?" Josh asked.

"How?" Deloise asked.

"This symbol. If you carve it into a person's skin, their soul can't enter the Dream."

Feodor took the photocopy and studied it.

"He won't be able to go into the Dream at all?" Josh asked. "Not even when he sleeps?"

"Neither body nor soul," Mirren said. "You understand . . . it's a forbidden act. To stop someone from entering the Dream . . . it's sacrilege."

"How will keeping him out of the Dream help?" Will demanded. "He'll just kill us when we're awake!"

"It'll keep him from staging," Deloise told Will. "Maybe if he can't enter the Dream, he'll lose interest in controlling Josh."

"Or maybe he'll sneak into the house and murder us while we sleep!"

Josh wondered if Will was right. Peregrine's interest had always been in determining the extent of Josh's powers as the True Dream Walker. He'd never borne her a particular enmity—although that would probably change after they turned his chest into scratch art.

"This appears to be from the Muzat School," Feodor said. "Impressive."

He held the page out to Josh, and she stared at the scratches. "We'd have to carve this into his skin? With a knife?"

"Josh!" Will protested in a near shout. His lips were pale with anger.

"Yes," Mirren said. "But . . . we wouldn't have to kill him."

Josh shook her head. "After what he did to us, I always thought it would be easy to kill him. But maybe it just isn't easy to kill someone."

"Maybe it shouldn't be," Deloise said.

"He's a murderer and a psychopath," Will said desperately.

Josh ran a hand through her hair. "I know," she assured Will. "I know exactly what he is."

Not yet, her mind said. *Not yet.*

She looked at her sister. "Can you live with using this symbol on him?"

"Being unable to dream could drive him mad," Mirren warned.

Deloise sighed. "He's already mad. At least this way he gets to live."

"Will," Josh said. "Can you live with it?"

She was almost afraid to ask, knowing how angry he was at her.

"I think we should shoot him in the head," Will said. "He *deserves* to die! How do you even know this symbol thing will work?"

"The Muzat School created a number of such symbols," Feodor told him. "The others have proven effective."

This information only enraged Will further. "I don't care!" he shouted. "He's criminally insane! Why can't we just kill him?"

"Because we aren't killers," Josh said.

Will gave her a look then that scared her. He wasn't the Will she knew, the one who had thought things through so carefully, who had been able to examine his own desires and emotions with such a rational eye.

"Josh, if you don't do this . . ."

He trailed off, and Josh didn't know if he couldn't think of a threat bad enough or just couldn't speak.

He's going to break up with me, she thought, *if I don't kill my grandfather.*

But she couldn't do it. Not even for Will. She had killed one person that night; she wasn't going to kill another.

She stood up and held the gun out to Will. "I can't kill him. If you can, that's your choice."

"Josh," Deloise said with alarm.

"Uh, is this a good idea?" Whim asked.

"It's a great idea," Will said, taking the gun from Josh. "I'll do it myself."

"Josh," Deloise said again. "Stop him!"

Josh shook her head. "It's Will's call."

Mirren put some distance between herself and Peregrine's body, and she drew Deloise away. When Whim started to step toward Will, Josh held out her hand to wave him off.

"What are you doing?" Whim asked.

Josh just held out her hand.

Will knelt at the top of Peregrine's head. He pressed the barrel of the gun to Peregrine's forehead, then changed his mind and put the gun in the old man's mouth.

Josh waited. Deloise watched through her fingers, and Whim jumped every time Will made any motion at all.

"Okay," Will muttered to himself. "Let's do this."

But he didn't do anything. Josh watched the gun tremble in his hand, the metal barrel clacking against Peregrine's teeth. From where she stood, Josh could see the lump beneath the back of Will's T-shirt—the scar from the skin graft he'd needed after their last encounter with Feodor. As much as Will blamed Feodor for his suffering, he and Josh both knew that Peregrine was equally to blame. He was the one who had manipulated them into entering Feodor's universe, knowing what they would face.

Still, the sight of the scar didn't make Josh willing to kill her grandfather. It just made her want to put her arms around Will and guide him away. It made her want to balance the universes once and for all.

Will repositioned himself, checking to make certain the barrel was pointed at the back of Peregrine's skull. He squared his shoulders and got a good grip on the handle. He took a deep breath.

He still didn't fire.

Josh had known he wouldn't. Well, almost known. She had been pretty sure. He'd shot at Feodor, but Feodor was already dead. For all Will had been traumatized, he was still a moral person under-neath, and he couldn't shoot a living man in cold blood any more than Josh could. She felt an unexpected pride that he couldn't pull the trigger, not even against a man who had hurt him terribly.

"Oh, my God," Whim burst out. "Just shoot him already! The suspense is killing me!"

Will's head snapped up, and his face was filled with rage and, beneath that, humiliation. "Can you shut up for one minute, Whim?"

"It's been like ten minutes!" Whim protested.

Will sprang to his feet, yanking the gun from Peregrine's mouth. "You know what? This isn't my problem." He shoved the gun into Josh's arms, and for an instant she fumbled it dangerously. "All of this is *your* fault," Will told her. "So you take care of it. I'm done cleaning up your messes."

His words filled Josh with a familiar rush of guilt and shame. He was right that the situation they were in was her fault—not completely her fault, but enough.

He stormed out of the file room, and Josh ran after him, hand-ing the gun to her sister as she passed. She heard a metallic slid-ing as Deloise removed the magazine.

"Will, wait!" she called, and she caught him on a landing be-tween staircases. "Please, wait."

He had tears in his eyes. "I can't do this anymore," he said, all his anger burned away. "Josh, I can't do this. I don't want to do this anymore."

"I know, I know. You don't have to do anything else." She tried to take his hand, but he was moving too quickly. "We'll go home and you can rest."

"No, I don't want to go home! I don't want any of it!"

He means being a dream walker, Josh realized.

"I almost shot a man!" he wailed. "I can't—I can't be part of this! It's changing me. It's . . . destroying me."

"Will," Josh said, "this is the end of all the craziness. I promise. We'll go get Haley back and then it will all be over."

"Over? Are you kidding? You just assured that it *isn't* over by letting Peregrine live! And I can't—" He pushed the hair out of his eyes, taking dizzy, pacing steps on the landing. Josh tried to hug him and he pushed her away. "No! Don't touch me! I don't want any of it! I'm sorry. I'm sorry. I can't be with you. I can't be part of any of it."

Josh didn't know what to do, and her own panic was making her hands tremble. *He doesn't mean it,* she told herself. *He'll calm down and see reason.*

"Ask me for something," she begged. "Anything. I'll do whatever you want—go to therapy, or quit dream walking for a while, or go on vacation."

He shook his head, and the way he looked at Josh without seeing her, as if she no longer existed to him, made her realize that she had already lost him.

"I just want my mom," he said hollowly, and he wandered up the next flight of stairs, away from her and alone.

Later, after they'd found an emergency kit with a syringe of morphine to keep Peregrine sedated, and after Feodor had volunteered to do the cutting, and after Josh, Whim, and Mirren had spent an hour holding the old man down and putting pressure on his new wounds, her friends tried to convince Josh that Will would come around.

"He's all hyped up on adrenaline," Whim said. "He just needs a day or two to chill out."

"Once he gets some perspective, he'll be glad he didn't kill Peregrine," Mirren insisted.

They meant well, Josh knew. But they were wrong. Will wouldn't calm down and he wouldn't forgive her, because in the end, she had been the one who hurt him the worst.

Only Feodor failed to try to convince her that everything would be fine.

Feodor knew better.

Thirty-one

Two days later, Will sat alone on the couch in the guys' apartment and watched the Accordance Conclave coverage.

"Joining us now," said the reporter on the television screen, "is noted political analyst Jobe Calmikterie. Jobe, is there any doubt about the outcome here?"

"None," replied a middle-aged man in an ugly suit. "Now that Mirren Rousellario has been exposed as a traitor, the only votes she's going to get will come from fringe lunatics and hard-core anarchists."

"Like mother, like daughter, eh?"

"That's right, Myssa. I doubt we'll even see a statement from her regarding the Accordance Conclave. If she has any sense at all, she's left the country."

"I'd shoot her if I saw her," Myssa agreed.

Her words added another boulder to the mountain of despair Will already sagged beneath. He and the others had returned from the Hidden Kingdom to find that every dream walker they knew believed Mirren was evil—even Davita, who proudly announced that she had been the one to show Peregrine how to access the Hidden Kingdom.

Josh explained to them that they had been victims of staging, and even though they all believed her, they seemed unable to connect the staging with their certainty about Mirren. Right now, the adults of the household were in the living room, watching the election results and cheering for Peregrine. Kerstel was wearing a homemade T-shirt that read, "Babies for Borgenicht!"

Mirren herself was safely tucked away in the Hidden Kingdom (the entrance to which had been moved), but she had sworn to return to the World once everyone stopped wanting her dead. Will didn't know how long that might take, given how high anti-Mirren sentiment was running.

Myssa the reporter was standing in front of a projected map of North America, talking about which districts had turned in results already. The districts in which Peregrine had won were colored lime green, centered on Braxton. The districts in which Mirren had won were meant to be colored orange, but so far none were, not even far away where Peregrine hadn't been able to stage dreams.

"As goes Rome, so goes the empire," Feodor had said when he'd predicted this outcome the day before.

Feodor was in Whim's bedroom with Whim and Deloise, building some sort of cage that he said would help them restore Winsor's soul. "Assuming her brain isn't mush," he'd added when he finished explaining that he thought reunification would be possible. Will expected it was all just another trick, but he'd given up trying to warn anyone.

"Even with twelve more districts left to report in, this election has obviously been a landslide for Peregrine Borgenicht and the Lodestone Party," Jobe said. "It's a shame that he isn't well enough to publicly claim victory and truly enjoy this moment."

"Obviously we're all sending well wishes and congratulations to the hospital."

After Feodor had carved Peregrine like a roast, Deloise, Josh, and Whim had carried him out of the Hidden Kingdom and done a dump-and-run outside a Braxton ER. The Lodestone Party was saying he had pneumonia, but according to Whim's underground sources, he was really in a psych ward, babbling incoherently and missing a hand.

"Five more districts have just reported," Myssa said, and another burst of lime green appeared on the map. "Oh—and here's a surprise! Greenland has gone orange!"

Jobe laughed. "Do they not have Internet up there? How far behind on the news are they?"

"Of the fewer than five hundred dream walkers in Greenland, slightly over one hundred voted for Mirren Rousellario and eighty-nine for Peregrine Borgenicht." Sarcastically, she added, "Now we've got a real race on our hands."

Will groaned. Bad enough that Mirren was losing; did the reporters have to enjoy it so much?

The apartment door opened, and Josh appeared, carrying several poster-sized sheets of what appeared to be copper. She stopped short when she saw Will.

Deloise had told him that Josh had killed Bash to save him and nearly killed herself in the process. In fact, Del insisted that Josh had died for at least a minute. She had been performing mouth-to-mouth while Whim did CPR when Will hit the activator and nearly destroyed the Hidden Kingdom.

Will felt nothing but guilt about any of it. Josh had killed Bash, and Will had killed Bayla, and neither of them had been able to kill the only person who needed killing.

The sight of Josh standing in the doorway sent a throb of pain through his heart, both because the wound of losing her was so fresh and because he still loved her so damn much. He knew that demanding she kill her grandfather had been irrational, yet he still felt angry that she hadn't done it, which was supremely hypocritical since he hadn't been able to do it either. And he hated her for having shown him that.

The truth was, whether or not they'd killed Peregrine had been immaterial to the state of their relationship. Will would have broken up with her either way, he saw that now. Distancing himself from her and the constant danger she inspired was the only chance he had to regain some of his sanity. He needed space, and quiet, and peace. He needed to feel safe in the World again.

Besides, Josh was Feodor's in a way she had never been Will's, maybe not even in a romantic sense, but in some deeper, more thorough way. Feodor and his memories had changed who she was, and Will didn't know her anymore. He didn't trust her.

Will had overheard them talking in the office earlier. They'd been speaking Polish, and very quickly, as if they had so much to say to each other.

Will didn't have anything left to say to Josh. He didn't even know what he was doing in this house anymore, except that Whim and Deloise and his adopted parents had all insisted he stay, and since he wasn't eighteen yet, he didn't really have a choice.

Now, as Josh fumbled with her sheets of copper in the doorway, Will just stared at her and said nothing. He pinched his lips shut against the desire to say, *I'm sorry. I take it all back.*

"Sorry," she babbled. "I was just going to— I can come back later."

"It's fine," Will told her, his voice cracking. "Do what you need to do."

She set the sheets of copper against the wall and closed the apartment door behind her. Still not looking at him, she said, "About . . . I was . . . hoping, I guess . . ."

So we're back to this, Will thought, remembering how difficult she had found it to talk to him when they first met.

"I didn't mean to . . ."

Back then, he would have helped her, coaxed her into finding the words she needed, reassured her that whatever she felt was okay. The urge to do so was still strong in him, as was the desire to hold her close and reassure her without words.

He didn't have the strength to do either.

Finally, Josh just muttered, "Sorry," again, and fled to Whim's room with her copper.

As soon as she disappeared, another round of guilt hit him. He knew what it must have taken for her to even try to start a conversation about the way things had ended.

I should have helped her. She was trying so hard.

But he was afraid that one forgiveness would lead to another, and by tomorrow he'd be neck-deep in nightmares and danger and science he didn't understand. Being alone was so much easier and less frightening. He turned up the volume on the television.

"And it's official!" Myssa declared. "Peregrine Borgenicht and his Lodestone Party have been voted in as the permanent form of government for the dream walkers of North America!"

Lime-green confetti rained down on the stage, and the station cut to a shot of dream walkers celebrating at the Dashiel Winters Building in Braxton.

Will leaned back on the couch and closed his eyes, and the cheers filled his ears.

"Long live Peregrine Borgenicht!"

Thirty-two

 Feodor broke into the nursing home at two in the morning, crawling through a window in the accounting office and taking the equipment elevator up to the third floor, which was useful because they had a lot of equipment. Besides the copper cage, Feodor required various osmium plates, a wealth of crystals and magnets, a massive negative ion generator, a water pump with ten yards of tubing, and five gallons of seawater. Not to mention the canister containing Winsor's soul.

"If we get caught," Whim whispered to Josh as they rode the elevator up, "what do you imagine the nurses will think we're doing?"

She shushed him.

In the relative safety of Winsor's room, they got to work.

Despite the fact that they were—hopefully—about to restore her soul, Josh still felt sick when she looked at Winsor, and even sicker when she had to remove her friend's blankets and stretch her out, corpselike, on the bed. Feodor said to take off her pajamas, but Whim glared at him and he admitted that rolling up her sleeves and pajama pants would do.

Josh and Whim wrapped Winsor's body in plastic tubing and turned the pump on so that the seawater circulated around her. The thought had crossed Josh's mind that this might all be an elaborate ploy to kill Winsor, and she was sure Whim had thought the same thing, but to what end? Feodor had nothing to gain from her death and everything to gain from creating goodwill with his captors. So Josh didn't protest when Feodor put an oxygen mask on Winsor's face and connected it to the negative ion generator.

They spent the next hour attaching crystals and magnets to the cage, using a roll of copper wire.

"This is too weird," Whim said, his voice low. "Is this even going to work?"

"Feodor says it will," Josh told him.

"But don't you know? Don't you remember?"

There are so many things I don't remember.

The memory of how Will had stared at her that day in the living room came back full force, filling her with shame and sadness. The expression on his face had been so closed to her. She'd desperately wanted to remind him of his promise to love her no matter what she had to do, but his stillness and silence had made it more than clear that he no longer cared about keeping his promises to her.

"No," she told Whim. "I don't remember."

They went back to work.

But as Josh attached crystals to the cage, she kept recalling their first encounter with Feodor and how physically damaged they had been when it was over. This time, she and Will were physically whole, but she felt that they had lost even more.

Maybe if they saved Winsor and got Haley back, things would get better.

When the crystals and magnets were in place, Feodor said they had to wait half an hour.

"For what?" Whim demanded.

"To prepare her body. If she is not prepared to receive her soul, it will flee."

They waited a terse half hour. Whim played Yahtzee on his phone, but Josh just leaned against the wall with her arms crossed over her broken heart and waited.

"If I may ask," Feodor said softly to her as time dragged by, "have you attempted to open an archway since we returned from the Hidden Kingdom?"

"No." She hadn't even thought about it.

"A most interesting ability," he mused. "And one I have never seen before."

"Well, don't get too excited. It seems to be all I'm capable of."

She hadn't told him about the egg, or the visions, or the little voice inside her that had woken up and whispered, even now, *You have to follow it.* She hadn't told anyone except to say that in the moment she was near death, she had tapped into her True Dream Walker powers briefly and healed Feodor and Katia.

"Oh, but I am excited," Feodor said. "And I believe this ability might mean a great deal."

Josh looked at him. He sat in the rocking chair but didn't rock, and even in the meager light of the parking lot lamp beyond the window, she could see his bemused smile.

"Tell me," he said, "have you ever broken Stellanor's First Rule of dream walking?"

Josh shivered.

"How the hell did you figure that out?" Whim asked, getting up from the floor.

Feodor shrugged. "I read it in a very old prophecy regarding the True Dream Walker."

"I've never heard that," Josh said.

He smiled coyly. "I expect I know quite a bit that you do not."

That was true. But . . .

"If I'm the True Dream Walker, then why is opening archways the only thing I can do?"

"Just because you haven't been trained to use your abilities does not mean they don't exist."

Josh's heartbeat quickened in spite of her mind's warning not to trust him.

"And I suppose you could train me," she said.

"I could," Feodor agreed.

Her first thought was that Will would never forgive her, but Will would probably never forgive her anyway.

Her second thought was of Haley.

"Nothing is more important than getting Haley back," she said, which was almost true. It was true enough.

As Feodor opened his small mouth to respond, Winsor gasped.

Whim shot across the room, and Josh and Feodor followed him to the bedside. Beneath her eyelids, Winsor's eyes darted around. Her fingers twitched.

"Quickly," Feodor said. "Remove the oxygen mask tubing from the ion generator and connect it to the outgoing valve on the canister, but don't open it! Reconnect the ion generator to the ingoing valve."

Whim and Josh worked on the tubing, Whim's hands shaking with excitement.

"Josh, place the small osmium plate in her mouth."

"What if she chokes on it?" Whim asked.

"She won't choke. Turn off the water pump. Whim, open the ingoing valve."

"What about the outgoing valve?"

"Not yet. With alacrity, Josh!"

Whim leaned over the bed to turn off the pump while Josh secured the plate in Winsor's mouth.

"Open the outgoing valve!" Feodor cried. "Now, now!"

Whim spun the valve handle on the canister. "It's open!"

He stepped back from the bed, and they all stared silently at Winsor.

She began to cough.

Her jaws moved, slowly at first, then faster, trying to force the plate out. Josh reached in to help her, and she retrieved the plate just as the door blew open and a nurse came in. She flicked on the overhead light and everyone froze except Winsor, who continued to cough. "What's going on in—"

She stopped short when she saw Winsor in the cage. "Mary mother of Jesus!"

Winsor's eyes opened, and they were blue again, blue and clear and alive.

"Winsor?" Whim asked. He yanked the cage off the bed and clasped her face in his hands.

"She's awake," the nurse said with a gasp. "Dr. Guyer!"

She went running down the hallway, shouting for the doctor.

"You did it," Whim said to Feodor, his expression awed.

Feodor crossed his arms over his chest and smiled smugly. "I believe the appropriate expression is, I told you so."

She's back, Josh thought, and she felt a sweet, tiny glimmer of hope. *We saved her.*

"Winny?" Whim asked. "Can you hear me?"

Winsor coughed again, and she looked at Whim with terror in her blue eyes.

"Say something," Whim said.

Winsor opened her mouth, lips trembling, and screamed.

"*SAAAAAM!*"

Thirty-three

The second time they entered Death, Mirren brought three silver coins with which to pay the boatman.

He took them and grunted, as he had the first time, but Mirren thought his grunt sounded less cranky than before.

She sat beside Feodor in the boat, and Josh sat across from them. Mirren thought Josh's eyes were still pink rimmed from crying and she never seemed fully present, but she looked a little lighter since they'd restored the souls in the canister to their bodies.

Well, three of the four. One soul's body had already died, so they were bringing that soul with them to Death.

Josh said Winsor had woken up screaming for someone named Sam and that one of the souls in the canister had belonged to a young man named Sam. Even Feodor didn't seem sure what to make of that.

In gratitude to Feodor for restoring Winsor's soul, Whim agreed to break back into Death instead of shooting him in the face, and they'd all driven out to Iph National Forest to perform the singing bowl ritual again. Will had played his bowls but refused to enter Death, and Feodor had played Haley's part.

Mirren was jittery with the anticipation of seeing him. Yes, she'd lost the election; yes, she'd had to retreat to the Hidden Kingdom; but at least she could have Haley back.

The excitement made her talkative, and she asked Feodor something she had been wondering about since their first visit to the afterlife.

"Feodor," she said, "the gods of the underworld called you by a name, *inumen*. What does it mean?"

He smiled enigmatically. She didn't know if he found amusement in her question or in his answer.

"It means *clown*," he said.

For some reason, the answer made her nervous.

Inside the temple, the lords of Death shone brighter than ever. Haley wasn't there; Mirren had thought he would be, that he would anticipate their return.

"Your Highnesses," Mirren said, falling into a deep curtsy. "We have returned the *inumen* and wish to exchange him for the hostage."

One of the gods rose to circle Feodor, examining him.

"Tell us your name," it said, "and die."

Feodor, who had not bowed to the gods, said, "I propose a new arrangement."

"Arrangement?" asked one of the seated gods. "Do you treat Death so callously?"

"Wait," Josh said, her eyes flashing with alarm.

Feodor ignored her. "While I was in the World, not only did I help these children stop a powerful evil, but I restored three souls to the bodies from which I had taken them, and I have brought you a fourth."

"What are you doing?" Josh asked. "Feodor, stop."

Mirren's pulse began to pound.

"Before I died," Feodor continued, "I trapped more than sixty souls in a pocket universe. When my universe collapsed, those souls, rightfully dead, were lost in the Dream. If you allow me to remain alive, I will bring those souls to you."

"No," Josh said. "No."

"Where is Haley?" Mirren asked desperately. She felt dizzy and sick, and she grabbed hold of Feodor's arm, but she couldn't stop him from speaking.

"Without my help, those souls will remain trapped in the Dream forever," Feodor warned.

"His name is Feodor Kajażkołski!" Josh shouted, but to no effect.

The golden beings conferred. Josh grabbed Feodor and spun him to face her.

"What are you doing?" she demanded.

Feodor gave one of his light little shrugs, but then he fondly touched Josh's cheek. "Silly American child. Do you think the dead can be dropped off like a package on a doorstep?" He made a *tsk tsk* sound. "We are each on a journey."

Josh stared at him wordlessly.

We all started to trust him, Mirren realized. *With his soft accent and his good manners and the way he helped Winsor. We forgot who he is.*

"Please," she begged him as the tears ran down her face. "We need Haley back. Please don't do this."

"Ah, Kapuścisko. Such a sweet boy."

"He can't survive here!" Mirren cried.

"No one can," Feodor said shrewdly.

The lords of Death returned to their thrones.

"Every month, on the night of the new moon, you must return, bringing with you three souls," the central figure said. "If you fail to do so, we will come for you."

"What about our friend?" Josh asked. "The hostage?"

"He will remain a hostage, so that you might remember that the *inumen* is your charge to control."

Mirren couldn't repress a cry.

"Please," Josh begged. "Please. Return our friend. I'll stay in his place."

"The bargain is struck," the golden figure said.

For the second time, Mirren found herself sitting on the forest floor, crying.

That night she lay in Haley's bed, wrapped in the familiar sights of his things, unable to sleep. Wearing the sweater he had given her, she wandered aimlessly around the room for a while, looking through old photos, shamelessly going through his drawers. In the closet, she found a classical guitar, and she sat on the bed for a while, strumming it. But the guitar sounded like she felt, discordant and sad, as if they had both given up on Haley's return.

Finally, she put the guitar away and got back into bed, pulling the comforter around her. She pressed her face into his pillow and pretended it was his shoulder.

As her hand slid beneath the pillow, she touched something smooth and cool.

She pulled out a page torn from a steno pad and folded into quarters. With frantic fingers, she opened it.

Mirren,
Build the Royal Trimidion.

Epilogue

On the far side of the temple of the golden beings, Haley stood among the masses of the dead and trembled. He longed for a cardigan to wrap around himself, some small protection from the needy eyes of the souls that wandered to and fro, staring at him with a depth of hunger their physical bodies had never known.

He slid down against the side of the temple and stayed there, curled in a ball, for hours. Although they'd broken into Death in the middle of the night, the sun had been high in the sky here. Now it began to set, and Haley watched his last measure of comfort vanish beyond the horizon. His muscles ached from shaking. He felt as if his moment of bravery had emptied him of all courage, and as night crept over the land of the dead, he gave himself over to helplessness.

I'm never going home. I'll never see Mirren again. I'll never see Mom again, or Will, or Whim. I'm going to die here, alone.

Finally he began to cry, pressing his hot face against his knees, cursing himself and his gallant stupidity. Some of the dead paused to watch—their expressions confused, as if they were witnessing a ritual they only dimly remembered—but after a time, Haley became aware of a figure standing over him, waiting with his arms crossed and his foot tapping.

Haley raised his throbbing head. Against the blazing sunset, he could only make out dark hair and a familiar figure, and it wasn't until he caught sight of the stranger's aura—hot-rod red and cobalt blue—that he realized the stranger wasn't a stranger at all.

"Hello, little brother," Ian said, and he grinned.

Turn the page for a sneak peek at
Kit Alloway's next novel

Dream Forever

Available March 2017

One

A corpse lay slumped on the floor in the center of the coffee shop, right in front of the holiday mug display. Customers stepped lightly around it as they passed from the counter to the cream and sugar station, their wet boots squeaking on the floor. The Christmas-caroled air smelled of ginger and cloves, and trays of frosted snowmen grinned from the display cases. Beyond the open doorway, shoppers thronged the mall hallway.

"Christmas nightmares," Josh said. "They come earlier every year." She glanced behind herself at Will—

But it wasn't Will standing behind her. It was Feodor.

He wore his usual expression—a mishmash of contempt and amusement—and his usual outfit, a white button-down shirt and high-waisted, pleated slacks, the creases ironed as crisp as the lines of his lips. Arms crossed over his chest, he waited patiently as Josh assessed the nightmare around them, as patiently as he had once collected souls in canisters, his congregation growing slowly, year by year.

Finally, though, he made a little fluttering gesture with his hand, as if to say, *Get on with it.*

Josh sighed and turned back to the corpse. Two months and she still expected Will to be at her side.

Stop thinking about Will, she ordered herself. *There's work to be done.*

The dead man wore blue jeans so dirty they looked black, broken-down shoes, and no shirt. Burst blood vessels stretched across his nose like networks of roots, suggesting years of hard drinking, but Josh doubted it was the bottle that had killed him. His entire chest had exploded, revealing a mashed cobbler of internal organs.

Josh knelt and touched his cold, stiff hand. This close up, he stank like a two-week-old steak. She closed her eyes and imagined the stone walls that protected her from the dreamer's fear.

Her mother had been the one who taught Josh to imagine herself surrounded by stone walls. They had begun working on the visualization when Josh was only eight—a year before she was even allowed to accompany Jona into the Dream. Now the image of white rock and gray mortar and the sense of security it provided felt as familiar as the weight of the plumeria charm she wore around her neck.

In her mind, she imagined using her fingertips to pick a well-worn cork from between two stones in the wall. When it popped loose, a waft of blue smoke slipped through, and Josh breathed it in, inhaling a taste of the dreamer's fear as she did so.

She will reclaim me, the fear whispered. *What has been promised must be paid. Tlazolteotl is hungry.*

Josh opened her eyes.

"What did you sense?" Feodor asked.

"This dead guy isn't the dreamer." Josh stood up and wiped imagined death germs from her hand. "She's over there."

Josh nodded toward a caramel-skinned woman in her fifties whose arms were strung with so many shopping bags that she was having difficulty pouring sugar into her coffee.

"And?" Feodor asked.

"And Tlazolteotl is coming to get her."

Feodor considered. "The name sounds Aztec. Try again. Try to see the shape of the nightmare."

Josh closed her eyes again, imagined those stone walls, pulled the cork from the hole, and breathed deep. Technically, she was breaking Stellanor's First Rule of dream walking: *Never let the dreamer's fear become your own.* There was a good reason it was the *first* rule: getting caught up in a dreamer's fear could render her helpless to the nightmare. But Josh had been breaking the rule almost since the day she'd learned it, and Feodor had a theory that her ability to do so was the key to accessing her abilities as the True Dream Walker.

She breathed in a big ole dose of fear.

That which you have lost you must give up. Tlazolteotl is hungry.

Tlazolteotl was somewhere in the mall, and she was coming closer. Josh tried to imagine what would happen when she found the dreamer.

She'll . . . what? Kill her? Eat her?

Strangely, what came to mind were the woman's packages.

But what does the corpse have to do with it?

Josh pictured the dead man, but he didn't fit with the images in her head. She just kept coming back to the packages.

Opening her eyes again, she saw that the woman was pouring creamer into her drink. One of her bags had knocked over a squeeze bottle of honey.

Tlazolteotl's going to steal her Christmas shopping?

Frustrated, Josh tried again. This time she thrust a fist through the imaginary wall, the stone crumbling around her knuckles. Blue smoke rushed through and billowed around her.

You have to follow it, Josh reminded herself.

She still didn't fully understand what that meant, any more than she understood why Tlazolteotl wanted the dreamer's Christmas shopping. But she'd first heard the words during a moment of wisdom, and she repeated them to herself when she was hoping for insight.

Now she waited, allowing her mind to show her whatever it wanted. From the darkness behind her eyelids, an image emerged, stepping out from the shadows and into the light of Josh's understanding. She saw Tlazolteotl—a huge, primal figure dressed in animal skins—coming into the coffee shop, grabbing the woman, opening the shopping bags, and thrusting her muzzle-like face inside, devouring the contents. Whatever was in those packages, it was more precious to the dreamer than her life, and Josh felt the chill of the woman's fear like a gulp of ice water.

Tlazolteotl is here. Tlazolteotl is hungry.

Josh moved before her eyes were open and managed to trip over the corpse at her feet. After jostling a table of ornaments, she found her footing and rushed through the coffee shop to where the woman was struggling to get the plastic lid back onto her drink. Her hands were shaking.

"Tlazolteotl is here," Josh said. "What's in the bags?"

"No," the woman begged. "Please. I can't."

"I need to know—"

"No!"

But Josh had already yanked one of the bags off the woman's wrist. She pulled the twine handles apart and looked into the pale pink paper bag.

At the bottom of the bag sat the woman's innocence.

Later, Josh wouldn't be able to recall exactly what she had seen. Perhaps innocence had no physical form. All she would remember was starlight the color of rose quartz and a sense of hope so grand it left no possibility for anything other than joy. Josh was still blinking when the woman grabbed the bag back.

"I can't lose it!" she shouted at Josh.

She ran out of the coffee shop, and Josh and Feodor ran after her. But Josh needed to close her eyes—*Someday, I'm going to figure out how to do this with my eyes open*, she swore to herself—so she took hold of Feodor's arm and said, "Lead me. Don't lose her!"

Trying to ignore her own motion and Feodor's voice calling, "Pardon! Make way for this young blind woman!" Josh went back to the stone walls. They stood close around her, like the walls of a well, and they were so real to her that when she began yanking stones out, they scraped her palms.

The blue smoke poured in around her, clouding her vision with the woman's terror. Josh felt the familiar burn of dreamfire. But she needed to see past the smoke, and she imagined herself crawling through the hole she'd made and out past the walls entirely.

On the other side, where the blue smoke had cleared, she saw the woman as a little girl in a pale green bathing suit, cowering behind the flimsy plastic curtain of a locker room shower. The outline of a man darkened the curtain, and thick fingers curled around its edge—

"No!"

Josh's own horrified scream snapped her back into her body. The shoppers who surrounded her stopped walking to stare, even the dreamer.

Josh ran to her, pushing startled shoppers aside. "You already lost it," she told the dreamer. "You lost it years ago."

"No," the woman said, beginning to push through the crowd again. "No!"

"Your innocence is already gone," Josh insisted. "Give it to her! Tlazolteotl can't steal what you offer freely."

"It's mine!"

"Don't make her take it!" Josh grabbed the woman by the shoulders and turned her so that they were face-to-face. "Listen to me! You have to accept what happened and let it go! She won't hurt you if—"

"I *can't*!" the woman wailed, and she tore herself away.

Behind them, something roared.

In the center of the mall food court, her head brushing the third-story ceiling, walked a giant copper-skinned woman. A curled gold bar pierced the septum of her nose, and enormous turquoise earrings hung to her shoulders. She wore an elaborate horned headdress and a red and green skirt, but her breasts were bare except for a multitude of beaded necklaces. Instead of a lower jaw, she had a muzzle, and when she opened it, she revealed a mouth full of dirt, blood, and very sharp teeth.

Tlazolteotl—the eater of sins.

"Oh, shit," Josh said.

The shoppers began to stampede away from Tlazolteotl, their screams drowned out only by the goddess's furious roar.

"I believe this would be an appropriate time to abort," Feodor said.

Each of Tlazolteotl's steps shook the floor. With a growl, she knocked a forty-foot-high Christmas tree onto a jewelry kiosk.

"I can still resolve it," Josh insisted, even though her first instinct was to run like hell. "Come on."

She dashed after the dreamer, shoving people left and right. They were only figments of the dreamer's imagination, after all. It didn't really matter if they got trampled or eaten. The only person who mattered was the dreamer.

Josh found her cowering under the escalator.

"You have to give Tlazolteotl the bags," Josh said. "It's the only way to satisfy her."

The woman shook her head and clutched the bags to her chest. "No, I can't. I'm not ready."

"You are," Josh insisted. "If you weren't, you wouldn't be having this nightmare."

For the last two months, Josh had been entering the Dream and diving into dreamers' fears. It hadn't been easy and it sure hadn't been fun, and if Feodor hadn't been there to keep an eye on her, she would have lost herself entirely on more than one occasion. But in witnessing so much fear, she had noticed a pattern: nightmares had purpose. They were almost designed like tests intended to force the dreamer to grow or evolve in some way.

You have to follow it, Josh thought again.

"Nightmare?" the woman repeated.

"Yes. And if you just let your innocence go—"

But she'd said too much. The woman must have realized she was dreaming and woken up, because the Dream shifted, sending Josh and Feodor spinning through space.

They landed hard on an evergreen forest floor covered in pine-cones, and the corpse from the coffee shop landed right between them, hitting the ground so hard it sent pinecones bouncing.

"Gross," Josh said. A hundred yards away, she noticed a pair of black bears climbing a tree. Squinting, she was able to make out two people clinging to the tree's upper branches.

This nightmare could wait—at least for a few minutes.

"There is only one explanation for how this body passed from one nightmare to another," Feodor said.

"It's a real corpse," Josh said, like a good student. It disturbed her that she sounded like Will used to, when talking to her. What was she becoming—Feodor's apprentice?

The body seemed grosser now that she knew it was real, and the fall hadn't done it any favors. The man appeared to be in his sixties, but he'd obviously lived a hard life: his hair was long and greasy, and his open mouth exposed missing and rotting teeth. Black tattoos that had faded to blurry ashen smudges covered his arms.

"I haven't heard about any dream walkers being lost in the Dream recently," Josh said.

"This man does not strike me as a dream walker," Feodor said, a note of elitism in his voice. "He stinks."

"Dream walkers can be alcoholics, too," Josh told him, thinking of Will again. But she was more than certain that Will wasn't drinking these days.

The man's chest appeared to have exploded from within. Ragged, torn flesh revealed the jagged ends of broken ribs and a meaningless mass of shredded organs that Josh couldn't identify. The cavity ran from the man's breastbone down nearly to his belly button.

"This is an unusual wound," Feodor admitted. With a fallen stick, he poked around between the ribs.

"Let's drag him out of the Dream."

Feodor made a *hmm* sound, but he seemed intrigued rather than irritated. Focusing her mind, Josh flung her arm out from her body and felt power soar through her palm and into the midst of the forest, where a shimmering archway formed.

She grabbed the corpse's legs and Feodor caught him under the shoulders, and together they carried him out of the Dream.

Josh tried to set him down gently, but the dead man made a *thud* when he landed on the archroom's white tile floor. *Kerstel's going to make me bleach this floor,* Josh thought regretfully, wishing she'd put a towel down first. But her irritation was overcome by the excitement of realizing she had been right: the dead man was real.

"Do you have a scalpel?" Feodor asked, getting to his knees beside the corpse.

"Why would I have a scalpel?" Josh asked. "Never mind—don't answer that." She sat back on her heels. "This wound is too ragged for a knife, and too big for a bullet. Maybe if he was shot from behind with a hollow-point . . ."

They were rolling the man over to check for a bullet entry point when Whim Avish walked in.

"Oh, sweet Mother Mary!" he cried, jumping back so fast his shoulder slammed into the door frame. "What am I walking in on?"

Josh was on her butt, pulling on the dead man's hips so that she could roll him. "Do you see a bullet wound in his back?"

"I don't know! Who is that guy?"

"We found him in the Dream."

Feodor, wedging his foot under the corpse's hips so he could get down on the floor and see beneath the man's torso, said, "I don't believe he's been shot, but it's difficult to tell. There's been considerable seepage of fluids."

"Stop talking!" Whim shouted. "And stop parbuckling him! Dear God—my eyes!"

Josh and Feodor let the corpse fall back onto the floor.

"Parbuckling?" she asked.

"It's a word!" Whim insisted.

Will Kansas stuck his head into the archroom.

Will met Josh's eyes without hesitation. He always did. Over the last two months, he had been unfailingly polite and unreasonably friendly. He had acknowledged Josh's presence, asked her to pass the salt, picked up her gloves when she dropped them once. Sometimes he even smiled at her, in a genuine, forgiving way.

It was awful.

"Whoa," Will said at the sight of the dead man.

Could anyone else tell how wrong his voice was? It sounded so natural, so casual, with just a hint of acknowledgment that they used to be more to each other than they were now. Josh had never thought she'd miss Ian's cold shoulder, but this was worse. Will wanted them to be friendly—to be *friends*. Josh just didn't know how to do that.

Work to be done, she reminded herself.

She tried to focus on the corpse in front of her. "All I can think is that someone stuck a bomb down his throat. But that would have messed up his back, too."

"If I'm not mistaken," Feodor told Josh, "I believe this is the heart. Do you see how it has ruptured? Both chambers of each lung seem to have burst."

Whim started gagging.

"Whim, can you please go call the Gendarmerie and tell them that we just pulled a corpse out of the Dream?"

"Yeah." Whim coughed. "I'm going. Gladly. Come on, Will."

Josh glanced at Will as he left the room. He gave her another one of those honest, kindly, understanding smiles.

Does he not miss me? Josh thought. *Is that what he's trying to tell me? Is that why he looks so good?*

He looked better than he had since they'd first met, now that he was in counseling and on anxiety medication. The circles under his cornflower-blue eyes were gone, and his previous pallor had been replaced by a healthy, ruddy color.

Breaking up with me was the best thing he ever did for himself, Josh thought.

That was her real fear—that his equilibrium and contentment weren't an act, that he was legitimately fine without her. Was he hiding his pain, or did he just not feel any?

Feodor made a little *ahem* sound, which was his way of laughing at her. "The corpse?" he said.

"I'm thinking," Josh told him.

"Perhaps you would like to think of something more relevant," he suggested.

After giving him her best glare, Josh returned to examining the body, and only moments later, she found something that drove all thoughts of Will from her head.

"Feodor," she said tightly. "Look."

At the base of the man's throat, near where the skin began to split, were numerous small cuts. They didn't appear to be part of the fatal wound—they were straight and clean. Several cuts intersected to form a triangle at the end of a long, straight line.

Feodor cursed softly in Polish.

"Is it . . . ?" Josh asked, even though she knew it was.

He sighed heavily. "Yes. Someone carved the symbol we used on Peregrine into this man's chest."

Two months earlier, Josh had been faced with the choice of either killing her grandfather or risking letting him live. She'd compromised and carved an ancient symbol into his chest, one that would prevent him from entering the Dream universe. The only people who currently had access to the symbol were Mirren Rousellario and Peregrine himself.

"But I thought the symbol would stop the wearer from entering the Dream," Josh said.

Feodor gestured to the dead man's ravaged torso. "Obviously, it did."

Josh sent Feodor upstairs to hide in the library—only a dozen people knew he was back from the dead—and then rolled the dead man up in a sheet. It was a good sheet, too, and she'd probably catch hell for using it, but she thought he deserved something nice. It seemed like the least she could do, after dragging him out of the Dream and landing him like a trout on the archroom floor.

A gendarme named Burnette arrived at the house to collect the body. The Gendarmerie were the approximate equivalent of dream-walker police, but they only dealt with issues that couldn't be taken to the real police. Josh was pretty sure pulling a corpse out of an alternate universe counted.

"You don't look surprised," she noted when she'd finished explaining how she'd found the dead man.

Burnette sighed. "Look, I wouldn't tell this to anyone else, and I'm trusting you to keep it to yourself."

Josh nodded.

"This is the fifth corpse we've pulled out of the Dream in the last six weeks."

"The *fifth*?" Josh asked, aghast.

Burnette nodded, blond curls falling into her eyes. "Looks like we have a serial killer. We still can't figure out how they're being killed. Our best guess is one of those shark knives that blows things apart with a burst of air."

Josh said nothing. She'd always wanted to use one of those knives—but not on a person.

"We've only managed to identify one of the bodies. Homeless guy."

Josh wouldn't have been surprised to learn that this man was also homeless, and suddenly the entire scheme clarified itself in her mind.

Peregrine is going to homeless men, offering them a meal or a place to stay, and then using them as guinea pigs to try to find a way around the symbol.

A sickening rush of guilt hit her so hard she reached out for the wall.

"You okay?" Burnette asked. "Why don't you sit down?"

Peregrine had done some despicable things in his life, but this ranked near the top.

How is it so easy for Peregrine to kill people and still so hard for anyone to kill Peregrine?

Josh's grandfather had been missing for six weeks. After staying in the hospital for two weeks, having the stump where his hand should have been treated and the cuts in his chest stitched, he'd snuck out and disappeared. No one had heard from him since. He'd been supposed to take the reins of the new dream-walker democracy, but since he hadn't showed up, the junta was still in charge while they tried to figure out what to do.

Josh didn't know where Peregrine could have gone. She'd hoped that his disappearance meant he'd died, but she'd never kidded herself. Now she had proof that not only was he alive, he was actively trying to reenter the Dream.

"Do you have any leads on my grandfather?"

Burnette's pen paused in its travels across her notepad. "Do you think he's connected to this?"

There was no way Josh could explain what she knew without admitting to the fact that she'd mutilated her grandfather, or without exposing her friend Mirren.

"I wouldn't put anything past him."

After helping Burnette carry the dead man to her vehicle, Josh went to find Feodor in the library, where he was browsing the family diaries. She told him what Burnette had said, and her own conclusions about Peregrine's activities.

"One cannot fault the man's tenacity," Feodor said when Josh was finished.

"Let's try to avoid complimenting him," Josh said.

Feodor shrugged. He had the most graceful, elegant shrug Josh had ever seen, a little ballet-movement of a shrug.

"He has overcomplicated the testing process," Feodor replied. "I would have experimented on animals in his position." He considered, tapping his lip with one finger. "Cats would have been of sufficient size."

Trying to ignore that thought, Josh said, "Glad to hear it."

"However, we may be able to use his thoughtlessness to our advantage. If we map out where each body was found, we might be able to pinpoint the archway from which he's operating."

Clever, Josh admitted to herself. "I'll ask Burnette if she'll send me the case file."

"Do you think she will?" Feodor asked skeptically.

"Sometimes people give me special access because I'm Peregrine's granddaughter."

That was only part of the truth. Josh had a reputation among dream walkers as a prodigy, and they were usually more than happy to bend over backward for her.

"Ironic," Feodor said, but he smiled at her in a way that made her feel like he saw right through her. "Unfortunately, triangulating the bodies will give us, at best, a rough idea of where Peregrine might be."

Not to discount the lives of the five men Peregrine had killed, but Josh had a larger concern. If he found a way back into the Dream, he was likely to hurt a lot more people. "What are the chances he'll figure out how to deactivate the symbol?"

Feodor considered. "I could do it. But then, Peregrine is not me."

"Well, that's reassuring," Josh said.

"However . . . the power of obsession to propel a man to acts of which he might not otherwise be capable should not be underestimated. I believe Peregrine will continue until he finds a way."

That was not reassuring.